# HIS GUILT

# HIS GUILT

## THE AMISH OF HART COUNTY

## Shelley Shepard Gray

AVON
INSPIRE

*An Imprint of* HarperCollins*Publishers*

This is a work of fiction. Names, characters, places, and incidents are products of the author's imagination or are used fictitiously and are not to be construed as real. Any resemblance to actual events, locales, organizations, or persons, living or dead, is entirely coincidental.

P.S.™ is a trademark of HarperCollins Publishers.

HarperCollins books may be purchased for educational, business, or sales promotional use. For information, please email the Special Markets Department at SPsales@harpercollins.com.

FIRST EDITION

*Designed by Diahann Sturge*

Library of Congress Cataloging-in-Publication Data has been applied for.

ISBN 978-0-06-246913-7 (paperback)
ISBN 978-0-06-267563-7 (hardcover)

17 18 19 20 21  LSC  10 9 8 7 6 5 4 3 2 1

*To Laurie Smith. Thank you for inspiring me in more ways than you can imagine! You are a blessing to me.*

Greater love has no one than this: to lay down one's life for one's friends.

JOHN 15:13 (NIV)

Whatever your past has been, you have a spotless future.

AMISH PROVERB

# CHAPTER 1

*Horse Cave, Kentucky*
*August 4*

He was watching her again.

As she handed her customer change across the counter of the Blooms and Berries nursery, Waneta Cain did her best to pretend that their newest employee was not inordinately interested in everything she did. He was simply observant.

Surely, it was just her imagination playing tricks on her anyway. Mark Fisher was probably trying to see how she handled the checkout counter. She used to watch Mr. Lehmann all the time when she'd first started at the nursery.

That had to be the reason.

"Thanks for your help, Neeta," Mr. Killian said, interrupting her thoughts. "I'd be lost without you."

"I'm simply glad I could help ya," she told the Englisher with a bright smile as he lifted his box of seedlings from the wide well-worn countertop. "See ya soon."

The man tipped his ball cap. "You sure will if I can't get these to bear fruit. Wish me luck."

"Good luck and good blessings, too." After helping him with the door, she let it close behind her with a satisfying *thunk*.

She chuckled to herself. That Mr. Killian was a terrible gardener but a frequent customer. She sincerely hoped that one day he would develop that green thumb he wanted so badly.

"Do you always act that way?"

A shiver coursed through her as she turned.

Meeting Mark's dark-brown eyes, which seemed to be studying her intently, she struggled to appear calm. "Like what?"

Mark stepped away from the row of metal shelves located in the back of the store. He'd been unpacking boxes and re-stocking shelves for the last hour. Methodically sorting and organizing merchandise while she helped customers. "Like they're your friends," he replied. "Like you're so happy to see them." Stepping closer, he lifted a shoulder. "Is that how you really are . . . or is that just an act?"

She didn't care for the way he seemed to be insinuating that she wasn't genuine. "It's not an act. Mr. Killian is in here a lot. He's nice. We are friends."

"He's English and must be fifty years old."

"I don't see how that matters. I can like people who are different than me."

"Maybe you can. But you were sure smiling at him a lot. Or do you do that on purpose? To make sure that he will return?"

His question made her uncomfortable, but his sarcastic tone made her angry. "I don't know why you are asking such things. I really don't like what you are suggesting. I'm not doing anything out of the ordinary or smiling at customers in any special way. I'm just being my regular self."

"Huh. So you treat everyone with smiles and kindness. You are friends with all sorts of people. Even people who are different from you. Except me."

"I've been perfectly amiable to you," she retorted. Except, of course, that was a lie.

"I don't think so," Mark murmured. "I've been here seven hours, four of them barely six feet away from you."

She knew that. She'd known exactly where he was every moment that they'd been together. "And?"

"And during all that time you've hardly said ten words to me. You sure aren't smiling at *me*."

She opened her mouth, closed it again. What could she say? He wasn't wrong.

Mark stepped closer, invading her space. She could see the fine brown hairs on his forearms now. Noticed that he hadn't shaved in a day or two.

"Is it because I was once taken in for questioning?" he asked quietly, his dark-brown eyes watching her, as if he feared she would run. "Or, is it just me? Do you not want anything to do with me, Waneta?"

Her palms were sweating. She fisted both as she tried to come up with an answer. He was right on all accounts. She was uneasy around him.

Fact was, Mark Fisher was a large man. Tall and well-muscled. He had a rough way about him, too. It was disconcerting.

Of course, she'd always felt uneasy around him. He'd been an angry teenager, always glaring and short-tempered with most everyone. After he finished school, he'd worked for a few people around town. Rumor had it that his brother, Calvin, had taken off soon after their mother did. Mark had even lived in Mr. Lehmann's home for a time, until he was taken in for questioning about Bethany's assault.

And after he was questioned, then let go for insufficient evidence, he disappeared for two years.

Now he was back.

Mr. Lehmann assured her that Mark hadn't done anything wrong, but a lot of people in the community still believed that he was the masked man who'd beaten Bethany Williams. It wasn't much of a stretch. Bethany had told lots of people that her assailant was over six feet tall and was very strong. But she also said that she wasn't able to identify the man.

Few other details had circulated after that. Then Bethany and her family moved up north, practically the moment she was released from the hospital.

Realizing Mark was still waiting, Waneta said, "I haven't spoken to you much because we don't know each other."

His eyes narrowed. "But that's not really true. We knew each other once. We did go to the same Amish school."

"You were ahead of me in school. We hardly talked then." He was only three years older than herself, but they were miles apart in terms of how they'd lived their lives. He'd also been the kind of boy she'd been a little scared of. He was rough and had always seemed so angry.

For a second, he looked dumbfounded. "So, you do remember."

"Of course I remember you and your brother, Calvin. Our school wasn't that big, Mark." Feeling pretty good about how self-assured she was sounding, Neeta folded her arms across her chest. "But that was a long time ago. Years have gone by."

"Yeah. You're right," he said slowly. "Years *have* gone by. Practically a whole lifetime."

He sounded so sad. She wondered what was going through his head. Did he regret hurting Bethany? And what had he been doing for the two years since it all had happened? Why had he even come back to Horse Cave? Surely, there were other, far better places to start over.

The door jangled as a couple came in. Like Mr. Killian, they were regular customers. James and Katie Eicher were Amish and lived on a large farm on the outskirts of town.

Glad for the reprieve, she smiled at them. "Hiya, Katie. James. How can I help you?"

Just as Katie was about to answer, her husband put a hand on her arm. "Go wait in the buggy, Kate."

Katie looked at her husband in confusion, then blanched when she caught sight of Mark. Without a word, she turned and walked back out the door.

When it closed again, James glared at Mark. "What are you doing here?"

Mark lifted his chin. "I work here."

"Is that true, Neeta?" James asked. "Did Henry actually hire him?"

"*Jah.* Today is Mark's first day." Unsure how to handle his anger, she cleared her throat. "Now, um, how may I help you?"

"Where is Henry?"

She looked around the room, which was a ridiculous exercise, seeing as it was perfectly obvious that Mr. Lehmann was not there.

"He's out back," Mark said, pointing to one of the four large greenhouses behind the retail store. "You want me to go get him for ya?"

"I don't want you to do a thing for me," James said. "I'll go find him myself."

Mark rocked back on his heels. "Suit yourself."

Neeta winced at his flippant tone.

James, however, looked irate. Pointing a finger at him, James said, "I'm telling you now, Fisher. You stay far away from my wife. Don't talk to her. Don't even look at her."

Instead of looking cowed, the corners of Mark's lips lifted. "Or what?"

"Or I'll do everything I can to ensure that you leave here for good."

Mark narrowed his eyes. "Are you threatening me?"

Ignoring Mark again, James turned to her. "I can't believe you are working in here with him. Do your parents even know?"

Before she could say that they did not, James strode out the door. It slammed in his wake.

For a good couple of seconds, Neeta stared at the door. She tried to calm herself, especially since she'd just realized that her hands were shaking.

Why was she so rattled? Was it because she was afraid of Mark Fisher?

Or because James's anger had been so scorching?

"You never answered him," Mark said from behind her, startling her out of her dark thoughts. "Do your parents know that you are working here with me?"

"*Nee.*"

"Why not?" he asked. "Is it because you're afraid that they'll want you to you stay far, far away from the dangerous Mark Fisher, too?"

Before she could answer, the door opened again. This time it brought in Mr. Lehmann.

He looked from Mark to her and sighed. "I came to check on how you two are doing after James Eicher's visit. It don't look like you're doing too *gut*."

"I'm fine, Mr. Lehmann," she said. "But, um, well, it's four o'clock."

"Which means it's time for you to get on home," he said with a kind smile. "Grab your things and get on your way. We'll see you tomorrow."

She smiled weakly as she turned toward the back storage room, where her belongings were stowed. For the first time since she'd started working at the nursery, returning to work filled her with dread.

She didn't trust Mark. Worse, she didn't trust herself when she was around him.

# CHAPTER 2

*August 4*

Mark exhaled as he watched Waneta Cain hop on her bicycle and ride down the driveway toward the main road that led into Horse Cave.

What was wrong with him? He'd been nothing but rude to her all day. He'd been so direct and angry, it was like he'd been picking a fight. Why had he acted that way?

After Henry turned the Open sign to Closed and locked the front door, he walked to Mark's side. "Care to tell me what's been going on between the two of you?"

"Not really." When Henry crossed his arms over his chest, obviously ready to stand and glare at him until he got the explanation he'd asked for, Mark dared to tell the truth. "All right. I'm pretty sure she's scared of me."

"Scared might be putting things a bit harsh, son."

As it always did, Henry's use of *son* eased him like little else did. Henry Lehmann was the only person Mark trusted.

He was also the only person with whom he could let down his guard. From the time Mark was old enough to care, Henry had believed in his worth, even when his parents hardly knew he existed. Even when his teacher looked at him warily, like he was about to steal something off the top of her desk.

Henry had also taught him about love and kindness. About steadfastness and loyalty, too. For that, Mark tried his best to give the sixty-year-old man honesty, even when it hurt to be so vulnerable.

"Scared might be harsh, but it's accurate," Mark said. "I meant to act better, I tried to act better, but after Waneta hardly looked at me for most of the day, something snapped. I said a lot of things I shouldn't have."

"Sounds like the both of you had a difficult day, then."

"No worse than you. My being here cost you customers, didn't it?"

Henry walked to the counter, opened the cash box, and started counting the bills. "If you're talking about James Eicher, it ain't no great loss. He doesn't come in that much anyway."

There was his answer. His presence was costing Henry money and that was no way to repay him for the job. Mark's pride told him that he should quit, not burden the best man he'd ever known. And certainly not take out his frustrations and anger on a sweet, nice woman like Waneta Cain.

But he had no other options for employment. No one else had wanted to hire him, and Mark had asked most everyone in the area. He needed employment and he needed the money it gave him if he was going to follow through on his goal of living in his old house and fixing it up into something special.

Henry squeezed his shoulder. "Stop fretting, Mark. I'm

sure you didn't say anything to Neeta that canna be soothed with an apology. Waneta is a nice girl with a fine heart. She'll come around. Other folks will, too. It just takes time."

He hoped Henry was right. "I'll try harder tomorrow."

"I reckon you're trying hard enough. Just relax and settle in. Once you show Neeta the real you, she'll like you fine. In no time, the two of you will be getting along like salt and pepper."

"You make that sound so easy."

Compassion filled the older man's light-blue eyes. "I suppose it won't be easy. But remember this. I'm not going to fire you."

"*Danke.*"

"I'm also not going to let you quit."

The older man looked like a bantam rooster, he was so fired up. "So you're saying that I've got no choice but to stick it out," Mark teased.

"None whatsoever," Henry replied with a trace of humor sparkling in his eyes. Handing Mark a silver ring of keys, he said, "Now, go out and lock up the greenhouses. Double-check that all the water hoses are turned off, too, if you please."

Taking the key ring, Mark exited the building and exhaled. The August sun was still burning bright in the sky, practically scorching the ground below. They really needed rain.

He rolled his shoulders, trying to ease the tense muscles around his neck. Maybe it was the weather that was making him so crazy. The ninety-degree heat, combined with the high humidity, was enough to make even the best of men feel out of sorts.

As he entered one greenhouse after another, he dutifully checked the hoses and picked up anything that he was sure was out of place. At the same time, he attempted to reconcile his reasons for returning to Horse Cave in the first place.

He hadn't had a good childhood here. His parents had been emotionally abusive and completely negligent. Though they were Amish, nothing about their way of life followed the *Ordnung*, the set of rules that governed everyday Amish life. Mark remembered the preacher or bishop visiting their home often.

After those visits, things would get better, then progressively get worse again. Looking back on those days, Mark knew his parents had done very little to help or provide for him or his younger brother, Calvin. He'd hated that. Had resented them, too. He and Calvin had been the hungry boys in the classroom. The ones with the dirty clothes and the homework never done.

As he'd gotten older, Mark tried his best to look after his brother, but his efforts were never good enough. By then, Calvin had changed. Gone was the hopeful boy who yearned for acceptance. In his place was someone who was conniving and desperate. He'd ignore Mark's efforts to get him to study, and spent most of his free time away from home.

Then, just when Mark thought their situation couldn't have gotten any worse, it did. One morning, after a particularly bad fight, he and Calvin woke up to their father sitting at the kitchen table alone. He informed them that their mother had left in the middle of the night, and she wasn't coming back.

When Calvin blamed their *daed*, their father hit him. Hard. Scared and fed up, his little brother left that day. He was barely fourteen.

From then on, it was just Mark and his father. Mark wasn't

sure why he stayed. His father had been angry and emotionally abusive. He'd stopped working, stopped going to
church. Eventually, he left the faith, and started being even
more self-destructive.

Mark began taking odd jobs to help pay the bills and buy
food. Henry Lehmann had always allowed him to work
around the nursery, sweeping and cleaning the greenhouses
and walkways on the property.

And though he kept going to church, and even met with
the preacher, much of their community distanced themselves even further from him.

His brother's leaving had nearly broken him. His mother's
departure, his father's abandonment of their faith and de-
scent into drug use, had left him shocked. However, it was
the church community's disregard for his needs that caused
the most pain. He'd never felt more alone.

But it was being suspected of assaulting Bethany Williams
that had shaken him to the core.

How had that happened? How was it possible that a girl
in their community had gotten attacked? And how come
Sheriff Brewer decided that Mark was the one who'd done
it? He'd spent most of his life trying to do the right thing in
the worst sort of circumstances. He finished school, tried to
take care of his brother. He'd even tried to take care of his
parents.

But after Bethany was assaulted, all that anyone seemed to
remember was that he'd been the kid with the dirty clothes,
messed-up family, and very little supervision.

The moment the charges were dropped and he was free
to leave the area, Mark finally came to terms with the fact
that Horse Cave held nothing for him. Not anymore. Maybe

it never had. He headed to Indiana and got a job in an RV factory near the Illinois state line. The work had been good and Mark was able to save a lot of money.

While he was there, he was able to let down his guard some. The men he worked with thought he was just like them: a young Amish man trying to make something of himself. Only when he was sitting in his apartment late at night did he allow himself to think of his childhood in Horse Cave. He'd remember the windy, hilly roads, the creeks, the abundance of trees, and the scent of wildflowers in the air.

He'd lost track of Calvin and had pretended his father didn't exist. The only person he kept in contact with was Henry, and that was because Henry had refused to give up on him. Only when Henry informed him that the small house he'd grown up in was now his—and mentioned that his doctor had been cautioning him to cut back on his seventy-hour workweeks—did Mark decide to return.

So, here he was. Two years later, but it felt like everything he'd been running from had happened just yesterday.

After locking up the last greenhouse tight, Mark squinted at the sun. He was going to be in for a long night. There was no way he was going to be able to simply walk around his house, yet again, dodging memories of his father. Knowing that his father was gone forever, and that nothing between them had ever been resolved, was hard to swallow. He supposed he'd always held out a sliver of hope that his father would one day seek him out and ask for his forgiveness. But that had never happened.

So, going home right away was out.

Instead, he would walk over to the salvage market, pick up a couple of things in the sale aisle, and stop by the library. Or maybe he would go to Bill's Diner. He'd been avoiding that place, knowing he'd see a lot of people in the community there. But perhaps it was time.

"You got everything locked up tight?" Henry asked when Mark walked back inside.

"*Jah*," he replied as he handed Henry his keys. "Everything is locked and the hoses are all off. I checked each one like you asked me to."

"Would you like to join me for supper? I've got some leftovers from last night's taco casserole."

Henry was a huge fan of creating his own casseroles out of leftovers in his refrigerator. After choking down something called pork chop surprise, Mark had sworn never to eat another one of Henry's suppers again. "*Danke*, but I thought I might go to the diner. It's liver-and-onion night. Want to join me?"

Henry grimaced. "I'll pass, son. No matter how I've tried, I never could abide it. You enjoy your meal, though, and I'll see ya at eight tomorrow, right?"

Mark nodded. "I'll be here."

Henry peered over the rims of his glasses at him. "I'll be here, too, son. See you then."

# CHAPTER 3

*August 4*

Whint do you think about going to Bill's tonight, Neeta?"
her mother asked practically the moment Waneta
walked in the back door. "They've got a mighty good special
for supper. Liver and onions!"

It took everything she had not to grimace. "It's been an awfully long day, Mamm. I was hoping to stay here and relax."

"But Daed and I have been sitting here all day, practically
just watching the hands on the clock move around. We were
hoping to get out a bit."

"Oh, Mamm." Waneta hid a smile. Her mother might have
been watching the clock, but Daed had most likely been far
more interested in his new book or napping. After his last
"episode"—which he seemed to have taken in stride, but
which scared her mother and Waneta half to death—Daed
was put on several new heart medicines, and they were taking a toll on him. Some days he seemed to be able to tolerate
them just fine; other times, they didn't seem to agree with

him at all. Except for his biweekly attendance at church, he rarely left the house anymore. He said his body simply preferred being comfortable in his easy chair.

Which was why Waneta knew that her father had definitely not been the clock-watcher parent that day. It had been her mother, who was still the most social member of their little family.

"Mamm, how did you find out it was liver-and-onion night at Bill's?"

"Ruth stopped by around three. She said she was going around five thirty, before the supper rush." Looking a little winsome, she added, "I believe Faith is going, too."

Her mother, Ruth, and Faith were best friends. As far as Waneta could surmise, they'd been best friends practically since birth. Ruth was married and lived just down the street; Faith's husband passed away almost five years ago.

All three had been new brides together and, later, new mothers. Still, whenever they got together, they acted like silly girls. They'd gossip and laugh, plan future meetings and work on sewing projects.

In short, they were lovely women. Devout and kind. Sweet and fun. But they also had the difficult habit of encouraging Neeta's *mamm* to do things that weren't possible—and rarely offering her a way to do them.

"Mamm, next time Ruth mentions that she's going out to supper, you ought to ask if you could go with her."

Her mother's eyes brightened, but she shook her head. "I couldn't leave your father," she whispered. Well, tried to whisper. Her mother had never really mastered that art.

"Sure, you could," Daed barked from his easy chair.

Waneta chuckled. "See?"

"But I don't want him to be lonely."

"He won't be lonely if you leave him for an hour or two to enjoy a meal with your friends at the diner, Mamm. He'll be okay. Plus, I'm home now. I'm going to have supper with him."

"You don't think we could get your father to go out to supper? It might be good for him."

"I'm fine, Gettie," he called out.

Waneta knew this was hard for her mother, this first time of leaving him home while she went out. However, she also knew that her mother was going to have to get used to doing things like this. Norman Cain's health wasn't going to get better; the doctors told the three of them that in no uncertain terms.

Gently, Waneta said, "You know Daed doesn't like to eat in public anymore. His hands shake. And he is tired by five or six each evening."

"But—"

"Mamm, like I said, I'm tired, too. I worked all day. I don't want to take Daed out to eat. I'm sorry."

Mamm swallowed hard. "Nothing to be sorry about, dear. You are right. I shouldn't make such a fuss about such things anyway."

Making a decision, Neeta turned to the bench by the back door where her mother had set her purse for as long as she could remember. Picking it up, she handed it to her mother. "It's almost five thirty. I bet neither Ruth nor Faith has started walking to Bill's Diner yet. Go down and ask Ruth if you can walk with her."

Her eyes widened. "I couldn't do that! It is rude." But even as she said the words, she reached for her bag.

"It might be rude if you didn't know those women so well,

but you know them practically better than me," Waneta teased. "Go on, Mamm. Go enjoy a nice supper out. I promise, Daed and I will be happy to relax together."

Though she was still clutching her black leather purse like a lifeline, her mother glanced into the living room. "Do you think he'll feel secretly sad that I'm leaving him?"

"I won't!" he called out.

"He's going to be as glad as I am that he's not eating liver and onions, Mamm. Go, now."

Her mother walked toward the door. "Maybe I'll bring you both some slices of pie."

"*Danke*. I will enjoy that. Pie will taste *gut*." Waneta made a shooing motion with her hands. "Say hello to Ruth and Faith for me!"

With a new set to her shoulders, Gettie walked out the door. Watching from the window, Waneta felt a lump form in her throat. This must have been what her mother felt when she had walked to school for the first time on her own. Waneta had felt both pride and a bit lost.

Change was hard.

When her mother was out of sight, Neeta went to check on her father. He had the paper opened on his lap, his reading glasses perched on his nose, and an amused expression on his face.

"That was quite an accomplishment there, daughter. I'm proud of you."

"You thought it was the right thing to do, too, *jah*?"

"Of course I did. Your mother worries too much."

"She loves you."

"I love her, too, which is why I'm pleased she got out of here for a bit. It's good for her."

"She'll have a nice time with Ruth and Faith."

He nodded. "I'll get a break, too. Your mother fusses over me all day long. Even when I'm sleeping." Looking mildly aggrieved, he added, "You know, she never has gotten the hang of whispering."

"Faith's daughter Grace once told me that her parents thought that Mamm would have made a great preacher, if women did such things. Her voice can sure carry."

"No one would ever sleep during her sermons. Ain't so?"

Perching on the chair next to him, she joked, "We might want to mention that to Preacher Eli next time he comes to call." Sharing a smile with him, she said, "Anyway, I'm glad Mamm went. She really loves liver and onions."

"Indeed, she does. But her going out wasn't about liver, child. It was about becoming a little bit more independent. It needed to be done." That smile was replaced by a look that was far more reflective. Maybe a little wistful, too. "It was time, don'tcha think?"

How could a question like that hurt so badly? Especially when she'd just been thinking the very same thing? Wordlessly, she nodded.

"What are you going to make me for supper, child?"

Even though she'd already told him, she said it again. "I thought I'd make some chicken, potatoes, and broccoli. Does that sound okay?"

"It sounds just fine, dear," he said as he closed his eyes. "Wake me up when it's ready."

Getting to her feet, Waneta walked to the kitchen, opened the refrigerator, and pulled out the package of chicken.

Around her, the house was dim and silent. Warm, even with the windows being open.

It was a summer evening. The kind, when she was a child, that she loved.

She'd loved spending the majority of each day in bare feet. Loved the feel of the sun on her skin; loved the air filled with the scent of freshly cut grass and her mother's roses.

But just like the seasons, her childhood had passed. She now had responsibilities and new worries. Things that only adults should worry about.

Things like her father's failing health, her mother's tentativeness about her looming independence. And, she supposed, her new coworker.

Why had God placed Mark in her life? What did He want her to do? Perhaps just as importantly, she needed to figure out what she wanted to do about him. Did she want to continue to keep him at a distance, doing her best to keep her conversation, and smiles, to a minimum? Or, did she need to grow up and remember that he deserved her compassion and kindness as much as anyone else in Hart County?

That was a lot to think about as she sliced potatoes and prepared the simple meal.

To her surprise, Waneta was still thinking about Mark when her mother came home, as she sat in her quiet room—and long after she would have been fast asleep. Unable to stop herself, she continually replayed their conversations in her head and wondered how she could have acted differently.

Suddenly, it all made sense. The Lord wanted her to make amends. To change her attitude toward Mark. She shouldn't have acted so distant toward him. She should have talked to him more, looked him in the eye. She should've been a whole lot nicer.

That was why she hadn't been able to think about hardly anything else.

Tomorrow, she resolved to try harder to be his friend.

# CHAPTER 4

Neeta, I didn't even tell you about the big news everyone was talking about last night," Mamm said as she slid two fried eggs onto Waneta's breakfast plate. Every morning without fail, her mother got up and fixed her a big breakfast. Just the way she had when she was a young girl.

Waneta couldn't count the number of times she'd told her mother that there was no need to do such a thing anymore. But it was now apparent that, while it might not be necessary for Waneta, her mother needed to feel like she was still doing something to take care of her, even if it was in this small way.

Taking the plate from her, Neeta added toast and a slice of sausage, then quickly closed her eyes and gave thanks. When she opened her eyes again, her mother was bringing her a fresh cup of coffee.

"Here you are, dear. Piping hot with two teaspoons of sugar. Just the way you like it."

After taking a grateful sip, Waneta smiled. "I don't know

how you do it, Mamm. Your *kaffi* always tastes better than mine."

Her mother beamed. "That's because someone else made it. Food made by other people always tastes better. That's why people go to restaurants."

"I think you may have a point, Mamm," she said with a laugh. "So, what was your big news? You look like you're about to burst."

Taking the chair next to Waneta, her mother's eyes lit up. "Mark Fisher was at the diner last night."

"Oh?" Quickly, Waneta took a bite of toast before she lost her appetite.

"Oh, yes. At first I wasn't sure who he was. But Ruth knew. She told me. And, she reminded me all about his attack on Bethany." Wrapping her palms around her own cup of coffee, her mother said, "I can't believe I had almost forgotten that. Why, I might have talked to him by accident!"

Never before had her mother's penchant for gossip bothered her like it did at that minute. It also made her uncomfortably aware just how judgmental she'd been at work the day before. "Mamm, Mark was proven innocent. He had nothing to do with Bethany getting beat up so badly. You shouldn't say such things."

"But don't you think the policemen got it wrong? Everyone who Ruth and Faith and I talked to last night think so."

Waneta could just imagine the conversations that they had! "Oh, Mamm."

Ignoring her moan, Mamm continued. "Just so you know, I think other people in town doubt his innocence, too. No one besides Lora, his server, said a word to him the whole time he was there. And I'm sure she only did because she didn't have a choice."

Neeta could just imagine how Mark had dealt with that. He'd probably borne the talk and glances like he had when James Eicher came into the store—with barely held stoicism. But underneath that? Now she knew, he had been hurting. What a horrible experience that must have been for him. He took himself out to supper after a long day of work, only to be treated like a pariah the whole time!

After praying last night and speaking to her mother now, Waneta was even more determined to show Mark a different side of herself. She might still be a little wary of him, but she certainly didn't fear him. She'd never worried yesterday that he would harm her.

"I don't think the policemen got it wrong," she said slowly. "I think he was in the wrong place at the wrong time, or maybe someone just wanted him to be guilty because of his family. Or, who knows? All I do know is that his past isn't any of our business. He grew up here, same as everyone else. We all need to give him the benefit of the doubt."

Her mother's happy smile faltered. "I must say I'm surprised. You sound awfully sure about this Mark Fisher, considering he's practically a stranger to ya."

"He's not a stranger. As a matter—"

Her mother interrupted. "Well, maybe I am being rather harsh." Frowning, she continued. "He was a sweet little boy, now that I think about it. Always trying so hard to care for his little brother."

"I had forgotten about that."

"Me, too," Mamm said as she stood up and poured herself a bowlful of cereal and milk.

Unlike Waneta and her father, her mother had always had a secret fondness for unhealthy breakfast options. She loved all kinds of children's cereal, Apple Jacks being her absolute favorite. A close second were chocolate Pop-Tarts, though she tried hard never to buy them.

Pop-Tarts were a sure way to make her happy, though. Neeta remembered her father bringing them home from Walmart whenever Mamm was in a particularly bad mood. They always brightened her spirits.

So did, she realized, Apple Jacks.

Now was her chance to tell her mother about her new work relationship with Mark.

Waiting until her mother had a mouthful of sugary cereal, she said, "Mamm, I've got something to tell ya. I'm working with Mark now."

Mamm set her spoon down and swallowed hard. "Say again?"

"Mr. Lehmann hired Mark." When the line between her mother's brows didn't ease, Waneta said simply, "His first day of work was yesterday."

"How do you feel about that?"

"To be honest, I was a little wary of him yesterday. But I feel better about him today. He seems nice enough." Okay, that was kind of a stretch, but there was a good chance that he could be nice, if she was nice, too.

"What did your father say when you told him?"

"I didn't tell him yet."

"Why not?" A bit of nervousness entered her tone. "He might have a weak heart, but he would want to know who you are around all day long. He worries about you, you know."

"I know." Her father worried about her waiting on strangers at the greenhouse, and used to ask her all kinds of questions about who she'd talked to while at work. He would have wanted to talk about Mark, too. Probably for a good long time. She hadn't been willing to do that. "I wasn't ready to talk about Mark yet," she said honestly.

"Was it because you are afraid of him? If so, I want you to quit right now. You can always find another job."

"I'm not afraid, and I don't want to work anywhere else," she said quickly, though just yesterday she'd thought about getting a new job more than once.

Now Waneta's reticence seemed so silly. After nibbling the last of her whole wheat toast, she stood up and washed her plate in the sink. "Speaking of work, I need to get on my way. *Danke* for breakfast. I appreciate it."

"You're welcome." Standing up, her mother picked up her bowl and brought it to the sink. "Don't forget your lunch."

Dutifully, Waneta went to the refrigerator and collected her small cooler. "*Danke*, Mamm. You are sweet to always pack my lunch."

"You know I don't mind helping you."

"I know. That's why you're such a good mother, and I hope to be just like you one day."

"Ack, Neeta. The things you say."

Glad to see some color back in her mother's face, she pressed a kiss to her cheek. "Now, don't worry about me. And please, don't worry Daed about my job. I'll talk to him when the time is right."

"Your father can handle anything if he needs to handle it. The Lord will help. Now, let's talk about this Mark some more."

"Sorry. I can't."

Her mother followed her to the back door. "Neeta, please be careful around this boy. He might not be everything you think he is."

"He's not a boy, Mamm. And he might not be everything you think he is, either."

"Well, this man, he might be up to no good. He might be biding his time or something." She snapped her fingers. "Then, poof! You are hurt."

"Or he might be simply trying to fit in and settle down. Now, I really must go. See you tonight." She smiled as she grabbed her tote bag and purse and hurried out the door.

It was a blessing that her mother didn't follow her.

After placing everything in the basket on her bicycle, she pushed off and headed to work. As she rode down the windy road, feeling heat already coming off the pavement, Waneta prayed that she wasn't being more optimistic about Mark than was wise.

And while she didn't think Mark was going to hurt her, she certainly was a long way from feeling comfortable around him.

She didn't know if she ever would be.

# CHAPTER 5

*August 5*

Waneta Cain was difficult to understand.

All day yesterday, she'd appeared to go out of her way to avoid him. She'd barely met his eyes; she certainly hadn't spoken to him unless she had to. As much as it had hurt, it was nothing more than he'd expected.

But today? Well, she was acting different.

Really different.

From the moment she greeted him in her robin's egg blue dress, she was a bright little ray of sunshine. She told him good morning. She not only didn't seem as tense around him, she even joked with him a bit.

He caught her studying him more than once, too, as if she wanted to know more about him. Not like she had yesterday. Definitely not like everyone at Bill's who stared at him last night.

No, today it seemed as if she had something new on her mind. He wondered what it was, and if she was planning to share.

He counted it as a personal blessing that the store was especially busy. He had too much to do to dwell on her abrupt change in personality.

Henry had told Mark when he'd arrived that morning to get ready to do a lot of running around, and he hadn't been mistaken. It was Friday, the beginning of the weekend. Lots of tourists came to Hart County on the weekends and stopped by the nursery on their way to tour caves or visit on the horse farms in the area.

Locals from Horse Cave and Munfordville stopped in, too. Blooms and Berries was not only known for its plants, shrubs, and gardening supplies but also for the large variety of local produce that they sold.

All three of them had been at customers' beck and call since they'd opened the door at eight. Because of that, Mark had only been treated to rude gasps and stares from a couple of people. Most just treated him with cool politeness. Being able to just do his job instead of feeling like he was an animal on display at the zoo was a relief.

The only bright spot had been when Preacher Eli had stopped by. Though Mark didn't feel as close to him as he did Henry, Eli had been instrumental in helping Mark reclaim his faith. He had an ease about him that Mark appreciated.

"Looks like you're settling in," Eli said when he brought a pair of gerbera daisies to the counter.

"I'm doing my best," Mark replied while Waneta rang Eli up.

"That's all one can ask for. Ain't so?"

"Mark is doing just fine," Waneta said with a smile. "I'm glad he's here."

Mark was surprised to hear her say that. After glancing at

her curiously, he held up the two plants. "Want some help carrying these out?"

Eli laughed. "I ain't that much older than you. If I canna handle two daisies, I've got a big problem."

Mark, Waneta, and the next people in line chuckled as he left. Once again, the preacher had brought light into a room with only a few words.

That light had stayed with Mark for the next hour . . . until Henry had appeared. "If any two people deserve a lunch break, it is you both," he said as he walked in the front door after chatting with a pair of farmers in the parking lot. "It's sure been busy."

"It has," Neeta said. "I'm glad. It always makes the day go faster."

"Indeed." Turning to Mark, Henry said, "You've been a big help today. It was nice to be able to count on you for all that heavy lifting."

Mark dismissed the praise. He hated being thanked for doing something that should have been a given for all of them. "You shouldn't be lifting anything at all," said Mark. "Especially not anything over twenty pounds. And neither should you," he added, looking at Neeta. "I don't know how you two have managed so well without me all this time."

"I wouldn't say we managed well," Waneta said. "You definitely have an easier time carrying around bags of mulch than I do."

"I should. Those bags are at least thirty pounds!" Mark exclaimed.

Henry laughed. "I'm old but not that old. And Neeta is stronger than she looks. But don't forget that we have Ben

Hilty coming in on Saturdays now. He's young and strong. We've put him to work from time to time as well."

"I don't know who he is."

"He lives over in Munfordville. Just turned fourteen. But he's eager to be of assistance."

Mark barely stopped himself from commenting on Ben's age. Fourteen was young, but not too young to share some burdens. After all, he'd been practically managing his whole house by the time he was thirteen.

Henry didn't seem to be perturbed by Mark's silence at all. Brushing his hands together, he said, "Let's stop worrying so much. Today has been *gut*."

"Indeed it has," Waneta said with a smile.

"I think it's time for you two to take your lunch break," Henry said as he took his place back behind the counter.

"Both of us?" Mark asked. Hadn't he just pointed out that Henry needed his help?

Waneta looked agitated. "Henry, we don't have to eat together. That doesn't seem fair to you."

"Nonsense. I'll be fine. I was managing this nursery for quite a while before you came along, girl." Making a shooing motion with his hands, he said, "Go on, now. Sit down and rest. Both of you. I'll see you in forty-five minutes."

Mark hesitated. "That seems too long for lunch. How about—"

"If I need help, I'll call ya," Henry said, his voice firm. "Now, go on. I'm tired of bickering."

Mark wasn't sure where to eat. Yesterday, he'd eaten his lunch in the storage room. But he'd been alone. Now, the thought of sharing that small space with Waneta seemed like it might be awkward, especially since she hadn't seemed all that thrilled about eating with him.

But if he didn't eat in the storage room, he didn't know where else to be.

"Come on, Mark," Waneta said as she walked toward the back door. "Mr. Lehmann is right. We deserve a break. But let's not eat in the storage room. It's so dark and cramped in there."

"Where do you suggest?"

"How about we go get our lunches and sit outside?"

Now his coworker was not only being friendly, she was trying to get them to spend time together. She wasn't being shy about it, neither. Feeling at a loss for words, Mark followed her. What was she up to now?

WANETA'S BODY WAS betraying her. Her heart was racing, her face felt flushed, and a fine sheen of perspiration was coating her brow. Though she was doing her best to pretend that she was no longer afraid of Mark, it seemed her body hadn't caught on to that idea. She hoped he didn't notice these sudden changes. If he did, it would be awfully embarrassing.

"Waneta?"

"*Jah?*"

"Care to share why you are looking like you are trying your best not to throw up?"

"I'm not about to throw up. And even if I was, I wouldn't want to share that information."

As they continued to walk toward the old picnic table in the back of the property, Mark kept darting concerned looks her way. "Is it me? Is the thought of being alone with me scaring you that much?"

"*Nee.*"

Since it was too late to back out from eating lunch with him, she hoped for both of their sakes that he just thought the hot summer day was getting the best of her.

As they sat down, he opened his mouth like he was about to ask something, but then closed it.

Yet again she was somehow making things worse between them instead of better. After putting her cooler on the worn metal picnic table, she silently blessed her meal and dug in.

Mark was moving far more slowly as he grabbed his own lunch, which looked like it was in an old Walmart bag. After he took a large bite out of his peanut butter sandwich, she felt pretty embarrassed. She easily had three times the amount of food that he did. Why had her mother packed so much anyway? No one needed that much food!

"I haven't eaten a peanut butter sandwich in years," she said. "Is it good?"

He shrugged. "Good enough. It was easy to make. That's all that counted early this morning." He took another bite.

"I know what that is like. I'm always running late in the morning." She swallowed as she opened her own container of leftover chicken and rice. Also in her cooler were four oatmeal cookies, two apples, and some macaroni salad.

As he peered into her cooler, his lips twitched. "You are such a tiny thing. I never thought you'd be such a big eater."

"I'm not." Though, of course, her sizable lunch said otherwise.

"Ah."

"I usually share my cookies with Mr. Lehmann." So, that explained two of the cookies. "And, well, I guess I'm always a little afraid of going hungry. This job is tough on an empty stomach."

"True enough."

Mark was just about done with his sandwich. She, on the other hand, had enough for several more people. It was a lot—even for her. She realized then that Mamm had been trying to feed Mark, too.

Pulling out the container of macaroni salad, she said, "Obviously I brought too much. Would you like this? And maybe an apple?"

He looked at it suspiciously. "Why?"

"Because I brought too much food and I thought you might still be hungry." Nudging the salad his way, she said, "Please, help yourself. You'd be doing me a favor."

He shook his head impatiently. "I meant talking to me. You said good morning and kind of smiled at me. Now here you are, eating lunch with me and offering me your food. Why?"

She wasn't really sure if it had more to do with concern for him or worry about how she felt about herself. She hoped she wasn't that self-serving, but at the moment she wasn't sure. Maybe she'd never been tested?

To buy herself time, she attempted to tease. "I didn't kind of smile. I did smile, Mark."

"Whatever. You know what I mean." Before she could answer, he blurted, "Is it because of your mother?"

"What does she have to do with me offering you an apple?"

"I saw her at Bill's last night. She kept eyeing me like I was going to either take her purse or yank her into a dark corner."

Because she could actually imagine her mother looking like that, she laughed nervously. "Surely, you exaggerate."

"Yeah. Probably. But I'm still asking you."

He had a right to be answered, too. "Maybe I just felt bad

about yesterday," she said at last. "Maybe I realized that I should have been more welcoming to you."

But instead of dropping the subject, he shifted, looking even more intimidating. "Only *maybe?*"

She was starting to hate how he wasn't letting her off easy. "Look, I'm not proud of the way I behaved yesterday. I was, well, nervous around you."

"Because of what you thought I did."

She nodded. "*Jah*. But also because you weren't friendly. You seemed angry and tense as well. But even though you acted that way, I know I should have been more welcoming. I hardly spoke to you at all and it was your very first day. I am sorry."

Immediately, his whole posture changed. He tensed up and his judgmental expression was replaced by a look of concern. "Are you still nervous?"

"*Nee.*" When he continued to simply watch her warily, she amended her words. "Actually, yes. I think I might still be a little nervous, but I'm trying not to be. I'll get better."

"I would never hurt you."

This conversation was most definitely not going in the direction she'd intended. Why couldn't they have simply eaten in peace? Meeting his gaze, she saw that his dark eyes seemed almost liquid. He was being sincere.

He was truly concerned that she could be afraid of him.

"I know you wouldn't hurt me," she whispered.

"Do you? Do you really?"

"I know I need to learn to trust you."

"I didn't hurt Bethany. The sheriff didn't just find me innocent, I *was* innocent, Waneta."

She figured that was a pretty important point. As she did

the night before, she imagined what life must have been like for him. He'd been accused of a terrible crime and had been asked to prove his innocence. Wasn't he supposed to have been presumed innocent until proven otherwise?

Done with the leftovers, she closed the container and placed one of the apples on her napkin. "I don't actually know you, Mark. I know who you are, and I remember you and your brother in school." She paused, then decided to lay everything out. "Even back when we were all little, I heard stories about your parents, too. I know they left the order. I heard they made a lot of mistakes. I also know that you are living in your old house. I can only imagine how hard that must be."

She paused again when she noticed that he seemed stunned by her words. "Even though I know all that, I realize we have much to learn about each other. Just like I don't know you very well, you don't know me."

He blinked. "That is true."

Now that they were finally making amends, she smiled slightly. "Mark, please believe me. I don't fear you. At all."

"I never thought you'd bring all of that up. You surprised me."

"I never intended to bring it up," she said. "I thought it would be rude. But just now, it felt like it would be rude not to bring it up. Since I like this job and we're going to be working together, I was hoping we could simply learn to get along. Can you forgive me enough to do that?"

"There's nothing for me to forgive," replied Mark. "And you are right. We don't know each other. I'd like to fix that, though."

She smiled in relief. "I'd like that, too."

Though he didn't exactly smile, he seemed to relax. Reaching out, he said, "Hey. Are you done with your fork?"

She looked at him in confusion. After all she'd just said, that is what he asks her? "I am."

"*Gut.*" He picked it up, opened the Tupperware container, speared two macaroni noodles, and popped them in his mouth.

She swallowed, felt her cheeks flush. "I could have washed that for you."

"It looked fine."

"But, I . . ." She didn't want to say the obvious, but didn't he think using her fork was, well, kind of personal?

"Are you sick?"

"*Nee.*"

"Then it's fine," he said as he speared a red pepper. "This is good, Waneta."

"*Danke.*"

"Did you make it?"

"*Jah.* My mother cooks a lot, but I made the salad."

He took three bites, then closed the container and put the fork on top of it. Now he was biting into the red apple she'd given him.

She bit into hers as well, tried to concentrate on the tart, sweet taste of the Gala apple on her tongue. But for some reason, she could only focus on how happy he looked eating his.

"I'd compliment you on the apple, too, but I think God had more to do with making it than you did."

She giggled. "You would be right. I love apples."

"What else do you love?"

Glad that the tension between them had broken, she leaned back and smiled. "Hmm. Well, I love walking in the woods, for one. Gardening, too. And snow, even though most people don't care for it much. Oh! And walking in Horse Cave. I love exploring the cave system. I think it's fascinating."

"You really like the outdoors, don't you?"

"I love it. Though my *mamm* taught me to cook and clean and sew, of course, I don't love those things all that much." Smiling at him, she said, "What about you?"

"What do I love?"

"Come on. If I'm sharing, you are, too."

"Okay, then. I love clean, fresh cotton sheets on my bed. I love silence in the house. I like dogs. I like hot, sunny days." With a wink, he added, "And macaroni salad."

"It seems we're at odds with each other, since I like the winter and you like the summer."

"We like different things, but I don't know if one would say we're at odds with each other. I hope not." After he threw his sack and apple core in the trash, he turned to her. "Thank you again," he said almost formally. "This was nice."

She realized he was going to go back into the store. "You're going back already? I think we still have fifteen minutes."

"It's early, but I don't mind. I don't want Henry to have to work by himself any longer. See you in fifteen minutes."

Alone again, she thought about her little speech, and how off guard he'd looked when she'd mentioned his parents.

She thought about his list of loves. Realized that they were all things she took for granted, things he'd most likely missed when he was a boy growing up in that house.

Then she thought about him using her fork and eating the food she'd brought.

And she wondered why she was so pleased that things had turned out the way they had.

# CHAPTER 6

*August 5*

**Y**ou are so foolish, Mark chided himself as he walked home Friday evening after work.

Remembering their lunch together, he grimaced. He'd finally had the opportunity to show how much he'd grown. But instead of simply eating lunch and talking about easy things, he'd delved into something far more personal.

Really personal.

What had possessed him to ask her about things she loved?

It had been obvious that he'd taken her off guard.

Then he'd gone and used her fork. He'd known doing something so personal and unexpected would make her uncomfortable. But he'd done it anyway.

Who in the world even did things like that? One would think he'd actually been in prison for the last two years, the way he was behaving. His parents might have done a lot of things wrong, but they had taught him the basics of getting along with others. He did know the correct way to behave.

If he didn't learn to apply some self-control around Waneta Cain, he was going to do or say something to make her wary enough to complain to Henry about him.

He wouldn't blame her if she did that, either. She had every right to complain if the new employee was making her uncomfortable. Then Henry would have to make a decision about whether to keep him on or not. And if it came down to choosing him or her?

Well, he knew who Henry would ask to stay.

Mark would be out of a job so fast, he wouldn't know what hit him.

He needed this job, too. He wanted to live in Horse Cave and fix up his old house. He wanted to show everyone in the area that he really was better than they believed him to be. He wanted to show himself that very same thing. He should be doing everything he possibly could to keep this job and make Henry glad he took a chance hiring him. He should be working hard and keeping his head down. Not acting too forward and familiar with Waneta Cain.

As he continued walking home, taking time to notice that several people were on their front porches and watching him walk by, he analyzed their lunch some more.

And realized that Waneta had actually stopped being nervous for a little bit. She'd even smiled at him, too. It hadn't looked strained, either. Instead, it had seemed genuine.

It had made him feel good inside. Almost too good, because it had even made him imagine that he could have a chance with her one day.

For a while there, they'd talked, and their conversation hadn't been stilted or full of long, awkward silences. Instead, it had been easy. Almost relaxed.

He'd felt something happening between them and it felt

an awful lot like acceptance. Acceptance was something he hadn't felt in years.

It also wasn't something that he'd experienced in a long time. Maybe that meant that they could eventually be friends. Maybe even more than friends.

"Mark Fisher, is that you?"

Stopping, he turned to see Lora Weaver walking right behind him. "Lora?"

She nodded and smiled, increasing her pace.

Mark didn't even try to hide his surprise. Lora had been his female counterpart in Horse Cave when they were growing up. Both of them had sad home lives that they tried desperately to keep hidden. Her father had taken off when she was just a toddler, ignoring both his marriage vows and promises to the church. His actions had left Lora's mom alone with four children, no income, and a fierce depression.

Lora used to shyly admit that on some days their mother never got out of bed. As the years passed, Lora took on more responsibility for her younger siblings and became bitter and angry during the week, and more than a little wild during the weekends.

She'd always said she was going to leave Hart County the first day she could, and never look back. She'd done that, too. She left when she was sixteen or thereabouts.

"I sure never thought I'd see you again," she said when she reached his side.

"I was just thinking the same thing about you. I canna believe you are here."

"I know." Looking sheepish, she continued. "I swore I'd never come back if it was the last place on earth. But, here I am."

"You moved back?" He didn't even try to hide his aston-ishment.

She lifted one shoulder. "I did. Fourteen months ago." Her voice drifted off. "I suppose everyone does things at one time or another that they never intended."

Though he agreed, he thought she was generalizing her return a little too lightly. Lora had been vocal about her disdain for their hometown.

But he didn't have any desire to hurt her feelings. "It's all part of life, I guess," he murmured. "Maybe."

"*Jah*. Maybe." When she smiled in a condescending way, he studied her. She was wearing dark-washed jeans and a snug-fitting black tank top. Bright-blue bra straps directed his eye to her shoulders. Worn rubber flip-flops were on her feet. Her toenails were painted dark purple and she had a couple of silver earrings in each ear. She looked good. Free-spirited.

Pretty much like any other English girl about her age.

And the complete opposite of Waneta. "Why did you come back? What happened?" he asked.

"That's the same question I was going to ask you."

"Henry told me that he'd heard that I inherited my parents' old house and decided to come back and live there."

She raised her eyebrows. "Really? I would have thought you would have wanted to stay as far away from there as possible."

"It's paid for." He also wasn't willing to give up on his life here. Though his home life had been so bad, there was still a stubborn part of him that kept hoping to make things better. It was how he'd survived his childhood.

Hearing from Henry had felt like a sign, too. He'd secretly

felt like the Lord was telling him that it was time to return to his past and make things better.

Maybe even transform it?

When he returned, he'd met with Preacher Eli and gotten baptized. Then he decided to transform the house, just like he'd been seeking to transform himself.

Then there was Henry. Henry needed him and Mark craved the man's love like a child craved a mother's arms.

Lora nodded. "Makes sense. Paid for is good."

"What about you?" he asked again, since she still hadn't answered his question. "Why did you come back? I thought you were long gone."

"I was." Her lips thinned. "It's a long story, but I guess it's enough to say that I discovered that the big world ain't all that easy." She paused. "But things have been good here. I'm working over at Bill's Diner."

"I was there last night. I didn't see you, though."

"I had the night off. You'll have to come back soon. I'll introduce you to the other waitresses there. Everyone's real nice."

"I'm glad you are happy at your job. Hey, where are you living? In your old place, too?"

"I am, if you can believe that. My youngest sister, Beth, is pretty much my mother's favorite. She married an Amish man and lives on a forty-acre farm. Mamm lives with her and helps mind their six *kinner*. My other sister Amanda lived in the house until she and her husband could afford a bigger place. So she gave it to me. I'm the charity case."

"What about your other sister? I forget her name."

Lora's expression shuttered. "Martha died."

"I'm sorry to hear that."

She lifted her shoulder again. "Her death is a long story."

"She get cancer or something?"

"*Nee.*" Sounding strained, she said, "In a nutshell, Martha managed to get into even more trouble than me. We all thought something bad would happen to her one day. We were right."

Martha's story reminded him of Calvin. And that, of course, put him on edge. He was trying to move forward. To make something of himself. To create a new reputation. Not rehash and relive all the bad ones.

Shoving his hands into his pockets, he awkwardly stepped back. "Well, ah, good to see you. I've been working all day and I'm a sweaty mess. I'd best be getting on home."

"I understand. Do you mind if we walk a little further together? I pass your street on the way to my place."

Her offer made perfect sense and Lora had been nothing but pleasant—unlike the majority of the people at Bill's last night. So he didn't understand why he suddenly felt uncomfortable. "Yeah, sure."

Looking pleased, she started walking. As he stayed by her side, she began pointing out different people's houses. He listened and looked with only the smallest bit of interest. He didn't remember most of the people she named. He wasn't sure what to do with the information she was handing him, either.

"That place now belongs to the Swartz family," she said. "Remember Daniel?"

"*Jah.* You had a crush on him something awful."

"Oh, that. That didn't mean anything."

"You sure? 'Cause I kind of remember you mooning over him one Sunday evening at a singing."

"I didn't." She laughed. "All right, you caught me. I mean I didn't moon over him too much."

He grinned, finally feeling more relaxed. "I'm glad you called out to me, Lora. This is the most relaxed I've felt in a week."

"Really? Now that's a shame. You always were so nice." Her gaze landed on him fondly before drifting to the street. "Unlike some people."

Wondering who she was referring to, he gazed at the street.

And saw Waneta riding her bicycle, her tote bag and little cooler in the basket behind her seat.

He froze, just as she glanced his way. Their eyes met for a long moment before she looked nervously at Lora, then turned her head as she rode on.

Seeing him with Lora had obviously made Waneta uncomfortable. He wondered if it was Lora herself or the fact that he was out walking with her.

"It must be pretty hard to go through life as perfect and holier-than-thou as Waneta Cain," Lora muttered.

Mark frowned. She'd stretched out Waneta's name so it had sounded awkward and almost like a whine.

"That ain't fair. She's a nice woman."

"Oh, she's nice, all right. Nice to the right people. Not nice to people like you and me."

"I work with her," he said. "She's been nothing but kind to me."

Hurt flashed in her eyes. "Really? Well, if she is, then that is surely an accomplishment. Waneta don't give too many people the time of day. Especially people she thinks are beneath her."

Mark hated that Lora was speaking so disparagingly about

her. "You're being awfully harsh. Waneta hasn't been like that to me. Henry Lehmann thinks the world of her."

"Huh. Well, she's looked right through me more than once. If she's treating you different, it must be because she feels sorry for ya or something."

He didn't like anything Lora was saying. Not the insinuation that Waneta wasn't kind. Not how she was implying that she wasn't as good a person as Waneta. "My house is down the street," he said abruptly. "See you, Lora."

Looking puzzled, she stopped and stared at him. "That's it?"

"*Jah*. I told you I was going home."

"Oh." As if she was summoning a smile, she said brightly, "Hey, you know what? It's Friday night. What are you doing for the rest of it? Want some company?"

He wasn't sure what she wanted from him, but he wasn't ready to give it. He knew he wasn't in the right mindset to tackle Lora's animosity toward Waneta. "*Nee*. I just want to relax. See you later, Lora."

Hurt filled her gaze. "Oh. Well, um, yeah . . . sure. Bye, Mark."

As he turned down his street, he glanced up at the sky. *What had that been about, God? Did you need me to remember my past and how far apart I was from Waneta?*

Passing house after house, most looking bigger and more cleaned up and taken care of than he remembered, he thought of something else. Maybe the Lord was telling him the exact opposite. Maybe He had brought Lora into Mark's life to show just how far he'd come from his childhood, both physically and emotionally.

No longer did he have to be judged by his past, or by factors that had always been out of his control. Instead, he could present himself to be the man he'd always hoped he could get to be. He could show people like Waneta just how much he had changed.

Now, that was a good thought. A promising thought. Something to give praise for.

Feeling almost happy, Mark walked up his steps, pulled out his house key, and grabbed the mail from the box on the edge of the porch. This was normal. He had nothing to fear but his memories. Everything was going to be all right.

And as for Lora? Well, he'd just have to do a little bit of praying and thinking about that. Maybe she'd been reaching out to him because she only needed a friend.

Or maybe she needed some guidance and he was the best person to offer it to her. If that was the case, he would do his best to be the person she needed him to be.

When he walked in, he released a ragged sigh. At least he was home alone now. For the rest of the evening, he was going to do his best to forget about everything but eating a big supper and relaxing on the back porch. It had been a hard, hot week.

But just as he was about to sit down and sift through the mail, he noticed that some cushions from his couch were displaced. The book he'd left on the side table had been flipped over.

Hurrying to the kitchen, he saw that one of the four chairs around the table had been moved. The paper and yesterday's mail was scattered on the counter as well.

Someone had been in his house while he'd been working and they hadn't been shy about letting him know that.

Who could it have been?

# CHAPTER 7

*Friday, August 5*

Stuffing her fingertips into the front pockets of her jeans, Lora watched Mark as he walked away from her. She tried not to let his refusal to spend more time together get her down. But it still did.

She wondered what had set him off. At first he'd seemed genuinely happy to see her. Then, in an abrupt turnaround, he acted as if he was embarrassed that he even knew her name. What had she done wrong? Had she pushed too hard to connect with him again? Though the girls at work didn't seem to mind when she asked them questions or shared personal information, it might have been too forward for a private man like Mark.

Or maybe it was that they'd both changed too much. Mark was even more subdued than he had been as a boy. Then, of course, she was now obviously no longer Amish.

That seemed like a better guess. Mark Fisher always had been so straight and upstanding. He liked to follow the rules and liked it when other people did that, too. She'd always thought Mark cared more than most about how things looked. He never had liked it when things were out of order.

Not even when he was just nine or ten years old.

No matter what his parents did and no matter how much he looked like he'd needed a few solid meals and a fresh change of clothes, Mark had always acted as if he'd come from the best, most proper family in the county. Well, he'd tried to pretend that, though everyone knew his home life wasn't any better than hers.

Maybe he was afraid renewing their friendship would taint him somehow. That being seen with her would ruin his reputation, such that it was. Lora hoped that wasn't the case, but she could see that happening.

Calvin used to joke about his big brother, saying Mark was rebelling by being everything good since their parents were so bad. Lora would roll her eyes at statements like that, but she'd secretly admired Mark for wanting to be someone better than the people who'd raised him.

She'd thought it was admirable, but not necessarily possible. 'Course, she'd also done her share of pretending when she was a child. She'd told herself that living in a broken-down house with a broken-down mother wasn't so bad. She'd even got real good at pretending not to notice the looks of disdain half the population of Horse Cave shot her way when she and her sisters would wander around town late at night, doing anything to avoid going home. Sometimes she found she could even ignore other kids' cruel taunts about her ill-fitting clothes and missing father.

But as far as forgetting . . . well, that had been another story. She still woke up once or twice a month in a panic, cruel words and taunts ringing in her head from people like Bethany Williams.

Even now, thinking about Bethany made Lora cringe. She'd had the face of an angel, and the ability to convince every adult in the county that her soul was just as pure. Lora knew from experience that it wasn't. Lora had been skilled at delivering snide comments under her breath. Her victims would be hurt, but would be too afraid of her retaliation to ever speak up.

Though she'd kept her opinions to herself, Lora had been sure that Mark hadn't been the man who'd assaulted her. Bethany had been too willful and erratic for Mark. He had avoided her at all costs.

Shaking her head, she shoved all thoughts of Bethany away. That was in the past and she was doing her best to focus on the present. She needed to continue to count her blessings. She was back in Horse Cave and she was doing okay.

When her sister Amanda had called to offer her the house, Lora hadn't even acted like she wasn't grateful. Losing Martha to a drug overdose had been horrible. Discovering that she'd been living in a dirty room in downtown Cincinnati the last months of her life had been a blow to all of them.

Now she and her two remaining sisters were trying their best to forge a new relationship together. She didn't have much in common with them, but they'd all learned how difficult it was to dwell only on each other's differences.

Even their mother was trying to make amends for the damage she'd done to all of them.

While Lora doubted she'd ever be able to completely forgive her, Lora was able to at least share a meal with her every once in a while.

When her house was in sight, Lora let her thoughts drift back to Mark. Reflecting on their conversation, she realized that Mark's demeanor had changed the moment Waneta Cain rode by. It was obvious now that he was anxious to put some distance between them.

What was it about Waneta that he admired so much? When Lora shared her feelings about the woman, Mark jumped to Waneta's defense like a Doberman.

Actually, he'd defended Waneta like someone who was a very close friend, mentioning all of her qualities again and again. It didn't seem like he agreed with anything Lora was saying about Waneta. It was as if he didn't remember anything about their past; didn't remember how the two of them used to walk home together with twin feelings of dread while girls like Waneta barely looked their way.

Could Mark really have forgotten the way Waneta and her friends would giggle at Lora and her sisters—when they weren't ignoring them? How Waneta had gotten new dresses and backpacks and school supplies all the time? How she'd brought enormous lunches in her pail every day? How she'd share only with her friends while he and Lora went hungry?

Surely, he hadn't forgotten that!

But it hadn't seemed to matter. It was almost like he was sweet on Waneta. Maybe he was, she realized with a sinking feeling. Maybe Mark had decided to set his sights up high and he didn't want to associate with people like Lora when he could align himself with innocent girls like Waneta.

Lora trudged up her front porch steps and took a seat in one of the three white wicker chairs that Amanda had bought when she lived there.

Only when she sat down did she notice poor Katie Eicher

gardening in her front flower beds. She was on her hands and knees, painstakingly pulling weeds in her vegetable garden. She looked hot, sweaty, and tired.

Like she usually did, except when she went to church.

James, her husband, was a bully. There really was no other name for it. Lora heard him yell at Katie often. He wasn't shy about it. He certainly never attempted to keep their private life private. For what seemed—to Lora at least—increasingly dumb reasons, James would deride his wife, put her down.

It was hard to hear and even more difficult to watch.

Looking over at her, Lora sensed that Katie was trying her best to get the gardening done before her husband came home. Remembering the pot of sun tea she'd made two days before, Lora went inside and filled two Mason jars with ice, the strong tea, and two generous spoonfuls of sugar. Then, before she thought better of it, she walked across the street.

Taking care to keep her voice relaxed and friendly, she smiled wide. "Hiya, Katie, I brought you a glass of tea."

When Katie looked up, Lora almost gasped. One of Katie's eyes was swollen shut. The skin surrounding it was black and blue. "Oh, Katie. That has to hurt," she said.

Gingerly, Katie pressed one hand to her face. "It ain't so bad," she said in a rush. "Is it?"

Not knowing what to say that wouldn't make Katie feel worse, Lora settled for holding out one of the jars. "Would you like some?"

"*Danke.* It's warm out here. I was getting thirsty." She took a long sip, then another one. "It's *gut* tea, Lora. You always do such a good job with that."

"It's only sun tea."

"Mine never tastes as good." Katie smiled, then seemed to

recall herself. "I had better finish up my chores. James will be home soon."

It was pretty obvious that her neighbor was worried about getting everything done before her husband returned. "Do you need some help?" she asked. She didn't mind. The work would also serve to help keep her mind off her conversation with Mark.

"Doing what?"

"Weeding?" Katie looked so surprised, Lora chuckled. "Just because I'm not dressed Amish and don't keep a garden don't mean that I've never tended one. I can pull weeds as well as anyone."

"Oh. Of course." Biting her bottom lip, Katie gazed at her garden. "Well, now . . . thank you, but I'll be all right."

"Do you not want my help? Or is something else bothering you?"

Katie pressed her hand to her face again. "I shouldn't really talk about it."

There was her opening. She needed to say something about her face. She needed to know that even though they weren't especially close, Lora cared and wanted to help. Kneeling down, she looked directly at her. "Katie, when did that happen? Last night or this morning?"

Keeping her eyes averted, she nervously pressed a hand to her cheek again. "This morning." Lowering her hand, she looked at Lora directly. "I guess it really does look bad. Ain't so?"

"I'm more concerned about how you are faring instead of how you look." When Katie seemed confused, Lora said, "Your cheek is really swollen and your eye looks worse than bloodshot. Can you see out of it?"

"Kind of."

"You know, something could be really wrong. Do you think you need to go to the doctor? If so, I'll help you get an appointment. I'll go with you, too."

She paled. "I don't need to see the *doktah*." Raising a hand, her next words tumbled out in a rush. "Please, don't worry. I'll be okay. Hopefully my face will look much better by Sunday."

Lora knew now that if Katie's swelling hadn't gone down or if her eye wasn't completely back to normal by church, then Katie would simply stay home. "I want to help you. Will you let me?"

"Help? With what?"

"With everything. Do you feel safe at home?"

Abruptly, Katie set the Mason jar on the ground. "I don't know what you mean."

Lora wasn't in the mood to go through the motions and pretend that Katie hurt her eye by walking into a wall or some other sort of nonsense.

But she also didn't know her well enough to be completely direct with her and say that she knew James hurt her. So she simply shrugged. "I think you do know what I mean, but if you don't want to talk about it, I understand."

Looking frazzled, Katie thrust the jar into her hands. "Here. Thank you for bringing it to me, but now I must get back to work."

"Just because you don't want to talk about your eye doesn't mean you can't drink my tea. Does it?" Attempting to smile, she said, "How about I help you weed for a while?" Scanning the garden, she said, "I'll take the row of squash."

"You had better not," she said in a rush. "James would get upset."

"Why? He doesn't want you to have help?"

"He wouldn't want me to have you in our yard."

Not even to weed? "Why is that?" she asked slowly. "Is it because I'm not Amish?"

If anything, Katie looked even more worried. "That is one of the reasons." After darting a glance down their empty street, she stepped toward her door. "Now, I'm sorry, but I really must go. Good-bye."

When she turned her back again, Lora felt as if she'd been rejected for the second time in less than an hour. It seemed that no matter what happened, she wasn't good enough company. Not even good enough company to pull weeds.

Feeling more tired than ever, she got back on her feet and carried the two jars back to her house.

After she looked inside, she looked around. It was still silent, too big, and empty. She had returned even though she'd promised herself never to return. And suddenly, it was too much. The quiet. The memories. The time. She needed a way not to think of it for a while.

Thinking a six-pack of beer and maybe a bottle of tequila would take the edge off, she stuffed a couple of bills in her back pocket and left again.

She didn't bother turning the lock. No one would come to her house unless they had no other options.

She was living proof of that.

# CHAPTER 8

*Sunday, August 7*

W hat did you think about Preacher Eli's sermon?" June Gingerich asked Waneta as they helped to clean the four long tables that had been set up to serve the church luncheon. "It was pretty forceful, don'tcha think? Preacher Eli doesn't usually sound so stern."

Waneta nodded as she considered her friend's statement. In her usual way, June had focused on the heart of the matter. "I thought he was going to start calling out names, he was so upset about how some folks were acting. It caught me off guard. I've hardly ever seen him without a smile on his face. Who knew he could be so solemn?"

"He's been solemn with me when I've gotten counseling," June said. "But he never seemed like he was actually mad at me." Lowering her voice, she added, "I overheard two women say that they thought he was treating them like naughty *kinner*. They really weren't happy."

"I know his sermon probably caused quite a few people to be uncomfortable, but I think his stern manner was necessary," Waneta whispered. After darting a look around to make sure no one could hear, she added, "After all, there are some people here who certainly do need a talking to. Forgiveness is something we should all take seriously. It's one of the backbones of our lives, after all."

"I hear what you're saying, but I don't think Eli was simply talking about forgiveness." After bending down to pick up a couple of stray napkins that had fallen, June lowered her voice. "I think he was actually talking about Mark Fisher. I think he was telling us that we should all try to forgive him."

After double-checking that Mark was out of earshot, Waneta nodded. "I think that's who Preacher Eli was talking about, too. Mark has returned and he wants to be part of our church community. It is wrong for some people to treat him like he has the plague."

June shook her head. "I hear what you're saying, but I think you are being a bit too generous, Neeta. What Preacher Eli said was shocking. He offended a lot of people. Why, I thought my mother was going to bite her tongue, she was trying so hard to keep her feelings to herself."

"Since all those ladies are currently gathering in a tight circle, I don't think she waited too long," Waneta said drily.

June shrugged. "Who can blame them?"

"Mark deserves forgiveness. I, for one, would hate to come back to my parents' *haus* with a cloud hanging over me. I really would hate to realize that nobody wanted me to be there, too."

"I would hate that, too. But what if they are right? What if he really is a dangerous criminal?"

Moving to the third table, Waneta shook her head. "He's

not. What you are hearing is merely malicious gossip. It doesn't have any truth to it."

"But what if it does? After all, a lot of people don't want Mark here. A lot of people whose opinions I respect."

"So?"

"So? Well, so many people can't be wrong."

Waneta felt a bit like she was on a sinking ship and trying her hardest to bail out the water with a measuring cup. But still, she had to hold firm. Mark needed support. "I think differently. So does Preacher Eli."

Leaning closer, June said, "A lot of people, me included, even worry about you working with him at the nursery. I don't have a good feeling about that. I'm worried you are going to really regret it."

"Please don't. I've worked with Mark a whole week now. So far, he's been a real *gut* worker. He's also been a lot of help. Mr. Lehmann needed someone strong and able to help him."

"I thought Henry hired Mark because he felt sorry for him."

Privately, she didn't think it mattered why Henry Lehmann hired Mark. Even if he had only hired him at first because he'd felt sorry for him, Mark had more than proved his worth, even during the few days he'd been there.

"June, what matters is that everyone needs to take Preacher Eli's words to heart. What he said was important. And true." She felt so passionate, her voice rose. "We all need to stop judging others and casting stones. We also all need to seek forgiveness. I've witnessed some people be unkind to Mark at the nursery. My mother said that everyone was looking at him and gossiping at Bill's, too."

After she wiped down the last table, June braced a hand on her hip. "You sure sound high and mighty on his account."

Stung by her tone, Neeta paused. "What is that supposed to mean?"

"It means, I never figured you would be attempting to go against the rest of us for someone like Mark Fisher," she retorted, dismay heavy in her voice.

"Mark can't help where he came from."

"My parents said that more problems are going to happen around here now that he's back."

"They don't know that."

"And you don't know that they're wrong, either." Sounding more sure of herself, she said, "Waneta, I think you should start looking for another job."

"June!"

"I'm only trying to help you," she said, then looked just beyond Neeta. "I'm only trying to make sure you are being cautious and careful."

It was more than obvious now that June hadn't taken anything from Preacher Eli's sermon to heart. "I think you are being judgmental. You are casting stones without a care about who they hurt. I think you are making a big mistake and that you are going to regret it," Waneta bit out, anger thick in her voice. "I look forward to the day you realize that, too."

"I guess you've made your choice," June said in a huff. "Now it's only a matter of time before he hurts you. When that happens and you realize how reckless you've been, come find me. We'll talk then."

Waneta stared in shock as June picked up two plastic containers filled with leftover lunchmeat and walked away.

What had just happened? One minute, June had seemed truly concerned. The next, they were going back and forth, debating Mark's character. No, it seemed they were debating their own characters, too. And their families'. How had everything gotten so bad so quickly?

"Do you want me to go talk to her?"

Startled, Neeta turned to find Mark looking directly at her, his dark eyes seeming to take in everything she was feeling. "How much did you hear?"

"Enough to know that I was the focus of your discussion. And enough to realize that she didn't agree with your perception of me."

"I'm sorry. June likes to share what's on her mind. She ain't always right, though."

"Don't apologize for her words. You can't take on how other people feel or make them change their minds if they don't want to."

"I guess not." Scanning the crowd, she searched for her best friend. She was nowhere to be seen. "I'm surprised, though. June is a really *gut* friend."

"I'm sure she is. But fear does strange things to people."

"Well, she shouldn't be afraid. There's no one in Horse Cave who is going to hurt her."

"If you're talking about me, you're right," he said lightly. "Thanks for standing up for me."

"I was standing up for you because it was the right thing to do. I'm frustrated about how much people don't seem to be able to let go of the past."

"It's understandable. The past can be a difficult thing to let go of."

Just as she was about to answer, Waneta saw her father

approach, her mother following about twenty steps behind. Bracing herself, she mumbled under her breath, "Here come my parents. Whatever they say, I want you to know I'm sorry."

Mark's eyes warmed just as her father said, "Neeta, your mother and I are about ready to leave. Are you?"

"Can you give me a couple of minutes? I was talking to Mark."

Her father smiled. "We've been talking, too."

They had? Fearing that she was just about to subject him to a whole list of invasive questions, Neeta eyed both men. "Were you discussing anything special?"

"*Nee*. We were only getting to know each other."

A flash of surprise entered Mark's eyes before he composed himself. "Don't look so worried, Neeta. Everything is fine."

Right then, her mother joined them. "Hi, Mark. We know each other, but you might not remember me. I used to help out at your school from time to time."

"I remember."

Her mother smiled. "Then you know that I'm Gettie Cain. Waneta's mother."

Before Waneta could give her mother a meaningful look, Mark said, "*Danke*. Nice to meet you as well, Gettie."

Then her *daed* shared a look with her mother and said, "Mark, do you have plans for the rest of the afternoon?"

"Not really. I had planned to work on the house. I'm trying to clean it out."

"*Jah*. I imagine that is a big job. But Sunday is for rest, not work. Why don't you come over and spend a few hours at our house? Stay for supper. We're barbecuing cheeseburgers today."

Mark was wearing an expression Neeta hadn't seen on his face before. He looked nonplussed. "W-Well . . ." he stuttered as he glanced in her direction. "I'm not sure . . ."

He was doing that for her benefit, Waneta realized. In case she didn't want him there. "I hope you accept," she interjected. "My father grills the cheeseburgers. They're very good. And my mother planted more vegetables than you can count, in pots all along the back porch and patio. The tomatoes and peppers have gone crazy! It's something to see."

"I bet," he said with a touch of humor in his voice. "Well, in that case, *danke*. I'd be happy to come over this afternoon."

Her father clapped his hands together. "*Gut*. Now, can we get along? I'm ready for a rest."

"I'll walk with you, Norman," her mother murmured. "Now that we don't have to worry about our Neeta walking alone, we can get on our way and she and Mark can follow whenever they are ready. Are you sure you're going to be able to walk home? I bet we could find someone to give us a ride in their buggy."

"I've got some problems getting around, but not that many problems," Daed snapped.

Waneta had been so wrapped up in her defense of Mark, she'd forgotten just how weak her father was. Feeling that familiar knot of nerves in her stomach, she said, "We'll follow in a few minutes. Or, we can walk with you."

"No need for that. I'll be fine. You just make sure you don't tarry too long."

"I'll make sure she gets home safe," Mark said.

"I know you will. *Danke*, Mark," her father said. "Waneta has a good head on her shoulders. She ain't going to trust you for no reason."

When they were out of sight, Mark turned to her. "What just happened?"

"You have just been subjected to tornadoes Norman and Gettie. They have a way of coming in and creating havoc wherever they may be."

"That's putting it a bit strong. Ain't so?"

"You are saying that because you haven't lived with them all your life. They have a bad habit of turning everything upside down in their path."

"It's impressive. Are you upset about this? I couldn't tell. I would have tried harder to put them off if you didn't want me to visit your house."

"I want you to come over, Mark." Realizing how she sounded, she said, "I mean, I know you don't have a lot of friends here yet."

"Ah. Now I understand." He smiled, but it was strained. "Are you ready now?"

"I am." She started walking before she said anything else that could have been taken two ways. "We don't live far. Just off Second Street."

"I know where you live."

"You do?"

He coughed. "Sorry. I meant that I'm assuming you live in the same house you always have. If so, I remember it."

"I live in the same one." Laughing softly, she decided to say what was no doubt lingering on both of their minds. "We're sure doing a good job of stepping into holes, aren't we?"

"We are, but we seem to be getting a little better."

Though she felt June watching her, Waneta smiled at him.

She couldn't do anything about June's worries and doubts. Nothing except hope and pray that they were unfounded.

# CHAPTER 9

*Sunday, August 7*

Mark had spent most of the previous day ripping out the linoleum that covered the first floor of his house. Someone—he wasn't sure whether it was his parents or whoever lived there before them—had covered up beautifully finished wood floors with industrial-grade linoleum.

Now that it was over twenty years old, it was yellowed and cracked. The edges next to the woodwork were peeling, too. When he'd first pulled up a corner, he imagined only finding cement underneath. Discovering a wood floor in good condition had been a nice surprise.

The hard physical labor had cleared his mind and allowed him to come to terms with the fact that someone had been in his house. But he had no idea who it could have been. He hadn't discovered that anything was damaged; nothing seemed to be missing, either. His stash of money was still exactly where he'd hidden it—taped to the bottom of his parents' old dresser.

For some reason, it seemed that the intruder had only wanted to examine everything. Mark imagined he had simply walked inside, fingered some of his items, then left.

That should have given him some measure of peace. Instead, because he couldn't figure out why anyone would want to come into his run-down house and inspect his few belongings, it had set him more on edge. He'd tossed and turned all night, half expecting to hear footsteps signaling the return of the intruder.

When he'd woken that morning to only the chaotic chirping of a pair of robins outside his window, he resolved to put those fears behind him. There was nothing he could do anyway. It wasn't like he was going to go to Sheriff Brewer and share his suspicions.

Instead, he had greeted the day with two strong cups of coffee and a short walk to the Bylers' home. They were hosting church this week.

The coffee, the almost cool morning, and the brisk walk had put Mark in a better frame of mind. By the time he arrived at the Bylers' and took his place with the other men on one side of their metal-sided barn, he felt almost at peace with himself. To his surprise, that sense of peace had stayed with him during the lengthy church service.

But as far as what was happening now?

Well, he could safely say that nothing in his life had prepared him for Norman Cain seeking him out when everyone was lining up to leave.

"Mark, stay and talk to me a while, wouldja?"

Towering over the smaller man with a far bigger reputation, Mark did the only thing he could do. He nodded.

While most everyone else passed them by, Norman sat back down. "You don't mind sitting for a spell, do you? My legs don't work like they used to."

"Of course not." He sat, too, turned slightly, and rested his elbows on his black pants.

"Let's wait a moment to talk. My ears don't work too good anymore, neither."

Nodding weakly, Mark settled in his chair and waited.

As passing seconds turned to minutes, his palms began to sweat.

Truth was, he knew all about how to sidestep conversations. He was a master at avoidance. He was extremely good at shielding his thoughts and making sure no one knew what he was thinking. All of those skills had developed because of the life he'd had at home.

He'd put them into good practice when he'd been accused of assaulting Bethany and had been taken in for questioning. The whole time Sheriff Brewer questioned him, he'd answered honestly but with no emotion. Looking back, he imagined that he'd probably sounded more interested in the weather than in Bethany's death.

No wonder Sheriff Brewer hadn't believed Mark at first. He'd kept him in the county jail for two nights while he and his deputy had gathered evidence and questioned other people. And later, when he'd told Mark he was free to leave, Mark had taken care to keep his face an expressionless mask. Though the sheriff had obviously not trusted him, he'd let him go.

But now?

Now he couldn't remember a time when an upstanding man like Norman Cain had gone out of his way to talk to him. It had to be about Waneta. Maybe he was going to chide him for not being nicer to his daughter?

Or was it something else?

When the barn was finally empty except for the two of them, Norman breathed in deep. "Feels *gut* to have room to breathe. Some days, I think I'm going to expire in these crowded barns."

"It does get warm," Mark agreed.

"What did you think of the sermons today?"

"I enjoyed them."

Norman looked pleased. "*Gut*! Me, too."

"Ah. Is that what you wanted to talk to me about? Church today?" Maybe Norman didn't want him there?

Norman waggled his hand back and forth. "Kind of." He shifted and raised his voice. "See, it got me thinking. Well, the sermon and Waneta's lecturing did. I decided we needed to invite you over for supper."

The invitation was so unexpected, he was sure he'd misunderstood. "Excuse me?"

Norman raised his voice even louder. So loud it fairly echoed among the barn's rafters. "I want you to come over for supper this afternoon, Mark Fisher! Join me, Gettie, and Neeta."

"That's why you wanted to talk to me?"

"*Jah*. What do you say?"

"I say, Thank you."

His brow puckered. "Is that a yes?"

Mark laughed as he stood up. "*Jah*, Norman. It is a yes, all right." After all, how could he have refused an invitation like that?

"Oh! *Gut*." After he struggled to his feet, he turned to

shuffle down the empty aisle. "Go find Waneta in ten minutes or so," he called out over his shoulder. "I need to go tell Gettie that you're coming over."

Watching Norman leave, Mark did something he hadn't done in a very long time. He laughed. Right there, in the middle of the Bylers' empty barn—he laughed until tears formed in his eyes.

LATER, AS HE walked by Waneta's side, Mark's good mood was still intact. She, on the other hand, seemed to become more and more nervous. They'd hardly said a word to each other for the last ten minutes. However, he didn't think it was because she still feared him.

No, he was fairly certain it was because she was trying to save him from her parents' nosiness. She was looking out for him. He'd tease her for being his defender if he wasn't so humbled by her intentions.

When they were about halfway to her house, she glanced up at him. "I suppose we should talk. I feel foolish walking without saying a word to each other."

"It's okay if you don't want to talk to me."

"Why is it okay? Do you not want to talk to me?"

He laughed. "Waneta, I'm walking by your side to your house. Obviously I don't mind talking with ya."

"My parents asked you to walk with me."

"I wouldn't be here if I didn't want to. You have to know that."

Looking sheepish, she smiled. "I do know that. You are a man with your own mind. I don't think you would ever do something you don't want to do."

"I've done plenty of things I didn't want to do. But this ain't one of them."

Her eyes widened at his blunt reply. "I never know how to respond when you say things like that."

"Say whatever you want, Waneta. I'm not going to get mad."

"When I'm with you, I feel all flustered. I don't know why."

He knew why. But he also wasn't willing to rehash their differences in backgrounds again. Determined to make an effort, he blurted the first thing that came to mind. "Do you have a pet?"

"A pet?" She wrinkled her nose. "*Nee.* Why?"

"I don't know. I thought you probably had one. Most people have pets."

"Not me. Do you?"

"*Nee.*" Now he was feeling flustered, too.

She smiled suddenly. "I guess most people have pets, except for the two of us."

He chuckled. "It would seem so. So, why don't you have one?"

"I don't know. I guess my family really ain't pet people." Looking a little defensive, she added, "A lot of people aren't, you know."

It was on the tip of his tongue to chide her for being so prickly. But then he remembered that he was attempting to build a conversation, not start an argument. "I was thinking of getting a dog," he blurted.

"You were?"

"Yeah." When he saw her raise her eyebrows, he asked, "Why are you acting so surprised?"

She pursed her lips. He thought he'd blown the conversation yet again. However, after a minute or so, she spoke. "I'm surprised only because I know that you work a lot. Dogs take a lot of time." She coughed. "I mean, I am assuming they do. What kind of dog do you want?"

He wasn't a liar, but he was starting to feel like one, since he'd actually never given what type of dog much thought. "It doesn't matter to me. I thought I'd go to the pound and see the dogs there."

"That will be so sad. They all need homes."

"I bet you're right," he said slowly. Just imagining dog after dog in cages, each one desperate to be let out, made a lump form in his throat. Why had he started this conversation anyway? "It will be hard to make a choice."

Blue eyes shining, Neeta added, "It's going to be wonderful-*gut*, though. Don'tcha think?" she asked, her tone wistful. "Mark, you will be rescuing a dog who needs a home."

Though she'd said his name before, she didn't say it often. Hearing his name on her tongue sounded good. "That will be wonderful. *Wunderbaar.*" Impulsively, he said, "You should come with me."

"What?" Before he could take it back, she stopped and stared at him. "You really wouldn't mind me coming with you?"

He shook his head before he remembered that he hadn't actually planned to get a dog. "If you'd like to come, I'd be happy about that. I'm sure picking a dog will be a hard decision."

"You are going to need to find one who won't mind being home alone during the day. I think a big dog, too."

"Why big?"

"Because you're big." Her eyes widened. "I mean, um, I just assumed a man like you would want a sizable *hund*."

He chuckled at her expression. "I guess I had a big dog in mind." Then, because he couldn't seem to stop himself from digging his hole deeper, he found himself doing something he'd never done before. At least, not in recent memory, anyway. "Well, maybe we could go get one in a month or so. After I get the floors in my house fixed up."

"The nursery won't be as busy in another month. I could probably get a Friday or Saturday off in September or October. You, too."

Liking that they were making plans so far in advance, he nodded. "We'll pick a weekend when there isn't church. That way I'll have all Sunday to spend with it."

"That's a *gut* idea," she said as they walked up her front porch. "Mark, *danke* for asking me. It sounds like a lot of fun."

"What is going to be fun?" her father asked.

"Mark is going to adopt a *hund* from the shelter in a month or two. He asked me to go with him to pick it out."

Norman looked at him in surprise. "I see."

Mark felt his cheeks flush in embarrassment. "That is, if it is okay with you, Norman."

If anything, her father looked even more taken aback. "Well, now," he murmured. "I guess it is." Still looking reflective, he said, "Neeta, go help your *mamm* in the kitchen for a few minutes. She's making iced tea and putting cookies on a tray for our guest."

"I feel bad about you going to so much trouble."

"It's no trouble at all, Mark," Norman said. "When people come over, my wife feeds them, whether they want to be fed or not."

"I'll be right back, Mark," Waneta said before walking into the house.

When they were alone, Norman gestured to one of the empty chairs that dotted the porch. "Have a seat and tell me about this dog you want."

"I, um, was just thinking about maybe getting a dog. I never intended to ask her to accompany me to the pound. It just kind of happened."

"That's the funny thing about our daughter. She inspires others to do all sorts of things they didn't intend to." Stretching his hands out in front of him, he chuckled. "You'd be amazed about the things she's encouraged me to do. Or maybe not."

"Like I said, if you'd rather me not take Waneta to the pound, I understand."

"You might understand. She would not. My daughter is a woman who doesn't change her mind."

"Yes, sir."

As if that settled that, Norman stretched his legs and crossed his ankles. "So, how are things going for you?"

"Work is fine," he said carefully. "I like the nursery. I know Henry pretty well and am glad I can help him with some of the heavy lifting."

Looking satisfied, Norman nodded. "Henry is a *gut* man. He don't hire fools, either."

Since he was obviously referring to Henry having also hired his daughter, Mark said, "No, sir."

"And your *haus*? How goes it there?"

Mark knew Norman was looking for honesty, so he gave him that. "It's been difficult. It needs a lot of work. I'm currently ripping out the old linoleum flooring."

"Pulling out old linoleum ain't easy. It's a difficult undertaking."

"It is, but it will be worth it, I think. I discovered oak floors underneath in good repair. After I work on them a bit, they're going to be really fine. They'll make the whole place look better, too. Fresh."

Norman raised his eyebrows. "Fresh. *Jah*, I can see how that might be the case. Won't that be fine."

Feeling more eager and less like he was sitting for an interview, Mark nodded. "I believe so. When I made the decision to move back there, I knew I needed to make a lot of changes. My insides need it."

"I can understand that. You might not like me saying this, but I've often thought of you and your brother. You two had a hard time of it."

"We did." There was no reason to pretend otherwise.

"Was it difficult to make that choice to come back?"

"At first, no. Hearing that I could live somewhere rent free, it felt real good. But making my way back here was hard. That house was not a happy place. Not for me, not for any of us, really." Exhaling, he said, "But if I've learned anything, it's that the house is just that. A house. The memories hurt, but I don't want them to define me."

Norman eyed him steadily for a long moment before slapping his hands on his knees and standing up. "I'm *verra* glad you came over today, Mark. Mighty glad."

"I appreciated the invitation."

"Well, now. I think it's time I fetched Neeta. I imagine she's helped her mother enough for now."

After Norman departed, Mark sighed in relief. He felt as if he'd passed a test. He wasn't sure what Norman Cain had been hoping to discover that had been lurking inside of him, but it seemed that whatever he had been looking for, he'd found.

Unbidden, twin feelings of pride and embarrassment filled his insides. He'd been accepted. Deemed acceptable. That affirmation also left him feeling pretty embarrassed. He was twenty-six. Far too old to be needing acceptance from Waneta's father.

Far too old for it to feel so gratifying.

"Mark, are you all right?" Waneta asked. She had just stepped out on the porch. Two tall glasses of iced tea were in her hands.

He mentally shook his head. "Of course." Coming to his feet, he took one of the glasses from her. "Have you finished helping your mother already?"

She shrugged off the question. "Oh, that. Mamm and Daed wanted me out of the way so Daed could talk to you in private."

"I thought that might be what happened."

"Well, you thought right. I let Mamm know I wasn't happy about that, too. They shouldn't be inviting you over just to ask you pesky questions."

"You shouldn't have worried about it. I can take care of myself."

"Oh, I know that. But making you sit and talk with him the moment you got here was rude. I hope he didn't offend you too much? Or, if he did, I'll be glad to talk to him."

"There's no need for that," he assured her. He liked that she was attempting to be his protector. However, while he might seek acceptance like a child, he surely didn't want or expect anyone to fight his battles for him.

She sipped her drink. "Supper won't be ready for a little while. Would you like to play cards?"

"I guess so." Actually, he couldn't remember the last time he'd played.

"What about Rook? Is that okay?"

He hadn't played that game in years, not since he'd played with other teenagers on Sunday night singings and frolics. "I like it fine."

She breathed a sigh of relief. "I'm glad. I'll go get a deck of cards. We can stay here or go inside."

"Let's stay outside. It's warm, but not too bad under the shade."

"Okay. Great." He was starting to realize that her nervousness stemmed from him being a man and her a woman and not that she was afraid of him.

That made him want to gentle his voice and be even more patient with her. "Go find the cards. I'll be right here. Waiting for you."

Cheeks blooming, she darted back into the house. Chuckling to himself, he set the glasses on the worn table, then got up and walked to the porch railing.

It was warm out but pleasant enough. Surrounding the porch were a variety of shrubs and flowers. Boxwoods, burning bushes, and a crabapple tree decorated the bed on the right side. On the left were lavender, daisies, and black-eyed Susans. They were unpretentious flowers, he supposed. But bright and cheery, too. They reminded him of Waneta, a person who was easy and pretty on the outside, but whose sweet and caring personality shone through. He wondered if she was the gardener in the family. If so, then she was responsible for the well-tended beds. They flourished under her guidance.

He supposed he would probably transform the same way around her. Maybe some of his wildness would be tamed, too.

It was a fanciful thought. It amused him, too—realizing that he was hoping there really was something between him and Waneta. He would help her in any way that he could. And she? Well, she would give him the care and stability that he'd always craved.

Just as he was about to turn back to the table and sit down, he spied a movement near the edge of the Cains' property. Mark stepped forward, braced his hand on the railing, and stared more closely.

Spied a bright white shirt, then focused on the figure standing in the center of a grouping of pecan trees.

Mark was about to call out to Waneta that he was going to check on something when the man stepped out of the shadows of the trees and into the broad daylight.

Curious, Mark walked down the steps. As his eyes focused, he drew to a stop. Stunned. It was Calvin. His long-lost brother.

Mark stepped forward. Everything inside of him was crying out to go to Calvin. Hug him tightly. Promise anything so he wouldn't take off again.

But then a couple of things became apparent. Calvin was not Amish. The blinding white shirt was a T-shirt. It was untucked over a pair of dark jeans. His dark-brown hair was cut short, almost like a military buzz cut.

Calvin was also staring at him intently. His arms were crossed over his chest, his legs slightly parted. His chin was raised. He looked for all the world like he was daring Mark to acknowledge him.

Even from that distance, Mark could tell that there was

nothing tentative about his brother's expression. It looked vaguely mocking. Derisive.

Almost taunting. Like he was daring Mark to come to him.

The door swung open then. "Sorry it took me so long," Waneta said in a rush. "I had quite the time finding two complete decks. Has that ever happened to you? Three of the card decks in our drawer were missing one or two cards. I couldn't believe it."

She was excited. Happy to play cards with him on the front porch. Here, at her house, where her parents had invited him to spend the afternoon with them. Where her mother was going to the trouble of making him supper.

This was his future if he wanted it. He could stay a little longer. Grab hold of Waneta Cain's goodness and her parents' acceptance into their life.

Or, he could make his excuses and go see his brother, who he'd once loved more than anything. The boy he'd tried so hard to protect but had failed. Who had never understood Mark, never even tried to understand his motivations for doing the things he had done. Who had left him and had never responded to his notes or calls. For years.

Who had come to find him, not at their house where they could sit and talk and try to figure things out. But at the Cains' residence. Lurking, too. Not even announcing himself and stepping forward. Stepping back into the community.

It was a hard decision. A difficult one.

But he knew what he had to do in order to survive.

Turning around, he smiled at Waneta. "I think everyone loses cards all the time," he murmured. "That's why card companies keep making more playing cards. Ain't so?"

Eyes bright, she smiled.

Mark loved her smile. Cherished it. If Waneta was his future and Calvin was his past, there was no choice. She represented everything he'd ever wanted.

*Calvin?* He was a reminder that everything he'd ever loved had caused him pain. He already knew what pain and rejection felt like. "You better deal," he said as he sat down next to her. "It's been so long since I've played, you're gonna have to walk me through the first game."

"I can do that. But eventually, you're going to be on your own. I'm a bit competitive when it comes to Rook, you see."

He laughed. "I'll pay close attention, then," he teased.

Though he still felt a prickling on the back of his neck, felt Calvin's unwavering gaze still watching him intently, Mark never looked out into the field again.

He didn't need to experience his past again to know that if he gave in, it would hurt.

Those memories were alive and well.

# CHAPTER 10

Calvin Fisher couldn't believe it. His own brother had just turned his back on him. Mark had looked him in the eye, then proceeded to pretend that he didn't exist.

After years and years of no communication, the first time Mark had seen him, he'd chosen to ignore him.

As that knowledge sunk in, Calvin stepped further into the shadows. He watched Mark sit down across from Waneta Cain, watched him lean back and relax. Just like he belonged at her house. Like he was comfortable there.

Across from him, Waneta was talking a mile a minute, all while fumbling with a deck of cards as she clumsily attempted to shuffle them. After dropping several on the ground, Mark bent down and picked them up. Then he reached for the remainder of them and proceeded to shuffle the deck neatly. As he did, Waneta gazed at him like he was doing something difficult. Then she said something to him that must have been extremely funny because Mark threw his head back and laughed.

Laughed! *Mark was laughing.* He was spending time with Waneta Cain, who everyone had thought was a cute girl but far too sheltered and sweet. Now she was an attractive woman and she had invited Mark into her home. And, from the way they were acting toward each other, it was apparent that he was courting her.

Courting, the Amish way.

The idea both sickened and amused him. His older brother was not only still Amish, he seemed to be thriving in the lifestyle. So much so, he'd decided to return to Horse Cave and claim their childhood home.

Even after everything they'd been through inside of those walls.

Calvin couldn't understand it, but then again, he'd never really understood how Mark thought. Mark was steady. He liked things to stay the same.

And he'd always been sure that his faith would save him and keep him from harm.

But it hadn't.

Calvin's body still bore plenty of scars and bruises from the many times God hadn't saved him from his father's anger or their mother's neglect.

From the time he'd reached eleven, Calvin had only been able to think about leaving Horse Cave. He couldn't wait to get far away from their dysfunctional parents. From their house that smelled like stale cigarettes and dust. From their slow-paced, backward way of life.

Not Mark. No matter how many times Calvin had talked to him about leaving together, even going as far as to list all the reasons why they should, his older brother had never agreed.

Calvin still remembered the day he'd cut his hair short, bought jeans and a pale blue T-shirt with the University of Kentucky insignia on it, and stared at himself in the mirror.

He'd looked different. In the new clothes, he'd felt different, too. Better. Almost taller. Definitely prouder.

Actually, he'd suddenly felt like he'd at last become the person he was meant to be. He'd felt like he'd suddenly had options. He could now be anyone he wanted. He could do things that had been forbidden. He could talk to people he wasn't supposed to.

He'd known then that whatever happened, his life could only get better. But instead of supporting his decision, Mark had yelled at him.

Said he was being stupid. Talked about how dangerous life was in the outside world. Like it wasn't dangerous in their own living room.

Being neglected and emotionally abused by two unhappy people had been awful. Going hungry and being cold in the winter had been miserable. Never knowing if their parents were going to be sober or drunk or high had been difficult, too.

But having a brother who refused to admit that their life was an essential tragedy had been painful as well. Calvin had needed him. But instead of getting support, Mark had only made excuses for their parents' actions.

He'd gotten so frustrated with him. Calvin wished that *he* was the older brother, that he'd have been able to shake Mark. To shake him so he would finally see reason.

Instead, all he'd ever gotten from Mark was another lecture.

It had been a difficult decision to come back to Horse Cave, but once he discovered that their father had died, he knew he no longer had anything to fear. Since then, he'd been driving through every couple of weeks, trying to come to terms with his past.

When he realized that Mark had moved in, he knew he had to do something. That house was half his, and he intended to make sure he got what was coming to him.

After looking around the place while Mark was out, he'd felt even more sure that he had made the right decision. The house was in better shape than he remembered. He was going to be able to get the money he needed out of it.

But now everything was messed up.

Finally, he made the decision to show himself to Mark but was unable to find him. It had never occurred to him that he'd still be going to church.

So he'd waited. But when Mark didn't return home around noon, he'd gone looking for him. It was lucky that he'd run into Lora. She'd been only too happy to tell him that she'd seen Mark walking with Waneta toward her house.

So he'd stood outside and waited. Waited to be noticed.

When Mark met his gaze, Calvin almost felt like crying. After all these years, he was at last seeing the brother he'd depended on and had looked up to. Well, who he'd looked up to until it had become apparent that he wasn't ever going to put Calvin's needs first.

But what did Mark do?

He turned around and ignored him. Just like he didn't matter. Just like he wasn't worth anything.

Just like he'd done all those years ago.

Obviously, it was time to make a new plan. Reuniting with Mark and working together to put the house up for sale wasn't going to happen now.

Anger at the situation sliced through his very being. Why was life so hard? Why was it all so unfair?

Turning down the street, he walked back to his motorcycle. It was a late model Harley Dyna. It was banged up and more than a little scratched and worn, which was why he'd been able to afford it. It ran like a champ, though. Every time it roared to life, it gave him pleasure. It was a fitting symbol of how far his life had come from these quiet hills in central Kentucky.

Rubbing his hand along the fender, he felt a small sense of peace overtake him. Tonight, he would leave, head back to the cheap hotel he'd spied on the outskirts of Bowling Green, and figure things out. But first he decided to visit Lora again. He needed to be around someone who was just as out of place in Horse Cave as he was.

"What's wrong, Calvin?" Lora called out from her front porch. "And where's Mark? I thought you'd be all smiles right about now."

Turning, he took her in. Today, she had her hair up in some kind of complicated braid. Her black eyeliner made her blue eyes stand out; and her plain white tank top and snug low-riding jeans were no doubt causing most men in the area to give her a second glance.

But what drew him to her the most was the air of hope that continually surrounded her. He didn't understand it; she'd had as hard of a childhood as he had. She should seem a lot harder. Tougher.

Instead, it always seemed as if she was waiting for something good that was just around the corner. It was going to be a hard day when she realized that there wasn't anything like that.

Walking toward her, he smirked. He was hurting inside, but she didn't need to know that.

Watching him intently, she tilted her head to one side. "What happened?" In a rush she asked, "Oh! Did you not find the Cains' house? It's the one with the black door and the stone—"

There it was again. That optimism that she clung to. Feeling almost like he was letting her down, he cut her off. "No, I found it."

"Then, what's wrong? Why aren't you with him?" Before he could answer, she shot off another rapid question. "Oh. Were they not back from church yet?" The corners of her mouth turned up. "You know how some of those old folks are. They never want to leave . . ."

"They were there." Now that he'd answered her question, Calvin was tempted to turn around. Ignore all of her questions. Ride his Dyna, find a place to hole up for the night. He needed some time to figure out what to do next. If Mark was going to pretend he didn't exist and actually was planning to live in the house instead of selling it, then he was going to have to think of some way to encourage him to leave. He had no choice. He needed his half of the money from the sale of the house.

But as Lora continued to watch him, he was tempted to change his plans for the night. She was staring at him like he counted. She was looking at him in the exact opposite way that his own brother had stared at him. Lora was looking at him like she was sure he had something important to say.

He didn't know if he did or not. But he knew he liked her thinking that he did. He stepped forward.

If he couldn't count on his own brother, then he was going to need an ally in Hart County. While Lora continued to watch him, he walked up the steps of her front porch.

She stood there. Her lightly tanned arms crossed over that white tank, the toes of one of her bare feet curling against the beat-up wood floor.

When he didn't say anything for a couple more seconds, she raised her eyebrows. "Are you gonna tell me what happened, or are we just gonna stare at each other all afternoon?"

"They were back from church. All of them were," he said at last. "And Mark was there. I saw him standing on their front porch with Waneta."

"So, what happened? What did he say when he saw you? Did he run down to say hi?" Smiling, she said, "I bet he gave you a hug. Mark always used to do things like that."

He had. Mark had hugged him when he got hurt and scraped his knees. When they'd had no food in the house. When he'd had bad dreams at night. "No, we didn't hug."

"Well then, what happened?" Her eyes widened as she snapped her fingers. "Oh no. Did y'all already get in an argument? If you did, I bet he'll come around. Mark always put up with whatever you dished out. Ain't so?"

Her Kentucky accent, mixed in with such a typical Amish phrase, almost made him smile. "What if I told you that I don't want to talk about it?"

Disappointment flared in her expression, but she tamped it down. "Then I'd say that you don't have to."

"You mean that, don't you?"

"Yeah," she said quietly. "If you don't want to talk about something bad, then I'm the last person who's going to try to make you change your mind. I don't like to talk about my bad, either. I'll see you later."

Lora was expecting him to turn around and leave. But he was starting to think riding an hour away sounded like a lot of trouble, especially when he was going to need to come right back tomorrow. "Maybe I don't want to leave right now."

As if she sensed a new tension brewing between them, she gestured to the pair of metal chairs behind them. "If you don't have anywhere else to go, want to hang out with me for a while?"

He pushed off from the column he was leaning against but didn't sit down. "What do you have in mind?"

Her body tensed. "Nothing. I thought we could just talk or something."

"I could do that . . . if you have something to drink. Got anything?"

"I got a couple of cans of beer."

Just as she moved to the door, he added, "You got anything else?" She was pretty, but if he was going to be dealing with his brother ignoring him, he was going to need a whole lot more than just a couple of cans of beer to get him through the night.

She frowned. "There might be an old bottle of tequila. I gotta check. I don't drink much anymore."

"Good thing I have some weed, then. You up for that?"

Lora shrugged. "Maybe."

"Maybe?"

"I haven't done that in a while, either." She stared at him closely. "You're upset about Mark, aren't you?"

"Not really," he said, though she spied some hurt in his eyes. "What's wrong with you? You don't look real happy to see me."

"Nothing's wrong. I just didn't plan on spending my afternoon like this."

"What did you plan on doing?" He smirked. "Bible study?"

After a short pause, she opened her screened door. "Of course not."

"Then what's the problem? I mean, it ain't like you've got any other friends coming over, right?"

A new shadow filled her gaze. "Right. Come on in and I'll show you around."

Calvin had no interest in seeing her house. All he wanted to do was forget things for a while. But since Lora was looking like she wanted to talk, not just hang out, he shrugged. "Yeah, sure. Show me around, Lora. Can't wait."

When Lora closed the door shut behind them and locked it, effectively shielding them from the rest of the world, Calvin Fisher finally relaxed.

This wasn't what he'd planned to do today, but it was better than hurting.

It was better than a lot of things he'd done.

# CHAPTER 11

*Monday, August 8*

This is going to be a nice change, ain't so?" Waneta asked Mark when he joined her at the outside checkout stand, just in front of the row of four greenhouses at Blooms and Berries. "I'm glad Mr. Lehmann asked us to work out here together. Usually, I man the cash register while you stock and carry."

Mark grinned. "I'm pleased about it, too, though also worried that you might get sick of me. I'm such a talker, you know."

She playfully nodded, since there was no doubt which one of them was the real conversationalist. "I might need to ask for earplugs or something so I can hear myself think."

"I'll try not to irritate you for a couple hours yet."

"I think you might be irritating me right now," she said with a wink. Then, realizing how mean that sounded, she said quickly, "You know I'm only joking, right?"

"Of course. You wouldn't hurt a fly on purpose." Looking pleased, he added, "I'm glad that you feel you can joke around with me now. It's fun."

"I think so, too." Actually, she was finding that spending time with Mark was always nice. They were becoming good friends. It was a pleasant surprise.

And, if she sometimes thought of him in some way other than just as a friend . . . well, he hopefully would never find out.

As Mark watched still more people park in the lot, he said, "Have you worked many of Henry's sidewalk sales?"

"Oh, *jah*. At least five or six. Mr. Lehmann holds two a year."

"What can you tell me about them?"

Thinking about the crowds of people that seemed to come in waves, each demanding seedlings as quickly as possible, she murmured, "Just be prepared. They're really popular and sometimes people ask for more than you can give."

"So I need to be prepared to let them down easily."

"*Nee*, you need to be prepared to be firm. Mr. Lehmann has a limit of no more than seven seedlings per person. Make all the customers stick to that."

"I'll do my best."

She almost giggled. Mark Fisher was a formidable presence. She might be becoming more comfortable around him, but that wasn't exactly the case with everyone in the county. She'd noticed at church on Sunday that while people were more cordial, they definitely were watching him with distant expressions. They still didn't completely trust him.

That made her think that people weren't going to argue with him.

Of course, everyone might not want to even come up to

the counter if he was there. And that could be a problem. Mr. Lehmann would lose business.

And how would Mark react to that? Not very well, she guessed. Maybe even worse than not well. Maybe he would even get really angry.

Then what would she do?

"Waneta?"

"I'm sorry. My mind drifted off." Pasting on a reassuring smile, she said, "Mark, please, don't worry about a thing. Everyone from all over Hart County comes for plantings and seeds. It makes the day go by fast."

"I can handle that. Thanks for letting me know what to expect."

Realizing that he didn't look all that happy, whether it was because of the change in routine or for some other reason, Neeta felt some of her earlier exuberance and optimism dim. "Do you want to work the register or bag?"

"It don't matter to me, Waneta."

"Why do you always call me by my full name?"

"I like it."

"That's the reason?"

"It's a good one, don't you think?"

"I suppose." She was starting to feel even more and more confused. "Though, I prefer *Neeta*. Hardly anyone calls me Waneta."

"I'll be different, then."

She smiled weakly. *"Jah."*

"You ready?" Mr. Lehmann called out. "I'm about to tell Ben to open the gates."

"We're ready," Mark answered.

*"Gut.* Off we go." Mr. Lehmann raised his voice as he

moved the little walkie-talkie close to his mouth. "Ben, open 'em up!"

Almost immediately, they heard cars pull forward in one gate and other folks walk through another gate that Ben had propped open.

Every person who strode forward seemed to have a mission in mind. They darted to and fro, inspecting seedlings and grabbing some of the small mini carts that Blooms and Berries kept for just this occasion. One of Mr. Lehmann's older employees was walking around and helping folks make decisions.

Less than five minutes later, they had their first customers at the counter. Waneta felt her stomach clench, half waiting for the two Mennonite women to refuse Mark's assistance.

But they purchased their items easily and even chatted with Mark while doing it.

Once they turned away with cheery waves, Mark leaned toward her. "It's going to be okay, Waneta. No one is going to be mean. But even if they are, I'll be able to handle it."

"You shouldn't have to, though. It ain't right."

"It isn't something that I can't handle. Besides, I knew what it would be like when I moved back here. I knew some people would have a real hard time with me being here."

"I just want to kick some people in the shin when they are rude to you, though. We are supposed to forgive . . . and there isn't even anything to forgive. You were proven innocent."

Mark looked like he was going to say something more, but two men and a pair of women walked up.

And so it began.

For the next several hours, she and Mark rang people up, bagged or boxed their purchases, and helped customers.

Mr. Lehmann offered to take their places at the counter so each could take a lunch, but by mutual agreement, neither wanted to leave the other.

The most Waneta was willing to do was run to take a quick bathroom and water break.

By three o'clock, the nursery was like a ghost town. Everyone who had wanted something specific had gotten what they'd wanted.

"You two did a real good job," Mr. Lehmann said. "You didn't even take any breaks, either. I'm obliged."

"I was glad to help, Henry," Mark said. "Now, how about you go home for the day? I can clean everything up."

"That ain't necessary."

"You hired me so you wouldn't have to work so hard. Let me help you."

"I'll stay and help, too, Mr. Lehmann," Waneta said with a smile. "We've got this."

But instead of agreeing, their boss fidgeted. "I'm afraid you are needed somewhere else, son." After a pause, he gestured toward the empty parking lot. "The sheriff just called me on my cell phone. He's on his way over. He . . . well, he wants to talk to you."

Mark nodded, but his face had become perfectly blank.

Waneta knew he was taken aback. She was, too. "Why does Sheriff Brewer need to speak with him?" she asked. "He's been working here beside me the whole time."

"I know, Neeta."

"Then what does he want?"

"Don't worry," Mark murmured. "I'll be okay."

"You keep saying that, but I don't believe it. And now look—the sheriff is bothering you for no reason."

"Settle down, Waneta," Mr. Lehmann said. "No one is in trouble. You are jumping to conclusions."

Realizing he was right, she nodded.

"It looks like he just arrived. What do you think I should do? Wait here or go over to meet him?" Mark asked.

Mr. Lehmann sighed. "Looks like he made the decision. He's walking over toward us right now."

Looking resigned, Mark started walking. "I'll meet him halfway."

"I'm sure it will go all right," Mr. Lehmann said.

Waneta felt so helpless. Mark looked like he had the weight of the world on his shoulders and didn't expect anyone to lend a hand. "I'll wait for you after we clean up," she called out.

"Don't," he said, his voice flat. "There's no telling how long this will take."

"I don't mind waiting." Trying to sound encouraging, she said, "Why, I bet the sheriff just has a question about your house or something."

But instead of seeming to make him feel better, he flinched. "I don't want you to wait, Waneta. No offense, but I'd rather not be talking to the sheriff while you are staring at us from across the way."

She was kind of offended. "I'm not going to just stand around and stare at you."

"Please, just help Henry clean up and then go on home."

"I can handle anything, and I want to help. To be there for you. I know I'm only a small-town girl who has been pretty sheltered, but I am stronger than I look."

He didn't hear her. He'd already walked away. Watching his back, she felt so hurt. After everything she'd been doing, how could Mark still not trust her?

"Listen to him, child," Mr. Lehmann said.

"But I don't want him to feel so alone. He doesn't have to tackle everything all by himself."

"Let him have some pride, Waneta," he whispered.

"There's nothing wrong with trying to help a friend," she countered. "And I am his friend."

"I'm glad you are. I can tell that he's thankful for it, too. But getting in the middle of this won't help him. He's going to be embarrassed if you discover whatever the sheriff is going to talk to him about."

"I'm not going to judge him," she blurted.

Looking over her shoulder, it was evident that Mark was in a deep, serious conversation with the sheriff. Both of their stances were rigid and whatever they were talking about looked intense. "Something bad must have happened," she whispered. "I wonder what Sheriff Brewer is telling him." A new idea struck her then. "Or, do you think he's talking to Mark about his past again?"

Mr. Lehmann looked concerned. "Waneta, here's the thing. Everyone needs to keep some secrets to themselves. He doesn't want you knowing about his past. He doesn't want you knowing about the sheriff talking to him. Let it go."

Not wanting to go against both Mark's and her boss's instructions, Waneta stepped backward. "If that's the way you feel, I think I had better just go on home."

His expression gentled. "Good, child. Yes, go home, and don't you worry about Mark none. Everything will turn out in due time."

Waneta supposed Mr. Lehmann had wanted to make her feel better with his words. But all they did was leave her

feeling empty, like she had only been half filled with information. What, exactly, did he mean "in due time"? Was he
thinking of a week? A month? Years?

Though of course he could have no idea what the future
held for them, she had to admit that she was uneasy about
how nebulous it was. She needed something to hold on to.

Turning, she grabbed her purse and the lunch she'd never
eaten and walked as quickly as she could toward the main
gates. The pace she was going at made her perspire, making
the dark-pink dress she was wearing stick to her back.

When she was just a few feet away, she couldn't help herself and looked over at Mark and Sheriff Brewer one last
time. They were in deep discussion. Mark did not look happy
and the sheriff looked serious and grim.

While it didn't seem as if Mark was in trouble, it was evident that something serious had happened that affected him.

Taking a peek at Mark again, she saw him flinch. His expression turned from serious to ravaged. He was in pain.

Something awful had happened. But from the way he'd
treated her questions, she feared that he'd never share it
with her.

If that was the case, it left her feeling like her heart was
breaking. Because how could she ever believe in a man who
kept so much of his life closed to himself?

How could she ever have a real relationship with Mark if
he refused to talk about whole parts of his life? If he didn't
trust her to support him, she wondered if there would be
other situations in the future that he might try to keep hidden from her.

She hoped and prayed she was wrong. That she was overreacting and that her inexperience in relationships was making her doubt things.

But if she was right? Well, she was going to have to resign herself to only being his friend. She couldn't give her heart to a man who was so wary.

At least, she didn't think she could.

# CHAPTER 12

*Monday, August 8*

Sheriff Brewer looked uncomfortable, shifting from one foot to the other. He pulled out a white handkerchief from a back pocket and mopped his brow. Then, at last, he continued. "So that is the reason I wanted to talk to you about this, Mark."

"Because you saw my brother, and you know that he's gotten into some trouble in the past."

"It is more than just a bit of trouble. He assaulted Lora Weaver last night before taking off."

Mark clenched his hands as shame coursed through him. Once again he was getting pulled into a family member's crimes and mistakes and he was feeling compelled to fix them. But how could he fix this?

"Is Lora going to be all right?" he asked quietly.

"I think so. She didn't want any medical attention. My deputy told me that she looks bad but should recover in a day or two."

"I am sorry that she got hurt. I hate that Calvin was the

cause of it, too," he said haltingly. "I don't know what to say. I didn't even know they were still friends."

"I don't know what their relationship is. All I do know is that he was at her house partying the other night."

"Partying?"

Sheriff Brewer looked at his notes. "When Deputy Beck entered Lora's house, it was obvious that she and Calvin had been smoking pot. The place was also littered with beer cans, too."

"I'm not saying that what they were doing was right, but it kind of sounds like you are pretty upset about something that two people over twenty-one are doing. Smoking marijuana is a pretty small crime, compared to some other things that have been going on around here."

"I agree. But it is still a crime. Assaulting her is a crime as well."

"Yes. Yes, of course."

The sheriff continued. "Deputy Beck searched the house. Lora was pretty emphatic that they weren't her drugs. That Calvin had brought them to her."

"I'm sorry to hear this. I haven't talked to him in years. I've heard rumors that he's gotten into some trouble, but I don't know the extent of it."

Sheriff Brewer scanned his notes again. "Hmm. Looks like Calvin has been arrested several times for drug and alcohol charges in Ohio, Kentucky, and Indiana." Looking at his phone he murmured, "Though it seems he's been questioned about some other matters."

Other matters. Mark felt his stomach sink.

Calvin had made a mess of his life. It was also obvious that he was planning to change his ways. Not from what he'd seen from a distance, at least. Feeling irritated and angry at the whole situation, Mark wondered about the timing of it all.

Why had Calvin decided to show up barely two weeks after he'd arrived back in Horse Cave? It wasn't like they had anything to do with each other. Not in years.

And what had he been doing with Lora Weaver? Mark had been under the impression that she was working at Bill's Diner and trying to get her life back on track. Was that rumor wrong, too?

But even that didn't explain why Sheriff Brewer had taken it upon himself to come talk to Mark about it in the middle of his workday. In front of half the town. It was almost like he had done it on purpose in order to sabotage all of Mark's efforts to fit in and be accepted in the community.

The worst of it was that Waneta had watched with worry in her eyes. It felt like all the progress they'd made had been erased and they were back where they'd started.

He hated that. He resented Calvin's interference, too. And the sheriff's visit to his place of work. Lashing out, he said, "You know I wasn't with Lora and Calvin, Sheriff. I wasn't at her house doing drugs. And as much as it pains me to say this, what Calvin does is no business of mine. I ain't my brother's keeper."

Sheriff Brewer nodded easily, like he completely understood. And, unfortunately, like he had nothing but time on his hands. After taking care to fold his handkerchief neatly again, he said, "Any idea why he's back here?"

"None. Like I said, I haven't talked to him in years." Unable to stop himself, he glanced over toward Waneta. She wasn't looking his way anymore. Instead, she was in deep conversation with Henry. It looked serious. "You already know this.

We talked at length about my family when you took me in for questioning for Bethany two years ago."

"People change. I thought maybe he had."

"If he did, he didn't tell me. I have not seen him."

"At all?"

That moment flashed back in his mind. Of sitting on Waneta's porch. Of her quietly flirting with him. Then, of him glancing up and seeing Calvin staring at him.

And Calvin staring at Waneta.

It had taken everything he'd had to not go over to Calvin and yell at him to go away.

He'd kept a tight lid on his self-control. If he hadn't, he would have opened himself to being hurt again—allowing himself hope that Calvin would want to see him again; that his brother might say he missed him. Or that he wanted to get to know him again.

Or that he'd wanted to say he was sorry for the things he'd done.

But Mark's heart, which had been stomped on too many times, guided him that day.

"I did see him recently. Yesterday. However, we didn't talk."

Sheriff Brewer's expression sharpened. "What happened?"

"I saw him from a distance." Haltingly, he added, "I think he wanted me to stop what I was doing and rush over to talk to him."

"But you didn't?"

Mark shook his head. "I ignored him. Turned away. The next time I looked up, he was gone." That was almost the truth, anyway.

"Where were you, if you don't mind me asking?"

Sheriff Brewer was a master at asking questions in that

slow, Kentucky drawl. He could look humble and sleepy while asking difficult and uncomfortable questions. Against his will, Mark felt his skin start prickling and his upper back start sweating.

"I was at Waneta Cain's *haus*," he said. Not because he wanted to share where he was, but because he knew he had no choice. Sheriff Brewer would find out anyhow.

"So she could vouch for you?"

"Vouch for what? I went to church on Sunday morning, then spent several hours with Waneta and her family that afternoon."

"And after that?"

"After that, I didn't do anything special. I just went home."

"Could Waneta or her parents vouch for seeing him as well?"

This was turning painful. So uncomfortable, he was wondering if he should be asking if he needed a lawyer. "I don't think any of them saw him," Mark said slowly. "Calvin was lurking near a cove of trees. He didn't want to be seen." Well, not by anyone but him.

Sheriff Brewer's expression brightened. "Lurking, you say?"

"Like I just said, Calvin didn't want to be seen by Waneta or her parents," Mark said, each word now tinged with frustration. "Only by me."

"Why do you think that is?" asked the sheriff.

"I don't know." Feeling even more frustrated, he said, "Look, I don't understand why you are asking me all of these questions or why you've chosen to talk to me here. Do you not trust me? Are you trying to make sure everyone here doesn't forget about my past?"

"None of those things." After the sheriff wiped his brow

again, he stuffed the white handkerchief in a back pocket. "I was hoping for your help, that's all . . .

"I would help if I could. I haven't kept up with Lora or Calvin, but even I had heard that she'd changed. The things you are saying are disturbing."

"I think so, too. She swore up and down that the drugs were his. If that's the truth, then I want to talk to him."

"Which is the real reason you are here," Mark said.

"I am. Drugs are a bad enough problem in Hart County without someone new coming in and bringing more. If he's bringing Lora pot, he could be bringing much worse to other people in the county. I aim to put a stop to it."

Mark swallowed. This conversation was getting worse and worse. Now he was not only worried about his reputation, but he was concerned about his brother . . . and how Calvin would feel if Mark had to be the one to catch him and bring him in. "If I see him, I'll let you know."

Sheriff Brewer visibly relaxed. "Thank you. I'm sorry to come here to see you, but I honestly didn't think you'd have a problem with it. I only wanted some answers as quickly as possible."

"So, you still believe I am innocent of Bethany's assault?"

The sheriff looked at him curiously. "Of course I do. I wouldn't have let you go if I wasn't a hundred percent sure you had nothing to do with it, Mark. I don't *believe* you are innocent, I *know* you are." After glancing in Henry's direction and tipping his hat, he said, "I came here to get answers. That's all."

Mark looked in the man's eyes and saw complete honesty there. The sheriff was telling the truth and asking him for help. And because of that, he knew what he needed to do. "I'll help you if I can. Calvin may be my brother by birth, but we don't mean much to each other anymore," he said, though he feared that wasn't the truth. "I want to stay here. I care about this community, too. I aim to settle in, marry one day and have children here. I don't want it to be a place where I'm worried about my brother hitting women or peddling drugs."

"I appreciate it." After handing him his card, he said, "Take this and call me if you find out anything. Anything at all."

"Yeah. Sure," Mark said.

After Mark stood and watched the sheriff's vehicle disappear, he walked back to Henry, who was standing alone at the checkout counter. "I'm sorry about that."

"Everything all right?" Henry asked.

"*Jah.*" He was tempted to say something more, but how could he? Waneta was just beginning to trust him. If he did say more, and Henry inadvertently told Waneta that Mark had seen Calvin creeping around her property, watching her and him, it would ruin every bit of the trust he'd gained from her over the last week.

"Though it ain't my business, I hope Sheriff Brewer was being fair with ya."

"He was." Clearing his throat, Mark added, "He had some questions about my brother."

"Calvin?"

"*Jah.* He fears Calvin has returned to Hart County."

Henry's brows furrowed. "*Fears* seems like a pretty strong word to describe a brother's return."

"It's fitting, though. I'm afraid he hasn't changed much over the years."

Henry's gaze sharpened. "You sound as if you know that for a fact. Do you?"

"*Nee.* I am only saying that because of what the sheriff said." That sense of unease he'd experienced earlier returned. Was he now being too cautious? Was he now judging Calvin based on a couple of rumors . . . just like so many people in the area judged him?

Henry's expression didn't smooth, but Mark didn't have any more time to worry about that because several customers came up needing help all at the same time.

Later, as he rang up one customer's seedlings and another's fruits and vegetables, Henry chatting with each one as if they were long-lost friends, Mark began to feel like he'd just made a terrible mistake.

Unfortunately, he wasn't sure who he'd just made that mistake with. Was it with the sheriff, Henry, or Waneta?

Or, maybe, it was with his brother. What if Calvin had changed after all?

What if he'd come to find him and had hoped that Mark would help him in some way? What if he hadn't wanted a thing, he'd only wanted to reconnect and Mark had turned his back on him? And then, feeling bad because his brother hadn't given him the time of day, Calvin had sought Lora Weaver out?

A slow line of dread filled him at the thought. Here, he'd been so upset and felt betrayed because he'd wanted the community to give him another shot. To give him a chance to prove that he was worth more than they'd ever believed him to be. What if he had done the very same thing to his little brother?

He hoped that wasn't the case. But if it was, he feared he had just made a terrible mistake that he was going to be paying for in the days and weeks to come.

# CHAPTER 13

*Monday Evening*

I don't understand why you think we need to talk again," Lora said as she led Sheriff Brewer and Deputy Beck to the screened porch located at the back of her house. "I haven't done anything wrong."

"Other than create a public disturbance and smoke pot?" Sheriff Brewer asked with more than a small amount of sarcasm in his tone.

Glad her back was to him, Lora grimaced. She hated that she'd messed up yet again. Though she now lived the majority of her days in a way she was proud of, she still sometimes slipped. She certainly had Sunday night.

That said, she wasn't sure why her actions necessitated not one but two visits from the sheriff. It seemed a little excessive. Because of that, she was worried. They knew something she didn't, putting her at a disadvantage.

But showing weakness wasn't going to help anything. It hadn't when she was a little girl, and it hadn't when she'd been living on her own in northern Kentucky. Her only option was to brazen it out. Otherwise, these men would continue to view her as weak and maybe even try to take advantage of her.

As they entered the cool and comfortable screened porch, she looked over her shoulder at them. "First of all, we already discussed this. I've apologized for causing a disturbance. And the pot is gone. You know that." Focusing on the deputy, she hardened her voice. "You walked through the whole place even though I said several times that I didn't have any in the house. After I told you again and again that it wasn't mine."

"You're right. The house was clear," the deputy murmured.

Honestly, the deputy sounded as if he had suspected there was a meth lab down in the basement. Huh. It seemed he thought even less of her than she'd imagined. She sighed. "You know what? If we were in Washington State or Colorado, a Baggie of pot wouldn't be a concern."

"But we aren't there, are we?" Deputy Beck asked.

Wincing, she closed her eyes. For some reason, hearing the derision in the deputy's voice hurt even worse than hearing it from the sheriff.

Probably because Deputy Eddie Beck looked so composed and perfect. He had a lanky build and tanned arms. His hair was bleached from the sun. She remembered hearing something at the diner about him being really outdoorsy. He liked to camp and hike, and fish and ski. He had clear light-green eyes and an easy smile. All the girls at Bill's fanned themselves when they saw him walk inside. He smiled and charmed them all. Not her, though.

No, he wasn't smiling at all. Instead, he was examining her in a professional way. Like she was a witness to a crime. Or a piece of evidence he needed to transport to the lab.

He was eyeing her exactly the way he had late last night, like she was simply one more person he had to talk to as part of his job.

Seeing his expression made her squirm inside. All of her bad decisions from over the last few years came rushing back. She'd thought the recent changes she'd made might have balanced them out, but they didn't.

Not at all. At least not to him. Had she come this far just to be viewed as a loser girl all over again? After gesturing for them to have a seat on one of the brightly colored chairs that her sister Amanda and her husband had purchased before moving away, she decided to throw out all her ideas of acting cool and aloof.

She was too scared and too nervous to put on an act. She also had too much to lose. She needed to be as open and honest with the sheriff and his deputy as she possibly could.

Once she also sat down in the comfy chair, she said, "What has happened? Did something else happen that I haven't heard about?"

"We'll talk about that, Lora. But first, how are you feeling?" Sheriff Brewer asked.

She shrugged. "All right."

"Your bruises look worse," Deputy Beck murmured. "Are you in pain?"

She was hurting, but it wasn't anything she couldn't handle. She pressed a palm to her bruised and swollen cheek. "I'm all right."

Shifting, he pulled out his phone. "Want me to find you a doctor? I can take you."

Lora was shocked. He was acting as if he cared about her. They both were. "I don't need a doctor. Like I told you last night, my face hurts, but my pride hurts worse."

The deputy stiffened. "Your pride? Why? Are you embarrassed?"

"Well, yes."

"You have nothing to be embarrassed about. Calvin Fisher is at fault. Only him. *Not you*," he added with emphasis. "He shouldn't have raised a hand to you. There is no scenario where that is okay."

He sounded so sure, so emphatic, she wasn't certain how to respond. Clearing her throat, she said, "Is that the reason y'all stopped by? Because you were interested to see how I was feeling?"

"No," Deputy Beck said.

After exchanging a look with each other, Sheriff Brewer spoke. "Lora, here's the deal. We know you had Calvin over here. We know you had your own little party. We know you fought and he hit you. And we know he left soon after." His voice hardened. "But what we don't know is where he is now."

"Like I told you last night, I don't know where Calvin is either."

"You positive about that?" Deputy Beck asked.

She hated this so much. Had they only pretended to care so she'd lower her guard? "I'm very positive." When his expression didn't change, she threw the remains of her composure on the floor. "Deputy Beck, it's obvious that you don't think very highly of me. I know we have completely different backgrounds. I know I've made a lot of mistakes in my life. I know I've even done things you would never even think about doing. But that doesn't make me a liar."

"I didn't say you were."

"It's pretty obvious that you don't believe me."

"It's not that I don't believe you, it's that I don't know what to believe." He flushed. "Cases like this are hard for me. I get too emotionally involved. I can't help it, though. I hate men who beat up girls."

"Even girls like me?" she whispered. Because she had heard it before. After she'd run away, she'd found herself in a whole lot of bad areas, surrounded by lots of people who were used to breaking rules. She'd gotten hurt before. Once, even bad enough to have to go to the emergency room.

But even there, the orderlies and nurses seemed to judge her. They'd stopped short of saying she got what she deserved, but they insinuated it.

Looking even more frustrated, the deputy sighed. "Lora—may I call you that?" When she nodded, he continued. "What I think about you has no bearing on us trying to do our job."

"Actually, I think it has everything to do with that. Everyone here in Horse Cave only sees me as the girl from the bad home who never made anything of herself."

"I'm not from here. I don't know about your past and I don't—"

She cut him off. "But I am trying to get better," she blurted, even though it was probably way more than either of the men cared about. "I got my GED. I even got some counseling when I lived up near Covington. So, even though I'm still making mistakes, I'm better than I was."

"Lora," Sheriff Brewer said slowly, "about last night—"

"I don't know why I messed up so badly. I guess I was feeling so bad about myself that I didn't feel like arguing when Calvin wanted to get high."

And just like that, she felt stupid all over again. Here she'd been asking them to see her as someone worthy of respect, as a woman who was working hard to turn her life around, but the proof was in her actions.

"So you joined him."

"Yeah, I did. But that doesn't mean I'm going to do that tonight or tomorrow or next week. I want to change." Thinking she sounded weak, Lora hardened her tone. "No, *I will change.*"

"Lora," Sheriff Brewer began, "you aren't in trouble. We came here to talk about Calvin."

"And I told you that I don't know where he is, Sheriff Brewer. Until he showed up in town a few days ago, I hadn't seen him in years. When he showed up, I was feeling kind of down. Though I knew better, I invited him in. It was a big mistake. Before long, we'd had too much to drink and started arguing about stupid things."

"Like what?"

"Like my sisters," she said impatiently. "Like his brother, Mark. Like a volleyball game we'd played in sixth grade. Then, when it was more than obvious that we don't have anything in common, that I don't even like him, I told him to leave." Releasing a ragged sigh, she tried to regain her composure. "And that is when he hit me," she said quietly. "He hit me because he said I was putting him down. Maybe I was."

"If you see him again, will you let us know?" Sheriff Brewer asked.

"Sure."

As the men stood up, the sheriff's phone rang. "I've got to get this. Meet me at the station," he said to the deputy.

"Sure, Pat." Turning to Lora, Deputy Beck said quietly, "I

like my job. I really do. But I hate when I cause people to get so upset. Sorry about that."

*He* was apologizing? "It's all right. You are just doing what you have to do."

He nodded as they continued their short journey to the front door. "Hey, there's something else I've been meaning to ask you."

"What?"

"How come you never wait on me when I go to Bill's?"

Because he was too cute. Because she hated that she noticed that he was so cute. "Have I not waited on you? Huh. I thought I had."

"You haven't. I would have remembered."

"Ah."

"Next time I come in, if you are working, can I sit in your section?"

She was nodding before she even realized it. "Okay."

"Thanks." Smiling at her, he said, "I'm looking forward to having a regular conversation with you."

Smiling weakly, she opened the door. "I guess I'll see you at Bill's, then."

"Hope so." He smiled again, before walking to his vehicle.

Leaving her feeling more than a little tongue-tied and befuddled.

# CHAPTER 14

*Wednesday, August 10*

Two days had passed since Waneta watched Mark have an intense conversation with Sheriff Brewer; two days after Mark essentially informed her that his business was none of her concern. She wasn't going to lie—hearing those words had hurt.

She thought they were friends. After he'd come over and they'd spent hours playing cards together, she felt that they were becoming closer, that he was feeling the same spark that she was.

But it looked like she was wrong.

Yesterday, she'd tried to encourage Mark to reach out to her. She teased and cajoled. She smiled and reminded him of how nice it had been to have him at her home. She was willing to do just about anything to get him to gaze at her in that warm, trusting way again. But nothing seemed to work.

Actually, all her references seemed to make him even more distant.

Therefore, in an effort to shield her heart, she was step-

ping back. Maybe she'd been wrong about him. Maybe he
wasn't simply scarred from his childhood and being unjustly
questioned. Or, maybe, it was something simpler than that.
Maybe he simply didn't like her as much as she liked him.

All she did know was that she was tired of trying to convince Mark Fisher that she was worth his time and trust. It
was time to treat him as she would anyone else. Like a coworker. Nothing more, nothing less.

Ironically, her new attitude caught his attention on Tuesday. He seemed confused by it. More than once he tried to
talk to her about her sudden coolness toward him. He looked
hurt when she didn't immediately smile and act like they
were best friends— which just made her more irritated. Was
he playing a game with her?

She even briefly wondered if everyone else had been right
and she'd been wrong. What if he had beaten up Bethany
after all? What if he was capable of forming friendships, then
randomly breaking ties with the ease of breaking bread?

If so, then she'd been a fool.

Now, this morning, just as she was getting ready for work,
her parents decided to jump into the fray.

"When is Mark going to come over again?" Daed asked
when he'd joined her at the kitchen table. "Have you asked
him over for supper yet?"

"*Nee.*"

"Why ever not? We asked you to."

"I know, Daed." She sipped her coffee and pretended to be
concerned about her list in front of her of things to do.

But instead of taking the hint, Daed only frowned. "Waneta, I told you that we liked Mark. Mamm and me like him
a lot." Smiling slightly, he added, "The man was good com-

pany for me, too. He doesn't act as if my mind is as far gone as my body. Not everyone sees that, you know."

What could she say to that? She didn't want to hurt her father's feelings or his waning social life. But she had to guard her heart. "Daed, as a matter of fact . . . Mark and I realized that we don't have much to say to each other anymore."

"How can that be? You two talked like magpies on Sunday."

Picking up her pencil, she crossed off another item on her list. "Things change, Daed. I think we're simply going to be work friends for now."

Her mother frowned as she bustled around the kitchen. When she walked over to pour Waneta's glass of orange juice, she said, "Neeta, I watched the two of you playing cards on the front porch."

"Mamm, you were standing at the window?"

"I'm not going to apologize for caring. Not especially when I watched Mark smile at you." Her voice softened. "It was a sweet smile, daughter. A tender one. It was obvious that he didn't just want to be your friend. He wanted to be more than friends with you."

That reminder stung. But so did his change of heart. "Just because he wants something more doesn't mean I do. It takes two, you know."

"I agree. But it also takes a willingness to want to get to know someone better. Ain't so?" her mother asked as she fussed in front of the oven again. "Neeta, if you two got in a little argument, you need to stop being so stubborn and get over it."

"Mamm, just a week ago, you were gossiping about him."

"That is true, and I feel badly about that," she said as she fussed with the edge of her apron. "I've done a lot of praying. And I took Preacher Eli's sermon to heart."

"We both did," Daed added. "You should, too."

Waneta barely refrained from rolling her eyes. "I hear what you're saying, but I can't live my life according to Preacher Eli's wishes."

"You should, though. Mark is a good man," Daed said. "Give him another chance. He needs a person like you in his life."

"I did give him my friendship. It wasn't a good decision, though."

"Why not?" her mother called out as she fried bacon. "What happened?"

This was really too much of a conversation to have first thing in the morning. But the timing was as much her fault as anyone's. All week, she'd changed topics every time her parents brought up his name.

After taking a fortifying sip of juice, she said, "I think he has secrets, Mamm. A lot of secrets." *There.* That should give her parents an understanding about Mark.

But instead of looking concerned, her mother chuckled. "Well, of course he does."

"Don't you find that a bit of a red flag?"

"Not so much. If you already knew everything about him, you two wouldn't have anything to learn about each other."

She was talking as if they were already a couple. They were absolutely not. "I don't want to be in a relationship with a man whom I canna trust."

Her father frowned. "Something happened that you didn't tell us."

"You're right. Something did."

"Now would be a good time to share, child."

She knew that tone well. It was too ingrained in her not to respond accordingly. "On Monday, right toward the end of the sidewalk sale, Sheriff Brewer came to Blooms and Berries. He looked serious and asked to talk to Mark privately. And when I tried to talk to Mark about it, he pushed me away. He said there was nothing for me to worry about. That it was his business, not mine."

Silence met her statement.

She swallowed. It was too bad that she had to burst their bubble, but she supposed she couldn't shield them from distressing news all the time. "Now do you see why I need to keep my distance?"

"I can see how it must have been an awkward moment," Mamm said. "I bet poor Mark was embarrassed!"

Wait a minute. Poor Mark?

Shoving a plate in front of her, Mamm said, "Here. Have a pancake."

That pancake looked like it would sink to the bottom of her stomach like a rock. But she knew better than to refuse it. Picking up a fork, she cut off a bite-sized bit and popped it in her mouth.

"No syrup?"

"You know I don't like syrup, Mamm. But thank you for the breakfast." Dutifully, she ate another bite. It tasted like cardboard.

After refreshing Waneta's coffee, her mother sat down to watch her eat. "This is only my opinion, but I think you need to be more understanding of Mark's past."

"Mamm, I did everything I could. He's the one who is

keeping me at an arm's length. He doesn't want to be close to me."

"Take another bite, child."

Feeling like she was growing younger by the second, Waneta did as she was bid. Chewing slowly, she watched the second hand on the clock above the sink make its way around the dial. She had about five more minutes, then she was going to be able to leave.

And what a blessed relief that would be!

After sneaking a piece of bacon off her plate and eating half of it, her father spoke. "Dear, do you remember when I told you that I didn't learn English until I was in seventh grade?"

She set down her fork. "*Jah*. You said it was difficult."

"It was harder than that. I went from only speaking Amish to having to learn to both speak and write English. I was frustrated with myself and more than a little resentful with my best friend, Arnie."

"Why was that?"

"Arnie's parents had taught him and his sister English on their own, years before. Arnie and Mercy sailed through all the lessons while I struggled."

Forgetting about the time, Waneta watched her father. He didn't often share stories about his past. Especially stories like this, about times that he had been struggling.

Leaning back, his eyes clouded. "I would mess up spelling simple words and struggled with having the most basic of conversations. Arnie and Mercy corrected and teased me. All the time. Other kids heard and decided to tease me, too.

"Here I was, thirteen. Strong, already used to hard work

and a lot of responsibilities on the farm—but suddenly I was being made to feel stupid and weak." He shook his head. "I didn't like it."

Pushing the pancake away, Neeta rested her elbows on the table. "You weren't stupid, Daed. You just had to catch up."

"What I'm trying to tell ya is that my struggles almost ended my friendship with Arnie. He never did try to understand why I was struggling so much. Instead of helping me, he teased me about all my mistakes."

"I helped him, though," Mamm piped up.

"*Jah*, she did. That's one of the reasons I fell in love with her." While Mamm blushed like the schoolgirl she used to be, Daed looked a little sheepish. "Even after all this time, I guess I'm still a little upset about all that teasing."

At last, Waneta understood the point he'd been trying to make. "You think that I'm not being sympathetic enough about Mark's past."

"No one at his house taught him how to have good relationships, dear," Mamm said. "No one taught him how to love. Instead of growing up in a home where he felt safe and protected, he grew up with parents who treated him like a responsibility they never asked for."

"Then his mother took off," Daed added.

Mamm nodded. "Not long after, his brother left him, too."

"And then Mark was accused of that girl's assault and the whole community chose to believe the worst of him," Waneta said quietly.

"I'm sure he ain't an easy man to be around," her mother murmured. "But wouldn't you rather choose to think that he just needs someone to care enough about him to teach him about love and relationships?"

"You're making me feel awful."

"I don't want you to feel bad, child. But, well, maybe be more patient with him. He cares about you very much. I know he does."

Standing up, Neeta rinsed off her plate, then pulled out her cooler from the refrigerator. Once again, it was heavier than usual. There was obviously a lot of extra food in there. "How did you know I was sharing some of my food with Mark? Did he tell you?"

Joining her at the sink, her mother said, "I knew because I raised you, daughter. You would never let another person go hungry if you could help it."

Turning, she wrapped her arms around her mother's waist and hugged her tight. "*Danke*, Mamm. You are the best mother a girl could ever ask for. Daed, you are wonderful-*gut*, too."

While Daed laughed, her mother kissed her brow. "You are a good girl. Now you'd best go or Henry ain't going to be happy." Looking at the clock, she said, "You're running a bit behind this morning, you know."

"*Jah*. You are going to have to pedal a little faster than normal to make up for your dawdling this morning," Daed said.

As Waneta walked out the door, tote bag in one hand, loaded cooler in the other, she had to laugh. Her parents were wonderful, that was true. But they definitely weren't perfect.

None of them were.

Yet another thing to remember.

SHE HURRIED DOWN the road to Blooms and Berries, hoping Mr. Lehmann wasn't going to be too upset with her. Hopefully, Mark got there on time and took care of most of the usual morning chores.

The nursery was quiet when she opened the retail store's door. Both Mark and Mr. Lehmann were sipping coffee and talking quietly in front of the main counter. Henry looked a little listless while Mark's expression was shadowed.

This was mighty unusual. Most days when she arrived, Mr. Lehmann was already busy with some task and usually had a list of chores waiting for her the minute she arrived.

"Oh, here you are, Neeta," he said instead. "I guess it is just about that time to open."

A terrible sense of foreboding settled inside her. What had happened now? She glanced Mark's way. Hopefully, he wasn't involved in another crisis.

"What's wrong?" she asked, hoping and praying that Mark was all right . . . and that he wasn't about to stonewall her again.

Mark and Mr. Lehmann shared a look. "Please, tell me," she pleaded.

"All right, then," Mr. Lehmann said as he stepped closer. After a slight pause, he blurted, "Amy Miller was attacked last night."

After dropping her things on the ground, she rushed toward him. Like most other Amish girls in the area, Neeta had known Amy for years. "What do you mean?"

"June found Amy injured in her front yard last night," Mark said when their boss looked like he couldn't get the words out. "Someone tried to rape her. When she fought back and screamed, he hit her several times. He knocked her out. She was unconscious when June came upon her."

Tears pricked her eyes. "Is . . . Is she okay now?"

Mr. Lehmann nodded. "From what I understand, she's shaken up and scared, but okay. As okay as she can be after such an ordeal." Looking at her sadly, he continued. "She's home and resting now."

"Thank goodness."

Mr. Lehmann nodded. "*Jah.* For sure. Her beau, Abraham, is mighty upset, however. He's already been at the sheriff's office, demanding answers."

"Demanding answers? She doesn't know who did it?"

"*Nee.* It seems the man had a mask on his face. Of course, when she came to, he was nowhere to be found. June didn't see him, either," Mark supplied, his voice carefully flat.

Waneta shuddered. "I can't believe that this happened in our town. Ag—" She stopped herself from saying again.

"*Nee*, you can say it. It happened again." Mark's eyes looked so dark they were almost black. "I'm surprised you didn't hear about it on the way here."

"*Jah*, I thought maybe you had heard the news and decided to stay away," Mr. Lehmann blurted.

"I didn't hear anything. My mother made me pancakes and wanted to talk. Then, I was so worried about running late, I didn't talk to anyone the whole way here. How did you both hear about it?"

"I heard at the diner this morning," Mr. Lehmann said. "It's all anyone could talk about."

"Henry told me as soon as I got here," Mark added quietly. His tone was stiff and awkward sounding.

Usually, Waneta would have asked Mr. Lehmann if she could leave and go right to see Amy. But the pain in Mark's eyes was so fresh, she didn't have the heart to leave him. Amy had a lot of people who would be surrounding her with concern and love.

But Mark? He only had Mr. Lehmann and her.

"I'll be sure to stop by Amy's house tonight," she said, taking care to keep her voice light.

"You sure you're okay with waiting so long?" Mr. Lehmann asked. "If you don't feel like working, I understand."

"I'm sure. I think I need to work." Eager to change the topic, she said, "Mark, did you get the cashbox ready or turn on the solar fans?"

After visibly gathering himself together, he shook his head. "*Nee*, but I'll go do that right now."

"I'll work on the cashbox, then," she said, just as two cars pulled into the parking lot.

She needed to take her mother's advice to heart and imagine what it was like for Mark. He was expecting the worst from her. That was what his wary, blank look was all about.

It looked like she was going to have to start making sure that she surprised him with how different she could be.

# CHAPTER 15

*Wednesday, August 10*

Mark felt like he was in the middle of a recurring night-mare. From the moment Henry had told him about Amy Miller's attack, he'd been in a daze. His thoughts were hazy. Scattered.

The firm hold he usually had on his emotions felt tenuous. Worse, he felt like he was on the verge of losing everything good that he'd found since his return. That was difficult to swallow. Were all of his recent blessings truly that fragile? He hated the idea that everything he was so hopeful about could vanish in an instant, before he'd even gotten used to them.

He felt paranoid, too. The timing of Amy's attack seemed too coincidental. He couldn't shake the idea that it had some-thing to do with him, like someone had used his return as an excuse to hurt an innocent woman.

Just as quickly, shame consumed him. How could he even be fixating on how this event affected him and his life? An innocent girl had almost gotten raped, and he was upset with how the community was going to perceive *him*. When was he ever going to be able to shed his past and not view everything from a tainted perspective?

For most of the morning, Waneta worked in relative silence by his side. She darted wary glances his way in between customers, most of whom were Amish and seemed to be trying their best to ignore Mark. Though she wasn't acting completely distant, she did seem to be acting a little quieter around him.

He was relieved when Henry eventually asked him to work on one of the flower beds in front of the store. Henry liked to have the beds filled with seasonal annuals and switched them out a couple of times a year.

As he dug holes and added a row of yellow chrysanthemums, Mark turned his thoughts back to Waneta.

He wished they were someplace more private. Then he could ask her why she seemed so distant. He needed to know what was behind her silence.

Was she acting reserved because he'd been so aloof all week? Or was it something darker? Maybe she was afraid of him again. Maybe she was afraid of whoever had attacked Amy. Maybe she was simply upset about what had happened. Any of those options seemed like a good possibility.

If they were, he wanted to be there for her. Comfort her as best he could. He cared about her, as much as he cared about Henry.

"Excuse me?" a woman in running shorts and tank top called out from the door. "Could you help me with these begonias? I just bought four pallets and I need some help getting them to my Jeep."

"Of course." Jumping to his feet, he brushed off his hands, then turned to the laden cart. When she pointed to where her vehicle was, at the bottom of a sloping hill, he realized it would be easiest to simply carry each pallet there. "Lead the way and I'll follow," he said as he picked up a tray.

"Thank you so much." When they started walking to her car, she chatted excitedly about her gardening plans.

Back and forth they went, Mark silently carrying flowers and bags of potting soil while the woman talked about her yard, the barbecue they were about to host, and her hope that the deer wouldn't eat everything before the party.

"What do you think?" she asked when they were making the final trek to her SUV.

"I couldn't say," he murmured as he placed her last two bags of mulch on the floor of her backseat. "Deer do pretty much whatever they like. Ain't so?"

When he turned to smile at her, she pressed her hand to her lips. "I'm so sorry. I've been rattling on about flower beds and parties like you are interested."

"I don't mind you telling me about your plans at all." Actually, as far as he was concerned, the lady could talk about barbecues and begonias all day long. The easy conversation had been a nice break from the worries of the day.

And sure enough, when he went back to finish the bed he'd been working on, his thoughts returned to Amy and Waneta.

At two o'clock that afternoon, Mark was back inside the store and they finally had a break from the steady stream of customers.

Since Henry was in his office, Mark decided it was the

perfect time to finally break the ice. But just as he was attempting to figure out the best way to bring up the subject, Waneta placed one cool hand on his bare forearm.

He looked at her in surprise.

"Sorry if I startled you. I just . . . well, I wondered, now that a couple of hours have passed, how you were coping with the news?"

Her touch, combined with her concern for him, was a soothing balm. An unexpected one. "I don't know. My mind is kind of a muddle right now."

"I feel the same way. The whole thing is just so horrible. I'm so worried about Amy." She rubbed her hands over her arms. "Who do you think would have done such a terrible thing?"

"I couldn't begin to guess. I only know it wasn't me."

"Of course it wasn't."

She sounded so sure. So resolute. Relief filled him. "You really believe that, don't you?"

"*Jah*. Don't you want me to believe that?"

"Of course I do. I just thought, you know, with my history and all . . ."

"Your history has nothing to do with what happened to Amy."

Though he was still concerned that Amy's attack actually did have something to do with him, he nodded.

Looking pleased that he was listening to her, Waneta continued. "As a matter of fact, Mark, I think you need to learn that there are some people in the world who only want the best for you."

"Is that right?"

"Absolutely."

*And is one of those people you?* He ached to ask that.

But how could he? It sounded like he was fishing for compliments. Or maybe it just made him seem really desperate. He changed the topic. "Did you ride your bike or walk today?"

"I was going to ride, but I got such a late start, I decided to walk instead. The later I leave, the more traffic is on the roads."

"Okay. I am going to walk you home tonight. I'll come get you tomorrow morning, too."

"Mark, that ain't necessary."

"It is. If some man attacked your friend in her yard, then you certainly aren't safe walking by yourself."

Her expression softened. "All right, then. You're right. I will feel safer."

Mark sighed. He was glad she wasn't arguing about her safety. "Since it's so quiet now, why don't you go eat?"

"Don't you want to eat together?"

"Henry didn't offer that today, Waneta. And I don't want to ask him, either. He's just as rattled about Amy as we are."

"Oh. Well, just to let you know, I brought you some leftovers. Rather, my *mamm* packed you some."

"Maybe you could leave them for me?" he asked gently. "I'll fish them out when it's my turn."

She nodded, then after making him promise to call if he needed help, she walked into the storage room.

Unable to help himself, he smiled. Maybe everything was going to be all right between them. She seemed to trust him again, and he was grateful for that.

Now he needed to make Waneta realize that he was someone she could depend on.

Maybe he could start walking her to and from work. It was a little old-fashioned, but he'd have the opportunity to have her to himself twice a day. There was a benefit to that.

*Jah*. Maybe he could start taking her to supper sometimes after work, too. Or they could set a date to get that dog. Then they'd have lots of reasons to see each other outside of work.

The door chimed.

Mark turned to greet the newcomer. "Afternoon. Welcome to Blooms and Berries. We've got plenty of—" He stopped abruptly as every muscle in his body tensed up. "Calvin."

His brother stepped closer. He was wearing dark jeans, a rust-colored T-shirt that had obviously seen better days, and a smirk. "Oh, so you do know me. I wasn't sure."

The comment stung, but he figured it was justified. Mark definitely had ignored Calvin when he was lurking in Waneta's yard.

However, his brother could have handled things differently. He should have been more open. Calvin could have stopped by the house any evening to talk to him since he'd returned. Instead, he'd been hanging out with Lora and avoiding the sheriff.

Now, here he was, coming to see him in the middle of a workday. Where Waneta would see him.

Mark wasn't ready for that. Calvin could ruin everything between himself and Waneta.

"What are you doing here?"

Calvin glared. "That's all you have to say?"

"No, but that's all I intend to say here. This ain't the place to have our reunion."

Looking around the large shop, he shrugged. "It looks good enough to me."

"Well, it ain't. This is Mr. Lehmann's place."

"You and Mr. Lehmann. Always so close. You'd think he was your flesh and blood."

Mark had spent many hours wishing Henry was just that. And because of his regard for him, Mark wasn't about to do anything to jeopardize Henry's trust.

Especially not talking with a brother who seemed to be itching for a fight.

Walking around the counter, Mark said, "Calvin, I do want to see you. I really do want to catch up. Why don't you come to the house after I get home from work? I'll be home by six or seven."

"That's all you've got to say?"

"For now? *Jah*."

Uncertainty flickered in his eyes before he glared. "You know, when we were growing up, I always thought you tried too hard to be something you weren't. Looks like that habit has only gotten worse."

It looked like they were going to have to talk right there anyway. "I did my best to look after you," Mark said. "You know I did."

"If you had really cared about me, you would have left, too."

"Someone had to look out for Daed. Look out for our home."

Calvin grunted. "Because Daed treated us so well and our house was such a great place."

"It was what we had." It was also more than he'd managed to obtain on his own. "Do you have better?"

For the first time, a hint of vulnerability clouded Calvin's features. "Not yet."

Another time, in another situation, Mark would have loved that answer. It would have signified that all the things he'd wanted his little brother to have had come to fruition.

But now, seeing him angry and agitated—almost looking for a fight?—he only felt wary and disappointed.

"I need to talk to you about the house."

"What about it?" Mark asked.

"It's half mine. The money we could get for it would be half mine, too."

It took everything Mark had not to show how disappointed he was. Calvin had sought him out for money. That was at the heart of their reunion. But even though he knew that, he couldn't push him away.

Feeling weary and far older than his years, Mark said, "Come over tonight and we'll talk. We can have supper together."

"Do you cook now?"

"I can grill a steak and put some corn and potatoes in the oven."

Just as Calvin looked about to answer him, Waneta and Henry came into the store. Each was looking at Calvin intently. Henry was obviously assessing him, taking in his T-shirt, jeans, and heavy-soled black leather boots.

Waneta was simply staring at him curiously.

Mark knew he needed to say something. But while he debated how to best handle the introductions, Waneta stepped forward.

"Calvin? You're back!" Her smile was tremulous.

For the first time since he'd walked in the door, his brother looked unsure of himself. If he wasn't so worried about what Calvin was going to say, he would have smiled. Waneta had that effect on a person.

"I'm surprised you remember me," he said.

She looked confused. "Why?"

"I left a long time ago."

"That's true. And you're obviously English now."

"I got rid of my suspenders the moment I got on the bus."

"Ah." Waneta looked more hesitant. Even a little nervous. Mark knew she wasn't taken aback by someone deciding not to join the faith. It certainly happened from time to time. No, she was wary because of his tone of voice. Calvin sounded snarky and belligerent.

"Like I said before, brother," Mark said. "I'll see you this evening. After I get home from work."

Calvin folded his arms over his chest. "I may not have time then."

Feeling deflated, he nodded. "Whenever you do have time to see me, I'll be there waiting."

"Still waiting, aren't you? Still waiting for someone to see the good in ya."

"He ain't waiting for that, boy," Henry said as he strode forward. "Your brother is a good man and always has been. But it is time you left. Unless you came in to shop, of course."

"I ain't shopping here."

"Then we got nothing to say to each other. Do we?" Henry said.

Waneta looked even more nervous. Her eyes kept darting from Calvin to Mark to Henry.

Mark walked to the door and opened it. "Come by the house later," he said again.

Two cars pulled into the parking lot. Soon they were going to have an audience. Mark feared that would spur Calvin's anger on.

As he walked to the door, Calvin glanced at Mark. "She's better-looking up close, Mark," he said loud enough for Waneta to hear. "No wonder you were panting after her the other day."

Mark's hand clenched. Really, it was all he could do not to shove him out the door.

Obviously glad to have gotten that reaction, Calvin laughed before turning, and kept walking as two customers entered the shop.

"May I help ya?" Waneta asked.

"We're interested in flowering trees."

Looking pleased to escape the tension in the room, Waneta walked them over to one of the greenhouses. The man who had just come in simply wanted to look around.

"What was that about?" Henry asked when they were standing alone again.

"I'm not sure."

"Did you know he was back?"

Mark nodded. Oh, yes, he'd known. He'd fooled himself into thinking it had been a secret he could keep a little longer, too.

It was now obvious that he couldn't have been more wrong. Calvin had returned for a reason and Mark feared that it had something to do with him, his anger, and maybe even Amy Miller.

# CHAPTER 16

*Wednesday, August 10*

Even at twenty-four years of age, rejection still hurt. As Calvin walked to the far corner of the parking lot where he'd parked his bike, he wondered what he had expected would happen. Had he really thought that Mark was going to drop everything, give him a hug, and announce that he was glad to see him?

Maybe.

He would have never admitted it out loud, but even after Mark had ignored him standing in the Cains' yard, Calvin still hoped that their next reunion would be different.

That's what love was. Well, what it was supposed to be, anyway. An emotion that overruled bruised feelings and past mistakes. Something so strong that it couldn't be taken away.

He'd been wrong.

He'd needed Mark's help, too. Things were getting worse with the gang he owed money to. They'd told him from the beginning that they didn't forget about debts that were owed. Now he owed almost as much in interest as the original amount he'd borrowed. He was in over his head. He was going to have to find some way to convince Mark to sell the house and give him half the money.

If that didn't work, Calvin was going to have to go another route. Think about using a bit of coercion. Maybe Mark could be convinced to pay him off so Calvin wouldn't disturb his new, little perfect life and sweet romance with Waneta Cain.

Weighing his options, he decided to head over to Munfordville. There were a couple of places there to eat that offered decent food for cheap.

Just as he pulled his key from his jeans pocket, a sheriff pulled up next to him.

For a split second, Calvin considered starting up his bike and running, but it was doubtful he'd make it far. Most likely all it would do was make things worse.

Therefore, he stayed put and stared at the sheriff, his expression carefully blank.

"You Calvin Fisher?" the sheriff said as he got out of his vehicle. He was both walking and talking slowly, like he feared Calvin was going to pull a gun out and start shooting.

"Yeah."

"I'm Sheriff Brewer. I have some things I need to talk about with you. Let's go down to the station. There's a place to talk there in private."

No way was he going to go to a sheriff's station if he could help it. "We can't discuss whatever it is right now?"

"In the Blooms and Berries parking lot? No."

"I'm kind of busy right now. I ain't in the mood to get questioned, especially since I didn't do anything wrong."

Sheriff Brewer narrowed his eyes. "I didn't say you did. You're not in trouble. But we do need to chat. It won't take long."

Calvin inserted the key into his cycle's ignition. "If I'm not in trouble, then I don't have to chat with anyone."

"I'd hate to force you to come with me." His voice had turned hard.

"And I'd hate to contact my lawyer. But I will if need be."

"You have a lawyer?"

He didn't. But he hated how the sheriff thought he wasn't good enough to get one. "Yeah. So, I'll be seeing you around." Facing his bike now, he exhaled. He'd done good. He'd held his ground but didn't lose his temper or make things worse.

Just as he climbed on and was about to punch the ignition, the sheriff spoke again. "I know you brought some drugs to Lora Weaver's. I know you hit her."

Though he knew he shouldn't take the bait, he said, "Did she press charges against me?"

"No, but she could have. You bruised her face pretty good. She could have been seriously hurt."

"If she didn't press charges, she ain't my problem."

"So you aren't denying any of my accusations?"

"No. I'm saying that I have nothing to say about anything."

"Lora told us that you have access to heavy drugs."

Why had she told them that? With effort, he choked back a laugh. "That's rich."

"Why do you say that?"

"I'm not saying I was there or that I know anything about drugs. But, come on. Lora don't need anyone to give her drugs. She can get them just fine on her own."

"You sound like you know a lot about her."

"I know that she's a sad sort of person with time on her hands. I know that whatever she's up to ain't my problem."

Sheriff Brewer nodded slowly. Then, just when Calvin was sure he was going to leave, he blurted, "What about Amy Miller, then?"

"Who's that?"

"Her name doesn't ring a bell?"

"Obviously not." Calvin didn't trust the way the sheriff's eyes brightened. "Who is she?"

"Oh, she's just an Amish girl who was assaulted last night. The man who attacked her was wearing a mask, so she can't identify him. We're going to have to rely on DNA."

Calvin knew his heart was starting to race. That was the real reason that the sheriff had been watching for him. It didn't have anything to do with Lora or a Baggie of pot. It was about the girl.

And DNA? What did that mean? Had Brewer planned on taking him in and swabbing his mouth or something? "That's real sad," he finally bit out. "But that girl don't have anything to do with me."

"Maybe. Maybe not. Calvin, I want to know what you were doing last night."

"I was in Munfordville."

"Any specific place?"

"Yeah. I was sitting on my bed, watching television in my motel room."

"And the name of this motel is . . . ?"

Calvin couldn't remember. It was just another run-down dive offering rooms for thirty-six dollars a night. "I don't remember the name exactly. Cave something. Or maybe it was Hart Hotel?"

"You don't recall?" Skepticism was thick in his tone.

"No, but it ain't like there are lots of places to choose from. Go ask around if you want."

Sheriff Brewer looked ticked. "I'll be doing that."

It was happening. He was going to get attempted rape or assault, or something, pinned on him. Just because he was a Fisher.

Or maybe Lora had been talking bad about him. Or Mark had.

That idea hurt like crazy but seemed possible. As the bitterness coated his insides, he lifted his chin. "Don't want to tell you how to do your job or nothing, but it sure sounds like you picked the wrong brother to question."

Sheriff Brewer straightened his shoulders. "Care to explain that?"

"What do I need to explain? Weren't you the cop who arrested Mark two years ago?"

"It was me. But I didn't arrest him. Only brought him in for questioning."

"Well, I could be wrong, but I heard that men don't change their habits about things like that. He could have returned and gotten back to his old ways."

Looking like he was smelling something rotten, Brewer said, "Now I've heard everything. A man turning on his own brother."

"If that's the worst thing you've ever heard, you should have stopped by our house growing up. You'd have learned then that nothing is off limits. Not for brothers, and not how parents can treat their sons. But, oh yeah, no one cared about us then. You only care about the Fisher boys when you need to pin a crime on somebody." While those words hung in the air, he let the engine roar to life.

As bitterness and regret filled his lungs, he roared out of the parking lot, practically daring the sheriff to follow him or give him a ticket for speeding.

But as he sped down the highway, no one was following him. Not the sheriff. Not his brother. Just his memories of the things that had happened in his house.

Turned out that he didn't need anything more to spur him on. He decided to ride until he got his emotions under control, and then head back to town.

There was something he needed to do. Something that couldn't be helped.

# CHAPTER 17

*Wednesday, August 10*

Waneta had been thankful that Mr. and Mrs. Johnson were so interested in organic produce. Standing in the vegetable greenhouse, surrounded by the scent of fresh herbs and row after row of peppers and tomatoes, she'd answered all of the couple's questions about growing tomatoes of their own.

After they purchased four plants and a green plastic watering can, she'd met Mark at the counter. He still looked upset.

For a moment, she considered not even mentioning Calvin's surprise visit, but she decided that would be wrong. Surely, it was better to identify the elephant in the room instead of pretending that it didn't exist?

"I didn't know your brother was back," she finally said, keeping it simple.

"Yeah. He arrived a couple of days ago."

His voice was flat, and Waneta was pretty sure that the

muscles in his neck had tightened. Every response that came to her mind sounded too trite.

Keep it simple.

She had almost elected to keep silent. But when she noticed just how upset he was—his dark eyes almost black, so filled with pain—she decided to say something. Even if it wasn't the right thing to say.

"He looks different than I remember."

A bark of laughter erupted from Mark. The opposite of joyful. It sounded dark and bitter. Frustrated.

"*Jah*. He surely does."

"I had heard he'd become everything English. I guess that rumor was true."

"I knew he would," he said slowly. "He . . . Well, it seemed he was never suited to our way of life. Never content. Always hoping for something different. Better."

Finally, he was opening up! Maybe he was realizing that he could trust her. Feeling hopeful, she said, "He found it, then. That's a good thing, right?"

"*Nee*. What he chose ain't better. It ain't anything close to that."

She'd been wrong, then. "I'm sorry. Obviously, I'm struggling with finding the right words to say."

He pressed a hand to his face. "*Nee*," he said softly. "Don't apologize. You haven't done anything wrong. I'm the one who is sorry. Seeing him upsets me. Seeing him around you upsets me even more. I never know how he's going to act. I never know what he's going to say or do. I'm afraid he's going to offend you or hurt your feelings." Looking down at his feet, he said, "Maybe even something worse. I don't know how to handle it."

She had no idea what he was referring to, but she couldn't

imagine that his brother could ever affect her that much. She wasn't a weak girl.

It was time he realized that. "You don't need to worry about me, Mark."

He paused, then said, "*Nee*, I do. He's erratic. He's saying and doing things that I don't understand." Rubbing a hand across his face, he added, "It makes me crazy." Looking around the empty space, with all the stock perfectly organized, he added, "You may not know this, but I like things in proper order. It sets my mind at ease."

"I actually have noticed that about you," she teased. "After all, you are the one who rearranged these shelves."

"I think it's a consequence of how we were brought up. Growing up, my parents never did what was expected of them. It made me want to be around people and things I can count on. But that's not really possible."

"Which is hard on you," she said, understanding him even better now.

He nodded. "Waneta, all that has been going through my head. Well, all that, and Amy getting hurt and Calvin returning. It's set me off. I know it's confused you, too. I'm sorry for the way I've been acting this week."

"You have been running a bit hot and cold."

"I have been. I'm a grown man, but I don't know how to protect myself from giving into these mood swings." After a pause, he added more quietly, "Or how to protect you from harm, period."

"You need to stop worrying about me so much. It's just me. Waneta."

"You are just you. But, don't you see? That means something. You mean something to me."

She didn't know whether to give him a hug or burst into tears. His words were heartfelt. So sweet.

Looking embarrassed, he said, "I guess it's pretty obvious that I like you. I want to get to know you better and I want you to get to know me better, too. But as hard as I try, it seems that I can't separate my past from the present. It taints everything I'm trying to do. I feel like I'm living in fear of you finding one more thing that will be the final straw. That will make you finally turn away from me."

His honest words made her pulse flutter. Again, she felt helpless by her naiveté. She wished she had more experience in relationships.

Since she didn't, she could only rely on honesty and hope it was enough for him. "I want to get to know you better, too, Mark. I don't know what secrets you're hiding, but I don't plan to judge you on either your past or your brother."

"You sure about that?"

She shrugged. She didn't feel sure about anything. Not his past, not her feelings, not even his scary brother. "Does it matter?" she asked. "Do we have to know everything about each other in order to have a friendship? Or to even have something more than that?"

He shook his head slowly. "*Nee.* But will you promise me something? If you do start feeling like you need more space from me, if you feel like whatever is happening between us isn't making you happy, tell me, okay?"

"Okay. I can do that."

His expression warmed, though she felt a new tension brewing between them.

"May I come over tonight?"

"You may, but why? Do you need something?"

Looking a little embarrassed, he said, "I want to call on you properly, like your parents would expect a suitor to act."

Knowing that he was right, that her parents would need to see him do everything that they expected, even if it was all slightly old-fashioned, given their situation, she nodded.

"Maybe they'll even let me take you out for an evening stroll. We can look at the fireflies."

"Maybe they will." She smiled, liking that idea.

Mark smiled, too. For once, his happiness even reached his eyes. "I better get to work, then. We'll talk later," he said before turning away.

She watched him stride over to Mr. Lehmann, chat with him for a moment, then exit out the back door toward the far greenhouses.

Watching him made her feel a little mushy inside. A little optimistic about their future.

It also made her wonder if everything between them was on the verge of falling apart . . . even if it had never really had a chance to begin yet.

"WANETA, WE ARE so glad to see you," Mrs. Miller said as she let her into their house. "I guess you heard about Amy?"

"First thing today. I'm sorry I didn't get here earlier. I had to work."

"We've had our share of visitors today. Poor Amy was so exhausted by the time the last group of young people left."

"Oh? Would you like me to come back tomorrow?"

"Of course not. You and Amy have been close for years." Her lips pursed. "Unfortunately, some of the men and women who stopped by only came over to get information. My Francis put a stop to that."

"I bet he did." Mr. Miller was stocky and had worked for many years up in the Michigan logging camps. He was big and burly and had no patience for people who didn't adhere to his standards.

"Amy just woke up from a nap. Her father has been sitting by her bed, watching her sleep."

"I'm sure he's been a great source of comfort."

"He has, but you can give him a break. Come along now." Two steps away from her daughter's door, she turned to face Waneta again. "You might want to prepare yourself, dear. Amy was pretty beaten up," she said just as she opened the door and led the way inside.

The moment Waneta saw Amy's bruised and battered face and arms, she wished she would have taken that advice to heart.

Amy wasn't just a little bruised. She looked like her attacker had slammed her face on the pavement. Cuts and stitches were on her cheek and above her eye. Her nose was swollen and her eyes were blackened.

Even more disturbing were the dark fingertip bruises around her throat and on her collarbone. Someone had gripped her hard. Really hard.

"Neeta," she said. "You came to see me."

Her voice was hoarse and rough sounding. And the expression in her eyes! She looked so sad.

Tears pricked Waneta's eyes as she darted forward. "Oh, Amy. I am so sorry."

"Me, too." Her bottom lip trembled before she glanced at her father. "But I'll be all right. God was with me today. That is why I wasn't hurt worse."

Standing up, Mr. Miller nodded. "What she says is true. Though she was hurt badly, the Lord helped her through it. The nurse said she's going to heal and be just fine. That was a blessing."

Waneta had a strong faith, but she wasn't sure how it was possible to look at anything that had happened as a blessing. Feeling at a loss for words, she simply smiled as Mr. Miller told Amy that he'd give the two of them some privacy for a half hour.

When the door closed behind him, Amy exhaled. "You had perfect timing, Waneta. I love my father dearly, but I needed a break from his hovering."

"I'm glad I came at this time of day, then. You are making me feel useful."

Shifting against her pillow, Amy tried to smile. "Glad I could help."

"I sure am sorry you were attacked. I bet it was scary."

"It was horrible. I'm still shaken up. I don't know how I'm ever going to be able to walk anywhere alone again."

"I bet you won't have to. Your parents and Abraham will no doubt keep a close eye on you for months."

"I think you are right. Abraham was so upset. When he first saw me, he looked like he couldn't decide whether to hold me close or go after Mark Fisher."

She was stunned. "Why would he want to go after Mark?"

Amy looked at her strangely. "Come on. You know why."

"*Nee.* I really don't. I heard you didn't see who attacked you." All at once, a horrible thought came to her. "Wait a minute. Was that not true?"

"*Nee,* it was true. The man had a mask on and I didn't

recognize his voice," she said weakly. "But we all know that Mark hurt Bethany. So I'm thinking that it must have been Mark who hurt me."

"He didn't!"

Amy stared at her. "If not him, who else could it be?"

Feeling like she was destined to continually stand up for Mark, who had done nothing to deserve such harsh treatment, Waneta said, "I have no idea, but I know it wasn't Mark. He didn't hurt Bethany, Amy. He was taken in for questioning and then released. Sheriff Brewer cleared his name."

"Well, it was someone I knew. I do know that much."

"How? What did he say?"

After glancing at the door to make sure it was shut, Amy whispered, "He yelled at me when he had me down on the ground. He said that he knew I dressed up and went to the mall and the movies with Abraham last weekend."

Waneta was surprised. Belatedly, she recalled that Abraham's parents hadn't minded him parking his truck in their field and that he and Amy hadn't been baptized yet. Technically, they were still in their *rumspringa*. "I had forgotten that you both still went out and did things like that."

Amy looked at her sharply. "'Like that'?" she repeated sharply. "You make it sound like we are doing something wrong."

"I didn't mean to make it sound that way," she said quickly. "I meant only that I'd forgotten that you still hadn't joined the faith."

"Still? Boy, now, that sounds judgmental."

"I'm not judging you." At least, she was trying not to.

"I hope not. Because there's nothing wrong with still going

out and experimenting with English ways. Abraham said we have time before we have to join the church."

"*Jah*. Of course." Feeling more uncomfortable, Waneta said, "Maybe the man who attacked you was English. He could have seen you at the movies and followed you home so he'd know where you lived or something."

"Maybe, but I doubt it."

"What did Sheriff Brewer think?"

"He isn't sure who it could be. But then, I didn't tell him about what the man said."

"Why not?" It was hard not to raise her voice. "It sounds important."

"Waneta, he might have told my parents!"

"They don't know that you've been going to the mall and movies?" Waneta was incredulous. Surely, neither Amy nor her parents were that naïve?

"Of course they don't know."

"But they know you and Abraham are still doing things like that . . . Right?"

Amy sighed. "*Nee*. They don't." Impatiently, she brushed a stray strand of hair away from her face. "Waneta, I don't know why we're even talking about this. What matters is that Mark Fisher is hurting people again."

Waneta stepped away. She felt like she was in an impossible situation, but she also knew that she had to do what was right. What was in her heart. "Amy, I feel sorry for you and I would have never wanted you to get attacked like you did. I will pray for your recovery. But I am friends with Mark now. I can't allow you to blame him for something I know he didn't do."

"Do you really *know* he didn't do it?"

"Of course."

"And how do you know he is so innocent, Neeta? Were you with him last night? Are you his alibi?"

She was tempted to say she was. Tempted to lie. But that lie could only blow up in her face. "I wasn't. But I talked to him about it this morning. He was really upset and shocked. Just like I was."

Amy looked at her curiously before understanding dawned. "You two are working together at the nursery, aren't ya?"

"*Jah.*"

"Then I'll tell you the same thing you just told me, Neeta. I am sorry for you. I hope this never happens to you. But if you continue to hang around him, chances are good that something will happen to you, too." Lifting her chin, she said, "I think I need to rest now. Can you see yourself out?"

"Amy, please don't be mad. You know I'm only trying to stand up for a friend."

"I thought *I* was your friend."

Since it was now obvious that Amy wasn't going to try to understand her point of view, Waneta started for the door. "I'm leaving now, but I really do think you are making a mistake about not telling the truth to Sheriff Brewer. You shouldn't lie about what that man said."

"You sound so holier than thou. I can't wait for the day when you realize that it was a mistake to be so judgmental."

Even bruised, Amy had an answer for everything. Feeling hopeless about the situation, she walked right from Amy's room to the front door and quietly let herself out.

She felt a little guilty. The right thing to do would have been to inform Mr. and Mrs. Miller that she was leaving, but she couldn't find the nerve to do it. She was too upset and distressed about everything Amy had said.

Walking back home, Waneta felt so isolated. For years now, she'd gone to work and gone home. Sure, she'd enjoyed many friends in the area, but she hadn't made time to do things with them in a very long time. Instead, she'd found her happiness with her parents and in her work at the nursery.

Perhaps that's why Amy's comments had stung so badly. Not only did Amy seem more than a little derisive about Waneta's choices, it seemed like she faulted Waneta for staying on the straight and narrow.

As she walked along, feeling the heat of the late-afternoon sun warm her shoulders and smelling the faint scent of honeysuckle in the air, she realized that she couldn't see anyone for miles.

The chill that ran down her spine caught her by surprise.

She realized that if someone did come out of nowhere and attacked her, no one would hear her scream. She'd have to fight him off on her own.

As she turned the corner and saw her house and her two neighbors' houses in the distance, she breathed a sigh of relief. She was safe, for now.

But her pulse was racing so fast, she was starting to feel like she soon wasn't going to be safe.

# CHAPTER 18

Someone had been in his house again. There was nothing blatant, just a couple of signs that stood out to him. A closet door left open that he knew he'd shut. Drops of water dotting the old stainless steel sink in the kitchen.

A bottle of Gatorade was missing from his refrigerator.

Mark wondered if his culprit had been Calvin or if there was another person in Horse Cave who was anxious to uncover all his secrets.

He wouldn't have been surprised if there was. He doubted it was Sheriff Brewer, but there were likely other people who were suspicious of him.

Maybe even someone like James Eicher, who'd acted so angry when he'd spotted him at Blooms and Berries on his first day at work.

He wasn't sure what the intruder had been looking for, however. He didn't have anything worth stealing and the house was so run-down that anything that was removed could be considered a blessing.

Ever since Mark had gotten home two hours ago, he'd been pondering the possibilities over and over. It was a futile exercise for the most part, however. There were too many people he didn't trust, and they no doubt felt the same way about him.

Bending down, he picked up another armful of worn and dilapidated linoleum that he'd pulled off the kitchen floor. At last, it was all removed. After he sanded and stained the wood floor, it was going to look terrific. Knowing he was responsible for the transformation would feel good, too.

Pushing open the back door with his shoulder, he carefully navigated the two steps down to the cement pad leading to the old garage, and at last dropped the offending materials in the pile.

His shirt was soaked with sweat. Was the temperature ever going to cool off? Stretching his arms, he bent from one side to the other. He needed the moment to relax before he went inside to shower, grab something to eat, then mentally prepare himself to return to the Cains' house.

Rolling his shoulders, he exhaled, attempting to ease the knots that had formed there as he thought about Waneta and the way she made him smile.

He wasn't sure exactly how to be the type of suitor Waneta needed, but he was certainly going to give it a try. He would do just about anything in order to make her happy.

"Hey, Mark!" Lora Weaver called out from the top of his driveway.

Turning to her, Mark tried to summon some kind of welcoming expression. He wasn't sure why she'd come over, though. They'd been friends when they were young, but it had been more out of necessity than a real liking for each other. Now it seemed like they were polar opposites.

"Hey, Lora," he said at last.

As he imagined her reasons for stopping over, the only one that made sense was his brother. And that made him stop. He needed to say something about Calvin hurting her. "I'm glad you stopped by. I wanted to talk to you about Calvin, and see how you were feeling."

She interrupted him. "What's this you're doing?"

Feeling confused, but willing to let her lead the conversation, he pointed to the pile of old flooring. "Working on the house. Pulling off old linoleum. It's a miserable job."

"I bet. What was underneath it? Concrete?" she asked as she walked closer.

Glancing at her face, he noticed that her eyes were red and there were faint lines of strain around them. Maybe the sheriff had been wrong. Maybe she'd been hurt worse than anyone realized.

But since her expression was so pinched, so earnest, he bided his time and continued talking about the house. "Actually, I found wood floors underneath. Oak in good condition, too." Unable to help himself, he rolled his eyes. "Only my parents would have placed linoleum over perfectly good hardwood."

She smiled tightly. "At least they cared about the place at one time, right?"

She had a point. "Yeah."

Reaching out, she fingered a yellowed, curled corner of linoleum. "Now that all this ugly flooring is out, I bet your place is going to look a lot better."

"Hope so."

"Of course it will. I mean, it couldn't have looked much worse," she joked.

Maybe it was because he was still stewing on the fact that someone had been inside, but her comment struck him as odd. "How do you know that?"

She looked at him curiously. "No reason. I mean, it's true, right?"

"It is true. But I'm wondering why you'd say such a thing. It ain't like you've been in here in years. Or have you?"

"Of course I haven't." Sounding hurt, she continued. "Why are you looking at me like I'm the one who put in all that ugly linoleum? I'm only making conversation."

"Someone came in my house today without my knowledge. I'm trying to figure out who would do such a thing."

"Well, it sure wasn't me." She rubbed her palms on the tops of her thighs. Today she was wearing a long beige cotton skirt, white T-shirt, and flip-flops. It was close to being what any girl of their acquaintance who was dressed conservatively would usually wear. It was far different than the tank top and tight-fitting jeans she'd been wearing the first time they'd talked.

He wondered if it was a coincidence, or if she'd dressed like that purposely in order to remind him of their past.

Just as quickly, he disregarded that idea. He really was becoming paranoid. He needed to get a grip on himself. But first he needed to bring up the subject she seemed intent to avoid. "Lora, I wanted to tell you that I'm really sorry that Calvin hurt you."

"You know it was Calvin?"

"*Jah*. Sheriff Brewer told me. He said that Calvin was partying over at your house a couple of nights ago."

"Partying is a strange word to describe it, considering that he hit me."

Mark flinched. He was not his brother's keeper, but even now old habits seemed hard to shake. "I really am sorry. I hope you are healing?"

"Yeah. It's all right." She tilted her chin toward the fading sunlight. "I'm still bruised, but the swelling's gone down."

Looking at the lingering discoloration on her cheek and around her eye, he felt even worse. "I really am sorry. I can't believe Calvin would hit a woman."

"It surprised me, too. But then, a lot of surprising things are happening around here these days."

"Like what?"

"Like me coming back last year. Like Calvin showing up. Like you courting Waneta Cain."

He didn't like the new, cool inflection in her voice. "I'm not going to talk about her with you."

"Why not?"

"You and Waneta are too different. You have nothing in common."

"Maybe she and I aren't all that different, Mark."

Waneta was sheltered, positive, and honest. At the moment, she seemed like the complete opposite of Lora Weaver, with her tainted past and hard edges. "I'm sorry, but I don't agree. Maybe one time you were alike, but you are very different now."

"You mean I'm very different than the girl I was." When he nodded, she lifted her chin. "Maybe you are very different than who you used to be, too, Mark. And maybe, just maybe, Calvin and you are a little like me and Waneta. Different on the outside but not so different in your heart."

Mark didn't know how to respond to that. Everything inside of him was wanting to refute her words, to tell her that she was wrong.

She sighed. "Calvin ain't here, is he?"

"*Nee.* I don't know where he is."

She looked puzzled. "Oh. I thought he was going to see you today."

"He did. But he stopped by to see me at work. I told him I didn't want to talk to him there. I told him to stop by tonight."

"Oh. Do you think he'll stop over?"

"I doubt it. He wasn't happy with me. He raced off on his motorcycle with a giant chip on his shoulder."

Lora gazed at him sadly. "He's kind of a lost soul right now."

Though he was more than ready to say something scathing, he knew she was giving him the opening that he desperately needed to learn more about his brother. "How can you say something like that, Lora? He hit you."

"Yeah, he did. I've forgiven him, though. I know he probably feels bad about it. I think he's in a world of trouble."

"I'm pretty sure that is the case. He always was a champion of making bad decisions."

"Maybe so, but I have a feeling that he's been reaping the consequences lately. He seems aimless and hurt."

"Hurt? By whom?"

"You." She shrugged. "Me. The world. I'm getting the feeling that he's afraid of something, too. You should try to help him."

Lora's words made much sense. They brought back feelings of guilt and loss. How many times in his life had he dropped everything to try to save him? He'd run to his defense in the classroom and on the playground. After church and at home. But all he'd gotten for it was pain and abuse.

Wasn't it right that he was putting himself first now? "I don't know how I can help him anymore. We're too different."

"You may be Amish and he's English, but that doesn't mean you can't love him still. You're brothers."

"I don't care that he's English. I don't even care that he didn't try to stay in touch after he left. But I can't be all right with the choices he's made."

Her open expression shuttered. "Well, now I understand."

"Do you?" he scoffed. "I kind of doubt it."

"You don't know what it was like, leaving the Amish like we did. Trying to make our way in the world when we had no idea what to do," Lora retorted. "It was hard, Mark."

"Life is hard. It don't matter what choices a person makes, if you make the choice to live, chances are better than good that each day ain't going to be easy."

Lora shook her head in obvious distaste. "No wonder Calvin never wanted to come back here. You are so sanctimonious."

"At least I'm not a drug addict."

"Oh, good point. Thank goodness you never did drugs. All you've done is beat women."

Mark felt his face and neck flush. He fought to show reaction, though he feared he was failing miserably. She'd struck a nerve, and they both knew it.

Before their conversation descended into an even lower level, he said, "I think it's time you left. Calvin ain't here and we have nothing to say to each other."

"*Jah*, I'll leave. But if I were you, I'd take care throwing all those stones of yours. One day someone is going to throw one back at ya. And it's going to hurt something awful."

Looking at her retreating form, Mark was fairly sure that he'd already had plenty of stones thrown his way. He knew because they truly had hurt. He had the scars to prove it.

As he went back inside, he pulled out his pocket watch and cursed under his breath. He now had less than fifteen minutes to shower and get to Waneta's house.

Food and prayer were going to have to come later.

Sometime much later.

# CHAPTER 19

*Wednesday night, August 10*

Waneta, I swept the porch and wiped down the railing out there, too," her mother said. "At least Mark will think we keep a clean house."

With exaggerated patience, Waneta said, "Mark has already been outside on the porch. He's not going to care how clean everything is."

Pressing her hands on her waist, her mother looked at her with a knowing expression. "He might, daughter. Men like clean houses, you know."

As if women did not.

It was all so silly. Honestly, her mother was acting as if she'd never had a man come courting before. She had. Several men from their community had sat on her front porch swing over the last few years. She'd never been as anxious about their visits as she was about Mark's, though.

Hmm. Maybe her mother wasn't acting all that out of sorts, after all.

Then, as she scanned the dining room table and saw two

platters filled with snacks and cookies, a pitcher of freshly squeezed lemonade, and a carafe of freshly brewed coffee, Neeta knew she hadn't been wrong. This was too much. Mark was going to be overwhelmed and she was going to be embarrassed.

"Mamm, he's coming over to sit on the porch swing. Not eat supper," she chided.

"He's a young man living by himself. Of course he's going to want some food."

"She ain't wrong!" Daed called out.

When her mother smiled at her, obviously pleased to have her opinion reinforced, Waneta gave in. There was nothing she could do about the refreshments now anyway.

"It does look real nice, Mamm. Thank you for going to so much trouble. I'm worried that you overdid it, though. You know how you get tired when you overexert yourself."

"Bustling around the *haus* from time to time is good for me." Clasping her hands together, she said, "Now, what are you going to talk about with Mark?"

Oh, but her mother was chewing on her last nerve. "I don't know. Whatever comes to mind, I expect."

"I think you should have something better in mind. Don't you?" She nodded encouragingly.

That was her mother's favorite habit. She asked questions in conjunction with either a nod or a shake of the head. When she was younger, Neeta had appreciated the signals; it gave her a very good idea about what response would make her mother happiest.

But now she only felt the not-so-subtle movements were rather amusing. "Mamm, I'm not going to have conversation starters prepared in my head for Mark. We work all day together and get along just fine." Okay, that was probably a bit of an exaggeration, but it was still true.

"Well, whatever you do, don't talk about work," she warned.

"Why not?"

"Because work isn't romantic."

That was true. Work definitely was not romantic. But she wasn't about to guide the conversation toward romance! "Daed, help me out here," she called.

"Sorry, Waneta, but I'm helpless when it comes to the ways of courting."

"Not really. You courted Mamm."

"*Nee*, it was more like I was wandering around town when your mother snagged me. I didn't stand a chance."

*Snagged?* Her seventy-two-year-old father just admitted that her mother snagged him?

"Oh! He's here!" Mamm said, smiling from her spot next to the front windows.

Sure enough, two raps accompanied her mother's announcement. Mark had arrived. And not a moment too soon.

"I'll get the door, Mamm," she said as she turned the knob. Hopefully, her mother would take the hint and leave before she said anything to embarrass Waneta.

"Hey, Waneta," Mark said. "I'm sorry I'm late."

"Nothing to apologize for. I didn't even notice the time."

"She means that in the best way possible, Mark," Mamm said over her shoulder.

"Mother—"

But instead of looking as uncomfortable as Waneta felt, Mark just grinned. "That's *gut* to know, Mrs. Cain. Otherwise, a man might be feeling a bit forgettable."

"Want some food?" Daed called from his easy chair. "Gettie's been cooking all afternoon for ya."

His expression went blank. "You have?"

It was too much. They were being so heavy-handed, he'd probably never come back. "You don't have to eat anything, Mark," she said quickly. "My mother just sometimes overdoes things."

"Actually, if you don't mind, I'd love something to eat. I'm starving. I didn't have time for dinner."

Giving Waneta a knowing look, her mother stepped closer. "Let me take you to the dining room and get you a plate."

*"Danke."* After sending an apologetic look Waneta's way, Mark walked to her mother's side.

When she was alone in the entryway, Waneta wondered what had come over her mother. Just a week or so ago she was gossiping about Mark and wanting Waneta to quit her job. Now she was practically planning their wedding. Had he really made such an impression on her when he visited?

Or, had Mamm truly taken Preacher Eli's words to heart and was practicing what he preached?

She was still dwelling on the changes when Mark came back out with a glass of lemonade in one hand and an overflowing plate in the other.

"Sorry about that," he said. "I really was hungry, though."

Now she was the one who was feeling like she needed to offer up an apology. "Nothing to apologize for," she said. "You just made my mother happy. And I wouldn't have wanted you to sit on the porch with me swinging while your stomach was growling."

"This is going to be the best meal I've had since, well, the last time I was here."

She laughed. "My mother is a fine cook. I'll pass on your appreciation."

Mark sat down with his plate of fried chicken, sauerkraut balls, pickles, and cheese and crackers. After chomping down on one of the pickles, he said, "I don't know what happened. The time got away from me."

"What were you doing?"

"I've been pulling up old linoleum. Then I had an unexpected guest."

"Was it your brother again?"

"*Nee.* Lora Weaver."

"Lora? What did she want?"

"To talk about my brother." Looking down at his plate, he ate another couple of pieces of chicken, then said, "Do you mind if we don't talk about either of them right now? I need a break."

Though she nodded, Waneta couldn't deny that she was feeling awkward all over again. It looked like he still didn't trust her. Why had he even wanted to come over if he didn't feel comfortable answering even the easiest question?

Minutes later, his plate was cleared. He stood up and rested it on the small table on the corner of the porch. After sipping his lemonade, he eyed her warily.

"Did I just make a mess of things?"

"By eating? Of course not."

"By everything. Inhaling my food. Showing up late. By doing what I just did."

"You've lost me, Mark. I don't know what you are referring to."

"Because I didn't explain myself. You look hurt."

"That's not how I'm feeling. I'm . . . well, I'm wondering what we should talk about."

"Anything you want to talk about is fine."

"Except your brother. Or Lora's visit. Or why the sheriff wanted to talk to you. Or Amy Miller's attack."

"You're right. I have a lot to learn about conversation. I promise I'm trying, though."

Remembering Amy's parting words about acting holier than thou, Waneta said, "I have things I'm working on, too, Mark."

His gaze warmed. It was obvious that he was grateful that she had let him off so easy. Kicking one of his legs out, he said, "So, did you end up going over to see Amy?"

"I did."

"I'm sure you brought her a lot of comfort."

"Not so much. We ended up arguing."

"What about?"

"About her. Me. And some things that don't matter."

"I guess you are getting as good as I am about keeping things hidden."

"Not really," said Waneta. "Though, I am finding it hard to be open and honest with someone who doesn't want to act the same way. I wouldn't say you've been difficult. But you do have me confused."

"I'm not surprised. I have been prickly about a lot of things, haven't I?"

"Yes. But that's your business, Mark. Not mine."

"No. I said I really like you, but now I'm not hardly giving you anything back. Ask me anything and I'll try to answer as best I can."

She was disappointed. She felt like he was making her do the choosing about delving into his personal life. It hardly seemed fair.

Instead, she kicked her legs out and said, "I remember when I was twelve and you were sixteen."

"Let's see. That means I was out of school and working for Henry."

"*Jah*. You were." She smiled softly. "I was walking home and was having quite a time carrying all of my things. I got to take Miss Edith's rat home for the weekend."

He chuckled. "I'd forgotten all about that rat. Everyone sure loved it."

"*Jah*, they did. I couldn't wait to be chosen to be the lucky girl who got to take the rat home. Anyway, when my weekend came, I had my hands full on the way home. I had a time juggling it all and kept stopping to catch my breath and rearrange my books, that cage, and my lunch pail. Then, just when you walked by, everything but the rat tumbled to the ground."

Remembering the moment as if it was yesterday, she looked at him. "I was so frustrated with myself and embarrassed, I almost started crying. But all you did was kneel down, pick up all my books, and offer to see me home."

"I wish I could tell you that I remember that afternoon, but I don't." Looking off into the distance, he said, "I'm even trying to remember why I would have been walking along that road at that time, when I was sixteen."

"It was because of Calvin. You used to walk Calvin home, which he constantly complained about."

"Oh, yeah." Looking reflective, he said, "I remember that day now. Calvin had just run off a couple of days before. I had forgotten until I watched everyone walk out the schoolhouse door and he didn't appear." Smiling at her, he said, "I didn't think you were ever going to let me hold that cage, Waneta."

"I didn't want you to. I thought you would take it from me."

"You thought I'd steal it?"

Oh, but he sounded indignant! "Maybe," she teased. "All I could think about was how much everyone else had wanted to take the creature home. But I was the one Miss Edith had picked."

He laughed. "Miss Edith would have never let Calvin or me take it home. She didn't trust us."

"With good reason. You took pencils."

He shrugged. "We needed pencils. It weren't like our father was going to spend his money on school supplies. Miss Edith knew that, too, but she never seemed to care."

Waneta gulped. This conversation strand wasn't going well, either. It was time to get to the point. "The reason I brought it up was because you said something to me when we were walking side by side."

"What did I say that was worth remembering?"

"You said that you'd never met another girl who tried so hard to be good." She was somewhat pleased that her voice didn't tremble when she said that.

But instead of looking touched by the memory, he pressed a palm to his face. Like he was embarrassed. "I was a jerk."

"You were a jerk a lot of the time, Mark," she agreed. "But not then. That day? You were kind. You also told me that the rat was probably going to have the best weekend of its life with me."

The corners of his mouth lifted. "I bet I wasn't wrong."

"I don't know if you were right or wrong. What's important is that I didn't understand what you meant back then. I do now. It was a lovely compliment."

"You are a nice person, Waneta. You've always been that way. You've got a good heart."

"You do, too."

"Not really."

"Why did you come back, Mark? Was it really because of the house?"

"Partly. But also because of Henry. He got a talking-to from his physician. The man said Henry ain't resting enough and needed to stop trying to do too much."

"So you came to help."

"I did. I know he appreciates you, Waneta, but he needs someone to take care of the hard labor and the heavy lifting. I aim to get him to let me do more and more as the weeks go by. I'm hoping that soon he'll only work a couple of days a week."

"He must be so glad you came back to help him."

"So far, I don't think so. Since I've come back, I've gotten the impression that everything around Horse Cave has started to fall apart."

"Hardly."

"Amy Miller was just attacked." He raised his eyebrows. "That wasn't good."

"I agree. But just because something awful happened since you returned doesn't mean we haven't had our share of drama around here from time to time. Believe me, bad things have happened in the county even when you were gone. Why, a girl was kidnapped and tied up in a basement over in Munfordville a couple of months ago!"

He sighed. "I hear you. But I still feel like I've given Henry a new set of problems."

"Even if you have, I hope you won't add them to your burdens. I think Henry can handle most anything."

"I think he can, too. But that doesn't mean he should have to." Mark took a deep breath. "Waneta, when Calvin showed up at Blooms and Berries, I was very upset."

She could tell that he was really struggling to hold on to his composure. And that he was trying his best to reveal his feelings in an honest and forthright way. It made her want to try to help him as much as she could, even though she feared she was hopelessly incapable of really helping a man who'd already suffered through so many personal tragedies.

"That was understandable," she said slowly. "You didn't want to see him."

"You're right. I didn't. And though that is something I haven't quite come to terms with, it wasn't the only reason I was angry with him." After taking a deep breath, he said, "It was because he was playing with me. Playing with all of us. I hate that he is involving you in his games."

"How so?"

"He could have come to the house at any time. But he was picking to come to the nursery because he wanted you and Henry to see him. He wanted other customers to see me talking to him."

"Why would he care about that?"

"He doesn't want to see me. He only wants me to sell the house and give him half the money."

"Would you do that?"

"On my good days, I think of course not. I don't want to leave. On my not so good days, I think that selling the house wouldn't solve either of our problems."

"And on others?"

"On other days? I want to pack up my duffel and take off. Get as far away from here as I possibly can."

"I hope you don't do that."

Some of the chill faded from his eyes. "You really mean that, don't you?"

"I do." After weighing what she was about to say for a moment, she decided to simply speak her mind. "Forgive me, but I think there's another reason you came back here, Mark. I think the Lord needed you to come back and deal with all the hurts and problems that have been plaguing you for so long. I think He knows you won't really be happy until you are able to look your brother, your house, and everyone who was so quick to judge you in the eye."

"That's easy to suggest but a lot harder to do."

She was just relieved he hadn't thrown her suggestion back in her face. "I bet it is," she agreed easily.

"And what do you think I should say to everyone? What do you think I should say to Calvin when I talk to him again?"

"I canna answer that." Even she knew one couldn't tell someone else that they needed to accept their apology or grant forgiveness. That had to be something that was decided on all by oneself.

"Waneta. You canna just offer me some advice? Tell me what you really think I should do."

"I don't know what words you need to say. But more importantly, I don't think I'm supposed to know them. Only you and God know." She squirmed under his gaze. "I know I'm probably not helping, but I wanted to tell you what I thought. I really do think God has brought you back here to heal."

His gaze sharpened. "What about you?"

"Me?"

"*Jah*. If the Lord wants me to see all the people I hoped I never saw again, and to make peace with them, too . . . what do you think He wants me to do with people like you?"

"Like me?" She could practically feel her skin turning a deep shade of pink.

"*Jah*," he murmured, still staring at her intently. "Waneta, do you think I should follow my instinct and see where our relationship leads? Or—" He stopped abruptly.

But she needed to hear his thoughts. "Or?"

"Or wait until everything in my life is peaceful again?"

She felt deflated and more than a little let down. "Mark, when you say things like that, I always find it confusing. I never know if you are teasing or being completely serious."

"I'm serious. I wouldn't joke about you and me."

"You sound mighty sure about that."

"I am. I waited too long to have a moment like this. There's no way I'm going to give it up without a fight."

She wasn't sure if he thought she would be fighting him or if everyone around them were.

But maybe it didn't matter. All that did matter was that they were now trusting each other enough to build the beginnings of a relationship.

That in itself was something for which to be grateful.

# CHAPTER 20

*Thursday, August 11*

He was in her station. Standing over by one of the back counters.

Lora studied Deputy Beck. He was dressed in a pair of faded jeans that were frayed at the edges, flip-flops, and a snug-fitting weathered gray T-shirt. He looked far different than he did in his usual khaki-colored uniform. Younger. Maybe even more approachable.

Bill's wife, Mia, had just seated him in one of the booths by the west wall. He was halfheartedly looking at the menu. And far more intently looking around the diner.

Instinctively, Lora knew he was looking for her.

The question, of course, was why. Had he felt the same little zing of awareness that she'd felt every time they'd talked as well? Or had something else happened and he needed to ask her about it?

"Are you going to go wait on our customer, Lora, or expect him to serve himself?" Bill said from the other side of the kitchen window.

"I'm going. Sorry, Bill."

"No apology needed. That just ain't like you, watching and waiting. You are usually far more eager."

She couldn't deny that. While most of the other girls who worked there were always dreaming about the day they worked somewhere else, Lora actually liked her job.

Here, at Bill's Diner, she'd found a home of sorts. Bill and Mia were good to her, making her feel like she mattered to them. She also felt a lot of pride in her work. At Bill's she felt in control. She knew how to manage her time and how to manage her customers. She was good at waitressing, too. She always got the most tips and the most requests from regulars for her section.

The other girls said it was because of her usual attire of snug tank tops and the way her dark-blond hair hung in waves down her back.

Lora knew her popularity was because she took care of her customers. Young or old, Amish or English, local or tourist, she made it her mission to make sure they were glad they'd come to Bill's.

Which was why it really wasn't like her to keep Deputy Beck waiting.

Grabbing a pitcher of water, she hurried over to him. "Hey, Deputy Beck. I'm sorry I kept you waiting. I guess I was asleep on my feet. Water?"

"Sure." He smiled up at her as she poured. "How are you today?"

"Just fine. You?"

"Not exactly terrific, but I'm all right, too."

His honesty made some of her professional armor falter. "I hope everything is okay."

"It will be." He smiled again. This time the corners of his eyes crinkled a bit.

She tried not to be affected. "Do you know what you want to order?"

"I can't decide." Studying the menu, he said, "What is your favorite? The tuna melt or the cheeseburger?"

"Both are good."

"Which one do you eat more often?"

"Neither of them. I usually get a salad or something."

"Ah. You're a healthy eater."

When did his order become centered around her? "I'm a girl who likes fitting into her jeans."

Lowering his menu, he slowly eyed her from head to toe. "I guess a server here does have to practice some serious willpower."

"If I didn't, I'd gain ten pounds every month."

"Nah, you'd just have to go running with me every morning."

It sounded like he was turning their acquaintance into a relationship. And the way he was smiling at her! It was so direct. Just like she meant something to him.

Nervously, she glanced behind her, hoping none of the other girls heard him talk to her like that. She wouldn't live it down for weeks. "Deputy, most people really like Bill's cheeseburgers. I don't think you could go wrong there."

"I'll have one of those, then. And a strawberry shake." He winked. "I'm living on the edge today."

In spite of how agitated she felt around him, she laughed. "I'll get that order in and bring you your shake in a jiffy."

"Thanks." He smiled, then started fussing with his cell phone.

When she turned, Lora realized her fears had come true. She'd been watched. The other servers, Mia, and Bill had watched the interplay between her and the deputy. All four of them were grinning like Christmas had come early.

Ignoring their speculative glances, Lora rushed back and turned in the order, then started scooping ice cream for the shake.

But just as she had known it would happen, Meredith joined her at the counter. "Boy, he never talks to me like that when I take his order."

"Maybe he's in a chatty mood today," Lora replied, hoping she sounded far calmer than she felt.

Then Christine came over, too, turned, and stared at him boldly. "Do you know him?"

No way was she going to share that he'd questioned her. "Kind of." As she added strawberry powder and a cup of milk to the blender, she lowered her voice. "Turn around, would you?"

Christine did as Lora asked. "What does 'kind of' mean? Have y'all gone out? Are you dating?"

If Lora had been sipping water, she would have choked on it. "No."

"Do you want to? Because it sure looks like he does."

Feeling even more flustered, Lora jabbed at one of the buttons on the blender. "I need to get this out to him and check on my other customers."

Meredith chuckled. "Okay. I get the hint. I was just going to tell you that I hoped you were. You'd make a cute couple."

If she only knew! Quickly, she poured the mixture into a tall glass and brought it to the deputy. "Enjoy the shake. Your burger should be up soon."

"No hurry. I'm fine just sitting here."

Lora smiled weakly as she checked on her three other customers, collected a tip from a fourth, and helped get the door for a mom holding a cranky toddler.

"Order up," Bill called out.

Getting the deputy's plate, she brought it to him. "Here you go, Deputy Beck. Enjoy."

"Any chance you can sit with me for a sec?"

"I'm working."

"I know. But if you get a break or something?"

Dread settled in. "Did anything else happen?"

"Beyond Amy Miller getting attacked? No." Looking at her intently, he said, "See if you can take a break, though, would you?"

In spite of herself, she nodded. Unsure of what to do, she checked on her only other customer, an older man who was one of her regulars. As usual, he was eating a dish of chicken fried steak while reading his book. Other than making sure his glass of iced tea was filled, he wasn't going to need anything for at least another fifteen minutes.

"Go sit down," Mia said.

Looking at her boss's wife, she sighed. "You heard?"

"Christine did, who informed me," she whispered. "Now, go sit down and take a break for fifteen. I'll keep an eye on Mr. Granger."

Out of excuses, Lora walked back to Deputy Beck's booth and sat down. He was about halfway through his cheeseburger. When he looked up at her, she smiled awkwardly. "I decided to take that break now. I have fifteen minutes."

"Good." After sipping some water, he leaned back against

the red vinyl seat. "I wanted to see how you've been doing since we talked."

She shrugged. "I've been all right."

"Honestly?"

"Deputy Beck, I'm not sure how to answer you. Are you here on business? Am I in trouble?"

"I'm here because I care how you're doing."

But why? "Well, in that case, I guess you could say I'm doing about as well as can be expected after embarrassing myself with Calvin Fisher."

"That's kind of a strange way of putting it."

"I hate that I let a couple of brothers make me feel so bad about myself that I relapsed. I'm stronger than that."

"*Both* Calvin and Mark?" Looking concerned, he said, "Was Mark at your house, too?"

"Oh, no," she said in a rush, wishing that she'd taken the time to think how her words were going to sound. "Mark didn't do anything. He just . . . Well, he reminded me that I was a lot different than him." And the perpetually perfect Waneta Cain. Practically squirming in her seat, she said, "As for Calvin? He was being like he always was—trouble. I simply allowed myself not to care for a couple of hours one evening." Pressing a hand to her cheek, she said, "I learned my lesson, though. And, before you ask, no, I haven't seen him since."

He studied her as he took another bite, chewed thoughtfully, then sipped the last of his shake. "You know, I actually didn't intend to talk about all that."

"What did you intend to discuss?"

"I don't know." He smiled suddenly. "Me? You? I was hoping I could find a way to get you to relax a little bit more around me. Then I could ask you out."

"Like on a date?" Oh, no. Had she just said that?

Grinning now, he nodded. "Guess I'm pretty bad at this, huh?"

"If you're bad at it, I'm worse. I don't have a lot of experience dating." She didn't have any experience with men doing the stuff they did in movies and books, where they picked her up at her front door and treated her like she was worth their time and money.

"Will you think about it?"

"Yes."

Looking pleased, he said, "In the meantime, I'm going to plan to have a bunch of meals here. Maybe I'll even try that tuna melt next time I come in. And a chocolate shake, too."

"If you keep eating like that, you're going to have to run morning and night."

"That's okay. I still haven't given up hope that I'll have company. Now, here's a question for you. How many times have you actually been inside Horse Cave?"

The sudden switch of topics made her laugh. As they chatted, his questions about the cave and the surrounding areas encouraged her to think about a lot of things she usually took for granted. Newcomers to the area were often surprised to learn that their town was actually built on top of an actual cavern.

"I've only been inside twice."

"That's it?"

"It was enough. It's not like Mammoth Cave; it's a dark and wet place."

Eddie frowned. "How come?"

She laughed again as she told him what she knew about the cave's history . . . even the rumors about how it got its name from outlaws who hid their horses deep inside. Eddie listened with interest, asking her all kinds of questions. Making her feel like she was interesting.

Later, when he left, she realized she'd never take conversations like that for granted again. They were too sweet. Too special.

# CHAPTER 21

*Thursday, August 11*

Mark had now called on Waneta Cain two times in two days. This visit had been just as successful as the first. Almost becoming a habit.

"Come back soon, Mark," Gettie called out from her front door, waving like she was saying good-bye to a long-lost relative. "Don't be a stranger."

Feeling a bit like he'd stepped into another man's life, Mark returned her wave, smiled at Waneta, then started home. In his arms were two bags of food. One was filled with leftovers from today's visit; in the other, a block of white cheddar cheese and a loaf of freshly baked bread.

"Everyone can do with fresh baked bread and some cheese from S&L Salvage, don'tcha think?" Gettie had said when she'd placed the bounty of food in his arms.

Overwhelmed by such kindness, he'd mumbled a barely coherent response. "*Danke*. I will enjoy everything."

"I know you will. You need to eat more, Mark."

Biting his lip, he turned to meet Waneta's eyes. They were bright with amusement. She shrugged and smiled.

After thanking Mrs. Cain again, he collected the items with pleasure. He was going to have fresh bread later that night, and a couple more cookies, too. Such food could never be taken for granted.

Now, as he walked along the street, he allowed himself to remember another time when he'd gotten such a gift. It had been when he was still a child, probably no more than eight or nine. It was the last day of school before Christmas break and everyone in the classroom had been so excited about the upcoming days off.

Everyone but him, he'd thought. Calvin had still been young enough to be hopeful about Christmas. He still believed that their parents were going to up and change and suddenly act like the other children's parents. Though Mark knew that wasn't going to be the case, he hadn't had the heart to burst Calvin's bubble. All it would do was make him sad and whiney, and Mark had enough to do without dealing with that, too.

Because of all that, at the end of the day he was the last child to leave the classroom. Just as he was putting on his coat, Waneta's mother walked inside.

"Mark," she'd said. "I'm so glad you are still here."

"How come?" he'd asked.

Her smile widened. "Because I have something for you." She held out a canvas bag with a little Velcro flap on it.

He'd taken it suspiciously. "What is it?"

"I made you some cookies and granola bars."

Opening up the flap, he saw at least two dozen individually wrapped snacks. The scent of chocolate, brown sugar, and molasses made his stomach growl. He knew that if he only ate one or two a day, he could make them last for the whole break. He could hide the bag in his backpack. No one would look in there and they'd be his secret.

But something felt strange about accepting it. "Did you bring everyone a bag?"

"*Nee*, Mark. Only you and Calvin."

"Did you already give Calvin his bag?"

"*Nee*." Looking at him directly in the eye, she said, "I thought you might want to give it to him later. Maybe on your way home."

Mark knew if Calvin got a tote filled with snacks, the first thing he'd do would be to tell their parents. Their *mamm* would probably just look at it in confusion.

But their father would be angry. He'd use it as a reason to get mad at the both of them. Would likely say that they'd been bellyaching about their home to the teacher or to the other kids.

Then they'd no doubt get punished.

He knew what he had to do. "I don't want them," he said, before walking out the schoolhouse door.

He could feel Mrs. Cain's disappointed look resting on his back, but he didn't pause to say anything. It was better if she thought he was mean and rude. That was better instead of poor and hungry.

"You ready, Calvin?" he'd asked, his voice sounding gruff, even to his own ears.

"*Jah*." With a smile, Calvin trotted to his side. "Guess what? Some of the kids said when they get home, they're gonna have hot chocolate and popcorn, on account of it being the last day of school before Christmas."

"Good for them."

Calvin scampered a bit to keep up with Mark's stride. "Do you think Mamm will have that waiting for us?"

"*Nee.*"

His brother's eager smile faltered. "You sure? Maybe—"

"That ain't how things are at our *haus*. You know that, Calvin. Don't pretend otherwise."

When Calvin's steps slowed, Mark breathed a sigh of relief. It was better this way. Better for Calvin to stop hoping for things that were never going to happen.

Mark shook off the memory, hating how it made him feel. If he could go back in time, he would have taken the cookies, of course. At the very least they could have eaten a bunch of them on the way home.

All refusing had done was make him sadder and angrier at the world. It hadn't changed one thing about his life.

WHEN MARK WALKED in his front door, he half expected someone else to be waiting for him. That seemed to be the case these days. People were popping up out of his past without notice. Causing him to react without thought.

However, the house was quiet. It was also dark, thanks to the fading sunlight outside. After lighting a kerosene lantern, he set the tote bags on one of the kitchen countertops and opened one of the windows that had a screen, just to encourage some fresh air.

Then he walked through each room in the house to make sure there were no signs of visitors while he'd been gone.

But like the kitchen, everything seemed peaceful and didn't look disturbed. He sat down on his bed and removed his heavy boots and socks. Then wiggled his toes, glad to feel the cool, smooth wood underfoot.

Feeling relaxed, he walked back into the living room and sat down in the lone chair there.

The chair was new. He'd probably paid too much for it. He should have either kept the furniture that his father had left behind, or bought something at a thrift store. But he hadn't been able to.

Actually, keeping the furniture that had been left behind hadn't even been a possibility. It reminded him too much of long evenings spent watching his father either drink or smoke himself into a stupor. Or of him standing in front of the chair while his father sat and yelled, blaming him for Calvin's leaving and his *mamm's* taking off.

No, he told himself sternly. One trip down memory lane was more than enough for one afternoon. He needed to concentrate on something else. Anything else.

But when he heard the footsteps at the front door, he stood up with a sense of relief.

It seemed he wouldn't be alone with his memories for the time being after all.

Opening the door, he braced himself for whoever was there.

But when he saw Preacher Eli, he couldn't have been more surprised. Instead of greeting him right away, he stood and gaped at him in confusion.

Preacher Eli was only three or four years older than himself. He'd grown up in Charm, Ohio, and had moved to Hart

County when he was twenty-one or twenty-two. His and his wife's families had helped them buy some rich farmland, the price of property being much less in central Kentucky than in northern Ohio. Since then, Eli had been a farmer and a popular member of the community.

Mark heard he'd become a preacher only the year before. It seemed that the Lord had been very wise when He'd guided Eli to be called. Eli was a gifted preacher and a kind man.

But Mark had never heard of him doing evening house calls.

"Is everything all right?" Mark said at last.

"Of course. I just decided to pay you a visit. I'm glad I caught you at home. I wasn't sure if you were inside. It looked mighty quiet."

"I just got home, as a matter of fact. Would you like to come in?"

"I would."

Little by little, good manners returned. He waved a hand inside. "Do you want coffee or a glass of water?"

"Water sounds good. *Danke.*"

When Mark turned to go to the kitchen, the preacher followed. Whistling softly, he said, "My, look at the floors. They are going to be very fine."

"I hope so. They're gonna take a lot of work, but they'll be worth it," he said as he got them both glasses of water.

"Are you planning to work on them this week? If so, I could come by with two or three men from my cousin's shop and help you prep them."

"Thank you. I would appreciate that," he murmured. It felt a bit strange to accept such help so quickly, but he couldn't think of refusing. Not when there was so much to do. "I had forgotten that some of your family owns a wood-working shop."

"One by one, we're all moving out here. We like Kentucky. I like to do carpentry from time to time as well. It makes for a nice change in routine from my usual preaching and farming."

Mark had always thought it would be mighty hard to be a preacher. Names were drawn by lots, and the job was assigned for the rest of a man's life. "The Lord has blessed you, for sure."

"He's blessed us all." Preacher Eli took a chair and stretched his legs out. "I came over to see how you were doing. Are you having a difficult time being back here?"

Well, that was surely blunt. But what could he say? *"Jah."*

Preacher Eli's eyebrows raised before he broke into a broad grin. "I'm glad you don't mind speaking the truth."

"You might not say that in a few minutes. I'm afraid it's been quite a trying day. I think I don't have any more space in my head to phrase things gently."

"It's my lucky day, then. 'Cause I surely didn't come over here for you to keep your answers from me."

"What questions do you have?" asked Mark.

"I'd like to know how I can help make your return easier."

"I'm not sure how you can do that. Not with Amy hurt and her boyfriend telling anyone who will listen that I attacked her."

Preacher Eli looked down at his folded hands. "Abraham is a hothead, to be sure," he said after taking a fortifying breath. "He's a bit confused these days, too."

"He ain't confused about his feelings for me. Everyone is talking about how Abraham thinks I attacked her."

"He's worried about his girl. When he settles down, his harsh words will, too." Before Mark could argue that point, Eli said, "Now, what about everything else? Are you liking your job?"

"*Jah*. I like it fine. Henry Lehmann is a good man."

"He's in poor health, though," said the preacher. "He tries to cover up his pain, but I fear it is getting worse."

Mark nodded. "I'm worried about that, too. I'm glad I'm there to help him."

"And to be with Waneta Cain, too, *jah*?"

Eli was a wily man, to be sure. Just as Mark had relaxed, he'd circled back to the one person who had him completely in knots. He would have appreciated being able to have this time to think about his feelings for her and keep them to himself.

But maybe that was the problem with his life at the moment? He was so conditioned to getting hurt, he kept everything to himself. That didn't solve all his problems, though. It made him seem unreachable to everyone that he thought he was trying to befriend.

He needed to let down his guard and share his worries and weaknesses. Only then would other people begin to trust him.

However, it wasn't easy. "I don't know what to say about Waneta," he said at last. It wasn't a great start, but at least he was trying.

Instead of letting Mark lead the conversation, Eli simply laughed. "There's nothing to say about Waneta, Mark. She is a lovely and faithful woman. That is enough to know about anyone. Ain't so?"

Not necessarily. "She is also too trusting."

"Of whom? You?"

That was exactly what he feared. "Maybe."

Eli reached out and squeezed his shoulder. "Mark, I am going to offer some advice. I'd like you to listen, but you don't have to accept it. Okay?"

He nodded.

Looking pleased, Eli leaned back in his chair. "Here's the thing. You can't walk backwards all your life. You also canna get very far if you are constantly looking over your shoulder and wondering if anyone is following you."

"I know no one is following me." That was part of his problem.

But instead of smiling, Eli's light-brown eyes narrowed. "You could not control what your parents did. You could not control how your father treated you. Or your brother."

That went against everything he'd been fighting. "But—"

"*Nee*. No buts. You need to come to terms with this, Mark, or it's going to eat you up inside. The fact of the matter is that you also could not help Calvin."

"You weren't around then. You don't know. He was only fourteen when he took off."

"I realize I came after he left, but I remember the pain in your eyes—even all these years later. I have talked and prayed with the other preachers in the area about you and your family, too."

While Mark attempted to process that, Eli continued. "You were only sixteen, Mark," he said, each word emphasized. "You were only sixteen. You were not a man. You were not in control. Stop carrying that guilt."

*Stop carrying that guilt.* Four words. Forcibly said. He swallowed hard. "Is that what you think I've been doing?"

"*Nee.* That's what I *know* you've been doing. You've been secretly apologizing for all kinds of things that weren't your fault and you had no control over." He stood up then.

Eli's relatively small stature—he was only five foot seven compared to Mark's six foot two frame—seemed to grow in size as he looked down at Mark. "You did not hurt Bethany Williams. You did not attack her. You did not attempt to rape her."

"I know that. I've been telling everyone that, too. But—"

"But you have acted like a man who was ashamed."

"I was ashamed of who I was," he said with some surprise.

"You are a survivor. You don't give up. You have a good heart. You are a good person. You are someone worth knowing."

"Thank you."

"*Nee.* Don't thank me for seeing the real you," Eli said with obvious impatience. "Go out in the world and let everyone else see the real you, too."

"Including Waneta . . ." *There.*

He finally got it.

But Preacher Eli shook his head. "*Nee.* Not including Waneta. She already sees the real you. That's why she trusts you and wants to be with you. I mean everyone else."

Everyone else. The entire population of Horse Cave. Everyone in Hart County. Even, it seemed, Calvin.

Feeling vulnerable, Mark said, "My brother came back. He wants me to sell the house and give him some money."

"Do you want to do that?"

"*Nee.* I want to continue fixing it up. Make it livable. It will be a nice place to live in eventually."

"I agree. It's big enough for a family, too."

"But Calvin might have a point. The house is half his, after all."

"Why is it half his? Because he was born?"

"Well, yes." Mark thought that was pretty obvious. "I mean, that's what is fair."

"But you've already learned that life isn't fair, right?"

"To be sure."

"Then why do you need to bend over backwards to help a man who doesn't have any interest in helping you even a little?"

Mark gaped. "That seems kind of harsh."

"I agree. It does. But that doesn't mean I'm wrong."

His bluntness hurt. But maybe Eli was correct. Everything that was right didn't always feel comforting. Standing up, Mark said, "Eli, this visit of yours sure packs a wallop. I feel a bit run over and damaged."

"I didn't mean to do that. But I did want to wake you up." Pointing to the window, he said, "There's a big world out there. It is filled with pain and hurt. To be sure. But it's also filled with opportunities and wonderful people. And love. If you dare to step out of your prison."

With those cryptic words still ringing in Mark's ears, Eli said, "Well now. I had better get on my way. I have one more visit to go before the sun disappears completely."

Walking him to the door, Mark said, "Hey, Eli?"

Eli paused. *"Jah?"*

"God knew what He was doing when He made you a preacher. You have a gift."

Eli smiled, his eyes lighting up, too. *"Danke,* Mark. Our Lord is good, to be sure. I am blessed that He has entrusted me with so much."

At the door then, Preacher Eli took his hat and left.

Leaving Mark feeling exhausted and energized, and with four words still ringing in his ears. *Stop carrying the guilt.*

He'd definitely needed to hear that, he realized as he went into the kitchen, unwrapped the block of cheese he'd brought home, and sliced a thick wedge. Then he sliced a piece of Gettie Cain's homemade bread. After making a small sandwich, he took a bite.

It tasted good. Tasted perfect.

And, perhaps, like he deserved it, too.

# CHAPTER 22

*Tuesday, August 16*

Mark had asked to come in late, and Mr. Lehmann had already shared that he wouldn't be working until early afternoon. He had a couple of doctors' appointments over in Bowling Green.

Therefore, Waneta was working at the nursery by herself. It was an unusual occurrence. Usually, her boss asked one of the younger boys who worked on the weekends to join her, if for no other reason than to help customers with lifting bags of mulch and carrying plants and shrubs to their vehicles. But, today, he hadn't been able to find anyone to work. It seemed a lot of people were traveling this week.

Waneta didn't mind being at Blooms and Berries alone, however. Actually, she was kind of enjoying the novelty. Since she was so busy caring for her parents and the house in the evenings, it was a rare experience to have time for herself. This slow day at the nursery was a good opportunity to sort out some things in her head.

In between helping the few people who had entered the

store, Waneta had constructed mental lists of things to tackle and other things to leave to God.

The first item had been Amy Miller. Waneta had come to realize that she wasn't going to be able to change Amy's opinion about Mark anytime soon. Since she was not going to simply stay quiet while Amy bad-mouthed Mark, it was necessary to give Amy space to recover. It had been a hard decision. She liked Amy very much. But that didn't mean she had to listen to Amy's mean comments.

Was Amy the first of many people she was going to have to distance herself from if she continued to fight for Mark's character? She hoped not, but it might very well be the case.

When the door chimed, she lifted her head to smile at the newcomers, glad to take a break from her thoughts.

Just as quickly, she stifled a groan.

James and Katie Eicher had returned, and James looked just as irritated by life as he had the last time he was there.

Remembering Mr. Lehmann's words, about how it wasn't necessary to like every customer in order to serve them well, Waneta stepped forward to greet them.

"James. Katie. Good day," she said pleasantly.

Katie's eyes warmed. "*Gut* day to you, too, Waneta. Is it hot enough for you?"

Waneta lifted up her foot, showing off her yellow rubber flip-flops, which matched her pretty daffodil dress. "It's so hot I decided to give my feet a break today. It was too hot to even wear tennis shoes."

"I bet," Katie said with a small laugh. "I've considered wearing flip-flops a time or two myself."

"Except that it ain't seemly," James said.

"Of course, James," Katie murmured, all traces of laughter firmly tamped down.

Oh, that James was just so mean to his wife! With great effort, Waneta kept her voice friendly and even. "What can I help you two with?"

"You can find a man to assist me."

It was becoming harder and harder not to glare. "I'm sorry, there's only me right now."

James looked around the shop. "Where is Henry?"

"He's not in this morning." She didn't think it was everyone's business what Henry was doing. "Now, did you come in for anything special?"

"What about Mark Fisher? Is he here? Or, did Henry finally get rid of him?"

"Mark will be in later," she said with rapidly evaporating patience. "Now, I'll be happy to help you with whatever you are looking for . . ."

"He's still an employee? Even after what happened to Amy?"

Though she was tempted to jump to Mark's defense, she kept her expression as neutral as possible. "Just let me know when you are ready for my assistance."

"I don't know what has gotten into everyone around here. First criminals are walking around unattended and now good Amish girls are running around, getting themselves into trouble."

That was the last straw. No longer caring if she was going to have to listen to one of Mr. Lehmann's lectures, Waneta pressed her hands to her hips. "Are you referring to Amy? I believe she was attacked near her house."

"If she was attacked there, it's only by chance. You know what she's become like. Wild."

"I saw her yesterday. She was hurt very bad. She most certainly didn't deserve what happened to her."

Katie rested her hand on James's bicep. "James, you know we didn't come in here to discuss Amy's accident."

*Accident?* Before she could stop herself, Waneta said, "I don't know if you could call her attack an accident. Some terrible man tried to rape her, you see."

James shook his arm free of his wife's clasp as he strode forward. "You don't know what you are talking about. I think you should stick to only discussing work."

That had been what she'd been trying to do! "I would rather you not speak to me that way."

"Good Amish girls are supposed to be biddable and demure. It's bad enough that you are working in a public place such as this. But now you are defending all sorts of people who shouldn't even be here."

"Are you saying that I'm not being a good person?"

He stepped forward, overwhelming her with his size. "I'm saying you should be watching yourself and being careful about who you speak to."

"Or what? What are you going to do?" Waneta asked, hardly aware that the door was opening.

"Or I'll make sure you will be disciplined."

*Disciplined?* She couldn't help it, she laughed. "James, what has gotten into you? Do you hear what you are—"

He grabbed her arm, yanked it hard. So hard, she knew her arm was going to be bruised and her shoulder was going to be sore. She cried out, "James!"

"Take your hand off of her," Mark called out as he rushed forward.

Instantly, James's hand lifted. He whirled around to face Mark. He stepped toward him, obviously looking anxious to fight.

But Mark ignored him. He walked right by James, moving with intent until he stopped directly in front of Waneta. "Are you all right?" he asked. "Has he hurt you?"

She realized then that she was trembling. "He didn't hurt me. But I'm glad you arrived. In the nick of time, too." She had the awful suspicion that James had been mere moments from doing something worse.

He rubbed her arm with his right hand. "I'm glad I got here when I did."

Just as she smiled at him, James's voice broke the moment.

"Look at you, Waneta. Standing there. Allowing him to touch you."

"You need to stop talking," Mark said. "Better yet, you need to leave. Immediately."

But James did not. "You've made your decision, haven't you, Waneta Cain?" he asked, his voice filled with sarcasm. "You've pushed aside what is right and proper. Instead, you've sided with the likes of him."

"James, I think it's time you left," a man who had entered the store called from the back of the room.

All of them turned.

Waneta breathed a sigh of relief. John Paul Schlabach and Matthew Yoder had just walked inside the shop and both of them were staring at James Eicher like he was the lowest sort of man.

"You watch it, John," James muttered.

John Paul strode forward, all two hundred and fifty pounds of him. "*No*, you watch it," he said. "You are causing a scene and frightening your *frau*. I don't know what is wrong with you, but I'm thinking you need to get your bearings. You're on the verge of losing control."

James froze as John walked to his side. "John Paul, you don't understand. Waneta here was acting uppity—"

"Now ain't the place," Matthew Yoder said as he moved to stand next to James on his other side. "Go on."

Without another word, Katie hurried toward the door. Her head was down and her shoulders slumped. She looked defeated.

Breathing like she'd just finished a marathon, Waneta watched Katie's departure. Part of her knew she should be feeling sorry for the woman, but she was too shaken by James's anger to feel much beyond relief. Her hands were shaking—her nerves were letting her know that the experience was taking its toll.

His hands in fists, James glared at all of them. "You are going to regret choosing a man like him over me." He turned to her again. "One day soon, when you are injured and hurt and lying on the ground forgotten, you will only have yourself to blame."

She was finding it difficult to breathe.

Moving closer to her side, Mark looked at him thoughtfully. "Are you threatening Waneta?"

"I don't need to threaten anyone," James countered, his expression triumphant. "I'm only predicting what will happen to any woman who trusts you. To any *person* who trusts you. You taint them. Hurt them. Always, sooner than later." With those parting words, he turned and walked out the door.

Waneta noticed that James's chin was up and his shoulders were pulled back. Just as if he'd made his point and he was proud about it.

The moment the door shut behind him, Waneta felt dizzy. "I need a minute," she mumbled as she hurried off to the storage room. She needed the dim, cool space in order to relax and regroup.

Once she was completely alone, she sank into one of the chairs. The tears that she had been holding at bay pricked her eyes as she wrapped her arms about herself. She had been really scared of one man in that room.

And it hadn't been Mark.

# CHAPTER 23

*Tuesday, August 16*

As he sat in Lora Weaver's kitchen, with its pale turquoise walls, sparkling white counters, and worn-out table and chairs, Calvin Fisher was reflecting on things.

It was kind of a new thing but unavoidable.

Every time he had an extra minute or two, his mind would drift back to his most recent conversation with Mark. Over and over, he continually revisited the words they'd exchanged. It hadn't been pleasant.

Actually, it had been a painful undertaking. Few of the things that they'd discussed had made him feel good. Most of it had left him feeling empty and filled with pain.

From the time he left home at the age of fourteen, he'd taken care of himself. It hadn't been easy. He'd quickly learned that there were a whole lot of people in the world who enjoyed taking advantage of young Amish boys.

But he had prevailed. He'd worked odd jobs, learned how to manipulate people, learned to control situations in order to get what he needed.

He'd also gotten real good at imbibing a variety of substances so he wouldn't hurt too much. So he wouldn't feel too much. Numbness, whether it was derived from a six-pack of beer or a handful of pills, had its advantages.

Until he'd returned to Horse Cave, he hadn't thought much about the type of man he'd become or the significance of his actions. All he'd cared about was that he was surviving while so many others were not. But now, after talking to Mark and hearing his goals for the future, after witnessing the way he was slowly earning respect in a place where no one had ever respected their family, Calvin was beginning to wonder if he'd gotten it all wrong.

Maybe he should have cared more about consequences.

Maybe he should have tried harder to stay sober and forced himself to confront all of the demons in his past. If he had, he could be more like his brother right now.

Was it too late? He didn't know. He wondered if even God knew.

"Calvin!" Lora said around a yelp as she walked into her kitchen. "Oh my word. You scared me, sitting in here in the dark."

"Sorry. I didn't think you'd mind. I had nowhere else to go."

"Actually, I do mind. I don't want you coming inside without me being here. It ain't right."

She was wearing a simple sundress today. It was some kind of complicated floral pattern, all done in faded shades of yellow and orange. It hung loosely on her, ending mid-calf.

He realized it was probably the most modest outfit he'd seen her wear. Her hair was brushed and it was confined in a ponytail at the back of her neck. Her skin looked fresh and clean. Maybe she had on some mascara, but nothing else.

She also was acting pretty mad. "What's wrong with you?"

"Do you really need to ask?"

"You still upset about me accidentally hitting you?"

"Of course I am."

Remembering how out of control he'd been . . . and how guilty he'd felt, Calvin could hardly look her in the eye. "I already apologized for that."

"Not really. Not enough."

"Give me a break, Lora, wouldja? I won't be here long. I just needed someplace private to hang out for a couple of minutes."

Her gaze sharpened but she said nothing, only pulled out a glass and a pitcher of water from the refrigerator. "Want some?"

"Yeah. Sure."

She poured two glasses of water and handed him one as she sat down in the other chair at her small table. "Why are you really here?" she said after draining half the glass. "And don't tell me it's to rest and relax."

Calvin noticed that her eyes were averted. Her voice was thick, and she was acting far differently than she had the first time he'd shown up unannounced. Like night and day.

"What is wrong with you?" he asked. "You're acting as if you don't even know me. Like we've never been friends. Like you and I weren't hanging out together just last week."

Her eyes flashed. "Calvin, don't act like the trouble is with me. You hit me—then ran off."

"I'm here now."

"You sure are," she said sarcastically. "After serving food for seven hours at Bill's, I walk into my own house to find you sitting at this table. Looking like you don't have a care in the world. Of course I'm going to be surprised and ticked off."

He figured she had a point. But if he conceded that, he'd feel obligated to leave.

And then where would he go?

Therefore, he fastened on to the one thing she couldn't dispute. "What do you mean, working at Bill's?"

"I work at Bill's Diner. Did you not even know that?"

He hadn't. He hadn't really thought about it. "You a waitress there?"

She nodded. Lifting her chin, she said, "I've had this job fourteen months now."

She'd kept the same job for fourteen months. For over a year. It hit him then that she'd been obviously counting those months. She was proud of herself. "So that's why you're so dressed up."

She looked down at her sundress and shrugged. "Why are you here, Calvin? You never said."

Knowing that he had to come up with a topic before she threw him out, he said, "I talked to that sheriff. He said he and his deputy talked to you."

"Yeah. Sheriff Brewer and Deputy Beck came over to see me the morning after we sat here and got drunk together." She frowned. "This place was a mess. At first, I thought he was going to arrest me because the living room smelled like pot."

"He didn't?"

"No. He did look around, though."

"Did he have a search warrant?"

"I didn't care. It wasn't like he was going to find anything."

Her expression tightened. "I was kind of out of it, Calvin. My face really hurt."

"What did you tell him about me?"

"That I had the beer but you had the pot."

Panic was setting in. "Is that it?"

Leaning up against one of those white counters, she sipped her water. "Yes," she said after a moment. "I mean no."

"Which is it?"

"I don't know."

"Lora, this is important. I'm afraid the sheriff wants to blame me for Amy Miller getting hurt." Then there was the whole drug thing. And maybe even his ties to the gang he owed so much money to.

"I don't know what you want me to say, Calvin. If you're asking if I told the sheriff or Deputy Beck that I thought you were trouble, I didn't." Looking at him coolly, she said, "But I didn't defend you, either."

"I thought we were friends."

After draining her glass of water, she turned on the tap and got some more. All while he stood there and fumed.

When she turned his way again, her expression was distant. Almost like she was stuck talking to a stranger. "Calvin, you and I have a past. We've also had some good times together. But that night we spent together was a mistake. You caught me at a weak moment."

"I didn't force you to do anything, Lora."

"I'm not saying you did. But I'm also not going to repeat it. Ever. I'm not like that anymore."

"You were the other day."

Looking incredulous, she said, "What do I have to say for

you to understand how I'm feeling? I regret letting you in my house. I regret drinking with you. I regret smoking pot with you. I regret our argument. I regret that I wasn't strong enough to stop you from hitting me."

Needing to distance himself from her words, he leaned against the opposite row of cabinets. "You're being dramatic."

"Maybe I am. But what I am sayin' is that you are toxic, Calvin Fisher. You've come back here after ten years. A whole decade. And you have nothing to show for yourself except some scars marking your body and an attitude that is selfish and mean."

"I had to leave home at fourteen. Don't you know how hard that was?"

"Boo. Hoo," she taunted, sarcasm thick in her voice. "Like you're the only person in Hart County who has had bad stuff happen to them."

Memories that he fought so hard to forget bubbled up to the surface. Suddenly, he smelled the dirt and mildew in the house. Smelled the stale liquor, the unwashed dishes. The empty cabinets. Heard his father yelling at him. At all of them. "You don't know what the inside of my house was like."

"Sure I do. But even if I didn't, I do know what your brother is like."

"What is he like?" he asked harshly. "Perfect? Stuck-up? Far too full of himself?"

"Maybe he has moved on. Moved forward."

Jealousy hit him hard. "Is that who you're trying to impress, Lora? My older brother? Just like when we were in school and you used to sidle up next to him and try to get his attention?" Ignoring her look of embarrassment, he stood up, too. "Just to let you know, he ain't never going to give a person like you the time of day. He's got his eye on Waneta Cain, who's so pure and sweet, it's amazing she doesn't melt when it rains."

"You need to leave."

"Oh, don't act so hurt. You didn't really think that a girl like you would ever be good enough for my high and mighty brother, did you? Mark Fisher would never want a girl like you. Especially not when he finds out everything you've done over the years."

"I am not trying to snag your brother."

"Oh, is it someone else, then? Someone good? Someone other people respect?"

He knew he'd hit the mark when she visibly flinched. "Get out of here, Calvin. Get out before I call the sheriff and tell him that I'm afraid of you."

"Don't worry. I'm leaving," he said as he walked to her back door and yanked it open. "But I'm warning ya, Lora Weaver. If you start thinking that you can change, you're in for a real surprise. People like you and me won't ever change. And we're never going to be good enough for the likes of Mark Fisher or Waneta Cain. To them, you and I are always going to be worthless. Trash."

Pain filled her eyes. "That's not true."

"Of course it is. We might be older and we might even be smarter. But some things never change. Not for people like us," he said quietly as he started walking.

He picked up his pace when he heard her cry. Knew he'd just hurt her badly.

If Calvin wasn't feeling so much pain already, he knew he'd feel terrible.

But all he felt at the moment was numb.

# CHAPTER 24

*Tuesday, August 16*

Only after Calvin disappeared from sight did Lora close the door. Then, because his words were still ringing in her ears, practically infecting her, she locked it and flipped the deadbolt for good measure.

She'd meant what she'd told him. He was toxic. His cruel comments and negative outlook infected her, made her doubt herself, made her doubt everything she tried to believe about herself.

Feeling sick, she downed another glass of water. One of her self-help books she'd been reading had advised doing that. Something about how water was cleansing. Lora wasn't all that sure if it was cleansing her insides or not, but she figured it was worth a try.

After all, she had plenty of water from the tap on hand.

Once she was calmer, she put Calvin's glass in the sink, then opened the two plastic sacks she'd set on the counter when she'd first seen Calvin in her kitchen.

One of the good things about working at Bill's was the fact

that servers often got to take home leftovers. Today, she'd brought home a carton of beef stew, some macaroni and cheese, and two slices of cherry pie.

After setting the cardboard containers in the refrigerator, she picked up a rag to clean up her counters. But they were as white and pristine as she'd left them that morning. She sighed in relief.

Another one of her books had suggested doing home improvements every time she had a craving for doing something that she shouldn't. She'd taken that advice to heart. A year ago, she'd repainted the kitchen a pale turquoise. The cheery color had instantly made each day feel more optimistic.

After that, she'd bought some industrial-strength cleaner that Bill had recommended and scrubbed and scrubbed her countertops. Now they were a squeaky-clean white. It was silly, but she felt like they were a symbol for herself. Under all the grime and mistakes, there were some good things. She just had to work on uncovering them.

On her days off, she was tackling the tile in her bathroom. One day she hoped it would look as fresh as the countertops. She didn't know if it was possible, but she was going to try.

If only she could make Calvin's words vanish so easily!

Still feeling off-kilter, she walked to the bathroom and stood in front of the mirror. Looked at her skin—she still had lines around her lips from smoking for all those years, a scar on her arm from the car accident she'd been in.

The shadows under her eyes.

Even though she was in a new dress and her hair was shiny and clean, she still had a long way to go to be untarnished.

Maybe Calvin was right. Maybe she was an idiot, forever

thinking she could change and that someone good and decent would think she was that way, too.

But just as she was about to turn away, she noticed something else. Her eyes were brighter. Her body was okay, too. She wasn't skinny and malnourished anymore. She looked healthy. Normal.

Why, if she didn't tell someone about all the things she'd done, they would probably never even guess.

She *was* better.

The phone rang. Running to her purse, she dug it out. Staring at the screen, she considered ignoring the call. What did the sheriff's office want from her now?

However, if she ignored it, then they would probably come find her again. She couldn't deal with another house call from them.

"Hello?" she said at last.

"Lora!" an unexpected voice said. "I was about to hang up. This is Eddie Beck. I'm glad you answered."

He was glad? She had no idea how to respond to that. "Hi, Deputy Beck," she said at last. "I, uh, was washing my hands. It took me a minute to grab the phone."

"Nothing to apologize for. And listen, I thought we had made it to first names by now. Haven't we?"

"Well, um . . ."

"My name is Eddie."

Oh, she knew. Now he was making her flustered. "I remembered." When he said nothing, she mumbled, "I mean, yes, we did make it to first names. Hello, Eddie." Great. Now she sounded like she was back in eighth grade. Her voice was sharp and she was fumbling over every word. "Um . . . did you need something?"

"I did." He paused, then blurted, "Sorry for the late notice, but is there any chance you are free right now?"

She gripped her cell phone a little tighter as despair settled into the pit of her stomach. What had happened now?

More importantly, why did the deputy think she had something to do with it?

Unless . . . it had something to do with Calvin? A handful of worse-case scenarios came to mind. Maybe he was watching her house? Maybe the deputy had just seen him leaving?

"Why? What's happened?"

"Nothing." He sounded taken aback.

"I don't understand, then."

"Well, you see, I've got the rest of the afternoon off. And, well, I don't know if you noticed, but for once it's not a hundred percent humidity. It's actually kind of bearable outside. Almost pleasant."

"It is nice."

"So, I wondered if you would like to go to Nolin Lake with me? There are some nice walking trails along the lake, and a great place for fried fish and burgers."

Her toes curled against the floor as the reason for his call sunk in. Deputy Eddie Beck wasn't calling to question her. Or to let her know that he saw Calvin walking out of her house.

He wasn't calling her for a business reason at all. No, it was personal.

Just to make sure she wasn't misunderstanding, she said tentatively, "Eddie, are you asking me out?"

He chuckled. "I guess I am, though I must be doing a really bad job of it if you have to ask."

"No, it is good. I was just surprised." She covered her phone with her palm and cleared her throat. Her voice sounded off. Hoarse.

"Surprised in a good way? Or bad?"

"In a good way," she replied, chuckling. "The best way."

"So is that a yes?" His voice was warm. Hopeful. "May I come pick you up in about a half hour? I promise, I'll be in my truck, not a police cruiser."

Feeling like she was in a daze, she nodded. Then remembered he was still waiting on the other end of the line. "Yes. A half hour is fine. I'll be ready. *Danke*." She shook her head. "I mean, thank you for the invitation."

"You're welcome, Lora. See you soon."

Only when she clicked off did she realize that Eddie had answered her in Pennsylvania Dutch, because she'd accepted in *Deutsch*!

Pressing her hands to her cheeks, she chuckled again.

And realized that Calvin couldn't have been more wrong. She could change. She could be more than she'd thought. She was worth it.

Even to people like Eddie Beck.

LORA WAS STILL feeling a lovely glow four hours later. She and Eddie had had a wonderful time. They'd walked along the shores of Nolin Lake, talking about sports, Eddie's basset hound, and her latest home improvement project.

They'd had fish-and-chips in a cute restaurant next to the docks. Then he'd kissed her on the cheek at her front door and waited until she got safely inside before going back to his vehicle. Just like a character in one of those romantic comedy movies she liked so much.

After she'd closed the door, Lora turned on the small light

in the hall and then peeked out the window while he started his car and pulled away. For the first time in her life—that she could remember anyway—she felt content.

She felt normal and cared for and almost hopeful about the future.

"You have no shame, do you?"

Stifling a scream, Lora whirled around. When she saw him standing in the doorway of her kitchen, pure panic set in. "What are you doing here?"

"Not a lot. Only waiting. Waiting almost an hour." Even in the dim light, his expression looked full of disdain. "You should have been home, Lora."

"You need to leave," she said in a firm tone. "You can't just come in here and wait for me."

"I need to talk to you. But it's obvious that talking ain't going to help you change your ways, is it?"

She was shaking now. Ruthlessly, she fisted her hands, hoping the slight pinch of her nails digging into her palms would give her the control she needed to have.

He noticed. A triumphant gleam entered his expression. He was glad she was afraid.

"It's been you, hasn't it?" she whispered. "You are the man who attacked Amy Miller."

"Amy wasn't behaving right. She was lying to her parents. Dishonoring her family."

"You wore a mask with her." Her voice was trembling. To her amazement, she realized that there was still a small part of her that was waiting for him to deny her allegations. To tell her that it hadn't been him at all.

But instead, his voice turned hoarse. "I had no choice. She would've been able to identify me."

His voice was calm and even. As if they were talking about the menu at Bill's. As if he was in complete control of himself.

But she recognized that look in his eyes. It was the same one that had appeared in some of the men's faces when she'd walked into homeless shelters late at night. Whether it was from drugs, alcohol, or derived from pure anger and hate, she knew it was going to only bring her pain.

Especially since she was afraid he had a very good reason for not wearing a mask. He didn't plan for her to be alive to identify him one day.

She stepped back toward the door.

"Don't," he barked.

But Lora knew better than to believe that obeying him was going to help her. She stepped backward again. Then, turned and ran to the door and pulled open the handle. She had to get away from him.

Just as she stepped through the threshold, he grabbed her shoulders and threw her down to the ground. She screamed as her head hit the hard linoleum floor while her shoulders grazed the inside of the doorframe.

"You won't ever learn, will you, Lora?" he asked as he pulled her inside.

She fought. Kicking and twisting, she screamed again as her back slid along the cool floor. Screamed as loud as she could, for once thankful that she didn't live on an acre of property on the outskirts of town. Surely, someone would hear her.

"*Nee!*" With a grunt, he hit her hard. Hit her mouth.

She tasted blood as her lips tore against her teeth. Pain ebbed from the cut, radiated through her head, making her feel disoriented. But still she fought back. With as much power as she could, she pushed at his shoulders.

He grunted before hitting her again. This time harder. Spots filled her vision, and she knew she was about to black out. But she'd been through far too much to simply give up. Since her body was weakening, she had to use the only thing left to her.

Her voice.

"You can't keep hurting women like this. You are going to be discovered. Then punished."

"By whom? Your police officer?" His voice was filled with sarcasm as he shifted to slam the door shut.

Effectively ending her effort to get away.

Dark acceptance filled her. She wasn't going to be able to run away. Or fight back. Or stop whatever he was about to do. Her body was hurting too much, her head was pounding too hard.

Therefore she glared at her attacker, letting all the disdain she felt for him seep into her expression. "You aren't going to get anything right, are you?" she whispered. "Eddie Beck ain't a policeman. He's a sheriff's deputy. And oh, yes, he will punish you for this. Of that I have no doubt."

Then all her words left as he grabbed her shoulders, shook her hard, then hit her again. And several more times after that.

# CHAPTER 25

*Wednesday, August 17*

"Mark, you don't need to start walking me to work. I'll be fine," Waneta said as they started down her driveway.

"Like I told you the other day, you mean something to me. Something important. I'm not going to take a risk with your safety."

Her heart melted. Mark made her feel feminine and protected. She knew she shouldn't yearn for such things, that she should want to feel independent and self-assured, but the last year had taken its toll. She'd been spending her life on autopilot, dutifully going from her duties at work to tackling her chores at home.

She'd known she'd been tired. She'd known she'd been emotionally exhausted, but she hadn't realized how drained she'd been. Mark's attentions and protective nature made her feel a little weak. More than a little warm and mushy inside.

She wasn't sure why God had decided that now was their time together, but she couldn't deny that His timing had been impeccable. Just when she'd needed someone the most, Mark had arrived in her life.

But that didn't mean she wanted to take advantage of his goodness.

"I could have ridden my bike, you know. If I thought I was in danger, I could simply pedal faster."

"You think a blue bicycle with a brown wicker basket is going to save you from someone trying to do you harm?"

"Maybe. Especially since I don't think I'm going to come to any harm."

"Since I don't want to hurt your feelings, I won't mention Amy Miller, then."

"Well, that's a sneaky way of adding your two cents," she said, though his comment *had* hit its mark. She was still shaken up by Amy's attack.

"I'm going to do whatever I can to make you take your safety seriously," he said as he moved her closer to the side of the road as a vehicle approached. "You mean too much to me to keep my feelings to myself."

As it slowed and veered around them, Waneta noticed that the driver had waved at them as he passed. No doubt he was thinking they were a sweet Amish couple walking together.

And maybe that's what they were. She had on a light-green dress with short sleeves, a white *kapp*, and rubber flip-flops. Next to her, Mark was in brighter colors, wearing a short-sleeved bright-blue shirt and black pants, set off by his straw hat. He was also carrying her lunch cooler.

"I feel a little like we're on our way to school and you're carrying my lunch," she teased.

"We're pretty close to that." Smiling, he said, "But that would have been nice, don't you think?"

"If we were younger and still in school?"

"If we could go back in time and take advantage of the opportunities the Lord gave us. If I had been smarter, I could have
courted you then. It would have saved me a lot of trouble."

She supposed he had a point. But as wonderful as it
sounded now, she doubted she would have been in the right
frame of mind back then to have been his sweetheart. She'd
been too sheltered and tentative about anything that was different than the narrow world she knew.

And Mark? Well, she didn't remember him acting this
way. He'd been restless and angry. Now, of course, she knew
why. Back then? . . .

She hadn't really wanted to know.

"I think we were meant to wait for each other," she said
softly. "Though it would have saved us some hardships, I
don't know if it would have saved us from a bunch of other
problems."

A muscle in his cheek twitched before he nodded. "You
know, I think you are probably right. This is our time. And
because of everything we've been through—not in spite of
it—I know we are meant to be together."

Now her insides felt like jelly. Mark really did say the
sweetest things. "Just for that, I'm going to let you share my
lunch."

He bent his elbow, pretending to groan, as if her cooler
weighed a hundred pounds. "I hope so, because if you intended to eat all this food, I'd be mighty worried about you."

"Are you sure you can carry that cooler without a problem? Your hand is awfully bruised."

"Oh, it's nothing. I just knocked it wrong when I was attempting to repair some old woodwork."

"It's more than nothing. It's mighty swollen."

He shrugged. "I'll survive. Or maybe Henry will feel sorry for me and make you do all the heavy lifting today."

"I'm stronger than I look. You forget that I did your job for years before you arrived."

"I haven't forgotten. You do like to boss me around."

She was giggling as he moved her to the shoulder of the road again.

"Careful, now," he murmured. "Some of these cars go by far too fast."

As the vehicle approached, Mark tensed. "This one don't seem— *Ah*, it's the sheriff."

Waneta stopped as they watched Sheriff Brewer's vehicle slow down beside them. The passenger-side window rolled down, revealing Deputy Beck.

"Morning," he said. "We were on our way to Blooms and Berries to speak to you."

"To me?" Waneta asked curiously . . . just seconds before panic set in. "Oh, no! Did something happen to my *daed*?"

After the vehicle stopped, the deputy got out. "Your parents are fine, Neeta," he soothed.

"Then what do you need?"

Sheriff Brewer's door opened and shut. "We were looking for Mark, not you."

Mark stepped closer to her. She wondered if he was trying to ease her concerns or allay his own. "What happened?" he asked.

"The side of the road isn't the best place to have this discussion," the deputy said. "We'd like to take you in."

"To the station?" Mark's expression turned stormy. "I think you need to explain yourselves right here first."

"Lora Weaver was attacked last night," Sheriff Brewer said.

"She almost died," the deputy added. "She wasn't found until this morning when she didn't show up for work and her boss got concerned."

"Who found her?" Mark asked.

The deputy glared at him. "I did. She was lying on the floor, barely breathing. Blood all around her. It's amazing she is still alive."

Imagining poor Lora, Waneta started shaking.

Mark curved his arm protectively around her. "Careful, now," he warned the officers. "There's a better way to tell a woman news like this. Bluntly on the side of the road ain't it."

"This was the way you wanted to handle it, though," Deputy Beck said. "As if you really cared."

Mark's expression turned to stone. "What are you saying?"

Before either of the officers could reply, Waneta raised her voice. "Who could have done this? Is Lora going to be all right?"

"The ambulance took her in. I sent a man out to fetch her sister," Sheriff Brewer said. "But she's unconscious. They're running some tests now to check for bleeding."

"So you don't know who did it?"

"We have some ideas," the deputy said quietly as he reached for his arm. "Now, it's time you came with us."

Mark jerked his arm away. "I had nothing to do with Lora getting hurt. I was friends with her."

"That wasn't what she said."

"When?" Mark said, his voice incredulous. "You just told us that she wasn't awake."

Ignoring Mark's retort, Deputy Beck shot off another question. "What were you doing last night?"

"I was working in my house."

"Alone?"

"Yes. Of course."

"How did you get that bruise and scrape on your hand?"

Staring at his hand, Mark flexed his fingers. "I was repairing some corner woodwork," he said slowly. "Wait. You really do suspect me, don't you?"

Sheriff Brewer stepped closer. "As much as it pains me to do this, I need you to come to the station with me, son."

Mark shook his head. "I told you I'd never allow you to put me through that again. I had nothing to do with Lora getting hurt."

Deputy Beck gripped his arm. "You can either get in the vehicle without arguing or we can slip some handcuffs on you."

Waneta shook her head. "*Nee*! Sheriff Brewer, don't do this."

"Deputy Beck is going to walk you back home, Waneta."

"*Nee*." Feeling frantic now, she rushed toward Mark. "I don't know what to do. How can I help?"

Pain filled his expression as he gazed at her. "Calm down, Waneta. I'll be all right."

"*Nee*, you aren't—"

"I promise, I'll be fine. See? I'm getting in the car now," he continued easily. "Go on home now."

"Mark, I canna just stand here and do nothing."

Looking even more grim, he said, "You won't. You'll be staying safe, which is more important. Go home, Neeta. I'll come over when I'm done."

Waneta stood helplessly as she watched Sheriff Brewer open the back passenger door and guide Mark in, then get in the driver's seat.

She was frozen as she stood by the deputy's side while the car pulled out and drove toward town.

"Is this yours?" Deputy Beck picked up the heavy cooler.

Seeing that cooler was the tipping point. Because it wasn't really hers. That food was for Mark and her to share. There was no way she was going to be able to enjoy it without him beside her.

Tears filled her eyes. *"Jah."*

"Waneta, we have a couple of choices," he said quietly. "I can walk you back home or I can call and have someone pick us up."

All she could seem to do was stare at him. Lora was unconscious. Mark had been taken in for questioning. None of it felt real.

He cleared his throat. "I'm sorry. I'm sure you are having a difficult time, but I need your help. I need to get to the hospital as soon as I can."

She didn't want to walk anywhere with him. How could he have thought Mark would hurt Lora? But standing on the side of the road wasn't an option.

"I don't want to go home. I'd rather go to work."

"Are you sure?"

*"Nee.* But, as you said, you need an answer. I gave you one."

A muscle in his cheek jumped. "Understood. Let's start walking, then."

She picked up her tote and began leading the way. She was hardly able to look at him, she felt so betrayed. Luckily, she and Mark had been almost halfway there when Sheriff Brewer and Deputy Beck stopped beside them.

If the deputy was upset about her silence, he didn't let on.

He simply kept looking straight ahead and matched his pace with hers.

When Blooms and Berries came into sight, her anger bubbled over. "Mark would never hurt Lora."

"He's only being taken in for questioning."

"When Sheriff Brewer questions him, he'll realize that Mark is innocent."

"Someone beat Lora Weaver badly. They need to pay for that."

Hating his tone, she whirled around to glare at him. "Is that what you are going to do at the hospital, then? Stand vigil by her bedside until she can give you a name?"

His light-green eyes looked like shards of ice. "I am going to sit by Lora's bedside because I can't bear the thought of her waking alone."

"You care about her—"

"Of course I care," he snapped. "Lora was beaten. She could slip into a coma. She could wake up and be blind." After a pause, he added, "The question is, don't you care, too?"

The force of his tone, together with his devastated expression, gave her pause. "Of course I care. I've known Lora for years."

"Did you really know her? Or did you just know of her?"

She heard something new in his tone. Almost like he was chastising her. "What is that supposed to mean?"

"It means that she was pretty alone here in this town. Every time I saw her, she was either working or home alone. She only mentioned having work friends. Or, maybe you just judged her on how she looked and on her past."

"If I did those things, I didn't do it intentionally."

He raised his eyebrows. "You sure about that?"

"*Jah*." At least, she thought she was. "If I have harmed her feelings in some way, I'll do my best to apologize. I'll make amends."

"I see."

His voice had an edge of sarcasm to it. She didn't know where his antagonism toward her came from, but she didn't appreciate it. Not under the latest circumstances.

Feeling hurt and worried and more than a little irritated with him and Sheriff Brewer, Waneta grabbed her cooler.

"Do you hear what I'm saying, Deputy Beck? I hope so, since I'm currently of the mind that you and Sheriff Brewer might be doing the very same thing with Mark Fisher." While he gaped at her, she said, "My place of work is right here. I'll see myself there now."

After turning, she rushed to the entrance.

When she got there, Henry Lehmann looked up from a garden supply magazine he was studying. "Waneta? What's wrong? Where's Mark?"

Finally, there in the safety of the store, she rushed to her boss's side and burst into tears.

# CHAPTER 26

The room Mark was in was all too familiar. Beige walls. Faded yellow, scratched linoleum tile on the floor. Three chairs made out of particle wood surrounding a metal table with an avocado-green vinyl top that was nicked and torn. The room smelled like he remembered, too. Vaguely of disinfectant and dirty shoes, with a good dose of sweat and starch mixed in.

As Mark shifted in his chair across from Sheriff Brewer, he figured that it was probably just as well that the environment was so familiar, since the participants were the same. After all, it had been just a little over two years ago when he'd sat in this very same place for almost the very same reason.

But instead of feeling scared to death and sure that Sheriff Brewer and the rest of Hart County, Kentucky, was out to get him, this time Mark only felt irritated with the situation.

And impatient.

He was impatient that their "meeting" was taking so long.

He needed to get out of the room and check on Waneta. He hated that she was at home fretting about him.

He also felt a deep sadness for Lora. He hoped and prayed that she would recover.

Across from him, Sheriff Brewer also seemed different. The last time he'd questioned Mark, he'd been intent, focused, and transparently sure of Mark's guilt. However, so far, he'd been rather apologetic. Almost as if he hadn't wanted to pick Mark up in the first place but hadn't had much of a choice.

Now he was sipping coffee and staring at a blank pad of paper. His left hand was playing with a pencil, twirling it between two fingers.

Mark wasn't sure why the silence had gone on so long, but he was getting bored with it. "You're left-handed?" he asked, just because the silence was getting to him.

Sheriff Brewer looked down at his hand, then stared at Mark in surprise. "Yeah. I am. Why?"

"No reason. I am, too."

Brewer dropped the pencil. "Used to be, lefties were a rarity. Now there are quite a few of us."

"I've noticed that, too. Even among the Amish."

"Still hard to find a pair of left-handed scissors, though." The sheriff flashed a smile before shifting in his chair. While the cheap material creaked and groaned beneath him, he seemed to get back on track. "We need to go back to what you were doing last night. You say you were working on your house's woodwork?"

"Yes."

"Now, why were you doing that again?"

"It shouldn't be that big of a surprise. You've seen my

house. What my father didn't neglect or ruin, four months sitting vacant did."

"Tell me how, exactly, you bruised your hand." As if he could tell that Mark was about to point out that they'd already discussed this in length, Sheriff Brewer raised his eyebrows. "Again, if you please."

"I hurt my knuckles refitting warped woodwork. I had a crowbar in one hand and was trying to pop the wood into the space. My hand slipped, and the crowbar bumped it."

"Bet that hurt."

It had, but it surely wasn't anything to complain about. Pressing his hands flat on the vinyl tabletop, Mark leaned slightly forward. "Sheriff, I ain't some naïve Amish man with a chip on my shoulder anymore. I know about evidence and fingerprints and DNA testing. I know you've already combed poor Lora's house for samples and maybe even checked her fingernails while she lay unconscious. You ain't going to find anything from me. I haven't been in her house and I haven't touched her."

"But what about Calvin?"

He inhaled sharply.

Sheriff Brewer had hit his target, Mark would give him that. He felt as if someone had kicked him in the chest, then decided to rest his boot there awhile. As he tried to regain his composure, the sheriff looked unperturbed.

He actually kicked his legs out in front of him, crossed his ankles, and took a sip of coffee.

"I canna answer for my brother," Mark said at last.

"Why not?"

"I haven't seen him in days."

"What day, exactly, did you see him last?"

Mark tried to recall the day. Was it last Tuesday? Friday? "Maybe Thursday or Friday of last week? I can't really remember."

"Why not? I would remember the last time I saw my brother."

"Perhaps your brother is the type of man you look forward to seeing. Mine is not." Before the officer could ask some inane question about why, Mark stared hard at him. "And we know why, too," he said. "Calvin is running with a bad crowd and is making poor decisions. I gave up parenting him when he ran away years ago."

"I've done some checking on him. A couple of informants from Louisville say he owes folks some money."

"Then he probably does." This was news to him, but not surprising.

"He hit Lora the other night. She told us that."

"I know."

"So . . ."

"I don't know what happened, Sheriff Brewer. I don't know what happened between Calvin and Lora at her house. I don't know what happened to Amy in her front yard. I don't know who attacked Lora in her house." Taking a deep breath, he let his frustration show. "All I do know is that I worked on my house last night and had the privilege of walking Waneta Cain to work this morning, when you and your deputy plucked me off the street. Waneta is no doubt scared, Henry is no doubt lifting too much at work, and Lora is in the hospital. I need to get out of here and be of use."

"You seem different now, Mark," the sheriff said slowly.

"That's because I am different. I'm better."

Sheriff Brewer stood up. "Can I give you a ride home?"

Mark knew it was as close to an apology as he was going to get for being questioned that morning.

With a burst of awareness, Mark realized he didn't actually need one. He was becoming confident enough not to need reassurance from everyone he knew to feel good about himself.

Maybe he really had come a long way.

"You can give me a ride to Blooms and Berries," he said with a smile. "I need to make sure Henry ain't overexerting himself."

Sheriff Brewer smiled. "Let's go, then."

WHEN MARK GOT out of the sheriff's vehicle, he wasn't sure what to expect. He doubted Henry Lehmann was going to treat him any differently, but he was the only person he felt sure about.

As for everyone else? Well, he knew some would look at him as the most obvious suspect in Lora's attack. He was prepared to deal with that. But if his getting picked up for questioning had ruined everything between him and Waneta, it was going to crush him. He knew now that he didn't just care for her. He didn't just like her, either.

He'd fallen in love with her. He held her in the highest regard, and he would be devastated if she didn't trust him anymore.

To his surprise, the shop was crowded. Mark didn't know why he was so surprised. It just felt strange that the rest of the world continued on while his own felt like it was lying on its side.

Mostly English customers were roaming the aisles. Some he recognized, a few he knew well enough to shake hands with and say hello. Waneta and Henry were behind the counter, working side by side. Ben was nearby, stocking and assisting.

Mark breathed a sigh of relief. He was really glad someone was helping them with the heavy lifting in the heat.

When he approached, Henry raised his head. "Mark. Good day."

Waneta was running a credit card and wrapping up a woman's purchases. Mark supposed that was the reason she hadn't turned to smile at him.

But his boss's expression looked carefully blank as well.

Mark's stomach sank. Could he not even trust Henry to believe in him?

"Good day," he replied softly. "I'm sorry I'm late."

"I expect you had good reason."

"I'm ready now. Where would you like me?"

"Go to the storeroom, wouldja? There's a new apron for you there."

Mark raised his eyebrows but did as he was bid. He really hoped that Henry wasn't trying to get him out of sight.

When he opened the storeroom, though, he literally gasped.

His brother, Calvin, was sitting on an upturned bucket, sorting seed packets.

"Hey," he said. "I had just about given up on you."

"Calvin." Feeling stunned, he stumbled over his words. "Does Henry know you're here?"

"Of course. I wouldn't be sorting seeds on my own."

That was Calvin. Ready with a flippant reply that hid the seriousness of the situation. Actually, he spoke like his showing up at Blooms and Berries made perfect sense.

It didn't.

As Mark thought about Lora's injuries, Waneta's friendship, Sheriff Brewer questioning him, then driving him here, he realized that Calvin's appearance in the storage room fit right in with how everything in their lives was going.

Nothing made perfect sense at the moment.

# CHAPTER 27

*Wednesday, August 17*

W hat are you doing here?" Mark asked.

Eyeing his brother, Calvin relaxed. Mark wasn't yelling at him or telling him to get out of his life. It was a small thing, but an improvement. "I heard about Lora . . . and that you were taken in for questioning. I figured you might need a hand."

In a move out of their childhood, Mark visibly got control of himself. After a few seconds, Calvin strode closer. "I've been worried about you. Where have you been?"

Wasn't that how it had always been? Even when he was in so much hot water that he could barely breathe, his brother still concentrated on him.

If he hadn't thought Mark would have taken it the wrong way, Calvin would have laughed. Instead, he got to his feet. They were the same height. Roughly the same build. Calvin hoped that would remind his brother that he wasn't a weakling needing to be looked after. "Where do you think I've been?"

"I couldn't even begin to imagine."

*Huh.* It seemed Mark wasn't attempting to act calm and nurturing after all. "You sound as if you've been imagining a lot of things, actually. What have you been picturing me doing, Mark? Maybe that I took myself over to Lora's *haus* last night and decided to beat her bloody?"

Mark's neck flushed, giving Calvin his answer. "You hit her before."

It was hard, but Calvin stayed steady. "You're right. I did. I hit her and apologized for it. It don't help that I was drunk and stoned, does it?"

"*Nee.* That was no excuse."

"You're right. It don't matter at all. I got mad, did something I was ashamed of, and hurt her in the process."

Mark just stared, his expression cool. "I still don't know where you've been."

"Because you don't need to know. But we do need to talk. That's why I'm here. Because we need to talk about some things."

"Actually, well, now ain't the best—"

"I get it, Mark," Calvin interrupted. "I get that you are never going to want to hear what I have to say."

"Hold on. I didn't say that."

But his pensive expression told Calvin otherwise. "We have a lifetime of hurts and mistakes that lie between us like a deep, dark pool. We are afraid to get closer because we don't know what we're going to find between us. Maybe we're afraid of drowning."

"I never thought you were the type of man to bring up metaphors."

Calvin smiled. "Really? Did you ever pay attention to what

I could do, Mark?" he asked softly. "Or was it easier to simply concentrate on what I couldn't do. What I didn't do."

"Don't make our childhood into something it wasn't. Of course I was never your buddy or your pal. I grew up having to take care of you."

"And I grew up knowing that you had to. How do you think that felt?"

Mark swallowed. "What does it matter? You're an adult now."

Choosing his words with care, he said, "It matters because I was your burden. When I left, I knew you weren't going to understand why."

"I know you got into a lot of trouble. I know you left me alone to take care of our father."

Calvin flinched. He'd conveniently given himself a dozen excuses and reasons that justified his leaving. More food for Mark. Less tension in the house. Mark could have more time for himself. Never had he thought that his brother had felt much more than relief at his departure.

"We might have too much between us to ever get along. But I need you to put our pasts behind us for a little while and give me a few minutes of your time." When Mark looked like he was about to push him off again, Calvin added quickly, "Call it giving me just a smidge of the Lord's grace."

"Don't speak of the Lord."

"How about you stop acting so high and mighty?"

Mark pressed his palms to his face. Then, looking weary, he sat down on the edge of a stack of wooden crates. "What do you want to talk about?"

"I came to Horse Cave to find you because I heard you got

the house. I wanted to convince you to sell it and give me half the money."

"I know. I haven't changed my mind. I'm not going to sell the house."

"Yeah, I figured that out. You don't think I deserve it."

Mark folded his arms across his chest. "Maybe I thought about that at first. But, really, the house needs so much work, I don't know how much money we would ever get for it. Or when it would sell. Then I would be back where I was—homeless. I can't live that way again."

Yet again, Mark's practical nature shamed him.

Or, maybe it was Lora getting hurt.

Until now, all Calvin had been thinking about was freeing himself from the gang. He hadn't considered all the consequences of his actions. Yet again. "I guess you're right," he said at last.

"Are you in a lot of trouble?"

"In trouble with the people I owe money to? Yeah. Some." Of course, that was a lie. He was in *a lot* of trouble, and out of ideas. There was a real good chance the gang wasn't going to let him live another two weeks unless a miracle happened.

"I don't have any extra funds to give you," Mark said. "Do you want to live back at home with me?"

He'd never imagined Mark would offer that. If Calvin wasn't so used to steeling himself against pain, he swore he would have started crying. He'd thought he'd lost everything.

"Thanks, but that place is never going to hold anything but bad memories for me."

Disappointment flickered in Mark's eyes before he steeled himself again. "So, is that what you wanted to tell me? That you came back here because you're in trouble?"

"Yeah. I mean, ain't that enough?"

Staring at him, Mark shook his head. *"Nee."*

"I don't know what else you want from me."

"Maybe I want you to listen to me for a change."

"And hear what?"

"That I'm sorry. I shouldn't have pretended not to see you when you first showed up. I shouldn't have acted like you were going to taint my relationship with Waneta." Looking exhausted, Mark sat down on a crate. "I guess I haven't changed all that much, after all. When we were young, I felt that I could never let my guard down. If I did, we'd get in trouble, or we wouldn't have any food. Or someone would want to try to separate us."

"You aren't wrong. You couldn't let your guard down. Our parents? Well, they weren't much good at parenting."

"They weren't much good at much," Mark corrected. "Anyway, lately, I've been trying so hard to rebuild my life that I had forgotten that I had to repair my past in order to do that. I should have put you first."

"I didn't come here to hear that."

"I'm glad you did, though." Optimism filled his tone. "Calvin, it's not too late. We can do that now. I want us to try to get to know each other again."

Calvin doubted he was going to live long enough for that to be possible, but he was willing to give it a try. "I want that, too," he said quietly.

When the storage room door opened, Henry Lehmann and Waneta Cain walked in.

Mark fairly jumped to his feet. "Waneta, hi," he said in a soft tone. "Are you all right?"

Crossing the room, she reached for his hands. "I am now," she said with a bright, blinding smile. "We just heard that Lora is awake!"

"Praise the Lord," Henry said. "The doctors think she is going to make a full recovery."

"That's wonderful news. The best," Mark said, smiling right back at her.

"We also heard some news, though this was a bit harder to hear," Mr. Lehmann said. "Lora told the deputy who her attacker was."

"Who?" Mark asked.

"James Eicher."

Waneta inhaled sharply while Mark pressed his lips together. "Have they picked him up yet?" Mark asked.

Mr. Lehmann shook his head. "I don't believe so. I was mostly concerned with Lora, though."

Waneta gazed up at Mark. "I'd like to see her. I don't want her to think she's all alone."

"I thought you'd want to get over there," Mr. Lehmann said. "I just called for a driver to take you and Mark to the hospital. He should be here within ten minutes or so."

Calvin cleared his throat. "Can I go, too?" Realizing he sounded like a little kid, he shook his head in dismay. "I meant, well, I'd like to join you."

Mark smiled. "If you want to join us, we'd be happy to have you come along."

"I want to."

Waneta turned to him and smiled. "Everything is going to be so much better now. I'm sure of it."

Calvin didn't speak, but he did glance at Mark. Relief shone in his eyes.

It was the same exact way Calvin was feeling.

LORA WAS SURPRISED to discover that Eddie Beck was still sitting at her bedside when she woke up from another long nap late that afternoon.

"You came back," she murmured, her voice thick with sleep.

"I did. After I went back to the office for a couple of hours, I told the sheriff that I wanted to come keep you company."

"That's sweet of you."

Taking her hand, he ran his thumb along her knuckles. "I didn't want you to be alone."

"I'm glad you're here."

He smiled, but the warmth didn't quite reach his eyes. He was worried. No doubt he was hoping for more information about James's attack. "Do you want me to talk about what happened now?"

"Do you mind? I know we already went through this once. Do you think you can handle telling me about the experience again?"

"Well, I can try. I mean, that's why you're here, right?"

Standing up, he leaned over and brushed a chunk of her hair away from her face. "Actually, no. I came back because I care about you, Lora. You are what is important to me."

He was so kind. He sounded so sincere. Her pulse quickened as she imagined them together. Then, just as quickly, she reminded herself that she was no doubt putting too much into his words. Why, he probably thought he should care about every person who lived in Hart County.

His eyes brightened. "Lora Weaver, never decide to start playing professional poker. I can read just about everything you are thinking."

"Even now?" she tried to joke. Her face was swollen and one of her eyes was almost shut.

"Especially now," he said as he brushed his hand through her hair again. "I'm not going to make you answer a bunch of questions or play games with you. I just want you to know that I'm here for one reason only. Because I want to be with you."

His words were so sweet. Soon, she knew she would treasure every word of their conversations, too.

But for now? She was too weak to do much except tell him what he needed to know. "Like I told you before, James was waiting for me when I got home from our date."

Pulling out his notebook, he flipped it open and started writing. "Tell me again what he was wearing. And what you remember him saying."

"It might take me a while," she warned. "I keep remembering everything out of order."

Pressing his lips to her brow, he whispered, "Take all the time you need. We'll talk about James, then we'll put it behind you and talk about something else."

"Such as?"

He chuckled. "Maybe I'll tell you a story or two, Lora."

Relaxing again, she started to talk. The words came easier now, maybe because she knew that their conversation wasn't about to end.

Like their relationship, it was only just beginning.

"YOU SURE ABOUT this?" Mark asked when they stopped in front of Lora's house two days later.

"Mighty sure," Waneta said. "When I told Lora that I wanted to be a better friend to her, I meant what I said."

Taking her hand, he squeezed it. "I know that. I just don't want you to walk home from her house by yourself."

"I'm going to go straight home, Mark. I'll be careful." Releasing his hand, she gave him a little push. "Now, off you go. You have supper plans with Eli."

He smiled. "We're going out for Mexican. Turns out he likes spicy food as much as I do."

"Enjoy yourselves. Now, I've gotta go."

After he gave her a hug, she raced up Lora's walk and rapped on the door. After a minute or two, Lora opened the door.

"Boy, Mark sure doesn't like telling you good-bye," she teased.

Waneta smiled. "He's sweet . . . but I think he's actually more worried about me walking home alone. I told him I'd be fine, though."

"He has good reason," Lora said as she slowly made her way into the small living room. "But don't you worry. Eddie is going to stop by in an hour. He can walk you home."

"*Danke.*" Watching as Lora curled up in her chair, her penguin pajama bottoms and worn T-shirt making her look like a teenager, Waneta said, "How are you feeling?"

"A little better. One of my sisters came over last night. She helped me take a shower."

Though she was still bruised, Lora seemed to be getting around better. "I think the swelling might have gone down a little bit."

"I think it has, too." Pointing to a stack of frozen vegetable bags, Lora said, "Who knew frozen peas and carrots would feel so good?"

"They are lifesavers. My *mamm* swears by them," Waneta added. "Now, how about something to drink? I can make you some tea. Or maybe something cold?"

Lora raised an eyebrow. "You're not going to let me do a thing, are you?"

Already on her feet, Waneta shook her head. "Nope. I'm going to pick things up, do some dishes, and wait on you as much as you'll let me."

"I can't let you do that."

"Sure you can," Waneta called out from the kitchen. "Because I want something in return."

"What's that?"

Hearing the note of worry in Lora's voice, Waneta walked back to her side. "I want to know all about you and that deputy," she said.

This time it was Lora who was smiling kind of awkwardly. "I like him a lot."

"I can't wait to hear all about how you two met."

"Does that mean I can ask about you and Mark?"

Waneta nodded. "*Jah.* Because we're friends now. I mean, if you want to be."

"I do," Lora said.

After sharing another smile, Waneta hurried back to finish making them both tall glasses of iced tea.

In no time, James would be caught and everything would get back to normal. God had given her a warm and solid relationship with Mark and a new friendship with Lora.

Surely, He wouldn't do such things unless He intended for things to settle down in Hart County.

At least, she hoped that was the case.

# CHAPTER 28

*Thursday, September 8*

Three weeks had passed since Lora Weaver had identified James Eicher as her attacker. When Sheriff Brewer and Deputy Beck went to his house to arrest him for assaulting Lora Weaver, they'd discovered his wife Katie bruised and battered on their floor.

James was still nowhere to be found.

Katie later said that the moment James had heard that Lora had regained consciousness, he'd burst into a terrible rage.

That was the first time she had realized what James had been doing. When she'd tried to stop him from running out the door, he'd beaten her.

No one had any real idea where James could be. Everyone in the county seemed to have a guess—yet some people were sure that James would be hiding in Horse Cave, in one of the narrow, needle-like branches of the cavern under the town.

Waneta figured James hiding in a cave was as good a guess as any. After all, the cavern was only about fifty percent explored. There were too many dark and unstable areas that were prone to either flooding or at risk for caving in.

At first she and most other women in the area were on pins and needles, sure James was going to pop out of the cave's entrance and seek vengeance on them all.

But that hadn't happened.

Actually, as the days passed and inched toward September, very little did happen, with the exception of Waneta growing closer to Mark and Calvin showing up every so often, sometimes even staying the night with his brother. Things were still awkward between them, but at least they were communicating and trying to patch things up. That was something, she supposed.

After practically shadowing Waneta everywhere for weeks, Mark had finally begun to give her more space. She was thrilled. She loved spending time with him, but she'd begun to feel a little claustrophobic.

She usually enjoyed riding her bike or walking by herself sometimes. But her parents had insisted she take her bike to and from work. Her father pointed out that it was a little safer. She was happy to do that, and had already ridden it two times that week.

Riding made her feel like things were back to normal again. This morning, she'd even taken a longer route than usual, enjoying the morning air against her face as she navigated the hills and windy roads around Blooms and Berries.

But now that she was about to leave work, she realized she had a big problem.

It was still in the place where she'd parked it, but both tires were flat as pancakes. How had it managed to accrue not one but two flat tires?

Walking to her side, Mr. Lehmann gazed at the wheels with an expression that would have been funny if Waneta hadn't been so despondent. He was a man who enjoyed getting around on his feet or by horse. He didn't hold a lot of appreciation for bicycles.

"Neeta, what do you want to do with this contraption? Wheel it home?"

She understood his tone. It had been a long day. Really long. Customers had come in sporadically and when they did, they all seemed to be upset by something. By eleven o'clock, Waneta had felt like she did not have another ounce of patience left for argumentative, hard-to-please customers.

Thinking she needed her long day to be over, she said, "Mr. Lehmann, could we put my bike inside for tonight?"

"For sure. But how will you get home?"

"I'll walk."

"I thought your parents didn't want you walking no more."

"They don't, but it can't be helped. Besides, before I got my bike, I walked here every day. I'm not about to call a driver to come get me."

"Of course not. Well, I'll lock this inside the storeroom and we'll figure out how to patch up the tires in the morning. Now, you should hurry home and get some rest. Tomorrow is sure to be a better day."

"I hope so. It couldn't get much worse."

He playfully shook a finger at her. "Don't say such things, girl. You're liable to jinx yourself."

Smiling at his joke, she grabbed her tote and cooler and trudged home.

By the end of the first mile, she was getting tired. Maybe

she should have gotten a driver after all? It was hot and humid, making each step feel exhausting.

Then there were her nerves. They seemed to be getting the best of her. Though it was still daylight, hardly anyone was around. She kept imagining someone was watching her, which was ridiculous.

Increasing her pace, Waneta kept walking. Sweat ran down her neck, making the fabric of her dress stick to her skin. When she began breathing heavily, she forced herself to stop. The last thing she needed was to get overheated. Releasing her heavy cooler, she pulled at the fabric of her dress.

Attempted to fan herself.

But it didn't do much good.

She was nervous and hot. Tired and imagining things. Why, even the sound of a twig snapping behind her made her nerves on edge! Just to prove herself wrong, she glanced behind her when she picked up her cooler again.

And saw James Eicher standing right there.

"James?" she sputtered. "What are you doing here? Have you been following me?"

At first, he seemed surprised to hear her address him. But then he glared at her. "Don't speak."

He needn't have worried. Waneta didn't think she could form another word if she tried. He looked as angry as ever. With a shiver, she wondered if he'd worn the same expression when he'd attacked the other girls.

She needed to do something. Her only option was to run. Tossing her cooler at him, she turned and started running as fast as she could. Dirt kicked up under her flip-flops as the rubber soles slipped and slid against the packed earth.

Before she could pick up her pace, a hand dug into her shoulder. Pulled her back. Hard.

"Don't turn away from me."

She twisted her head to meet his gaze as his fingers pressed deeper into the soft area right above her collarbone. "Stop, James. You are hurting me."

"You need to learn to listen, Waneta."

Eyeing him closely, she knew she had to act fast. He was strong. She hadn't been able to outrun him. Her only option was to keep him talking until someone saw them. "Who do I need to listen to, James? You?"

Fire lit his eyes as he visibly struggled for control.

Attempting to pull her shoulder from his grasp, she said, "You need to go home. Leave me be. Accosting women on the street ain't good. The sheriff has been looking for you, you know."

Without warning, he slapped her hard.

She reeled back. Just as she was on the verge of losing her balance, he pulled her toward him, his grip on her upper arms now. They dug into her skin, his nails cutting her, stinging. Leaving her no choice but to bend to his wishes.

Looking into his eyes, Waneta realized that though he was angry at her, his eyes looked clear and calm. He knew exactly what he was doing. He'd planned for this.

Still holding her close, he spoke. "You were perfect. You were everything a proper woman should be. But then you ruined yourself. You became tainted."

She shook her head.

"You've accepted men into your life whom you shouldn't have even looked at. He ruined you."

"You're upset with me for being friends with Mark? After everything you've done, you are casting stones?" she asked, not even trying to hide the disdain in her voice. "You are being ridiculous."

"Don't speak to me like that."

"I wouldn't be talking to you at all if I could help it." Looking pointedly at his hands on her arms, she said, "You are the one who sought me out. Drop your hands, James."

"Drop my hands?" Jerking her hard, he shook his head. "You don't understand, do you? This isn't going to end with me saying I'm sorry and walking away. You are going to have to be punished for the things you've done."

*Not going to end.*

*Punished for the things she'd done.*

He was going to hurt her. Just like he'd hurt Lora Weaver. Just like he'd gone after Amy. Just like he'd beaten Bethany Williams two years ago.

"Why did you do this?" she whispered. "Why have you been terrorizing women? What possessed you to bring so much pain to all of us?"

"I haven't terrorized anyone. I've only been delivering consequences that the preachers or the deacons should have handed out all along. But they didn't. Preacher Eli only talked about forgiveness! Forgiveness don't mean anything, not really. Vengeance is what counts." He dropped his hands, giving her some relief . . . until he stepped closer, crowding her space.

Hardly allowing her to see anything but him.

"Someone had to do it. Ain't so? What's been going on isn't right. Women are forgetting their place. Tainting our way of life. Disrespecting our traditions."

She shook her head. She knew right then and there that she needed to speak from her heart. To voice how she felt. He wasn't going to let her go. He wasn't going to let her walk away from him.

He was going to hurt her the same way he did Lora. The same way he did the other women. He was taller. He was stronger.

She had no one nearby to help her.

She could only hope to survive. Finally, at long last, she realized that she wasn't alone, though. In fact, she never had been. God was always with her. He had directed this moment and He was the one who would help her get through it.

That knowledge gave her the strength she needed to continue. Even though she felt uncertain, she was strong. Strong enough to handle anything that came her way.

Feeling more assured, Waneta knew it was time to fight back. "Only God can deliver vengeance. You know that."

"He needed my help."

"*Nee.* He needed you to follow His word. But you have ignored him. Instead of helping others, you've been hurting. You've been doing terrible things. Shameful things."

The skin around his lips pinched and turned white. The expression in his eyes pained. It was obvious that she had struck a nerve.

Gathering her courage, Waneta said, "What does Katie think of you? She can't be proud. No wife would be proud of a husband who harms other women." Before he could answer, she said sarcastically, "Or, does she merely fear you? Did you break your vows to her, James?"

For the first time, he looked flustered. "I am keeping my

vows," he said, taking hold of her arms. "I am preserving our family's honor."

She didn't even try to hide the disdain she felt for him and his convoluted reasoning. "You are doing a great many things, but you are surely not doing that."

Without warning, he tightened his grip on her arms. Shook her hard. "You will say no more!" he yelled. Eyes darting left and right, he added, "Stay silent."

Then, just as abruptly, he released her with a push.

Struggling to keep her balance, Waneta scanned the area. Though it was rarely crowded, in the past she'd always seen at least one or two other people in the vicinity. There had to be someone in the distance who she could call out to.

But the fields surrounding them were empty. And all she could see were freshly shorn fields of grass, the distinctive Kentucky-blue tinge, reminding her that she was close to home but alone.

Though she knew the Lord was with her, she yearned for someone to help her. "God, please," she begged silently. "I'm so scared." She looked around, half hoping the Lord would have made someone strong and fierce appear like a Viking of old.

Unfortunately, it didn't happen.

But she did feel His presence and His belief in her. She wasn't alone.

Standing a foot away, James was glaring into the distance, breathing hard. He seemed just as off balance as she felt. Though he was physically stronger, he wasn't without weaknesses.

It was time to help herself. Even if she failed, even if she died at his hands, at least she'd go down fighting.

She needed to take advantage of his weak moment. Kicking off her flip-flops, she turned and started to run.

She'd barely made it five steps before he grabbed her again, jerking her backward. Crying out, she pulled away and kicked his shin.

He grunted. One of his hands slipped. When she kicked him again, he shoved her shoulder while the fingers of his other hand dug in deeper.

She cried out and pushed at him as hard as she could.

James retaliated by slamming her to the ground. She fell back. Her right hand tried to temper her fall, but it was useless against the force of his shove. A bone snapped in her hand as her head hit the pavement. Bells rang in her ears as warm liquid coated the back of her head.

Pain reverberated through her body as she opened her eyes and tried to focus. Then realized he was on the ground next to her. His hand was on the collar of her dress.

The sound of ripping fabric rang in her ears.

Whether it was for her own good or because she simply had no more to give, her eyes slipped to half-mast. Her vision became blurry.

She was only aware of the heat of the dirt against her back, the smell of the earth and the grasses. The pounding in her head, the pain in her arm, and the knowledge that James Eicher was finally going to be triumphant.

He was at last going to be able to succeed with her where with everyone else he had failed. He was going to rape her. Violate her.

She was not going to be able to fight him anymore. He was too heavy. She was not strong enough. The knowledge didn't give her any peace, but the clarity did allow her to look ahead. She was simply going to have to survive it. Somehow, some way, with God's help, she was going to have to overcome this moment.

Surviving was better than dying. It had to be.

Just as her vision clouded again, a voice rang out.

*"James!"*

She knew that voice. She'd come to trust it—and the man it belonged to—with her entire being. "Mark?" she whispered. Though the pain was making her vision blur, she tried to focus on what was going on. Mark was running toward them, his brother just steps behind. James cursed and grabbed a handful of her hair, pulling her toward him.

She gasped.

"Move away from her!" Calvin called out.

Immediately, James released her. He scrambled to get to his feet, but he was too slow. Mark and his brother grabbed hold of him and dragged him to the side. James grunted and swung his fist as Mark and Calvin systematically worked to subdue him. Curse words flew. It happened within seconds, time seeming to stand still.

Dust and dirt flew up, coated her skin, stung her eyes. She needed to move. To get out of the way. Though she felt as if her body weighed a thousand pounds, she struggled to sit up.

Just as a third person, a woman, came to her side.

Lora Weaver.

"No, no, just stay still," she whispered. "You're badly injured."

She was also still alive.

Overcome, Waneta started crying.

Lora wrapped an arm around her. "You are safe, Waneta Cain," she whispered before pulling back to give her space. "He's not going to hurt you anymore."

Waneta was so grateful, she tried to form words. However, it was a challenge. Her mouth felt dry, her throat was bruised and felt swollen.

Brushing stray strands of hair from her face, Lora shook her head. "*Nee*, don't talk. There's no need. Everything is going to be all right now. Help is on the way."

But she had to speak. She had to say what was on her mind. She had to at least try. "Lora," she whispered. Pleased that she had been able to get that word out.

Lora leaned closer. "*Jah*? What is it, honey? What do you need?"

"To thank you for being here," she whispered before sinking into oblivion.

# CHAPTER 29

*Thursday, September 8*

Mark had always thought that no moment in his life could be worse than the time he'd been forced into the back of a sheriff's cruiser and brought into his office for questioning.

He'd been wrong.

Though that had been a terrible experience, it had been about himself. He'd known that he was innocent. He'd also known that he was tough enough to be able to survive whatever happened in that interrogation room. After all, he'd survived worse things at home.

Those feelings were nothing compared to how helpless and lost he felt as he stood to one side while Deputy Beck applied pressure to Waneta's head wound and barked orders into his police radio. Lora Weaver was kneeling beside him, holding Waneta's hand and whispering to her.

Mark had no idea if Waneta could hear anything. Her eyes were still closed and her body looked limp. He was tempted to kneel next to her as well. He ached to be the one to promise her that she was safe. He wanted to be the person who could ease her fears by holding her close and reassuring her that she was no longer fighting James by herself.

But he was just as afraid that his touch wouldn't comfort her at all. She could very well flinch at it. James Eicher might have caused Waneta as much damage emotionally as he did physically. It was better to wait.

Glancing down the road, Mark watched Sheriff Brewer cuff James and lead him to his vehicle. As he watched James's smug expression, Mark let other, darker thoughts consume him. Maybe he should stand at the ready, just in case the sheriff needed some help. Mark would be only too happy to subdue him again.

Stuffing his hands in his pockets, he decided to do none of those things. The sheriff didn't need his help, and Waneta was being soothed and taken care of by Deputy Beck and Lora until the ambulance arrived.

What Mark needed to do was calm down.

If that was even possible.

As if she sensed his attention, Lora glanced at him and exhaled. He nodded, letting her know that he understood. She needed to be near Waneta for as much her sake as Waneta's. They had both been through too much to be apart.

Turning away, he saw his brother. Calvin was bent over, his hands braced on his knees. He looked just as torn up by what had just occurred. He was still breathing hard and looked pale. Even though he'd acted so world-weary and tough, his brother looked like he was just as stunned by the latest developments as Mark was.

After checking again to make sure that Waneta didn't need anything that he could provide, Mark walked toward his brother.

"What?" Calvin asked when he got close.

"Nothing. I was only making sure you were okay."

"I'm a grown man who has been living on my own for years, Mark. Of course I'm okay."

"I know that." He was embarrassed now. "I know you probably don't care how I'm feeling, but I'm pretty shaken up. I thought we hadn't gotten here in time."

Calvin's belligerent expression cleared. "I'm pretty shaken up, too."

"It's amazing that we got here. What if we hadn't gone to the diner? What if Henry hadn't worried about Waneta walking home by herself? What if we hadn't run as fast as we did?" Mark knew he was on the verge of tears, but he didn't care. The images that were coming to mind were too upsetting.

But then Calvin reached out and gripped his arm. "Don't go there, Mark. What matters is that all those things did happen." He laughed softly. "You know what? My faith has been wavering for years, but us finding her had to have been the Lord's doing. There's no other explanation."

Mark couldn't disagree. He'd spent his day off working on the house and mowing the Cains' lawn. Then, when Calvin had shown up, they'd gone to Bill's Diner to eat. They'd been placed in Lora's section, one booth down from Deputy Beck.

The deputy's appearance had spooked Calvin. At first, he hadn't wanted to stay, but Mark held his ground. Only when he pointed out how the deputy only seemed to have eyes for Lora did Calvin settle down.

But just as they finished their meals, Lora walked toward them, a worried expression on her face. "I'm worried," she said. "Mr. Lehmann just called and said Waneta was walking home by herself because someone had slashed the tires on her bicycle."

Mark had shaken his head. "*Nee*. She wouldn't walk home by herself. She promised me she wouldn't."

"But she did."

Exchanging a look with Calvin, Mark threw a twenty on the table and ran outside.

It had been Calvin who had suggested that they cut through two farmers' properties to get to the back road that Waneta usually walked or rode her bike on. Side by side, they'd jumped fences and ran like lightning through pastures.

That was how they'd found her just in time. Lora and Deputy Beck arrived less than five minutes later. But those five minutes had made a big difference for Waneta. Mark could hardly imagine what might have occurred if he and Calvin hadn't gotten there when they had.

"I'm real glad we found her," Calvin said, bringing Mark back to the present. "And we did find her, brother. That's all that matters."

"Thank you," Mark said.

"For what? Helping Waneta?"

"For being here. For coming back to Hart County and not leaving again. Even when I didn't want you to be here. Thank you for not giving up."

Calvin appeared to look like he was going to argue that point, but then he shook his head wearily. "You're welcome, but we both know my reasons for reaching out to you weren't good. Especially not at first."

"All that matters is that you are here now."

Mark could hear sirens in the distance. In seconds, the ambulance would arrive. Probably more police cars, too. Eventually, Waneta would go to the hospital and Sheriff Brewer or Deputy Beck would want to talk to both him and Calvin.

This rare moment between the two of them would be gone. "What else is on your mind?" Mark asked, because Calvin kept looking at him curiously.

"You know what it is. I'm trying to wrap my head around what I just saw. I'm fairly stunned."

Mark knew Calvin wasn't speaking of James's attack. No, he was referring to how Mark had fought James. Remembering the anger that had been coursing through him made him uneasy. "Because . . . " he asked, not wanting to give anything away.

"Because you got right there on the ground and attacked James. I didn't think you had that in you."

Mark examined his brother carefully, just to be certain that Calvin wasn't pulling his leg. When he realized that he was being completely sincere, Mark didn't know whether to be offended or find humor in his reaction. "Are you really that surprised that I was defending Waneta? What did you think I would do? Ignore what was happening?"

This time Calvin looked a little shamefaced. "Probably not. But I didn't think you would attack like you did. You went at him with great, ah, vigor."

"Vigor?"

"It's an appropriate description."

"Not hardly."

"Come on. You were tough. As tough as you needed to be."

Well, he supposed that was true. Mark grinned. "I tell you what, Calvin. Only you could manage to make me feel like laughing at a time like this. Seriously, though, I'm grateful for you. And Lora. And Deputy Beck. I couldn't have helped Waneta and captured James on my own. Together, we got him."

"Now it's my turn to feel shocked," Calvin said. "You don't need to thank me. I wouldn't have wanted to be anywhere else. I'm glad I was there."

"What are you going to do now?"

All trace of humor faded from his face. "I had intended to disappear. The gang I owe money to ain't going to forget about it."

"Do you still intend to do that?" Mark hated the thought, but he knew he couldn't stop him from leaving.

Calvin shook his head. "I think I might talk to the sheriff about my options."

"Really?"

"Yeah. I know a lot of people who are in fairly high positions in a couple of gangs in the state." He shrugged. "Maybe there's a way to use that to my advantage. Then I might actually have a chance."

"I hope so."

"Me, too."

Two cruisers were now parked nearby. Mark turned and watched as Sheriff Brewer talked to the EMTs, knelt down to say something to Waneta, who was now awake, then directed the deputy to put James in the back of one of the vehicles.

Then the sheriff turned to Mark and motioned for him to approach.

"Looks like you're on," Calvin said.

"Yeah. Wish me luck."

"You don't need it, Mark. You are the hero today."

That statement was ringing in his ears as he resolutely walked toward Sheriff Brewer. "Sheriff."

Sheriff Brewer held out his hand. "I just talked to Eddie. As you know, he used to be an EMT. He thinks Waneta is going to be okay."

Mark exhaled. "Do you know if anyone went to go fetch her parents?"

"Lora thinks one of the servers at the diner went to go get them."

Feeling relieved, he took a deep breath. "Waneta will be glad about that."

"Now that she's awake, I know you probably want to go sit with her, but can you tell me what happened?"

As Calvin joined them, Mark quickly relayed Lora's announcement at the diner and what he and Calvin had decided to do. He briefly described their fight and how Deputy Beck was able to take over the moment he arrived on the scene.

Sheriff Brewer looked from one of them to the other. "You spending time together now?"

Just as Mark nodded, Calvin said, "Yeah." Then he gestured to the two officers standing next to the vehicle where James was sitting. "What's going to happen to him?"

Sheriff Brewer pursed his lips. "Justice," he said after a pause.

As Mark walked back to Waneta's side, he breathed a sigh of relief. No woman in Hart County was going to be in danger anymore.

At least not from James Eicher.

# CHAPTER 30

*Thursday, September 8*

After Waneta had regained consciousness, Lora moved to the side. Deputy Beck and the EMTs had taken Waneta's vitals, started an IV, and loaded her into the ambulance.

After the sheriff spoke with Mark and Calvin, he and another officer left the scene.

Soon after the ambulance workers arrived, Mr. and Mrs. Cain showed up. Bill and Mia had obviously left the diner and picked them up.

As they took in the scene and spoke to one of the policemen, their eyes had filled with tears. They'd approached the ambulance with shaky steps, the policeman hovering over them.

Mark had stepped out of the ambulance and hugged them both before guiding them to a spot where they could speak to her. Then, as if he couldn't bear to be separated from Waneta any longer, he'd climbed back into the ambulance just before it headed to the hospital, lights flashing.

It was obvious Mark and Waneta were a strong couple

now. Mark had saved her today, but she had saved him weeks ago when she offered him trust and her friendship. No longer would either of them have to walk through life alone.

Lora hadn't been standing by herself the whole time. Calvin had lingered for a while. He'd even spoken a couple of words to her, but it was obvious that neither of them was comfortable around the other anymore. After mumbling something about being glad everyone was all right, he darted off.

Soon, the other vehicles left.

Now only she and Deputy Beck lingered.

Well, actually, he wasn't there lingering at all. He'd been busy taking samples of dirt and grass. Every so often he would bend down on one knee, peer at something more closely, then put it into a plastic bag.

He'd also darted curious looks her way several times.

She'd been tempted to offer to help, but she knew it was police business. She was also a little afraid that if she broke the silence, he would ask her to leave. She didn't want to do that.

Finally he straightened, put the last of the dirt samples in an envelope, and walked over.

"I'm about done here. Do you want a ride?"

She did, but she was suddenly feeling awkward around him. He had to have a lot to do, and she would just be in the way. "I'll be okay. It's only a ten-minute walk for me from here."

"Are you sure? My truck has air-conditioning, though it probably won't cool off until I pull into the station's parking lot."

*Huh.* It seemed he was feeling just as tentative as she was. Just an hour ago, she'd hopped into his truck when he'd torn out of the diner parking lot.

Feeling a little amused by how they were acting, she raised her eyebrows. "So you're asking me to sit in a hot truck with you?"

"I am, but what I'm really asking is if we could spend some time together."

Her pulse jumped. She wanted to hope. Wanted it so badly, especially after he'd stayed at her side for hours in the hospital.

However, he'd distanced himself since then. He'd called her, but their conversations had centered on her health. He hadn't asked if he could stop by her house. And today was the first time in a week that he'd gone out to eat at the diner when she was working.

Common sense told her that he was busy, trying to locate James and see to his other responsibilities. But there was another part of her that feared that he'd simply grown tired of her. She'd misjudged far too many people for most of her life to expect too much from him.

That was why she looked at him curiously. "Do you have some questions for me about James?"

"Nope."

"Oh. Well, then . . ."

After a moment, he smiled. "Lora, are you really going to make me say it?"

Say what? "I'm afraid I am. I have no idea what's on your mind."

"Really?"

"You ain't making things any easier, Deputy Beck."

"Eddie. You called me Eddie on our date. Remember?"

Biting her bottom lip, she nodded.

"And before you start questioning anything else, I'm just

going to say the words. I like you. I want to get to know you better."

Staring into his eyes, Lora wished for a lot of things. She wished she was a whole lot more accomplished and a whole lot more innocent. She wished they'd met another way and that he hadn't had to investigate her.

But most of all, she wished that she was confident enough to believe that none of those things mattered.

"I like you, too. But do you really think something between us could work out?"

He pulled his ball cap off his head, then put it back on, this time backward, with the bill at his back. "I do. Why don't you?"

She could see his eyes better now. He looked sincere. She knew he was sincere. But that didn't mean she trusted a future with the two of them together. "You know why," hating that she was stating the obvious. "We're pretty different."

"Yeah, we are." He grinned. "I don't have pretty, long blond hair and legs that go on forever."

She was pleased he thought she was pretty, but she needed to know that they had something more than that. "You know what I mean."

"Would you believe me if I said I don't care that we're really different?"

"I would believe you, but I'd also say that you're being naïve. Our differences are going to matter one day, Eddie. To you, and also to your friends and your family."

"Before I accept what you're saying and leave you alone, let me ask you one thing . . . Are you done?"

Done? "I don't understand what you're asking."

"You've already accomplished a lot. You got your GED.

You have a good job and people like you there. You've had the courage to return to Horse Cave even when you knew coming back wouldn't be easy. You survived a brutal attack, and you were brave enough to help Waneta. Could you have done all that two years ago?"

"*Nee.*" Two years ago she'd been living with a jerk and trying to save up enough money to go out on her own.

"So you're different than you used to be." Slowly, he smiled. "That's why I'm asking you, are you done growing and changing?"

"No."

"I'm not done, either. That's why I don't want you to start telling me about all the ways we are different, because we are going to be different people next year. Maybe even next month."

His reasoning was a bit optimistic. But then she remembered Mark Fisher. He'd been accused of beating a woman, then practically shunned. What if he'd given up?

She knew that answer. He'd still be struggling like Calvin was. And what a waste that would have been. "You know what? I think I would like that ride, Eddie."

His gaze warmed. "My reasons swayed you, then?"

A lot of things did. Hopes and dreams swayed her. But she didn't think he needed to know that. "Yep. You are a very persuasive man."

"Good." Glancing at his phone, he said, "Let me take you home, then I've got to get back to work."

It was time to take a chance. "You know, I'm not working tonight. And I don't just work in a diner. I can cook pretty good, too. Would you like to come over for supper?"

"It might be late. Close to seven."

"It might not be fancy, just a casserole with two sides."

Opening the passenger door for her, he nodded. "I'd like that."

She left the door open while he walked around because the inside of the vehicle was really hot. But after everything that had just happened, it didn't matter to her at all.

# CHAPTER 31

*Thursday, September 15*

Sharing a bemused look with her mother, Waneta inspected the small olive tree beside the couch, which Mr. Lehmann had sent over. "This is mighty nice. I don't believe I've ever seen an olive tree before."

"Me, neither. It's pretty with its silver leaves. It will look mighty nice in the garden."

"And in the kitchen in the winter, since Henry said that it can't take the cold."

Her mother fingered the leaves. "No offense to your boss, but this is a strange sort of gift, don't you think? He gave you a tree that bears olives, which you don't eat; and it requires a lot of time and attention, which you don't have to give."

Waneta had just been thinking the same thing. "I don't understand it, either, but maybe one day I will."

"That's the spirit, dear. Yes, indeed, one day you'll understand why you have an olive tree."

"You girls worry too much about things that ain't important," Daed said. "All that matters is that Waneta is safe and sound."

"She's safe, but I don't know about sound. She still has a broken wrist and more bumps, cuts, and bruises on her than any girl should ever have."

"I'm going to be okay, Mamm," Waneta said softly. Just as she had for the last week.

Her mother resituated the pillow under her cast. "I hope so."

"I know so. Now, please stop worrying so much. You heard what the doctors said. I need to rest for two weeks, but then I can go back to work, at least part-time."

"I'm going to make sure you do rest, daughter," Daed said as he got up to answer the knock at the door. "And I'm going to make sure your visitor knows not to get you too riled up as well."

Curious as to who could be visiting now, Waneta watched her father open the door in an almost spry manner. If there was a silver lining to all that had occurred, that had to be it, she surmised. Her father was moving around better than he had in years. It seemed he liked being as needed as she did.

"Ah, now. Look who has returned," Daed said. "Mark."

Staring at him, Waneta felt her cheeks heat. "I didn't know you were planning to stop by today."

"I wanted it to be a surprise," he said.

"Really?" She wondered why. He had to know how much she liked being around him and it was obvious that her parents adored him.

"We were all just admiring Waneta's new olive tree," Mamm said.

Walking over, Mark knelt on the floor next to the couch

and smiled. "I told Henry that flowers might be just as appreciated, but he was fixated on this olive tree. He said olive trees symbolize good fortune and prosperity."

"In that case, I'll try even harder to take good care of it," she joked.

"I'm sure you will." Turning to her, he reached out and ran his thumb along her cheek. "Now, how are you doing today?"

His voice was low and sweet. And his touch? Well, she couldn't deny that she liked his attentions. "Better now," she whispered.

Tracing the line of her eyebrow, he said, "Sure?"

Hardly aware of anything but his loving glance and touch, she nodded.

"We are going to go outside!" Mamm announced from behind them. "You know what? We might even go for a little walk."

"A long one," Daed said. "So don't you worry about us."

Mark's lips twitched as her parents bustled out the door. "They are two of a kind, your parents."

"Indeed. They're the best kind, though. They have been so wonderful these last couple of days."

"Good." Rubbing her cheek, he focused on her again. She felt his gaze traipse from her hairline to her cheek to the cast on her wrist. "Waneta, I don't know what I would have done if you hadn't survived."

"We won't ever have to know. You and Calvin got there in time."

Releasing a ragged sigh, he nodded. "I know you're right. I keep hoping if I tell myself that long enough, I might even believe it." After climbing to his feet, he looked down at her. "Any chance you have enough room on this couch for two?"

"There's plenty of room, if you don't mind my feet on your lap."

"How about I hold your head in my lap instead? I've got some things I want to talk to you about."

Since she didn't care where he was, as long as he was close, she simply smiled. Then laughed as Mark tried to resituate her without harming her ribs, head, or arm. When he had at last repositioned her to his liking, she stared up at his handsome face. "What did you want to talk to me about?"

"I've got some updates for you. First of all, it seems my brother has nine lives. He talked his way into some kind of situation with some kind of government agency. He's going to do some undercover work for them."

"What does that mean? Where will he be? Do you think that's safe?"

"To answer your questions, I don't know, I don't know, and finally, I don't know." Smiling at her look of surprise, he shrugged. "I'm okay with not knowing and you should be, too."

"Really? Why?"

"Because at least we'll know he's on the straight and narrow and alive. That's a positive thing."

Relaxing against him, she nodded. "You're right. I'm glad for Calvin."

Running a hand up and down her good arm, he continued. "Now, are you ready for the second piece of news?"

"*Jah.*"

"You sure? It's big."

"I'm lying down. I should be able to handle it."

"All right, then, but brace yourself."

"Mark! What is it?"

"Lora and Deputy Beck eloped last night."

She gaped. "Surely not."

"Oh, *jah*." He chuckled. "She called the store to tell me so no one would worry when she wasn't around for the next week." Looking pleased as punch, he said, "Right now, they are on their honeymoon in Gatlinburg."

"I'm amazed. But I kind of think it's fitting, too. Lora never was the type to play by the rules."

"For what it's worth, she sounded really happy."

"That's worth a lot. I'm glad for her." Waneta still felt bad whenever she thought about how she never really did have much to do with Lora. That was going to change, though. They'd been through far too much to go back to being distant acquaintances.

Smiling up at him, she sighed. "I'm real glad you came over, Mark. You are filled with good news."

"I'm not done yet." Looking a little awkward, he said, "I have one more thing to share."

"Really? Who is this bit of news about? Henry?"

The smile vanished. "No. Me."

"You?" she teased, then tensed. "Wait a minute. Did something happen?" All kinds of worst-case scenarios came to mind. "Is Sheriff Brewer mad at you? Or did something go wrong with your job? Or your house?"

Grinning, he shook his head. "The answer is no. Four times."

"Mark, don't play games."

"All right, then. Here's my news, Waneta. I've fallen in love with you."

"Oh!"

"Yeah, oh. And since I have fallen in love, I decided I had better talk to you about that."

She felt like laughing and crying. "What . . . What did you want to talk about?"

"Well, first, I'm going to have to ask you not to keep me in suspense. Do you love me, too?"

"You know I do."

Raising her hand, he kissed her knuckles. "*Jah*. I do know you do. You were there for me when practically no one else was. You've defended me when most didn't think I deserved it. You've taught me to trust again. To believe again."

"I don't know if I did all those things, but I do know that I'm better with you, Mark Fisher."

Leaning down, he brushed his lips against her forehead. "Now, I have something to ask you, and I want you to think about it long and hard before you answer."

She pretended to brace herself. "All right. I'm ready."

"Will you marry me, Waneta Cain?"

She didn't need to consider it. She sure didn't need any more time to pass. "Yes."

He sighed dramatically. "You just promised me that you'd think on this for a while."

She was injured. She was so weak and sore that she was lying with her head in his lap instead of sitting by his side. She was also younger than him. And far shyer than he'd ever been.

But there was one area where she was far and away his superior.

And that was believing in the two of them.

"I just promised to marry you, Mark Fisher. That trumps everything else."

"Does it, now?"

"Very much so. And that means, it's time for you to do one thing."

"Which is?"

Looking into his eyes, she smiled. "Kiss me."

Next thing she knew, Waneta was sitting in his lap. Her arms were looped around his neck. He was holding her with care . . . and kissing her like he didn't intend to stop anytime soon.

As she relaxed against him, Waneta sincerely hoped that was the case.

After all, they had a lifetime of happiness to look forward to.

## About the author

## About the book

## Read on

Insights,
Interviews
& More . . .

# Meet
# Shelley Shepard Gray

The New Studio

IN MANY WAYS, my writing journey has
been like my faith journey. I entered
into both with a lot of hope and a bit of
nervousness. You see, I didn't get baptized
until I was in my twenties and didn't first
get published until I was in my thirties.
Some people might consider those events
to have happened a little late in life.
However, I feel certain that God knew each
took place at exactly the right time for me.

To be honest, these days I rarely stop to
think about my life before I was a
Christian or a writer. I simply wake up,
drink my coffee, and try to get everything
done that I can each day! I feel blessed to
be a part of a large church family, to have
my husband and children, and to enjoy a

busy career. But every so often, someone will ask why I write inspirational novels. Or why I write at all.

Then I remember how it felt to knock on a minister's office door and tell him that I wanted to be baptized; and how it felt the very first time I wrote "Chapter 1"—both felt exhilarating and nerve-wracking.

Perhaps you are a little bit like me. Maybe you, also, developed your faith a little after some of your friends or family. Maybe you, also, began a new job in a field that you didn't go to school for. Maybe you started on a journey where you weren't sure you were going to be a success or even fit in.

Or maybe, like me, success wasn't what you were hoping to attain. Maybe it was a matter of following a power bigger than yourself. If so, I'm glad I'm in good company. I'd love to know your story, too.

Now I have been a Christian for almost thirty years. I've been a published writer for about half that time. Both journeys have not always been easy. Both have been filled with ups and downs. Yet, both have given me much joy, too. I'd like to think that anything worth having takes some hard work. It takes some time to grow and mature, too.

And because of that, I am comfortable with the fact that I'm still on my journey, one morning at a time.

With blessings to you,
Shelley Shepard Gray

# Letter from the Author

Dear Reader,

A long time ago I decided that the characters in my books would be people I would want to know. I figured if I was going to be spending hours and hours every day with them, sometimes for months at a time, I might as well like them! Usually, this plan works well for me. As I write my pages or rewrite scenes, I find myself rooting for my made-up people. Then I began this novel.

To be honest, even after I wrote the first seventy-five pages or so, I didn't like any of them, except Waneta—and I wasn't even particularly thrilled about the way she first treated Mark. And Mark! I felt his pain, but I felt he kind of had a chip on his shoulder, too. As for Lora and Sheriff Brewer and Deputy Beck and Calvin? I found every single one of them frustrating!

One day, as I was staring at all my notes, the magazine pictures, the map of Hart County, and a blinking cursor on the computer screen, I came really close to deleting the whole thing. Then I realized that all those characters had become real to me. They were real, imperfect, flawed, full-of-mistakes characters. However, they were also tenacious—and filled with such hope that I knew I couldn't give up on them.

That's when I knew I had a book worth writing.

When I finished, I realized that these characters were a lot like me, maybe even like most people. I'm imperfect. I make mistakes. However, each day I try to be a better person. I rely on my faith and people I love for guidance. Maybe you can relate a little bit?

I sincerely hope you enjoyed Mark's and Waneta's story! I hope you grew to love their characters as much as I did. If you have time, drop me a line! I'd love to know what you thought. The next story in the series is called *The Gift* and it takes place right around Christmastime.

Until then, I wish you many blessings. Thank you for giving this book a try!

With my best,
Shelley Shepard Gray

# Q&A with the Amish

One of the reasons I enjoy writing novels featuring the Amish is because I live in Ohio near several Amish communities. One community is just an hour from my house! Because of this, I've had the opportunity to visit different Amish communities several times a year, both in Ohio and Kentucky.

Over time, I've been blessed to know several Amish ladies well enough to call them friends. Because of this friendship, they were kind enough to let me interview them about everything from faith to canning to learning to drive a buggy. I hope you'll respect their privacy and understand that I won't be using their names, only their initials. I also am not listing the community where they live.

Enjoy the interview! Even after all these years, I learned something new!

**Shelley:** *What were some of your favorite childhood activities? Are they different from generation to generation?*

**B:** Yes, I'm sure they are different from generation to generation. We liked to play croquet in the summer. Nowadays, it's a lot of volleyball. We also played a lot of board games and cards, like Uno, Rook, and Phase 10.

**J:** Growing up on the farm I always enjoyed outdoors work, being around the animals, helping with the garden, and putting in hay. Our family always had ponies and riding horses, which we enjoyed. I would say some things have stayed the same. Most Amish children have a pony during their growing-up years. Not very many families are doing farming anymore, so that has changed some things, but children help do yard work, help in the house, do dishes, etc. Of course, there are those few that are spoiled and don't do much to help.

**Shelley:** *When did you learn to sew and quilt? Did you learn from your mother? Did your daughters enjoy sewing and quilting, too?*

**B:** Yes, I learned to sew from my mom, but I didn't do much of it before I was married. It was easier to let my mother do the sewing and I do the other work, because I didn't really like it.

After I got married, I sewed. I also didn't like to quilt at first but really like it now. One daughter really liked to sew and quilt and the other one didn't like it; she liked working outside.

J: I was taught to sew as a teenager. I was left-handed so I kind of learned by myself as my mom was right-handed and it was hard. My daughters taught themselves and from watching me. They learned at an early age, and they like to sew lots more than I do. Quilting is not so much a hobby anymore; the young generation are not all taught to quilt.

**Shelley:** *What about canning and gardening? What do you like to can? Has the process changed much over the years?*

B: I like to can green beans, four different kinds of pickles, applesauce, and apple pie filling. We freeze the corn and peaches. We also can a lot of pizza and pasta sauce.

J: Our family has always done a lot of canning and gardening. I enjoy it very much. I like to can most anything. I do my own sauerkraut. We also grow a lot of popcorn. My garden is always bigger than most other people's. There are Amish people who do not have a garden and will just buy at produce stands, etc. For me, gardening is relaxing and is very much a stress reliever.

**Shelley:** *How does your faith guide your life?*

B: By reading the Bible and praying. Also attending church.

**Shelley:** *Driving a horse and buggy looks hard to me. Was it difficult to learn to do that?*

B: Usually, we learn with a tame horse. Some horses don't like big trucks. They sometimes jump towards the ditch. You have to have the lines tight, then they can't do too much. ▸

**Q&A with the Amish** *(continued)*

**Shelley:** *Do you have favorite recipes that you like to make for other people?*

**B:** Yes, I make coffee cake for coffee breaks with friends. I also like to try new recipes.

**Shelley:** *Has your community changed much over the years?*

**J:** Our community has changed a lot, with hardly any farmers left. Most people live on smaller properties, anywhere from one acre up to ten acres. Some have more land and will do some hay crops. Along with no farms, people have more time for leisure activities and will spend time camping, spend evenings around campfires with friends, go out to eat, and spend more time with family, etc. As times change, rules change. We have generator power for washers, sweeper fans, sewing machines, etc. Also solar power for some.

We also have a lot more youth gatherings, volleyball, and singings. Most people are accepting of changes. There are always a few that hang on to the old ways.

**Shelley:** *What was Amish school like?*

**J:** For me, going to school in the 1970s and 1980s, we always talked Amish during school. Then in the seventh grade we got a new teacher and everyone had to talk English. Wow, that was hard! We knew enough English to get by before that, but I suppose we probably did not always use the proper words.

Now all children must speak English at all times during school. Now most children know English even before school, as people have more contact with the English and often have friends they get together with. Our children went to public school with approximately twenty-five to thirty other Amish in their grade when starting kindergarten. As time went on and more Amish schools were built, some would drop out of public and go to Amish school. Also, a few do homeschool.

I always felt an education was important, as children should be taught as much as possible. Unfortunately, not all Amish feel that way. Some families are very strict and send their children to Amish schools only. Over all, our Amish schools are good; but, then, we do have some that have a share of problems with students and teachers.

**Shelley: *What might surprise others about the Amish?***

**J:** That I don't think our way of life is hard at all. It is a blessed life, being close to nature, which God created. God is good.

Others might be surprised that not many people in some communities are farmers. We have a lot of woodshops, sawmills, welding shops, grocery bulk-food stores, variety stores (like Walmart), too. We also have sewing shops and fabric stores. All are owned and managed by Amish.

Also, if you want, you can buy all your Amish clothes. You don't have to make them. We also like to shop at Walmart and Aldi. Also Kohls!

Something else some might find surprising is that we would pay a driver to take us on vacation. A lot of Amish own houses in Sarasota, Florida, and will spend the winter months there.

And some Amish youth, when they turn eighteen, will sometimes buy a car and drive, but most of the time will sell the car after a time and become a member of the church. Most parents do not approve but will allow the child to stay at home with the family. There are some (few) parents who will not allow their child to stay at home if they have a car.

**Shelley: *Thank you both so much for doing this interview with me! I loved learning more about you and your families. I think my readers will enjoy learning more about the Amish, too.*** ◡

# Questions for Discussion

1. What is your first impression of Mark Fisher? Would you have reacted to him the same way Waneta did? Why or why not?

2. What did you think about Mark's reasons for returning to Horse Cave? Would you have returned?

3. While writing this novel, I discovered that I enjoyed developing the secondary characters as much as Waneta and Mark. Who in the book did you enjoy getting to know?

4. One of the themes in the novel was forgiveness. I spent a lot of time thinking and praying about what it means to forgive others and oneself. Mark touched my heart because he carried so much guilt for things that he was not responsible for. Could you relate to his guilt?

5. I really enjoyed writing about Lora Weaver, most especially, her relationship with Deputy Eddie Beck. How do you think her relationship with the other characters influenced them? Who in your life has influenced you in an unexpected, positive way?

6. The following scripture verse from John guided me while writing the novel. Have you ever had the opportunity to overcome a great many obstacles for a friend? How did it alter your relationship? *John 15:13 (NIV) Greater love has no one than this: to lay down one's life for one's friends.*

7. I found the Amish proverb *Whatever your past has been, you have a spotless future,* when I was about halfway through writing the book. I had to smile because it seemed to speak to almost every character in the book! What do you foresee happening with Mark and Calvin in the future? What about Waneta, her parents, and Lora?

8. *His Guilt* is the second stand-alone novel in this six-book Hart County series. If you've also read *Her Secret,* what do you think of the series so far? ❧

# Can't Get Enough of the Residents of Hart County? Here's a Sneak Peek at *The Gift,* a Christmas Novel from Shelley Shepard Gray,

*Coming November 2017 from Avon Inspire*

*We walk by faith, not by sight.*
—2 CORINTHIANS, 5:7

*Enjoy today. It won't come back.*
—AMISH PROVERB

### November 28

Crack!

Susanna Schwartz knew of only one thing that could make a sound like that. A rifle. Someone was shooting nearby. Right by Highway 218.

*Crack. Ping! Ping!*

That sounded closer. Though it was nerve-wracking, she tried to calm herself down and concentrate on driving her buggy home. What she needed to do was simply make some sense out of what she was hearing.

Yes. That was it.

She exhaled. First of all, it was Thanksgiving weekend, the first weekend of the hunting season. At least, it was back in Ohio. Maybe a hunter wasn't paying ▶

attention to where he was going? That had happened all the time back in Berlin. Boys and men would get so excited about tracking their turkeys and deer, they would forget where they were going.

Though her heart was beating so fast, she forced herself to remain calm. No good would come of her getting in a tizzy. If she did that, she'd upset the horse, and then she'd really be in trouble.

But when the crack of a rifle reverberated in the air again, this time far more closely, fear took over. Star whinnied and attempted to pick up speed.

"Steady, Star," she called out. "Easy, girl. It'll be all right."

She hoped it would. At the moment, she wasn't so sure about that. At the moment, everything about her decision to drop off her little sister, Traci, at a girlfriend's house seemed like it had been a bad idea. Why couldn't their parents have told her to stay home?

The snow had picked up. It covered the empty highway in a thick blanket and made driving her buggy almost difficult. The metal wheels had already slipped and slid several times since she'd begun the journey.

She just wished it hadn't gotten so dark so fast. She really wished gunshots weren't piercing the air.

Feeling her pulse start to race, Susanna attempted to calm herself. Don't make things worse by imagining things, she cautioned herself. Focus on what is happening now, not what could be.

That was good advice, too. She didn't need to borrow trouble or let her mind drift toward flights of fancy. She needed to remain calm and keep Star's lines firm and steady.

When Star whinnied again, jerking her head to the right, she tightened her grip on the leather straps. "Easy now, Star," she called out, hoping and praying that the taught lines and her voice would calm the mare before she lost control.

But it was too late. As if she could sense the danger, Star neighed in alarm. Jerked to the right. Then, as another *crack* reverberated through the air, the horse picked up speed.

Heart racing, Susanna leaned forward, holding on to the bench seat with her left hand while trying to retain her grip with her right. "Whoa, Star!"

Her cry did no good.

The buggy wobbled, its metal wheels sliding precariously on the black asphalt covered in ice and snow.

12

The muscles in her arms strained as she attempted to gain control. A slow burn raced up her forearms and biceps as she pulled the reins.

Star scrambled, the horseshoes clattering on the ice and snow.
*Ping!*

Terrorized now, Star kicked her legs. The action forced one of the lines to the buggy to snap. Seconds felt like minutes as the buggy jerked and slid. Star pulled away.

Susanna cried out. Screamed as the buggy slid and rocked precariously on its metal wheels. Grasping the seat as tightly as she could, she tried to pray. Tried to think.

Suddenly free, the buggy skidded toward the center of the road. What to do? What to do?

She grabbed the brake. Attempted to pull. But she might as well have been clutching air. The buggy spun, then slid toward the other side, racing toward the ditch.

She was going to crash. Desperately, she tried to focus on where she was. But between the frost on the windshield and the sleet and ice falling in thick sheets around them, there was no way to tell. Everything was distorted and out of focus.

Crying now, Susanna closed her eyes, held on to whatever she could, and prayed. Prayed as hard as she could. Prayed like she never had before.

And as the conveyance tumbled into the ditch, crashing into a thicket of trees, the force of the impact threw her toward the door. She was thrown out, landing on her side, her arms barely bracing her. She'd gotten out. She'd survived.

But as the snow and ice fell against her skin, stinging like sharp pellets, Susanna wondered if that was enough.

"*Jah.* There you go," a soft, masculine voice whispered by her side. "Come now, give it a try again. Open your eyes."

Wondering what was happening, Susanna willed herself to try to do as the soothing voice bid. But it was hard. Her head was pounding and each of her eyelids felt like they weighed a hundred pounds. Then, too, her skin felt cold. So cold. Freezing. Unable to help herself, she moaned.

A warm hand glided across her cheek. It paused, then stroked her cheek again. It was soothing. Almost reassuring. ▶

"Ach. I know it's hard, girl. But give it another go. *Jah*?"

She tried again. It was dark, but there was a flickering light nearby, and the low beam of a flashlight on the ground. The beam reflected the white from the snow, making the area seem brighter . . . and vaguely foreign.

Blinking to focus. Then stared into the light-blue eyes of her rescuer.

"Green." He smiled, revealing a slightly crooked incisor.

*Green?* She blinked. Inhaled through the pain to attempt to get her voice.

"*Nee*. Don't talk. There's no need for that," he murmured, pulling back enough for her to see more of his features. His wide brow. The line of his jaw. The chunk of dark-brown hair mixing in with dark, thick eyebrows. "A car stopped just up ahead. Wonder of wonders, it was Lora, a friend of mine. She's calling for an ambulance. You should stay still until they come."

His words made sense. Until she remembered what had just happened. Where was she? The buggy? Her horse? Had Star been hurt? Was she somewhere nearby, cut or injured?

Panic engulfed her. "Star?"

"Star?" He turned a puzzled eye to the heavens.

Unable to do anything else, she, too, looked above.

"*Nee*, I don't see no stars out. 'Course, it's a bad night out here. Ain't so? Sleeting and spitting snow. Miserable weather for Thanksgiving." Shifting in his crouch, he smoothed the blanket over her. "Good thing I had this, though. We need to keep you warm."

His words, though he had completely misunderstood her, reminded her of where she was. It was Friday night, the evening after Thanksgiving. She'd been driving back from dropping Traci off at a new friend's house. She'd gotten a late start back because they'd invited her inside for a slice of pumpkin pie.

While she'd been inside, the wind had changed direction. That change had turned the lightly falling snow into hard pellets of deadly ice. Right about that time, darkness had fallen, enveloping her and Star in a thick, soupy world. She'd had to slow Star's pace so her hooves wouldn't slip on the asphalt.

Then those shots were fired.

"Shots?" she blurted, though her voice sounded hoarse and distorted, even to her own ears.

He frowned. "I reckon you will have to get some shots, but maybe not." When she parted her lips, desperate to make him understand, he started talking again. "You'll be all right in no time, though," he said with a reassuring smile. Don't doubt that. Good enough to start your Christmas baking . . . Ah, here's Lora. Let me see what she says."

He stood up abruptly, shaking off one of his boots. "Did you call for an ambulance?"

"I did better than that. I called my husband," the English woman said, her voice drifting slowly toward Susanna. "And thank the good Lord I did, too. Eddie was so worried when he'd tried my cell phone a couple of minutes ago and I didn't answer. Anyway, I told him about the accident. He dispatched an ambulance from the radio in his car. He should be here any second, too." Lowering her voice, she whispered, "How's she doing?"

"Don't know. She seems sluggish and she's talking nonsense."

"She probably has a concussion."

"*Jah.* I thought that, too. That said, she's talking and her eyes are open. So, that's good, right?"

"I think so. So, who is she? Do you know? Has she said anything? Do you know what happened?"

"I ain't been having much of a conversation, Lora. So far, all she's been doing is asking about stars and shots. I haven't even gotten to introductions yet."

The woman's chuckle echoed through the air. "Honestly. The things you say."

"Hey, now . . ."

"You know I'm only having a bit of fun with you."

"At my expense . . ."

"Go on, now. You wait for Eddie. I'll join her. Poor thing, lying alone on the pavement." Smiling softly, she stepped closer, then knelt down on the pavement beside Susanna. "Hi, there. I'm Lora Beck," she said softly.

"Hi," Susanna replied, taking in the attractive woman's golden hair falling way past her shoulders, her brown eyes, green turtleneck, jeans, and puffy down coat. ▶

**A Sneak Peek** *(continued)*

"I know you're worried, but don't be. My husband is a cop. Well, a sheriff. Well, a sheriff's deputy," she amended, her tone easy and light. She paused before gently wiping Susanna's face with a soft cloth again. "Anyways, he's on his way. So's an ambulance. I know you're cold and hurting, but hold on a little longer, okay?"

It took effort, but Susanna answered. "'Kay."

"If you're talking, that's a good thing." Leaning closer, Lora smiled. "That guy is so silly. He was acting like you don't know what's going on, but you're gonna be all right, aren't you? I bet you're gonna be just fine."

Before Susanna could attempt to answer that, the sound of sirens filled the air. Help was on the way. Thank the good Lord for that!

Closing her eyes, she allowed her mind to relax. At the moment, it didn't really matter where this man had come from, did it? Or why shots had been fired.

Only that she'd survived.

There would be time enough to figure out who everyone was and how they came to be near her when her head wasn't pounding, her body didn't feel beaten, and she wasn't freezing cold, lying on the hard pavement.

At least, she hoped and prayed that was so.

### Two weeks later

"I'm so glad you are nice," a sweet-looking blond woman said as they joined the buffet line after the three-hour-long church service. "I didn't think you would be."

As the statement registered, Susanna felt her smile falter.

She should have been used to comments like this by now. Unfortunately, they still hurt.

While the teens in the area hadn't seemed to have a bit of trouble accepting their thirteen-year-old sister, Traci, all the adults seemed to have a grudge against her family.

Try as they might, none of them could figure out exactly why.

Though her twenty-year-old sister, Amanda, was sending her a warning look, Susanna realized that she had gotten more than a little tired of being in the dark.

But maybe it was time to get some answers? "I'm sorry if I've done something to offend you," she replied in as conciliatory tone as she was able. "But if you could tell me what I've done, I'll attempt to make things better."

The woman looked taken aback. "You haven't done anything."

"No?"

"*Nee.* I mean, not besides the obvious."

Nothing had been obvious to her. "I'm sorry, but I'm still not following you."

The blonde flushed. "You know . . . the way you treated the Vance family. Well, your parents."

Now she was even more confused. "We didn't 'treat' them any way at all. I've never even met the Vance family. All my parents did was put an offer on the farm when they put it up for sale."

"Indeed, y'all did. And for a good price, too."

There seemed to be a hidden jab underneath that comment. However, it was just as evasive and confusing.

Since she couldn't think of a way to get better information without sounding like she was picking a fight, Susanna decided a slight change of subject might be in order. "It's been hard to put my best foot forward, what with my accident and all."

"Ah. Yes. We did hear about that. It must have been so scary."

"It was. It was one of the scariest things I've ever been through." Right up there with sitting in a hospital waiting room while her mother had emergency surgery.

"It's a blessing you weren't badly hurt."

"I agree." Physically, she was better. Mentally? Well, that was another story. Almost nightly, she woke up in a cold sweat, reliving the sound of gunshots reverberating through the snow. Of Star panicking and getting hurt.

When she'd woken up in the hospital, her mother had been sitting by her side. Her face had been stark white, the only color being the ring around her eyes. She'd been crying for hours.

Susanna had sustained a concussion, a colorful array of bumps and bruises, and some really awful scrapes on her arms and hands. But miraculously, nothing had been broken.

It truly had been a blessing in the midst of so much pain.

The doctors had kept her another day, then they'd sent her home with firm warnings about taking things easy. ▶

**A Sneak Peek** *(continued)*

That hadn't been hard to agree to. She'd felt as if . . . well, as if she'd been thrown from a moving buggy. Every part of her body ached.

Then, too, there was the grief she felt for Star. Star's leg had been injured in her frantic bolt. The sheriff who'd come out to the accident had to put her down right on the side of the road.

Though Susanna knew she couldn't have done anything differently, Star's loss hit her hard. They'd had her for years, and she was such a steady, sweet-natured horse. Susanna felt like she'd let Star down. Almost as difficult to bear was the knowledge that her father was now going to have to buy another horse and buggy. It was a costly expense that she knew they couldn't really afford. Not after they'd used the majority of their savings to purchase the farm.

Days after Susanna had returned home, she'd caught a terrible cold. She'd been so feverish and sick, her family hadn't even gone to church.

Now, here it was, almost a week later. They'd come to church, but though some people were cordial, others—like this woman in line—were far more standoffish.

She'd been so excited to finally make friends. Unfortunately, it was starting to be fairly evident that even the upcoming Christmas holiday wasn't inspiring many people to become more cordial.

After scooping a small amount of pasta salad onto her plate, Susanna tried to think of something to say that could smooth things over. So far, nothing was coming to mind.

"I heard that you thought someone shot at you," a dark-haired woman on the other side of the blonde said.

Though it would be better to hold her tongue, that had never been Susanna's strongpoint. "I didn't *imagine* I heard gunshots. I *know* I did. Someone was firing a rifle in the dark."

"How can you be sure?" she asked. "Did they find any casings?"

"Not that I'm aware of."

"Your buggy wasn't actually hit, was it?"

"*Nee.* But the gunfire scared my horse."

"Shame, that."

"*Jah.*" It had been a shame. Actually, so much about their move to Kentucky had been a disappointment.

18

"Though our first weeks here have been eventful, I'm looking forward to celebrating Christmas here in Kentucky," Amanda chimed in, in that friendly way of hers, which she'd mastered around the age of four. "Hart County is so different, but I'm sure we'll enjoy the holidays very much."

The woman's posture eased. "I'm glad you are settling in. Now that you all are getting out and about, I suppose we'll get to know each better."

"I imagine we will," Amanda said with an angelic smile. It was another move she'd mastered. She'd been born with golden blond hair and bright-blue eyes. She was striking. Very pretty.

She'd always been everything that Susanna never had been. She was bright, while Susanna's appearance was more burnished, with her brown hair and green eyes. Vivacious and eager, while Susanna had an unfortunate habit of blurting whatever was on her mind.

Well, at least Amanda was succeeding where Susanna seemed to be floundering.

"Would you girls like to sit with us?" the blond woman asked. "My name's Rachel, by the way."

"We would. *Danke*, Rachel," Amanda said before Susanna could say a word.

"But of course. We want to do everything we can to help ease your transition here." Smiling far more warmly at Amanda, Rachel gestured to one of the long tables near the end of the driveway. "I'll save you both a seat. You are okay eating outside, aren't you? It's a little chilly, but since the sun is out today, it's better than being back in the barn. It can get stuffy in there."

"Oh, I agree," Amanda said with an even brighter smile. "Eating outside in the fresh air is *wunderbaar*. Come January, we'll all be stuck inside for weeks."

"*Jah*," Susanna agreed. When Rachel and Amanda both turned to her, obviously hoping to hear something interesting or cute, she only smiled awkwardly. "It's good to appreciate good days, the weather is so unpredictable." Of course, she realized that she was talking about so much more than the weather.

As they followed the other women out of the barn and over to a long table situated in the sun, Susanna scanned the crowd, especially the group of young men sitting near where all the food was set up. ▶

"Hey, Amanda? Do you see any man that looks like my description of my savior?" The paramedics had told her that the man who rescued her asked not to be identified.

She'd thought that odd. Her father had, too. But her mother pointed out that the man might be afraid that they would do something to embarrass him or something. Some people didn't like to be thanked.

Susanna had been really hoping to catch sight of her rescuer today. Before church, when all the young people were milling around, she'd carefully looked at each man's face. But so far, no one looked like that burly man with the pale-blue eyes and ruddy complexion.

Amanda shook her head. "It's too bad you don't remember more about what your mystery man looks like."

"I had a concussion and it was pitch-black outside. I was kind of otherwise occupied," she said with a grin. "I did remember his light-colored eyes, though. I know I would remember them. They were so light, one might even think they were gray."

"Maybe we can ask Rachel and her friends if they have any idea who the man was."

"That's a *gut* idea."

When they joined Rachel, the rest of the table was already full. After smiling at everyone again, Susanna took a bite of her chicken and concentrated on learning more about the ladies.

First there was Rachel and her mother, Ava, and Rachel's daughter, Ruth. Then there was Charity, the woman in line who had dark hair. Sitting near her was her sister, Beth. At the end of the table was Maggie, who didn't say much but seemed to listen and watch all of them intently.

"Do you like your new home?" Charity asked.

Susanna looked at Charity more closely. It sounded to her like the question had a double meaning, but she couldn't imagine what that could be. Shaking off the sense of unease, she nodded. "We do. It's plenty big and has two bathrooms, which is always good when there are three girls in the house," she joked.

If she had known them better, she would have explained how much bigger their house was, compared to the small duplex they'd lived in back in Berlin. The purchase of this farm in Kentucky was a dream come true for all of them. From the time she'd been a child, Susanna had hardly seen her father. In order to support them, he'd managed a wealthy Englisher's farm. Because of the distance away, he'd even slept in a small suite of rooms in the back of one of his barns four or five nights a week.

While he was working, their mother took care of her, Amanda, and their little sister, Traci. Susanna knew her mother was lonely, and they all missed their happy, hardworking, affectionate father. But she also had learned not to complain or wish for anything different. They were blessed to have each other.

But then about a year ago, two things happened that changed everything. First, their mother contracted a series of illnesses, eventually being in bed for almost a month with mononucleosis. She was exhausted and tired and their father worried about her terribly.

The second thing that happened had been both a hardship and a blessing. The gentleman their father worked for passed away—and had left a sizable amount of money to their father. Enough money for Daed to buy a farm of his own.

That money, combined with the money he'd saved, had been an answer to a prayer . . . until he realized how very little it would buy in Holmes County, Ohio. The land there was expensive. That's when Daed hired a real estate agent and started searching for another place.

Which brought them to the Vances' property.

All that was why she hated to apologize for her father being so tough in his negotiations for that farm. If it had been more expensive, they would still be in their duplex, waiting to find the perfect piece of land for them.

But it sure didn't seem like anyone they were sitting with was interested in hearing their side of the sale. As the minutes wore on, everyone looked increasingly uncomfortable.

"What, um, Susanna means to say is that we are sure we will be mighty happy here," Amanda said, for once sounding as tentative as Susanna. "We feel blessed that the house came up for sale when it did."

But if anything, the mention of being blessed seemed to bother everyone even more. Rachel exchanged glances with her girlfriends. ▶

Sipping her coffee, Susanna was starting to wish they'd simply gone home right after church. She'd much rather be sitting in their family room reading than navigating her way through this awkward conversation.

Deciding to finish as quickly as possible, she took a big bite of macaroni.

Obviously deciding to smooth things over, Amanda smiled at everyone. "Can any of you do my sister and me a favor? You see, when Susanna got in the accident, a local man came to her rescue. We don't know his name, though Susanna does remember quite a bit about what he looked like."

"That's intriguing. Was he Amish?"

Susanna nodded. "He was. He was so kind, too. I kept hoping that he would stop by our house and say hello, but that hasn't happened." She shrugged. "But maybe he didn't know my name, either."

"That's probably true. There are a lot of Amish in the county, now. It ain't like it used to be, when we all knew each other and our horses, too."

Susanna began to relax. Maybe this was going to be all right. She just had to keep from taking offense at every imagined slight.

The women smiled at each other. "Describe him the best you can. Then I'll start bringing likely men over," Charity said with a smirk.

Susanna could just imagine how awkward that would be! "*Nee*," she said quickly. "There's no need for that."

"Come on. It will be fun. What's the benefit of sitting with people who know everyone if you don't put us to good use?"

Amanda grinned. "She has a point, Sue."

"All right. You're right." Smiling awkwardly, she said, "Well, the man was large."

"Fat?"

"Oh, *nee*. He was built large, like a football player. Tall, too."

"What color were his hair and eyes?"

"He had on a knit cap, but his eyebrows looked kind of brown."

"Dark or light brown?"

She had to think for a minute. "Light brown. I think."

"And his eyes?"

"That, I remember," she said with a smile, pleased at the game.

22

"Blue." Remembering something else, she said, "Oh, and he had fair skin."

"So you were rescued by a tall, hefty man with light-brown hair, fair skin, and blue eyes."

"*Jah*. He had a deep voice, too. Kind of scratchy, but I could be wrong about that."

She felt a new kind of tension as the other women exchanged glances. "What? Any ideas?"

Charity nodded. Rachel look pained.

"What did I say?" Susanna asked. "Is something wrong?"

Again, everyone looked awkwardly at each other.

"You all are starting to make me worried," Amanda joked. "What is wrong?"

"Nothing, except the man you are describing sounds an awful lot like . . ." Charity looked around, then pointed to a trio of men standing by the barn. "Him."

"Who?" Susanna got to her feet and turned. Staring at the men.

Just then, one of them looked directly at her. His gaze was solemn and blue. His fair-colored cheeks were scruffy. He had on a thick wool coat, but even in the company of other men who were bundled up, he stood out. It was him!

He blinked as he obviously recognized her, too.

She smiled.

Oh, but this was wonderful! At last, she was going to be able to thank him in person.

"Susanna, sit down," Amanda said.

"I can't. That's him," she said as he started walking their way. "Ladies, thank you! I've been so worried I wasn't ever going to be able to thank him properly."

Just then she noticed that the other women still weren't smiling. "What?" she whispered. "What is wrong?"

"You really don't know who he is, do you?" Rachel asked at last.

"I know he saved my life. What's his name?"

"That is Neil Vance."

"Neil *Vance*?"

As if reading her mind, Rachel nodded. "That very one. Your family bought his family's farm." ▶

**A Sneak Peek** *(continued)*

She felt like every bit of food she'd just consumed was now lodged in her windpipe. "That is quite a coincidence."

"It's something, all right. Because your parents didn't want to pay a fair price for the farm, they are all living in a relative's tiny older house. Everyone is trying to make ends meet. Barely. And at Christmastime, no less."

"Instead of a coincidence, I think we should call it ironic. That's more fitting. Ain't so?" Charity asked to the table at large. "Neil Vance saved Susanna's life, just days after her family practically ruined his." ❧

Discover great authors, exclusive offers, and more at hc.com.

Key Northern Posts
of the
Hudson's Bay Company

30°W.

70°N.

GREENLAND

ELLESMERE I.

Grise Fjord

DEVON I.

Baffin
Bay

Lancaster Sound

esolute

ERSET

Arctic Bay

BORDEN PEN.

Pond Inlet

ort Ross

BAFFIN I.

Davis Strait

Gulf of Boothia

Igloolik

Haven

Pangnirtung

60°N.

Repulse Bay

SOUTHAMPTON I.

Foxe Channel

Frobisher Bay

Cape Dorset

Lake Harbour

Cape
Fullerton

Coral Harbour

Hudson Strait

esterfield

Inlet

Chesterfield Inlet

Erik Cove

Port Burwell

Ungava
Bay

Rankin Inlet

George River

Eskimo Point

Cape Smith

Povungnituk

Fort Chimo

George R.

Hamilton Inlet

Hudson Bay

Port Harrison

Rigolet

Cartwright

Churchill

North West
River

Goose Bay

Belcher Island

York Factory

Fort Severn

Great Whale River

Great Whale R.

50°N.

Weenusk

Fort George

Mingan

CAPE HOPE I.

Eastmain R.

Fort Albany

CHARLTON I.

Eastmain

Rupert R.

Albany R.

Rupert House

60°W.

Moose Factory

Tadoussac

# BY THE SAME AUTHOR:

# MERCHANT PRINCES

# MERCHANT PRINCES

## COMPANY OF ADVENTURERS
### Volume III

## PETER C. NEWMAN

**VIKING**

**VIKING**

Published by the Penguin Group

Penguin Books Canada Ltd, 10 Alcorn Avenue, Toronto, Ontario, Canada M4V 3B2

Penguin Books Ltd, 27 Wrights Lane, London W8 5TZ, England

Viking Penguin, a division of Penguin Books USA Inc., 375 Hudson Street, New York, New York 10014, USA

Penguin Books Australia Ltd, Ringwood, Victoria, Australia

Penguin Books (NZ) Ltd, 182–190 Wairau Road, Auckland 10, New Zealand

Penguin Books Ltd, Registered Offices: Harmondsworth, Middlesex, England

First published by Penguin Books Canada Ltd, 1991

10 9 8 7 6 5 4 3 2 1

Book design by V. John Lee

Design adaptation by René Demers

Maps by Jonathan Gladstone/J.B. Geographics

Production editing by Jane McNulty

Printed and bound in Canada on acid-free paper ∞

**Canadian Cataloguing in Publication Data**

Newman, Peter C., 1929–

Company of adventurers

Partial contents: v. 3 Merchant princes.

Includes bibliographical references and indexes.

ISBN 0-670-84098-X (v. 3)

1. Hudson's Bay Company – History.   2. Northwest, Canadian – History – To 1870*.   3. Fur trade – Canada – History.   I. Title.

FC3207.N49 1985              971.2′01              C85-098658-3 rev
F1060.N49 1985

British Library Cataloguing in Publication Data Available

American Library of Congress Cataloguing in Publication Data Available

For DOUG BEARDSLEY, the poet;
JIM PAUPST and GEORGE SZASZ, the healers;
and GEORGE WHITMAN, the knight-errant—
who helped in bad times.

And for my daughter LAUREEN NEWMAN,
with love.

PRO PELLE CUTEM

*"The working of great institutions is mainly
the result of a vast mass of routine,
petty malice, self-interest, carelessness, and sheer mistake.
Only a residual fraction is thought."*

— George Santayana

# CONTENTS

*Lesser Slave Lake post, September 26, 1891*

# PROLOGUE

*To be a Bay man was like belonging to a*
*religious order that now only bottles brandy —*
*but had once touched the hand of God.*

THE PRIORY AT THEYDON BOIS in Essex, northeast of London at the far side of Epping Forest, is more than six centuries old, and feels it. It was, until the lands of the Roman Catholic Church were taken over by the state, occupied by a devout brotherhood of Benedictine monks. Its floors slope towards lopsided windows set three feet deep in stone alcoves; carpets are worn thin from generations of pacing; the air seems stale and heavy, though the visitor senses not so much decay as the weight of history.

The only functioning monument to the priory's original purpose is a crypt, below the main vestibule, that leads into an underground passageway connecting the building to the nearby abbey. Every Sunday morning the priory's owner still makes the subterranean journey to read the lesson for local parishioners. The priory's furnishings are a decorator's nightmare of crossed Zulu swords, narwhal tusks, abandoned harps, boulle cabinets, overstuffed sofas (which Queen Victoria might have envied), George Chinnery canvases of early trading sequences in Canton, Shanghai and Hong Kong, plus the obligatory hunting scenes (hounds, foxes, splashes of blood) that decorate almost every upper-class Englishman's hearth.

This is the home of Sir William "Tony" Keswick, the Hudson's Bay Company's last merchant adventurer.

An imposing presence, Keswick (pronounced Kezzick) turns out to be more than six feet tall, with a ruddy complexion and the commanding air of an Imperial Army brigadier, which he was. He appears to be the ideal British aristocrat—a cross between a *Punch* cover and a bulldog. Although he is eighty-four and his periwinkle eyes have grown watery, he retains an aura of authority.*

"Look here," Sir William exclaims by way of introduction, showing me his passport, "I'm the only Englishman who officially lists his occupation as 'Merchant Adventurer.' Gets me into awful trouble crossing borders, particularly in the Orient. 'Merchant' is easy; that means someone prepared to lay his hands on anything. But 'Adventurer'—the customs people have trouble with that. Still, I love being an adventurer—the romance of it, to risk everything, to make things go."

Three decades (1943–72) a director of the Hudson's Bay Company and for nearly thirteen years its Governor, Keswick regards his time with the Canadian trading giant as the highlight of a crowded and audacious life. "I adored the HBC," he sighs. "I'd have done anything for the Company, within reason—or without reason. It was a wonderfully romantic concern, and its people would have cut off their hands to help. We British are fanatically romantic about our history. The magnificent Prince Rupert was the Company's first governor, our great Duke of Marlborough the third. The second—the Duke of York—gave it up only to become King of England. I've seen the minute book in which the Duke apologizes for not being at the next board meeting because he has just taken on the throne. I mean, that's absolutely honey to a Briton. You'd pay a dollar more for your twenty-dollar share if you could get that thrown in—even if it has no practical merit!"†

Keswick's claim to being a merchant adventurer is not entirely based on his time with the HBC. In 1886, his Scottish grandfather took over the firm founded by Dr William Jardine, who with his partner, James Matheson, had in 1832 established Jardine, Matheson, the company of piratical Far Eastern traders and opium dealers that

---

*I keep trying to forget the briefing by a mutual friend that while Sir William is indeed a distinguished merchant adventurer, he is also a very careful man. So careful, I was told, that he has buttons on the flies of his trousers—just in case the zipper sticks.

†Not only a romantic but a mischievous romantic, Sir William named his middle son John Chippendale Keswick because the boy was conceived in a Chippendale bed. The husband of Lady Sarah Ramsay and a successful merchant adventurer in his own right (he is chairman of Hambros Bank), the younger Keswick is still known as Chip.

became the far Pacific's most princely hong, and later the model for James Clavell's Noble House and Taipan. The Keswicks have run it ever since, and Sir William himself was a director and chairman of Matheson's, the London affiliate, for thirty-two years.

WE TALK INTO THE AFTERNOON, and several cups of tea have grown cold between us when Keswick starts rambling on about his great heroes— Hannibal, the Carthaginian general whose army used elephants to cross the Alps, and Sir Edward Peacock, the Canadian-born financial Merlin with whom he sat on the board of the HBC—then briefly switches to his favourite villains: Moses and Cromwell. "They were such negative boys—always telling us *not* to do things."

I bring the conversation around to the Hudson's Bay Company and remind him that I have come to see The Chair. No outsider has ever seen it. Keswick hesitates, then motions me to follow. We climb to a small room on the priory's top floor. Sturdy and slightly oversized with a straight back, The Chair has a large upholstered seat. We stand very still, looking at it and at one another. On The Chair's seat, Keswick has reproduced in perfect needlepoint the Governor's Flag of the Hudson's Bay Company, with its intricate design that includes a fox, four beavers and twin elk rearing up on their hind legs. I can't resist looking at the former Governor's hands. They are ham-like, his fingers so thick that he cannot close them in repose; the joints are swollen and bent by arthritis. Embroidering that seat must have been excruciatingly awkward and required angelic patience, a quality not usually associated with merchant adventurers.

Keswick breaks the silence. "I'd never done anything like this before, but found gros-point needlework very soothing," he says. "One can think while working, with no ulterior motive . . . I used to do it after hunting, have tea, then come up here . . . Took me a year . . . Soothing, what?"

We both know he's fibbing. There are easier hobbies to soothe the soul. But not the soul of this Governor of the Hudson's Bay Company, one of its greatest, who was so upset about leaving his post (because he chose not to preside over the Company's departure from England) that he spent most of a year stitching this chair, working out his sorrow and his frustration. "I was and am in love with the old Company," he admits, as he leads me downstairs. "I don't know why one is so sentimental, really."

We part. "You're talking to a fanatical son of a gun," he shrugs.

I would never have guessed.

Keswick turns away, and says to nobody in particular: "Takes a hell of a lot of killing, the Hudson's Bay . . ." and shuts the door firmly behind me.

THE MEMORY OF THAT BRITTLE AFTERNOON at Theydon Priory stuck with me during the writing of this third and final volume of my Hudson's Bay history. Tony Keswick's enduring passion for the Company was by no means unique. Some of its bachelor officers willed it their savings; one woman executive confided to me that she loved the HBC more than either of her husbands. Even the grumblers, fed up with their long, slow lives in some dreary posting, would vow that they were damn well going to "retire early"—after only thirty-eight years in the service.

The one emotion the HBC never engendered was neutrality. In Canada's North, many Inuit and Indians insisted its initials should really stand for the Hungry Belly Company, while their women denounced it as the Horny Boys' Club. No one touched by the Hudson's Bay Company's Darwinian will to survive remained unaffected. To be a Bay man was like belonging to a religious order that now only bottles brandy—but had once touched the hand of God.

BY 1870, WHEN THIS VOLUME BEGINS, the HBC's feudal empire was starting to unravel, its halcyon days buried with Sir George Simpson, the Company's great instrument of thrust and thunder, who had served as its viceroy from 1821 to 1860. It was under his Napoleonic direction, exercised from the belly of a birchbark canoe, that the HBC reached its apogee, spreading its mandate across a private empire that encompassed a twelfth of the earth's land surface.* In 1870, the Company's landholdings were sold to the newly confederated Dominion of Canada for £300,000 plus title to seven million acres, its trading monopoly having been disrupted by the influx of settlers eager to till the rich soils of the Canadian plains. Following a brief interregnum, the HBC came under the spell of Donald Alexander Smith, the acquisitive Labrador fur trader who settled the first Riel Rebellion and eventually rose not only to preside over the HBC, the Bank of Montreal and Royal Trust but also became the dominant financier of the Canadian Pacific Railway and the man who hammered in its last spike. Having lost one empire, the Hudson's Bay Company moved to

---

*For a chronicle of Simpson's reign, see *Caesars of the Wilderness*, Chapters 9, 10, 14.

consolidate another, establishing its dominant influence over Canada's Arctic, organizing the trade in fox pelts, and eventually manning more than two hundred posts in the Canadian North. In western Canada, the retail trade was channelled into half a dozen downtown department stores that eventually became the nucleus of a mammoth merchandising operation, currently composed of 540 outlets with 38 million square feet of space, selling goods worth $5 billion a year. There were other ventures, too, such as the HBC's entry into merchant shipping during the First World War, when nearly three hundred vessels flew the Company's flag, running the gauntlet with essential food supplies and ammunition to France and Tsarist Russia, a third of them sunk by torpedoes en route.

Between 1920 and 1970, when the Company's charter was finally transferred to Canada, turf wars raged between the HBC's patrician British Governors and the Canadian Committee's Winnipeg-based Good Old Boys. At times the internal struggle was more important to these memo-warriors than trying to modernize the Company, but the HBC did expand into oil as well as urban real estate. It captured control of such significant retail chains as Zellers, Fields and Simpsons. In 1979, Kenneth Thomson purchased three-quarters of HBC's issued shares—more than anyone else had ever held—for $641 million cash.

The second half of this book deals with the HBC's boardroom politics, as vicious and fascinating an end-game as was ever played out in the wild fur country. Under its new owner, the Bay lost more money than it had netted in the three previous centuries and came very close to foundering. The drama of that downfall and subsequent resurrection, revealed here for the first time, concludes the HBC story and this book. This volume's final section features the first intimate profiles of Lord Thomson—Canada's wealthiest individual—and his son and heir, David, who easily rank among the world's, not just Canada's, most fascinating capitalists.

IN THE ACKNOWLEDGEMENTS that follow the main text, I have briefly touched on some of the research trails I followed to complete this book—mainly in the stillness of the Canadian Arctic and the buzz of the City, London's financial district, where the Company was born. I particularly remember being at Moose Factory, near the bottom of James Bay. First scouted in 1671 by Pierre Radisson, it seemed to be populated by ghosts. I spent most of my time in the Company cemetery, walking among the tombstones and the crosses, twisted into crazy angles by the permafrost. It was beginning to snow a little and as I stood in front of a tilted marker that proclaimed, "Sacred to the Memory of Peter McKenzie of Assynt Scotland, a Chief Trader in the Service of the Honourable Company," I sensed the spiritual presence of the fur traders who had lived and died here. I felt them silently staring at me, their faces like those haunting slashes of pigment Vincent van Gogh used to portray the Borinage miners: flat eyes, prominent cheekbones, looks that betrayed not a glimmer of duplicity but deep accusation. They were dead men from a dead culture, their deeds and misdeeds long ago consigned to the dustbin where Canadians store their history.

They were dead men, but they wanted to know why their lives had prompted so little attention, why their names had been ignored even in that crowded corner of obscurity reserved for Canada's heroes. They had, after all, done everything that was expected of them and more. But the phantoms quickly vanished, and I walked back through a gathering snowstorm to the Hudson's Bay store. There I spotted a twenty-dollar bill, with a note attached to it: "This is to cover the cost of 2 knives stolen from your store 13 years ago."

That night I joined a burr of Bay men, trading yarns. They were drinking to remember the good old days, then drinking some more to forget them. These were the men who would gladly have sold the Bay blankets off their beds to maintain the Company's reputation. They missed the fur trade because it had been less a business than a way of life, an escape from the restrictive codes of civilization. Now it was finished, and so were they.

Somebody mentioned George Simpson McTavish, an HBC Factor who had spent forty years at the Company's most isolated posts. To break his seclusion, he had domesticated a mouse and discussed in great earnestness each day's events with the friendly rodent. McTavish always travelled with a loaded pistol, not as a defence against attack, but to shoot himself in case he broke a leg on the trail and couldn't get back to his post. That's lonely. Nothing ever happened to McTavish, except that the mouse died, but I couldn't get him out of my mind, trekking across some screaming stretch of wilderness, wondering when he might have to put the gun in his mouth.

Canada's back country, where the original HBC held sway, was populated by many such "ordinary" men and women. They spent their lives in that obscure killing-ground of the soul the poet Al Purdy called "north of summer." Concealment of emotion was their chief article of faith—and nobody ever waved goodbye.

Thinking and writing about these "ordinary men" I had grown

to admire so much, my memory twigged to a line in Shakespeare's *Henry V*, after the battle of Agincourt, when the King requests a list of the English dead. "Edward the Duke of York, the Earl of Suffolk, Sir Richard Ketly, Davy Gam, Esquire; none else of name," replies the King's herald.

"None else of name"—history's most devastating epitaph—yet it fits most of the hard cases who lived and died here, on the margin of the known world, in the service of the Company of Adventurers.

Defining the gravitational pull of that benighted Company has been my obsession over the past decade. In the pages that follow, I have tried to explain that fatal attraction—to chronicle how the Company's quirky behaviour played such an essential role in determining Canada's history, geography and national character.

# LABRADOR SMITH

*Sir Donald Smith in 1895*

# CHAPTER 1

# THE MAN WHO BECAME A COUNTRY

*Who is Smith? What is Smith? . . .*
*Why, Smith is not a name, but an occupation!"*
—Thomas Wilson

IF THEY REMEMBER HIM AT ALL, most Canadians retain only a vague folk memory of Donald Alexander Smith as the centrepiece of their country's most famous historical photograph. He is that bearded gentleman in the stovepipe hat awkwardly hammering home the last spike of the Canadian Pacific Railway at Craigellachie, a hastily erected caboose-town in Eagle Pass of the Monashee Mountains on November 7, 1885.

But from there the fuzzy public memory ends.

He had, after all, been neither head of the CPR (that was George Stephen) nor the railway's builder (William Van Horne), and the reason for his prominence during that improvised ceremony was as mysterious at the time as it appears in retrospect. Typically, he said not a word at this most memorable of his life's occasions; he just bashed in that big nail.

Although he spent considerable energy cultivating the myth of being an enigmatic presence in crowded landscapes of his own choosing (or even making), in retrospect, there was nothing very profound or mystical about Smith—or the faith he worshipped: his own pocketbook. The institution he served during an astounding seventy-five-year association was the Hudson's Bay Company, which he transformed from a haphazardly linked collection of wilderness outposts into a profitable commercial enterprise.

In terms of modern Canadian history, Smith was there at the creation. His roster of accomplishments, self-serving as they may have been, distinguishes him as a giant among the decision-makers who transformed Canada from colony to nation. Preferring to dominate events from behind the scenes rather than directly confront rivals, Smith staged a dazzling sequence of commercial and political *coups d'état* that made him the richest and most powerful Canadian of his day. He became the role model for his peers. Smith won every available public honour, including two university chancellorships, the close confidence of four Canadian prime ministers (each of whom he betrayed), the friendship of two British monarchs, a knighthood and a barony for which he chose the tongue-paralysing title: "Baron Strathcona and Mount Royal, of Glencoe, co. Argyll, and of Mount Royal, Quebec, Canada."

No one felt neutral about Smith. "As a Canadian," proclaimed the Very Reverend Daniel M. Gordon, Vice-Chancellor of Queen's University, "I am grateful to God for the large service He has enabled Lord Strathcona to render for Canada." In contrast, W.T.R. Preston, then chief Liberal organizer for Ontario and a close observer of his methods, wrote: "The Smith syndicate was entirely responsible for using [the] Canadian Parliament for the most improper purposes that ever became operative among a free people."

Smith's catlike career enjoyed endless reincarnations. Each move irrevocably led to another opening, with Smith propelling himself from one opportunity to the next without a touch of diffidence or backward glance:

> The last of the great historical figures associated with governance of the HBC, Smith spent most of three mind-numbing decades as one of the Company's Labrador fur traders before being anointed last Chief Commissioner, first Land Commissioner, and, for a tense quarter of a century, London-based Governor. The first apprentice-clerk to attain such exalted rank, Smith turned out to be an indifferent administrator, but he did move the Company away from its genesis in bartering animal pelts to real estate, transportation and the beginnings of retailing. He thus ensured the HBC's survival after the Company lost its trading monopoly when the Dominion of Canada purchased the original land grants in 1870. Smith was fully as significant a figure in the HBC's history as that great Caesar of the Wilderness, Sir George Simpson, who had governed the operating arm of the Company during four adventurous decades from his express birchbark canoe.
>
> For forty-two years a director of the Bank of Montreal, as well as its second-largest shareholder, and for seventeen years its president, Smith

turned the Bank into Canada's most profitable and North America's safest financial institution. At the same time, he treated the Montreal as a private financing instrument for his various ventures—Canadian history's fattest piggy bank.

A director of the CPR and member of its executive committee for thirty-two years, Smith took little interest in its building or operation. But as anchorman of the road's private- and public-sector financing, Smith had the fiscal perseverance that allowed completion of the Confederation-fulfilling project. Patriotic as it may have appeared, this effort did not force Smith to stray too far out of character. As one of the railway's main shareholders, he benefited mightily from the stock's extravagant long-term rise. Members of his syndicate purchased CPR treasury stock for their own accounts at twenty-five cents on the dollar and grabbed control of the Canada North-West Land Company, which sold 2,200,000 acres of the Crown land granted the CPR as a construction incentive.

Smith's most successful railroading venture had nothing to do with the grandeur of the CPR. Along with three partners, he invested a borrowed $250,000 in the bankrupt St Paul, Minneapolis and Manitoba Railway, which, following a decade of stock manipulation and minimum construction, increased in value to a cool $60 million. Even considering the gutter ethics of late nineteenth-century railway promotion, acquisition of the St Paul earned pride of place as the most shameless of swindles.

Along the way, Smith became founding president of the Royal Trust Company, now Canada's largest trust. He co-owned a textile mill at Cornwall, Ontario, and a rolling-stock manufacturing plant in Montreal; his will documented many other discreet but significant holdings.

Smith's political influence equalled the impressive impact of his commercial activities. His crucially timed intervention settled Louis Riel's Red River Rebellion; his personal vote defeated Sir John A. Macdonald's second Canadian administration; he served eighteen years in the House of Commons, much of that time as the powerful pro-consul for western Canada—known in Parliament as Minister for the Hudson's Bay Company.

Some of Smith's more positive legacies included recommendations that led to formation in 1873 of the North West Mounted Police, predecessor of the Royal Canadian Mounted Police, and to the founding of Canada's reserve army. Convinced that it was a sin for a Scot to die rich, he became one of the most generous and creative philanthropists of his age, helping establish Montreal's Royal Victoria Hospital and significantly expanding McGill University. He won the admiration of a grateful British Empire by personally donating a regiment of Canada's best horsemen to help fight the Boer War and by funding the start of Lord Baden-Powell's Boy Scout movement. He gave away more than $20 million and left many benevolent Canadian and imperial legacies, including funds for a leper colony and plans for the so-called All-Red Transportation and Telegraph route that was supposed to circle the globe.

The first HBC executive to evaluate correctly the agricultural potential of the fur country, Smith foresaw that much of the Prairies would become fertile farmland. To position the HBC (and himself) as recipients of the revenues from sale of those acres, Smith became one of the principal promoters of immigration responsible for settling the West.

Smith spent eighteen years as Canada's High Commissioner to the United Kingdom, quickly becoming as influential in Britain as he had been in Canada. He bankrolled and became chairman of Burmah Oil and the Anglo-Persian Oil Company, the innovative energy firms that later spawned the giant British Petroleum. At the personal behest of Winston Churchill, then first Lord of the Admiralty, Smith's companies guaranteed security of oil supply for the Royal Navy as it prepared for the First World War.

It hardly seems possible that any man could have engaged in so much activity in a single lifetime, since until the relatively advanced age of forty-nine Smith was fully occupied by the mundane business of trading furs with Indians in a remote corner of Labrador, then justifiably known as "the world's jumping-off place." Part of the explanation for Smith's long roster of achievements was the extraordinary stretch of his life. Donald Smith was born in 1820, the year of George III's death, and arrived in Canada within months of Queen Victoria's accession, while the odd soldier who had fought under Wolfe or Montcalm on the Plains of Abraham still tottered along the streets of Quebec. He died in his ninety-fourth year on the eve of the First World War. His crowded lifetime spanned Canada's evolution from wilderness to urbanization. He headed west when the buffalo still roamed the plains, and died just before tanks rolled into the fields of France.

It was an astonishing life of significant tenures:

75 years with the HBC
42 years with the Bank of Montreal
32 years with the CPR
23 years with the St Paul Railway

18 years as Canada's High Commissioner in London
18 years in the Parliament of Canada
15 years as president of Royal Trust
6 years as chairman of Burmah Oil and Anglo-Persian Oil
4 years in the Manitoba Legislature.

Smith of course held most of these positions simultaneously. He had the knack of switching from one business to another, from yet another enterprise to politics and back again, without any derailment of consecutive thought or action. In 1905, for example, he was at one and the same time Governor of the Hudson's Bay Company, president of the Bank of Montreal, director and executive committee member of the Canadian Pacific Railway, president of Royal Trust, Canada's High Commissioner to Britain, chairman of Burmah Oil and the Anglo-Persian Oil Company, all the while remaining a major influence in Canadian and British public affairs and masterminding recruiting efforts in Europe to populate the Prairies. Not that 1905 was a particularly busy year—and he was eighty-five at the time.

Smith's compulsion to increase his wealth and expand his power when he already possessed a surfeit of both baffled and disturbed his supporters and critics alike. His contemporaries shared a sense of disquieting inevitability about Smith's amazing career. Considerable as they were, his accomplishments seemed less man-made than imposed by a force of nature. He was like the first rain of a monsoon season: nothing much could stop or pacify him.

Thomas Wilson, one of his many political opponents, best summed up the puzzle of Smith's obsession when he demanded, during a Manitoba by-election campaign: "Who is Smith? What is Smith? Is the palladium of our destinies to be entrusted to a Smith? What has a Smith done that he should seek to grasp the Ark of the Covenant with the one hand and with the other wrestle for the sceptre of the Almighty? Smith! Why, Smith is not a name, but an occupation!"

UNLIKE THE CHRONICLES OF MOST PUBLIC INDIVIDUALS, Donald Alexander Smith's life and times were impossible to separate. He so frequently advanced his career along with whatever historical forces he happened to be commanding or diverting at the time that he eventually stopped differentiating between his personal ambitions and the national interest. In his mental calculations these diverse objectives could be joined in a singular path: his own.

That intuitive leap had curious consequences. It meant that while at the beginning of his career Smith was driven by the same devils that push any self-respecting swashbuckler, he eventually came to see himself as an instrument of the national will, convinced that his personal success and the nation's destiny were inextricably linked. He failed to recognize any conflict of interest between the public good and his private benefit. According to this self-imposed credo, the consequences of his decisions could flow either way, there seldom being any difference in the spelling of the name of their ultimate beneficiary.

At first glance, this monumentally self-centred view of the world appears to collide with the fact that during most of his life Smith sought to advance the estate and well-being of the Hudson's Bay Company. Not necessarily. For many years Smith was the largest individual shareholder of the Company, so there was in this, as in his other endeavours, little absence of common cause.

Not only did Smith hypnotize himself into following such dubious logic but others began to believe it too. McGill historian John Macnaughton wrote of Smith in his later years: "That old man *was* Canada. In him, the whole history of our country, from the mink-trap and birch-bark canoe, down to the grain-elevator and ocean-liner, lived and breathed and moved and walked about. . . ."

Smith's egotistical approach was not unusual for his day. "God helps those who help themselves" was less an anachronistic cliché than an eleventh commandment. The myth, perpetuated in the simpleminded Horatio Alger books of the late nineteenth century (really one book rewritten a hundred times over), that thrift and hard work secured wealth, which in turn guaranteed virtue and godliness, had ignited the ambitions of a generation. Since it was clearly God's design that the virtuous become wealthy, to gain riches meant gaining Divine Sanction. Anything to be nearer, my God, to Thee.

Having thus created his own fiscal universe and a self-sustaining ethic to go with it, Smith seemed genuinely puzzled when he was accused of bribery and corruption. He wished to be remembered as a man who had never sinned and indeed had been intrinsically incapable of sinning. Yet he virtually invented insider trading, and doublecrossed both his political allies and one-time HBC comrades in the field. He regarded his House of Commons seat as a patriotic trust and refused to accept his Member's salary. But he was tossed out of Parliament for bribing voters, and the success of his syndicates depended directly on bribing politicians. As the British social historian Jan Morris noted, "All his life Smith was attended by a detectable aura of double-dealing . . . he was . . . without many principles but admirably resourceful."

Even in an age when the slightest evidence of business ethics was considered a sign of dotage, Smith's juggling of loyalties was breathtaking in its scope and audacity, outrageous in its absence of accountability or sound auditing practices. "Apart from their illegibility, Smith's letters reveal a man pre-occupied with politics, railways, steamboats, furs, and lands—in that order," concluded Alan Wilson, who studied Smith's surviving correspondence. "Many of his reports would appall a modern business practitioner by their lack of sufficient data, of attention to detail and sufficiently regular review. . . . For one who had close relations with some of Canada's leading bankers, he had a curious distaste for accountancy in his own administration."

That careless approach to detail was hardly startling. When the burden of a nation's future rests upon one's shoulders, who has time for balance-sheet trifles? The notion of an individual personifying a civilization now seems bizarre in any context outside an insane asylum. Yet in Victorian times the idea was not that preposterous. Those who, like Smith, subscribed to the efficacy of the British Empire—and it then ruled a quarter of the world—saw the expanding arc of their authority as a means of elevating mankind. Smith believed that immigrants hailing from anywhere in the British Isles were endowed with a very special mission. It was perhaps best described by the Earl of Carnarvon, a Secretary of State for the Colonies, who mused that in the far reaches of the Empire there were "races struggling to emerge into civilization. . . . To them it is our part to give wise laws, good government, and a well-ordered finance. . . . This is . . . the true strength and meaning of imperialism."

The concepts of parliamentary government, the value of gentlemen's clubs, fiscal stability, free trade, chivalry, Rudyard Kipling and the supremacy of the Royal Navy were all part of Smith's gospel. Canadian reaction to his imperialistic sermons was divided into predictably opposing viewpoints. Canadian nationalists of the time— a minority, then as now—believed this message was nonsense, that their burgeoning new country could find strength and identity only by cutting its cross-Atlantic apron-strings. The young nation's business and political Establishments preached just as fiercely that the only way for Canada to attain international stature was to expand the British link by gaining influence within the Empire's highest councils. Despite his Scottish origins and Presbyterian roots, Smith was an acknowledged leader of the second faction, behaving like a born-again Anglophile yet being fiercely (if somewhat patronizingly) proud of his rarefied brand of Canadianism.

Constantly cultivating the reclusion of a great man in the service of an all-consuming mission, Smith was stubbornly uncommunicative in an age when business tycoons pranced across front pages, dispensing avuncular advice and dropping marginally relevant comments. Smith stayed mum. He knew how to wait and he had a nose for power. Whatever nefarious fiction (or truth) might be written or repeated about him, he realized how valuable it was to allow legends to marinate undisturbed—that however useful a reply might be, silence was even better. He destroyed nearly all his early papers and was seldom interviewed. He managed almost always to take the credit for his achievements without bearing the burden of his failures. "There were always others willing to accept the responsibility," noted W.T.R. Preston. "He developed his power in this direction into a science. He never allowed himself to show resentment. So far as possible he avoided arousing thoughts of reprisals in the hearts of his opponents. However the end might justify the means, the reason for the means was not in evidence—his hand was never visible."

Portentous and solemn, terminally obscurantist in his manner of speech, Smith, as one contemporary observer put it, kept "his own counsel, his sixpences, the Sabbath, and everything else he could lay his hands on." George Stephen, first president of the CPR and his closest business associate for forty-eight years, once confided to a friend about Smith: "What a strange creature he is, so Indian-like in his love of mystery and secretiveness." Smith was obsessive about not committing incriminating facts to paper. Even though he and Stephen spent most of a half-century cutting the youthful Dominion's important business deals, nearly went bankrupt together, and ultimately fathered Montreal's essential philanthropies, Smith wrote Stephen few letters, preferring to discuss important issues personally, even if it meant crossing the Atlantic to do so.

Because the first three decades of his career were spent in the Labrador wilderness, cut off from the events in which he longed to play a part, Smith developed a need for self-assertion that never left him. But instead of signalling what he was doing through public displays or pronouncements, he simply acted and allowed others to catch up with him if they could. His formative years, insulated from the kind of lively discourse that prepared men for the anterooms of power, led Smith to distrust words, written or spoken. He developed a sense of boldness that required no validation from others. If there was one quality that characterized everything he said and did, it was aversion to revealing his innermost feelings. "He loved the solitude of a crowd, a privacy of mild light, from which he shone benevolently on

*North West River, in the Labrador wilderness,*
*where Smith spent more than twenty years of his early career*

all alike and upon no one in particular," wrote Professor Macnaughton, who also noted that "his really fine manners" were "more impenetrable and isolating in their lubricant defensiveness than crocodile's scales."

Smith's appearance helped create the air of some enigmatic Old Testament prophet who spoke in public so seldom that his occasional pronouncements were given more weight than they deserved. His imperturbable composure served him well during financial negotiations. Because Smith was photographed only after he left Labrador, the record of his physical aspect is almost entirely that of his later years—grey-bearded, tall and slight, elegant yet wiry, all bone and gristle at a time when distended bellies were regarded as a sign of affluence. His body language was a lexicon of military precision, but his most marked physical features were those bristling eyebrows, hiding eyes of feral flint. His sight had been injured early by snow blindness and the intensity of his gaze lent his glance a telescopic effect. One of his characteristic gestures was to turn his hands outward, showing the insides of his wrists, then to lean forward in a semi-bow that granted others in the room permission to speak—without having uttered a word himself. Whenever he did condescend to say something, there was little head-nodding for emphasis and nary a quiver in his meticulously trimmed beard. He lacked any flash of wit or mischief and left the task of abusing his enemies to underlings.

His solemn manner and demand for unquestioning obedience had their roots in instincts Smith acquired during his sojourn in Labrador. It was there that he learned to husband his energies and ration his emotions; survival often required both. Compliance with orders was equally important because dereliction of duty, however minor, could place human life at risk. The stern code of behaviour implanted during those formative years never left him. Work, to Smith, was less an occupation than a compulsion; his operational code was the maxim: "To rest is to rust."

THE KEY TO UNDERSTANDING DONALD ALEXANDER SMITH is the Scottishness of the man—Scottish to the marrow of his soul, despite his English airs and Canadian domicile. Like all good Scots, he knew how to maximize the authority of pursed lips and disapproving glances, how to parlay endurance into salvation, and, above all, how to fight.

The Scottish clans had always been fighters—against the Romans, the Anglo-Saxons, the Danes, the Anglo-Normans, the English—and, when there was no one else to fight, one another.* Scottish soldiers served as mercenaries of French kings, German princes and Scandinavian knights, and provided the human cannon fodder used in the defence of the wilder margins of the British Empire. "Scotland's history," the noted military writer John Keegan has observed, "is bloody with battles ... and her national heroes ... are men of the sword. The military ingredient of Scottish life goes deeper than that. For to the Scots ... war has been something of a national industry."

---

*Of the Scottish clan wars, Andrew Strome Carmichael-Galloway, Bannerman to the 30th Chief of the name, has noted that there were MacDonalds and Campbells who hated one another in the west; Armstrongs and Carmichaels who hated one another in the south; Mackays and Gunns who hated one another in the north; Lindsays and Ogilvies who hated one another in the east; MacGregors in the centre whom everybody hated, and Douglases who hated everybody everywhere.

That bellicose nature was a useful trait Smith and his fellow Highlanders enlisted in the service of the Hudson's Bay Company. Sparse of speech but swift in action, they had temperaments perfectly suited to the fur trade—the meld of perseverance and self-sufficiency, of endurance and courage that Donald Smith epitomized so perfectly. It was their gravity of demeanour and curiously rolling gait, their gloomy cast of countenance and habit of being close with money and emotions—their determination that even moments of pleasure or splendour must appear accidental—that was the Scottish way.* Scotsmen like Smith embraced the burden of hard work as Calvinism's earthly path to salvation. They were theological hybrids— Presbyterian Jesuits who believed that a fixed dose of piety could be exchanged for a prescribed sprinkling of grace.†

With all that self-righteousness burning inside him, Smith could never forgive himself for having taken up with Isabella Hardisty, then another man's wife. It had happened in Labrador under perfectly understandable circumstances, and his own marriage to Isabella lasted sixty-one years, but the whispers never let up. As late as 1888, two decades after Smith had left the North, Sir Henry Tyler, president of the Grand Trunk Railway, confided to Lady Tyler that Smith's "wife is said to have another husband." Smith grew so desperate to quell such rumours that at nearly every important juncture of his career, he remarried Isabella—no fewer than four times.

An equally serious source of guilt was Smith's sly betrayal of his fellow fur traders. Although he had been one of their number for most of three decades and they had entrusted him with their savings and with representing their case for better working conditions to the London board, Smith instead struck a deal that allowed the Company to acquire for next to nothing the traders' legitimate 40-percent share of profits. The once proud partners were reduced to ill-paid

---

*"The Scots," observed R.B. Cunninghame Graham, one of their wittier essayists, "fornicate gravely but without conviction."

†Scottish puritanism knew few limits. Canadian novelist Hugh MacLennan recalled that Sir William Dawson, the renowned Scottish-educated geologist who became principal of McGill University in 1855, once led fifty-seven other members of the congregation out of the Presbyterian church on Montreal's Stanley Street when the minister dared install an organ. The choir had previously used only a tuning-fork to pitch their hymns, and Dawson was convinced that the new musical instrument would sully the austere purity of the service.

*Lady Strathcona*

employees, shut out from revenues generated by sale of the land they and their predecessors had claimed and protected for two centuries.

All in all, Donald Alexander Smith may have been the most intriguing rogue in Canadian commercial history—a distinction that covers a lot of territory. Certainly, he was the most successful.

*Donald Smith at North West River, Labrador, 1860*

# CHAPTER 2

# GROWING UP COLD

*"A man who has been frozen and roasted by turns every year must be the tougher for it, if he survive it at all."*

—Donald A. Smith

DONALD SMITH'S PEREMPTORY ARROGANCE was particularly galling to those aware of his inconspicuous beginnings. He was born on August 6, 1820, at Forres, a storied Scottish trading town in that brooding countryside where Shakespeare's Macbeth and Banquo encountered the prophetic trio of witches. One of three sons and three daughters, he was much less influenced by his father, a shopkeeper clinging to solvency with alcoholic indecision, than by his mother, Barbara Stuart, the feisty and admirable Highland dame who brought up the family.* "Her voice was low, and she disliked loud noises," her son remembered. "She set great store by courtesy and good manners, and our bonnets were always off in her presence. She insisted on scrupulous cleanliness in house, person, and apparel, and herself set an example of perfect neatness in dress." Among other things, she taught young Donald to recite metrical versions of the Psalms then popular in Scotland, one of which he repeated "without error, pause or confusion" on his deathbed.

While his elder brother attended the University of Aberdeen and studied medicine at Edinburgh (he became a doctor on the northwest

---

*Alexander Smith, the father, was a brother of George Stephen's mother; Barbara Stuart was a Grant on her mother's side, distantly related to Cuthbert Grant, the Métis leader who staged the massacre at Seven Oaks. (See *Caesars of the Wilderness*, Chapter 7.)

frontier with the East India Company and a major in the Army Medical Corps), young Donald was articled to Robert Watson, Town Clerk of Forres. He spent most of his time hand-copying documents, but apprenticing to succeed Watson was far too humdrum a prospect to enlist his energies or talents. He was much more excited by the arrival on retirement leave of his mother's brother John Stuart, a doughty former Nor'Wester who had been second-in-command during Simon Fraser's daring exploration of the Fraser River in 1808 and later served as a Chief Factor with the HBC. Stuart promised to recommend the youngster to George Simpson, the HBC's all-powerful overseas Governor, and Donald set out on foot from Forres to Aberdeen, where he caught a London-bound schooner. Armed with his uncle's letters of introduction to Simpson and other influential Montrealers, Smith sailed for North America on May 16, 1838, aboard the *Royal William*, a 500-ton timber-trade windjammer. Just before leaving, Smith wrote to his mother, breathlessly enumerating the wonders of the British capital: "I have already visited the West End of town, walking all the way from the Mansion House, where the Lord Mayor resides, to Hyde Park, where the aristocracy are to be seen riding and driving. . . . Here the trees and flowers are a good month in advance of ours in Scotland, or at least in Forres. Had I been in the Park an hour later or earlier, I should have been rewarded by the spectacle of Her Majesty. The Queen and the Duchess of Kent, her mother, drive every day, I am told; so I shall hope to enjoy the privilege."

Much of Smith's fifty-day voyage was spent studying the only reference book aboard, Francis Evans's *The Emigrant's Directory and Guide*, which stuffily advised: "Canada is a country where immigrants should not expect to eat the bread of idleness, but where they may expect what is more worthy to be demonstrated as happiness—the comfortable fruits of industry." Smith landed in Montreal at a time when nationalist stirrings had reached their culmination in the Papineau rebellion, and his vessel passed the steamer *Canada*, carrying the last of the *Patriotes* of the 1837 uprising to Bermudan exile. British North America then had a population of 1.2 million, with most of the lands north and west of what is now Ontario belonging to "The Governor and Company of Adventurers of England Tradeing into Hudsons Bay." Montreal was a crude bush settlement numbering scarcely 30,000 inhabitants, its only patch of sidewalk being in front of the Cathedral of Notre Dame. On dry days, blinding limestone-powdered wind eddies made walking difficult, while rain turned the streets of the hilly town into mudslides that made getting about all but impossible. McGill College consisted of a medical faculty staffed by only two part-time professors.

*Donald Smith in 1838*

Smith walked upriver to Lachine, where Simpson administered the Hudson's Bay Company's 170 trading posts, scattered not only across the Prairies to the Pacific but also down to the Oregon Country, through half a dozen future American states, south to San Francisco, and as far west as Hawaii. The young Scot was hired at "£20 and found" a year and assigned to counting muskrat skins in the Company warehouse.*

---

*At the time, apprentice-clerks worked five-year terms at a gradually increasing salary that culminated at £50 in the final twelve months. If their records were acceptable, they could then sign up for another five years at £75. A third contract with a £100 maximum was offered to the best of them, followed, after a total of at least fifteen years of loyal and efficient service, by a chance to be promoted to a Chief Trader's and, eventually, Chief Factor's commission. These two ranks were eligible for shares in the Company's annual profits that ranged as high as £2,000. Retired commissioned officers received half-pay for seven years. All HBC personnel were granted free board but had to buy such basic goods as soap and boots from Company stores, at a one-third discount. They were responsible for providing their own bedding and room furniture. Typical yearly food rations consisted of 240 pounds of flour, 20 pounds of tea, 120 pounds of sugar, 10 pounds of raisins, and 5 pounds of coffee or cocoa per person. Their annual liquor allowance was two gallons each of sherry, port, brandy, rum, Scotch whisky, and all the lime juice they could drink.

*Montreal in 1838, the year Smith arrived*

The initial drudgery in the Lachine warehouse was a useful lesson for Smith in learning how to differentiate the various qualities of pelts, and he soon graduated from muskrat to grading beaver, marten, mink and otter, learning to judge the value of a silver fox by the number of white hairs in its glossy patina. Buoyed by his uncle's introductions, he spent a memorable evening mingling with some of Montreal's leading citizens, including his host, the international financier Edward Ellice, HBC Arctic explorer Peter Warren Dease, Duncan Finlayson, then about to leave for his new assignment as Governor of Assiniboia at Fort Garry, and Peter McGill, chairman of the Champlain and St Lawrence Rail-road and president of the Bank of Montreal. The Forres apprentice would leave Lachine soon afterwards and not return to Montreal permanently for another thirty years, but the memory of the sweet adrenalin of social acceptance he had experienced that brief, magic evening never left him.

The circumstances of Smith's departure remain mysterious. One version involves Frances Simpson, the Governor's vivacious wife, twenty-six years younger than a husband who spent most of his time away on inspection tours. According to a fellow apprentice, the lonely Mrs Simpson, who "took a friendly interest in the 'indentured young gentlemen'. . . was attracted by the simplicity and gentle address of the new-comer's manners." They seem to have enjoyed an innocent flirtation, the odd boating excursion on Lake St Louis and several cups of tea. Harmless it may have been, but the Governor was not amused. He called Smith into his office soon after his return and was heard shouting that he was not about to endure "any upstart, quill-driving apprentices dangling about a parlour reserved to the nobility and gentry." Smith was abruptly banished to the Company's career purgatory, the King's Posts district at Tadoussac.

Owned by the French Crown before 1760 and mainly by British monarchs thereafter, the seven tiny trading locations had been leased in 1830 by the HBC, which also rented the more easterly Seigniory of Mingan. Trade was slow because most of the territory had been beavered out and the Company did not enjoy the monopoly there it had elsewhere. Assignment to the region was regarded as an un-welcome alternative to being fired.

Tadoussac itself was one of the oldest trading points in North America; this was where Jacques Cartier had obtained his furs in 1535. Summers were cool and damp, the winters bitterly windy; nothing disturbed the rugged, sterile geography—certainly not the huddle of huts in the hollow of a mountain without even the presump-tion of a stockade, near the confluence of the broad St Lawrence and the deep Saguenay. That was the Tadoussac of Smith's initial assign-ment. He spent seven of his most unhappy and unproductive years in the area, trading principally for fox, marten and sable pelts with the Montagnais Indians, who paddled down annually from the Quebec-Labrador plateau. "You would have to travel the whole world over to find a greater contrast to the Scotch than these same Indians," the young trader wrote home. "If civilisation consists in frugality and foresight, then the Montagnais are far worse than dogs, who at least have sense enough to bury a bone against an evil day. In some of their lodges even before winter has properly begun their rations have come to an end. Everything about the place has been swallowed that can be swallowed, and starvation stares them in the face. They stalk in the tracks of a solitary caribou, and in their excitement forget their own hunger, but this does not make their families forget theirs. The caribou eludes them. They wander farther afield and at length bring down a bear. They cut him up and return to find their families dying or dead, which is what happened last month near Manwan Lake."

Smith tried to keep his spirits up by reading such classics as Plutarch's *Lives* and Benjamin Franklin's *Correspondence*, but often he found himself scanning every line of outdated copies of the Montreal *Gazette* and Quebec *Mercury* left behind by travellers. At this point he also suffered a strange "second sight" experience, dreaming that Margaret, his favourite sister, on a sickbed in Forres, was muttering "Donald! Oh, Donald" with her dying breath. Letters that reached him later revealed she had indeed died, of smallpox, on January 12, 1841, at the very hour, allowing for difference in longitude, of Smith's nightmare.

Eventually placed in charge of Mingan, the most remote of the King's Posts (opposite North Point on Anticosti Island) and an even more dreary locale than Tadoussac, Smith incurred the wrath of Simpson, who arrived for a surprise inspection in the summer of 1845. The post's account books, which to Simpson were the Company's secular bibles, were far from satisfactory. Following his visit, the Governor sent the young clerk this devastating assessment: "Your counting house department appeared to me, in a very slovenly condition, so much so that I could make very little of any document that came under my notice. Your schemes of outfits were really curiously perplexing, and such as I trust I may never see again, while letters, invoices and accounts were to be found tossing about as wastepaper in almost every room in the house . . . if you were but to give a few hours a week to the arrangement of your papers your business would be in a very different state to that in which I found it."\*

Smith hoped to redeem himself by submitting a neater set of accounts the following season, but on September 29, 1846, his house burned down. He had been briefly away on an errand, and one of his assistants had salvaged most of his belongings. With the Company records destroyed, Smith turned so despondent that he descended into a highly uncharacteristic public display of anger and frustration. According to eyewitnesses, he danced around the still-burning pyre of the tiny post, feeding the flames with his clothes and private papers, cackling incoherently: "Let them go, too, if the Company's goods have gone!"

The following winter he suffered from snow blindness and feared he might become permanently sightless without medical attention. Not bothering to wait for official permission, he boarded the HBC's Montreal-bound supply ship *Marten* and reported his condition to Simpson. The Governor immediately ordered an eye examination. When the attending physician found no clinical problem, Simpson

---

\*Smith's successors at the various King's Posts where he had kept the books had similar complaints, and the originals in the HBC Archives are scrawled with frustrated notations such as "Hang Donald S.!" or "Damn Donald Smith, I cannot make head or tail of this!" But there is evidence that Smith, rather than being careless, was beginning to exercise his penchant for secrecy and that the accounts were kept in a code to which he alone had the key.

accused his clerk of malingering, then interrupted his catalogue of Smith's perfidies in mid-flight to offer him another chance.

It was not a typical Simpson gambit. Smith had now been with the Company most of a decade. He was twenty-eight and had done little to distinguish himself. Yet Simpson must have sensed a potential in the intense but sensitive young Scot that Smith himself probably didn't recognize. At the time, the HBC was busy trying to revive its Labrador district, partly to counter competing freebooters moving in from Newfoundland and also to prevent nomadic Indians from evading their Company debts as they migrated from one post to the next.

Simpson's business acumen was attracted by that mammoth, frigid Labrador peninsula for precisely the reason no sane man wanted to go there. For its latitude, it was the coldest place on earth. Mercury froze in thermometers. Snow fell early and deep; it stayed so long that winter stretched over nine months. To survive in that harsh climate, animals had to grow extra thick, tight pelts that fetched premium prices at the HBC's London auction house. As early as 1828, a Company trader named William Hendry had sailed up the Ungava coast from Moose Factory in James Bay as far as Richmond Gulf and explored an overland route into Ungava Bay. Two years later, Nicol Finlayson established Fort Chimo about thirty miles above where the Koksoak River flows into Ungava Bay. There he waited twenty months for the local Naskapi to appear. When they finally did, Finlayson described them as "the most suspicious and faithless set of Indians I ever had to deal with . . . they must be sharply dealt with before they are properly domesticated." The primitive tribe, then numbering less than three hundred, suffered from having no internal political structure—no chiefs, no social organization larger than the family, no ritual ceremonies to facilitate trade, no formal alliances with any other groups. They were subsistence hunters, living off migrating caribou, and it was mainly their addiction to the HBC's rum and tobacco that prompted them to become trappers. As trade expanded, Simpson opened Fort Nascopie on the northwest arm of Lake Petitsikapau (near present-day Schefferville) and purchased from some Quebec merchants their post at North West River on Esquimaux Bay (now known as Lake Melville) about halfway up the eastern Labrador coast.

Just before Smith came to Lachine with his eye problem, word had reached Simpson that Chief Trader William Nourse, then in charge of that faraway region, had been incapacitated and badly needed medical attention. The Governor directed the "malingering" Smith to leave immediately at the head of an emergency winter relief party to North West River. Although he had come out of the bush seeking solace for bruised eyes and for an even more seriously damaged ego, Smith now found himself with a challenging option. The bristle of his Scottish nature had been touched: if Simpson was mean enough to issue such an order, Donald Smith was too proud not to obey it. Accompanied by a young HBC clerk named James Grant and three Iroquois boatmen, Smith accomplished the thousand-mile journey in record time, almost starving to death along the way and being lost for extended periods in snowstorms. It was the toughest physical ordeal of his life. Years later he refused to dwell on the details, though it is known that two additional Indian guides hired along the way starved to death.

Once in Labrador, Smith found Nourse paralysed, the victim of a serious stroke. While Grant stationed himself at North West River, Smith took temporary charge of the smaller but more strategically located post at nearby Rigolet. The North West River station (near modern-day Goose Bay airport) was tucked into a clearing on the shore of a 110-mile-deep salt-water gash in the frowning eminence of the unexplored Labrador coast, with mountain ranges rolling out of both horizons. Rigolet sat nearer the Atlantic, at the mouth of the rocky gorge that joined Hamilton Inlet to Esquimaux Bay. The unpredictable riptides of those treacherous narrows had already claimed many an over-confident vessel, including the British man-of-war *Cleopatra*. Smith placed the gravely ill Nourse aboard the annual supply ship, and by September his successor, Chief Trader Richard Hardisty, had arrived from Montreal. Smith was promptly relegated to his earlier rank of clerk, though he was delighted to welcome his new superior and especially his accompanying family. Hardisty, who had served in Wellington's army as an ordnance officer in the Peninsular campaign and the Battle of Waterloo, came to Labrador accompanied by his Mixed Blood wife (Margaret Sutherland) and their lively daughters, Isabella, Mary and Charlotte.*

While the Hardisty family moved inland to live at North West River, Smith remained at Rigolet. Under his direction, the little station became more than the mother post's maritime outlet. He met

---

*Each of Richard Hardisty's six sons joined the HBC, with varying degrees of career success. The best known of the sextet was his namesake Richard, who rose to the rank of Inspecting Chief Factor and in 1888 was appointed the first senator for the old Northwest Territories, representing the district of Alberta. Richard's granddaughter Isabella, known as Belle, married James Lougheed, himself named to the Senate for the Northwest Territories in 1889 and knighted in 1916. One of Senator Lougheed's grandsons, Peter Lougheed, was the longtime premier of Alberta.

head-on the marauding free traders who were attempting to lure the Naskapi to their shore trading posts, ranging far back into the fur country to finalize his trades and claim *de facto* exclusivity over a territory outside the HBC's Charter.

Though he could move fast on snowshoes, Smith acquired few of the proficiencies of frontier life. He was a terrible shot, attempting to down birds by firing without first taking the trouble to aim, and there is a record of his bagging a lone wolf, which he noted proudly in a letter to his mother. He never learned to ride, though he introduced the first horses to Labrador, and could not properly handle a canoe. He very nearly drowned when a kayak he was attempting to paddle overturned after only a few yards. "I went straight home and took a glass of wine," he later recalled, confessing, "the only time, by the way, I ever tasted liquor by myself." Yet he could be brave, too, and when the *Marten*, sailing out of Rigolet, ran aground, he personally commanded the rescue boats that saved cargo and passengers— though not the captain, who committed suicide rather than face the wrath of the HBC Governor.

By the autumn of 1850, Smith was writing letters directly to Simpson, not exactly disparaging Hardisty's efforts but clearly implying that the Company might expect better returns from the district if a younger Chief Trader from, say, Forres, were in charge. For his part, Hardisty seemed genuinely impressed with Smith, recommending him to Simpson at every turn. These exchanges produced results in 1851, when Hardisty requested permission to leave Labrador on furlough the following year. As soon as it was agreed that Smith would temporarily replace the older man (though still in his rank of clerk), he grew bolder in his criticisms. He wrote to Simpson that Hardisty was much more suited to a great inland post than to the actively competitive Labrador situation and criticized the Chief Trader for not seizing the local commerce more energetically. He openly attacked Hardisty's slackness in the face of increasingly vicious competition and criticized his plans for diverting staff and funds to improve some of the local Company posts. None of this backbiting seemed to disturb Hardisty. "He is all fire, and indefatigable in his endeavours to promote the interests of the Company," he wrote to Simpson about Smith, "and having a thorough knowledge of the business carried on in this district, I consider him in every respect competent to succeed me. . . ."

On July 8, 1852, only four years after arriving in Labrador, Smith was formally promoted to commissioned rank and placed in charge of the Esquimaux Bay District. "I have much confidence in your energy and desire to turn the business to good account," Simpson wrote, adding an important codicil, "but trust you will adopt a greater degree of regularity and system than characterized your management at Mingan. You no doubt remember that on my visit to that place while you were in charge, I had occasion to note what appeared to me a want of method and punctuality in your household arrangements, as well as in the shipping office business. I now revert to this matter in the most friendly spirit with a view to putting you on your guard against a repetition of such a ground of complaint which in your present more important charge might be productive of greater injury. . . ." Smith took the admonition under advisement and moved out of the barren clapboard hut at Rigolet to the much grander Chief Trader's residence at North West River, which boasted a winter fireplace and a summer veranda.

The senior Hardistys departed alone. Their youngest daughter, Charlotte, had recently died, while Mary had wed an HBC clerk named Joseph McPherson and moved away to Kibokok, a small post northwest of Rigolet. Isabella, who was twenty-three when she first arrived in Labrador, had shortly afterwards married James Grant, Smith's companion on the long overland trek from Montreal. Because there were no clergy in that empty place, the ceremony was performed by the bride's father. He had no official authority to do so since he was neither a clergyman nor sanctioned to perform marriages by his HBC commission because Labrador lay outside the Company's Charter territory. Such country marriages were routinely performed by anyone or no one, requiring only the consent of the couple involved. James and Isabella had a son named James Hardisty Grant in 1850 but shortly afterwards separated when, as Donald Smith explained, Isabella's husband exercised "no command of his passions." Just before Richard Hardisty left Labrador, Isabella and Smith decided to marry and went through an informal ceremony on March 9, 1853. The presiding official at that wedding was none other than the groom himself. Smith later claimed that he had been appointed a lay preacher by the Governor of Newfoundland and thereby had properly sanctioned Isabella's first *real* wedding (to himself), making an ostentatious fuss about the illegitimacy of her previous match.

The following year saw the arrival of Margaret Charlotte, Isabella and Donald's only child. To everyone's embarrassment, including his own, James Grant remained at the post another two years. Smith did his best to undermine his rival's career, complaining to Simpson that young Grant "has [very] much to learn before becoming an experienced trader, his long residence at North West River having been anything but advantageous to him, as while there he had little or nothing to do with the trade, and literally got no insight into the manner of keeping accounts which beyond a blotter or an invoice, he was rarely, if ever, permitted to see." In the same letter he lied to the Governor about his own romantic involvement: "It is just possible these remarks might lead to the supposition that I myself have been an unsuccessful suitor, but the case is so far otherwise that up to the present time I have not been so presumptious [*sic*] as to aspire to the hand of any fair lady."*

It took Smith seven years to acknowledge his marriage in correspondence with Simpson. Even then he referred to having wed a "Miss Hardisty" rather than any "Mrs Grant." Although it was a routine event in the bush ethic of the time, the episode was magnified and made infinitely more wicked by the rub of Donald Smith's Presbyterian conscience—a flexible instrument that failed to censor some of his far more questionable pecuniary ploys.


DURING HIS TWENTY YEARS in Labrador, Smith developed the cold insensibility that allowed him to betray political and business associates at will. The pressures that made him one of the most frigid, class-conscious aristocrats of his era had their origins here in Smith's lonely treks through the boreal wilds of Labrador, apparently forgotten by the glittering world he had barely glimpsed before his exile. He never admitted that there might have been a dramatic event to blame for his bitter turn of spirit. All he would say was that Labrador had toughened him. ("A man who has been frozen and roasted by turns every year must be the tougher for it, if he survive it at all.")

The Naskapi who traded in Smith's territory experienced grave difficulty adapting their lives and seasonal cycles to the white man's requirements. Their main source of food was the enormous herds of caribou migrating semi-annually across their turf. The Naskapi had to stalk the animals through deep snow, which required infinite patience and great skill—until, of course, the local HBC posts supplied them with guns and powder. These made the hunt relatively simple: so simple, in fact, that the old skills were quickly lost, and the hunters soon could not survive without weapons. Their independence had

---

*James Grant left Labrador and the HBC in 1855, moved to New York, remarried, and became a successful stockbroker. His son with Isabella used Smith's name and was mentioned in Smith's will, but when the family left Labrador, he lived apart from their household.

*Naskapi women and children at the turn of the century*

been broken. "Because the HBC controlled the supply of ammunition," the late Dr Alan Cooke of the Hochelaga Institute pointed out, "the Naskapis were obliged to spend part of their time trapping furs, mainly marten, whether or not they preferred to hunt caribou. When they abandoned their traditional techniques of hunting caribou for the new technology of guns and ammunition, they gave themselves into the traders' hands. There was no return."

The Naskapi were further endangered because the marten-trapping and caribou-hunting seasons coincided. The marten is one of the few woods animals that carries almost no edible meat, so the Indians were caught in a vicious circle: they could hunt caribou—their sustaining food supply—with guns and ammunition that the traders would provide only if they turned in good marten skins. But they couldn't keep themselves alive long enough to trap the pelts because that diverted them from pursuing the caribou. This dilemma could be avoided if the local HBC trader was understanding and advanced them the necessary ammunition, assuming that over several seasons he would come out ahead. (One such Company clerk, Henry Connolly, himself part Indian, did just that and found himself reprimanded for having been too generous in his allotments.)

During the winter of 1843, three families of Naskapi numbering twenty souls starved to death within sight of the HBC's Fort Nascopie, then managed by Donald Henderson. Three winters later, three dozen more Naskapi died, and in the winter of 1848 there was mass starvation in the area. Most of this was caused by Henderson's denial of enough ammunition to the local hunters. Henderson eventually left the service; but word of the disaster had spread, and Simpson demanded an explanation. As Alan Cooke observed: "Indians starving to death was, of course, regrettable, but the loss of hunters in a sparsely populated region that produced valuable furs was a serious matter. . . . During the space of six years, a 'proud' and 'independent' population of 276 persons had been reduced to about 166, with what hardship, misery and sorrow, and with what effects on family and social life no one today can imagine or understand."

These tragic events at Fort Nascopie had taken place before Smith's arrival, but there is evidence that he was directly involved in the subsequent famines of the mid-1850s, the worst of them all. For one thing, it was well-documented knowledge within the service that "no matter how poor the post might be, Donald Smith always showed a balance on the right side of the ledger." At this time he was trying to make the best possible impression on Sir George Simpson and his principals in London by maximizing fur returns at any cost. During the 1857 deliberations of a British Parliamentary Select Committee studying the HBC, a letter was tabled that former Chief Trader William Kennedy had received from a Company clerk at Mingan. "Starvation has, I learn, committed great havoc among your old friends, the Nascopies, numbers of whom met their death from want last winter; whole camps of them were found dead, without one survivor to tell the tale of their sufferings; others sustained life in a way most revolting, as [sic] using as food the dead bodies of their companions; some even bled their children to death, and sustained life with their bodies!" In another undated note, Kennedy's correspondent stated that "a great number of Indians starved to death last winter, and———says it was———'s fault in not giving them enough ammunition." Since these blanks appeared in the Committee's final report, Smith's name was not officially linked with this harrowing episode, but he was in charge of the region at the time, and because of the very tight control he maintained over trade expenditures, it is not unreasonable to assume that the famine, which wiped out so many lives, was his direct responsibility.

Smith's own reminiscences of Labrador mention few specific Indians; the natives were simply there, like trees or the wind. As the HBC's Chief Trader, he was North West River's community leader and that often meant medical duties as well. He achieved modest success treating wounds with a pulp made from the boiled inner bark of juniper trees, a method authenticated by Lord Lister, who introduced the principles of antiseptics to surgery in 1865.*

At night, the vast Labrador stillness was interrupted only by the hoot of a hungry owl, the subdued yelp of a dreaming dog or, during spring breakup, the thud and groan of heaving ice. Smith stayed up late, writing to his mother, reporting on each day's events even though his letters could be sent out only once a year via the HBC's supply ship. That vessel also brought Smith annually from London issues of *The Times*, which he carefully perused over breakfast—each newspaper exactly one year after publication. On Sundays he held religious services with his household, HBC staff, and a dozen or two Indians as the congregation. "To-day we all assembled for prayers in Mrs. Smith's parlour—every mother's son scrubbed and brushed up to the *n*th— even old Sam, who looked positively saint-like with a far-away expression, although he was probably only counting the flies which were buzzing on the window pane," one of Smith's clerks later recalled. "We sang three hymns, I coming out particularly strong in the Doxology."

To provide his family with a proper diet, Smith sent to the Orkney Islands for hardy seed grains, poultry, and cattle and to Quebec for horses, sheep, goats, and an ox. On seven painstakingly cleared acres, fertilized by fish offal, he grew cucumbers, pumpkins, potatoes, and peas, ripening more fragile fruits and vegetables in a large greenhouse. Charles Hallock, afterwards head of the Smithsonian Institution in Washington, was exploring "bleak and barren Labrador" when he happened on Smith's farm. "Then the astonished ear is greeted with the lowing of cattle and the bleating of sheep . . . ," he wrote of his visit in *Harper's New Monthly Magazine*. "In the rear of the agent's house are veritable barns, from whose open windows hangs fragrant new-mown hay; and a noisy cackle within is ominous of fresh-laid eggs. . . . Donald Alexander Smith, the intelligent agent of the post, is a practical farmer, and, by continued care and the

---

*Fifty years later, Smith, now Lord Strathcona, delivered a lecture on his primitive but effective techniques to medical students at Middlesex Hospital in London.

employment of proper fertilizing agents, succeeds in forcing to maturity, within the short summer season, most of the vegetables and grains produced in warmer latitudes." To complete the tableau, Smith built a two-mile track from his house to the farm—Labrador's first road. In summer he would take Isabella for sundown outings aboard his ox-drawn carriage.

North West River hosted another distinguished visitor in 1860, Captain (later Admiral) Sir Leopold McClintock, then in command of HMS *Bulldog*, a Royal Navy survey ship, who had gained prominence during the search for the Franklin Expedition. His log provides one of the few physical descriptions of the Labrador Chief Trader at this point in his life: "Smith ... was about forty years old, some five feet ten inches high, with long sandy hair, a bushy red beard, and very thick, red eyebrows. He was dressed in a black, swallow-tail coat, not at all according to the fashion of the country, and wore a white linen shirt. . . . His talk showed him to be a man of superior intelligence." McClintock in later years told Smith that he had foreseen at the time of the visit "Labrador won't hold this man. . . ."

To prove his worth to Simpson, Smith not only reported unprecedented fur-trade returns but began diversifying the district's sources of revenue, expanding into a salmon fishery (and eventually cannery), exporting barrels of seal oil, and even sending out rock samples for geological tests. "I believe," he predicted, "that there are minerals here which will one day astonish the world."* The most beneficial consequence to Smith of these activities was that the fishery, which involved shipping the iced or canned salmon to England, gave him an excuse for corresponding directly with HBC headquarters in London, bypassing his aging benefactor, Sir George Simpson. The Company eventually formalized this arrangement by separating Labrador from its Lachine administration, so that Smith now reported to London on all his activities. In one of his last letters, Simpson warned his ambitious protégé against being heavy-handed trying to impress his British superiors: "When you want to bring any point strongly under notice, it will have a better chance by putting it in a few clear and appropriate words than by spinning out the theme so as to make it look important by the space it occupies on paper."

Smith ignored that advice and his letters grew embarrassingly verbose. As soon as he felt a promotion might be in the works, Smith

---

*Simpson ignored the rocks, but Smith proved to be correct. The area he pinpointed as having valuable mineralization later proved to contain a huge iron-ore body, as well as lesser quantities of titanium, lead, zinc, nickel, asbestos, columbium and uranium.

did what he would always do in later life: he remarried Isabella. This particular wedding, performed either by an itinerant missionary or a visiting sea captain, must have been staged so that Smith could not only salve his conscience but also specifically refer to the sanctioned ceremony in his London correspondence.

He was appointed Chief Factor shortly afterwards at the age of forty-four, and in 1864 decided to take his first home furlough in twenty-six years. After visiting his mother, who was now almost blind, he hurried to London and spent the balance of his leave trying to ingratiate himself with the bigwigs at the HBC's Fenchurch Street head office. He met the Governor, Sir Edmund Walker Head, his deputy, Curtis Miranda Lampson, Eden Colvile, a future Governor, and most of the other important Committeemen. "Smith, the officer in charge of our Esquimaux Bay District," Colvile reported to Lampson, " . . . gives a good account of our affairs in that region, where he has been stationed for many years. As he is just the sort of man you would like to meet, shrewd and well-informed upon every topic relating to that *terra incognita* of the British Empire, I have asked him to dine with us on the 14th." Lampson, in turn, had been predictably charmed by the visitor who from now on was a marked man in the Company's future planning. There was one small hitch. As was their custom, on the eve of the departure of the supply ship (which would carry Smith home), the Company directors proposed hearty toasts to the well-being of its Commissioned Officers. But when he was called on to reply, Smith had vanished. Overcome by a fit of shyness, the Labrador trader (who had known he would be requested to speak and had prepared his notes) could not face the distinguished gathering, afraid that he might somehow blot his copybook. It was the first public evidence of Smith's well-deserved reputation as a clamshell.

Smith was back in North West River by August 1865, but the visit had transformed him. He now knew there was still a chance for him to participate in the great events of his time. Despite his geographical isolation, Smith's reading of the Company's prospects was amazingly accurate. Perhaps because he had never been there and had no vested interest in the HBC's main fields of operation in the West, he could clearly see that the future would not run with the buffalo hunters or fur-trade canoes but with the oxcarts and ploughs of settlers come to claim new lives in the new land. "I myself am becoming convinced that before many decades are past," he wrote to a friend at the time, "the world will see a great change in the country north of Lake Superior and in the Red River country when the Company's licence expires or its Charter is modified. . . . You will understand that I, as a

Labrador man, cannot be expected to sympathize altogether with the prejudice against settlers and railways entertained by many of the western commissioned officers. At all events, it is probable that settlement of the country from Fort William Westward to the Red River, and even a considerable distance beyond, will eventually take place and with damaging effect to the fur trade generally."

Within a year, the newly self-confident Smith had decided to visit Boston, New York and Montreal. Ostensibly, his trip was to view the sights of the city he had left twenty-seven years earlier. "The object I most wanted to see . . . ," he explained, "was the Victoria Bridge, which is truly one of the wonders of the world, and gives Montreal an unbroken railway communication of 1100 miles. . . ." In reality, he was seeking belated acceptance in the milieu he felt had suddenly become accessible to him.

The most important part of his trip, at least in retrospect, was a call on his cousin George Stephen. The son of a Banffshire carpenter, Stephen had emigrated from Scotland at twenty-one to become a clerk in his cousin's Montreal drapery business, in which he eventually purchased a controlling interest. He studied banking and had become associated with some of Montreal's leading entrepreneurs. The cousins' initial meeting was hardly propitious. The Smith family had gone shopping, and Donald had purchased a gaudy crimson carpet-bag for his Labrador journeys. Later, he wouldn't discuss his encounter with Stephen, but when Isabella was asked whether his cousin had been happy to see Smith, she burst out: "Really, why should Mr. Stephen be glad to see country cousins like us—all the way from Labrador? I wish . . . [my husband] had waited until he had met Mr. Stephen before buying that red carpet-bag. But he wouldn't let me carry it and the rest of us waited outside." Still, Stephen did condescend to introduce his country cousin to friends at the Bank of Montreal and leading members of the city's shipping circles. All the talk was about domestic electricity, still considered a risky innovation, William Gladstone's surprising eloquence in the British House of Commons, Alfred Tennyson's latest verses and the prospects for Canada under Confederation, then only a year away.

Smith reluctantly returned to North West River, but mentally he had already left Labrador behind. Simpson had died in 1860, and his successor, Alexander Grant Dallas, had transferred the Company's North American headquarters to Red River, closer to its main field operations. Since Smith was already in charge of the Labrador District, all that remained in Lachine was direction of the relatively minor Montreal District, which included the King's Posts along the St

Lawrence as well as trading forts up the Ottawa and Mattawa rivers. After the retirement on June 1, 1869, of the Montreal District's Chief Factor, E.M. Hopkins, "Labrador Smith," as he had become known in the Company's service, was appointed to the job.

And so Donald Alexander Smith came out of the wilderness at last. He was forty-nine years old, his skin permanently blackened by two decades of snow tans, his nerves as taut as those of a sprinter about to start his championship turn.

Montreal by then had a population of about 100,000, its streets had been paved and its harbour dredged, and the city (North America's tenth largest) was becoming an important rail and steamship terminus. Smith fitted in as if he had never left. "I called to-day to pay my respects . . . ," reported a startled HBC Factor shortly after Smith's arrival, "and was suprised to find him so affable and assuming, with no trace of the ruggedness you would associate with the wilderness. You'd think he had spent all his life at the Court of St James instead of Labrador. . . ." One reason Smith was treated as an equal by members of the city's financial élite was that in a modest way he was already one of them. During most of his time in Labrador he had put away virtually his entire HBC earnings (arriving in Montreal with a grub-stake of $50,000), but starting in 1853 with the purchase of two shares, he had also quietly been accumulating stock in the Bank of Montreal. Coincidentally, George Stephen had been doing the same thing, and within the next four years the two cousins would become the Bank of Montreal's second-largest shareholders.

Overnight, Smith seemed to be launched on the urban business career that had been his long-postponed dream. Then a confluence of circumstances intervened and hurled him into the vortex of a strange rebellion gathering momentum halfway across the continent.

*Donald Smith in 1871*

*Louis Riel, about 1885*

# CHAPTER 3

# Bringing Louis Riel to Heel

*Louis Riel remains the perfect martyr of the prototypical Canadian tragedy: a well-meaning yet deluded mystic who died prematurely by pretending to be sane.*

THE COUNTRY WHOSE HISTORY Smith was about to affect still seemed more an idea than a reality. Canada in 1869 consisted of Nova Scotia, New Brunswick, Quebec and Ontario (the latter two minus their present northern areas), plus the huge but nearly empty western territories then in the process of being acquired from the Hudson's Bay Company.* After protracted negotiations, the Canadian government had agreed to purchase Prince Rupert's original land grant for £300,000 ($1,460,000) through a loan guaranteed by the Treasury of the United Kingdom. In addition to receiving cash, the HBC was granted unhindered trading privileges and 45,000 acres around its 120 trading posts as well as the right to claim, during the ensuing fifty years, one-twentieth of the fertile land (about seven million acres) between Lake Winnipeg and the Rocky Mountains. The transfer that would extinguish the HBC's long-coveted monopoly rights was to take effect on December 1, 1869.

In the decade after Confederation, most of the 3.6 million citizens of the new Dominion scratched for a living in rural isolation; only 390 square miles were occupied by two dozen embryonic towns and cities.

---

*For details, see *Caesars of the Wilderness*, pages 361–75.

Montreal was the largest at 100,000 people, with Quebec and Toronto competing for second place at about 60,000 each. Across the broad continent west of the Lakehead, there was almost nothing. "The plains were as thousands of years of geological and climatic change had made them," wrote W.L. Morton, the bard of western Canadian historians. "The grasses flowed, the prairie fires ran in the wind; the buffalo grazed like cloud shadows in the plain; the buffalo hunt raised a flurry of dust in the diamond summer light; the rivers sought the distant sea unchecked; summer made green, autumn bronze, winter white, spring gray. . . . What had been wrought . . . lay unchanged until it became the setting for the last frontier."

Because the HBC had for two centuries kept nearly everyone who was not a Company employee out of its domain, the new Canadian West remained in the public mind a territory not far removed from those mysterious hunks of geography labelled on ancient charts "Here Be Dragons." Returning missionaries and the odd free spirit had brought out fragmentary reports of the land's contours and habitability, but it was the American, not the Canadian, West that attracted most settlers. The larger population base of the United States, its better climate and the mood of egalitarianism that characterized the self-confident republic made it a good place to start new lives. The notion of upward mobility still seemed foreign in Canada, which remained trapped in perpetuating vestiges of the British class system.

Canada's West was isolated more because of the absence of transportation facilities than as the result of geography. There were only three means of entry: by ship to York Factory through Hudson Bay; by Red River cart northward from the headwaters of the Mississippi River in Minnesota; or by canoe along the historic fur-trade routes from the upper end of the Great Lakes. Local HBC post managers had from the beginning been encouraged to live off the land, but except for the tracts of cultivation at Red River and a tiny spread at Cumberland House, the pioneer trading post opened by Samuel Hearne in 1774, only a few kitchen gardens had taken root. That began to change with the report by John Palliser, a Dublin-born explorer and buffalo hunter who was commissioned by the Royal Geographical Society to report on the region's potential. He not only defined a fertile land crescent across the prairie and noted deposits of coal and other minerals but also explored six passes through the Rockies for possible future railway construction. His optimism was somewhat tempered by the conclusion that no railway could be built across the treacherous bogs north of Lake Superior; the Red River settlement would have to be provisioned from the United States, via Chicago and St Paul.*

By the late 1860s, Red River's inhabitants, including the offspring of the dispossessed crofters from the Scottish clearances, had turned the fifty-mile area around the HBC post at Fort Garry, near the junction of the Red and Assiniboine rivers, into a relatively prosperous, if insular, community of about ten thousand souls. Half were proud buffalo hunters descended from the mixed marriages of voyageurs and HBC clerks with Cree, Saulteaux, Blackfoot, Chipewyan, Dogrib and Slavey women. Their spiritual centre was the grey stone cathedral in the parish of St Boniface, presided over by the shrewd Roman Catholic bishop, Alexandre-Antonin Taché. The tiny village of Winnipeg at the edge of the HBC fort had grown into a miniature business centre, with half a dozen saloons, hotels and stores, supplied by the Red River cart brigades that maintained the link between Fort Garry and St Paul.†

Red River's hermetically sealed world revolved around the Hudson's Bay Company's Canadian headquarters at Fort Garry, its busy compound enclosing the Governor's residence, storehouses, clerks' and officers' quarters, sales and trading shops, the powder house and a scatter of outbuildings. Here in summer came the Indian canoe flotillas, loaded to the gunwales with pelts. The trading chiefs—big men with deliberate limb movements and the rhythmic lope of hunters—would hump the fur packs through the fort gates, eager to acquire guns, blankets, copper kettles, and the increasing range of household goods brought over by the HBC from England. Most summer days, Red River carts would be pulling in from St Paul or pulling out, their ungreased wooden wheels screeching in the sunlight, to supply the HBC's outposts along the North Saskatchewan River all the way to Fort Edmonton. They would return three months later bulging with the inland fur harvest.

Inside the fort, where each arrival and departure was accompanied by the yelps of a swirling chorus of mongrels, the walls had been painted scarlet, yellow and orange to offset the monotony of nature's blues and greens. Local courts sat here, as did the district's

---

*For the founding of Lord Selkirk's colony, see *Caesars of the Wilderness*, pages 137–89.

†The first saloon was opened in 1859 by "Dutch George" Emmerling, who arrived with a barrel of whisky and sold the diluted rotgut at sixpence a shot. The sleazy emporium was eventually purchased by Robert Atkinson Davis who promoted it as "a haven of warmth, rest and billiards." Davis reluctantly quit the saloon business in 1874 to become Manitoba's fifth premier.

administrators, ruling for half a century through an insipid body known as the Council of Assiniboia, headed by the resident HBC Governor, its roster padded by tame Company appointees. James Ross, an English Mixed Blood who had gone east and graduated from the University of Toronto before returning to Red River, complained sourly about "the incubus of the Company's monopoly—the peculiar government under which we *vegetate*—it cools our ardour—destroys our energies—annihilates our very *desires* for improvement."

Even William Mactavish, the HBC's incumbent Governor, declared himself disgusted with "the greedy London directory" and the "arrogant Dominion Government," since neither had exercised the courtesy of informing him directly about the impending changes of circumstance. Although negotiations agreeing to terms that would surrender the HBC lands and monopoly had been concluded in London on April 9, 1869, by November of that year Mactavish had still not received notification of the transfer. In the absence of reliable information, rumours swept the HBC compound, so that Mactavish's already difficult position became untenable.*

The Edinburgh-born Mactavish had joined the Company as an apprentice in 1833. He was trained mainly at York Factory and worked his way up through the accounting department with few operational commands until he was promoted to the HBC's highest overseas office. A dreamy yet disenchanted Highlander, Mactavish was an amateur phrenologist who believed that a person's character could be read by the shape of his or her skull. He had accepted the governorship of Assiniboia under protest and later lamented he would rather have served as "a stoker in hell." His unhappy tenure was made all the more agonizing by the fact that he was suffering from advanced tuberculosis and had to expend most of his waning vitality fighting the awful lassitude inflicted by the disease. As a result, no matter what the provocation, no matter how seriously the Company's authority was challenged, Mactavish retreated into a stupor of inactivity and apparent indifference. Yet had Mactavish been the most enlightened and energetic of men, neither he nor any other Bay official

---

*He said little publicly about the impending transfer, which would terminate his authority, and his official journal is equally reticent on the subject. Mactavish expressed his real feelings in a letter to his brother, Chief Factor Dugald Mactavish, in Montreal. "I will not speak of our dignity," he wrote, "but it is more than flesh and blood can bear that we who have conducted the government of this country for years, with a view to the welfare and best interests of all classes of the inhabitants, should be summarily ejected from office, as if we were the commonest usurping scoundrels."

*Métis at camp on the prairie, 1858*

could have turned back the gathering storm at Red River.

The tiny settlement, with little of the required infrastructure to provide channels for common cause, housed almost as many factions as families. A small but vocal Canadian Party led by Dr John Christian Schultz, a militant Protestant and publisher of the local paper, the *Nor'Wester*, demanded union with the Dominion; equally loud were the proponents of immediate annexation to the United States. There were Irishmen fulminating against everything British, Highlanders trying to replicate their ancient clannish ways, even importing nightingales to make themselves feel at home, and agents of Napoleon III* vainly resurrecting wispy dreams of French empire along the vanished trails of the *coureurs de bois*. The best-organized Red River grouping was that of the Métis. They were united by concern for the buffalo herds, their main source of income and pride, which had been relentlessly gunned down and dangerously thinned out. The magnificent beasts were often shot solely for their tongues, that commodity when pickled having become a delicacy in fashionable European restaurants. The advance of agriculture and decline of the fur trade—the main market for buffalo meat in the form of pemmican—threatened their livelihood. They were restless and they

---

*The French Emperor had dispatched Norbert Gay, an army captain, to Red River to "report on the situation," because a majority of its population was French-speaking and its political future seemed uncertain. Although Gay did little spying, he helped train the Métis buffalo hunters into a formidable fighting force.

were angry. They had opened up this country and now saw little future on their home turf. Their temperament was much too volatile to turn in their guns for the restraints of urban domesticity. Since they recognized that evolving circumstances would neither restore their past nor validate their future, the Métis decided to draw on their French and Indian roots to fashion a peculiar world of their own—a new nation, *their* nation, on the edge of civilization.

TROUBLE CAME FIRST in the form of Colonel John Stoughton Dennis, a United Empire Loyalist and cavalry veteran commissioned by William McDougall, Minister of Public Works in Sir John A. Macdonald's first administration, to chart the new territory. He arrived at Red River unannounced in August of 1869, four months before the transfer was due to take place, charged with making a survey so that the unoccupied Red River lands could be subdivided in a radically new pattern. The land had traditionally been laid out according to the Quebec seigneury style, with long, narrow rectangular lots fronting on the Red and the Assiniboine. Most of the farms occupied about four hundred feet of riverbank, then arched two miles or so through fields and woodlands to the drier prairie soil, where "hay privileges" were shared with neighbours. Ownership was based on original HBC and Selkirk grants or, more often, squatters' rights.

Following instructions from McDougall, Colonel Dennis and his military surveyors began to lay out square townships designed for large-scale grain production from ploughed land. As practical as that may have sounded to Ottawa bureaucrats busy preparing the way for occupancy by ambitious newcomers from Ontario, the system ran directly counter to the Métis way of life and farming requirements. On October 11, a survey party led by Captain Adam Clark Webb unexpectedly arrived at the hay privilege of André Nault. The distraught Métis sent a messenger to fetch his cousin, Louis Riel, who came at the gallop with fifteen unarmed but defiant companions. An elegant and remarkably self-possessed gent with a high forehead overhung by clusters of black curly hair, Riel theatrically placed his foot on Captain Webb's measuring chain and solemnly declared: "You go no farther." The surveyors eventually went away and nine days later the Métis formed a committee, based on the old buffalo-hunt governments, with the twenty-five-year-old Riel as secretary. He quickly emerged as the group's real leader.

At this point, onto the stage of western Canadian history stumbled William McDougall, former minister of public works, now designated first lieutenant-governor of the Northwest Territories. Picked for the Red River assignment mainly because Macdonald considered him pompous and inflexible enough "to keep those wild people quiet," McDougall was one of the Prime Minister's more serious miscalculations. Known as Wandering Willie because he had served so many political faiths, McDougall turned out to be as stupid as he was pompous—not an easy accomplishment.

When McDougall's caravan, consisting of sixty carts loaded with his official entourage, relatives, fox-hunting dogs and an ornate vice-regal throne of state, arrived at the customs house in Dakota Territory on October 30, McDougall was handed a note from Le Comité National des Métis de la Rivière Rouge, refusing them entry into Rupert's Land. Three days later, an unarmed Riel, riding at the head of more than 120 armed followers, seized Fort Garry, explaining to a compliant Mactavish that his purpose was to prevent bloodshed and guard the fort against unspecified dangers. Although the HBC Governor was confined to quarters, there seemed to be remarkably little hostility between him and the rebel leader. McDougall later accused the Company of opening the fort gates to the Métis and welcoming the invaders.

Viewing the escalating pace of events with increasing alarm from Ottawa, Sir John A. Macdonald hastily dispatched two messages. The first went through the correct political channels to the HBC in London, pointing out that since McDougall was being denied entry to Red River, the land purchase would have to be postponed until peaceful possession could be assured and advising the Company not to expect its £300,000 payment until the official transfer could take place. His second letter was to McDougall, telling him to stay put. "I hope," cautioned the Prime Minister, "no consideration will induce you to leave your post—that is, to return to Canada just now. Such a course would cover yourself and your party with ridicule, which would extend to the whole Dominion."

Encamped on the American side of the border and unaware of the postponement, McDougall was determined that the transfer date as he knew it would not go unnoticed. On the afternoon of December 1, he drew up a bogus royal proclamation. "Victoria, by the grace of God, of the United Kingdom of Great Britain and Ireland, Queen," it began, then appointed, of all people, "our trusty and well-beloved William McDougall" to hold supreme governmental authority over the disputed territories. That night, in one of the great comic turns of Canadian history, McDougall had his carriage driven through a twenty-below blizzard into Canada. He was accompanied by seven puzzled functionaries and two pointer dogs casting curious glances to left and right as they approached the ceremonial moment. Then, having reached the courtyard of an abandoned HBC post, McDougall ostentatiously positioned himself in a proper Nelsonian stance and, while one of his minions unfurled a Union Jack and another held a guttering lantern, sonorously read his proclamation to the empty prairie sky. He stood there, the parchment in his mittened hands, baying at the polar moon. The winds blew, the dogs howled, the functionaries snickered into their beards—and McDougall basked in the glow of his self-anointed glory.

The absurd deed done, the nocturnal caravan, led by the pair of bounding pointers, quickly headed back to the warmth and safety of its temporary American quarters, satisfied with a long night's work well done. It had indeed been an occasion to remember: the night the Honourable William McDougall finally stepped over the slippery line between pomposity and idiocy. McDougall's document carried the weight of no authority. He had none of his own and had counterfeited the Queen's imprimatur. His impetuous act turned the federal government into the object of frontier hilarity.

None of this bothered the Ottawa emissary (thereafter known as "*Silly* Wandering Willie"), who actually expected Macdonald to reward him for his "prompt display of vigour [that] will inspire all inhabitants of the Territory with respect for your Representative, and compel the traitors to cry, 'God Save the Queen.'" The Prime Minister ignored McDougall's bluster, angrily denounced him for having "done his utmost to destroy our chance of an amicable settlement with these wild people," and recalled him to Ottawa. Before leaving, McDougall appointed the surveyor, Colonel Dennis, as his "Lieutenant and Conservator of the Peace" and ordered him to clear the rebels out of Fort Garry—in effect inviting Dennis to launch a civil war. McDougall also dispatched copies of his worthless proclamation to Fort Garry, so that Mactavish and the Hudson's Bay Company would be officially aware they had just been deposed. The HBC Governor, his chest on fire with advanced tuberculosis, was beyond caring. He spent most days sitting alone at his deserted council table, coughing and staring into space.

Red River did have an effective government, and Louis Riel was at its head. When the Métis leader called a community meeting to establish the terms of his provisional administration, English-speaking delegates asked Mactavish whether he still considered the HBC to be Red River's prevailing authority. The gravely ill Governor advised them that McDougall's mission, however foolishly conceived,

*Métis family with Red River cart on Main Street, Winnipeg*

would soon terminate his powers, and that since he was "a dead man," they had better construct a government to maintain peace.* Riel named himself President of the Provisional Government of Rupert's Land and the North-West (then the world's second-largest republic) and raised over Fort Garry the new Métis flag (a golden fleur-de-lis and a green shamrock on a white ground).† To emphasize his authority, Riel transferred the new Government House furniture that had been prepared for McDougall's arrival to another part of the fort, which became his office as chief of state.

The rebellion, if that's what it was, had been achieved with force but no bloodshed. With the subtlety of a seasoned politician, Riel had drawn enough consensus from the diverse elements of the colony to govern Red River. While the Canadian government dithered, American annexationists were quick to realize the potential of the situation, offering Riel flattering entreaties and generous cash donations if he

---

*John Bruce, a local magistrate and president of the National Committee, later testified that Mactavish had told him McDougall and his successors should be resisted because Canada's taking possession of the territory was "an injustice to the people and to the officers of the Hudson's Bay Company, since the Government had given them no part of the £300,000 paid for their country."

†The fleur-de-lis was the proud standard of Samuel de Champlain, the Father of New France. The shamrock was added to recognize the treasurer of the Métis Governing Council, a professional Irishman named W. B. O'Donoghue, who taught mathematics at St Boniface College.

would throw in his republic's lot with the Stars and Stripes. Insignificant as Red River was, Washington politicians recognized it as the ideal entry point for a takeover of Canada's West—and eventually the entire continent. "The tendency of North American events is plainly towards the consolidation into one great nation," chirped the New York *Sun*. "From the Polar Sea to the Isthmus of Darien, there will in time be only one national government—that of the United States. Who among us can say that ours is not a glorious destiny or reflect without exultation that he is an American citizen?" Macdonald understood these sentiments all too well, lamenting that while he would gladly neglect the West for the next half-century, if Englishmen didn't go there, Yankees would. Something had to be done fast to bring Riel's upstart republic to heel.

SUCCESS BY INADVERTENCE did not figure prominently in Labrador Smith's cunningly conceived career path, but at this pivotal moment in Canadian history Sir John A. Macdonald's ignorance intervened to place the still-obscure fur trader at centre stage. Sir George Simpson, who for most of forty years had operated the Hudson's Bay Company as a private preserve out of his headquarters at Lachine, just west of Montreal, had such an enormous personal impact on Canadian public life that Macdonald quite naturally assumed the secretive Company was still run out of Montreal, even if he no longer knew who was in charge. That had not been true since Alexander Grant Dallas, Simpson's successor, had moved the headquarters to Red River in 1860 and had himself been succeeded by William Mactavish four years later. Ensconced in Montreal for less than a year, Smith had Company rank only of district manager, and his department was the HBC's smallest and least typical, taking in eastern Canada and Labrador. The Prime Minister had never met or heard of Smith, but it was a normal reflex for him to call on the highest accessible HBC official to help settle troubles on the western front in what was, after all, still Company territory—particularly since he had been recommended by George Stephen. Smith, who had never even visited a Company post west of Lachine, was the last man on earth to try to set Macdonald straight. As he later explained, it was no part of his duty "to volunteer to correct any man's opinion or delusion unless it were in the general interest."

Summoned to Ottawa on November 29, 1869, Smith was closely questioned by Macdonald on the difference in attitudes between the HBC's London head office, anxious to complete the transfer and get its money, and local Company officers reported to be encouraging the insurrection. Not averse to involving himself in a situation he knew nothing about, Smith laid much of the blame on the government for not securing Governor Mactavish's co-operation before dispatching McDougall to the territory. To counter claims that the HBC was helping the rebels, he insisted that adjustment of the present difficulty would be of great advantage to both the Company and its field officers, then delivered a patriotic sally he must have known would please the Prime Minister. "If no settlement occurs," said he, "there will be no transfer, and if there is no transfer of the territory, law and order and property will be at the mercy of the most lawless members of the community until the Americans step in and annex it."

Macdonald interrupted to ask Smith whether he would go to Fort Garry and help settle the dispute, and later the same day sent a memorandum to Joseph Howe, the cabinet minister in charge of the Red River negotiations, praising Smith: "I am now strongly of opinion that we should make instant use of D.A. Smith. In the chat I had with him to-day he took high ground, declared himself a staunch *Canadian* and lost no opportunity of emphasizing his own complete impartiality as well as the desire of the Company to effect a speedy settlement of this unhappy business. If the Hudson's Bay officers are implicated in fomenting the disturbance, Smith can, from his position, discourage them. . . ."

Smith was shortly afterwards appointed Dominion Commissioner to Inquire into the North West Rebellion and charged with endeavouring to arrange some system of concerted action in the pacification of the country. The term "pacification" correctly identified his real mission. He was to use the moral suasion of the royal proclamations he carried with him plus whatever bribes might be necessary to create a political movement that would oppose and, if possible, overthrow Riel, laying the groundwork for future negotiations, not with any puppet administration but directly between the citizens of Red River and the Canadian government. Smith left Ottawa on December 13, accompanied by a brother-in-law, Richard Hardisty, and Dr Charles Tupper, one of the Fathers of Confederation and former premier of Nova Scotia, now a prominent Tory Member of Parliament. Tupper (after 1879 Sir Charles) came along ostensibly to inquire into the whereabouts of his son-in-law, Captain D.R. Cameron, who was serving on McDougall's staff, but was probably included by Macdonald as his personal spy. The party took the fastest route available—by train to Toronto, Chicago, St Paul, and the end of steel at Breckenridge, Minnesota (the last miles aboard the St Paul and

Pacific Railway), then by stage and canvas-covered sleigh to the Canadian border.

They met McDougall on his way back to Ottawa and were briefed on the horrors of Red River. But what Smith recalled most vividly about that trip was the fertile land along the tracks of the St Paul and Pacific, the bankrupt railroad originally chartered to reach Oregon on the Pacific Coast. For Tupper, one of the more curious moments of the journey was Smith's unexpected attack of megalomania. The fur trader, less than a week after taking on his government assignment (and less than two weeks after anybody in Ottawa even knew his name), demanded to be named a member of the august Privy Council, then Canada's highest civilian honour. When Tupper pointed out that, if sanctioned, this should have been done before they had left Ottawa, Smith stopped at the next telegraph post and wired the suggestion to Sir John A. Macdonald, who just as quickly turned him down. The trio fought their way across the frigid plain towards Red River, stopping to rest and warm up at Fort Abercrombie, where the landlord took them to his shed. Six woodland caribou were standing there, like horses in stalls, frozen stiff, and the Abercrombie cook hacked off a hindquarter for the travellers. After leaving his royal proclamations at an HBC trading post along the way, Smith arrived at Red River on December 27.

He was received civilly enough by Riel, but when asked to promise he would not try to upset the provisional government's legality, Smith declined and was detained for most of the next two months in a cramped room at Fort Garry. Allowed an unlimited flow of visitors and using his well-connected brother-in-law to recruit the right people, he persuaded several of the settlement's moderates to support Ottawa's intentions of integrating Red River with the growing Dominion. When persuasion failed, Smith had at his disposal several thousand dollars to bribe wavering Métis, credits to hand out at HBC stores for winter supplies, and jobs as tripmen for next summer's canoe and cart brigades. Realizing that his support was beginning to drain away, Riel demanded that Smith demonstrate the legitimacy of his mission by showing him the royal proclamations. Smith dispatched Hardisty to fetch the documents. Métis raiders tried to stop him, but some of the Smith converts escorted Hardisty to the fort, spreading the word that there was among them a fully accredited representative of the Canadian government and Queen Victoria with important news for Red River citizens. Riel could not refuse Smith's demand that everyone be brought together the next morning to hear his message.

JANUARY 19, 1870, DAWNED SULLEN AND COLD, the sun hugging the horizon
as if hesitant to venture into such frigid surroundings. It was twenty
below zero Fahrenheit, and the wind snarled across the flat landscape,
obliterating most points of reference with snow. The good burghers of
Red River came, more than a thousand strong, to hear the Ottawa
emissary. They arrived aboard horse-drawn sleds swathed in buffalo
robes, on snowshoes or by puffing dog trains from the outer settlements and gathered in a field inside the fort. They lit small fires,
stamping circles in the snow to keep the blood flowing, and, as the
temperature dropped, tucked mittened hands inside their HBC blanket
capotes for extra body-warmth—or indulged in some liquid glow. The
steam of their breathing had almost obscured the enclosure by the
time Riel and Smith climbed onto a hastily erected platform to begin
the historic proceedings.

For five hours Smith read aloud from various documents, his
words faithfully translated by Riel, including the text of the original
commission to the misguided McDougall, proving that the Prime
Minister's original emissary had acted entirely on his own. Smith
read the lengthy proclamation from Sir John Young, reiterating the
Governor General's wordy pledge that the "Imperial Government has
no intention of acting otherwise, or permitting others to act otherwise
than in perfect good faith towards the inhabitants of the Red River
district of the North-West. . . . The people may rely upon it that
respect and protection will be extended towards the different religious
persuasions; that titles of every description of property will be carefully guarded; and that all the franchises which have existed, and
which the people may prove themselves qualified to exercise, shall be
duly continued or liberally conferred." Except for the occasional mild
tiff between Smith and Riel about which papers should be promulgated, the mutual respect that seemed to flow between the two men
impressed members of the audience. By mid-afternoon, the sun was
settling into the southwest, and the cold had become intolerable; the
small boys who had been collecting wood to keep the fires aglow were
too chilled to continue. The meeting was adjourned to ten o'clock the
next morning.

On the following day, lectured at for another five hours, the
crowd—except for the Métis riflemen patrolling its edges—started to
swing towards Smith. It wasn't so much anything specific he said or
promised as the cumulative effect of his documents, their carefully
drafted and often stilted phrases demonstrating the fact that central
Canadian politicians really did care about Red River's welfare. And it
was Smith himself, looking fully his fifty years, the leathered skin

reflecting his two decades in Labrador's primitive fur trade, who made his arguments persuasive. He told them, as if it were a hard-wrung confession, that he was married to a Hardisty whose mother had been a Red River Sutherland, and that his own mother was a Grant, related to the great Métis leader, Cuthbert Grant. He seemed somehow incorruptible in his dour Scottishness, the tiny beard-icicles bobbing to the rhythm of his earnest pledges. He kept reading all those long documents, with their high-sounding cadences, transmitting the subliminal message that anyone taking this much trouble to sound officious had to mean it. He read a personal greeting from Queen Victoria (delivered through Lord Granville, the Colonial Secretary) assuring his listeners they would enjoy the same status as British subjects in any other part of Canada. At the end of that interminable second day, Smith set aside the dreary documents and spoke from the heart. "I am here to-day in the interests of Canada," he intoned, "but only in so far as they are in accordance with the interests of this country. . . . As to the Hudson's Bay Company, my connection with that body is, I suppose, generally known; but I will say that if it could do any possible good to this country I would, at this moment, resign my position in that Company. I sincerely hope that my humble efforts may, in some measure, contribute to bring about, peaceably, union and entire accord among all classes of the people of this country."

Not eloquent, exactly, but after ten hours of mind-numbing proclamations, at least genuine, and Smith was cheered for his effort. A chastened Riel now took the stage and moved that a convention of twenty Métis and the same number of English-speaking representatives meet to consider Smith's commission and draw up a list of rights for submission to Ottawa. When a listener objected that his statement cast doubt on the legality of Smith's documents, Riel replied matter-of-factly that the Bay man's commission was valid and that it should be implemented. Riel's agreement to set up a constituent assembly outside the sponsorship of his own purview meant that Smith had achieved precisely the breakthrough Sir John A. Macdonald had recognized as the crucial element in any solution: that Canada be able to negotiate directly with representatives of Red River instead of Riel's unelected and radical provisional government. Three delegates to the Ottawa talks were eventually elected and a Bill of Rights framed under which the people of Red River were willing to become part of Canada. Riel was chosen—by representatives of the entire community this time—to continue as head of the provisional government. As a sign of good faith, he later released most of the Fort Garry prisoners, including HBC Governor William Mactavish, who left for his ancestral hearth in Scotland.*

A few days before Smith was due to leave for Ottawa to report on his mission, Red River's fragile tranquillity was shattered by a series of bizarre blunders. A hundred English-speaking malcontents from Portage la Prairie, west of Red River, marched towards Fort Garry determined to hang Riel. Norbert Parisien, a young Métis they had taken prisoner, escaped, snatching a double-barrelled shotgun, and started running across the frozen Red River. When Parisien encountered a popular young settler named Hugh John Sutherland, who happened to be passing by, he shot him in the chest. His pursuers, seeing the mortally wounded Sutherland, recaptured Parisien and kicked him to death. Members of the rowdy, now bloodied gang, including a boisterous Irish Protestant drifter named Thomas Scott, were arrested by Riel's riflemen. Not much was known about the twenty-eight-year-old Scott because there wasn't that much to know. He was one of those marginal frontier characters who substituted racial and religious prejudice for personal motivation and had spent the past year cursing and harassing the Métis. Once in the Fort Garry jail, Scott jeered at the guards, insulted their religion, called them cowards, and at one point physically attacked Riel. The situation deteriorated to the point where Scott's guards could no longer maintain discipline and bluntly told Riel they would shoot *him* if he didn't execute Scott. The Métis leader's more militant followers were already angry that he had ordered the release of so many other prisoners, and Riel had to find a way of quickly reasserting his authority. Scott was brought before a court martial, found guilty of insubordination and sentenced to death. When Smith pleaded with Riel not to spoil his bloodless record with a senseless execution, the Métis leader shrugged and replied, "We must make Canada respect us."

At noon on March 4, 1870, the Reverend George Young, a local Methodist pastor, led the terrified Scott to a ditch outside the fort. His hands were bound, he was blindfolded, and a firing squad of six Métis shot the trembling Irishman in the chest. When Scott was heard moaning, François Guillemette, one of the executioners, pulled out a revolver and at close range put a bullet through his left ear; it came blasting out through his mouth. Refused burial at Red River's Presbyterian cemetery, Scott's body was placed in a rough coffin and taken to a shed, where, according to George Young, five hours after the

---

*Mactavish reached Liverpool on July 21, 1870, and died two days later.

execution he was heard still pitifully moaning, "Oh, let me out of this. My God, how I suffer!" Riel dispatched two guards to deliver a *coup de grâce*. Scott was buried inside a deep hole in Fort Garry's stone battlements, but a year later when his remains were being disinterred for transfer to a proper graveyard, diggers found his coffin empty— except for the rope that had been used to tie his hands at the execution. According to one report, just before the original burial, Scott's body was removed from the coffin by a Métis guard named Elzéar Goulet, weighted down with chains, and dropped through a fishing-hole in the Red River ice. "The secret of Thomas Scott's burial will likely never come out . . . ," Alexandre Nault, whose father was one of Scott's executioners, told the Winnipeg *Tribune* in 1961 on his eighty-seventh birthday. "An oath was taken never to tell."

Scott's lively ghost harmed no one more grievously than Louis Riel.* The many shots that killed the Irish renegade destroyed any chance of peaceful transfer of the HBC lands. Dr Schultz, leader of Red River's rabid pro-Canadian party, toured Orange Ontario brandishing a rope that he claimed had bound Scott's hands during the execution and a vial of the martyr's blood.† Schultz and others whipped up public outrage, demanding revenge on those the *Globe* in Toronto labelled as desperate, depraved, devilish Papists. In Quebec, Riel and his praetorian guard of Métis were raised to the status of folk heroes—champions and victims—of French Canada's crusade against Anglo-Saxon bigotry. It was one of the many ironies of the situation that only five days after Scott's execution, Bishop Taché arrived in Red River bearing word from Sir John A. Macdonald of a general amnesty and the promise of welcoming Red River into Confederation as a province, to be called Manitoba. Riel immediately released all remaining prisoners and prepared to join Confederation. The trio of Red River delegates—a priest, a magistrate and a store clerk—left for Ottawa to negotiate the terms of what became the Manitoba Act, passed into law on May 12, 1870. It included nearly all of Riel's demands, such as guarantees for the French language and Catholic religion, and set aside 1.4 million acres for the Métis, preserving their precious river lots.

---

*After Louis Riel was hanged for treason in Regina on November 16, 1885, one of the jurors at his trial admitted, "We tried Riel for treason, and he was hanged for the murder of Thomas Scott."

†Volunteers must have provided refills, since Schultz freely sprinkled the blood on the handkerchiefs of tearful women at the climax of his melodramatic lectures.

CANADIAN
ILLUSTRATED NEWS

VOL. 1.—No 25 |          MONTREAL, SATURDAY, APRIL 23, 1870.          [SINGLE COPIES, TEN CENTS.
                                                                    [ $4 PER YEAR IN ADVANCE.

THE TRAGEDY AT FORT GARRY, MARCH 4, 1870.—SEE PAGE 394.

*Execution of Thomas Scott at Fort Garry, March 4, 1870*

DONALD SMITH DEPARTED RED RIVER a changed man. No longer the obscure fur trader, he was hailed as the heroic peacemaker of the North-West. His report on the events of the past three months recommended, among other reforms, recruitment of a permanent paramilitary force to maintain law and order in the North-West. Smith's future was assured. It was whispered that even Benjamin Disraeli, the British Prime Minister, kept a copy of Smith's submission on his desk to show visitors how such documents should be drafted.

On his way back to Montreal, Smith had a memorable encounter with James Jerome Hill, a one-eyed St Paul entrepreneur (born at Rockwood, Ontario), who was on his way to assess Red River as a location for future business opportunities. Hill had arrived in the Minnesota capital as a teenager and immediately became part of the steamboat scene, at first providing fuel, then becoming a partner in some of the operations. An aggressive and unpleasant deal-maker, he tended to intimidate people with the stern look of his one good eye, the other having been lost in a youthful archery accident. Hill and Smith had heard of one another by reputation and it didn't take them long to find a common interest. The two men shared a wilderness meal and spent the night in a tent, trading dreams, discussing the need for a railway to link Red River with the civilized world.

Back in his HBC office, Smith was besieged by cablegrams from London soliciting his counsel on the Company's future affairs. Treated as the HBC's overseas chief operating officer, he was shortly afterwards promoted to President of the Northern Department (a new title for William Mactavish's former position) and transferred to Fort Garry. Smith's most urgent priority was to meet with his northwestern Chief Factors and Chief Traders, gathering in late July at Norway House near the upper end of Lake Winnipeg. This was to be the last of the great Northern Council meetings to be held at Norway House, initiated by George Simpson half a century earlier. It was here, seated around the great oak table where they had traded so many quips and empires, that the Hudson's Bay Company's seasoned veterans first met their new viceroy. The understandable hesitation of pledging loyalty to this awkward stranger who had mysteriously been promoted over their heads gave way to respect as Smith conducted the meeting with the same resolute dignity that had marked his debut as an orator at Red River. In the end, the HBC field hands empowered him to represent them in negotiations with London for their rightful share of the £300,000 transfer fee. After the meeting, Smith went by canoe to Fort Alexander, a post on the southeast side of Lake Winnipeg ninety miles from Fort Garry, originally built in 1792. There he impatiently awaited arrival of the troops Sir John A. Macdonald had dispatched to claim the North-West.

To appease the anti-Riel backlash and assert Canada's authority, the Prime Minister sent an army detachment to Red River under the command of Colonel Garnet Wolseley, a prematurely stuffy Anglo-Irish officer then serving as Deputy Quartermaster-General in British North America. The contingent, numbering 2,213 officers and men (a quarter of them British regulars) and 700 voyageurs, was officially described as a "benevolent constabulary," but its prevailing mood was that of a punitive military expedition. The sentiment was appropriately caught in Wolseley's private journal. "Hope Riel will have bolted," he confided to its pages, "for although I should like to hang him from the highest tree in the place, I have such a horror of rebels and vermin of his kidney that my treatment of him might not be approved by the civil powers." A vintage hawk who, as a viscount and field marshal, would later command the British Army, Wolseley loaded the soldiers and their equipment aboard 140 boats and heaved them across the mudpie labyrinths west of the Lakehead. The Manitoba historian Reverend R.G. MacBeth was being restrained when he described the task as "more suitable for aquatic animals than for human beings." The agony of strong-arming the heavy equipment across forty-seven punishing portages lasted ninety-six days, and at times the lead and last boats were as much as 150 miles apart. After Smith joined the Wolseley troops on their way through Fort Alexander, they marched in battle formation towards Fort Garry.

Pleased with the passage of the Manitoba Act and still brimming with Victorian ardour, Riel had planned to welcome the British troops in elegant fashion. Elaborate arrangements were made for bonfires and salutes on the south bank of the Assiniboine, with Riel himself presiding at the turnover ceremony at the head of a hundred crack Métis cavalrymen. Expecting to benefit from the general amnesty granted by Ottawa, the Métis leader had even drilled a guard of honour for Wolseley's inspection when the British colonel reached Fort Garry. For once, he seemed alone in his faith. Reports began to arrive that many of the Canadian volunteers were Ontario Orangemen boasting they would avenge Thomas Scott's execution by lynching the papists and watching them squirm. That was enough for most of Riel's lieutenants, who began drifting away, mumbling excuses about going home to check on relatives.

By sunrise, only Riel and O'Donoghue were left in the fort, pacing its echoing battlements, peering through the rain, trying to decide which way to turn. They lowered the brave Métis flag, suspecting it would never fly again. Wolseley's 60th Royal Rifles could easily be spotted stumbling unprotected through the mud, and Riel must have glanced at Fort Garry's thirteen silent cannon with something close to regret. The two men escaped through the fort's front gate barely ahead of the troops, scurried to the river, which they crossed on a raft hastily fashioned out of fence posts tied with their sashes. Riel cut the cable of a nearby ferry to prevent pursuit, but he needn't have bothered. Colonel Wolseley was too busy strutting around the fort, firing royal salutes, raising the Union Jack, boasting how he had routed the "banditti." Deprived of their quarry after the hardship of their long march, the troops took out their frustrations on the local Métis, looting their homes, raping their daughters (including seventeen-year-old Laurette Goulet, the child of a Riel supporter, who died after being assaulted by four drunken soldiers), and murdering most of the provisional government's ministers. Elzéar Goulet, a member of Scott's court martial, was chased into the Assiniboine and stoned until he sank and drowned. Another of the men who determined Scott's fate was left for dead on the American side of the border, while a third, François Guillemette, was shot.*

Riel himself had initially escaped to the United States but soon returned, still anxious to assist in Manitoba's transfer to Canada, and even helped organize the Métis to counter an abortive invasion by a band of Fenians from the States. Macdonald didn't want Riel arrested because that would have played badly in Quebec. But he didn't want him casually strolling around Red River, either, because Ontario's Orangemen still had a price of $5,000 on his head. Resorting to the political ethic of his day, the Prime Minister eventually sent a bribe of $1,000 (supplemented by £600 from Smith) through Archbishop Taché to get Riel out of the country. On February 23, 1872, he was unceremoniously escorted outside his "country" under police protection.

And so the Red River Rebellion ended in both victory and defeat, its objectives achieved, its founding spirits shot or disowned. Ironically, Red River's ostensible liberators had inflicted far more moral and physical damage than the rebels themselves. Most of the regular troops departed five days after they arrived; it was the last British military operation in North America.

---

*Ambroise Lépine, who presided at both the trial and the execution, was convicted of murder in 1875 and sentenced to be hanged. The Governor General, the Earl of Dufferin, commuted his sentence, and Lépine died in 1923 at the age of eighty-three in rural Saskatchewan.

As the HBC's presiding officer, Smith stayed on to head a re-constituted Company government that ruled Red River until McDougall's permanent successor arrived. The new lieutenant-governor of Manitoba and the Northwest Territories was a sensible Maritime lawyer-politician named Adams G. Archibald, who had been Macdonald's first Secretary of State and now would negotiate the first two treaties with the Indians of the North-West.

"I yield up to you my responsibilities with pleasure," said Smith.

"I really do not anticipate much pleasure on my own account," said Archibald.

With that insipid exchange the Hudson's Bay Company finally surrendered its bountiful monopoly over the largest empire ever ruled by a commercial enterprise.

A DETAILED ANATOMY of the Red River Rebellion and the North-West uprising that followed in 1885 is beyond the scope of this book— except as Louis Riel was manipulated by and influenced the Hudson's Bay Company. His tragic saga, particularly the 1885 trial for treason, when he refused to hide behind a justified plea of insanity that might have saved his life, is Canada's most enduring myth. A compelling rebel in a nation of cloying conformists, Louis Riel remains the perfect martyr of the prototypical Canadian tragedy: a well-meaning yet deluded mystic who died prematurely by pretending to be sane.

Riel's dominant characteristic was his sense of ambiguity. Caught between Métis nationalism and Victorian loyalty, he could never let go of either emotion, trapped in a polarization of his own making. He was constantly trying to overthrow an entrenched Anglo-Saxon hegemony in order, as he paradoxically kept insisting, to gain "our just rights as British subjects." In one moving address after passage of the Manitoba Act, the Métis leader was glowing with *bonhomie* as he praised his followers for bowing to the Queen—the same Queen whose forces were at that very moment marching west to destroy him. "I congratulate the people of the North-West," he said, ". . . on having trust enough in the Crown of England to believe that ultimately they would obtain their rights." The man's fundamental dichotomy was symbolized even by his dress: during eight months as President of the North-West Republic, Riel received visitors wearing hand-sewn buffalo-hunt moccasins—and a formal Victorian frock coat.

Had it not been for Scott's execution, Riel would have been elected the province's first legal premier and could justifiably have claimed to be the Father of Manitoba. But in Canada, civic monuments are erected to functionaries, not rebels. Riel's resistance had salvaged the French element in Canada's North-West and in the process bestowed on the Métis a degree of self-confidence and self-assertion they had never before possessed.

Riel has inspired idolatry and contempt in equal measure, being condemned by English Canadians as a traitor who deserved to be hanged, while Quebeckers still worship him as a victim of Anglo-Saxon racial and religious prejudice.* Hartwell Bowsfield, a York University historian, best summed up the heroic revolutionary's contradictions: "He was a man of intelligence and authority who was mentally unstable; a reasonable protester against legitimate grievances who turned fanatic and dictatorial; a gentle man whose name became associated with violence even though he himself never took up arms; a simple man of great personal appeal who developed grandiose pretensions as a spiritual and political leader; a visionary and an erratic religious mystic who inspired unquestioning faith in the Métis people."

That faith was unrequited because Louis Riel's conflict was as ancient—and as contemporary—as Canada itself: a clash between the semi-articulated *collective* demands of the Métis and the stubbornly held *individual* rights of English Canadians.

---

*Honoré Mercier climbed to power in Quebec on Riel's execution. Ironically, in 1990 the bridge named after Mercier became the focal point in Indian-French disputes. Mercier used Riel to get at the Conservatives in Quebec and at the Tories in Ottawa. Where did it get his descendants?

*Louis Riel standing trial after the North West Rebellion, 1885*

*HBC steamer North West at Edmonton, 1896*

# CHAPTER 4

# THE GREAT FIRE CANOES

*The* Northcote *may or may not have been the first warship to fight an engagement in waters thirty-six inches deep — twice the depth of a children's wading pool. But she was the only man-of-war ever to proceed into combat with a billiard table as armour.*

DONALD SMITH RULED THE NORTH-WEST for only eight days—and his main public edict was to close the saloons at night—but he was the perfect transitional figure between the Hudson's Bay Company's two centuries of sullen monopoly and its transformation into a dominant but vulnerable commercial enterprise. He differed from every other senior Bay man in the territory because his heart was not in the West; his Labrador background made it easy for him to deal unemotionally with the new circumstances. He came to the job with enhanced credibility through his diplomatic triumph at Red River, moved by restless aspirations for his own and the Company's advancement that had not been in evidence among the HBC's overseas managers since Sir George Simpson's day.

The first sign of the Company's reduced status appeared when Colonel Wolseley called for tenders to supply stove-pipes for the barracks of the remaining army volunteers. The HBC submitted a high bid, assuming it would get the business automatically. A local merchant named James H. Ashdown sent in a much lower quote but lost the contract when Smith convinced army officers the newcomer wasn't equipped to do the job. Once the HBC got the contract, Smith discovered there were no tinsmiths on his staff and ordered Ashdown to do the work under HBC auspices. When Ashdown refused, Smith asked the colonel to force the fellow into line. Wolseley cancelled the

HBC's contract instead and asked Ashdown (who went on to found western Canada's largest wholesale hardware house) to produce the stove-pipes at his original bid. The minor incident reflected the competitive new world in which the ancient fur-trading company would have to operate.

Smith's initial order of business was to settle accounts outstanding from the Red River Rebellion. It was typical of their corporate ethic that the HBC's London Pooh-Bahs viewed Louis Riel's agonizing struggle on behalf of his people strictly as a bookkeeping entry. The uprising had disturbed the business of the Company, and now it was claiming refunds from the Canadian government for missing fur stocks, lost trading opportunities and six months' interest, at 5 percent, on the delayed transfer payment of £300,000—a total of £32,508, not counting the amounts Smith had paid out in bribes. It took a dozen years to settle the dispute, and the Company received very little cash because Ottawa subtracted the costs of surveying its territory, but the claim hurt the HBC's already poor reputation. "A corporation has no conscience," observed Captain W.F. Butler, Wolseley's intelligence officer, whose familiarity with the West produced its most evocative early literary portrait, *The Great Lone Land*. "From a tyrant or a despot you may hope to win justice; from a robber you may perhaps receive kindness; but a corporation of London merchants represents to my mind more mercenary mendacity, and more cowardly contempt of truth and fair play, than can be found in the human race."

Despite such condemnation, there were some genuine worries about the HBC's loss of stature. The Company had become vital in the daily lives of the North-West's Indians. Natural gathering places, its trading posts were the natives' only source of the barter goods that made wilderness life more bearable—the guns, blankets, axes and other items they had grown to depend on. "The sudden withdrawal of the Company's operation from any part of the Indian country will cause widely spread misery and starvation and the consequent disorders and embarrassment to the Government which spring from such scenes," William Mactavish, Smith's predecessor, had warned, "nor can any other company . . . be in a position . . . to supply the Indian tribes with the requisite regularity with those necessaries of life at present provided them. This is the secret of the Company domination—its existence is a necessity to the Indian." That was true enough, but the fur trade itself was in a highly volatile state. Felt hats made from Canadian beaver had enjoyed a momentary fashion revival in the 1860s. The headgear took the shape of wide-brimmed adaptations of the "wideawake," a name invented by the humour magazine *Punch* for a hat that had no nap. But now the new seamless silk toppers were much more in vogue, having been worn by the Prince Consort, the Prince of Wales and President Abraham Lincoln. Although there was continued strong demand for specialty pelts from North America, London's fur industry was turning towards other, less expensive sources, and to nutria, the skin of coypu rats, being harvested in Brazil and Argentina by the million. The most immediate impact on the North-West was the final downgrading of York Factory, which for two centuries had been the flourishing centre of the North American fur trade. By 1875, the headquarters of the HBC's Northern Department had been moved to Fort Garry and the magnificent tidewater depot was reduced to a regional trading post.

That shift drew attention to the staggering realization that a full century after James Watt had perfected his steam engine, the Hudson's Bay Company was still depending on a primitive transportation system of horse- or ox-drawn carts, birchbark canoes and York boats. Apart from the immense manpower expenses, which were mounting now that the Métis no longer thought of themselves as slaves, use of such primitive technology meant that it took the Company four years to realize returns on invested capital. As one frustrated shareholder exclaimed at the Company's 1871 annual meeting, "Gentlemen, this Company has not been very celebrated for doing things in a hurry. It is really very much like Rip Van Winkle waking up in the year 1871 and finding out that steam engines and steam boats will be of advantage to the trade."

Right on cue, Donald Smith wrote to William Armit, the HBC's secretary, on November 6, 1871, recommending that the fur trade's cost structure be streamlined by the use of steamboats along the North Saskatchewan River, its main traffic artery. That would radically reduce costs and, ideally, bring the furs out in a season or two instead of four seasons. On top of these benefits, Smith recognized the possibility of perpetuating the Company's monopoly over western Canada, this time by controlling its commercial traffic flows.

The Hudson's Bay Company decided to relaunch itself as a prairie shipping line, using a brand-new fleet of what the Indians quickly dubbed Fire Canoes.

INCREDIBLE AS IT NOW SEEMS, an awkward but sporadically effective flotilla of sternwheel steamboats for a time supplied the Canadian

*Steaming down Main Street in the* Assiniboine *during the Red River flood of 1897,*
*Emerson, Manitoba*

West. These ships, chugging along at a respectable five knots, became
a common sight in what everyone then—and now—assumed to be a
landlocked prairie. They not only carried the materials of the fur
trade (two or three trips in the high-water season easily handled the
cargoes previously consigned to the large and expensive brigades of
carts and fleets of York boats) but quickly branched out into ferrying
the necessities of the new civilization being born on the Prairies.
Ploughs and scythes, tea and bacon, threshing machines, and their
accompanying pioneers crowded the decks and cabins.*

The perky vessels' steam whistles could be heard up to Edmonton
on the 1,200-mile flow of the North Saskatchewan River; along the
South Saskatchewan past Saskatoon to Medicine Hat and beyond; on
the Assiniboine, from Fort Pelly and Fort Ellice to Lake Winnipeg;
and up the Red to Fargo in Dakota Territory, which had connections
to the railway networks of the northern United States.†

By 1879, seventeen ships, not all owned by the HBC, were regularly
employed on prairie rivers. Getting there was all the fun. Constant

---

*Passenger fares aboard the HBC boats from Fort Garry (Winnipeg) to Edmonton were
forty dollars one way for cabin space, twenty dollars for a perch on the open promenade
deck. Freight was carried at four dollars a hundredweight.

†See the map on page 102 for details of the prairie steamboat routes.

stops had to be made for cordwood to fire the boilers.* The flat-bottomed sternwheelers, difficult to control under the best of conditions, didn't so much travel the river routes as bounce their way through them. New obstructions were always being encountered, or a bumping acquaintance with old ones was being renewed. Flood times were the worst because the surging waters hid dangerous rocks and made the keelless vessels impossible to steer. Occasionally a bold skipper would take advantage of the high water to invent a shortcut. On May 10, 1873, Captain Alexander Griggs was en route to Fort Garry aboard the *International*, carrying a large liquor consignment for the Hudson's Bay Company. He had to reach the border by midnight or his cargo would be liable for a new tariff. Cursing the day's delays and gazing at the waters spilling over the banks of the Red and flooding the plain, Griggs "coolly turned the boat out of the bed of the river," as reported later in the *Manitoban*, "and made a short cut over the prairie ... thereby reducing the distance very materially and gaining the Customs House" in time.†

Summer low water was a much more common problem. Ships' captains, mostly recycled wharf rats from the Mississippi River trade, often ordered crew and passengers overboard to help push or warp the vessels through shallow sections. Warping meant literally walking the ship over an obstacle. This was achieved by using four strong spars hinged to double derricks on either side of the bow. When aground, the vessel could lift itself over the obstruction by the manipulation of ropes running through these derricks to turn the poles into stilts. One skipper was exaggerating the shallowness of the river only slightly when he yelled at a settler who was dipping his pail into the Assiniboine, "Hey! You put that water back!" Stuck in the ankle-deep backwaters of the North Saskatchewan above Cumberland Lake, Captain Aaron Raymond Russell of the *Marquis* ordered his crew members overboard with picks and shovels to dam every creek flowing out of the main channel. The extra inches obtained this way made it possible for him to tiptoe his way downstream to deep water.

---

*Finding it could get tricky. The HBC's *Lily*, desperate for firewood, pulled into the tiny enclave of Red Deer Forks when her crew noticed two Métis log cabins whose owners were out hunting. In minutes the buildings had been dismantled, their timbers loaded, and the ship was hastily puffing her way along the Saskatchewan.

†Another example of overland navigation was the *Assiniboine*'s astonishing sweep down the main street of Emerson, Manitoba, to rescue and bring relief supplies to Red River flood victims in 1897.

"We go from one bank to the other," complained Lady Dufferin in August 1877 when she and her husband, the first Governor General of Canada to tour the West, were aboard the *Minnesota* on their way to inspect the Red River settlement, "crushing and crashing against the trees, which grow down to the waterside; I had just written this when I gave a shriek as I saw my ink-bottle on the point of being swept overboard by an intrusive tree. . . . The consequence of this curious navigation is that we never really go on for more than three minutes at a time. . . . Our stern wheel is often ashore, and our captain and pilot must require the patience of saints." Later that day Lady Dufferin saw another ship, the *Manitoba*, approaching in the dark. "It looked beautiful," she reported, "with two great bull's-eyes, green and red lamps and other lights on deck, creeping towards us; we stopped and backed into the shore, that it might pass us. It came close and fired off a cannon and we saw on the deck a large transparency with 'Welcome Lord Dufferin' on it, and two girls dressed in white with flags in their hands; then a voice sang 'Canada, Sweet Canada,' and many more voices joined the chorus, and they sang 'God Save the Queen' and 'Rule, Britannia', and cheered for the Governor General as they began to move slowly away disappearing into the darkness."*

During the viceregal visit, Lady Dufferin hammered in the last spike of western Canada's first railway, a primitive four-mile-long, narrow-gauge tramway built by the Hudson's Bay Company where the waters of the Saskatchewan roared down the Grand Rapids to Lake Winnipeg. The wilderness link provided horse-drawn wagons to handle goods en route between Edmonton and Fort Garry, bypassing the steep limestone canyon where the river dropped almost a hundred feet in three miles, causing painfully long portages. For a

---

*"O Canada," with music by Calixa Lavallée and words by Adolphe-Basile Routhier, was not written until 1880, and not widely sung outside Quebec until the early years of the twentieth century. Its use as the national anthem was approved by Parliament in 1967, and it was officially adopted in 1980 under the National Anthem Act. Lavallée, who had served as a bandsman with the Union forces in the U.S. Civil War and favoured U.S. annexation of Canada, spent much of his adult life in the United States and died in Boston in 1891. Routhier was a judge of the Superior Court of Quebec from 1873 who later became chief justice of that court and was knighted. In English-speaking Canada, a popular national song for many years was "The Maple Leaf Forever," written in 1867 by Alexander Muir, a Toronto teacher. Its emphasis on the Britishness of Canada tended to rule out its use in French Canada. The English translation of "O Canada" now in use is a modified form of the words written in 1908 by R. Stanley Weir, an author of legal texts and later judge of the Exchequer Court of Canada.

time, using a specially trained white horse, the little railway actually ran itself. Trains consisted of a car laden with the merchandise being trans-shipped, followed by an empty carriage. At the height of land, a platform was built the same height as the cars. Having been taught the drill, the animal would pull the two carriages up from one or the other terminus, slip out of its own harness, walk onto the platform and into the empty car, which would then glide down behind the load to the end of steel, banked to provide an automatic brake.

Once this barrier was conquered, the prairie ships grew in size and appointments. Captain Peter McArthur's *North West* boasted a five-thousand-dollar grand piano and two bridal chambers. First-class passengers aboard the *City of Winnipeg* dined in soft leather chairs in a carpeted and chandeliered Grand Saloon. According to the *Manitoba Free Press*, one of their number was so overcome by the ambience— and presumably the booze—that he "was trying to waltz across the deck with an umbrella . . . for a partner." Inevitably, the intoxicated passenger made one uncalculated twirl and "without trying, waltzed off most beautifully into the river."

THE FIRST STEAMSHIP ON THE CANADIAN PRAIRIES was a prototype of the bizarre fleet that was to follow. The *Anson Northup*, which arrived at Red River from Georgetown, Minnesota, on June 10, 1859, was ninety feet long and twenty-two feet wide, though she had a draft of only fourteen inches. She looked like a log cabin mounted on a washbasin with a toy smokestack stuck in the middle, but she could carry fifty tons of cargo as well as passengers, and her arrival caused great excitement. "Horses with buckskin riders, oxdrawn two-wheeled carts from the fields, and cautious Indians clad in feathers, leggings, and moccasins streamed to the fort landing," wrote Ted Barris in *Fire Canoe*, the definitive study of prairie steamboats. "Children thronged at the riverside to see 'an enormous barge, with a watermill on its stern' emerging from the wilderness like a demon churning up water and spitting sparks. The few carriages available rushed to the scene with flounced and furbelowed ladies attended by bearded gentlemen in tall hats—the [HBC] Governor's entourage."

The Hudson's Bay Company reacted by purchasing the *Anson Northup* through a dummy U.S. company and later bought a slightly larger sister ship, the *International*, reasserting its transportation monopoly by raising rates to prohibitive levels on goods carried for its competitors. The monopoly was broken in the spring of 1871 by the sudden appearance on the river of the much larger *Selkirk*, which could carry 125 passengers and 115 tons of freight. Owned by J.J. Hill, the St Paul entrepreneur Donald Smith had met on his way back from settling the Red River Rebellion, the new venture represented enough of a challenge that Smith negotiated a partnership deal that gave the two men control over a new entity called the Red River Transportation Company, which secretly granted the HBC a one-third preferential freight rate. It became so profitable that 80-percent dividends were not uncommon. Within four years, grain was being exported by Manitoba farmers, adding further impetus to improve a transportation system that was already handling more river traffic than moved along the Mississippi between St Paul and St Louis. When the competing Merchants International Steamboat Line launched the *Manitoba*, Red River Transportation Company captains proved that subtlety was not their long suit. Acting on orders from Smith, on June 4, 1875, the skipper of the *International* rammed the *Manitoba* abreast of her stacks and sank her.*

The HBC's own shipbuilding adventures verged on slapstick. First to be completed was the *Chief Commissioner* (named for Smith), launched on May 7, 1872. Her draft turned out to be too great to navigate her intended route along the Saskatchewan, so the ship was reassigned to Lake Winnipeg, where the absence of a keel made her wallow too violently to be of much use. Another HBC ship sank the following summer near Grand Rapids, a day into her maiden voyage. The next project was an expensive (£4,000) steel-hulled vessel built at the Clyde shipyards of Alfred Yarrow & Company for reassembly in North America. The *Lily* was fast and she was beautiful; but an anonymous marine architect had designed her draft four inches too deep, and the North Saskatchewan's margins for error were so narrow that this was enough to keep her out of practical service. After many modifications the *Lily* finally fought her way up the South Saskatchewan nearly as far as Medicine Hat, hit a submerged rock, and sank.†

---

*Jerry Webber, the captain of the *Manitoba* and other sternwheelers, was known mainly for the fact that he kept a tame raven with red ribbon tied around its wings on his bridge.

†The best-known skipper on the South Saskatchewan was the appropriately named Horatio Hamilton Ross. He built eight ships (including the *O'Hell*) and sank them all. His most famous encounter was with a bridge in Saskatoon, which the local paper correctly described as "the greatest marine disaster in the history of Saskatoon." At the wheel of the 130-foot SS *City of Medicine Hat* and aware that spring flooding had raised river levels, Ross was navigating carefully under the city's bridges, even removing part of the smokestack to

The Company's most durable vessel was the *Northcote*. Launched in 1874, she was 150 feet long, had a 30-foot beam, and drew only twenty-two inches—about the same as a loaded York boat. Her boilers and high-pressure engines had been brought all the way from Cincinnati and could produce 39.72 horsepower. On her maiden voyage, the *Northcote* made it to Carlton House after only ten days' steaming, recouping her cost in one trip. On July 22, 1875, she reached Fort Edmonton with a cargo that had left Fort Garry only thirty-three days earlier, turned around after three days in port, and was back at Grand Rapids on August 5. Later seasons were less successful because of low water levels and trans-shipment delays from Fort Garry.

This lack of reliability plus steep insurance premiums and the unwillingness of the Canadian government to help remove some of the more obvious hazards to navigation gradually cooled the Company's shipping ardour.* The fleet was eventually folded into two independent transportation companies that allowed the HBC preferential freight rates with no need for further capital expenditures. The arrival in Winnipeg on October 8, 1877, of the *Selkirk* pushing a barge that carried the West's first locomotive signalled the terminal phase of the Prairies' brave steamships.†

---

lower the height of his ship's superstructure. But the *Medicine Hat*'s rudder snagged in some telegraph wires, and the ship was impaled on the 19th Street pedestrian bridge just as a few head of cattle were being herded across. The cattle stampeded, as did their keepers, and, according to an onlooker, everybody aboard the ship "scrambled up onto the bridge to safety, except the engineer. He popped out of the engine room and jumped into the water. By the time he reached the river bank, he had drifted a mile downriver, the current was so strong. . . ."

*The premiums were high both because river beds were strewn with rocks that seemed drawn to the flat-bottomed hulls and because the ships' stacks emitted live sparks. Every riverbank farmer knew that if his barn or haystack caught fire, it was far more profitable to let it burn and claim the insurance than attempt to fight the blaze.

†The engine was the *Countess of Dufferin*, named after the wife of the Governor General who visited Manitoba that year. Five years old when Joseph Whitehead, a pioneer railway construction man, bought her, the locomotive was built at the Baldwin yards in Philadelphia and had been in the service of the Northern Pacific. After arriving in St Boniface, the *Countess* was put to work by Whitehead building a southbound line along the east side of the Red River to Pembina, where a connection would be made with the U.S. railroad to St Paul. The little locomotive ended up on the scrapheap at Golden, B.C., after working for the Columbia River Lumber Company. In 1908 R.D. Waugh, later mayor of Winnipeg, found her there and persuaded the lumber company to donate her to the Manitoba city. The CPR hauled her back to Winnipeg and restored her to become a municipal historic artifact.

*The* Selkirk *delivering the West's first locomotive, the* Countess of Dufferin, *at Winnipeg, October 1877*

But the HBC's sternwheeler *Northcote* had one more great adventure in store. She went to war.

When Louis Riel returned to Canada from his dispiriting American exile in the summer of 1884, the Métis of northern Saskatchewan enlisted his fervour in what was to be the bloodiest expression of agrarian protest in Canadian history: the North West Rebellion of 1885. Apart from acting as principal provisioning agent for the troops dispatched by the Canadian government to quell the uprising, the Hudson's Bay Company's main contribution was to charter the *Northcote*, at $250 a day, to Major-General Frederick Dobson Middleton, the blimpish, walrus-moustached former commandant of the British military college at Sandhurst, who had been placed in charge of the Canadian militia. Riel and his shrewd field marshal, Gabriel Dumont, were massing Métis warriors and their Indian allies at Batoche, a small farming community on the South Saskatchewan River southwest of Prince Albert, while the *Northcote* was being used by Middleton's staff to ferry troops across the river at Saskatchewan Landing to help relieve the siege at Battleford.

On April 23, 1885, the ship was assigned the dangerous task of carrying ammunition into the war zone, towing two barges loaded with ordnance supplies behind her. Middleton's plan to oust the Métis, snugly dug into their rifle pits at Batoche, called for the *Northcote* to provide an amphibious second front for his land attack. Aboard the saucepan-bottomed wooden tub was one of North America's ace Indian fighters, Arthur "Gat" Howard, late of the Connecticut National Guard, who had been seconded to the militia contingent because of his marksmanship with the hand-cranked, multi-barrel Gatling gun. In addition to this rapid-fire weapon, which had never been used in Canada before, the *Northcote* carried a nine-pound cannon mounted on her weather deck, and thirty-five sharpshooters lined her railings. That arsenal was formidable enough, but it required armour for protection, not an easy commodity to come by in these parts. The *Northcote* may or may not have been the first warship to fight an engagement in waters thirty-six inches deep— twice the depth of a children's wading pool. But she was the only man-of-war ever to proceed into combat with a billiard table as armour. On her way downriver, the HBC vessel had passed the plundered homestead of Gabriel Dumont, and the *Northcote*'s crew protected her gun emplacements with his billiard table and two-inch-thick planks torn from his barn door. The table was reinforced with Dumont's mattress and bags of oats, not to mention his washing machine and his wife's sewing machine.

And so the *Northcote* steamed to war, a floating apparition sure to dismay her friends and comfort her enemies.

Middleton had arranged to rendezvous with the ship at a loop in the river just above Batoche, near Gabriel Dumont's ferry crossing. The plan was to launch a co-ordinated assault, his land forces marching to the fanfare of their bugle boys, while the *Northcote* would provide a diversion by sailing towards the centre of the Métis position to the hoot of its three-note steam whistle.

The *Northcote* had firepower of a kind and armour of a lesser sort, but she had no camouflage. It is not simple to hide a 150-foot ship, chugging through a 3-foot-deep river on the plains of Saskatchewan. Métis scouts reported on her every lurch downstream, and on the morning of May 9, when she rounded the final bend of the river, her crew was greeted with concentrated fire from Métis troops lining the banks. Her captain promptly assumed his battle station by lying prone on the wheelhouse floor, doing his best to guide the ship's wheel— with several of its spokes shot off—by peeping through a rifle hole. As

*The* Northcote *before the Battle of Batoche, 1885*

the *Northcote* reached the ferry terminal at Gabriel's Crossing an hour early, Dumont ordered the ferry cables, normally slung high above the river, lowered astern and ahead of the ship, crippling her manoeuvrability. The forward motion of the vessel when she hit the taut wire sheared off the smokestack and most of the pilot-house, loading spars and steam whistle, disabling the prairie warship but allowing her to drift onto a sandbank below Batoche.

Thus ended the HBC vessel's Gilbert-and-Sullivan naval engagement, but the doughty and awkward steamboat, having successfully run a five-mile gauntlet of murderous rifle fire, was still more or less afloat. Certainly her presence had been intimidating enough for Louis Riel to pray, "O my God, I pray you, in the name of Jesus, Mary, Joseph and St. John the Baptist, grant that you use the cable of our ferry to upset the steamboat; that we may have the provisions, the useful things the boat contains, the arms and the ammunitions."

After the Battle of Batoche, the *Northcote* was beached at Cumberland Lake in a meadow opposite the Pas River, a bullet-scarred hull the only evidence of her brief moment of glory. She died nineteen years later, the victim of evangelical zeal. A Catholic priest who discovered that local teenagers were using the *Northcote*'s cabins to flirt away long summer evenings persuaded the HBC's Cumberland House manager to give an Indian named Jimmy Greenleaf enough coal oil to torch the proud ship's remains.*

Completion of a railway link between Winnipeg and St Paul in 1878 brought Red River's commercial water traffic to an effective halt, though one ship, the *Grand Forks*, didn't make her final run until 1909. There were still three vessels operating on the North Saskatchewan as late as 1887, and the *North West* ran a tramp service along the river for another dozen years.†

One by one the ships disappeared. Their final resting place was seldom at dockside. They died where they had lived, at river bends or at the edge of rapids. They were left to sink where they had rammed their final rock or crunched into their last riverbank. Eventually, their superstructures disintegrated into driftwood, and their rusting remains were blanketed by the shifting sands and weeping willows.

---

*According to Ted Barris, the *Northcote*'s bell "now beckons a congregation to the Duck Lake Anglican Church each Sunday; while a hundred miles away the Gardiner Presbyterian Church—now Fred Light's tiny museum in the old town of Battleford—houses the *Northcote*'s three-tone steam whistle. And three feet of *Northcote* deck plank functions as a . . . cribbage board in one Prince Albert living room."

†Only the *Keenora*, converted from steam to diesel during her career and restored by the Marine Museum of Manitoba, now survives. Of the scores of passenger steamers of the inland waterways of the West, only four sternwheelers—the *Klondike* and *Keno* in Yukon and the *Moyie* and *Sicamous* in British Columbia—remain.

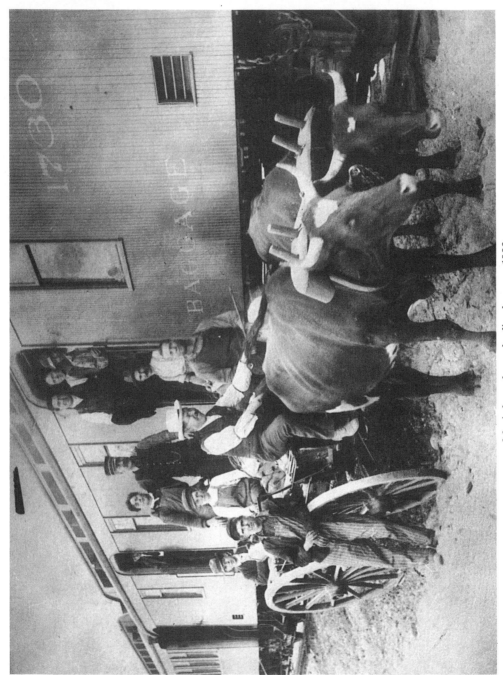

*Manitoba settlers unloading baggage, 1880s*

# CHAPTER 5

# PROGRESSION AND BETRAYAL

*"Fine promises butter no parsnips."*
—HBC trader James Lockhart

TRAVERSING THE STILL UNOCCUPIED WEST by steamboat and canoe, on foot and snowshoe, aboard sleighs and buckboards, Donald Smith spent most of a decade after the Red River Rebellion and the subsequent surrender of the HBC's monopoly holding the Company together long enough to transform its core business from fur trading to real estate. Apart from laying down a drastically altered operational code in line with the HBC's new competitive environment, Smith's main concern was to deal with the increasingly strident demands of the Company's wintering partners for their share of the Canadian government's £300,000 cash down payment on Rupert's Land.

According to the 1821 and 1834 Deed Polls, which set down the rules of their engagement, Chief Factors and Chief Traders were not employees but partners. To them belonged 40 percent of the Company's equity, divided on a share basis according to rank, and they were thus entitled to the same proportion of its net profit. This was not some form of earnings incentive; the dividends plus a modest subsistence allowance represented their sole income. Having suffered through many downturns in fur prices, they seemed entitled to participate in the Company's cash windfalls. They argued convincingly that Rupert's Land was available for sale mainly because they and their predecessors had legitimized and expanded Charles II's original land grant through right of occupation. They felt particularly deserving because the transfer to Canada, which had destroyed the monopoly that made the fur trade so profitable, was bound to endanger their livelihood. At least one favourable court judgment had upheld the basis of their claim. When the Company's headquarters building on Fenchurch Street was sold at a profit five years earlier, London's Chancery Court had ruled the wintering partners were entitled to two-fifths of the proceeds, since the original purchase price had been paid out of the fur trade's gross income. Using that precedent, the overseas officers also claimed two-fifths of the $450,000 the Company had recently been awarded for giving up its Oregon territories to the United States.

When these points were raised by his Chief Factors and Chief Traders at the Northern Council meeting held at Norway House in the summer of 1870, Smith promised to make their case in London. Even if he was a stranger, the field men thought they recognized in the man they appropriately nicknamed "Labrador Smith" a colleague who had connections with the powerful and who could salvage their estates. "Our immediate destiny is in your hands," one of the Chief Factors pleaded with him. "You know our life—you know how arduous our labours are. In nearly every instance they involved long servitude, separation from friends and relations, many hardships which we feel more sensitively as time wears away. . . . These might be, as they often are, borne cheerfully even for a long period, were the prospects of retirement on an adequate competency in sight; but failing this hope, they are almost insupportable."

Sir Stafford Northcote, who was named HBC Governor when the Earl of Kimberley resigned to become Lord Privy Seal in the Gladstone government, balked at sharing the £300,000 award, insisting that the value of the wild land had not been improved by the fur traders' activities. In fact, Northcote enjoyed little manoeuvring room. For the first time in its long history, the Hudson's Bay Company was no longer controlled by the London Committee. Since the sale to the International Financial Society in 1863 there were no more "sleeping partners" who could be counted on to vote automatically with the directors on the conduct of the fur trade.* Instead, the stock was actively traded on the London Exchange, and annual meetings were swayed by whatever coalition of shareholders emerged on any particular issue. These new-style investors, hard City men with long pedigrees but little sense of history, felt no allegiance to the traditions

---

*For details of this transaction, see *Caesars of the Wilderness*, pages 369–373.

of the Company; their only concern was to increase stock yields. During some of the early years after the end of the Company's monopoly, net revenues had been so paltry that winding up the HBC and splitting up its assets seemed entirely appropriate—but no one was quite certain how such an ancient royally chartered enterprise could be extinguished.

Smith spent the summer of 1871 in London advancing his officers' claims. Even as he was arguing their case, he was haunted by that train ride he had taken eighteen months earlier on his way to Red River, through the fertile farmlands lining the railway tracks north and west of St Paul. With the HBC about to receive title from Canada to seven million acres of what was the northward extension of that rich soil, he was convinced of something most of his Chief Factors only vaguely suspected: that furry animals would not be the main source of the Company's profits much longer. He realized that where buffalo roamed, cattle would one day graze, and had ascertained that much of the land about to come into the Company's possession was favoured with two more hours of sunshine a day during the wheat-maturing season than other farming areas. But that was only the beginning of Smith's vision. He knew that to switch the prairie economy from fur to grain would require large-capacity transportation—a railway network, initially down to St Paul, Minnesota, and eventually right to the Pacific. Reverting to character, Smith merged his own aspirations with the country's future and turned the combination into a personal mission. He became determined that in some as yet unpredictable way he would participate in construction of a railway across the Canadian West.

Although he was only two years out of Labrador, circumstances had conspired to place Smith at the vortex of a historic transformation. Despite his very recent promotion, he suddenly commanded enormous leverage within the councils of the HBC. The Red River incident had made him all but indispensable in rearranging the Company's overseas affairs. He had proved during his long Labrador stewardship to be a capable fur trader, worthy of the Company's confidence. In his dealings with Riel he had gained the respect of Canada's Prime Minister, the confidence of the North-West's settlers, and the trust of the HBC's officers. Having accomplished all this so quickly, Smith began to sense that his destiny was not on the gumbo streets of Fort Garry or even in the relatively sophisticated offices and curtained salons of Montreal. It was in London, among the patricians of Empire transacting the world's important commerce, that he wanted eventually to claim his roost.

As a first step, Smith set out to ingratiate himself with the Hudson's Bay Company's directors, especially Governor Northcote, a seasoned political juggler who had honed his skills as secretary to Prime Minister William Ewart Gladstone, President of the Board of Trade and Secretary of State for India. He intended to show Northcote and the HBC Committeemen that he was really one of *them*, that he had the Company's best long-term interests at heart rather than the dispensable concerns of the wintering partners. He did this by suggesting a workable compromise to resolve the fur traders' demands that they share in the government's £300,000 payout. Northcote later won shareholder approval for the scheme, which provided the winterers with a one-time payment of £107,055. It also guaranteed continuation of their 40-percent equity position and perpetuated their 40-percent share of trading profits. In return, they had to sign a new Deed Poll that specifically exempted them from proceeds of future HBC land sales.

Having expected little, most of the fur traders were pleased with the suggestion, particularly the cash, since the service then had virtually no pension provisions. When he returned to Montreal, Smith was feasted by the outback veterans, who presented him with a silver serving set worth £500. Only a few of the more astute characters realized that Smith had signed their professional death warrants. By giving up future land profits, the one-time lords of the forests had been rendered powerless and poor. The appropriately grateful London board showed its appreciation by immediately promoting Smith to Commissioner at a generous annual £2,000, and a year later to Chief Commissioner, with a healthy salary increase.

The Factors held desultory discussions about resigning to establish a new independent fur-trading company and several retired on the spot. Among those who quit in disgust was Chief Trader Roderick McKenzie. "If we had insisted in participating in the sale of lands there might be some hopes of a certain remuneration for our services, which under the present régime with all the expense is very doubtful," he wrote to a colleague in the Peace River country. Another senior trader, James Lockhart, noted: "It is all very well for Donald A. Smith, with his £2,000 secure annually, to puff the new arrangements. But 'fine promises butter no parsnips,' and you will all find yourselves fooled. . . . For your sake and the sakes of a few other true friends of mine still in the service, I hope things may turn out all right, but I do not expect it, and would advise you to do as others have done, i.e. send back their commissions with the note, 'Declined with thanks.'" Still, under pressure from Smith, most of the traders signed the fateful Deed Poll.

Northcote, by then Lord Iddesleigh, returned to British politics in 1874, becoming Chancellor of the Exchequer and later Foreign Secretary in Lord Salisbury's second ministry. He was succeeded in the HBC Governor's office by George Joachim Goschen, later first Viscount Goschen, who had attained a Bank of England directorship at the age of twenty-seven and had more recently served as first Lord of the Admiralty in the Gladstone government. Instead of trying to offset bad times by branching out into retail stores or aggressively pursuing government contracts, the HBC under Goschen withdrew into a form of suspended animation. He tried sporadically to revitalize the fur trade; but initial progress in land sales was slow, and revenues dipped so steeply that HBC stock prices in London slipped from £38 to £12. One of his few positive contributions was to strengthen the HBC board by recruiting Sir John Rose, partner in the London merchant banking house of Morton, Rose & Company, who had served as finance minister in Macdonald's first Canadian government and had since become the country's unofficial ambassador to London's financial district.

The trio of patrician governors—Kimberley, Northcote and Goschen—who ran the Hudson's Bay Company between 1868 and 1880 raised its social profile but accomplished little else. The Company's unostentatious headquarters in a former silk warehouse of the East India Company on Lime Street had only a tiny permanent staff that was made up of the corporate secretary, an accountant, a warehouse keeper, a few shipping clerks and some fur graders. Governors presided over fur auctions two or three times a year but measured annual time spent on HBC affairs in hours rather than days. The head office's budget, which in 1870 barely exceeded £13,000, had *dropped* by £2,000 thirty years later. Once a month or so the Committeemen would meet in the Governor's office to debate policies and prepare for the semi-annual gathering of shareholders (still quaintly referred to as General Courts of Proprietors), held at the London Tavern or the City Terminus Hotel. Even when these assemblies were stormy, the election of directors was customarily confined to approving candidates from the Governor's house list, and most Committeemen contributed little beyond their physical presence.

INTO THIS VOID STEPPED Donald Smith, the freshly minted head of the HBC's North American operations. The fur department, which had been without strong leadership since the death of Sir George Simpson in 1860, had suffered during the decade of neglect, and badly needed Smith's brand of energy and dedication. Curiously, it didn't get it. Smith's heart was no longer in the fur trade. Since leaving Labrador he had participated in grander events and had expanded his personal agenda in too many new directions to be drawn back into daily concern with the messy business of buying pungent pelts and selling them on a reluctant market. He did manage to keep the fur trade going, but he continued having trouble with its mundane bookkeeping details (as he had had while a youthful clerk), failed to maintain his inspection timetable to outlying districts, and allowed the HBC infrastructure to slide into dilapidation. "The Chief Commissioner cares nothing and hopes nothing from the fur trade," complained Chief Trader Lockhart.

Despite his preoccupation with more weighty issues of state—politics and railways—Smith's position at the head of the HBC's Canadian operations required him to live and work at Red River, which had been incorporated as Winnipeg in 1873. In the spring of that year Smith purchased Silver Heights, a comfortable mansion in the St James district, where he could spend time with his wife, Isabella, between trips to Montreal, Ottawa, London and St Paul.

Captivated by the potential of real-estate speculation, Smith resigned his fur-trade posting in the spring of 1874 to become the Company's first Land Commissioner and moved his main office to Montreal. He was succeeded as head of the fur trade by a cheerful nonentity named James A. Grahame, a Chief Factor then in charge of Victoria and the Western Department's sub-commissioner. His main historical legacy seems to be that his beard was even longer than Smith's. When he switched responsibilities to what was then the more junior posting, Smith made certain he preserved his valuable privilege of reporting directly to London. In a circular letter to Chief Factors and Traders announcing his decision, Smith added a telling postscript: "It may not be out of place for me here to add that I shall informally give my attention to the personal interests of my friends connected with the service who have investments with 'private cash' in my hands. This latter, as you are aware, having throughout been entirely independent of my relations to the Company as their Commissioner. . . ."

Here was the first hint of Donald Smith's most daring gamble—and the source of his betrayal of his one-time fur-trade colleagues. He had not only deluded them into giving up their share of the HBC's land sales profits but he also intended to buy control of the Company right out from under them—using their money to do it.

The scheme that made this possible had originated with Sir George Simpson. As overseas Governor, he had helped the Company's thrifty backwoods Factors invest their earnings. He eventually controlled a large block of funds, adding to his clientele such churchmen as Alexandre-Antonin Taché and Henry Budd, and the famous plainsman James McKay. As early as 1848, when Smith was still in Labrador, he had started buying shares in the Bank of Montreal and later in the Hudson's Bay Company. His reputation for shrewd money decisions attracted fellow Factors, who turned to him for investment management after Simpson's death. By the early 1870s, Smith was running thirty-seven trusts with considerable financial leverage—a fact the Bank of Montreal recognized in naming him a director. Whenever one of his investors retired or wanted to withdraw from the money pool, Smith would pay out the capital and agreed-upon 3-percent annual return, but purchase the shares for his own account. He eventually became first president and chief shareholder of the Royal Trust Company, specifically established to handle these transactions, which were quickly making him very rich. Smith used these funds— plus his generous credit lines at the Montreal—to purchase large blocks of HBC stock at depressed prices when termination of the Company's monopoly triggered a market panic. Smith, who was all too aware of the HBC's underlying land values, could thus pick up stock at £9. (Within his lifetime those shares would become worth more than £130 each—an increase of 1,300 percent.*) These strategically timed purchases and his subsequent dealings in HBC stock confirmed Smith as Canada's father of insider trading. Granted, there were no laws against using privileged information to play the stock market in those days, but Smith abused the system mercilessly—and deliberately didn't share his knowledge with the fur traders whose financial destinies had been entrusted to him.†

---

*That capital gain does not take into account the Company's generous dividend payouts. Between 1872 and 1911 the HBC's entire capital stock was repaid to shareholders six times over in special bonuses. To maximize returns on the profits generated once the real estate started to move, the nominal par value of shares was reduced and the difference paid out in cash directly to shareholders. In the fifteen years after surrender of the HBC's monopoly, for example, HBC shares were written down from £20 to £13, with £700,000 distributed to stockholders.

†At about this time Smith also purchased major equity interests in the Paton Manufacturing Company of Sherbrooke, Quebec, a spinning and weaving mill, and the Cold Brook Rolling Mills Company of Saint John, New Brunswick.

"WHERE EVERY MAN'S A LIAR—that's where the West begins!" That anonymous boast, quoted by Prairies historian Grant MacEwan, caught the exuberant spirit and somewhat less glorious reality of history's greatest voluntary migration. The movement of new settlers into the West didn't really begin on a mass basis until the last half-decade of the nineteenth and the first decade of the twentieth centuries, but the people who eventually occupied fifty-eight million acres of the Canadian plains were driven by a common motive. What lured them was less rumours of fortune than the personal freedom they might gain. Here, as ploughs creased the startled land, came the supreme blessing of a new start. Men and women could till the good earth and make fresh lives without having to face an entrenched aristocracy, established church or preordained political order.

All they had to pledge was their youth, strength and endurance—and it certainly wasn't easy, freedom or no. Settlement of the land was painfully slow. It was delayed by absence of railway transportation, an economic depression triggered by the collapse of American financier Jay Cooke's debt-burdened Northern Pacific Railway, the casual gait of government surveyors and the HBC's determination to get a better deal. Under the original Deed of Surrender, the Company could retain about 45,000 acres around its major posts and had the right to claim, over fifty years, one-twentieth of any township within the Prairies' "Fertile Belt"—the desirable agricultural tracts enclosed by the American border, the Rockies, the North Saskatchewan River, and (on the east) Lake Winnipeg and Lake of the Woods. That amounted to a valuable seven million acres, but no one seemed certain how the HBC's actual acreage within each township should be chosen.

The Dominion Land Act had established a survey system based on the American model, with each township divided into thirty-six square sections of 640 acres each (plus road allowance) to ensure that farms would be large enough for commercial wheat production. Originally the HBC lands were to be chosen by lot or chance, but Smith prevailed on the government to allocate the same pattern of sections in each township. Purchasers of HBC land were allowed fairly generous terms: a down payment of one-eighth the market price, with the balance payable in seven annual instalments at 7-percent interest. (A similar arrangement spread over five years applied to town lots.) In a typical ten-year period (1879–89), the HBC sold 514,009 acres and had to repossess all but 195,150 acres when breaking the land broke the farmers instead.*

---

*To the HBC went Sections 8 and 26 in every fifth township, and in all other townships all of Section 8 plus the southern half and northwest quarter of Section 26. Of the remaining

Although Smith had lobbied for the job as HBC Land Commissioner, his record in that office was no more impressive than his time as head of the fur trade—and for the same reason. His interests had grown too diverse. He was too deeply immersed in railway manipulation and politics to devote his prime energies to being the Company's chief real-estate agent. Typically, the Hudson's Bay Company sat on its land, allowing prospective buyers to make bids but doing very little to promote sales. No effort was made to lure railway builders towards its territory, and London even turned down the opportunity of acting as paymaster, on Ottawa's behalf, for the newly created North West Mounted Police. During Smith's tenure, little farmland was sold. He did open a land office in Winnipeg, though he himself stayed mostly in Montreal, and successfully auctioned off town lots in Winnipeg and Portage la Prairie. The urban plots, measuring fifty feet by a hundred, were sold at the equivalent rate of $7,000 an acre.*

An enduring mystery of this interregnum in his career is why, as the HBC's senior representative in North America, Smith didn't even attempt to convince his British principals that they should take advantage of the HBC's primacy in the North-West. Although he was right at the centre of the action, in charge of the HBC's most future-oriented department, he did little to expand the Company's revenue base and nothing to involve the HBC in railway construction. Smith put up a small hotel at Portage la Prairie, built a few grist mills, and began operating a ferry service across the Assiniboine at Fort Ellice—and that was the full extent of the HBC's diversification during his stewardship. Asleep at the edge of the rapidly awakening new territories, the HBC land department under Smith's direction gave up its head start by default and lapsed into a period of ill-tempered hibernation. It was typical of the HBC's mentality that while great opportunities were being lost, the Company was concerning itself mainly with such fusty detail as setting rates on the Fort Ellice ferry. Crossing tariffs were

---

sections, two (29 and 11) were set aside as educational endowments, and all even-numbered sections were reserved for homesteads, available to heads of families for a nominal ten dollars plus the requirement of carrying out specific improvements. The odd-numbered sections were reserved for later sale at one dollar an acre, with a limit of one to a customer. When the CPR claimed its land grants, the odd-numbered sections four deep on either side of the tracks became railway property.

*The HBC presented fifty acres to the new Government of Manitoba as sites for office buildings. The first sale from the HBC's 500-acre Fort Garry Reserve was to the Canadian Pacific Hotel Company for $838 per lot; the first land sale, 640 acres near Emerson, Manitoba, was to William McKechnie for six dollars an acre, or $3,840.

minutely differentiated at twenty cents for a cart with one horse or ox and thirty cents for the same vehicle drawn by two animals. Foot passengers were charged a straight eight cents.

As the Canadian historian Michael Bliss astutely noted in his epic history of Canadian business, *Northern Enterprise*, "If ever an organization had a head start on the commerce of an area it was surely the Hudson's Bay Company in the lands that became western Canada. If the Company of Adventurers of the 1860s and 1870s had been as shrewd and supple as its founders had been two centuries earlier, it would have diversified and adjusted its organization to exploit the new order being brought about by Canadian expansion. It would have dominated, if not monopolized, trade and development in the new West. It would have been a leader in transportation—one of the Company's historic strengths." Bliss is right. Although the CPR was built by a syndicate in which Smith was a dominant influence, there is no record in the HBC archives of any suggestion by him that the Company become involved in railways.

The inevitable and hardly surprising conclusion is that, once again, Smith applied his self-serving code to the situation and chose the CPR instead of the HBC as his favoured instrument. The railway, at least in those years, must have seemed to him an attractive personal investment with the possibility of unlimited perks for early shareholders; the HBC, on the other hand, was only his employer, and it would be another decade before Smith would hold enough stock to control its policies. For more than forty years he lived with a deepening conflict of interest between the two organizations—at first in terms of which group would build the railway and later in terms of whose land he would try harder to sell. This meant appraising the conflicting geographies of the two companies: the HBC's infrastructure glued to the rivers that had once been highways for the fur trade while the new population centres followed the ribbons of steel. When he eventually became the dominant shareholder of both, Smith was free to balance the land-sales policies of the CPR and HBC, which at least in their time frames were complementary rather than competitive. Interested in building up traffic along its new tracks, the Canadian Pacific was anxious to sell its land sooner than the Hudson's Bay Company, which regarded real estate as part of the price for surrendering its monopoly and was determined to obtain top dollar, no matter how long it had to wait. Certainly it was no accident that by 1914, the year of Smith's death, only one of the fifteen prairie towns with HBC department stores (Fort Qu'Appelle) was not served by CPR trains.

*Charles John Brydges,*
HBC *Land Commissioner, about 1889*

It took five years for Smith to lose his patience with the land business. When he finally decided to resign in 1879, his departure was applauded by the London board, fed up with his inability to keep the books straight. "Looking to the small amount of work connected with the accounts of the Land Department it was hoped that the details would have been promptly and regularly rendered," HBC Secretary William Armit had scolded, "but as the Committee are again disappointed in this respect, they direct me to state that a minute was passed directing your special attention to the matter and calling upon you to render the accounts in question regularly." Smith had grown exasperated by the slow pace and bureaucratic nature of the Land Department. Real-estate sales seemed to be in remission until the advent of the railroads, and title transfers of the few acres that were sold could be handled by clerks. Smith was by now more of a railroader than a Bay man and for the next four years occupied no official post with the Company.

It was a sign of the times that he was succeeded as Land Commissioner by a railwayman, Charles John Brydges, who had been general manager of the Grand Trunk and general superintendent of government railways under Alexander Mackenzie's administration. A confidant of leading Canadian politicians, a good friend of Sir John Rose, who was about to be appointed the HBC's Deputy Governor, Brydges carried himself with an air of righteous enthusiasm. "His arrival in Winnipeg," observed historians Alan Wilson and R.A. Hotchkiss, ". . . was like that of a great administrative juggernaut. Extensive surveys began in prospect of a 'Manitoba Fever'; new administrative, legal, accounting, and advertising machinery emerged; contracts for supplies to Indians and the North West Mounted Police became competitive; new hotel and milling facilities enhanced the value of HBC lands; a subsidiary bridge company for the Red and Assiniboine rivers at Winnipeg was formed; the retail stores were reorganized under new men, not those only 'accustomed to the barter system with the Indians'; supervision of barge and steam transport of goods and passengers was wrenched from the hands of 'incompetents'; and, finally, executive operations were permanently moved from Montreal to Winnipeg in November 1880. Within a year the HBC was recognized as the most reliable source for information on settlement and commerce in Manitoba and the North-West Territories." This was good news to everyone but Smith, who didn't want any successor showing him up. He had refused Brydges the courtesy of a briefing and didn't even pass on his correspondence files, though the new Commissioner discovered unpaid seven-year-old HBC tax bills in Smith's desk.

At the same time as the business tempo in Canada was picking up under Brydges, a similar transformation was taking place at the Company's head office. With Goschen's return to politics in 1880, the energetic Eden Colvile was appointed Governor. He stood out from his twenty-four predecessors in two important respects: he understood something about the fur trade and he had actually visited Canada's North-West.

The son of Andrew Colvile, who had served the HBC for most of three decades as Deputy Governor and Governor in the mid-1800s, the younger Colvile had been sent to Rupert's Land as Associate Governor in 1849. Only eight years out of Eton and Cambridge, he had apprenticed brilliantly under Sir George Simpson's direction and became a lifelong HBC enthusiast. He turned head office into a far more interventionist agency and was determined to rid the Company of Donald Smith's corrosive influence. Colvile's love of the Company made him distrust Smith, who had so cavalierly mishandled his last two appointments, and the British Governor specifically instructed Brydges to displace the vestiges of Smith's authority and to downgrade the Fur Commissioner, James Grahame, so that he could be responsible for the entire North American operation.\*

Unlike Smith, who regarded life in Winnipeg as a necessary but melancholy inconvenience, Brydges threw himself into community activities, becoming head of the Manitoba Board of Trade, chairman of the Winnipeg General Hospital, head of the local Anglican church's building committee, and president of the Manitoba Club, the exclusive gentlemen's watering-hole incorporated only eight months after the city itself.† Brydges succeeded in altering the local image of the HBC as a distantly run, shadowy presence. His spans across the rivers (inevitably known as "Brydges' bridges") drew people from east and south of the city to the Company store, and he even persuaded municipal politicians to site the terminus of the city's first streetcar line on HBC property.

Between the summers of 1880 and 1883, Winnipeg, by then known as the Bull's Eye of the Dominion or the Chicago of the North, exploded into a land boom. Some 1,300 lots were sold in Winnipeg alone, with other townsites at Portage la Prairie, West Lynne (adjoining

---

\*For his part Colvile returned some of the lost grandeur to the Company by acquiring a flotilla of impressive ships to serve its West Coast operations directly from England. Pride of the fleet was the graceful tea clipper *Titania*, then the world's second-fastest vessel—next only to the *Ariel* and faster than the *Cutty Sark* or the *Thermopylae*. Two hundred feet long, she made the 14,000-mile journey from Victoria to London in a record-breaking 104 days. Built in 1866 by Robert Steele at the Steele yard on the Clyde, she was designed by his brother, William Steele. Basil Lubbock, the authority on clipper ships, said of *Ariel* and *Titania*: "[They] carried all before them in the tea races, besides being the most beautiful and yacht-like merchantmen that ever sailed the seas." Flying the Company's pennant for six years, the *Titania* was luckier than most of the HBC's Pacific squadron—the *Labouchere*, *Lady Lampson* and *Pacific*, which all foundered on the intertidal rocks of the West Coast.

†No other Canadian private club has symbolized so directly the concentration of economic authority in any province, institutionalizing its decision-making process from the beginning. Membership in the Manitoba Club, according to W.L. Morton, remained "the symbol of success and the Club itself the centre of the informal exchange of opinion and information—access which marks the 'insider.' " If you were male, that is. E.H. Macklin, an early member who served for many years as general manager of the *Winnipeg Free Press*, explained during a Club debate on whether or not to admit women that he gloried "in the progress women have made. I rejoice in the liberty they enjoy. I would extend that freedom to embrace the granting of every privilege they might ask, every wish they might express, save one, the privilege of admission to the Manitoba Club. I appeal to you, preserve one little spot on this planet where the swish of women's skirts and the music of their voices are not heard. . . . It would prove a great boon to many of us who for an hour or two every now and then want to live the simple life." Women members (and Jews) were finally admitted in 1974, though neither group has since taken much advantage of the privilege it took only a hundred years to achieve.

*HBC land sale advertisement, 1882*

and later absorbed by Emerson) and Rat Portage (Kenora) filling up equally fast, while in a single year (1882) some 341,588 acres of farmland worth $2,235,308 were sold—sixteen times the previous annual total. "The office now is like a fair," Brydges happily reported to London, "and the people stand in a row waiting their turn to reach the counter. It is like the crowd at the entrance to the pit of a London theatre. . . ." and two months later, "Bedlam let loose was a mere incident to the scene in our office. . . . I never saw Winnipeg in such a state of frantic excitement."

The boom quickly degenerated into a speculative frenzy; Winnipeg's streets "were more crowded than Broadway." The initial lake shipment of Manitoba grain was delivered by James Richardson & Sons in 1883. The Harris Company of Brantford, Ontario, established its first Winnipeg agricultural implement dealership in 1878 and signed up seventeen agencies across the West. One of the main real-estate investors was Donald Smith. He used the knowledge he had gained as the HBC's Land Commissioner to purchase properties on his own account, even utilizing Bain & Blanchard, the HBC's Winnipeg legal firm, to negotiate the contracts. Not surprisingly, he chose the lots within the four-mile belt along the Assiniboine, then thought to be the most probable route of the CPR being built by a syndicate to which he belonged. He also invested in the new CPR hotel. He not only obtained a $15,000 loan from the Company to purchase the hotel property but also demanded that Brydges turn over to him gratis two of the HBC's most desirable town lots. Brydges refused, and, fearing an end run, wrote to London recommending against the grant.

Preoccupied as he may have been with his railroading schemes, Smith had no intention of losing touch with the Hudson's Bay Company's intimate corporate affairs and never ceased expanding his stockholdings. He hired spies inside Brydges's office to keep him informed of the Land Commissioner's correspondence with London and even rented space in the new Winnipeg real-estate building to keep a personal eye on who came to call on Brydges and for how long. "I am satisfied that there has been a long pending scheme to wreck the H.B. Co. and buy it up as a wreck," Brydges complained to London about Smith, "and there is much chagrin & disgust that the scheme did not succeed. Mr. Smith has been very outspoken in denouncing the trade operations of the Co as at present conducted, and his friends talk very openly & very publicly in the same way. He has talked in that sense to me several times but I have simply listened. His course is altogether too sinuous."

Smith resented the confidence Governor Colvile had placed in Brydges, even though he had done little to deserve it himself. An honest man enthralled by his mission to breathe new life into the Company while helping to nurture the new West he had come to love, Brydges recognized early how essential it was for the Company to assume community leadership.* "Armed with ... [a] sense of the Board's confidence, he seldom hesitated to set his mark upon every aspect of the Company's operation... ," concluded historian Alan

---

*Brydges had a romanticism of his own. He claimed a link to the old barony of Chandos, whose holders owned Sudeley Castle, since the Civil War of the 1640s one of the great ruins of the English countryside.

Wilson. "He operated from instinct and mandate as if he were Chief Commissioner, not Land Commissioner—and as if it were *his* task to create a new image of the Hudson's Bay Company as a citizen of the Canadian North West." Even when the Manitoba land boom fizzled and the HBC had to repossess property worth $900,000, Brydges managed the negotiations without harming the Company's reputation.

The clash between Smith and Brydges finally came into the open over the railways clawing their way towards Winnipeg. The Grand Trunk, Brydges's former employer, had been trying hard to discredit the CPR on world money markets, and, despite his vigorous denials, the Land Commissioner got some of the blame. More seriously, Brydges became involved in the controversy over location of the CPR, whose engineers favoured crossing the Red River at Selkirk instead of Winnipeg because of spring flooding dangers. Brydges offered the railway twenty acres of prime land for a station and lobbied so strenuously and so successfully on behalf of the Winnipeg route that he permanently alienated not only Smith but also Charles Tupper, then federal Minister of Railways and Canals, and Sandford Fleming, the railway's chief engineer, who was also a director of the HBC.*
Brydges supported the strong representations of Winnipeg business leaders against the CPR's branch-line monopoly and recommended the HBC grant city land to the Northern Pacific, an American railroad, to offset Canadian Pacific's influence. He gradually found himself with many local friends but just as many—and much more powerful— distant enemies.

The first hint of Smith's counter-attack was in a private letter Brydges received from Governor Colvile alleging irregularities in some of the Winnipeg land sales. The issue was brought up by Smith at the Company's 1882 shareholders' meeting, and a committee was struck to investigate the charges—specifically, that Company officials, including Brydges, had personally profited from buying fifty-six Winnipeg lots, eleven of which were later resold for almost the total

---

*A Scottish immigrant, Fleming surveyed routes for four pioneer railways, lithographed the country's first large-scale surveyor's maps, designed Canada's first postage stamp (the three-penny brown, featuring his drawing of a beaver, which turned the animal into a national emblem), wrote an interdenominational prayer book, founded the Royal Canadian Institute, laid the Pacific cable between Vancouver Island and Australia, was chancellor of Queen's University for thirty-five years, and served as an influential HBC director for more than a quarter of a century. Frustrated by trying to run trains across a country where every town set its own clocks, he invented standard time, which divided the earth into twenty-four fixed zones of fifteen longitudinal degrees each. Canadian territory, spanning a quarter of the earth's day, was divided into five time zones.

purchase price. Except for HBC Deputy Governor Sir John Rose, the committee members—including Sandford Fleming and HBC Secretary William Armit—were solid Smith partisans, but even they found nothing to condemn Brydges for except the vague charge of having "erred on the side of prodigality." They recommended that HBC land auctions should be held only once a month with firm upset prices, and that no Company land be sold within five miles of the railway right-of-way. Like Smith, Fleming had a double loyalty to the HBC and CPR, and, like Smith, he usually came down on the side of the railway. "I do not believe in mixing up our land sales with anyone else," Brydges objected. "The proposal puts the whole matter in the hands of the CPR." Sir John Rose's report totally vindicated Brydges. The Deputy Governor had even gone to the trouble of personally examining the cancelled cheques for all the transactions involved. As he wrote to Sir John A. Macdonald, "We . . . trace all these reports & complaints . . . to Donald Smith. He has evidently a great enmity towards [Brydges]. . . ." None of the specific accusations against Brydges were ever substantiated, and he was even awarded a cash bonus of £1,500 to compensate for the mental stress he had suffered.

Smith wouldn't let up. At the 1883 General Court he revived the accusations as if no investigation had been made, and despite Rose's defence of Brydges (which filled thirty pages of transcription) the Land Commissioner remained under a cloud. After verbally approving the Company's annual report, most of the shareholders departed the meeting. These included some of the Committeemen, who assumed that, as was the custom, their re-election would be routinely based on the "Governor's list." Instead, Smith got up and proposed his own Committee slate, which included himself and one of his financial allies, the noted barrister Charles Russell, later Lord Russell of Killowen and Lord Chief Justice of England. A surprised Colvile called for a secret ballot, and when the votes had been counted, thirteen of the fourteen shareholders still present—everyone but Smith—supported the Governor's list. But if Smith didn't have the numbers, he had the weight. His ballot represented 4,000 shares, far outnumbering the other votes. Smith took his seat on the board, and when questioned by *The Times* about his successful *coup d'état*, he piously declared, "My long connection of 40 years with the Hudson's Bay Company and being, perhaps, the largest registered holder of the shares on the books of the Company, should offer to my fellow proprietors some guarantees that I am unlikely to take any course prejudicial to their interests."

A more incisive summary of the dubious manoeuvre was the

verdict of Shirlee Smith, a close student of the Company's history and until the autumn of 1990 Keeper of the HBC Archives in Winnipeg. "Smith's actions were certainly unethical and probably illegal," she wrote, ". . . but two of his great strengths were strategy and timing. He now had a seat on the London Committee and was thus in a position to have an even greater say in the Land Department." And he did. At the following shareholders' meeting he championed a resolution appointing two directors (himself and Fleming) to form a subcommittee in charge of supervising Canadian affairs. Smith insisted that Brydges would have to report directly to the new subcommittee as well as to the London board. Poor Brydges must have known the trap was closing on him, but he agreed to go along with the scheme, only to find that Smith never would see him, even when they were both in Winnipeg at the same time—and would then complain that Brydges wasn't accountable enough.

When Sir John Rose died suddenly in the summer of 1888 while stalking deer on the Scottish estate of the Duke of Portland, Smith's last critic on the HBC board disappeared, and he moved immediately to have himself named Deputy Governor. Within a week of his appointment, Smith returned to his campaign of harassment, forcing Brydges on the defensive by repeatedly asking him to justify his work and his salary. Sensing disaster, Brydges wrote to his friend Sir John A. Macdonald to complain that Smith's behaviour had "every appearance of a desire to worry me out." But it was too late. On January 17, 1889, a tired and exasperated Eden Colvile retired as HBC Governor, and Donald Smith was "elected" in his place. With the retirement of Colvile most management traditions were cast aside. Never again would an HBC Governor "take charge of the hammer" at the Company's fur auctions. The very day of the takeover, Brydges was sent a letter dispensing with his services.

Thus ended the feud between the conscientious Charles John Brydges and the fur trader turned autocrat who, during fifty-one years in the service, had advanced from muskrat grader at Lachine to Governor of the Company of Adventurers. Brydges didn't live long enough to receive his termination notice. On February 16, 1889, while inspecting the Winnipeg General Hospital, one of his favourite philanthropies, he died of a heart attack. The correspondence between the two men provides a telling example of Donald Smith's pettiness. He was indeed, as the *Dictionary of National Biography* noted in his entry, "A good hater . . . resenting the success of other men's ideas."

WITHIN THREE YEARS OF ASSUMING the Governorship, which he was to hold for the next quarter-century, Smith had packed the board with money men who would do his bidding. Because he was both Governor and the Company's largest shareholder, the semi-annual meetings became more subdued affairs, particularly since he treated net land revenues as profit, which he distributed annually as dividends. Now that he was in charge, he could apply his thrifty policies freely on the expense side of the ledger, cutting the budget of the Land Department in half, for example.

Smith dismissed the fur trade as a doomed enterprise run by ill-starred eccentrics too stubborn or too ignorant to accommodate themselves to their fates. Although the proceeds of the fur trade kept the Company alive until the western land boom, that once buoyant commerce had deteriorated drastically since its heyday. Fur prices hit a twenty-year low in 1876, but trade was bolstered by diversification into new varieties. Instead of concentrating on beaver, the Company shipped out twenty-four categories of pelts, including muskrat, marten (Canadian sable), lynx, mink, otter, skunk, ermine, wolverine and seal, and muskox and buffalo robes.

Between 1876 and 1878, fur prices at London auctions declined by half, and wheat surpassed fur as Manitoba's leading export. Because the Company suffered continuing losses in the mid- and late 1870s, the Chief Factors and Traders who depended on dividends for their livelihoods were threatened with having to serve at their own expense. They retaliated by organizing themselves into a quasi-union called the Fur Trade Party to demand an annual guaranteed minimum dividend of £200 a share—but quickly grew quiescent when London offered £150. The oldtimers' feeling of abandonment was best expressed by Chief Factor James L. Cotter, descendant of an Irish baronet, who had been a Bay man for thirty years, mostly at Moose Factory.* "I . . . see no prospect of ever being able to retire on anything beyond a mere pittance," he wrote to a fellow Factor. "My health is delicate, and I could not now go at anything else in the way of business; so I am beset with difficulties and anxieties on all hands. . . . We work as if at the pumps of a sinking ship. It is a strained and unhealthy state of mind."

---

*Cotter also took the first pictures of the Hudson Bay area with a homemade camera, a tradition carried on by his grandson, George Cotter, who is the HBC's best contemporary documentary film-maker.

*HBC trader grading fox, beaver, mink and other pelts at Fort Chipewyan, 1890s*

Money was not the only problem. Although the fur trade enjoyed another fifty years of impressive activity, these hardy traders who had so diligently manned and maintained the HBC's land preserve felt dispossessed. The comforts, sophistications and relatives they had left behind in Scotland, England or the populated parts of Canada had become as disconnected from them as the rapidly changing contours of the once-immutable landscape of Rupert's Land. They had nowhere to turn. "While competent in the woods, I was inferior to John, the H.B. Co.'s messenger boy, in city life," complained George McTavish, a York Factory Chief Trader on a visit to Victoria. "My greatest fear was that I should display my ignorance, be laughed at and taken advantage of if I asked the price of everyday necessities, say a box of matches. When my old schoolmate, Arthur Robertson, secured a place for me at the festive board of Miss Coates on Fort Street . . . I was as a fish out of water. The table talk was unintelligible to me."

Chief Commissioner James Grahame, who had succeeded Smith in charge of the fur department, was replaced in 1884 by Joseph Wrigley, a vaguely connected Yorkshire businessman who proved so ineffective that he managed to give banality a bad name. The first Commissioner with no background in the fur business, he was hired strictly as an overseas agent to enforce London's will. And London's will under Smith's direction dictated that the fur traders be deprived of their 40 percent of the Company's profit. Wrigley promptly called a meeting of all the Chief Factors and Chief Traders—the Northern Council—for August 30, 1887, at the Queen's Hotel in Winnipeg.

They came from as far away as the Arctic Circle and the verdant forests of the Pacific slopes, the historic hovels around Hudson Bay and the modern if still primitive shops of the southern Prairies. There was great excitement as they journeyed to the Company's Canadian headquarters because there were rumours this would be the very last time the Northern Council, which had traditionally ruled their professional lives, was to meet.

The Winnipeg that greeted them was less a frontier settlement grown large than a commercial entrepôt, the hustling metropolis of the West, close to the height of its importance. The Grain Exchange was being organized—later to include the Bawlfs, Bells, Roblins, McMillans, Galts, Mitchells, Atkinsons, Spinks, McBeans, Hastingses, Maulsons, Richardsons, Parrishes—and the new grain families were busy spawning their fortunes. The thriving community had not only its own private banks (Alloway & Champion was the biggest) and the West's best bordellos (on Annabella Street) but also a theatre and opera house (at the corner of Notre Dame and Adelaide) and even a telephone exchange (560 subscribers, with a special long-distance hookup to Selkirk, twenty-two miles away).

As they gathered for that final time, an anonymous photographer snapped a group portrait (*overleaf*), revealing the fur traders as large but not fat. They have few double chins, no flabby, swollen bellies—just rib-cages as solid as if held together by barrel hoops. They boast trim beards and wise country eyes. The British poet Stephen Spender once remarked that for him the division between the past and the present was the French Revolution because he always imagined that before it, everyone wore fancy dress. The photograph catches that *fin de siècle* quality—the quandary of being out of one's place and time, knowing the world is wrong but being unable to change it. At one level, the picture evokes the sombre mood of men attending their own funerals, awkward in their Sunday suits, trying to position their age-dappled hands as if to show how very hard they had toiled. But a second look reveals these hard-etched faces glowing with a touch of swagger, the pride of having practised the continent's ancient commerce and survived.*

---

*Among those in attendance was Canada's least-heralded explorer, Robert Campbell (the big beard to the right of the door-frame), who had explored most of Yukon and once had snowshoed 3,000 miles from Fort Simpson on the Mackenzie River to Crow Wing, Minnesota, on the Mississippi. He was extraordinarily robust and seems never to have been ill. The day before Campbell died in 1894, at the age of eighty-six, he placed his hand on his forehead and declared in a puzzled tone, "I have a pain here. I suppose that is what people call a headache." It was his first and his last.

*The Northern Council at their last meeting, Winnipeg, August 30, 1887*

The meeting dealt with such mundane problems as the Northern Department's scale of allowances, which carefully equated rations to rank, so that, for instance, an Ordinary Interpreter would receive three pounds of tea a year, a Mechanic five pounds, an Apprentice Postmaster eight, a Postmaster ten, an Apprentice Clerk fifteen, a Clerk twenty and a Commissioned Officer thirty. Wrigley confirmed the traders' worst expectations that not only would this be the last Northern Council meeting but that no new commissions would be issued to those who had entered the service after the 1870 land transfer. That meant it was only a matter of time before their partnership with the Company would be dissolved. They would have to give up their 40-percent ownership and become bureaucrats instead of proprietors. "This very startling information threw a wet blanket over the entire Service and produced in many cases very unfavourable results in the Company's interest," reported N.M.W.J. McKenzie, a junior trader at the time. "The only interest the majority of their servants have had since then was their weekly, monthly or annual salary."

Wrigley was replaced within two years of the Winnipeg meeting by a Smith servitor named Clarence Campbell Chipman, a former secretary to Sir Charles Tupper. He closed down posts, hounded veteran traders out of the service, and dropped the apprentice plan that had kept the fur trade fuelled with new energies. "Here was a great scatteration, a breaking up of family ties so to speak," lamented N.M.W.J. McKenzie.

In 1893, Smith—speaking through Chipman—abruptly terminated the vestiges of the Deed Poll and extinguished the former wintering partners' equity positions. Some of the Chief Factors bewailed their fate ("I have waited so long for promotion, and have worked so hard to make and keep affairs prosperous, that I have lost heart and do not care what is done," wrote J. Ogden Grahame); others became angry ("The *fiat* has gone forth and Attila is to ravage and destroy the handiwork of the 'Company of Adventurers,'" fumed Roderick Ross). But they all knew who was to blame.

Reduced from patriarchs of the forests to supervised employees, the winterers at last realized how the colleague they had so fervently hoped would champion their cause had betrayed them. A Factor named Duncan MacArthur summed up their rage when he termed Donald Smith "the prince of humbugs and probably the worst enemy the Company ever had."

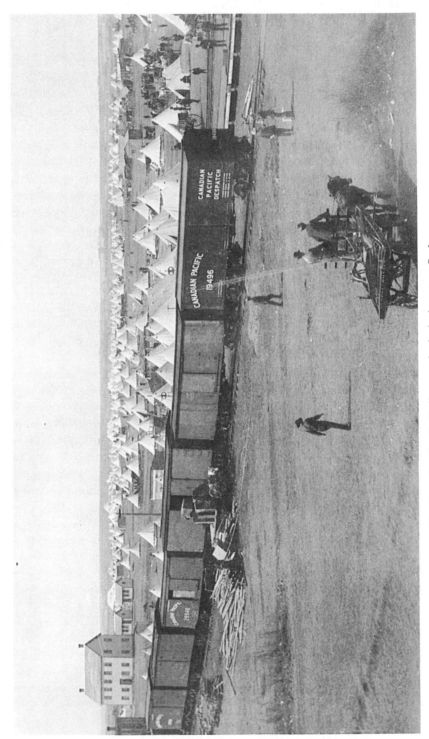

*The Canadian Pacific Railway and colonists' camp at Saskatoon*

# CHAPTER 6

# STEAL OF EMPIRE

*Smith vacillated in his support between the Conservative and
Liberal parties, equally disloyal to both and trusted by neither.*

THE PUZZLE OF DONALD SMITH'S straining for most of three decades to
promote himself within the Hudson's Bay Company's hierarchy,
rising to head its fur and, later, land operations, then treating these
highly coveted positions as minor annoyances was explained by his
obsession with having control of the Company instead of trying to run
its functional parts. More to the point, at this midstage in his career
Smith was preoccupied with politics and railways, faster and financially much more rewarding paths to power.

In contrast to most of his contemporaries, who sought wealth as an
avenue to political influence, Smith recognized that in the primitive
environment of his time it was infinitely easier to parlay political
connections into lucrative private ventures, often supported by the
public purse. "For forty years his personality stands out in every
political crisis in the Dominion," noted W.T.R. Preston, one of
Smith's many political foes. "He has had far more to do with the
defeat and victory of political parties since Confederation than all
other influences combined. . . . On many important occasions Parliament, without being aware of the fact, simply registered his decrees."

Smith's view of public life paralleled his approach to business. He
believed political parties were no different from commercial
corporations—handy conveyances to be boarded and abandoned at
will, according to which one best served his personal purposes at any

given moment. Smith was aware of no conflicts of interest in his adroit manoeuvrings between the private and public sectors because *his* interests never conflicted; they were, one and all, designed to advance his fame and his fortune. "His philosophical disposition to accept the inevitable never deserted him," noted Preston. "His standard of political honour was not high, but it served."

Smith vacillated in his support between the Conservative and Liberal parties, equally disloyal to both and trusted by neither. He once complained that he would not consign ownership of his grandmother's toothbrush to the ordinary politician—even if his own record proved the understatement of that taunt.

The buccaneering that characterizes developing economies found its most virulent expression in Canadian railway promotion. By 1915, when major construction ran out of steam, Canada had 40,000 miles of rails, built with government cash, subventions or bond guarantees worth more than $1.3 billion—plus the giveaway of 65,000 square miles including some of the finest wheat-growing land on earth. Yet despite these extravagant provisions, every mile of every track was privately owned. Financing a new railway usually meant its promoters would set up secretly controlled construction companies, then negotiate inflated contracts with themselves, collecting hefty profits at both ends of each deal. At the same time, they would award themselves bloated debenture offerings in return for artificial corporate services, reducing their balance sheets to rivers of red ink. They would then turn to Ottawa and demand subsidies to cover fiscal overruns, either bribing ministers to ensure bailouts or threatening to embarrass the government by halting construction—or both.

And yet the railways did get built, and they provided the essential infrastructure for the transcontinental economy, yanking an embryonic Dominion into the new century. The railways' promoters and operators became folk heroes, Canada's version of the great American robber barons—reviled and envied, riding about in their ornate private cars, gesturing with fat cigars, collecting old masters and young mistresses. Apart from the obvious chicanery in the link between politicians in power and these railway manipulators, the industry corrupted the electoral process itself. Railways and politics in nineteenth-century Canada became interchangeable black arts, only marginally more ethical than piracy on the high seas.

DONALD SMITH'S DEBUT in Canadian politics followed his successful arbitration of the Red River Rebellion in 1870. He contested and won the Winnipeg and St John seat in Manitoba's first provincial election and was simultaneously appointed to the executive council of the Northwest Territories. Unhappy with its municipal status as a "police village," Winnipeg in 1872 requested the right to incorporate itself as a city, but the new provincial legislature adjourned without dealing with the issue. Feelings ran so high that when enactment of the measure was delayed by Dr Curtis James Bird, a local physician who had been elected the legislature's Speaker, he was lured out of his home on a phony nocturnal house call and waylaid by constituents who dragged him from his sleigh and poured a bucket of tar over him. Popular outrage had been roused by a belief that Bird was helping Smith oppose incorporation so that the HBC could avoid paying city taxes. Insinuations of corporate favouritism were fanned by the fact that the province's first lieutenant-governor, A.G. Archibald, lived on Company property and his successor, Alexander Morris, toured his domain aboard HBC steamers. Before Manitoba's first bank was incorporated in 1873, the Company acted as the provincial treasury and repository for funds collected by customs officers. This official status, added to the retroactive bitterness over the HBC's long monopoly, had jelled into an enduring resentment of the Company and all its works. Dr John Christian Schultz, the charismatic leader of Manitoba's pro-Canadian movement, summed up popular sentiment when he labelled the Hudson's Bay Company "a curse to the country."

The act of incorporation was finally passed in the closing days of 1873. Winnipeg's original street surveys followed the Métis river lots and boundaries of the HBC's Land Reserve, its five-hundred-acre holding around Fort Garry.* The settlement's muddy alleys ("a mixture of putty and bird-lime") had been graded and planked, but there was nothing tame about Winnipeg's roughneck inhabitants, who turned the settlement into Canada's closest approximation to the American Wild West. The gin mills and mug-houses were there, as were the prostitutes brazenly auctioning off their sexual wares. "Winnipeg and Barrie are the two most evil places in Canada," went a typical report of the time.

Smith sponsored few initiatives in the Manitoba Legislature mainly because he was hardly ever there. Quickly growing dissatisfied with the constraints of provincial and municipal venues, he won the

---

*Winnipeg's original coat of arms featured a buffalo, a steam locomotive and three sheaves of wheat. This was slightly fanciful, since the buffalo had long vanished from the city's environs, the first train would not arrive until 1878, and there would be no substantial grain exports for another five years.

Prairie Territories
of the
Hudson's Bay Company

Steamboat Routes

Canadian Pacific Railway

250 miles

400 kilometres

JBG91

55°N.

95°W.

Nelson R.

Norway House

L. Winnipeg

Grand Rapids

Dauphin R.

L. Manitoba

Winnipeg R.

Lower Fort Garry

Red R.

to
St. Paul

Pembina

Upper Fort Garry (Winnipeg)

Portage la Prairie

Brandon

Assiniboine R.

Fort Ellice

Fort Pelly

L. Winnipegosis

Flin Flon

Cumberland House

Cumberland L.

The Pas

Fort Qu'Appelle

Qu'Appelle R.

Regina

Moose Jaw

105°W.

Prince Albert

Batoche

Saskatoon

Duck Lake

Carlton House

Battleford

South Saskatchewan R.

North Saskatchewan R.

Frog L.

Fort Pitt

Fort Edmonton

Calgary

Bow R.

Oldman R.

Medicine Hat

Lethbridge

115°W.

50°N.

Selkirk federal seat in 1871 and held it in the next three campaigns.*
He showed no favouritism, being elected twice as a Conservative and
twice as a Liberal. The contests were hard fought, with boozing and
brawling part of each run-up to election day and axe handles across
the head frequently used to persuade dithering voters. Smith's margins of victory, ranging from a high of 196 ballots in 1872 to only 9 in
1878, reflected the bitterness of these contests.

The first Manitoba representative to arrive in Ottawa, Smith
didn't take his parliamentary career too seriously and spent little time
in legislative pursuits; debating the fine points of new laws was not a
profit-producing enterprise. But from the moment he walked into the
House of Commons, Smith knew that within the shifting alliances of
that resplendent chamber there was significant personal authority to
be gained, and he intended to grab it. The great issue of 1871 was
British Columbia's entry into Confederation. The twelve thousand
white residents of the former HBC territory and British colony had
decided to enter Confederation as Canada's sixth province on condition they be linked to the rest of the country by a railway within ten
years. The only regular passage across the Rockies north of the forty-
ninth parallel was by HBC-owned pack mules. The animals, fitted
with *aphareos* (Mexican-style pack saddles), gathered at the Punch
Bowl, near what is now Jasper, to transfer loads and passengers.†

The entrepreneur who first undertook to build a railway across the
Canadian West was Sir Hugh Allan, yet another Scottish immigrant,
who had expanded his Montreal shipping line into the North Atlantic's largest merchant and passenger fleet. Allan had most leading
Conservative politicians, including Sir John A. Macdonald, Sir John
Rose and Sir George-Étienne Cartier, in his pocket and regularly
obtained lucrative subsidies and mail contracts for his maritime
operations. Named to the Bank of Montreal board, Allan also expanded his coal and steel interests, and built himself Ravenscrag, a
magnificent house on a fourteen-acre estate on Mount Royal that had
originally been owned by the greatest of the Nor'Westers, Simon
McTavish. Modelled on a fifteenth-century Tuscan villa, the house
had thirty-four rooms including an imposing ballroom complete with

---

*The constituency Donald A. Smith represented was known as Lisgar in his time. In
1891 the name was changed to Selkirk. Some sources list Smith as Member for Lisgar,
others for Selkirk.

†HBC packtrains, numbering three hundred or more animals, were led by a guide
followed by a bagpiper and an HBC Chief Factor, who usually carried a Bible and a
bottle of gin in his saddlebags, consulting both along the way.

a minstrels' gallery to accommodate a large orchestra. From the estate's seventy-five-foot tower Allan could scan the horizon for glimpses of his steamers returning from their weekly run to Glasgow or setting off to supply the sloping riverbank settlements along the St Lawrence. (These luxurious surroundings contrasted harshly with conditions at Allan's east-end Montreal cotton mill, which employed ten-year-old street waifs who didn't earn enough to buy shoes in winter.)

When the Macdonald government decided to honour its railway commitment to British Columbia, Sir Hugh Allan was the logical choice to head the construction syndicate. His lawyer, John J.C. Abbott (later Canada's fourth prime minister), incorporated the Canada Pacific Railway Company to take advantage of Ottawa's offer to grant the builder $30 million in cash and fifty million acres of land, plus an undertaking to extinguish Indian title along the way. Donald Smith was originally recruited as a member of Allan's syndicate to ensure the Hudson's Bay Company's co-operation in gaining use of its existing infrastructure through western Canada, but his name was not included in the final offering memorandum. To guarantee that he would be granted the Pacific railway charter under Ottawa's generous terms, Allan pledged secret subscriptions of $100,000 to Macdonald's 1872 campaign fund and even arranged for his Merchants' Bank to cancel $80,000 of Macdonald's personal debts.

The great Pacific Scandal that followed, one of the most thoroughly documented instances of bribery in the country's political history, involved more than $500,000. Its least subtle manifestation was the telegram Macdonald sent to John Abbott, the Allan lawyer, at the climax of the 1872 campaign: "I MUST HAVE ANOTHER TEN THOUSAND. WILL BE THE LAST TIME OF CALLING. DO NOT FAIL ME. ANSWER TODAY—J.A. MACDONALD." Abbott consulted with Allan and hastily replied: "DRAW ON ME FOR TEN THOUSAND DOLLARS." When the Montreal *Herald* published these and other incriminating documents, a royal commission was established to investigate the bribery allegations. It found the Tories guilty as charged. Macdonald had won the 1872 election with a dismal margin of only two seats, and his government seemed doomed—unless he could somehow retain Parliament's confidence. Macdonald quickly realized the fate of his administration hung on one vote, that of Donald Smith. "Upon you and the influence you can bring to bear," he wrote to the HBC executive, "may depend the fate of this administration."

Smith was in Fort Carlton, halfway from Fort Garry to Edmonton, on an inspection trip at the time, but immediately rushed back to Ottawa. He set a record of only five days returning to Fort Garry, six hundred miles to the east. Angus McKay, then a fifteen-year-old HBC apprentice, witnessed that mad dash across the Prairies. "We first noticed a cloud of dust on the big salt plain near Humbolt [*sic*]," he wrote in his journal. "Then we saw a buckboard, a Red River cart and a bunch of loose horses, driven by two men on horseback. When they met our freight train [of Red River carts], they stopped for a few minutes to ask questions while the men changed a tired horse for a fresh one, driving on again and leaving the tired one on the prairie. [Smith] was strapped crossways on his breast with wide strappings and onto the seat of the buckboard to prevent his falling out when asleep. It was the fastest journey ever made between Carlton and Winnipeg with horses."

Smith was in his seat when the Commons met on October 23, 1873. He hoped that Macdonald might take this occasion to grant Louis Riel the amnesty that had originally been promised and to pay back the $3,000 Smith had spent bribing the Métis leader and his followers during the 1870 Rebellion. The debt was long overdue, and Smith rightly maintained that he had been carrying out Ottawa's instructions, but had to pay the money out of his own pocket because there were no banking facilities in Red River at the time. The Prime Minister never disowned the debt, but he didn't honour it either. He was all too aware of how precarious the Conservatives' political situation was and that if word of any amnesty or payments to Riel leaked out, he would lose his remaining support in Orange Ontario.

The Prime Minister's cronies buzzed around Smith, trying to ensure his support, and eventually arranged a private meeting between the two men. Macdonald had been drinking for most of three days and took exaggerated offence when Smith calmly requested repayment of his loan and then advised the Prime Minister to confess his political sins and ask the country for forgiveness. Instead of trying to appease his western MP, Macdonald dared him to make the Riel bribe public, boasting with the false courage of the bottle that he could win Ontario in another election, no matter what Smith said about him. That barely coherent bombast was followed by a stream of woozy obscenities, as the Prime Minister worked himself up into red-faced ferment and finally passed out.

The performance didn't impress the puritanical Smith. He let it be known he would probably go against the administration but agreed to postpone his final decision until the night of the vote. Smith met with a sobered-up Prime Minister two days later, on November 4, and yet again asked for his Riel money back. Macdonald wearily agreed, had Smith write out an invoice, and promised he would be paid $3,367.50 the following morning. (Smith had characteristically added an interest charge.) The two men parted warily, as if they had not yet taken the full measure of one another.

The Commons session that evening was jammed with so many political ward heelers and lobbyists that they were crowded into the space on either side of the Speaker's dais. The busiest spot on Parliament Hill was the bar in the Commons basement, as MPs used any excuse to sneak away and toast their fortunes or drown their sorrows. *

At five minutes after one on that moon-washed autumn night, when the question on the government's amendment to the non-confidence motion was put, Smith finally rose to speak. The House of Commons hushed as its members tried to size up the enigmatic "member for the Hudson's Bay Company," the penthouse of his eyebrows masking any signal of his intentions. Barely four years removed from the Labrador wilderness, Smith was about to determine whether Canada's founding ministry would survive. He began hesitantly, as if suddenly aware of how far he had come and how much depended on his decision. He condemned the Liberal Opposition for establishing a case against the government on the basis of purloined letters and telegrams, defending the sanctity of private correspondence. He meandered on about Manitoba's need to have its own railway, then seemed to harden in his discourse by declaring that the Prime Minister had certainly not taken Sir Hugh Allan's money with any corrupt motive. That satisfied the Tory Whip, who led a troop of relieved Government benchers to the bar, where they lifted tumblers charged with champagne "To the health of Donald A." It wasn't long before they were chanting "Rule, Britannia!" and "God Save the Queen" — the echoes of their ribaldry drifting up to the Commons floor.

---

*There has never been anything unusual (then or now) in having drunken MPs on the floor of the Commons, but tactics in those days were slightly more crude. Whenever the sozzled members got excited, they would throw parliamentary papers (or, on one occasion, firecrackers) into the air, mimic roosters, dogs or bagpipes, perform jigs up and down the aisles — or just go to sleep. An inebriated James Domville, president of the Maritime Bank and MP for King's, New Brunswick, is on record in Hansard as having addressed the Commons with the fly of his pants open, and Colonel C.J. Campbell, the MP for Victoria County, Cape Breton, once prostrated himself at the feet of the Speaker, bellowing a drunken challenge for anyone in government, on Parliament Hill or from the whole universe to come and fight him.

There the mood had changed. Donald Smith had turned sour. "I would be most willing to vote confidence in the Government," he said, baiting the trap, "if I could do so conscientiously." Then, with that special brand of righteousness reserved for middle-aged Scots with long beards, he pronounced his verdict: "For the honour of the country, no government should exist that has a shadow of suspicion resting upon it; and for that reason, I cannot give it my support." A page hastily whipped down to the bar to inform the revellers: "Donald A. has gone over to the Grits." Members rushed back to vent their fury at the treachery of their colleague from Red River.

The Commons was adjourned without a recorded vote, but the government knew it was beaten and resigned the following afternoon. As Sir John A. Macdonald walked out of the chamber that momentous night, he turned to one of his cronies and remarked with bitter bite: "I could lick that man Smith quicker than hell could frizzle a feather." In the parliamentary basement, the Liberals now had their own bellies to the bar, singing "Sir John is dead and gone forever," to the tune of "My Darling Clementine."*

Behind Smith's switch in allegiances was a web of motives that became clear only in retrospect. Charles Tupper, in an 1877 speech at Orangeville, Ontario, described the HBC executive's 1873 tactics: "Mr. Smith was a representative of the Hudson's Bay Company and he had been pressing a claim on his Right Hon. friend [Macdonald] for public money; Sir John had been holding back, and Mr. Smith came to the conclusion that it would be just as well to jump the fence if there was to be a change of Government. But Mr. Smith was a canny man; he held back and sat on the fence and watched the course, certainly not in the interests of his country, because he did not want to jump too soon and find that he had jumped into a ditch. But, when he came to the conclusion that the Government was going out, he made the bolt,

---

*Ironically, Macdonald's last act before leaving office was to implement one of Smith's recommendations in his report on the Red River Rebellion: creation of a North West Mounted Police to rid the plains of American whisky pedlars and proclaim Canadian sovereignty. (In the summer of 1873, twenty-two Assiniboines were massacred by the rotgut traders in the Cypress Hills of what is now southeastern Alberta.) Their first commanding officer, Lieutenant-Colonel George French, head of the Canadian Militia Gunnery School at Kingston, treated his troops more as a cavalry regiment than a police force. That impression was heightened by their first uniforms: red jackets modelled on the British Army's red coats, cut to resemble those of Hussars, black breeches with red stripes as worn by the British cavalry, lances like those carried into battle by the doomed Light Brigade in the Crimean War, and pillbox hats held on with chinstraps—later replaced by Texas Ranger stetsons.

and he (Dr. Tupper) had no doubt but that he had had a great deal of reason since for congratulating himself on having jumped as he did." But beyond such strategic considerations was Smith's ambition to build the Pacific railway himself. In their wonderful *Lords of the Line*, popular historians David Cruise and Alison Griffiths unlock the mystery. "The key to Smith's actions most likely lay in the awarding of the Pacific railway contract, in which he had a clear personal interest. Certainly no one knew better than he the potential wealth of the northwest, and he wasn't anxious that the lush Red River territory be entrusted to the whims and self-interest of Hugh Allan. . . ." That imputing of motives rings true, but it doesn't do full justice to Smith's baser side. There was yet another reason for his betrayal of Macdonald.

By aligning his syndicate with Jay Cooke's Northern Pacific, Allan had virtually guaranteed that his Canada Pacific Railway Company would have to utilize an extension of the American promoter's railway from the international boundary to Winnipeg. Cooke had for years wanted to expand the Northern Pacific into Canada, and this would have been his ideal opportunity. But a competing syndicate, led by Smith and including his cousin George Stephen, had already applied for a railway charter to serve the link between the border town of Pembina and Winnipeg—just sixty miles away. Smith was also protecting his private investment in the Pembina venture.

In the 1874 election that followed, Smith ran as a Liberal supporting Alexander Mackenzie, the Sarnia stonemason who became Canada's second Prime Minister.* Smith's political antics had begun to concern London. The HBC Governor pointedly wrote to James Grahame, the Company's Canadian Chief Commissioner: "We are now simply a trading corporation and wish to confine ourselves to our own business, cultivating the most friendly relations with those in authority, but taking no side with one party or another. . . ." Smith paid no attention to such admonitions and won his seat with a 102-vote margin. At one meeting, local Tories, furious at his defection, pelted him with raw eggs until he was unrecognizable. "Few figures in political history apart from Benedict Arnold . . . have incurred the opprobrium directed at the member from Selkirk," noted the business historian Gustavus Myers.

---

*Mackenzie's background contributed to his reputation as Canada's most close-mouthed Prime Minister. While he was working as a stonemason, a hunk of cut stone weighing more than a ton dropped on his toes. He uttered not a sound—and during his five years in office said very little about anything important.

Back in Ottawa as one of Mackenzie's most influential advisers, Smith began to lobby for his Pembina charter. The Liberal Prime Minister had assumed the Public Works portfolio himself, determined to build the transcontinental railway as a government enterprise without increasing taxes or pledging incentives to greedy promoters.

At about this time, Smith's interest quickened in an awkwardly named relic of American railway speculation called the First Division of the St Paul and Pacific line. That preoccupation dated from his first meeting with James J. Hill, the Canadian-born entrepreneur from St Paul, Minnesota. The two men had tented together in 1870 when Smith was returning to Ottawa from settling the Red River Rebellion. They had jointly acquired the Red River Transportation Company—possibly the most profitable steamship line in North America.* Now that their shipping monopoly was threatened by the advent of railways, Hill came to Ottawa early in 1876 and stayed with Smith at the Bank of Montreal's residential "Cottage" on O'Connor Street. He had arrived late in the afternoon of St Patrick's Day in the vanguard of a fierce blizzard, and the two men talked for most of two days about what could be done. Their thoughts quickly turned to the First Division of the St Paul and Pacific, which had gone bankrupt and was being reorganized by a trustee, John S. Kennedy, and the line's receiver, Jesse P. Farley. The main bondholders were six hundred Dutch investors, headed by Johan Carp, who were owed $28 million. Hill knew they had become disillusioned by long-overdue payments and were open to offers. The two promoters agreed that Hill would obtain more details about the insolvent property, reach a realistic estimate of what salvage price the Dutch might accept, and put feelers out to the railway's receiver.

Smith had frequently travelled aboard the unfinished St Paul and Pacific on his way to and from Red River. Seldom out of bankruptcy, the ravaged company maintained the link between St Paul and Breckenridge with an increasingly decrepit railbed. By 1873, the right of way was littered with rotting ties and twisted remains of collapsed

---

*With their partners Norman Kittson and Captain Alexander Griggs, Hill and Smith had turned the Red River Transportation Company's monopoly into a formidable cash cow. Although it discounted HBC transportation invoices by one-third, helping to maintain the London firm's oligopoly in the area, the transportation company still turned such a huge profit that annual dividends of 80 percent were not unusual. One of Smith's critics calculated that regular freight charges along the Red River Transportation Company's three hundred miles of slack navigation cost customers double the rates paid for taking grain across the Atlantic and that freight could be sent the length of the Mississippi for half as much.

bridges. The tracks were a crazy-quilt of fifteen different types of rail, all made of iron instead of steel so that passage of a train made the whole rusty works tremble. Several stretches could be crossed only by handcar. James J. Hill's investigation revealed that despite its grotesque physical plant, the road was still an immensely valuable property. He discovered that an investment of only $5.8 million (most of which could be borrowed from the Bank of Montreal) would be enough not only to buy out the Dutch bondholders but also to complete the tracks to St Vincent, a town on the international boundary, which was the cut-in point for the 2.6-million-acre state grant that the woefully underfinanced railway had never been able to trigger. The road also had an exclusive charter to build up to the Canadian border. Because most of the land in the grants was in counties that were now well settled, Hill estimated that the bankrupt railway's real-estate assets alone were worth at least $20 million.

To complete the deal, Smith enlisted the cousin, George Stephen, he had first met while still a Factor in Labrador. Stephen had meanwhile become president of the Bank of Montreal and a dominant figure in Canadian finance. He was sufficiently interested to visit Amsterdam, where he obtained an option to buy the Dutch bonds at a third of their nominal value. He then arranged to have the Bank of Montreal underwrite a loan to take out both the railway's mortgage holders and the Netherlands group, while Smith, Hill and their partner Norman Kittson rolled their Red River Transportation Company shares over into railway stock. In 1878, the Smith-Hill-Stephen-Kittson partnership won clear title to the line and renamed it the St Paul, Minneapolis and Manitoba Railway. They put up only $283,000 in cash for what turned out to be a bonanza. Within a decade the railway would be worth $60 million and over the next thirty years Smith and his partners received an estimated $500 million in interest-bearing securities, not including dividends, from the once-defunct property.

The full potential of the renamed St Paul line could only be realized with completion of the Canadian link to Winnipeg. Prime Minister Mackenzie had promised to build that branch line to provide citizens of the newly incorporated province of Manitoba with outside access. Construction was painfully slow, but by the spring of 1878 the Pembina Branch was snaking the sixty miles to the American border. The first spike had been driven on September 29, 1877, in St Boniface when the Governor General, Lord Dufferin, and his wife had each driven a silver spike into the first tie. The viceregal couple had been entertained by Smith at Silver Heights, his estate outside Winnipeg.

*George Stephen*

"It is impossible to describe to you," Dufferin wrote to Mackenzie about that visit, "all that Donald Smith has done for our comfort. Had he been a great Duke in the old country receiving the Queen, he could not have made greater assertions, — in fact, I am quite vexed about it as the expense of his preparations must have been very considerable, and they quite exceed what we needed, for instance, he has built a large Reception Room, and two offices for the Colonel and myself, which are quite equal to those at Rideau, and in the minutest details has forgotten nothing. . . ."

Stephen had lobbied the Prime Minister hard to allow his St Paul syndicate to lease the new line, but Smith's participation in the project was a complicating factor. The Liberal leader knew that no undertaking with the Smith name attached to it would be approved by Sir John A. Macdonald and his Tories, who remained so angry with Smith that they left the House of Commons *en masse* whenever he rose to speak. When Mackenzie introduced the bill to lease the line on March 18, 1878, he not only left out Smith's name but also pointedly denied that Smith had any connection with the project. The Opposition Tories quickly turned the routine bill into a major issue, with Macdonald insisting that the legislation was a fraudulent measure because it would only "put money in [Smith's] own pocket."

Mackenzie used his Commons majority to ram the lease through, but it was vetoed by the Tory-dominated Senate. Smith informed the Prime Minister that if the roadbed could not be legally leased, his syndicate would be happy merely to rent running rights. When Mackenzie approved that compromise, Macdonald could no longer hold himself back. In a stunning attack on Smith, the Tory leader commended the Senate's action, "which would put a stop to their [the government's] bargain with the honorable member for Selkirk to make him a rich man and to pay him for his servile support."

Smith rose in the Commons the following afternoon (the last day of the session) to defend his honour. The House was all set to prorogue for a general election, but the Selkirk member's question of privilege halted the proceedings and turned Parliament into a rowdy day-care centre. When George Brown, founding editor of the Toronto *Globe* and at the time a Liberal senator, described the scene that followed as "the most disgraceful in the annals of the Canadian House of Commons," he was indulging in understatement. Members' shouts escalated from "liars" to "treacherous liars" and many cruder epithets that Hansard reporters chose to ignore. Just as the Commons was on the verge of bedlam, the sonorous knock of Black Rod, the parliamentary official whose entry signals termination of sessions, could be heard. The Speaker, trying to invite him in, as protocol demanded, could not make himself heard, so the poor man kept on knocking. "Finally . . . Black Rod entered," reported W.T.R. Preston, then a parliamentary page. "He bowed, as usual. His lips moved, but no sound reached the frantic House. The Speaker stood up and evidently made an announcement. He was not heard—the 'Faithful Commons' continued to shout at one another with unabated fury! Finally, with what dignity he could muster, the Speaker stepped down from the dais, the Sergeant-at-Arms shouldered the mace, and preceded by Black Rod, they slowly made their way to the lobby leading to the Senate. The Cabinet followed, and then as excited a mob as ever disgraced the House of Commons. . . ." Preston himself was caught up in the swaying, belligerent crowd and at one point found himself pushed against Smith, just as "Tory members reached out to strike his grey top hat."

As usual, Sir John A. Macdonald had the last word. The final insult recorded in Hansard during that stormy parliamentary sitting was attributed to Macdonald. "That fellow Smith," he declared, "is the biggest liar I ever met!"

The Liberal government's final official act was to grant Smith, Stephen and their partners the ten-year running rights on the Pembina

Branch line they had requested. It was soon connected with their St Paul, Minneapolis and Manitoba tracks, giving them a monopoly on western Canadian freight. In the election that followed, which easily returned Macdonald to power, the Tories singled out Smith as a special target. "Now, Sir John, if you want that prince of old scoundrels 'Smith' beaten, use your influence to get William Ogilvie to consent to run . . . ," advised John C. Schultz. "Donald Smith has I think lost just about the last vestige of character he ever possessed here, since the accounts of the closing scene of the House have come to hand. . . ." Smith's challenger turned out to be an even more formidable choice, Alexander Morris, who had been a minister in Macdonald's first administration and served as Manitoba's first chief justice. When Morris pointed out his opponent's obvious conflict of interest between what was best for land sales in Manitoba and best for him as one of the proprietors of the St Paul, Smith reacted with a dose of righteousness improbable even for him. With a straight face he explained that "the primary object of the railway was for the benefit of Manitoba and not for the purpose of making money."

Realizing that his re-election bid was in serious trouble, Smith tried to enlist the organizational assistance of J.H. McTavish, a popular HBC Factor, but London head office firmly directed Winnipeg to "keep the Company neutral . . . the Fur Trade officers must take no part in the election as such." Smith attempted to protect himself by pretending he was politically independent,* pledging that he had "no favour to ask and nothing personal to desire from any Government" and would "support only such measures as are conducive to the advancement of Manitoba. . . ." Just in case this high moral ground might prove too slippery, Smith transferred several gangs of Métis who were on the Company's payroll to his riding and ordered twenty-six HBC families to be temporarily moved into his jurisdiction, then bribed them to vote for him. Even these outrageous manoeuvres barely turned the trick. He won the election by a hair's-breadth margin of nine votes. On the night of his modest victory, as his cheering supporters led him through Winnipeg's main streets, the salute guns of Fort Garry boomed happily in the background. Smith was magnanimous in his triumph: he donated $750 to the Knox Church Building Fund.

A petition charging Smith with bribery and corruption was immediately filed, but when it was heard before Mr Justice Louis

---

*Which, in a way, he was—his sole allegiance was to himself.

Bétournay in the Manitoba Court of Queen's Bench, Smith was confirmed in his seat. That verdict was tarnished by the fact that Smith held a four-thousand-dollar mortgage on Bétournay's house, granted at highly favourable terms. When the decision was over-turned, a by-election was called for September 10, 1880. Smith ran as an independent, bolstering his political stance with bribes that to-talled more than $30,000. But the voters refused to be bought. Smith was decisively beaten. His subsequent comment to James Cole, an HBC Factor who had acted as his campaign manager, easily ranks as Canadian history's longest snort. "I am sorry to say," Smith com-plained, "that a majority of the intelligent electorate of my late Selkirk constituency have, in the exercise of their undoubted privilege and the right to choose the most fit and proper person available for the purpose of representing them in the Dominion Parliament, seen fit to reject my own humble, not hitherto unacceptable person."

"The damn voters," shot back the more succinct Cole, "took your money and voted against you!"

"You," intoned Smith, "have properly expressed the situation."

HIS POLITICAL CAREER TEMPORARILY ABANDONED, Smith could concen-trate on his long-standing ambition to be a fiscal animator—and personal beneficiary—of building a railway across Canada. His in-volvement with that project was to be the central public accomplish-ment of his life, forever perpetuated in the history books by the photograph of his driving in the last spike. Because it was the CPR that finally destroyed the HBC's dominance in western Canada, its con-struction, at least as briefly summarized in the pages that follow, is part of the Company's history. Smith had resigned his post as the HBC's Land Commissioner in 1879, but he continued buying up stock. By 1883 he had become the HBC's dominant shareholder and a year later was appointed, along with Sandford Fleming, to head a Cana-dian subcommittee that controlled the Company's overseas operation—all this before the CPR had been completed.

The building of that railway probably ranks as Canada's greatest achievement. "A new current was in motion within the mainstream of human history," wrote Ralph Allen in his evocative *Ordeal by Fire*. "The railways opened up a new caravan trail for the restless, the driven, and the questing and led them to the heartland of Canada."

By 1880, all the elements of Smith's career seemed to combine in pushing him to join his cousin George Stephen in becoming a decisive figure in the railway's realization. A fringe benefit of the Minnesota railway venture had been to provide Stephen with an opportunity to view the West at first hand. He had travelled over the St Paul's rickety tracks in the autumn of 1877 and was then driven north to Silver Heights, where Smith and Stephen discussed the railway project's future. "The immensity of the treeless Prairie landscape affected him deeply, indeed disoriented him, as it does most people when they see it for the first time," W.L. Morton wrote of Stephen's reaction. "He could at last imagine what Smith had all along been telling him—that people would come to this emptiness, that they would survive and prosper, and that the railway would be the instrument of this population—that it would bring the population to its lands, and those people would provide it with its future earnings."

Because the revelation of his association with the project would have killed its chances, Smith was deliberately kept in the background, but it was his determination that proved essential in financing the epic venture. He had roused Stephen's interest in both railroading and the great North-West, and though the cousins both tended to hoard their emotions too much to develop an easy friendship, theirs was an enduring partnership.

Stephen was unassuming in private and invisible in public. He loathed the circuitous mouthings of politicians but knew how to rent them—and occasionally buy them. He believed devoutly that man's salvation lay in hard work and besting one's enemies. His only recreation was fishing, and he owned the rights on two rivers to prove it, the Matapédia (later sold to the Ristigouche Club in New Brunswick) and the Mitis, where he regularly cast a most beautiful fly. He was a tall man, thin, with a hangdog look and brooding eyes that, complemented by his droopy moustache, endowed his face with a cast of melancholy wisdom. His position as the Bank of Montreal's president together with his experience in reviving the St Paul line made him a natural choice when the newly re-elected Sir John A. Macdonald began his search for a syndicate to build the long-delayed transcontinental railway. "This was the climate in which the CPR Syndicate was eventually formed," noted Pierre Berton in his lively history. "For all the controversy served to illuminate one fact: there was now available a remarkable group of successful men who had experience in both railway building and high finance. In the summer of 1880, the Macdonald government was looking for just such a group. It was John Henry Pope, the homely and straightforward minister of agriculture, who had first drawn his Prime Minister's attention to the St Paul associates.

" 'Catch them,' he said, 'before they invest their profits.' "

And "catch them" Macdonald did, with as generous a mark-up as was ever offered any businessman not selling snake-oil. According to W.T.R. Preston, it was "the most stupendous contract ever made under responsible government in the history of the world." To complete the transcontinental tracks from North Bay, Ontario, to Port Moody, at the head of Burrard Inlet in British Columbia, within ten years, the syndicate was granted an eventual $206 million in cash, subsidies and stock guarantees in addition to 25 million acres in land grants, with the shortfall in fertile acreage made up in other regions.*

According to John Gallagher, a historical researcher, when all the tax benefits and value of the land exchanges are taken into account, the CPR received gifts from the country worth $106,300,000. The CPR's authorized history, written by its publicity manager, John Murray Gibbon, was called *Steel of Empire*; a more appropriate title might have been *Steal of Empire*.

The new Canadian Pacific Railway syndicate, granted its charter on October 21, 1880, included George Stephen, James J. Hill, J.S. Kennedy (the New York banker who had acted as trustee of the St Paul), Duncan McIntyre, who controlled the Canada Central Railway running between Ottawa and North Bay, Sir Stafford Northcote, twenty-second Governor of the Hudson's Bay Company, and Richard Bladworth Angus, yet another Scot with a nose for money, who had been named the Bank of Montreal's general manager when he was only thirty-eight.†

Building a Pacific railway was the dominant issue in Canada's fledgling Parliament for thirty years. One CPR lobbyist boasted that whenever the Speaker's bell rang for a division, there were almost always more MPs in his apartment, swilling free liquor and puffing complimentary cigars, than anywhere else in Ottawa. The CPR directors dispensed bountiful "bonifications," as they preferred to call

---

*Between 1893 and 1930, the CPR sold 23 million acres worth $178 million.

†Unlike most of his confrères, Angus rejected the offer of a knighthood—twice—though he was a founder of the prestigious Mount Royal Club and his neo-Romanesque home was ample enough to eventually house McGill University's Conservatory of Music. His great hobby was cultivating orchids. One of his daughters married B.T. Rogers, founder of British Columbia Sugar, amalgamating what became two great Canadian fortunes. Angus, along with Stephen and Smith, dominated the Bank of Montreal for most of four decades, raising its asset base from $38 million to $350 million. Angus was its general manager from 1869 to 1879 and president from 1910 to 1913; Stephen served as vice-president and president between 1873 and 1881; Smith occupied the same positions from 1882 to 1905.

*William Van Horne*

them, to smooth parliamentary obstacles. Most of these bribes were in the form of CPR share options deposited in secret bank accounts.*

From the beginning the railway was difficult to finance. Most of the government's largess was scheduled to kick in only after completion targets had been met, and most sophisticated international investors had been disillusioned too often to gamble again on North American railway bonds. Stephen at first could not get any stock exchange to list the CPR shares, and by December of 1881, Stephen and Smith were already forced to borrow on their own signatures $300,000 in working capital from the Bank of Montreal.

That same month, the railway's prospects brightened considerably with the recruitment of William Cornelius Van Horne as the CPR's general manager in charge of constructing the rail line. His assignment was to lay twenty-nine hundred miles of track through a sparsely explored land mass, across the Rocky Mountains and around Lake Superior, stretches that even daring railroaders considered impass-

---

*At the CPR's incorporation, the company directors sold to themselves at least 200,000 common shares at twenty-five cents each. Stephen's holding of 31,000 shares later produced a net dividend income (in equivalent 1990 dollars) of $3.9 million a year, and Smith's was at least as large.

able. During the 1881 construction season, only 161 miles of road across the flat prairie had been completed, and the entrenched staff of British engineers resented the intrusion of the fat Yankee with the big cigars who cursed like a spike driver and seemed immune to sensible objections to his outrageous demands. "We did not like him when he first came to Winnipeg as general boss of everything and everybody," J.H.E. Secretan, a CPR surveyor, complained to his diary. "His ways were not our ways . . . he told me that if he could only teach the section men to run a transit, he wouldn't have a single damn engineer about the place."

Van Horne boasted that he would lay five hundred miles of track in 1882. By train and steamer or on horseback he ranged the Prairies—firing, hiring, ordering people and obstructions about. The snow had not left the ground when ten thousand men and seventeen hundred teams of horses began to push the rails westward, advancing two, three, and even four miles a day—once as much as twenty miles in three days. By the end of the 1882 season, 417 miles of track had been completed. When construction was held up by an engineer's refusal to drive his locomotive over a swaying trestle, Van Horne climbed into the cab himself.

"Well, if you ain't afraid of getting killed, with all your money, I ain't afraid either," reasoned the reassured driver.

"We'll have a double funeral—at my expense, of course!" Van Horne shouted back across the lurching engine as it successfully pirouetted across the deep divide.

Even tougher to cross were the two hundred miles along the north shore of Lake Superior. It is a land drowning in its own juices, with muskeg, quicksand and matted spruce forests making any kind of orderly traverse impossible. One particularly bitter stretch of muskeg cost $750,000 to cross, swallowing the tracks seven times along with three locomotives. To the east, between Sudbury and Cartier, a lake had to be lowered ten feet to secure a foundation for tracks, and three miles of curve were needed to go around Jackfish Bay, although the straight jump across the water was less than half a mile.

The unexpected ruggedness of the terrain rapidly drained the company's treasury. The normally placid Stephen was beside himself with worry and at one meeting with Smith despondently predicted the railway would go bust. "It may be that we must *succumb*," Smith calmly replied, "but that must not be as long as we individually have a dollar." The Macdonald government grudgingly advanced another loan of $30 million, but within six months Van Horne sent Smith a coded cable with the blunt message: "HAVE NO MEANS PAYING

*CPR tracklayers and boarding cars in which they ate and slept*

WAGES, PAY CAR CAN'T BE SENT OUT. UNLESS YOU SEND IMMEDIATE RELIEF, WE MUST STOP." Stephen begged Macdonald for an additional $22.5 million, and even though the Prime Minister at first told the CPR president he might as well ask "for the planet Jupiter as for more money," a bill for the further extension of funds was hastily presented to the Commons. The Liberal benches exploded with outrage, their critic charging that for six months a year the new railway would become "an idle, ice-bound snow-covered route," while party leader Edward Blake predicted its mountain section "would not pay for the grease on the axles."

The Tories finally rammed the extra loan through, but caucus demanded a dividend for their support. It took the form of humiliating Donald Smith by forcing him to agree, the story went, that he would run for Parliament in a future election not merely for the Conservatives, the party he had betrayed in 1873, but as a personal admirer of Sir John. As the CPR's troubles became more serious, Smith had emerged more and more into public view. "He was the great controlling spirit in all the principal business of the syndicate," Preston wrote of Smith, who officially became a CPR director in 1883 and remained the most influential member of the board's executive committee for the next thirty years. He was more or less reconciled with Macdonald over a bottle of Scotch at a 1883 meeting arranged by Stephen. In his typical self-centred way, Smith reported that the Prime Minister felt better for it: "I know—without his saying it—that he is today a much happier man."

Stephen hurried off to London and by pledging Smith's and his own personal credit was able to negotiate a £77,000 loan, which would tide them over until the government's guarantees were formally approved. "Once again the partnership of company and government, the partnership of Donald Smith, John A. Macdonald, and himself, had triumphed," Donald Creighton wrote of this moment in *The Old Chieftain,* the second volume of his magnificent Macdonald biography. "They were all Scotsmen, all Highlanders, all, ultimately, sons of the same river valley. . . . He remembered the river itself, winding on-ward, peat-black between the high banks, and brown, like old ale, over the shallows. He remembered the great rock which had given the Clan Grant its rallying-place and its battle slogan. The rock of defiance. Craigellachie. . . . He took a telegraph form, addressed it to Donald Smith in Montreal, and wrote a message of three words only: 'Stand fast, Craigellachie!' "

Less than a year after the $22.5-million bailout, the CPR was on the verge of bankruptcy again. Stephen and Smith borrowed yet another $650,000 from the Bank of Montreal. By March 1885, they were pleading for another one million dollars to provide Van Horne with construction funds for one more month, but even their Bank of Montreal credit facilities had been exhausted, and to try tapping another bank would have triggered panic. The desperate situation prompted from Smith a totally unexpected retort: a short, declaratory sentence. "It's to the government, or to the penitentiary," he told Stephen, who had lapsed into his customary silence.

It was, of course, to the government that the CPR turned because, as one of the railway directors correctly pointed out, "The day the CPR busts, the Conservative Party busts the day after." Whatever his personal feelings, Macdonald didn't dare ask his followers to approve yet another loan. He was on notice that at least three cabinet ministers would resign if he allowed the insatiable railway to feed at the public trough one more time. At a dispirited directors' meeting, Smith and Stephen agreed to see what credit they might raise from their personal possessions. Stephen stood quietly by in the study of his $3-million house as evaluators assessed his paintings, statuary, cutlery, furniture, linen and imported piano. But the CPR president didn't have to surrender these luxuries. His railway was saved by Louis Riel.

WILLIAM VAN HORNE LATER CLAIMED THE CPR should erect a monument to the Métis leader, and he was right. Since fleeing Canada, he had spent time in a Montreal lunatic asylum, become a naturalized

*Chief Poundmaker (left) and Gabriel Dumont*

American citizen, and taught in a Montana mission school. When settlers along the South Saskatchewan River became radicalized by Ottawa's insensitivity to their demands, they joined forces with local Indians and Métis who invited Riel to champion their cause. Once back on Canadian soil, he declared, "The time has now come to rule this country or perish in the attempt." Riel's exile had transformed him from the dreamy statesman of Red River into a hectoring, hard-edged prophet, preoccupied with theological theories. Riel spent little time on political or military strategy, formulating instead new catechisms and decreeing such oddities as new names not derived from pagan gods for the days of the week. He declared Bishop Ignace Bourget of Montreal his new Pope and himself a Messiah.

The rebellion, which was backed by Big Bear's and Poundmaker's Cree warriors, grown aggressive with the frustrations of lost land and impending starvation, as well as the Métis demanding aboriginal title similar to that granted their Manitoba cousins in 1870, was masterminded by Gabriel Dumont. Grandson of a voyageur, illiterate yet fluent in six languages, a crack shot, permanent chief of the buffalo hunt and head of the first local government between Manitoba and British Columbia, Dumont was a worthy predecessor of Ernesto (Che) Guevara, the Argentine revolutionary who perfected modern guerrilla tactics as Fidel Castro's lieutenant. Appeals to Ottawa having been either ignored or rejected, Riel set up a provisional government at Batoche, a fording place on the South Saskatchewan River thirty-seven miles southwest of Prince Albert, and appointed Dumont his adjutant-general. In a preliminary skirmish at nearby Duck Lake, Dumont's Métis easily routed a North West Mounted Police detachment from Fort Carlton, killing twelve constables and several volunteers. A dozen whites were massacred at Frog Lake; Battleford was ransacked by Chief Poundmaker; local HBC posts were looted and burned; lodges of Assiniboines were already marching east; and the powerful Blackfoot nation was threatening to join in.

In Ottawa, Stephen and Smith were back in their customary pose, palms outstretched for yet another government handout. The CPR had run out of payroll money and notes worth $7 million would be maturing by June 1885. Failure to redeem them would push the company into the bankruptcy courts. In British Columbia, a band of three hundred strikers demanding back wages was being held at bay by the NWMP, and the company's stock was in a free-fall on the New York and London exchanges. On March 26, Macdonald gave Stephen the hard news that the federal treasury was shut tight to any further CPR grants or guarantees.

That also happened to be the date of the battle at Duck Lake, and as word of the massacre was flashed to the Dominion's capital, everything changed. Having barely prevented the Métis takeover of Manitoba in 1870, Macdonald knew he had to move fast or the Métis leader might have the entire North-West up in arms. Yet there seemed to be no practical way of enforcing the federal power; Riel might as well have been on Mars.

William Van Horne, who was in Ottawa to backstop Smith and Stephen, announced that if the government put two batteries of men in his care, he would guarantee to have them on the Qu'Appelle River, next to Riel's encampments, in twelve days. Forty-eight hours after the Prime Minister agreed to the daring scheme, CPR trains were pulling into Ottawa to load the soldiers. Singing "The Girl I Left Behind Me," the men marched to the station for one of the most remarkable train rides in Canadian history. Macdonald had been right. There *was* no practical way to move the militia west; the railway's Superior link was incomplete, with four gaps totalling eighty-six miles yet to be filled in. Much of that country was nearly impassable for lone hunters; to move more than three thousand men with supplies, ammunition and heavy artillery pieces across these quagmires seemed impossible.

*Canadian soldiers travelling west to put down the North West Rebellion, 1885*

Van Horne routed trains across temporary rails laid only hours earlier and at each end of steel loaded the troops into hastily fashioned freight sleds, feeding the soldiers steak and roast turkey to keep up their spirits. Fifteen years earlier it had taken Colonel Wolseley ninety-six days to move his volunteer army from Toronto to Red River. Van Horne's army made it in seven, and two days after that they were safely on the banks of the Qu'Appelle. By mid-April, the entire force was in place except for one Halifax battalion, and the troops moved into battle. Dumont's brilliant hit-and-run tactics at Fish Creek had won the initial encounters, but only two hundred Métis sharpshooters remained to face the full onslaught of more than eight hundred soldiers at Batoche. Riel had refused to heed Dumont, who had advised continued guerrilla warfare. Instead, the Métis were placed in siege formation; without any artillery, they had no chance. The four-day battle ended with Dumont fleeing to Montana while Riel surrendered to three Mounted Police scouts.*

True to form, the Hudson's Bay Company reacted to the battle by trying to exploit its profit potential. Immediately after the Duck Lake

---

*The Métis leader was at first to be taken to Winnipeg for trial, but when he reached the CPR main line at Moose Jaw his party was rerouted to Regina for what, it was explained, were judicial reasons. The real reason was that under Manitoba law, prisoners had the right to demand half the jury be French-speaking. The Northwest Territories, where Regina was located, had no such provision.

massacre, the Company ostentatiously placed itself at the disposal of the Dominion authorities and assured Minister of Militia and Defence Adolphe Caron that it would provision his forces in the battle area. Trade Commissioner Joseph Wrigley set the tone of the HBC's patriotic contribution when he sent an urgent letter to Chief Factor Archibald McDonald at Fort Qu'Appelle, the field force's main jumping-off point. "All supplies furnished by you to the Military Expedition," he ordered, "must be charged at wholesale prices . . . get receipts!" By the end of hostilities, the Company submitted bills for $2 million, which included a $96,000 profit. The HBC then claimed a further $207,115.84 for damaged buildings and stolen furs but collected only $163,768.54.

In gratitude to the nascent railway for transporting the troops west, Parliament voted to authorize the guarantee of a temporary $500,000 loan. It wasn't much, but it was enough to save the line. An impatient creditor was about to push the company into receivership. When Van Horne and a group of CPR executives got the news, they went wild. "We tossed up chairs to the ceiling; we tramped on desks; I believe we danced on tables. I do not fancy that any of us knows what occurred, and no one who was there can ever remember anything except loud yells of joy and the sound of things breaking." Soon afterwards Parliament guaranteed most of a final $35-million issue of mortgage bonds,* and Stephen hurried over to London where Lord Revelstoke, head of Barings, the famous merchant banking firm, purchased the balance.

Because Smith was forced by political circumstances to stay under cover during much of the CPR's construction, it was Stephen and Van Horne who got most of the public credit for the project's completion. But a few years later before a London audience, Sir Charles Tupper, who as Macdonald's minister of finance had been in the centre of the bargaining, declared that "the Canadian Pacific Railway would have no existence to-day, notwithstanding all that the Government did to support that undertaking, had it not been for the indomitable pluck and energy and determination, both financially and in every other respect, of Sir Donald Smith."

CHOSEN TO HAMMER IN THE CPR'S LAST SPIKE, Smith had travelled west aboard his private railway car, *Matapedia*, as part of a small train that

---

*At this crucial moment, Smith reportedly presented Lady Macdonald with a necklace worth $200,000 to influence her husband to grant the new loan. Stephen later confirmed the "bonification" but stoutly maintained it was "a personal gift."

included Van Horne's *Saskatchewan*, a baggage car and the engine. As they puffed across the country, crews were racing to lay the final links through Kicking Horse Pass. The rails from east and west were due to abut at Eagle Pass, a forlorn spot in the Monashee Mountains that Van Horne had named Craigellachie, after the clan stronghold of Smith's and Stephen's ancestors in Moray.

In the United States, comparable last-spike ceremonies had inevitably included fireworks, marching bands, extravagant speechifying, free liquor for construction crews and gold-plated spikes. At the last-spike ceremony of the first transcontinental U.S. railway at Promontory, Utah, two gold and two silver spikes had been driven into polished laurel cross-ties. Telegraph offices along the line were manned, their specially wired keys left open so that an account of the hammer blows could be heard across the country. In contrast, the Craigellachie celebration was to be a very Canadian occasion with no pomp and little ceremony. A discarded boxcar had been set aside to serve as a temporary railway station. From the Pacific side arrived a mixed work train, and a small party of labourers gathered to watch the final spike being driven home. Lord Lansdowne, then Governor General, had commissioned a silver spike for the occasion, but Van Horne was his usual practical self. "The last spike," he decreed, "will be just as good an iron one as there is between Montreal and Vancouver, and anyone who wants to see it driven will have to pay full fare."

On the misty morning of November 7, 1885, Major A.B. Rogers, who had found the pass for the railway through the Selkirk Mountains, held the tie bar under the final rail in place for the ceremonial finish. Smith's first feeble blow merely turned the designated spike's head, bending it. Roadmaster Frank Brothers yanked it out, replaced it with a new one, and Smith carefully tapped it home. Alexander Ross, the hunchback photographer from Winnipeg, took his famous shots, but except for a thin cheer there was little rejoicing. The only sound that reverberated in that historic canyon was the thump of Smith's maul. For a long moment there was silence, as if those present were remembering all the anguish that had led to this moment. "It seemed," recalled Sir Sandford Fleming, the CPR director who had first suggested the practicability of a transcontinental railway twenty-five years earlier, "as if the act now performed had worked a spell on all present. Each one appeared absorbed in his own reflections."

Smith said nothing. Van Horne gruffly allowed that "the work has been done well in every way." But it was the conductor of the little train, now cleared to head due west, who pronounced the ceremony's

*Donald Smith hammers in the last spike, November 7, 1885*

most dramatic line when he shouted: "All aboard for the Pacific!"*

It was a moment that changed Canadian history. Louis Riel, whose two rebellions had unintentionally opened up the West, was hanged for high treason in Regina nine days later, clearing the way for prairie settlement. The closed world so jealously guarded by the Hudson's Bay Company for two centuries was now irrevocably breached. The spider's web of waterways and prairie trails, worn out

*The engine that pulled the train west was scrapped and the *Matapedia* burned on her trucks at Princeton, B.C., in 1925, but Van Horne's private car has been preserved by the Canadian Railroad Historical Association. The maul used by Smith to pound in the last spike was last seen in the basement of his Montreal house being used to break up coal lumps for the furnace. There is considerable controversy about the fate of the last spike, but in a letter to the author dated March 10, 1989, the present Lord Strathcona explained what happened: "The last spike was an ordinary nail and is still in place. The 'one-from-last' spike was bent and pulled out. Small pieces were cut out and incorporated into spike-shaped diamond brooches for Lady Strathcona, Lady Shaughnessy, and the wife of the Governor-General. In the Shaughnessy one, an emerald has been put in place of iron. We still have a slightly larger brooch with iron disc. The 'one-from-last' spike, with pieces cut out, was presented by me to the CPR at a centenary ceremony on condition it was put on display. It is on permanent loan to the Transport Museum in Ottawa, probably still sitting on a teak block made by me." Craigellachie itself never of the wilderness by decades of Red River carts hauling goods from Fort Garry to Edmonton, from Qu'Appelle to Battleford, and on westward to Red Deer Forks and all the way to Peace River Junction, had been rendered obsolete in a day. The great HBC installations at Fort Carlton and Fort Pitt shrank to inconsequence.

By throwing most of his energies into financing the CPR instead of enlisting the HBC's London board to sponsor or at least propose a joint venture for the railway through its former territory, Smith threw away the Company's future as a major player in the evolution of Canada's modern economy. "The Canadian Pacific Railway," Michael Bliss pointed out in his *Northern Enterprise*, "was created by westerners and fur traders. But not by the Hudson's Bay Company. The fur-trading concern was not able to maintain the monopoly it gained in 1821 or use its advantages to diversify into new lines. . . . New men, some of whom began as pipsqueak fur traders challenging the mighty Company, became the key to the Canadian Pacific—in alliance with one of the HBC's own former Factors. The former fur traders organized the CPR syndicate and built the road after central Canadian capitalists had bungled the job and given up. They succeeded without the help of the Hudson's Bay Company, and by their success they put it permanently in the CPR's shadow."

The first scheduled transcontinental left Montreal for Port Moody on June 28, 1886. Its engine was draped with flowing silk ribbons as the Pacific Express pulled out of Dalhousie Square Station to cheers and a fifteen-gun salute. It completed the 2,907-mile journey in 139 hours, just over five and a half days. Once it became fully operational, the CPR plugged Canada into world trade. The Silks—non-stop express trains hurtling eastward from Vancouver—provided a link for consignments of Oriental textiles dispatched from Hong Kong and Siam to Montreal and on to London. The dream of a North West Passage had been achieved at last—even if it was a century late and over land instead of water.

---

prospered and was all but abandoned after the Second World War. Its tiny train station was closed, though location of the last-spike ceremony was landscaped for a 1985 centennial re-enactment. The CPR did not bother to maintain the site, and in January of 1990, the railway company withheld permission for the final run of its last transcontinental passenger train to pull in at Craigellachie. Told they couldn't stop, the crew decided to throw a wreath off the train at the appropriate spot. But when the engineer slowed down, he forgot to notify the rest of the crew, and nothing happened. "They didn't tell us they were going to let us throw it off," explained a befuddled employee. If Paris was worth a mass, Craigellachie was worth a stop—but no one at the CPR cared.

AN EXHAUSTED GEORGE STEPHEN retired to England and turned the CPR over to Van Horne, who transformed it into an integrated transportation system, building grain elevators, hotels and steamships, as well as infusing the railway with the same gusto that had allowed him to build it in the first place. He later threw railways across Cuba and Guatemala but his first loyalty was to the CPR. "Building that railroad," he said on the day he renounced his American citizenship, "would have made a Canadian out of the German Emperor." *

On the way back from the last-spike ceremony, Van Horne had sprung a surprise on Smith. Without the elder man's knowledge, a spur line had been built from Winnipeg to his country house at Silver Heights. Smith and his party of railway executives were so busy talking no one paid any attention when the engine was being driven in reverse until they were almost pulling up to his house. "Now, there's a very neat place," Smith remarked, looking increasingly puzzled. ". . . who is it that has Aberdeen cattle like that? I thought I was the only one. This is really very strange . . . I must be going crazy; I've lived here many years and I've never noticed another place so exactly like Silver Heights." The mystery was explained when the conductor called the stop: "Silver Heights!" For once, Smith was overwhelmed. Proud of his homestead, he had raised a small herd of buffalo there and entertained four governors general. Smith could never do enough for his visitors. When the Marquess of Lorne, the Queen's son-in-law then Canada's Governor General, came to visit, the façades of Silver Heights' main buildings were transformed into a copy of Inveraray Castle, the viceroy's ancestral home.

Success of the railway had converted the trio of capitalist desperados who had built and financed it into high-Establishment figures. Queen Victoria honoured Stephen with a baronetcy while Smith and

---

*One of Van Horne's favourite ploys was to test future employees with his cigar trick. When a firm of cut-rate tobacconists had capitalized on his fame by calling a five-cent brand the "Van Horne," he ordered several boxes of the leafy horrors, removed their bands, and mixed them with expensive perfectos in his humidor. Prospective employees, wishing to acknowledge his reputation as a connoisseur, would inhale the tarry mixture, then ecstatically compliment him on the "delightful aroma." They could only smile icily at Van Horne's crude guffaw that followed his explanation. He once hired a man mainly because he had butted one of the dud cigars after his first whiff and demanded: "How much does the stable boy charge you for these things?" During Van Horne's final illness, his doctors limited him to three cigars a day. He meekly agreed. But by next morning he had a box of specially rolled two-foot-long perfectos brought to his bedside, and so puffed contentedly the prescribed three a day, four hours each, until he died on September 11, 1915.

Van Horne were dubbed Knight Commanders of the Order of St Michael and St George. By 1887, Smith was named the Bank of Montreal's president, having become one of its dominant share-holders, second only to Sir William C. Macdonald.* Smith ran for Parliament as a Sir John A. Macdonald supporter in the 1887 election and sat as a largely quiescent MP for the next nine years. During that period, he took some time out to savour his accomplishments and become a significant philanthropist. He donated at least $2.5 million to McGill University, of which he became the chancellor, directing that some of the funds be used to provide for the admission of women.† Together with Stephen, he financed the building of the Royal Victoria Hospital in Montreal and donated two ships to Dr Wilfred Grenfell's mission in Labrador.

To display his wealth and influence properly, Smith built a mansion on two properties at the corner of Fort and Dorchester streets. The exterior was brownstone, brought from the Ontario Credit Valley, and the front door opened onto a magnificent three-storey, $50,000 mahogany staircase, carved by artisans who dovetailed all the parts so that not a single nail was used in its construction. The second-floor ballroom was overlooked by a marble balcony to accommodate the musicians. Smith understood little about painting, but his private collection included works by Raphael, Titian, Gainsborough, Reynolds, Romney, Constable and Millais. The dining-room opened into a garden for summer receptions attended by more than two thousand neck-craners.

Below stairs and out of hearing was a row of eight rooms for more than a dozen maids and flunkeys, including an English butler, inevitably named James. Fitted more by temperament than by birth for the aristocratic life, Smith ruled his household with humourless mastery. Once, while he was eating breakfast with Dr Grenfell, he watched the lamp under the hot-water kettle falter and die. When the missionary wanted to relight it, Smith stopped him and angrily summoned the butler. "Remember, James," he said, "you have only certain duties to perform. This is one. Never, under any circumstances, let such an omission occur again."

Smith was a snob to the point of keeping a private guest tally

---

*Macdonald was a Prince Edward Islander who had amassed a fortune selling tobacco during the American Civil War.

†In his honour, McGill's first eight female graduates, who received their Bachelor of Arts degrees in 1888, called themselves the "Donaldas."

categorizing his visitors according to their social rank. The impressive roll call included a future king and queen of England, a prince and princess, eight dukes, seven marquises, twenty-one earls, six viscounts, six governors general, seven prime ministers, twenty-seven provincial premiers, four archbishops, seventeen bishops, fourteen chief justices, twenty-nine supreme court judges, thirty-one mayors and fifty-eight generals. The tally even separated this last group into forty-seven generals of the Imperial Army and eleven commanders of colonial troops. The future king and queen were George V and Queen Mary, who came to Montreal as the Duke and Duchess of Cornwall and York. On that occasion, Smith not only refurnished their rooms but had a special balcony built off the second floor so that the royal couple might have a better view of the fireworks display lighting up the top of Mount Royal in their honour.*

Through Smith's involvement with the building of the CPR he had become a significant figure on the world's financial stage, and in his corporate dealings he now reverted to concentrating his wiles and energies on the Hudson's Bay Company. Within three years of the last-spike ceremony he would become the Company's Deputy Governor and, less than twelve months later, its Governor.

---

*According to Freeman Clowery, the former archivist at the Bank of Montreal, Lady Strathcona presented the Duchess with a spray of maple leaves fashioned of gold, diamonds and pearls that had been made by Henry Birks & Sons for $1,600.

*Red River carts with furs at Calgary, 1888*

*Lord Strathcona, Canada's High Commissioner to the United Kingdom*

# CHAPTER 7

# CANADA IN A SWALLOW-TAIL COAT

*Becoming a peer of the realm was no trifling matter. So Smith did what he always did on such watershed occasions. He remarried Isabella. The secret ceremony . . . reunited the bride and groom (then seventy-seven) for the fourth and final time.*

DURING THE TROUBLED WINTER of 1895–96, there were whispers that Donald Smith would become Canada's sixth Prime Minister. Mackenzie Bowell, the fusty Ontario Orangeman who occupied the nation's top political office at the time, governed with a degree of incompetence that decisively distinguished him among the uneven quartet who succeeded Sir John A. Macdonald. In his bumbling way of dealing with nearly every issue threatening the still fragile Dominion, Bowell demonstrated an unerring instinct for his own jugular. His inability to manage the ordinary business of government, much less such politically charged issues as the Manitoba Schools Question, prompted seven ministers, half his cabinet, to walk out and demand a new leader.

Smith, who had by then been the loyal Tory member for Montreal West for most of a decade, was immediately nominated for the job. "There is one man, and one man alone," declared Sam Hughes, MP for the Ontario riding of Victoria North, "who can save the Liberal-Conservative Party from falling to pieces, and also who can command the respect and confidence of the whole country, and that is Sir Donald A. Smith." The cry was taken up by others, but the Hudson's

Bay Company Governor, ever faithful to his creed of self-advancement, saw no point in tying his future to the leadership of a party that had the smell of a dying political movement. Still, he used the occasion to help manoeuvre circumstances that would help him realize what was, to his way of imperialistic thinking, a more attractive alternative: appointment as Canada's High Commissioner to the Court of St James's.

Since that office was held by Macdonald's veteran lieutenant, Sir Charles Tupper, Smith made a great show of eschewing personal ambition and with mock modesty helped lever the holder out of the post he wanted to occupy. "I have no claim [to the prime ministership]," he humbly insisted, "while such a statesman as Sir Charles Tupper is alive and active, and prepared to assume the burden should the latter prove too great for Sir Mackenzie Bowell." Tupper rushed back to face the thankless task of leading his party into its disastrous electoral confrontation with Wilfrid Laurier. When Smith began to lobby him hard for the London job, the new Prime Minister, delighted at the prospect of having an ocean between himself and his one-time nemesis, undertook to appoint the HBC Governor High Commissioner, though the neophyte diplomat was seventy-six years old.

True to form, Smith followed his standard procedure whenever faced by an important career move: he remarried Isabella. Using the excuse that he had mislaid his marriage certificate, on March 9, 1896, he and his wife went through their third wedding ceremony in the Wall Street office of John Stirling, Smith's New York lawyer. Staged to put an end to whispers about the couple's murky marital past, this masquerade only drew attention to Smith's relentless sense of Presbyterian guilt. Tupper served only ten weeks in office before being beaten by Laurier, but on April 24, 1896, he appointed Smith to London and in a touching move also named him a Privy Councillor, the title Smith had coveted when the two men had ridden together to Red River twenty-six years earlier.

The British posting was Canada's most important (indeed, only) diplomatic appointment, but its occupant was under few legal, partisan or economic constraints. Sir Alexander Tilloch Galt, the railway promoter who became Macdonald's finance minister and later served as Canada's first High Commissioner, used the prestige of the office to help finance exploitation of the coalfields his son had discovered on the Belly and Little Bow rivers near Lethbridge in southern Alberta. Tupper himself held the posting while still a member of Macdonald's cabinet and regularly returned home to fight election campaigns.*

Although he served as his country's ranking representative in the glittering capital of history's greatest Empire, the High Commissioner devoted most of his time and energy to more mundane pursuits, acting as Canada's main immigration recruiter, chief financial facilitator and manager of the national debt. London was the centre of world trade and finance, while Canada's money markets were still too primitive and much too modest to capitalize the new Dominion's rapid expansion.

The 1896 election spawned a new age in Canada. The once vital era of Macdonald, which had sputtered to a dreary conclusion after the death of its guiding spirit, was replaced by the tantalizingly optimistic "ministry of all the talents" headed by Wilfrid Laurier, the forceful yet pragmatic nationalist who was to govern Canada for the next fifteen years. Suddenly, everything seemed possible. The new Prime Minister personified the young nation's hopes with his assertion that the twentieth century belonged to Canada.† Laurier didn't agree with Tupper on very much, but it didn't take the Liberal Prime Minister long to decide that Smith, who had spent most of two decades subverting the Liberal cause, was far less dangerous in London than back in Canada. The Hudson's Bay Governor, who also retained his presidencies of the Bank of Montreal and Royal Trust and his seat on the executive committee of the CPR, was quickly reappointed by the new government. Smith, who as a youth sixty years before had worshipped British royalty from afar, could now participate in history's grandest festival of Empire, Queen Victoria's

---

*The post has gone ever since mainly to superannuated politicians. During the Second World War it was occupied by former Liberal organizer Vincent Massey, who later became Canada's first native-born Governor General. While in London Massey vividly recalled receiving a letter from a worried British housewife with a unique complaint. "A Canadian soldier on leave has visited my house," she wrote. "As a result both my daughter and I are pregnant. Not that we hold that against your soldier, but the last time he was here he took my daughter's bicycle which she needs to go to work."

†Even if he didn't really say it. The closest Laurier came to coining that aphorism was during his Canadian Club speech in Ottawa on January 18, 1904. "Canada has been modest in its history, although its history is heroic in many ways," he declared. "But its history, in my estimation, is only commencing. It is commencing in this century. The nineteenth century was the century of the United States. I think we can claim that it is Canada that shall fill the twentieth century."

Diamond Jubilee, celebrated in the shimmering summer of 1897.

The Empire on which the sun dared not set then encompassed more than a quarter of the earth's land surface occupied by 372 million people, whose representatives came to parade for their Queen. "There were Rajput princes and Dyak headhunters," rhapsodized Jan Morris in her epic *Farewell the Trumpets*, "there were strapping troopers from Australia. Cypriots wore fezzes, Chinese wore conical straw hats. English gentlemen rode by, with virile moustaches and steel-blue eyes, and Indian lancers jangled past in resplendent crimson jerkins. Here was Lord Roberts of Kandahar.... Here was ... Wolseley, hero of Red River, Ashanti and Tel-el-Kebir.... That morning the Queen had telegraphed a Jubilee message to all her subjects.... The occasion was grand. The audience was colossal. The symbolism was deliberate. The Queen's message, however, was simple. 'From my heart I thank my beloved people', she said. 'May God bless them.'"

And He did. The forces that held the British Empire together seemed at times to be more theological than political. True adherents felt little confusion about what to believe or how to behave: God, Queen, Union Jack and family were the icons that mattered; being patriotic, disciplined, uncomplaining, frugal, chivalrous, stiff-upper-lipped and not too expert in any one thing (the cult of the all-rounder reigned supreme)—these were the coveted virtues. "The British as a whole," Jan Morris astutely observed, "would have been shocked at any notion of wickedness to their imperialism, for theirs was a truly innocent bravado. They really thought their Empire was good ... they meant no harm, except to evil enemies, and in principle they wished the poor benighted natives nothing but well." The passion in which the Empire was held is difficult to exaggerate. Typical was the story of Warburton Pike, an Englishman who had graduated from Rugby and Oxford but spent most of his adult life trapping, hunting and hiking in the Canadian wilderness. An archetypal imperial adventurer who took many risks exploring the outer edges of the northern tundra, he never forgot his British roots. Fifty-four when he reached home to enlist shortly after the outbreak of the First World War, he was rejected as too old. Pike was so upset he hiked to Bournemouth, walked into the sea, and plunged a knife into his heart.

At this high noon of Empire, the pervasive influences of what O.D. Skelton, the great Canadian public servant, called "the dervishes of Anglo-Saxondom" were in full and glorious flight. The Jubilee was pure light opera, with Edward Elgar writing the score and Rudyard Kipling the libretto. British society had little conception of

*Lord and Lady Strathcona in London*

how to treat the slightly awkward representatives of their newest "self-governing colony." One London matron who had condescended to include colonials at her garden reception addressed a special request to the Canadians suggesting that Wilfrid Laurier and his party kindly appear in their "native costumes." Canadians at home found themselves caught up in the fever of the occasion, with local parades, fireworks, floral arches across main streets and patriotic speeches. "As a warm darkness fell on the exhausted town that evening," June Callwood wrote of the elaborate Jubilee celebrations held in London, Ontario, "fireworks spelling VICTORIA hung for a long, poignant moment in the black sky. People watched it sputter out and were transfixed. It seemed something important had happened to them, to the whole country. It felt like a flowering, a future greatness just opening to enfold them all."

The Jubilee rewarded Smith with a royal accolade. Summoned to Windsor Castle, he received a barony from Queen Victoria. Becoming a peer of the realm was no trifling matter. So Smith did what he always did on such watershed occasions. He remarried Isabella. The secret ceremony, held according to Anglican rites at the British Embassy in Paris, reunited the bride and groom (then seventy-seven) for the fourth and final time. That requisite guilt-pacifier out of the way, Smith set about finding a title, crest, motto and coat of arms appropriate to his elevated rank. The crest was easy: a beaver gnawing at a maple tree. The motto was one exquisitely apt word: "PERSEVERANCE," the coat of arms a canoe paddled by four HBC traders, and a hammer with nail to symbolize the last spike. But the title proved more difficult. Queen Victoria usually referred to him as "Your Labrador Lordship," but Smith finally settled on a characteristically convoluted moniker—in the words of Burke's *Peerage*, "Baron Strathcona and Mount Royal, of Glencoe, co. Argyll, and of Mount Royal, Quebec, Canada"—in tribute to both his Canadian domicile and the large estate he had recently purchased in western Scotland.*

The freshly minted peer's love of Empire knew no bounds. In a speech during the launching ceremony of the steamer *Mount Royal* at Wallsend in the summer of 1898, Strathcona laid down some new definitions. "I do not," he trumpeted, "care to speak any longer of Canada and the other countries constituting the Empire, as Colonies. They are constituents of an Empire, one and indivisible. They are English quite as much as is Great Britain, and to remain so to all time is the desire of Canada and all other possessions of the Empire."

Strathcona and some of his more imperialist-minded friends conceived the idea of girdling the globe with telegraph wires and a transportation service, to be known as the All-Red Route, that would link railway lines with accelerated British steamship schedules. Telegrams, mail, people and merchandise could then move aboard conveyances inviolably British. Express timetables called for a twenty-knot service across the Atlantic, with sailings from Liverpool to Halifax taking only four days. "The All-Red Line," declared Sir Sandford Fleming, one of the project's enthusiasts, "would, in some respects, resemble the spinal cord in the human body; it would prove to be the cerebro-spinal axis of our political system, and give origin throughout its length to many lateral groups of nerves ... through which would freely pass the sensory impressions and the motor impulses of the British people in every longitude." Using a slightly more comprehensible metaphor, Strathcona's doctor once remarked to his patient just before a heart examination, "Now we must attend to the All-Red Route, my Lord." Strathcona tried hard to promote the project, but the fact that it would have required government subsidies of more than $100 million considerably cooled the ardour of its supporters. The Hudson's Bay Company Governor turned his attention to more practical pursuits.

---

*The *Strath* in Strathcona is the Gaelic equivalent for *glen* or *valley*. The difference between being just plain Donald Smith and becoming Lord Strathcona was most visible in the new peer's signature. The Bank of Montreal at that time issued its own currency, bearing the printed autograph of its president. As Donald A. Smith he had signed his name unobtrusively, the neat, tiny letters taking up only thirty-nine millimetres on the banknote; the bold new scrawl, *Strathcona*, could not be contained in its alloted space, spreading over ninety-five millimetres and jutting into the bill's margin.

THE SECOND-STOREY WINDOW of the Canadian High Commission on Victoria Street glowed through London's nocturnal smog into so many long evenings that passersby nicknamed it "the Lighthouse." Here Strathcona spent eighteen years, occupied with the business of his life. While he placed the HBC's affairs at the top of his agenda, actively participating in the Company's daily management and ongoing policy formation, his energies were dispersed in many directions.

He sat in his office, signing cheques, justifying accounts, writing letters (always by hand, because he considered typewritten correspondence a breach of courtesy): to the Queen's Chamberlain, asking for special seats at a royal ceremony for a visiting politician; to an old fur trader at Temiskaming, thanking him for a box of lightly salted deer tongues; to another former HBC Chief Factor, forty-three years in the service, bitter about having to live out his days with no Company pension; to his cronies at the Bank of Montreal, requesting them to approve a loan to help James J. Hill "fight off the Harriman forces."* His cable messages flew around the world. He bargained for tea and silk shipments from Yokohama and sent timber to the Orient; he settled Lewis crofters in northern Saskatchewan and sold Labrador sable to Chinese aristocrats; he tied down a Canadian company that would give him a monopoly on salt production; he shipped flour from Vancouver to Fiji; he arranged for the Bank of Montreal to underwrite the bonds for construction of the New York "El"; and he approved plans to expand the HBC's department store in Vernon, B.C. The work never stopped, and even if being Governor of the HBC was his dominant concern, he seemed frantic to keep expanding his reach, as if he could never have enough money, power or prestige.

Calculation of an individual's private wealth was not a suitable topic for public discussion in Victorian England, but Strathcona arguably ranked as one of the Empire's richest men. His vast holdings of HBC stock returned record dividends; the Bank of Montreal, with himself as its second-largest shareholder, was Canada's most profitable bank; and the CPR shares that he had purchased for $25 or less appreciated to $280 in his lifetime. Besides holding these highly visible directorships and major stock positions in these companies, he enjoyed similar arrangements with Royal Trust, the Canada North-West Land Company, the Canadian Salt Company, the Commercial Cable Company, the Great Northern Railway, the Minnesota Imperial

---

*Although he was offered a thousand dollars a share by E.H. Harriman for his Northern Pacific Railway stock, Strathcona stuck with his old friend Hill, rescuing him from bankruptcy—and he didn't even send Hill a bill for use of his proxy.

and Colonial Finance and Agency Corporation, the London & Lanca-
shire Fire Assurance Company, the Manitoba South Western Colonization Railway, the New Brunswick Railway Company and the St Paul,
Minneapolis and Manitoba Railway. He was also an important shareholder of Barings, the London merchant bank he helped rescue after
the 1890 crash. Strathcona continued to use the Bank of Montreal
(which during his term as High Commissioner was hired as Canada's
chief fiscal agent abroad) as his private cash dispenser and in his first
nine years in London did not surrender the bank's presidency. In
1905, on his eighty-fifth birthday, Strathcona decided it might be time
to give the young bucks a chance. He allowed himself to be named
honorary president and was succeeded by Sir George Drummond,
who was only seventy-six. Drummond in turn was followed five years
later by Richard Angus, then a spry seventy-nine.

The High Commissioner still returned regularly to Montreal
(once estimating he had crossed the Atlantic at least a hundred times),
but his heart belonged to London. Although he had long ago achieved
life's highest social and economic peaks, Strathcona continued to
labour like a man possessed, with no detail small enough to escape his
fussy attention. More pathetic than admirable, his devotion to duty
finally affected his health—though he always remembered the warning of a leading London physician, Sir Andrew Clark, that for him to
stop work would be fatal. After one of Strathcona's bouts of illness, Sir
Thomas Shaughnessy, then president of the CPR, reported in mock
serious tones to an Anglo-Canadian gathering in London that "yielding to the earnest entreaties of his physician . . . [Lord Strathcona]
has decided to relax his energies. He has succumbed to the united
pressure of his medical man, his family, and his friends, and has been
induced to promise to leave his office at 7.30 each evening instead of
7.45." During a holiday in rural England, Strathcona began dictating
letters to his newly hired secretary early Sunday morning. The assistant politely but firmly declared he could not work on the Sabbath.
The High Commissioner courteously agreed to indulge the young
man, then spent most of the day impatiently pacing his room. Promptly
at midnight he woke the startled clerk with the command: "The
Sabbath is over. We must make haste with those letters!"*

---

*Such work habits were not new. Dr Wilfred Grenfell, the Labrador medical missionary,
noted how he had been granted an appointment to see Smith at Hudson's Bay House, on
Montreal's St Peter Street, one Christmas Day. "I still remember vividly the deserted

His daily office labours done, Strathcona spent most evenings hosting or attending dinners and receptions at the Athenaeum Club, the Imperial Institute, and the Savoy or Westminster Palace hotels. As these and other venues proved insufficiently exclusive for the grand scale of the High Commissioner's hobnobbing, he eventually acquired seven houses and did most of his own entertaining. In Canada he had retained his magnificent dwelling on Dorchester Street in Montreal,* Silver Heights near Winnipeg, with its buffalo pound, and Norway House, his stone mansion at Pictou, Nova Scotia. In London his first town residence (at No. 53 Cadogan Square) was replaced by the much larger five-storey Grosvenor Square house (No. 28). As his country residence, he at first leased Knebworth in Hertfordshire, the ancestral home of the Lyttons (of *Last Days of Pompeii* fame) where Oliver Cromwell had met in solemn conclave with his followers to consider how England could rid itself of a tyrant king and a corrupt parliament. He later purchased Debden Hall in Essex and the Inner Hebrides islands of Oronsay and Colonsay, which included a beautifully sheltered manor house built from the ruins of a priory. But his most impressive property was the magnificent mansion he built in Black Corries of Glencoe, the rugged 64,000-acre estate he purchased in the west Highlands of Scotland, near Ballachulish. The place had an ominous background, and Dickens said that part of Argyllshire was "perfectly terrible."

Strathcona loved taking friends on grouse shoots in the Highland wilds, but his more serious entertaining was focused on pet causes. "Lord Strathcona presides most afternoons and every evening at some meeting or another," noted Gaspard Farrer, a young London merchant banker who moved in his circle, "and speechifies with great aplomb on art, music, medicine, science, university extension, French

---

streets . . . the silence and entire absence . . . of any living thing," he later told a friend, "and at last the great, towering portals of the world-famous Company's offices. I climbed the steps with no little trepidation, and the bell startled me, when its echoes rang out, as if in some long-deserted haunt of men. Finally, the great door swung open, and there stood, quite alone, the smiling old gentleman, apologizing for keeping me waiting."

*The Smith mansion was sold in 1927 to Lord Atholstan, publisher of the *Montreal Star*, who converted it into a home for elderly Presbyterian ladies from good but bankrupt Montreal families. In 1941, the contents were auctioned off and the following year the mansion was demolished to make way for an office building.

*Lord Strathcona's mansion on Dorchester Street, Montreal*

Employment, and every other interest that is glad to enlist the dear old gentleman's presence—and purse." Strathcona's most elaborate social function was the reception he threw for the four-hundredth anniversary of Aberdeen University. Named Lord Rector of the university in 1899 and later Chancellor, he realized there was not a hall on campus large enough to seat the 4,500 graduates and dignitaries invited to attend. He had a temporary building erected at his own expense on a three-acre site that could accommodate 2,500 at dinner and 4,740 in rows of chairs for the official ceremonies. Since no Scottish caterer was equipped to handle such a mob, he imported 650 waiters and their equipment (including 25,000 plates and 12,000 glasses) from London by special train. The actual graduation ceremonies and handing out of honorary degrees proved an anticlimax because by the end of the day the badly ventilated building was so fogged with cigar smoke no one could see which of the platform notables was speaking. When Andrew Carnegie, the American robber baron, couldn't make out the notes for his convocation address, he stopped in mid-sentence and explained, "I have given the eloquent speech which I had prepared, and from which I had hoped to elicit your cheers, to the myriad-mouthed press, and you will read it there in full tomorrow morning." Carnegie never did officially get his doctorate because when he walked up to Chancellor Strathcona, who was presiding, for his "capping," the two elderly men, who had started from nothing to reach this pinnacle, looked into one another's eyes and, moved by the emotions of the moment, shyly hugged one another instead of going through the degree ritual.

As he became ever richer, Strathcona turned himself into one of the Empire's more imaginative philanthropists. On top of the usual donations to hospitals and various funds for the unemployed (it then being cheaper to do good works than pay good wages), he also provided seed money for the establishment of Major-General Sir Robert Baden-Powell's Boy Scout movement and helped finance Captain Joseph Bernier's explorations of Canada's Arctic coast in the steamer *Arctic*. He purchased the auxiliary barquentine *Discovery* used by Captain Robert Falcon Scott in his Antarctic exploration of 1901–4, assigned the vessel to the HBC's northern trade for five years, then donated her to the Boy Scouts.* All requests for funds were placed on a silver tray, and every Sunday Strathcona would fish out a dozen or so. Those that satisfied his strict tenets of being "properly deserving" received a donation. One exception to this ritual occurred when an arrogant tramp appeared at his office and ordered the secretary to inform the High Commissioner that he was the son of the man who had driven young Donald to Aberdeen when he had left home to sail for Canada. Given a £5 note, the tramp was back the next day. When he was announced, Strathcona quietly told his secretary, "Give the gentleman another five pounds and tell him he need not return. You may add that his father did not drive me to Aberdeen. I walked."

Besides granting him automatic access to the Empire's most distinguished soldiers and statesmen, Strathcona's peerage made him a member of the Imperial Parliament. Until 1910 the Lords and Commons exercised equal constitutional powers, and the upper chamber contributed Prime Ministers of the realm into the twentieth century. It was two years before Strathcona made his first speech in these august surroundings, and when he did, it was on a curious subject. On June 28, 1898, he introduced a bill to legalize in the United

---

*She was later docked at the Thames Embankment in London as a memorial to Scott and moved to Dundee in 1986.

Kingdom colonial marriages with sisters of deceased wives. It was a quirky, rather risky topic for him to champion, and Queen Victoria, who resented such excursions into ecclesiastical law, was quick to take offence. "His Labrador Lordship," she pointedly remarked, "should be the last to meddle in these matters." Strathcona was careful to point out that his proposal would leave untouched marriages to brothers' widows and wives' nieces, but even though the Lords passed the bill, the government refused to take it up in the Commons.

His slightly strained relations with the royal household improved on Queen Victoria's death in 1901 and the succession of her eldest son, Bertie, the fifty-nine-year-old Edward VII.* The two men struck up a friendship so close that Edward treated the HBC Governor almost as a member of the royal household, referring to Strathcona as "Uncle Donald" and consulting him on matters of state as well as personal finance. Edward fondly remembered his 1860 tour of the Canadian provinces as Prince of Wales, particularly the great canoe pageant staged for him by the HBC's overseas Governor, Sir George Simpson, at Lachine.† But what had really won the heart of the British Monarch and most of his subjects was Strathcona's magnificent gift of Empire, the regiment of rough-riders he personally donated to help the British fight the Boer War.

THE APPOINTMENT OF JOSEPH CHAMBERLAIN, an impatient Birmingham screw manufacturer, to the Colonial Office in 1895 had hardened the face of British imperialism. A dandy who sported a monocle, Chamberlain didn't just preach white supremacy—he actually believed in it. The main flashpoint for the inevitable counter-thrusts that followed his sabre-rattling was South Africa, a pivotal outpost along the Empire's eastern trade routes. It was occupied by "black pagans" and, among others, intractable Huguenots from Holland, Germany and Belgium known as Boers (and later as Afrikaners) who had gradually withdrawn inland to the Transvaal and Orange Free State, while in the nineteenth century the British settled in the Cape Colony, Natal and Rhodesia. A major gold strike in the highlands near Johan-

---

*Victoria, who died in the arms of the Kaiser at eighty-one at Osborne House, her beloved country seat on the Isle of Wight, had become a powerful force for perpetuating the status quo in her country's life and exemplified it in her own, having her husband's shaving water taken to his room every day for four decades after his death.

†For a description of this unique ceremony, see *Caesars of the Wilderness*, pages 357–58.

nesburg disturbed the uneasy equilibrium, and a pre-emptive strike by the Boers into British territory on October 11, 1899, served as a declaration of war. British troop commanders, most of whom had not evolved their tactics much beyond the stolid battlesquares of Waterloo, were easily outmatched by South Africa's territory-wise opponents, who did battle in everyday clothing, elected their officers, and knew the contours of every gully in the veld. By winter, the proud British battalions, still rigidly close-advancing into battle to the wail of bagpipes, were in disarray.

Canada's defence force at the time consisted of a weak militia commanded by British generals, with eight steelclad Royal Navy cruisers patrolling the coasts. Although Laurier had responded to Chamberlain's 1897 plea that the colonies come to the aid of Mother Britain in times of need by declaring "Let the watch fires be lit on the hills and Canada will be the first to respond!" the Canadian Prime Minister now felt much more ambivalent. Henri Bourassa, the Quebec activist who later founded *Le Devoir*, resigned from the Liberal party to protest Laurier's intention of dispatching Canadian troops to the African killing-ground. Watching his adopted country dither, Strathcona decided to act. On the last day of 1899 he offered the British War Office a mounted Canadian regiment, recruited, armed and payrolled at his own expense. This grand one-million-dollar gift, Strathcona's most deliberately spectacular gesture, caught the public imagination on both sides of the Atlantic.

The patriotic troop of 540 mobile scouts was placed under the command of Colonel Sam Steele, the most impressive of the young North West Mounted Police officers who had helped establish law and order during construction of the CPR and the Klondike Gold Rush. Recruiting quotas for Strathcona's Horse were oversubscribed several times in five days, some 600-odd Arizona cowboys willing to supply their own guns and horses having been turned down. The final roster included many a renegade British aristocrat along with former army officers glad to serve as privates (known as "gentleman-rankers"), at least one fugitive from the law of the United States, as well as cowpunchers, bushwhackers, whisky-priests and the toughest frontiersmen Steele could find. When this motley assembly was inspected at an Ottawa march-past by Governor General Lord Minto, he complained to his diary of "the useless ruffians, the halt, the lame and the blind." The regiment may not have pleased Minto's fastidious Sandhurst standards, but other Ottawans, especially the young girls, loved these wild-eyed soldiers of fortune, colourfully clad in stetsons,

*Colonel Sam Steele and a detachment of North West Mounted Police at Beavermouth, British Columbia, 1885*

high yellow boots, and charcoal-hued greatcoats. As the troops journeyed by train to Halifax they were cheered at every stop before embarking for the long journey to the front.

Never at a loss to capitalize even on his patriotism, on the very day his soldiers sailed for Cape Town, Strathcona began to apply pressure on Chamberlain to make an important change in his barony, which, according to accepted custom, would have descended to his eldest son. Since he and Isabella had only a daughter (Margaret Charlotte, who had married Dr Robert Howard of McGill), he wanted to have a change made so the title would remain perpetually in the family. The adjustment required proclamation of a royal decree, and Chamberlain replied, through a letter to Sir Charles Tupper, that "there were great difficulties in the way of such an unusual grant." These problems were magically resolved by the intervention of Sir John McNeill, a Victoria Cross winner in the Maori War of 1864 and a friend of Strathcona's (they first met when the Scots officer was on Wolseley's staff at Red River), who now served as an equerry to the royal household and arranged for the required patent to be issued in the summer of 1900. It must have been a happy coincidence that shortly afterwards Strathcona purchased his Hebridean islands (Colonsay and Oronsay) from Sir John for £30,000.

In South Africa, the Canadian irregulars quickly gained a well-deserved reputation for matching the Boers' own guerrilla tactics with commando raiding parties and daring thrusts to sever the enemy's supply routes. Steele's contingent looked hopeless on the parade square, but in the field, where mobility, courage and innovation counted, no one could match the Canadians. Originally hardened by their ability to survive on their home turf, they had been toughened by their commanding officer's brutal approach to discipline. When half a dozen of his soldiers complained they were suffering from piles, for example, Steele ordered them to gallop bareback for five miles to burst the source of their complaints. "Of all the regiments, British or Colonial," reported London's *Daily Express*, ". . . Strathcona's Horse among the Boers were the most dreaded, and, strange to say, the most respected." Strange indeed, because Steele's men were reported to have lynched some Boer prisoners, and when a British officer remonstrated, they threatened to lynch him, too.

On the way back to Canada, Strathcona invited his regiment to London, where King Edward presented its battle colours, pinned each man with a medal, and rewarded Steele with the Victorian Order. Strathcona later dined the entire unit at an elaborate banquet. "The occasion of his own toast being drunk," trumpeted *The Times*, "produced the wildest enthusiasm, the officers and men springing to their feet, making the roof echo with their ardent cheering." At a special reception for officers in the great drawing room of the Savoy Hotel, attended by the Empire's leading dignitaries, Strathcona launched into yet another laudatory address, but Steele would have none of it. "He arrived a bit tight and grew tighter," recalled Agar Adamson, one of Steele's subalterns, "insisting on making a speech in the middle of which Lord S. pulled him up and said that they would have speeches on other occasions. He insisted upon continuing, in the middle of which [Steele] wanted to pump ship. He left the table . . . lost his way, and found himself in a kitchen, on the stove of which he relaxed nature. He then returned, and wound up being sick on the carpet." Despite such lapses, Steele was given important Canadian army commands and Lord Strathcona's Horse fought with distinction in both world wars and Korea.*

---

*During the 1980s, the regiment, now armoured and 500 strong, fielded Canada's last ceremonial cavalry troop consisting of a configuration of fourteen horses and eighteen men as riders and equipment personnel. It was saved from extinction by another Scottish-born philanthropist, Alan Graham, head of Calgary's Cascade Group.

Revered as the Empire's pre-eminent visionary, Strathcona became London's favourite colonial character. Ever courteous, more British than the British, painfully anxious to please, Strathcona as he grew older caused minor protocol problems for his London hostesses. He could never quite remember the proper precedence. One regal maven complained that "it was very difficult indeed to persuade him to 'stand in the order of his going.'" But the highly publicized generosity of his South African contribution had earned Strathcona wide repute and rescued the Hudson's Bay Company from social oblivion. "He is Canada in a swallow-tail coat," marvelled A.G. Gardiner, editor of the London *Daily News.* "You talk with him, and it is as if Canada stands before you, telling her astonishing story."

*Donald Smith, Lord Strathcona*

*Canadian advertisement for British immigrants at the turn of the century*

# CHAPTER 8

# THE RECKONING

*Too weak to stand or even to read his own remarks, he sat before a representative gathering of the Company's shareholders like a stuffed effigy of himself — mute, barely emitting any vital signs, yet still there, the Governor and a Bay man to the end.*

THE BOER WAR HAD CRACKED THE MIRROR of imperial glamour. While the British could claim a military victory, it had been achieved in a sequence of senseless slaughters. The Empire finally had to mass 450,000 troops to crush 35,000 elusive Boer warriors. In the process, the invaders ravaged the countryside, burned the Boers' farms, and imprisoned their families in detention camps. There, 20,000 women and children died, some of the youngest casualties being victims of ground glass mixed into their morning porridge. The conflict put an end to the naïve Victorian notion of "gentlemen's wars," and Britain's "splendid" isolation now became real. At the same time, technological change was making the grip of Empire less tight. Electricity began to take over from steam, and Marconi's transatlantic wireless transmissions shattered dreams of cable and telegraph monopolies.

Few of these momentous changes disturbed Lord Strathcona's personal world. His already spectacular financial prospects changed only for the better. The CPR was finally realizing its traffic potential, the Bank of Montreal was setting new profit levels, and the somnambulant Hudson's Bay Company became one of the London Stock Exchange's most fashionable investments. While trade in furs faced an uneven future, the Company's landholdings took on new significance. Since 1898, settlers had been funnelling into the Canadian West in ever-increasing numbers, and as they became successful farmers, even more were attracted. The influx triggered a land rush. Three million immigrants settled the barely inhabited Prairies before the outbreak of the Great War. Land values doubled, then doubled again. By 1903, the HBC was able to sell nearly 400,000 acres to willing homesteaders at five dollars an acre, though Strathcona would live to see the price quadruple to more than twenty dollars.

As land values soared, stock quotations shot up. The *Economist*, which hadn't thought about the HBC for thirty years, noted that the Company was showing "remarkable vitality in its old age." Share prices moved from £20 in December 1889 to £129.5 in November 1906, while dividends reached 24 percent and rocketed up to 50 percent—their highest level since 1688—though even at 50 percent this worked out to only 3.1 percent on the par value of the stock.*

Instead of sharing some of this new-won affluence with the field hands whose efforts had created and maintained the HBC's land empire, at the Company's 1904 annual meeting Strathcona delivered these worthy veterans the *coup de grâce*. He proposed that a pension plan be established (paying a top annual rate of $1,500 to Chief Factors with thirty years' continuous service) but specifically excluded aiding those who were already retired. Not only were the former traders to be deprived of any sustaining income but the £50,000 left in the Servants' Pension Fund after abrogation of the fur partnerships by surrender of the Deed Poll in 1893 was absorbed into general corporate revenues. When retired Chief Factor Roderick MacFarlane complained, urging Strathcona "to aid in doing the right thing by those . . . [who] have suffered many hardships, and endured many privations in the performance of their onerous duties in the interior," his pathetic appeal was dismissed with a curt note pointing out that it was really quite useless to trouble the board with correspondence relating to a period with which the existing Hudson's Bay Company had only "an historical concern."

That brutally dismissive phrase relegating more than two centuries of steadfast dedication by generations of loyal employees to the oblivion of "historical concern" served as the corporate epitaph to the HBC's fur traders, if not the fur trade.

---

*A fringe benefit of the fortunes made from the rise in value of HBC stock was the founding of Dublin's renowned Abbey Theatre. Forerunner of the Little Theatre movement and the first state-subsidized stage in any English-speaking country, the Abbey was able to open in its own building in 1904 thanks to £1,300 in HBC stock profits donated by Annie Horniman, a London theatre manager.

It seemed an easy, if heartless, decision because the land boom kept accelerating. When Rudyard Kipling came back from a trip to Medicine Hat (where he had seen flares of natural gas blazing like torches) and reported the town had "all Hell for a basement," Strathcona quickly realized the underground potential of mineral rights and ruled that the HBC would henceforth retain them on all the lands it sold. The High Commissioner's interest in speeding up the already hectic pace of land sales was not limited to his mandate as Governor of the Hudson's Bay Company. He was also a controlling investor of the Canada North-West Land Company, formed in 1882 to acquire five million acres of the original CPR land grant. In case emigrants to Canada failed to enrich his purse through purchase of a homestead, there was always the shipping line. During Strathcona's London tenure the CPR, in which he remained a dominant shareholder, established steamship connections between Liverpool and Montreal. The new fleet immediately became part of J.P. Morgan's North Atlantic maritime cartel, which was estimated to have extracted from newcomers to North America a surcharge of $44 million until U.S. courts broke the back of the trust in 1911. Canadian Pacific vessels used in the service were already subsidized by the Canadian government. Yet both Sir Richard Cartwright, the Liberal Minister of Finance (and later of Trade and Commerce), and his Tory successor, Sir George Foster, substantially increased these subventions, then enacted regulations that only goods travelling to Canada on steamships sailing directly to Canadian ports would be eligible for preferential British tariffs.

The rush to Canada was partly the result of the propaganda flooding Great Britain. The new Dominion was variously described as "the dutiful daughter of Empire," "a hunter's paradise," "the wild and woolly west" and "the land of golden opportunity." "It little mattered . . . if the Rocky Mountains sometimes penetrated into Saskatchewan or that no foothills ever dotted the fictional landscape," noted R.G. Moyles and Doug Owram, who have studied the promotional literature, "or whether the intrepid hero really could, simply by 'turning to the right-hand seek the rugged haunts of the grizzly bear . . . or, by turning to the left, ride after the buffalo on his own undulating plain.' . . . It was best that nothing be too specific or accurate; that setting be an *impression* only, an impression of a 'great wilderness' where . . . 'the red man and the buffalo roamed at will, and the conventionalities of civilised life troubled them not.' " Settlers' guides were distributed on British street corners; every railway station featured a poster glorifying some aspect of Canadian agriculture. Adventure novels of the period even hinted at erotic murmurs in the grain fields. ("Caleb would stand for long moments outside the fence beside the flax. Then he would turn quickly to see that no one was looking. He would creep between the wires and run his hand across the flowering, gentle tops of the growth. A stealthy caress—more intimate than any he had ever given to woman.")

The reality faced by immigrants was very different, of course: after the Atlantic crossing, cramped into steerage bunks, to be unloaded, cattle-like, in Halifax or Quebec; then the climb aboard wooden railway cars equipped with cookstoves but no mattresses for the long journey west. There the newcomers were dumped onto the flat, slough-pitted prairie to scrub for a hidebound life. But at least their fate was their own, and within the cycle of the seasons they cultivated the virgin soil, bought an ox, then a horse, built a house, made a life. Out of their labours emerged not only a new land but a new nationality.

Much to the surprise of almost every official involved (except Strathcona, who had been on the ground and appreciated the area's rich potential), the Prairies turned out to be almost as good as advertised. Even better, when Charles Saunders, an inspired cerealist working at a federal experimental farm, perfected a strain of wheat that required two weeks less to ripen than the standard Red Fife and produced top-quality flour. Even earlier, the prairie had been producing more than 100 million bushels of wheat, and as farmers consolidated their holdings, villages, towns and eventually cities simmered up. The local HBC trading posts were quickly overshadowed by general stores, train stations, grain elevators and bank branches—opened by young clerks sent west from head offices in Montreal and Toronto with a thousand-dollar bill pinned inside their coats to provide the initial capital. "There isn't a tinhorn gambler left in Nevada," exclaimed an American journalist after touring the West. "They're all selling town lots in Canada!"

Winnipeg came fully into its own. By 1911, it was Canada's third-largest city, and, at the height of the land boom, Winnipeg's hotel accommodations were so hard to come by that proprietors charged travellers willing to sleep on stairways a dollar a night. By 1904, Winnipeg's railway yards had grown into the world's largest—and busiest—with as many as 1,800 cars shunted through per day. While the city's North End became the centre of immigrant cultures, mansions of Winnipeg's rapidly expanding merchant class were thrown up on the south bank of the Assiniboine, forming Wellington Crescent and its environs, where many of the leading figures in Winnipeg gathered. They included, over the years, the Aikins family, the

*Lord Strathcona unveiling a plaque on the Fort Garry Gate
during his visit to Winnipeg in August 1909*

Allans, Alloways, Ashdowns, Bawlfs, Drewrys, Eatons, Galts, Heim-
beckers, Heubachs, McMillans, Nantons, Oslers, Pitblados,
Richardsons, Rileys, Searles and Sellerses.

In the summer of 1909, when Lord Strathcona paid his first visit to
Winnipeg in two decades, the local business establishment turned out
in force. They organized a two-mile triumphal parade from the
Canadian Pacific railway station to Government House, under arches
and banners glorifying (and exaggerating) his connections with the
city. Giggles of maidens dressed in white spread flowers before his
carriage, and the crowds cheered at the very mention of his name. It
was a marked contrast to his first furtive visit forty years earlier, when
as Donald Smith he had slipped into town and was promptly placed
under house arrest by Louis Riel. Strathcona enjoyed the celebration
but could not find it in himself to forgive Winnipeggers for having
voted against him in the 1880 federal election. When a local deputa-
tion asked him for a million dollars to help establish the Selkirk
Exhibition, he politely heard them out and said he would give his
decision on his return through Winnipeg from a journey to the
Rockies. On his instructions, the CPR scheduled that arrival to bring

his private coach into the Winnipeg station at midnight. The organizers were on the platform, but no one was invited to enter his darkened and shuttered railway car.

Such incidents aside, Strathcona, assisted by W.T.R. Preston, who had been appointed Commissioner of Immigration for Europe by Laurier, threw himself into the recruitment drive for new Canadians with typical enthusiasm—and was almost arrested for his trouble. Not satisfied with trying to boost emigration from Britain, he visited Hamburg to preach the gospel to German booking agents. They seemed impressed that a British lord had taken the trouble to address them, but the German authorities, particularly anxious not to lose any farmers, had a different reaction. The Minister of the Interior, Count von Posadowsky-Wehner, officially complained about the visit to the British government, threatening to arrest the High Commissioner if he ever returned. "The arrogance of the Canadian, Lord Strathcona, and the utter disrespect shown by him for the laws of the Empire in publicly conducting his emigration propaganda on German soil in the very teeth of the authorities, demand that vigorous representations should be made at once to the British Government . . . ," editorially thundered the *Hamburger Nachrichten*. "Apart from the weakening of the Fatherland which the success of such propaganda entails, the attempt to lure our fellow countrymen to this desolate, sub-arctic region is, upon humane grounds alone, to be denounced as criminal."

SHORTLY AFTER THE TURN OF THE CENTURY—only a few decades too late—the Hudson's Bay Company nervously began to develop retail stores. Although there had been a tiny tuck shop for local customers in a corner of the compound at Fort Garry since 1830, it was not until twenty-eight years later, during the Fraser Gold Rush, that the Company opened, in Victoria, its first real store.* In 1881, a modest drygoods, hardware and grocery emporium was built at the intersection of Winnipeg's Main and York streets, and there the Company stubbornly remained for forty-five years while most of the city's commercial development took place several crucial blocks away at

---

*Other small outlets, mostly glorified versions of the original trading posts, eventually appeared in Vancouver, Kamloops, Vernon and Nelson in British Columbia; at Pincher Creek, Edmonton, Calgary, Lethbridge and Fort Macleod in Alberta; at Prince Albert, Battleford, Yorkton, Fort Qu'Appelle and Whitewood in Saskatchewan; at Shoal Lake, Portage la Prairie, Deloraine and Lower Fort Garry in Manitoba; and at Kenora, Fort Frances, Fort William and Mattawa in Ontario.

*An early HBC retail store, at Peace River, Alberta*

Portage and Main, later Canada's best-known intersection. Sensing that the HBC was not intending to capitalize on Winnipeg's remarkable growth, in 1905 the Toronto-based T. Eaton Company opened a magnificent five-storey department store at Portage Avenue and Donald Street—the latter, ironically, named after Smith. Spread over 6.5 acres and using all the latest merchandising techniques, it employed beautifully groomed high-stepping delivery horses that were soon the talk of the town.

Eaton's had revolutionized the Canadian retail trade by selling merchandise strictly for cash with a satisfaction-or-money-back guarantee. A militantly Methodist abstainer who drank buttermilk instead of water because he didn't believe merchants should patronize anything that was free, the chain's founder, Timothy Eaton, had established a reputation for scrupulously honest dealings. Among other things, he had eliminated the so-called wet sales. This was a shabby trick used by merchants of the day to market fabrics by pretending they had been slightly water-damaged on their way across the Atlantic and could therefore be purchased at unbelievable savings. The merchandise was actually old stock nobody wanted to buy that had been carefully sprinkled with salt water from barrels kept specifically for that purpose in the storekeepers' basements.

In contrast to Eaton's innovations, the HBC persisted in its parsimonious and conservative ways, losing trade to rambunctious new competitors throughout the West. That lassitude was best expressed by Strathcona at the Company's 1908 annual meeting. When shareholders objected that little effort was being expended to turn existing trading posts into attractive sales centres, the Governor haughtily replied that this was unnecessary because "the Hudson's Bay Company by their dealings, their administration, and their management in the past . . . acquired a prestige, which is not possessed by others in the West. . . . The name of the Hudson's Bay Company is an advertisement of itself, and our stores do not require so many embellishments." If this had ever been a fact, it certainly wasn't true now. New immigrants, who constituted the overwhelming majority of prairie customers, had never heard of the HBC; many of the oldtimers, who knew it only too well, had unsettled scores with the Company and would gladly have walked or ridden miles to shop elsewhere.

THE FIRST SIGN OF CHANGE, though it seemed a natural and not particularly important appointment at the time, was the election in 1907 to the HBC board of Leonard Cunliffe to replace the retiring Sir Sandford Fleming. An important City animator involved with the financing of Harrods department store, Cunliffe did what few other British HBC directors of the day had ever done: he went on a Canadian inspection tour, accompanied by Harrods' resident impresario and managing director, Richard Burbidge. It was Burbidge who had converted a modest groceria into the world's largest department store, with, eventually, 220 departments and 20 acres of selling space. Under his influence, Harrods became recognized as a social rendezvous, with bevies of elegant dogs chained outside its entrances, waiting for their owners who were shopping or relaxing at one of three watering holes: a Georgian-style Gentlemen's Club done up in rich mahogany, a Ladies' Club in the Adam style, with figured satinwood and windows of stained glass, or the palm court tearoom, which featured its own orchestra. Burbidge was also known for engaging daughters of the nobility to model fancy underclothes. Paid £20 a week, debutantes considered the assignment quite a thrill.*

Cunliffe and Burbidge returned from Canada shocked by the inadequacy not only of the HBC's pitiful retail outlets but also by the

---

*Among other innovations, Harrods pioneered the use of department-store escalators, with attendants stationed at the top of the first flight to serve jiggers of cognac to anyone flustered by the ride. Harrods' cable address was, and remains, EVERYTHING—LONDON. The store much later became part of the business

absence of any administrative structure capable of capitalizing on the prairie boom. There was nothing particularly outrageous in their carefully worded report except its unmistakable subliminal message that Lord Strathcona was running the Hudson's Bay Company into the ground. The few stores that had been opened were so badly stocked and so poorly operated that they were turning over their merchandise only once every twelve to forty-eight months, and their accounting techniques were a century out of date. Strathcona's determination to govern the firm through a centralized London bureaucracy only vaguely in touch with Canada's startling new realities and, above all, his unwillingness to mobilize the HBC's financial resources to modernize its operations made it crystal clear that only the Governor's removal from effective authority could revitalize the Company.

Strathcona was yet again trapped in his own myth. He genuinely believed—as he always had—that what was beneficial for him personally would naturally benefit the Company. That may briefly have been true when both the man and the HBC were on their earlier growth curves, but the ever-increasing land-sale revenues and his own fattening purse had lulled the Governor into a false sense of corporate security. From his own narrow vision, it may have made sense to minimize expenditures on stores and to concentrate on marketing land. But such a shortsighted approach also meant that the Company was forfeiting its future. If current trends and management continued, the Hudson's Bay Company would have been virtually out of business the day it sold its last acre.

The most devastating condemnation of Strathcona and his methods was contained in an unpublished history of the HBC, written by Philip Chester, who was named the HBC's first General Manager for Canada in 1930 and had access to all the records. "Company policies were not changed by [Strathcona]," Chester alleged; "in fact he accentuated that [policy] of taking every possible dollar out of Canada, as he apparently believed the Deed of Surrender committed the Company to a slow, lingering death, which would come about when the acreage it had received as part of the purchase price of its monopoly had been sold. He established for himself a network of spies among employees in Canada, which contributed to denuding the organization ... of good administrators and managers. The vital

---

empire of the mysterious Egyptian billionaire Mohamed al-Fayed, who grew so enraptured with his possession that he vowed it would remain in his family for a thousand years. He announced that when he died he would be mummified and laid to rest in a tomb atop Harrods.

qualities of restless energy and expansion of the Simpson era were crushed by apathetic policies, and as civilization gradually pushed the Fur Trade into the North, the Company left the rich opportunities of a growing Canada to its young and aggressive competitors. In those years Canada became a nation and enjoyed great economic and social expansion, but the Company failed to meet these favourable circumstances, and the natural opportunity to become a great mercantile Company in Canada was lost."

While Strathcona was ensconced in the Governor's chair and still the Company's largest single shareholder, not much could be done to dislodge him. But in 1910 a powerful stockholders' alliance was formed to combat his regressive policies by challenging his sway over the HBC's board of directors. After a London court of appeal had ruled that receipts from the sale of HBC land were a return on capital and therefore not liable to income tax, a group of City financiers associated with the American interests of J.P. Morgan started to put pressure on Strathcona to increase the number of outstanding HBC shares so that they could participate in the potential growth of the company. At the 1910 annual meeting the Morgan interests won four out of the nine directors' seats, gaining significant influence. Thomas Skinner, a financial adviser to the Canadian government, a director of the CPR and the Bank of Montreal, and chairman of the Canada North-West Land Company, was promoted to Deputy Governor, along with the four Morgan representatives:

> Robert Molesworth Kindersley, chairman of the merchant bankers Lazard Brothers & Company and Whitehall Trust; he was also a director of the Bank of England, and managed large private shipping interests. Within five years he would be elevated to Governor of the Hudson's Bay Company.

> Vivian Hugh Smith, a partner of Morgan, Grenfell & Company, later Lord Bicester, who served as Governor of the Royal Exchange Assurance for forty-two years and was one of the City's most distinguished financiers.

> Richard Burbidge, the managing director of Harrods, who immediately obtained the HBC's British goods purchasing account (at 2.5 percent commission) and had his second son, Herbert, appointed Commissioner of the Company's stores. Harrods was also granted exclusive rights to merchandise HBC furs, the first time the pelts had been offered publicly in London since the Company's founding in 1670. The only other display of the Company's products had been at the Colonial Exhibition of 1886.

William Mackenzie, the Ontario-born teacher-turned-entrepreneur who was founding chairman of Brazilian Traction and president of the Canadian Northern Railway, completed from Halifax to Victoria in 1915. He was the first Canadian-born director and revelled in the honour.

This powerful quartet's first decision was to divide the HBC's operations into three separate departments, each with a new commissioner, in charge of the fur trade, land sales and retailing. The Company's stock was split on a ten-for-one basis and its capitalization doubled through issuance of 200,000 cumulative £5 preferred shares, which raised £1 million for store expansion. To advise on overseas growth, a fledgling Canadian Committee was appointed consisting of three eminent Winnipeg businessmen, Sir Augustus Nanton, George Galt and Sir William Whyte, a retired CPR vice-president. Almost at once they got down to the business of transforming the Hudson's Bay Company into a modern corporation. Construction of a major chain of department stores was commissioned, starting with Calgary and Vancouver in 1913. By the end of that year, the HBC had fifteen sales shops in operation, with $5 million invested in expanding the facilities.

Strathcona continued to occupy the Governor's majestic office, but the Company was beginning to slip away from under him.


AS TOUGH AS OLD PEMMICAN, Strathcona had finally begun to betray signs of his advanced age. During his 1909 Canadian visit when he had been on a buggy tour of the Okanagan Valley, the horses stumbled while going downhill and his carriage overturned. Both of the driver's legs were broken, but the eighty-nine-year-old High Commissioner survived intact except for a slightly strained arm. The same summer when he was back in England, a Royal Navy flotilla sailing up the Thames fired a salute salvo that exploded too close to Strathcona's eardrums. He was temporarily deafened and grew cranky and even more fusty than was his habit. When he heard that W.H. Duff-Millar, Agent-General for New Brunswick, had ordered a ceremonial uniform for a royal reception, he personally tracked down the tailor, walked into his shop and, waving his cane for emphasis, insisted that work on the garment be stopped immediately because provincial agents-general had no official standing and were not entitled to special dress.

In the spring of 1910, feeling poorly and having reached the great age of ninety, Strathcona reluctantly offered Laurier his resignation. The Prime Minister just as reluctantly accepted it and officially announced the High Commissioner's retirement at the Dominion

*Lord Strathcona visiting missionary Father Lacombe in Edmonton, 1909,*
*after being thrown from his carriage in the Okanagan. (His right arm is in a sling.)*

Day banquet in London the following summer. The resignation having been offered and accepted, nothing more happened. There was an election in the air, and neither of Canada's political parties wanted to press for the old man's departure. Any partisan demand for the High Commissioner's scalp would have left the offending politician open to Strathcona's wrath and the possibility of financial aid to his opponents. And so Strathcona was able to stay on through a simple stratagem: neither of Canada's political parties wanted him back because each was fearful of his possible support of the other.

Laurier had earnestly tried to accommodate Strathcona's every whim during the fifteen years of their political partnership. But in 1911, as the Liberal Prime Minister faced his toughest election campaign, advocating support for a reciprocity agreement with the United States, Strathcona remembered the one disagreement of their relationship and publicly came out against Laurier's trade scheme.*

---

*Strathcona was still nursing his recollection of the time the heir to the throne had visited Canada and stayed at his Montreal residence. When the royal party left for the West, Laurier would not allow the High Commissioner to attach his private car to the

Laurier's subsequent electoral defeat brought the Conservatives back into office under Robert Laird Borden. That pleased Strathcona because one of the new Prime Minister's first decisions was to order construction of three dreadnoughts as Canada's contribution to the Royal Navy. Borden and Strathcona had first met during a London visit by the then Opposition Leader two years earlier. "[Lord Strathcona] was most kind and attentive in every way," Borden later recalled. "I was struck at that time with an almost pathetic earnestness in the discharge of even the minor duties of his office. . . . He was in evidence on every occasion. He met us at the station upon our arrival in London; he regularly called upon us at our hotel; when I left to visit Paris, I found him (to my great astonishment) waiting for me at the hotel door early in the morning in order to accompany me to the train. On that occasion he reproached me for not having given him formal notice of my departure; and he seemed to feel that his failure to attend would have been almost a disgrace." Once in office, Borden reappointed Strathcona—now in his ninety-second year—unaware that the old man had turned his mind to one final project.

STRATHCONA'S LAST ADVENTURE, historically his most significant, ensured that in the decisive run-up to the First World War the Royal Navy would have adequate fuel reserves to take on the Kaiser's fleet.

Strathcona had been interested in petroleum exploration since it was reported to him that a CPR construction crew drilling for water in southern Alberta had struck gas. Besides retaining the Company's rights to minerals found on the lands it sold, he also instructed the new Canadian Committee to search for oil. Not much happened at first, but Strathcona was rewarded with a rich geological sample of oil seepage formations found near what is now Norman Wells in the Northwest Territories.* Through his Scottish connections, the High Commissioner had meanwhile obtained control of Burmah Oil, a firm founded in 1886 by Glasgow engineers who pioneered the extraction of oil from shale. The company's deposits up the Irrawaddy River in central Burma were not particularly extensive, but at least they were under British control.

---

royal train—even though Strathcona promised to ride along only as far as Calgary. Another, more weighty reason for umbrage involved Laurier's enthusiastic support for construction of two transcontinental railways, the Grand Trunk Pacific and the Canadian Northern, that cut into the CPR's earnings.

*Located on the Mackenzie River, the little settlement did eventually strike an economic oilfield and still produces a million barrels of crude a year.

That suddenly became important as development of marine engines fired by oil instead of coal began to revolutionize the world's navies. The Royal Navy had continued to act as the guardian of the Empire, protecting garrisons "on every rock in the ocean where a cormorant could perch," as the parliamentary reformer Sydney Smith had caustically observed. The silent service's self-esteem remained unaffected by the Boer interlude. Admiral Algernon Charles Heneage habitually removed his jacket while reciting his morning prayers because he considered it unthinkable for a uniformed British officer to fall on his knees. Another salty character, Admiral Sir Robert Arbuthnot, was such a martinet that when, shortly after he passed command of his ship to his successor, a seagull defecated on the foredeck, a chief bosun's mate deadpanned: "That would never have happened in Sir Robert's day." The navy's progressive element, led by the First Sea Lord, Sir John Fisher, was more concerned with transforming its obsolete coal-fired vessels to oil. Coal engines took eight hours to flash up and some ships took days to coal; oil propulsion was faster, more efficient, produced less telltale smoke and nearly doubled the effective action radius of warships.

The Royal Navy's predicament was that 94 percent of the world's oil supplies were under Russian or American control, with Royal Dutch/Shell and the Rockefeller-dominated Standard Oil interests uneasily sharing the western oligopoly. Apart from the tiny Burmah Oil operation, Britain's only potential petroleum source was Persia (modern Iran), where William Knox D'Arcy, the wealthy developer of the Mount Morgan goldfield in Australia, had obtained a sixty-year oil exploration concession for only £20,000 and 10 percent (later 16 percent) of net profit. He risked most of his fortune drilling the concessions, but his Polish and Canadian field crews reported only dry holes. Afraid that D'Arcy would be tempted to join the Shell or Rockefeller cartels, a delegation headed by Fisher secretly called on Strathcona and asked him to become chairman of a reconstructed and refinanced major oil consortium that would combine the Burmese and Persian properties.* Briefed on the strategic significance of the Royal

---

*D'Arcy had in fact been negotiating with both rival concerns. At one point Shell had hired a freelance master-spy identified by British Intelligence as Sidney George Reilly to intercept D'Arcy during talks he was holding with the Rockefellers aboard a Rothschild yacht anchored off the French Riviera. Reilly dressed up as a priest and, inveigling his way aboard the vessel on the pretext he was collecting money for a nearby orphanage, took D'Arcy aside and on behalf of Shell offered to improve any Rockefeller offer.

Navy's maintaining defensible oil supplies, Strathcona immediately agreed to help finance the new oil firm and become its chairman.

A new Anglo-Persian syndicate was hurriedly incorporated, D'Arcy was pushed aside, and at least £1.5 million was personally contributed to the oil hunt by the HBC Governor. He received 75,000 shares for his trouble, and by the very act of agreeing to become chairman of the highly risky enterprise provided the credibility required to raise more exploration funds. The joint venture struck oil at Maidan-i-Naftun soon afterwards and quickly outlined a major oilfield. At the personal urging of Winston Churchill, then First Lord of the Admiralty, Strathcona signed over the Persian concessions to the British Crown for £2.2 million, guaranteeing the Royal Navy twenty years of oil at a price that Churchill estimated saved British taxpayers enough money to have paid for construction of all its pre-war dreadnoughts. The Anglo-Persian reserves fuelled the fleet that gave Britain the edge at sea over Germany in the First World War. "It was not as a mercantile company that I looked upon it," Strathcona explained, "but really from an Imperial point of view."*

BY THE SUMMER OF 1913, Strathcona looked and acted his ninety-three years. The old man's proud chin no longer jutted out before him but looked more like a man-made jaw in which the paraffin was melting. Ethel Hurlbatt, the Warden of McGill's Royal Victoria College, who met him at the time, poignantly recalled his "detachment of manner, as if he had already passed some boundaries of time and space beyond his fellows, and while occupied and keenly interested and ceaselessly concerned with work and duty and service, [he was] really alone with himself."

On June 13, 1913, Labrador Smith presided for the last time over the Hudson's Bay Company's annual Court. Too weak to stand or even to read his own remarks, he sat before a representative gathering of the Company's shareholders like a stuffed effigy of himself—mute, barely emitting any vital signs, yet still there, the Governor and a Bay man to the end. The news was all good: £300,000 had been invested in the building of larger stores in Calgary, Vancouver and Victoria; the year's dividend declaration of £5 on each share of £10 value set a

---

*The Anglo-Persian Oil Company eventually grew into British Petroleum, the $50-billion London-based petroleum giant that now ranks as the world's third-largest oil multinational. In January 1975, Burmah Oil sold its 21.5-percent interest in British Petroleum to the Bank of England for $426 million.

modern record; land was being disposed of at an unprecedented $20.06 an acre, and 4,032,860 million acres were still to be sold.*

The High Commissioner's final public function was the giant Dominion Day reception he had given every July 1 at Queen's Hall. He tirelessly shook 2,300 hands, but his voice, never very strong, had given out. "The whole scene was exceedingly beautiful," noted the Reverend J.W. Pedley, a visitor from Canada. "The great hall with its brilliant illumination, its fine decorations . . . its orchestra discoursing the sweetest music, and crowded with the elite of London's social life . . . all arrayed in their best, flashing with jewels and adorned with knightly orders, presented a spectacle of light and color and animation, which was not only charming but wonderfully impressive." A month later, Strathcona decided on a lightning visit to Canada to inspect his latest investment, the Ritz-Carlton Hotel in Montreal. His wife, Isabella, herself a frail eighty-nine, had always accompanied him everywhere, but, having suffered several mild strokes, was not feeling healthy enough to go along. When Strathcona gently reminded her that he might not be well enough to return, she insisted on going to Euston Station so she could see him off. He last saw her there on the platform, lifted by four young men, gazing directly into the window of his private carriage, waving her fond farewell.

On the morning of November 7, after walking her Yorkshire terrier in Grosvenor Square, Lady Strathcona collapsed. Her cold developed into pneumonia, and she died five days later. Her husband of sixty years—and four weddings—was devastated. His grief caused him to make a fatal mistake: he stopped working.

Ten weeks later, on January 21, 1914, in his ninety-fourth year, Lord Strathcona died of "great prostration and heart failure." Incredibly, on his deathbed he was still worrying about the legitimacy of his marriage to Isabella, as if unwilling to carry the burden of that imagined sin to his grave. His two physicians, Sir Thomas Barlow and William Pasteur, signed a legal declaration with a firm of London solicitors testifying to his last words.†

---

*A further million acres had been sold by 1923, with most of the balance of the land-bank moved in the following two decades. By 1954, the HBC had only 18,250 acres in its inventory; the last major parcel of fifty acres was donated to the University of Victoria by the Company in 1961 when Richard Murray was Managing Director.

†"Lord Strathcona," the affidavit stated, "said he knew he was dying and asked us to come close to the bed and listen to what he was going to say. . . . He said his wife's first marriage was performed by a man who had not the legal power to do it in that district. The man to whom his wife was first married was called Grant. Grant treated her so

In their tributes, Strathcona's contemporaries attempted to outdo each other with purple praise. "We need not fear exaggeration in speaking of Lord Strathcona," declared Sir Charles Davidson, Chief Justice of the Quebec Superior Court. "In especial degree has he enriched and uplifted Canadian life. May we emulate even if we cannot in the mean while at least reach to the lofty standards of his public and private careers." Sir William Peterson, the principal of McGill University, had little trouble topping that. "Duty was his guiding star," he said of Strathcona, "duty and conscience. We ought to be glad, too—ought we not?—in our day and generation, that Canada can boast of him as a man of unspotted integrity." Even Sir Wilfrid Laurier seemed overcome by grief. "Since Sir John Macdonald's time I do not know that there has been any Canadian who, on departing this life, has left behind him such a trail of sorrow as Lord Strathcona. . . . He came as a simple clerk to the Hudson's Bay Company, and from that station he rose step by step until he became . . . at first in fact, and afterwards both in fact and name, the governor of that historic company, a position which he held to the last day of his life." *The Times* summed up his amazing career most succinctly: "With no advantages of birth or fortune, he made himself one of the great outstanding figures of the Empire."

The Dean of Westminster had suggested the High Commissioner's remains be preserved in a sepulchre in the Abbey among Britain's most distinguished sons, but Strathcona had stipulated that he wished to rest beside his beloved Isabella at Highgate Cemetery in North London.* Still, the Abbey was the scene of his funeral, a state occasion of grand proportions attended by the Empire's noblest citizens. His coffin, carried in to the sombre cadence of Chopin's funeral march, was followed by a single wreath of lilies and heliotrope orchids. Attached to it was a card from the Dowager Queen Alexandra: "In sorrowful memory of one of the Empire's kindest of men and the greatest of benefactors."

By the time he died, Lord Strathcona had outlived most of the

---

badly that life with him became impossible. They separated. Before Lord Strathcona married his wife he consulted several persons including Sir George Simpson . . . and they all advised that [he] would be justified in marrying her. The domicile of Lord Strathcona being Scotland and he being a Scotchman he had no doubt about the validity of the marriage. The marriage was subsequently repeated in New York. . . ." Oddly, his last Paris marriage, the only one accompanied by full religious rites, was not mentioned by the expiring peer.

*Thus sharing the graveyard with Karl Marx (1818–83).

violent animosities he had created as Donald Smith. Yet his carefully drafted will perpetuated many of his earthly quarrels. Although the document was a model of philanthropic generosity, spreading funds across three continents, it never once mentioned Winnipeg. The former fur trader's snobbery also extended beyond the grave. His legacy establishing a leper colony was conditional on a strict entrance test: only leprous English gentlemen of good standing might apply. More than $25 million—the bulk of his estate having been distributed to family members before his death—was dispersed to McGill, Queen's, Yale, Cambridge, and Aberdeen universities, as well as a dozen poor divinity schools and underfunded hospitals. He left small inheritances (£50) to a number of HBC traders and set up the Strathcona Trust for Physical and Patriotic Education in the Schools, which still operates from Ottawa.

The will's strangest revelation was an obscure paragraph that stated: "I remit and cancel the debts owing to me by (1) the estate of the late *Right Hon. Richard Cartwright*, (2) the estate of the late *Lieut.- Colonel William White*, one time Deputy Postmaster-General of Canada, (3) the *Hon. George E. Foster*." Cartwright had been the Liberal finance minister who made his reputation denouncing politicians who had sold their souls to the CPR syndicate, yet shortly after formation of the Laurier government he became highly sympathetic to the railway and later authorized huge handouts to Canadian Pacific steamship lines. Foster, a former professor of Classics at the University of New Brunswick, who had risen to be minister of finance in five Tory administrations, had similarly helped out the CPR while in office; the favours procured from William White were never revealed, though the CPR received many valuable mail contracts during his tenure. The heirs of the three men could now officially keep Strathcona's bribes— but only at the cost of sullied family reputations.

IT HAD BEEN A HELL OF A RUN. The minor HBC clerk who began his career for "£20 and found" had during his seven and a half decades with the Company not only preserved it and drastically altered its character but, unlike most of its modern Governors, had also become a pivotal figure in Canadian history. Here was a man of little privilege, unbridled ambition, and the mindset of a conquistador. For a time, he personified his country.

# II QUEST FOR A NEW EMPIRE

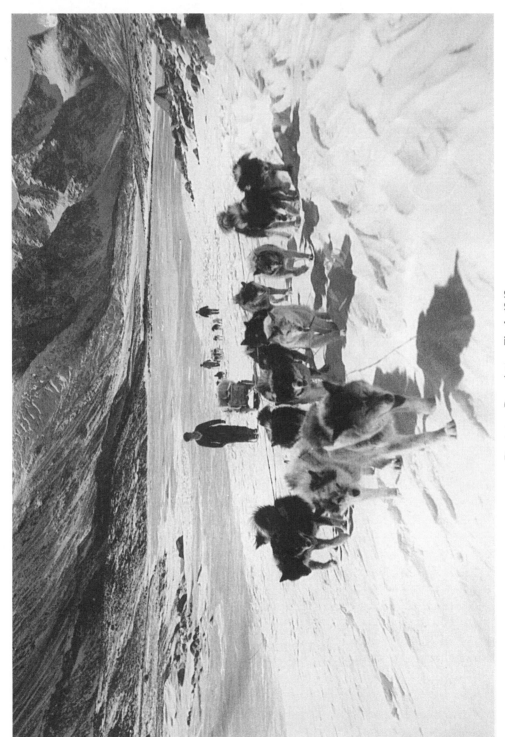

*Dog team, Pangnirtung Fiord, 1943*

# CHAPTER 9

# ON THE TRAIL OF THE ARCTIC FOX

*"Most masters of the Company's posts is lak kings. . . .*
*Yo kin be birthed and died without [their] consent*
*but dat's 'bout all."*

—Annie Redsky

HAVING LOST ITS EMPIRE in the western Canadian plains, where the influx of railways and settlers had reduced its influence to the kind of commercial competition for which the HBC had little skill and less stomach, the Company set out to establish a new kingdom on Canada's northern frontier. Many things about this frigid realm were radically different: the climate and terrain; the pelts the Company traded (Arctic fox, not beaver); the aboriginal people who did the work—Inuit instead of Indians; and the animals that fed and supplied the hunters—seal and northern caribou rather than deer and buffalo. But nearly every other aspect of the Hudson's Bay Company's shift north had an equivalent in its earlier sweep west.

The move into the Arctic took place mostly in the twentieth century, but, as in the plains, the Company had been operating successfully on the fringes of its new spread for most of two hundred years. While the pace of its expansion was at the speed of a funeral slow march, the HBC eventually prospered in the harsh new environment—as it had in the Prairies—but only as long as it could maintain a monopoly. Eventually, the HBC became the dominant retailer in each region, its initial customers being mainly the aboriginals whose way of life its presence had robbed of self-sufficiency.

In both places, the Company's expansion was essential to its own—and Canada's—future. During its western and northern hegemonies the HBC exploited a territory that was commercially untouched. Just as its slow but persistent move across the continent laid down the matrix of subsequent prairie settlement, its invasion of the land mass North of Sixty carved into that bleak landscape the lines of human traffic that would become its permanent pattern of habitation. Of the fifty main population centres in the modern Northwest Territories, three-quarters had been former fur-trading stations. As in the West, the Company served to protect Canada's sovereignty from outside, mainly American, pressures, not by heroic gestures or patriotic deeds, but simply by being there.*

"For at least 150 years," William Watson, a professor of economics at McGill University, noted, "the Hudson's Bay Company dominated the northern economy, both as a monopsonist [the only buyer] in the market for furs and a monopolist [the only seller] in the market for finished goods. There can be little doubt that it was The Bay—and not northerners, whether white or non-white—that was best served by this system." A simpler rationale for the Company's domination of the North was offered by Bob Chesshire, a veteran Bay man in charge of its fur-trade department in the 1940s. "At one time," he said, "we dispensed all the welfare in the Arctic, and the Government took the position that since we had a monopoly, we could bloody well provide the relief. I told them that was all right but that we only had a monopoly because no one else could operate in the damn country."

Except for explorers trying to find the North West Passage, or each other, Canada's far northern reaches had remained almost entirely outside the white man's purview until the nineteenth century, with only the whalers or the occasional missionary, looking for new positions, daring to break its silence. First to appear were the Moravians, who in 1771 established a mission at Nain, on the Labrador coast. Members of the world's oldest Protestant church, founded on the teachings of Jan Hus, the Bohemian martyr burned at the stake by Catholic persecutors in 1415, these dedicated men of God provided solace and support where little was available.†

---

*Canada's claim to ownership of the mainland portion of the Northwest Territories was based on its inclusion in the 1870 transfer of the HBC's charter lands to the recently formed Dominion. The islands of the Arctic archipelago were ceded to Canada through the British Colonial Office in 1880 "to prevent the United States from claiming them, and not from the likelihood of their proving of any value to Canada."

†Early missionaries had some unexpected problems with their gospel, which claimed that those who obeyed the Ten Commandments would go to heaven, where it was very beautiful, while those who sinned would go to hell, where it was very hot. To the

By the 1890s, Canada's North had become an area of intense theological competition, with various denominations attempting to carve out spiritual monopolies. There is a documented story of Father Henri Grollier, OMI, racing Archdeacon James Hunter down the Mackenzie River in the winter of 1858–59 to evangelize new districts around Aklavik. (The Catholic beat the Anglican.)

With Roald Amundsen's epic 1903–6 east-to-west journey across the roof of North America, the 400-year quest for the fabled Passage came to an end. The Arctic became, if not more accessible, at least less mysterious and more frequently visited. As more southerners ventured beyond the tree-line, they encountered the Inuit.* Because the white man entered a climate that defied his own survival, he had to manufacture a set of myths to account for the ability—and willingness—of the Inuit to endure. Such mythologies were expressed in many dubious ways, but the underlying message from those early contacts was that the people of the North were happy campers, frolicking in the snow—"Nanooks of the North" done up in polar-bear pants, their children playing with litters of photogenic puppies in cute igloos. "The Eskimo makes his or her appearance with a smile," wrote the northern expert Hugh Brody in a devastating parody of this silly stereotype. "[He] is an eternally happy, optimistic little figure; a round, furry and cuddly human with a pet name; a man or woman who amazes and delights our European representatives with innocent simplicity. Gorge themselves as they might on raw meat and blubber, a stereotypical Eskimo of the impossible north wages his battle

---

preachers' shivering listeners, hell didn't sound so bad. When Father Pierre Henri, the Catholic missionary at Pelly Bay in 1935, told his flock about how Jesus Christ had once walked on water, he was surprised to find they were singularly unimpressed. When the good Father asked why, a member of his congregation replied, "What's so difficult about that? We walk on water all winter."

*"Eskimo" is the Indian (most likely Montagnais or Naskapi) name for the northern aboriginals. It was the designation originally used by whites because a Jesuit in 1611 had heard Indians refer to the northerners as *Eskimantsiks*, a derogatory term meaning "eaters of raw flesh." It is used in this chapter only when authors or resident HBC Factors refer to the aboriginal population by that word. Inuit, the more contemporary term, simply means "people." (Inuk is the singular of Inuit.) Canada's 25,000 Inuit are divided into eight tribal groups: Labrador, Ungava, Baffin, Iglulik, Caribou, Netsilik, Copper and Western Arctic. They speak a common language, Inuktitut, which has six dialects. Dwellers in the Western Arctic have in recent years coined a new word, "Inuvialuit," to distinguish themselves from other Inuit. Those who live in Northern Quebec (Ungava) are "Taqramiut" (people of the shadow); they call the aboriginal citizens of Labrador "Siqinirmiut," people of the sun, which rises in their land first.

against environment in astonishing good humour." Brody also pointed out the difference between Inuit and Indians: "The 'Eskimo' smiles from the sidelines; the Indian is cunning, warlike and stands in our way. This distinction between the two peoples is a geographical and anthropological myth, but the double stereotype has nonetheless persisted. . . . The one at war with nature, the other with settlers."

Other observers have noted differences in their philosophical approaches to life, with the Indians tending to be more introverted and generally less mischievous. One example: for a time during the 1950s many Indians and Inuit suffering from tuberculosis were lodged at a hospital near Moose Factory in northern Ontario. "The Eskimos were very smart," recalled J.J. "Woody" Wood, a local HBC Factor. "They never complained but could get their point of view across. When there was an economy drive, the cook kept serving spaghetti. Nobody said anything, but I remember one supper hour when the hospital was unusually quiet. As the nurses started making their rounds again, they found everything—the light fixtures, toilet bowls, door knobs—decorated with spaghetti. That was a creative protest and very unlike anything the Indians might have done." Stuart Hodgson, the first resident Commissioner of the Northwest Territories,* notes that one of the main differences between the Indians (Dene) and the Inuit is that Dene settlements or camps are usually along a lake or river, whereas the Inuit are seldom far from salt water.

Inuit survival had a lot less to do with mischief or good humour than with an environment that daily stretched the limits of human endurance. Generations of men and women grappled with the exigencies of a frozen world that held out no advantage, except that it was home. The many historical instances of starvation, cannibalism and infanticide were eloquent evidence of how agonizing it all had been— the numbing cold, the constant quest for sustenance, and the unremitting search for shelter and for driftwood for cooking fires.

---

*A Grade 8 dropout and successful union organizer, Hodgson was an improbable appointee to head what was, before his arrival, a colonial old boys' club, the Northwest Territories Council. (During his union days he headed an organizing drive for the International Woodworkers of America in Newfoundland, where union-busting goons nearly killed him. He was terrified by his narrow escape. The next morning, when he looked into a mirror, he found his hair had turned white. Only later did he realize that in his nervousness he had put toothpaste instead of Brylcreem on his head.) During his dozen years as Commissioner (1967–79), when he actually lived in the NWT, Hodgson shook up the council and left a permanent and enlightened imprint on the North. "The Arctic does funny things to you," he once observed. "It's a jealous lover and it *doesn't* forgive."

To cheat nature they had to be tough. E.J. "Scotty" Gall, a veteran HBC Arctic trader, recalled that while building a boat at Tuktoyaktuk, he once saw his Inuk assistant pull nails out of the hardwood planking with his teeth. That story may or may not be true, but Father Frans Van der Velde, the veteran Arctic missionary, reported that an Inuk used his teeth like a third hand. The Inuit developed quite extraordinary ways to deal with their surroundings. While the wind that howls across the flat tundra prevented them from using such primitive communication methods as yodelling or Tibetan "far-away singing," they learned to *feel* movement a horizon away, so that they could communicate with arm-signals at great distances.

Until a version of Cree syllabics was introduced by the Reverend E.J. Peck in 1894, the Inuit had no written language, transmitting their myths and history through songs, stone carving and elders' recited memories. The half-dozen dialects of their spoken language catch the underlying sophistication of their culture. They use different words when addressing dogs or people, and some verbs possess a dozen tenses, so that instead of merely a past, present and future there are a near and a distant future, an imperative, a negative past and present, an interrogative, a subjunctive and so on. Many words describe snow because its exact condition is so important for hunting or trekking.*

In the early days, Inuit lived entirely off the land and sea, lighting fires by rubbing driftwood or striking bits of pyrite together, fashioning cooking pots out of soapstone, and making garments from sealskin with needles of goose or gull wing bones. Driftwood and whalebone were carved into harpoons; fish strips were frozen into thick, smooth packets to build sled-runners—providing basic rations in emergencies. No part of an animal was wasted. Seal windpipes were used as snow-house windows, ptarmigan bladders made children's balloons, fish eyes were snacks—a munchy Arctic version of Smarties. Inuit in the Western Arctic lined the hoods of their seal jackets with wolverine fur because frost won't stick to it. But the main source of nourishment, clothing and equipment was the caribou. Like the buffalo of the plains and the deer of the forests, the animal was a walking emporium, its skin used for tents, clothing, sleeping bags, ceremonial drums, hunting bags, gloves and buckets; its antlers turned into bows and arrows, thimbles, sled handles and anchors. Its

---

*Some of the more common are *igluksaq*, which is snow suitable for shelter-building on long journeys; *pukak*, a powder snow; *ganik*, falling snow; *piqtuq*, snow being blown about by a blizzard; *mauya*, soft, deep snow.

migration cycles fitted in with native life (or vice versa). Herds of caribou moved like great quadruped tides from the margin of the boreal forest to the edge of the Arctic Ocean, migrating between their rutting and calving grounds, involuntarily feeding man and wolf along the way. While he was stationed at Baker Lake in the 1920s, Archie Hunter, who spent thirty-five years with the HBC, watched the caribou go by: "One could look across Baker Lake by telescope to the rolling land around the mouth of the Kazan River and, at first, see nothing," he recalled. "Then, as the glass was focussed, what appeared to be a sea of antlers came into view and then the caribou themselves. The hillsides seemed to be moving. In whichever arc the glass was turned there were the animals, thousands upon thousands of them. One old native told me of watching a caribou herd during the fall migration which took three days to pass where he was camped."

The herds are supposed to have originally numbered a hundred million, and as late as 1907, the naturalist Ernest Thompson Seton estimated Canada's caribou population at thirty million, though both figures were probably exaggerations. According to calculations compiled for the Fourth International Reindeer/Caribou Symposium, held at Whitehorse, Yukon, in 1985, the North American caribou count had by then declined to between 2.3 million and 2.8 million animals, of which only half the herds were increasing in number. The gradual decimation of the life-sustaining critters was bad news for all but the Company. "The sooner the caribou are gone the better . . . for then more food-stuffs can be imported and the natives will be forced to trap and become fur producers or starve," a trader told Philip Godsell in 1934. Godsell, who himself spent two decades in the Company's northern service, abhorred that attitude, commenting in his memoir, *Arctic Trader*, that it was "a case of the Indian and buffalo over again. As long as the caribou are plentiful the Eskimo is independent of the white man but once the caribou are gone he becomes nothing but the white man's slave."

The Company attitude of encouraging the Inuit to become dependent on its goods was reminiscent of Sir George Simpson's edict, outlined in an 1822 letter to the HBC's London Committee: "I have made it my study to examine the nature and character of Indians and however repugnant it may be to our feelings, *I am convinced they must be ruled with a rod of iron to bring and keep them in a proper state of subordination, and the most certain way to effect this is by letting them feel their dependence upon us.*" J.W. Anderson, who spent his life with the HBC in the Canadian North, had a more thoughtful approach. "There is an optimum period in the dealings of any primitive people with the

*Inuit using a traditional
muskox- or caribou-rib bow drill*

white man," he concluded. "This might be described as the period of time when the aborigines have sufficient of the white man's material civilization to ease the *burden* of life, but yet not enough to disrupt their *way* of life—muzzleloading guns instead of bows and arrows; twines and lines for fish nets and snares, instead of tree and willow roots . . . steel traps instead of deadfalls. And one must not overlook those undoubted and perhaps harmless comforts, tea and tobacco, two of the greatest amenities we have given to the original inhabitants of Canada." The Inuit reached that turning point in the middle of the twentieth century; their treatment ever since has been a patronizing mixture of neglect and manipulation. But in the lexicon of villains that most Inuit feel have threatened their way of life, government ranks first, the missionaries second—and the Hudson's Bay Company a distant third. This is not because the HBC was particularly benign but because it was interested in selling them goods, not—as was the case with Ottawa and the churches—in converting them to new ideologies or ways of living.

THE HUDSON'S BAY COMPANY moved into the Far North with the founding of Fort Churchill south of the Arctic Circle early in the eighteenth century, but its commerce was with the Cree arriving from woodlands to the south. The only trade with the Inuit was from Company sloops irregularly dispatched into the upper reaches of Hudson Bay to barter harpoons, knives and lances for sealskins and whalebone. "So fond are these poor people of iron-work, that they lick it with their tongues before they put it by; indeed, I have seen them so transported with pleasure as to fall into dreadful convulsions," reported Andrew Graham, with his usual style of operatic exaggeration, after leading one of the earliest expeditions out of York Factory. The first regular trading station set up specifically to deal with the Inuit was Fort Chimo (Kuujjuak), at the south end of Ungava Bay, established by Nicol Finlayson in 1830. Not much business developed because the aboriginals had few items worth trading, but the Bay men hunted beluga whales and set up other whaling stations along Hudson Bay's east shore. In 1860 alone, twenty-three hundred white whales were harpooned off the Little Whale and Great Whale river posts, but within a decade overkill had ruined the hunt.

European whalers had been active in Davis Strait since the early eighteenth century. In pre-petroleum days the bowheads' blubber was valuable as a lighting oil and lubricant, while their baleen (horny tissue in the mouth with the consistency of human fingernails that allows whales to filter food from the sea) was used instead of spring steel or celluloid in many applications, including buggy whips, umbrella ribs and stays for women's corsets. Whale tongues were an exotic delicacy, and whale oil was so valuable that the profit from a pair of harpooned animals was enough to pay for a new ship. At the peak of the east-coast hunt, in the decade after 1820, some 750 vessels took part, landing more than eight thousand whales. The commerce was so lucrative that men spent their lives in pursuit of the huge mammals; one Scottish harpooner named Peter Ramsay died of old age aboard the *Erik* while on his fifty-sixth annual whaling expedition into Baffin Bay. It was a rough trade. Interminable tedium alternated with moments of mortal danger as crews scrambled to answer the cry, "*Thar she blows!*"

"It was not some primitive blood lust which prompted these sailors to endure the intense danger and prolonged monotony of a whale hunt," Daniel Francis wrote in his *Arctic Chase*. "The whalers probably served the most commonplace of masters, the need for a living wage. Today whaling is widely regarded as a slaughter of the innocents, but the men who engaged in it believed themselves simply to be doing a job—more perilous than most, less lucrative than many. Like those who engage in any task demanding skill, physical endurance, and bravery, the men had a fierce pride in their work, and popular writers found it easy to transform them into folk heroes." Only very occasionally did a whaler mildly lament the nature of his calling, such as this entry in the log of Captain William Scoresby, one of the most successful hunters: "There is something extremely painful in the destruction of a whale . . . yet the object of the adventure, the value of the prize, the joy of the capture, cannot be sacrificed to feelings of compassion."

As the business grew more competitive, the whalers began to set up shore stations to process the oil and to afford themselves the chance of profiting from a second summer in the whaling grounds. Tiny communities sprang up at Cape Fullerton in Hudson Bay and in sheltered coves such as the eventual sites of Pond Inlet and Pangnirtung on Baffin Island. It was at these makeshift camps that the first prolonged contacts between whites and Inuit took place. The Inuit found most ships' captains happy to barter almost any item aboard their vessels for polar bear and fox skins. The whalers hired the aboriginals to help man the harpoon boats and to trap for furs that could be taken back and sold at highly profitable rates, while the Inuit were, for the first time, exposed to the iron-and-steam-age goods of their employers. Eager to acquire axes, pots, copper kettles, blankets, knives, needles and guns as well as the steel traps that allowed them to catch the animals whose pelts boosted their "gifts" from the white men, the Inuit came to treasure the imported wares. Having acquired rifles and inherited the clinker-built harpoon boats left behind by the whale hunters, the relatively small number of Inuit involved with the hunt gradually moved away from their traditional emphasis on the seal hunts to seek fur-bearing land animals, impatiently waiting for more white men to appear with more goods.

The trade grew even faster on the continent's west coast. The first whaling ships into the Beaufort Sea were a fleet out of San Francisco, and when one vessel—the *Grampus*—came back with twenty-two bowheads worth $250,000, even more whalers followed. A wintering station was set up at Pauline Cove on Herschel Island, a rocky outcrop northwest of the Mackenzie Delta, and soon as many as six hundred whalers were living there, trading with the Inuit. Unfortunately, that exchange, which went on for two decades, was not limited to food and fur. From late September to early July the ships were frozen in, with

*Whaling ship, the* Era, *being prepared for spring whale hunt,*
*Cape Fullerton, 1904*

most of their crews gradually dispersing to aboriginal settlements that
had sprung up nearby. Unlike their east-coast counterparts, the western whalers distributed large quantities of liquor to the local population and participated in such uninhibited sexual orgies that a
disgusted witness described Herschel as "a paradise of those who
reject all restraint upon appetite and all responsibility for conduct;
when a dozen ships and five or six hundred men of their crews
wintered here, and scoured the coasts for Eskimo women. I do not
think it extravagant to say that the scenes of riotous drunkenness and
lust which this island has witnessed have probably rarely been surpassed." Another observer noted that "when girls were not obtainable, wives were enticed away from their husbands, or men induced to
rent out their wives." On August 7, 1903, two North West Mounted
Police constables were finally posted to Herschel to enforce order, but
they mainly collected customs duties in response to the HBC's complaints that the whalers were introducing cheap goods into the region.

By 1910, kerosene had taken the place of whale oil and the
whalebone-structured corset had gone out of style, driving the price of

baleen from a high of fifty dollars a pound to forty cents.* After trying to survive by slaughtering fleets of walrus and sea otters, the whaling crews departed the North, leaving behind an Eskimo population with a taste for European goods that the Hudson's Bay Company was only too happy to satisfy. Because the Company proceeded at its usual snail's speed, accomplishing in a decade what should have taken a season, former whaling skippers quickly established themselves as private traders. The most notorious of them was Captain Christian "Charlie" Klengenberg, who in his autobiography boasted about one of his typical commercial encounters with the Copper Eskimos: "They were so innocent a people of so long ago that I had not the heart to take advantage of them in trade, so all I took was most of their clothes and stone cooking pots and copper snow-knives and ice picks for steel knives and frying pans and a supply of matches. They had no raw furs with them, but their garments would be useful for my family and some of my rascally crew." Klengenberg, who had arrived in the territory from Denmark as the cabin boy on an American whaler, turned his ship, the *Maid of Orleans*, into a floating department store, serving, among others, the many Mixed Blood sons and daughters he had sired along the Arctic coast. One of his most popular items was trading rifles for furs, but the weapons lasted a long time. When the resourceful captain found there were few repeat customers, he rose to the occasion by handing out steel rods which, he explained, should be used to clean out the gun barrels. After a few applications, the rifles wouldn't shoot straight. Not unexpectedly Klengenberg was standing by, ready to sell replacements. When the Company persuaded the police at Herschel Island to ban the Danish swindler from the country, he begged to be allowed to take his ship on one more round, so he could supply his extended family. The local police inspector placed Constable Slim Macdonald aboard the *Maid* to make sure the trade was limited to the captain's relatives. When the ship returned to Herschel in the autumn without the constable, Klengenberg lamely explained that the policeman had unfortunately fallen overboard off Rymer Point on Victoria Island. There were no witnesses and the Dane was never charged, but his northern exploits— and Herschel's evil legacy—had come to an end.

The mainland sector of the Western Arctic, which lay to the south

---

*Whaling, on a reduced scale, has continued to the present day, with the magnificent animals' various body parts providing a fatty base used in the manufacture of margarine, fertilizer, food to fatten ranch-bred mink, and a special grade of oil used to lubricate the guidance systems of intercontinental ballistic missiles.

and east of Herschel Island, was far more accessible than the sub-Arctic regions on Canada's east coast because it had the Mackenzie River for a spine. With the connecting Liard, Peace, Athabasca and Slave river systems, the Mackenzie's drainage basin covers an area the size of Western Europe, most of it within relatively easy access— especially during the four precious months when the rivers aren't frozen. Though North of Sixty, this was mostly Indian, not Inuit, country and had been a highly profitable fur-trading preserve ever since Alexander Mackenzie's downstream dash to tidewater in 1789, because the frosty climate prompted its woodsy creatures to grow thick fur.* By the 1880s, the HBC had put steamboats on the Mackenzie and the Athabasca, with the *Grahame* running from Fort Chipewyan to Fort McMurray, where the Clearwater and Athabasca rivers meet, while the *Wrigley* served the lower Mackenzie. By then the HBC was maintaining eleven trading posts in the area, with Fort McPherson, less than 150 miles south of the Beaufort Sea, its northernmost installation.† The area's commercial potential received a big boost when a CPR branch line linked Edmonton to Calgary, and Waterways (part of the present location of Fort McMurray) became the Company's regional transportation terminus. The HBC ships looked like awkward floating verandas, with picket-fence rails around their decks, but they fundamentally altered the area's human geography. To push the trade northward, roads were built bridging the Mackenzie's only navigation hazard—the sixteen miles of rapids south of Fort Smith.

Accommodation aboard these early northern "fire canoes" was even more primitive than on their prairie counterparts, as attested to in this diary entry of Elizabeth Taylor, an early traveller down the Mackenzie. She had originally been assigned the *Athabasca River*'s best stateroom but was bumped to an ordinary cabin by an HBC Factor. "Mine, a single, had a hay tick only as furniture, no toilet articles whatever, and no bedding," she noted with mounting dismay. "I unpacked my blankets and went to bed. Had just settled for the night when a big drop fell on my nose and then another. I got up, spread the mackintosh over the slats above, and lay down again. But from the pattering above me, I saw that I should soon be deluged, so I rose,

---

*For a detailed description of Mackenzie's magnificent journey, see *Caesars of the Wilderness*, pages 59–62.

†Founded in 1840 by an HBC explorer named John Bell, the first white man up the Peel River, Fort McPherson became known for the longevity of one resident Factor, John Firth, who was in charge from 1893 to 1920 and died there in harness in 1939.

balanced myself uncertainly on the edge of the berth, and untied my bag of camping things, placed a frying pan under the leak, and tried to sleep again. But the leaks came faster and faster, and in fact I spent the entire night in warfare with the waters."*

A later passenger, on the sternwheeler *Fort McMurray*, was Jean Godsell, who went down the Mackenzie on her honeymoon in the 1920s. The ship was loaded with Mounted Police inspectors, priests, trappers, traders, card-sharps, Indians and "Improved Scotsmen," as she facetiously called the Mixed Bloods. The captain, decked out in gold braid and brass buttons, was constantly on the bridge, bellowing orders to crew members who paid absolutely no attention, except occasionally to bellow back some appropriate obscenity. The newly married Godsell spent most of her time with husband Philip in the *Fort McMurray*'s "Bridal Suite," which consisted of "a number of sacks of flour upon which we spread our bedroll; a dirty tarpaulin, stretched on hoops of willow, being our only protection from the snow flurries and fall rains which frequently beat down upon the heavily laden craft." The ten-day journey to Fort Smith allowed Mrs Godsell time to ruminate on the HBC outports she passed along the riverbank. "The unutterable loneliness of these little outposts of civilization—clinging like birds' nests to the riverbank, a hundred and fifty to two hundred miles apart—strikes one forcibly. Cut off for nine months of the year the life is one of extreme solitude yet, at boat time, they manage to surround themselves with somewhat of a gala spirit."†

Despite the relative ease of entry afforded by the Mackenzie and the predisposition of local Inuvialuit towards European trade goods, the HBC delayed its move into the far reaches of the Western Arctic until the second decade of the twentieth century, when it opened posts at Herschel Island, Baillie Island, Bernard Harbour on Banks Island, and Aklavik in the Mackenzie Delta. Even then, trade at these outstations grew slowly, easily surpassed by the busy commerce developing along the Mackenzie. In the Central and Eastern Arctic,

---

*The Company stopped carrying passengers on the Mackenzie in 1948.

†A few years later, while stationed with her husband at Fort Fitzgerald, Jean Godsell created a scandal when she publicly beat up the wife of an RCMP corporal who had been spreading gossip about her. "Blinded by a curtain of flaming red, I reached out, caught her by the coat-collar and smashed my fist in her face," she recalled with obvious relish. "For the next few minutes, I thrashed the snivelling creature within an inch of her life, and sent her crawling and moaning back to the barracks with the warning that if, on any future occasion, she as much as dared mention my name this would be but an infinitesimal sample of what she would get the next time."

whaling had also vanished, with the *A. T. Gifford* making her last voyage into Hudson Bay in 1915. As if masterminded by some benevolent deity, the decline of whaling coincided almost exactly with a dramatic rise in demand and price for Arctic fox. It was a time when furs ceased being strictly an extravagance, becoming much more popular and affordable. The fox pelts were fashionable not so much as garments but as trimmings—collars, muffs, neckpieces, and floor-length stoles that dripped with heads, tails and paws. White fox was ideal for the purpose because, unlike beaver or muskrat, it had a luxurious appearance without being unduly expensive and could be dyed almost any colour, with light grey, beige and black most in demand.

Although the market for Arctic fox was firmly established by the turn of the century, it took the Hudson's Bay Company the usual decade to react. Finally, in 1909, at Erik Cove on the south shore of Hudson Strait, which its vessels had been traversing for 240 years, the Company established its first Eastern Arctic post dedicated to trade with the Inuit. A treeless notch at the top of the Ungava Peninsula, the tiny harbour had been visited three centuries earlier by Henry Hudson and named Wolstenholme, after one of his financial backers. The HBC Factor placed in charge of the new venture was Ralph Parsons, who would quickly become a dominant force in the Company's northward expansion. Born at Bay Roberts on the west shore of Newfoundland's Conception Bay, Parsons was schooled at the local Church of England academy, then went to Labrador as tutor to an HBC Factor's children. He joined the Company himself as an apprentice at Cartwright in 1898 and spent six years commuting between Rigolet and North West River, the wilderness posts once managed by Donald Smith. Given only a week's notice to get the expedition to Wolstenholme organized, Parsons arrived at the desolate spot aboard the Company's supply ship *Pelican*, and after instructing his accompanying carpenter to start building the post, set off in a dinghy with two Inuit boys to seek customers. Finding none, they put in for the night sixty miles along Hudson Bay's east coast, and while they were asleep their boat and provisions were washed away by the tide. They had no choice but to walk back across hilly terrain, circumventing the fiords that serrate the coast. The rocky ground cut to shreds first their boots and then their feet. Staggering along the tundra for four days, exhausted and starving, the two boys gave up (but were rescued later) while Parsons was reduced to crawling on all fours as he approached Wolstenholme. He waited at the new post a full two years before the first customers showed up. "Snowing fast, very tough wind," he noted in his journal on April 20, 1909. "This place should have been called

*Advertisement in HBC catalogue, fall-winter 1910–11*

'Windhome' or something worse. Great place for a lunatic asylum, that sort of thing would *pay*." Once the Inuit found Parsons, the trade grew briskly, and by the summer of 1911 he felt confident enough to establish the Company's first Baffin Island post at Lake Harbour on the opposite side of Hudson Strait. Within the next eighteen years, Parsons inaugurated a dozen more posts (including Cape Dorset, Pangnirtung, Pond Inlet and Port Harrison), and a further twenty HBC stores were opened while he was in charge of the Eastern Arctic.

Parsons ruled over an immense empire with the righteousness of a latter-day Cromwell. The Company was everything to him, not just his job but his religion. He even made sure that the licence plates on his Newfoundland-based automobile always bore the numbers 1670, commemorating the year of the HBC's founding. He married Flora May House in 1918, and they had a son born the following year. After his wife died in childbirth the year after that, Parsons never remarried and wore a black tie for the rest of his life. "He was naturally reserved, independent, self-controlled," recalled Archibald Lang Fleming, first Anglican bishop of the Arctic, who knew Parsons intimately. "He also had amazing powers of detachment and never appeared to be surprised no matter how unexpected or absurd a report or incident might be. These qualities enabled him to rise step by step in the company's service until he became Fur Trade Commissioner in charge of the whole extensive and complicated transportation system. . . . He raised the whole tone of the fur trade. He was ruthless in his determination to stop drunkenness and immorality, not perhaps because of any deep religious conviction, but because he knew that these spelled ruin to both trapper and trader." Reflecting on that same single-track mentality in less kindly fashion, Captain Henry Toke Munn, who had run a trading post at Pond Inlet before being bought out by the HBC, commented in his memoirs: "The Company is a hard taskmaster and Parsons serves it with cold-blooded efficiency. He had been a Company trader at Lake Harbour, on Baffin's Island, for some years, and knows the Eskimos well, but I do not think he has ever understood them. He neither likes nor dislikes them, but regards them merely as instruments to serve the great Company."

THE HBC'S NORTHERN COMMERCE expanded gradually, with the Inuit trading in polar bear pelts, Arctic wolf and weasel skins, white whale hides (processed into shoe laces), the occasional find of mica (used for electrical insulators) or garnet crystals from Lake Harbour, eiderdown from Cape Dorset, and sealskins, used to make school satchels, boots and windbreakers. But such items were all incidental to the fox. The sharp-eared, fluffy animal that fed mainly on the remains of caribou brought down by wolves or the leavings of seal caught by polar bears lived everywhere north of the tree-line, often wintering on floes. Unlike its more wary red or silver cousins foraging in the forested south, the Arctic fox is less clever than it looks. The animal's most noticeable feature is its tail, a portable Linus blanket that can be used in close encounters to blind attacking predators but more commonly serves as a heating pad when the fox is curled up against the cold, guarding its exposed nose and footpads from the frost, acting as both a wrap and a respirator. Before the white man's arrival, the Inuit had little use for fox pelts because they are too flimsy for clothing. Their only application was as a hand or face wipe—a kind of furry Kleenex—or for trimmings on children's clothes. The foxes' meagre back legs, their meatiest part, provided little nourishment.

Too curious for its own good, the Arctic fox has an unerring instinct to investigate any physical change within its field of vision. Trappers tell of foxes watching from a distance while they are setting a trap; the moment they're out of sight, the animal is already poking at it, often the victim of its iron jaws. If the fox doesn't freeze to death in the trap's deadly embrace, trappers kill it by diverting the animal's attention with an outstretched hand and when it lunges, hitting it across the snout with a snow knife, so that the stunned animal can then be removed from its leg-hold.*

Valuable and relatively simple to catch though the white fox was, it had one drawback as a staple for the Inuit trade: its appearance in the North was subject to irregular birth rates, peaking quadrennially according to the life cycle of the lemming, the fox's main diet. HBC posts would collect five thousand pelts in a good year and a hundred in a down-cycle season.† Since the Inuit had become dependent on the white man's goods, the fox trade became essential. But few realized how fundamentally the switch from hunting to trapping would disrupt their traditional society.


BEFORE THE HUDSON'S BAY COMPANY moved into the North, Inuit life had followed specific seasonal patterns based largely around sea animals. Frozen water was a form of liberation because dog teams could whiz sleds along its smooth surface at much faster and safer speeds than over the fissured terrain of the tundra, allowing families to visit one another and to hunt together. Summers were spent at temporary fishing camps established at river mouths where the Arctic char wiggled towards their spawning grounds. The catch was stored for dog food; then, within a month, the hunters were out in their kayaks, after seal. In October there was fishing from stone weirs at river mouths and seal hunting through breathing-holes in the ice. Much of this catch was used to fuel dog teams during the inland hunt for migrating caribou. Since the average Inuit family and its dogs con-

---

*An alternative trapping method was used in capturing wolves and even polar bears. Small seal bones were filed to sharp points, then bent into a U shape, the ends loosely tied together with sinew, and the whole thing wrapped in a piece of meat, which was allowed to freeze. A wolf would gulp down the package; once inside its stomach, the meat would thaw and the bone would spring out, piercing the animal's stomach, causing a speedy death.

†A record 30,000 white fox pelts were exported from the Canadian North by the HBC in 1943.

*Inuit hunter with frozen seal at Igloolik*

sumed forty pounds of meat a day, this often caused a serious logistical problem. An inland Inuk had to kill at least two hundred caribou annually to keep his family and dogs alive. The constant search for food in a land with severely limited resources meant that each family had to hunt over a large area. Except for the temporary shelters thrown up to hold the traditional family reunions early each autumn, there were few real settlements or communities. The Inuit lived on the hunting trails or in temporary, widely dispersed fishing and seal-hunting camps. Inuit life was nomadic, coastal (except for the caribou forays), proud and independent.

In those early days, the Inuit lived in small, related family groups sprinkled along the coastline, and their visits to HBC posts were usually limited to two a year. In the dead of winter, the head of each family would arrive alone by dog team to trade and renew his essential supplies; in summer, whole families would come to greet the annual HBC supply vessel and mingle with kinfolk. Like the whaling ships, the Company's posts were there providing goods, but their presence was incidental to the seasonal rhythm of Inuit existence. As the fur trade accelerated, such HBC supplies as rifles, hatchets, needles, matches, tea and tobacco became necessities instead of supplements, and everything changed. To satisfy these essentials, the Inuit had to abandon their subsistence mode of life and concentrate on the only "cash crop" there was: fox pelts.

This shift from the primary role of hunter to trapper involved a radical switch in the aboriginals' sense of self-worth. Unlike trapping, hunting—especially of seal and polar bear—was a test of manhood, a dignified and courageous occupation in which each family celebrated the day's bounty. To be a hunter was to be an *Angut*—"a Man, preeminently." The fox had to be trapped in winter when fur was at its prime, which meant abandoning most of the seal and caribou hunts. That in turn meant not only having to change social customs but also having to buy from the HBC the clothing and tools previously obtained as byproducts of seal and caribou kills. To maximize their trade and retail selling opportunities, the HBC encouraged the concentration of the Inuit into villages or settlements. The location of few HBC posts was chosen by aboriginals; sites were picked for their proximity to safe supply-ship anchorages and their nearness to areas where the abundance of Arctic fox promised profitable commerce. At least once, the HBC moved whole Inuit communities to their trading posts; in 1934, fifty-three Inuit volunteered to be transferred (with their 109 dogs) from Cape Dorset, Pangnirtung and Pond Inlet to Dundas Harbour on Devon Island in the High Arctic, where the Company had set up a new store.*

THE FIRST PRIMITIVE POSTS RALPH PARSONS planted in the Eastern Arctic—consisting of a trading store, twin warehouses and a staff house (which was the only heated structure)—set the physical pattern for the HBC's northern presence over the next four decades. The buildings were makeshift, slapped together and not insulated. Painted or limed white on the outside, with green trim and black roofing (changed to red in the 1930s), the compounds stood out from those of such later arrivals as the Royal Canadian Mounted Police, who customarily occupied quarters in two tones of grey, and most mission-

---

*Later mass transfers, based on Ottawa's absurd excuse of using the Inuit presence as a symbol of Canadian sovereignty, occurred between Port Burwell and Coral Harbour on Southampton Island and from Port Harrison to Resolute on Cornwallis Island and Grise Fiord on Ellesmere Island, well north of any other habitation.

aries, who chose brown. The inside walls of the HBC stores were unpainted and there was no attempt at decoration except for the Coleman lamps and dog chains suspended from the ceiling. Merchandise was divided into three categories: provisions (flour, cornmeal, jam, baking powder, sugar, tobacco, tea, candles and matches); dry goods (canvas and duffel, tartan shawls, mirrors, toys, yard goods and the utilitarian panties known as "joy-killer bloomers"); and hardware (rifles, ammunition, files, traps, knives, pots, pans, hand-powered sewing machines, and coal oil or kerosene). Since few customers could read, colours were important in arranging the displays: five-pound tins of HBC tobacco were bright red, while the cheaper Ogden's brand came in light green; red-label tea was stronger than the green-label tea; red boxes held 12-gauge Imperial shotgun shells while blue boxes were used for Dominion shells, yellow boxes for rifle cartridges, and so on.*

Because stores were unheated and even on warm winter days indoor temperatures hovered at a chilly -20°F, the Bay men attended them only at trading time and seldom removed their outdoor clothing. They learned to sign counter-slips while wearing hairy caribou-skin mittens and standing in their deerskin boots on dogskin mats. "I'd go in there and stay as long as my feet didn't freeze," recalled Scotty Gall. "It was so cold that nail heads on the inside walls were coated thick with frost and if there were too many people in the store, you couldn't see anything because of their condensed breath. In those days we seldom dealt with fine articles, mostly trading in bulk items. Because it was too cold to use scissors, we'd premeasure and cut the calico into six-yard lengths." No glass goods were safe in the frosty environment, and one trader recalled that the approach of winter was heralded by the popping of ketchup bottles. The only vaguely fresh vegetables offered were potatoes, brought in aboard the annual supply ships by the barrelful. The official reason stores weren't heated was that coal (at a hundred dollars a ton) was too expensive; the real reason was that the Company wanted the Inuit out trapping foxes instead of relaxing around a welcoming warm stove.

Much like the Indians' stories of dealings with the HBC, too often the folk memory of the Inuit recalls the trading relationship with the

---

*These basic stock lists were gradually expanded to include accordions, axes, blankets, ostrich-feather boas, beads, boots, buttons, belts, tailor-made cigarettes, dresses, gingham, harmonicas, hats, mitts, needles, fish and mosquito netting, paints, perfumes, prepared and canned foods, snowshoes, soap, spectacles, sweaters, tents, toboggan boards, towels, tools, twine and waders.

Company as a simple exchange: fox pelts for goods. It was in fact a more complicated transaction, with each side slyly certain it was exploiting the other. The Inuit wondered why the white men wanted the perfectly useless fox and polar bear pelts, since neither could be made into warm or comfortable coats. The Bay men, on the other hand, knew only too well what these "worthless" furs were fetching on the London auction market. In 1923, for example, a .30/30 Winchester rifle sold for twelve skins, even though "the market value of a rifle was not much more than a single white fox pelt."

The actual swap was relatively uncomplicated.* When an Inuit family arrived to trade, they were lodged in what the HBC managers called their "Eskimo Kitchen," a small room adjoining the staff house where the visitors warmed themselves, and enjoyed a "mug-up" of tea and hardtack. When the trader felt the family might be ready to go into the store, he would casually inquire whether they had trapped lots of foxes. "The man would answer, in the old Eskimo manner," recalled Duncan Pryde, who served eleven years with the HBC before being elected a member of the NWT Council, "always belittling himself and his own efforts. 'Well, I've only got a few skins—really poor—hardly worth bothering to show the trader,' and then as likely as not he would bring out some of the loveliest hides you could ever wish to see. The Eskimos really enjoyed the trading. A man and his wife might come in with ten white foxes worth $200 . . . and we would know we were in for a long session in that frigid room. They would look all around the store as if they had never seen it before, and they would wander around—not that we minded, but all the time we would be getting colder and colder even though we were dressed like the Eskimos, in a full set of skins."

The Bay men had been schooled in how to detect faults in pelts such as rubbed shoulders in an animal that had suffered from fleas and had scratched itself too vigorously. Fur that was too flat indicated the fox had spent part of the winter in a burrow, instead of running about improving his coat's condition. "These fellows in the early stores worked under very poor conditions, often at night holding a coal-oil lantern in one hand, the pelt in the other," according to J.J. "Woody" Wood. "The customer might owe you a thousand dollars and be your best trapper, so you had to be psychologically very careful about what you said and what credit you gave. But whenever we overpaid for furs, we'd get a hot letter from Winnipeg." After the price was agreed to,

---

*This was in sharp contrast to the complicated ritual of Indian-HBC trading, as described in *Company of Adventurers*, pages 191–96.

*Les Manning, manager of Coppermine HBC post, trading with Inuit hunter, 1949*

trading tokens were placed on the counter and, as goods were chosen, they were withdrawn to make customers aware of how much each purchase was worth and how much they had left to spend.*

The quality of the HBC's early trade goods reflected the Company's monopolistic priorities. "It sold good rifles and traps, the best flour, tea and ammunition—all the items needed for a successful trapping expedition," noted Al Hochbaum, the Manitoba artist-naturalist who became one of the HBC's liveliest critics. "But otherwise there was much junk on the HBC's store shelves—bargain-basement stuff that wouldn't sell in Toronto or Montreal. Why, over the long trek, did they bring in frying pans so thin that food burned, or canvas tents so fragile that the wind whistled through and the insides became wet after only a light rain? Peter Arvelek once told me at Rankin Inlet that the frypans were thinner than the beer can he was holding." It was

---

*These tokens, matches or wooden sticks and brass, copper or later aluminum coins, had no monetary value outside the stores. (In 1926, the HBC's London Governor ruled that cash should be substituted for tokens at all HBC posts, but the order was ignored in remote areas and tokens were still being used in Ungava, for example, until the 1960s.)

one of the very few retailing relationships anywhere in which the merchant decided what goods his customers needed and how much they should be charged. The hunters who had been turned into trappers were gradually becoming consumers in a market economy that allowed them little freedom of choice.

Apart from having to trap for a living, the very idea of bartering for the goods they wanted was a new discipline for the Inuit. Their tradition allowed everyone to take whatever the reluctant land would yield; the notion of private property, money or material possession lay outside normal thought or discourse. In the pre-HBC period, Inuit society followed a pure form of communism (in the sense of a social order in which property is held in common), with protection and survival of the group (which usually meant family) being far more important than any one man's or woman's wishes. The Inuit were so determined to play down any sense of individualism that they would periodically exchange dwellings. Such a communal approach was essential on the tundra or when aboard some errant floe where all the available food had to be shared or someone could starve. But once the Company moved in and established its stores, individual possessions became a status symbol, and the basis of Inuit society was compromised. "The new barter economy—furs in exchange for the goods of civilization—made life harder instead of easier, more complicated instead of more simple," wrote Diamond Jenness, an early student of native cultures. "The commercial world of the white man had caught the Eskimo in its mesh, destroyed their self-sufficiency and independence, and made them economically its slaves."

THE RELATIONSHIP OF HBC TRADERS with the Inuit had its furtive aspects, too, and no part of that interchange was more carefully hidden from view—or more open to misinterpretation—than the sexual liaisons between them. The Bay men's perceptions of these sensual assignations varied according to their own experiences. "It was the accepted thing to do when I was up there as a kid," recalled Scotty Gall. "You went to the husband and asked for the wife, and you paid him in goods or ammunition and her in so many yards of calico or whatever she wanted." Chesley Russell, on the other hand, who spent from 1921 to 1960 in the HBC's northern service, claims none of it ever happened. "The Eskimos were just as jealous of their women as we are, and never traded off their wives to anybody," he insisted. Certainly, there was much gossip among the Inuit about the Bay men's sexual appetites. "They are not only in the North to make money but they're in it for a fast buck and a good piece of action, but they always forget they're dealing with human beings."

Cecil "Husky" Harris, the HBC Factor at Poorfish Lake on the edge of the tundra, had three Inuit wives at the same time and even visited Winnipeg with them all in tow, staying at the Empire, then known as the Hudson's Bay Hotel. "Harris' wives were quite a mixed lot," reported his colleague Sydney A. Keighley. "One was old and ugly, one was young and pretty, and one was very short and very homely. Eventually he decided to limit himself to one wife and he chose to keep the old, ugly one, who was the mother of his three children. Alfred Peterson bought the young, pretty one, and George Yandle bought the short, homely one. I never managed to find out what sort of price he got for them." Gontran de Poncins, the French adventurer who spent the winter of 1938 at the HBC's King William Island post, remembered asking Paddy Gibson, the local manager: "What would happen if I asked one of these Eskimos for his wife?"

"Very likely he'd let you have her."

"Without a word? Without any—er—bargaining about it?"

"Oh, quite! In the first place, it's done. And then, you see, it's something of an honor. The fact that out of them all you, a white man, picked her, would make the rest think more highly of her. And so far as the husband goes, of course he'd expect something in exchange. . . ."

"And suppose I asked for her several days running?"

"That wouldn't upset him. He might say to you, 'Tomorrow: I want her myself tonight.' But chances are that you could have her. And her husband and the rest would sit round in the igloo, laughing and chatting about you. The husband would be congratulated upon having made a rich friend. Probably he would let the others talk on while he dreamt of the things he'd get out of you."

No Bay man was more explicit in his sexual confessions than Duncan Pryde, whose exploits once prompted him to boast that "every community should have a little Pryde." Stu Hodgson could vouch for that reputation. "Duncan took on all comers," Hodgson recalled. "One time, I had a party travelling with me and I arranged to pick him up at one of the far northern settlements. I couldn't find him. There were thirteen houses near the beach. Suddenly Duncan came running out of the twelfth and said, 'Wait a minute—I have only one more to go,' and he dashed into the thirteenth. The local missionary came along, wringing his hands, saying, 'Please take him with you.' When we left, I am sure it was the first peaceful night he'd had in three weeks."

"Of all the Bay men who came north in the last sixty years,

Duncan Pryde was probably the best linguist and he gained an immense amount of respect among Inuit people," recalled Gordon Wray, an HBC veteran from Baker Lake who later became the Territories' minister of tourism and economic development. "But he destroyed himself because he did something that I don't believe he should have done. He wrote a book about his sexual dalliances, and mentioned names. He was forced out of the North, and people said they would kill him if he ever went back to the Central Arctic. He broke the rules. He was taken into Inuit life in ways that very few white men ever are, and he used it for his own personal gain; he broke the code of silence, and by using people's real names embarrassed a lot of people. Last I heard he was in London. He had lost an eye in a bar fight and was driving taxi."

Each tale of sexual liaisons under the polar moon may have tallied with specific moments and local circumstances, but the notion that Inuit women could be bought and that they couldn't wait to climb into the white men's beds distorts the rigid Inuit code of sexual ethics. Marriage was—and is—at the core of Inuit society. Men and women depended on one another not only for love and moral support but to carry out the division of labour so essential to the functioning of the Arctic family unit. Spouse-sharing did take place in the hunting days as a way of formalizing the sustaining alliances required for survival—less an expression of sexual licence than an essential social mechanism. "Far from being the casual and promiscuous affair that it is generally pictured to have been, 'wife-trading' was a very serious matter to the Eskimos," observed the American sociologist Ernest S. Burch, Jr. "We now know that it was an integral part of their system of marriage, which also included polygamous as well as monogamous forms of union. Both 'wife-trading' and polygamy, once thought to be manifestations of 'anarchy,' turn out to have been components of a complex but well-ordered system." An exception was "putting out the lamp"—a game played to relieve the tension of long winter nights. Nude couples shuffled about in their host's *iglu* until, at a given signal, they embraced the nearest person of the opposite sex.*

"My experience with Inuit on the land suggests that it is difficult for one man to exist without a woman," reminisced Commissioner Hodgson. "The man builds the snow house, looks after the dogs, hunts, traps, looks after the equipment and handles all of the chores outside the home. As the hunter goes, so goes the family. The woman

---

*And yes, in the early days Inuit did rub noses because kissing was considered unsanitary. The smaller and flatter a girl's nose, the more desirable she was deemed to be.

does everything else: prepares the food, raises the family, makes the clothes, keeps the home, skins the animals, prepares the skins and so on. One can't make it out on the land without the other."

"There are those that will tell you that the Hudson's Bay men were rapers and pillagers and there are those who will deny it ever happened. The real truth lies somewhere in between," Wray has pointed out. "Baker Lake is my home, and there are young and middle-aged Inuit whose features and mannerisms relate them to well-known HBC men. As a Bay clerk in a northern post—and I was one—you were, to a certain extent, the lowest caste or the lowest member of a caste system among the white community. There were two reasons for this: almost all of us were very young, seventeen, eighteen, nineteen, while most of the other white people were professionals in their thirties and forties—missionaries, government administrators, managers, Mounties and so on. We had nothing in common with the other white people in the community. So the HBC clerks would gravitate to Inuit their own age. Most of us were Scots, and we very easily assimilated into Inuit society; it wasn't the other way around. All our friends were young Inuit men and young Inuit women, and naturally a lot of us had girlfriends. I mean, there was nothing else to do.

"As a result, we became much more in tune with the goings-on within the Inuit community and because we were, that caused even more resentment among the older whites. There was this unwritten rule that the whites would stay together and have their own little parties and mix with the Inuit only when business dictated it. And so that put us down even more at the bottom of the totem pole to the point where we wouldn't be invited to their get-togethers, whatever. Almost always the relationships we developed were with people our own age who were Inuit. I'm now forty years old and I came north when I was eighteen. This talk about people swapping wives and Inuit giving you wives, I never saw that. Inuit men were very jealous of their wives, and in fact a lot of the murders in the old days that went unreported were caused by jealousies. I'm not saying that it didn't happen, but it was rare. Even then, it was often done with sets of preconditions, and I don't think it was as loose as everybody made it out to be. But the Bay boys clearly had a bad reputation, no question about that. In fact, most self-respecting Inuit girls wouldn't go to the Bay staff house until it was dark."

The Company had many informal rules against its employees marrying Inuit women and on May 8, 1940, issued a policy directive to that effect that included a remarkably muddle-headed paragraph on the subject: "The Board also discussed the question of the line of demarcation to be drawn as between 'native' and other women, Fullbred Indian and Eskimo women would obviously be classed as 'natives', but the distinction to be applied as between these and half-breeds and other women whose blood-relationship to 'natives' is more remote still, would appear to be a problem."

The young clerks served a five-year apprenticeship and learned to speak Inuktitut before being promoted to junior traders; if found incompatible with their surroundings, they were quietly dismissed. What they achieved upon promotion was a combination of freedom and responsibility. "So here we were," wrote J.W. Anderson about his first posting, which received mail twice a year, "on our own in the far interior, with no doctor and no means of communication with the outside world. We had to be prepared for all the hazards of life—fire, flood, famine, sickness and sudden death. This dependence on our own resources, and particularly inner resources, comes as quite a shock to the fur trade novice, though for my part I had made my peace with the country and its hazards during my first winter at Moose Factory." Anderson was fortunate compared to a trader named Charles Duncan, stationed at Payne Bay, where ice conditions were so bad it took two years to deliver a telegram notifying him of his father's death in a car accident.

WHETHER OR NOT IT HAD ANY CONNECTION with stories of nocturnal goings-on, the northern service was the HBC's most coveted posting. For an employee of an enterprise steeped in history, being an Arctic hand revived memories of the HBC's glorious genesis on Hudson Bay, and even though they were strictly a twentieth-century addition, the northern stores were often referred to as the Company's "founding department." Running an Arctic post was curiously similar to being captain of a Royal Navy ship-of-the-line, constantly at sea. The Company's headquarters in London and Winnipeg were belittled as "home ports" where uncomprehending desk-bound "admirals" schemed to produce irrelevant, bureaucratic red tape. The naval analogy was heightened by the HBC's insistence on dressing up its Factors in blue blazers with Company crests stitched on left breast pockets and special caps to exhibit the wearer's rank. An interpreter's or junior clerk's headgear had only a red enamel HBC flag on it; the flag on senior clerks' hats was surrounded by a cluster of gold leaves; post Factors or managers (as they were called after 1930) sported the flag and the cluster plus another spread of gold leaves (known as scrambled eggs) on their caps' peaks. "It was really the comradeship that bound us together," recalled Scotty Gall. "You felt you belonged."

Resident Factors derisively referred to anyone living South of Sixty as "on the Outside" and it was part of their rigid belief system that while they themselves spent most of their waking hours cursing the Company, any outsider who dared to agree with them did so at his own—often physical—peril. "The northern traders' loyalty had to be seen to be believed," noted Bob Chesshire, who was in charge of the northern posts during much of the transitional period to modern stores. "In some ways, it was a dangerous type of loyalty, because the Company could do no wrong, according to these oldtime Bay men." Bill Cobb, a Newfoundlander who joined the HBC as an apprentice clerk and retired thirty-seven years later as Deputy General Manager of Northern Stores, agreed: "God was the Company—and the Company was God. Let some outsider criticize the HBC and their life was in jeopardy." The Bay men knew no other life. When Cobb was at Rigolet in Labrador, the HBC employed a local cooper named Jim Deckers. He had spent his entire career making barrels at the post without ever bothering to collect his salary, though he had repeatedly been told there was a large savings-account balance available to him. "When the time came for Jimmy to retire," Cobb remembered, "he got quite upset and asked Ralph Parsons, 'Is that money you told me about still there?' " When he was assured that it was, Deckers offered to buy the cooperage, just so he could keep working there. The Company allowed him to stay on the job till he died, and he never did collect his accumulated pay.

An HBC Factor named Jimmy Bell was known as a character, even among the oddballs who populated this frozen outback. He served much of his time at Arctic Bay near the top of the Borden Peninsula on Baffin Island, where he devoted himself mainly to eating. He could gulp down ten pounds of seal meat at one sitting with no effort at all, and as one observer described the process, "it disappeared into him just as if he were a polar bear." Bell soon began to *look* like a polar bear, so that his 350-pound frame had to be lowered into his peterhead boat by block and tackle. Eventually transferred to Cape Dorset, Bell started to lose weight and vomit blood. He was diagnosed as having stomach cancer, but before leaving Dorset he told a companion that he wanted to be buried in the North. "When I die," he vowed, "my spirit is going back to Arctic Bay. That's the place I really love most. . . ." And that was exactly what happened. Although Bell was eventually treated at a Winnipeg hospital, where he died after six weeks, and was buried in a nearby urban cemetery, from the moment of his death, Bell's ghost began to appear in the Arctic Bay staff house. Doors opened mysteriously, footsteps were heard in empty rooms, shadows moved along the walls, noises and moans sounded for no explicable reason. One night, the HBC trader who had taken Bell's place heard his kitchen dishes rattling, and, finally fed up, he yelled out, "Leave the goddamned dishes alone, Bell, and get the hell out of here!" That made Jimmy so mad he bounced the dishes right out of their cupboards. The phenomenon was eventually reported to the RCMP, which carried out a formal investigation, but they couldn't get their ghost. Bell's old shack had to be abandoned in favour of a new post building.

The hardy stock that produced such dedicated eccentrics had previously generated the HBC's advance across the Prairies. They were hard-bitten Scots whose loyalty was beyond question even if their Company-supplied equipment was often beyond salvage—wilderness men who had more muscle than imagination and less introspection than courage. "They called us North Sea Chinamen," recalled Scotty Gall, proud to be one of them, "because we took the work cheaper than anybody else and we stayed with it. We were tough little guys; they could beat us into the ground with a hammer, and we'd spring up again." Recruited as youngsters in the Orkneys, Hebrides and Highlands, they signed on for twenty dollars a month to serve the HBC by day or night, pledging to protect with courage and fidelity the property of the Company with their lives if necessary. The youngsters could be sent anywhere within the HBC's domain, but North was where they all wanted to go. Apart from the adventurous aspect of these postings, advancement was faster and the Arctic posts were far more informally run than the western or even sub-Arctic stations. Philip Godsell, who left an entertaining account of his twenty-year HBC service, was posted to Norway House not long after arriving in Canada. Although it was located three hundred miles north of Winnipeg, Norway House was not considered a northern post and was run in the old-fashioned way. "We lived in a sort of semi-feudal state," Godsell later reminisced. "At regular hours the bell rang and we paraded to the messroom. Here, with much pomp and ceremony, presided the bewhiskered Donald McTavish, and although we were literally in the back of beyond, woe betide the person who appeared at table unshaven or without a white collar on. Once only I appeared with a spotted scarf knotted around my neck. Hardly was I seated ere I found myself transfixed by old Donald's astonishing and disapproving gaze. A string of expletives crackled off the old man's tongue as he demanded to know whether I considered they were all barbarians in this country. . . . I was forthwith ordered to proceed to my room and put a collar on." As late as 1912 at York Factory, HBC employees had to swear oaths of allegiance that obliged them "never to purchase any fur excepting for [their] personal use, and never to betray any business information that might come into [their] possession." The local cook, a marvellous, earthy Mixed Blood named "Lame Annie" Redsky, best summed up the HBC's operational code: "Most masters of the Company's posts is lak kings. . . . Yo kin be birthed and died without [their] consent but dat's 'bout all."

THEIR DOMAINS WERE VAST IF NEARLY EMPTY, but within these icy realms the HBC traders were kings. They acted as their subjects' shopkeepers, meteorologists, bankers, dentists, doctors and welfare officers as well as father confessors and, until the RCMP arrived, administrators of justice. "When I was in charge of a post," declared Cornwallis King, who spent forty-one years with the HBC in the Northwest Territories, "if orders were good, I carried them out. If not, I handled them in my own way. I was willing to be judged by results. Sometimes the orders from England were absolutely idiotic.* All right for London, perhaps, but no good in the Mackenzie River District fur trade. I did not look for credit for myself. If my own decisions brought the desired results, I let the honour go to the district manager. We were above money considerations. *We were the Company* [emphasis added]."

The Company kept a fairly tight rein on its employees, with regular visits by district managers and inspectors, but the most potent self-regulator was the journal in which every Factor was obliged to document his daily rounds and business transactions. Until the advent of radio and air travel, these diaries, kept in duplicate and forwarded annually to Winnipeg and London, were treated extremely seriously, so much so that on the inside cover of each journal there was pasted this admonition: "Your ability to keep this book in a neat and intelligent manner will be an indication of your character and ability as Post Manager." Some Factors grew bored and exasperated with trying to describe each day's largely repetitive activities. When Pierre Mercredi ran Fort Resolution on Great Slave Lake, one of his jobs was to haul firewood with a team of oxen named Bill and Tom. For twenty-one days his journal carefully noted the weather, how much wood was moved and so on. Each entry was virtually identical,

---

*London's suggestions included turning seal meat into dog food, processing Chesterfield Inlet mud into cement and building their famous boot-chewing machine. The traditional way to soften sealskin for boot-making was for Inuit women to chew the pelts until they were flexible enough to be sewn. This eventually wore their teeth down to the gums, which caused them great difficulty in eating. The HBC's Development Department built a device to soften the hides. It was based on the principle of an old-fashioned clothes wringer and had brass teeth mounted in it. One of the contraptions was actually installed at Port Burwell, but it didn't work.

and finally he could take it no longer. On the twenty-second day, his journal notation was reduced to two words: "Tom Balked."

The Company handled its staff with hard-fisted parsimony. "It was a pretty primitive existence," recalled Bill Cobb. "The furniture in staff houses was mostly home made, and some of the post manager's houses were real shacks." Architecturally, the worst example was the post manager's house at Repulse Bay on the Melville Peninsula. For reasons known only to himself, George Cleveland, who built the structure, reversed its windows so that they opened *into* the house and the windowsills sloped inward. That meant winter storm-windows had to be uselessly attached on the inside, allowing condensation to run into the rooms, where it froze. Local Factors vainly complained for decades that every winter at Repulse Bay was a nightmare, but the faulty building remained in place.

To cheer up post managers' wives, who began to move north in the 1930s, the HBC allowed them to pick their own staff-house colour scheme. One stir-crazy lady painted the ceiling of her living-room black, a foot-wide border at the top of the walls white and the rest of the surfaces a shocking pink; another applied various combinations of mauve and yellow. These early Company installations had no indoor plumbing, and there were serious logistical problems with outhouses. Any hole dug into the frozen ground caused the permafrost to thaw and the opening to widen, so that eventually the whole flimsy structure would sink into its own cesspool. When William Duval, a Cumberland Sound free-trader who had become a hermit, died, the Inuit, who had liked the strange white man, thought he deserved a proper Christian burial. There being no wood in the area to build a coffin, they interred him in the only wooden structure available: his own outhouse.

One area of significant discretion granted the Factors was the amount of credit they could allow various customers when Arctic fox prices were low and times turned bad. The problem was that no one could explain the basic laws of supply and demand to Inuit whose lives had come to depend largely on their ability to harvest furs. When fox prices at international auctions were at their lowest, the trappers worked extra hard because it took more pelts to obtain the supplies they wanted. That, of course, turned the classical supply/demand equation upside down, since conventional wisdom would have required the trappers to hold their goods back until the market turned up again. Understandably, they had little idea of what governed the price of a fur that seemed worthless to them—but that the white men wanted without being able to decide exactly what it was worth. Stuart Hodgson recalled how he once tried to explain the fluctuation in muskrat prices to an Indian on the Mackenzie.

"One day this fellow came up to me and said, 'Commissioner, how come I only get twenty-five cents for my rats?'

" 'Well, I'll tell you, it's like this. There's a guy in Paris by the name of Christian Dior, and one day he decided women would wear H-form dresses, which meant using short-hair furs for trim. So orders went out to the London fur auction houses to buy seal, and the Bay told its post managers to set a lower price for long-hair muskrat.'

"The Indian listened to the long-winded explanation with a stony expression, and shot back: 'Yeah, I know all about that. But how come I only get twenty-five cents for my rats?'

" 'Because that's all they're worth.'

" 'Well, why didn't you say so in the first place?' "

Because market prices and fox populations were both cyclical, on many occasions Inuit came into the HBC posts with no furs to trade or not enough pelts to obtain significant store credits. Some, if not most, of the HBC Factors responded with compassion, or at least as much compassion as was allowed within the limits of their headquarters-imposed credit lines and quantities of available supplies. But the extent of the HBC's generosity in those hard days before there was a federally sponsored welfare system remains an issue of active controversy. Charlie Watt, the Inuk who became a Canadian senator in 1983, has defended the Company. "When things were not going well, as they often did in those days ... the Hudson's Bay Company dispensed assistance to widows and people in need. Inuit were given per family per week: eight pounds of flour, half a pound of tea, half a pound of lard, half a pound of baking powder, two pounds of molasses or two pounds of sugar."

Others disagree. When he was Grand Chief of the Grand Council of the Cree of Quebec, Billy Diamond charged there was a graveyard ninety-five miles south of Rupert House on James Bay where twenty families had starved to death because the local HBC store would not give them credit. "The Bay *would* grubstake people," Stuart Hodgson maintained, "but they also kept good records and never lost a dime." Bernie Weston, a private fur trader wise in the ways of the North, argued that the HBC did carry starving people in off-season fur droughts, but that those who were helped later had to sell their pelts at whatever prices the Company set, even if it was less than they could get from competing traders.

Peter Ernerk, a former president of the Keewatin Inuit Association at Rankin Inlet and one of his people's more youthful spokesmen, put it this way: "The Hudson's Bay Company was necessary in our time as a trader of furs. It got rich from the native people in the North as well as throughout Canada and took advantage of the native people, especially in the area of furs, handicrafts and carvings. Inuit got very little return for their goods. It also lacked hiring native people, although this situation has improved in recent years. When I was growing up in Repulse Bay, which is my home town, I felt that. On the other hand, the Company provided a service which no one else was able to provide. So, from that point of view, it was positive. The Company's staff also acted as jack-of-all-trades besides being traders. They provided medical supplies and also acted as para-medical doctors. This was good."

Gordon Wray, the former Bay man who married an Inuk, is not as harsh in his assessment. "The missionaries were the ones who really changed people's ways and thinking," he claims. "When we joined the HBC, they said: 'The only way you can serve your customers is to understand that customer.' That's why they forced us into learning to speak local dialects and how to run a trapline. They made our lives hard because they wanted us to understand the people we were serving. But they never tried to change the Inuit in terms of how they did things or how they thought or to stop the drum dances or any of that stuff.

"The old people still have a lot of respect for the Bay. Some of it was out of fear, there's no question, but also some of it was genuine respect because the Bay appeared at a time when the Inuit were in trouble; there was a lot of starvation. The Bay was seen to a certain extent as having saved a lot of Inuit people because the Company appeared on the scene with better hunting equipment that allowed them to get more food and they did a lot of early medical stuff. But there was a sort of a safety net around that didn't exist before. So among the old people, you'll never hear a bad word said about the Hudson's Bay Company. The younger people are a different story. To them it was just another store. But not among the older people. The Bay is much more than just a store, it's part of their life, part of their culture almost."

Within two decades of its decision to seek a new empire in Canada's Arctic, most of the Company's infrastructure was in place and its business was reaching new levels of prosperity. Unaware that they were destroying aboriginal traditions in the process, the Factors who pioneered the HBC's northern service pointed with pride to the Inuit they had rescued from starvation. Closer examination revealed it was mainly the families of reliable trappers who were granted most of the store credit—and that the real reason for subsidizing them was that dead customers paid off no debts.

*Colin Fraser (left) and Sir Patrick Ashley Cooper (right) at Fort Chipewyan, December 1932*

# CHAPTER 10

# KILLING THE COMPETITION

*To open up a store against the Bay, that was heresy.*
*Why, you were committing an act against God.*
*It was God who gave the Hudson's Bay that land!"*

— HBC Trader Bill Cobb

THE WORLD OF THE TWENTIETH CENTURY was not smaller, but it was faster. When Guglielmo Marconi tapped his first wireless telegraphy signals across the Atlantic in 1901, it was only a matter of time before prices at London auctions were instantly being flashed to posts in Canada's beaver swamps. Ever dependent on fickle fashion, the HBC faced the most serious threat yet to its long-established trading system, with independent operators able to move in and out of fur categories and, by taking advantage of the new advances in communication, turn over their capital several times a season. Installation of regular telegraph services shattered what was left of the Company's monopoly because it demystified the fur trade by allowing everyone access to the latest market information.

At the same time, economic prosperity had returned to North America and stocks of luxury furs diminished as not only elegant women rushed to buy the glamorous garments but also men, driving the new open motor cars, wrapped themselves in enormous coats that made them look like pregnant mountain goats. "Growing numbers of fur buyers and traders, many of whom were Americans, were drawn into the Canadian north seeking new sources of supply," noted Arthur Ray, a University of British Columbia historian who specializes in the fur trade. Canada's northern edges—though not yet the Arctic—were being opened up through the Klondike gold rush and construction of

*Advertisement for HBC supplies for Klondike gold rush*

railways towards Port Nelson on Hudson Bay and into the Peace River country. Traders and merchants poured into the Mackenzie River Valley and Great Slave Lake territory so fast that the hamlet of Fort Resolution eventually boasted six retail stores, and Fort Chipewyan on Lake Athabasca counted more than a dozen fur-trading posts clustered around the HBC's historic fort. Because these newcomers enjoyed much lower overheads and were not subject to decisions made by boards of directors on the other side of the world, they cut deeply into the HBC's established business. At the same time, consignment and mail-order houses appeared in Canada for the first time, buying and selling furs on commission, allowing competitors quick and simple entry into the trade.*

---

*The impact of these innovations forced the HBC in 1920 to abandon its 250-year-old policy of auctioning only its own furs and to begin moving consignment pelts as well. Competitors opened alternative auction houses in London (C.M. Lampson & Company and A.W. Nesbitt), New York (New York Fur Auction Sales Company), St Louis (International Fur Exchange), Winnipeg (Fur Auction Sales Company), Vancouver (Little Brothers), Montreal (Canadian Fur Auction Sales Company) and Leipzig (G. Gaudig & Blum).

Occasionally, the HBC deliberately—and deviously—competed with itself. John Montague of North West River in Labrador recalled, with a touch of humour and an exaggerated accent, how he had once been fooled into selling to an "independent," with unexpected results: "I remember one time for sure when I had quite a little bit of fur and there was this feller come from Cartwright. Martin he was, Jim or Frank, I fergits now. I thought this feller was a fur buyer, not from HBC at all. I took my fur to HBC and they priced it. I took my fur to Martin and he didn't offer me quite as much, but I sold it to 'en anyway because I wanted to encourage him to come back. After he was gone I found out he was buyin' fer HBC. That was wonderful funny." But more often, the competition was real, and it nearly drove the Company's fur business to the wall.

First to follow the HBC into the Mackenzie district was Hislop and Nagle, which eventually opened twenty-four posts between Athabasca Landing and Arctic Red River, built three steamships, and even had its own sawmill and engineering shop. James Hislop, a mathematician and civil engineer from Pictou, Nova Scotia, had gone West as a surveyor on the Pembina Branch of the CPR and later moved to Edmonton. His partner, Edmund Barry Nagle, was a millwright who had served with the St Hyacinthe Infantry Company during the Fenian raids and had taken part in Métis buffalo hunts out of Fort Garry before joining Hislop in Edmonton. "They were considered outlaws at the time, because the Hudson's Bay Company behaved as if it still had a monopoly," noted Jordan Zinovich, who studied the history of the enterprise. "When Mrs. Nagle arrived at Fort Resolution, the HBC Factors and their wives would not talk to her. She was so socially ostracized that she had to bring in a 'professional friend' from the Outside." After harvesting fur worth $200,000, Hislop and Nagle in 1913 sold out to the Northern Trading Company of Edmonton, which eventually manned thirty-two small posts, obtaining financial sponsorship from London's A.W. Nesbitt and temporarily diminishing the HBC trade. When Nesbitt went bankrupt in 1919, Northern was pushed into receivership. A group of Winnipeg auctioneers led by Max Finkelstein and fronted by Colonel J.K. Cornwall (the celebrated Alberta entrepreneur known as Peace River Jim) obtained control and moved its headquarters to Fort Smith, but it never fully recovered and went bankrupt in 1931; the HBC picked up its remaining assets.

Lamson and Hubbard Corporation, Boston's leading fur dealers, arrived in Canada right after the First World War, erecting a dozen outlets on the Mackenzie and two short-lived Arctic posts at Chesterfield Inlet and Baker Lake. The firm moved in like an invading army, or rather navy, launching an impressive sternwheeler (the SS *Distributor*) that shuttled between Fort Smith and Fort McPherson, two other steamers, a pair of large gas boats, several gas-powered tugs and a fleet of fifty twenty-ton scows. Within six years its heavy overhead sank the firm, with the HBC yet again absorbing the pieces. Several smaller trading outfits tried to buck the Company, but none succeeded. The most tragic attempt was that of a group of retired British naval officers who incorporated the Sabellum Trading Company in 1911 and for the next dozen years dispatched trading vessels to Baffin Island. One of their ships, the *Erme*, was blown up by a German submarine; another, the *Vera*, a forty-four-year-old wooden Cowes-built racing yacht, proved comically unsuitable for Arctic voyages. Sabellum managed to land only one representative on Baffin, an elderly stone-deaf gunnery officer named Hector Pitchforth, who starved to death in his ten-by-fifteen-foot shack at Cape Kater on the isolated Brodeur Peninsula during the cruel winter of 1927. The following year Sabellum sold its few belongings to the HBC.*

THE ONLY SERIOUS LONGTERM RIVAL faced by the HBC in the North was Revillon Frères of Paris. Like that of the Nor'Westers who had challenged the Company's hegemony a century earlier, Revillon's assault lasted for most of four decades and was led by far more enterprising spirits than the bureaucratic duffers who inhabited the HBC's middle management. Exactly like the Nor'Westers, Revillon ultimately failed because it expanded too fast, and its backers—unlike the Hudson's Bay Company, which had put aside adequate financial reserves and enjoyed access to guarantees from the Bank of England —were unable to withstand long periods of financial drought. A successor firm to the veteran (1723) French furrier François Givelet, Louis Victor Revillon's company had revolutionized the industry. It broadened the market by selling fur coats through drygoods shops. Instead of purchasing all its pelts from wholesalers, it established its own trading outlets to obtain the raw product from Russian and Canadian trappers. At the turn of the century, Revillon purchased a string of Mackenzie River posts from Colonel Cornwall, and also

---

*Another inglorious venture backed by British interests was the Arctic Gold Exploration Syndicate, inaugurated by Captain Henry Toke Munn, formerly of Pond Inlet. Munn persuaded Lord Lascelles and others to back him in seeking gold on Baffin Island, mainly by showing them art photographs he had taken of some "naked Inuit girls reflected in pools."

*Lamson and Hubbard employee R.D. Ferrier*
*guarding winter supplies for Little Red River post*

established half a dozen stores on the north shore of the St Lawrence and up the Labrador coast.

Revillon's assault on Hudson Bay, planned for the summer of 1903, was predicated on impressing local trappers by installing one of its prefabricated stores beside nearly every HBC outlet. The necessary staff and material were gathered in Montreal and loaded on the *Stord*, a Norwegian-built merchant ship, which promptly ran aground at Pointe des Monts in the Gulf of St Lawrence. To get into the Bay before freeze-up, Revillon chartered the 820-ton *Eldorado*, then employed on the London-Liverpool run, whose skipper, Captain William Berry, had never ventured beyond England's coastal waters. He successfully crossed the Atlantic, picked up the *Stord*'s crew and cargo, then somehow muddled his way through Hudson Strait. The crew and passengers, numbering forty-seven, included Revillon's Montreal representative, a Monsieur d'Aigneaux, who was travelling with his wife, daughter and a governess, a doctor, four clerks and fourteen Quebec carpenters hired to erect the stores. Drawing a deep sixteen feet and carrying 1,450 tons of cargo, the *Eldorado*, her decks crowded with sections for the prefabricated buildings, lumbered into Hudson Bay bound for Fort George on the eastern shore of James Bay. After several close calls, the ship rammed a reef nine miles out of the settlement. "When the tide fell, she listed so badly that her decks became almost vertical," Third Engineer George Venables wrote in his journal. ". . . So serious were matters now that the captain insisted that the ladies, child, and other passengers should go in boats to Fort George, so as to be safe. It was well this was done, for on the Wednesday [September 2, 1903] a terrible storm came on, the ship bumped up and down on the cruel rocks, and finally tore a great hole in her bottom, through which the water rushed in volumes. We saved what food we could, and, with some clothes, got away to an island ere the doomed vessel was lost."

Donald Gillies, the HBC Factor resident at Fort George, counted the four dozen survivors and quickly realized his spare supplies would feed them for only two days. He lent them boats and advised them to hurry south to Charlton Island, where an HBC steamer, the *Lady Head*, was due to leave for London. After a hazardous passage the *Eldorado*'s crew reached Charlton the day after the steamer's departure—which was lucky, because the *Lady Head* was shortly afterwards wrecked on Gasket Shoals. The unhappy travellers made their way down to Moose Factory in borrowed HBC lighters, then had to travel five hundred miles up the Moose and Abitibi rivers before they reached civilization. It was a harrowing journey. "When we got up each morning," wrote Venables, "it was invariably to find that the blanket with which each person was provided was a solid piece of ice, as hard as iron, and we had to get it thawed and free as best we could. . . . We endeavoured to bake some of the flour into cakes each night; but as we had no baking powder you can imagine what the result was like. Our rations at best did not run to more than half a cake each per night, and we began to feel very weak and ill from being so underfed and so much exposed." When they came out of the bush at New Liskeard, without having lost a soul along the way, a correspondent for the Toronto *Globe* who interviewed the survivors wrote that they had portaged their "lifeboats" around the rapids through a terrain "as unknown to the party as if it had been in the heart of Africa."

The mishap set back Revillon's Hudson Bay venture, but by 1908, with supplies brought in on the 2,500-ton icebreaker *Adventurer*, Revillon had seven posts on line, including a dock and warehouse at Strutton Island in the lower bay. The *Adventurer* was eventually wrecked in Hudson Strait, but not before she helped erect other Revillon posts at Baker Lake, Repulse Bay and the Belcher Islands.*

---

*Revillon commissioned the explorer/film-maker Robert Flaherty to shoot *Nanook of the North* on the Belchers and at Port Harrison during the winter of 1920–21. The first documentary of its kind to achieve world-wide distribution, the movie was an instant hit, so much so that Americans marketed a new brand of ice-cream called Nanook, while Germans sold Nanook ashtrays. Brilliantly shot and edited, the film helped perpetuate the stereotype of Inuit as happy victims of their environment.

The French concern eventually operated forty-seven Canadian trading posts, mostly concentrated in the northwest. The firm's huge warehouse in Edmonton, its stock supplied from Montreal aboard a special twenty-six-car freight train, became the West's largest department store, offering everything from food products, china, fabrics and farm equipment to bronze bells and missionaries' chasubles. Revillon was soon doing annual business in excess of $5 million, including supply contracts for the Indian treaties and Mounted Police on the Peace and Yukon rivers, but like the HBC it had great difficulty supplying some of its western land posts. To move goods from Edmonton to Hudson's Hope on the Peace River, for example, required taking them by sleigh in January as far as Athabasca, where they were stored for the rest of the winter. In spring they were poled over by scow to Lesser Slave Lake, where they were stored again until the primitive road to the Peace River became passable. That oxcart passage was followed by another scow expedition to Hudson's Hope— the entire one-way journey having taken eight months.

It was typical of the Bay men that, although they had lost their official monopoly in 1870, they still behaved more than a generation later as if they owned the country. "Only those who have worked for the Company," explained Philip Godsell, "can understand the feeling that existed against the average opposition trader, and the perhaps misguided sense of loyalty which would, literally, cause a Hudson's Bay man to push even his own brother to the wall if he happened to be trading in opposition to the 'Gentlemen Adventurers.'" Bill Cobb, who traded against Revillon, echoed the thought. "To open up a store against the Bay, that was heresy. Why, you were committing an act against God. It was God who gave the Hudson's Bay that land!" he recalled in mock anger forty-eight years later, adding, "I laugh about it now, but that's the way I felt—and still do, to some degree."

In the field, competition between the two firms quickly turned vicious. Startled Inuit and Indians were treated to the sight of the only two white men in their settlements childishly squabbling over each pelt, spying on one another, outbidding each other's prices. It became standard practice for HBC Factors to decree that any trapper caught trading with Revillon could no longer sell to the Company. The Cree sensed this was a potent threat; their name for Revillon was *Tustowichuk*—the "people between them and the Company." The French firm's post managers complained that their customers refused to trade in the daytime lest they be spotted by the HBC traders, who had ostentatiously trained telescopes on their competitors' front doors. Even at night, exchanges at the Revillon posts had to be carried out behind drawn blinds.

Revillon's first managers were mostly retired French army and navy officers and superannuated bureaucrats, more familiar with wine vintages than the crude ways of the Canadian frontier. They underestimated their opponents and patronized their customers. The Bay traders derisively referred to Revillon as "the Frenchmen" and were not above delivering some low slurs. One Christmas at Moose Factory, a Revillon trader was celebrating alone while there was a big party at the Bay post. The Anglican missionary R.J. Renison, later an archbishop, who was visiting Moose Factory, urged the Bay man to go over and invite his rival. After grumbling about the idea for most of a morning, the Factor, a humourless Scotsman, agreed. But the Revillon man didn't show up. When Renison demanded to know how the invitation had been issued, the burred reply was: "I just asked him who won the Battle of Waterloo—any goddamned Frenchman should know that." Revillon eventually switched to recruiting in Dundee, Scotland. It signed on good men—at forty dollars a month, all found, twice the wage offered by the HBC—but its traders could not compete in the down cycles of the fur trade. Wallace Laird, who was one of them, claimed that he had never been at a Revillon post "that showed a profit. The cost of goods was so high . . . that a generous mark-up was still not sufficient to keep the posts out of the red."

By the spring of 1925, Revillon's owners initiated discussions with the HBC on a co-operative agreement that would reduce expenditures of both concerns. The contract, signed on July 17, 1926, was in fact a takeover, with the HBC agreeing to acquire 51 percent of Revillon Canada for up to $918,000 during the next eight years. Ralph Parsons was named the HBC's representative director on the Revillon board; the French firm had Canadian assets of $2,981,214 and current liabilities of $879,642 at the time. There was no doubt about the HBC's motives for the takeover. "Arrangements should be definitely made, for the fixing of the prices of Furs and Merchandise at all Posts affected directly, or indirectly, by the competition of Revillon Frères," stated an internal memo prepared for the HBC management. "These prices can be fixed periodically by the District Managers concerned, with Revillon managers. Competition between the companies for employees will be eliminated; thus eliminating salary increases unwarranted for any reason, other than the possibility of injury being done to our trade by a transfer of an employee."

Revillon continued to operate into the 1930s as a quasi-independent entity. By then an exasperated Jean Revillon was writing to the HBC Governor: "After more and more consideration on the subject, we came to the final conclusion that the active management of the Hudson's Bay Company's Trading Posts: i.e. Mr Parsons and his subordinates, were so deadly opposed to any competition held out against the Hudson's Bay Co., even though this competition be afforded by the Revillon Frères Trading Co. in which the Hudson's Bay Company holds the majority of shares, that they did everything in order to crush Revillon Frères Trading Company and the conclusion reached was that it was preferable for this Company to have a single owner."

When the Bay argued about the price it would pay for his firm's remaining assets, Jean Revillon didn't hide his anger: "We have good grounds to claim that the present state of Revillon Frères Trading Company is due to mis-management on the part of your Winnipeg office," he wrote to the HBC Governor. "The co-operation in the North, which was an important factor of our 1926 Agreement, and carried most weight towards our acceptance of it as far as our interests were concerned, was not lived up to by your managers. The results have proved disastrous. . . . The assets of the Revillon Frères Trading Company have been stripped and laid bare to the bone, which has been a wise policy on your part, as it certainly favours your claim when establishing the price of shares." By this time, net assets had been reduced to $1,158,000, and the HBC purchased all of Revillon's outstanding shares for $380,000. Liquidation of the French firm's Canadian holdings was completed during 1937, with twenty-two of its seventy-three employees joining the Bay.

There then followed a bizarre mop-up operation. The HBC didn't intend to stop at having beaten its rival; the Company wanted to obliterate Revillon's every trace, so that no other freebooter would again be presumptuous enough to assume the North belonged to anyone but the Company of Adventurers. When Revillon decamped, one of its district inspectors, a former French naval captain named Jean Berthe, decided to remain in the Arctic as an independent trader. A highly civilized Parisian with a wry sense of life's absurdities, he found pleasure in the eternal solitude of the Ungava Peninsula and, gathering a few trading supplies, settled near Burgoyne Bay, on the south shore of Hudson Strait. The Hudson's Bay Company panicked. Determined to hound the Frenchman out of the North, Fur Trade Commissioner Ralph Parsons placed three of his toughest subordinates—Alex Stevenson, John Stanners and Bruce Campbell—in charge of mobile trading posts codenamed U-X, U-Y and U-Z. The outfits were dropped at locations near Berthe's camp and loaded into peterhead boats, so that as soon as the French trader made a move in any direction an HBC post could immediately be set up near him to undercut his trades.

They chased him for three months and finally cornered Berthe at Payne Bay, where the Bay men erected their instant shop to head off the Inuit trappers. After two seasons of mounting losses, the French naval captain departed, his purse empty but his dignity intact.*

The Revillon episode was a turning point. The Company won, but the cost had been high. The North, like the West, could not much longer remain the private preserve of any commercial enterprise.

---

*A happier tale was the adventure of the American biologist Clarence Birdseye, who purchased Revillon's abandoned post on Sandwich Bay, near Cartwright in Labrador, for a fur-farming venture. He watched the catch of native fishermen freeze in -50°F weather, the moment the fish were taken out of the water. "Months later, when they were thawed out," he noted, "some of those fish were so fresh that they were still alive!" Applying similar techniques to meats and vegetables, he gradually perfected the famous frozen food products that bear his name.

*Horse-drawn wagon with Lamson and Hubbard fur shipment, Edmonton, 1922*

*The Nascopie at Port Burwell, 1937*

# CHAPTER 11

# THE *NASCOPIE* CHRONICLES

*"Signifying many things to many people and, on occasion, everything to a very few,* Nascopie *acquired a unique personality endowed with almost human characteristics."*

—Henny Nixon

CHIEF AGENT OF CHANGE in the Canadian North was not a man or a company, but a ship. On July 10, 1911, Lord Strathcona had commissioned construction of a 2,500-ton supply vessel from Swan Hunter of Newcastle-on-Tyne. The coal-burning *Nascopie*'s unique design—her stern cut away like a yacht from above the waterline, a semicircular hull and undercut bow, every steel plate reinforced and slightly curved to deflect the ice—fitted the vessel ideally for the treacherous journeys that would earn her pride of place among the ships that altered the perception of Canada's northern geography.*

Not precisely an icebreaker—though often used as one—the *Nascopie* was designed to open a seapath by sliding over the ice, then shattering it under her own weight. She had a bottom as smooth and rounded as that of a racing shell and no bilge keel, so that ice pressure around the sides would lift rather than crush her. Her bow was fitted with a "shoe"—a sturdy casing riveted to the keel plate that occasionally allowed her to batter ice formations until a crack appeared wide enough to sail through. "Signifying many things to many people and, on occasion, everything to a very few, *Nascopie* acquired a unique

---

*The *Nascopie* took her name from the Montagnais designation for the local tribe of Ungava and Labrador Indians, whose own name for themselves was *Nenenot*— "true men."

personality endowed with almost human characteristics," wrote Henny Nixon, an Ottawa maritime historian.

After her maiden voyage across the Atlantic, the *Nascopie* was employed in the Newfoundland seal hunt before setting off on her first voyage into Hudson Bay and the Eastern Arctic. When she arrived at the Charlton Island supply depot near the bottom of the Bay, local natives, astounded at *Nascopie*'s size, got balls of string to measure her 285-foot hull, and later they would stretch out the twine and explain to friends up the coast that the great new ship was "as long as that!" At the end of her 1915 voyage, with the Great War presenting new problems, the *Nascopie* was assigned to the Brest-Murmansk-Archangel supply run and armed with a three-pounder Hotchkiss, a gun built in 1857 to help quell the Indian Mutiny. The ancient weapon's range was uncertain, but it made as much noise as a six-incher. On June 14, 1917, when the *Nascopie* was attacked by the German submarine U-28 off Archangel, she drove off the boat with four well-placed shots. Later that year, command of the *Nascopie* was assumed by Captain Thomas Farrar Smellie, one of the few mariners who had master's papers for both sail and steam. For most of the next thirty years he sailed the largely uncharted waters of the Canadian North, turning his ship and himself into a legend. "There may have been some 'luck' about it," wrote Roland Wild, the *Nascopie*'s lively biographer, "but the happy partnership of Captain and ship was based on a much surer foundation. These partners knew one another, they each had sturdy beginnings; you could say they had each been built by craftsmen, each knew the qualities and endurance of the other—they were as one, not Captain and ship, but a unit."

The *Nascopie* made thirty-four trips to resupply the HBC's Eastern Arctic and Hudson Bay posts, bringing back furs, mail and rotating personnel, serving an area then not otherwise accessible. She went about her risky business in waters virtually unmarked by navigational aids, sailing through latitudes where compasses were useless because of underwater iron ore deposits and proximity to the north magnetic pole. In parts of Hudson Bay, the earth's magnetism is so powerful that compass needles point nowhere except down; at the entrance to Pond Inlet, the earth's variation is more than 100 degrees, so that ships have to be steered 10 degrees east of north to be heading west. Available maps were so amateurish Captain Smellie once complained that if he followed the Admiralty charts at his disposal, his ship's position would be 150 miles inland. The distances the *Nascopie* had to cover in the brief season of open water between the widely dispersed HBC posts were immense; each trip averaged 10,500 miles—

*Captain Smellie (right) aboard the* Nascopie, *with fur-trade head Ralph Parsons, 1933*

Arctic Bay, then the northernmost of the HBC outposts, was 2,800 miles by sea from Montreal.

Each voyage was an adventure. Smellie was tough; he had to be. A steward who served under him recalled a hazardous climb to the bridge as the ship, battered by blizzards and waves higher than her funnel, seemed ready to pitch-pole. The steward managed to reach the captain and shouted in his ear: "Would you like anything to eat?"

"Bowl of soup!" Smellie yelled back.

The steward laboriously climbed down to the galley, was instructed to carry the bowl not on a tray but in the hollow of a napkin held by its four corners, and climbed back up to the bridge, almost losing the soup and his life in the process. Feeling that he had been miraculously spared from the elements to fulfil his mission, he proudly presented the still-steaming brew to his captain. Smellie took one look at the soup bowl and bellowed: "*Where's the spoon?*"

THE *NASCOPIE*'S JOURNEY NORTH from her berth in Montreal quickly became a ritual. Her decks, noisy with penned sheep, chickens and pigs bound for traders' skillets, also carried an occasional milk cow. Her holds bursting with supplies, the vessel was so overloaded that shipping officials and Smellie had to play an unusual game. "When the Port inspectors made their routine check before departure," Roland Wild observed, "the Captain would show them the port side first, and give a vague kind of opinion that the ship must be listing to port, since the Plimsoll Line was invisible. When the inspectors repaired to the starboard side, the ship must have suddenly listed to starboard, for there was little sign of it there either. . . . Rather than order the ship to be unloaded of a hundred tons or so of vital cargo, they [the inspectors] seemed to have arrived at a remarkable conclusion: the *Nascopie* was a ship that listed on both sides at the same time." Fully loaded, the ship would sound her siren and, her pennants flying, cast off lines and steam half-astern to midstream. With all the ships in harbour blowing their salute whistles, the *Nascopie* would puff proudly out to the St Lawrence and set course for Labrador. Aboard would be not only HBC executives and post replacements but also red-coated Mounties, explorers, geologists, missionaries, doctors, nurses, postmasters and government administrators of every description.

The ninety-day voyage was a race against tides and weather. None of the three dozen or so ports of call had a dock, so the ship anchored off each post while goods were loaded and unloaded from wooden scows. This could be tricky. The HBC's Archie Hunter recalled putting into Chesterfield Inlet on a rough day: "When we arrived no one from shore dared venture out to meet us, with the exception of one hardy soul. Out he came battling the white-capped waves in a Lac Seul canoe until he finally made it to the ship. I still remember his introduction of himself, 'They call me Crazy Mac but you ought to see the rest of them ashore.' "*

The fox pelts were brought aboard in bales of one hundred, stamped with each trading post's name and a silk-cloth destination label that read: "Beaver House, Great Trinity Lane, London, England." The day of arrival was very special as the residents of each settlement read their annual ration of mail. Then the stevedoring started. "At every port where we stopped," complained Ernie Lyall, an old Arctic hand, "we had to work with the crew and hump cargo all the time. I think that's about the time that 'Heavy Bloody Cargo' got tacked on to the HBC initials." Local Inuit would help out, and some remembered the magic of those occasions. "The sight of these great vessels entering the world where we lived made thrills go

---

*Crazy Mac had by this time been north with the HBC for fifteen years without a furlough. He left that season aboard the *Nascopie*, got off at Halifax, and promptly married a bishop's daughter.

*The* Nascopie *loading at Charlton Island, 1933*

through our hearts," recalled Alootook Ipellie, a Frobisher Bay artist and carver. "This was during high tide and everyone worked as a unit, just like a circus setting up the big tents and other things to get ready for the opening night. There was laughter among the people, a sign of happiness which never seemed to stop as long as the ship stayed." The traders themselves held a less romantic view. The second-best day of the year was when the *Nascopie* arrived, they said. The best was when she left.

By early September, winter would begin to set in and the stops became shorter, the unloading even more frenzied. Smellie once steamed for an hour past the largest iceberg on record: an ice island a hundred feet high and ten miles long. In those pre-radar days he had to "smell" the presence of ice in fog or in the dark, and his ship didn't always stay out of harm's way. Smellie had three spare propellers on board, and whenever one was damaged, he would back his ship onto some deserted northern beach at high tide, wait for a tide shift, then change props. Heading north through Baffin Bay or into the riptides of Hudson Strait, ships had no protection from the grey swells, mountains of water thirty feet high, claiming the ocean for themselves.

THE *NASCOPIE*'S IMMEDIATE PREDECESSOR was the *Pelican*, a former British man-of-war and slave-chaser, purchased by the HBC in 1901. The 290-ton auxiliary sloop also beat off a German submarine (on August 26, 1918, off Cardiff) and continued in the Company's service until 1920. She was joined in 1905 by the *Discovery*, the heavily reinforced exploration barquentine that carried Captain Robert Falcon Scott's 1901–4 expedition to the Antarctic, which made the last annual supply voyage to York Factory in 1914.

Many a brave Company crew undertook the annual supply voyage, and the HBC even fought a major naval battle to protect its sea lanes, but many more vessels departed than returned.* The last HBC sailing ship to ply the Bay, the three-masted barque *Stork*, went down in a storm off Rupert House in 1908. Ice crushed the *Bayeskimo*, while the *Bayrupert* piled up on Hen and Chickens Reef, on the Labrador coast.† The fifty-six-ton *Fort Churchill*, a ketch that arrived at York Factory in the late autumn of 1913 with a load of coal from Falmouth, England, was left unattended at anchor some distance up the Nelson River. She vanished during a three-day easterly gale, only to be found two years later washed up on one of the Belcher Islands.

The potential for east-west trade across the top of North America was first demonstrated in 1930. The HBC's schooner *Fort James* (built in Shelburne, Nova Scotia, as the *Jean Revillon*) had sailed out of St John's to spend two winters frozen in at Gjoa Haven on King William Island. When the HBC's western-based supply ship *Fort McPherson* pulled in and anchored near her, it was the first time the North West Passage had been bridged—even if by two ships—since Amundsen's history-making crossing of 1903–6. In 1934, when the *Fort James* was transferred to the Company's western division, she went through the Panama Canal and eventually back into the North; she got as far east as Cambridge Bay—only two hundred miles west of her 1928–30 wintering place. Had she closed that short gap, the *Fort James* would have been the first vessel in history to circumnavigate North America. Both the *Fort James* and the *Fort McPherson* as well as the *Fort Hearne* were later wrecked in Arctic gales.

The Company's maritime experience in the Western Arctic wasn't much luckier. After several sinkings of chartered and pur-

---

*For details of this epic sea engagement, see *Company of Adventurers*, pages 120–25.

†The HBC manager at Wolstenholme had put away his salary for years to purchase a piano, which went down with the *Bayeskimo* in 1925. Two years later he had saved enough to order a replacement, only to have it sink aboard the *Bayrupert*. He found a new hobby.

*The* Baychimo

chased vessels, the HBC decided in 1920 to build a ship specially designed for the job, the auxiliary wooden schooner *Lady Kindersley*. Her ribs were mounted so close together that with planking and sheathing the hull had an overall thickness of nearly twenty-two inches, while her bow was reinforced with thick metal sheets. She sailed out of Vancouver on June 27, 1924, carrying not only a year's worth of HBC re-supplies but also a powerful government radio transmitter, due to be installed at Herschel Island. Imprisoned by the floes and hummocks off Point Barrow, *Lady Kindersley* had to be abandoned after a month of attempting to free herself.

Other ships were assigned to the west-coast run, but few hulls could withstand the battering of the ice around Alaska's northern coast. Originally built as a Baltic coaster and taken by the British as part of German post-war reparations, the HBC's supply ship *Baychimo* was the largest vessel to trade in the North West Passage. The 1,500-tonner successfully completed nine expeditions to the Company's eight Western Arctic posts, but on her return journey in 1931 she got stuck in ice off Point Franklin, near Point Barrow. Since she was carrying a million dollars' worth of fur there was no question of abandoning her, but when the vessel seemed in danger of being crushed, Captain S.A. Cornwall ordered the crew to set up a temporary shelter on shore, two miles away. Although some passengers and HBC officials were flown out by rescue planes, the captain and sixteen of his crew retreated to their makeshift dwelling to await a change in the weather, so that they might free their ship. On November 24, a blizzard howled in. It turned so ferocious the sailors had to close off their little dwelling, huddling together for warmth and comfort, taking turns sitting next to the gasoline drum that had been converted into a stove. When they dug themselves out three days later, the *Baychimo* had disappeared. She was seen a few months after that drifting alone through pack ice by an Inuk travelling from Herschel to Nome.

Two years later, the *Baychimo* was boarded by Isobel Wylie Hutchinson, a Scottish botanist bound for Herschel aboard the schooner *Trader*. The ghostly *Baychimo* had been sighted twelve miles off Wainwright, and the *Trader*'s captain had brought his little vessel alongside. "A strange spectacle the decks presented," Hutchinson later noted in her journal. "The main hold was open to the winds, but its half-rifted depths still contained sacks of mineral ore, caribou skins, and a cargo of various descriptions. . . . Writing paper, photographic films, ledgers of the Hudson's Bay Company, typewriter ribbons—all were here for the taking! In a wooden crate was an unsullied edition of *The Times History of the Great War* in many tomes. Charts of all seas of the world lay scattered upon the decks of the pilot-house. . . . A breakfast menu tossed in the doorway indicated that the crew of the unlucky ship were at least in no danger of starvation, for there was a choice of some six courses."

The *Trader*'s first mate determined that the *Baychimo*'s engines were in perfect condition and that all she needed was to have her spare propeller mounted before she could sail away under her own steam, but the weather closed in and the visitors scrambled off the doomed vessel as fast as they could. The sightings continued. In 1936 Captain Parker of the cutter *Northland* pulled alongside, and in 1961 she was spotted by a party of Inuit between Icy Cape and Point Barrow. A DEW Line supply superintendent from Vancouver named Don Roderick reported seeing her off Cambridge Bay in 1965. That any ship—manned by ghosts or men—could survive the awesome force of the polar ice pack for three decades seems beyond reason, but the HBC's *Baychimo* did just that, and since no one actually saw her sink, she may be out there still . . .

SCOTTY GALL, THE HBC TRADER who had been one of the last crew members to get off the *Baychimo*, reacted to his ship's fate with the typical aplomb of a good Company man. "Pity," he said. "She still had twenty bales of fur on her." Gall was back north six years after the *Baychimo* disappearance on what would turn out to be the greatest sea

*Scotty Gall on the schooner* Aklavik, *1937*

adventure of his career. In the spring of 1937, the Hudson's Bay Company decided to establish a connecting link between its western and eastern operations by building a trading facility in the Central Arctic at the bottom of Somerset Island on Bellot Strait. The new outpost was to be named Fort Ross, after the two British naval officers, uncle and nephew, who had first explored the area in the 1820s and 1830s. The *Nascopie*'s itinerary called for her to pick up some Inuit families at Arctic Bay for resettlement at Fort Ross, then rendezvous with the small (thirty-ton) schooner *Aklavik* at the eastern entrance of Bellot Strait. *

No steel-hulled vessel had ever entered these waters, and no ship of any kind had been here since the visit of Leopold McClintock, the

---

*These were the same Inuit who had been uprooted from their homes at Cape Dorset, Pangnirtung and Pond Inlet by the HBC in 1934 and taken to Dundas Harbour, where the ice turned out to be too rough and thick for either sled or boat travel. In 1936, Dundas Harbour was closed and the Inuit were transferred to Arctic Bay. Now they were being displaced again.

Irish-born Royal Navy captain who found documents and relics indicating the fate of the Franklin expedition while on an 1859 sledge journey from his ship, frozen in near the entrance to the strait. Bellot Strait, where Fort Ross was to stand, had been discovered by Joseph-René Bellot, a French naval sub-lieutenant, poking around the North mainly because he was in love with Sir John Franklin's widow, Jane, and hoped to gain heroic status by finding her husband's remains. Barely navigable, the strait was an important link in the North West Passage, dividing the Arctic archipelago from the North American continent. Scotty Gall, who spent forty-three years in the Company's northern service, had learned his navigation in the Mackenzie Delta. "I knew where all the reefs were; I'd hit every one," he remembered. "Some of the Scotsmen who came north were linguists, others studied the Inuit. I was much more interested in finding out how the aboriginals can travel without any navigation aids. I came to believe they have an inherent sense of direction, reading the sun, wind, snowdrifts or the lichen on rocks." It took Gall twenty years to hone his own instincts and crossing Bellot Strait was his greatest test.

The passage is twenty miles long and often less than a mile wide. Eleven-foot tides flood in from its western end, causing an eight-knot current. Just as he was steering the *Aklavik* into the strait, his engine (a 35-h.p. Fairbanks-Morse) failed; he replaced a faulty fuel strainer just as the little ship was about to run aground. The motor sputtered to life, but it would operate only at half speed. "The current was running pretty fast," Gall recalled, "and I couldn't get much way-on, so I turned the boat around, pointed my nose into the current, which gave me more control against side-slips, and we went through the Bellot backwards!"*

At noon on September 2, 1937, Gall traded his cargo of furs for supplies aboard the *Nascopie*, then anchored at Depot Bay, just off the Fort Ross site. The transaction made Gall the first man in history to have turned the North West Passage into a commercial reality. He was

---

*Known as a crack navigator, Gall also had the reputation of being the worst cook among the HBC's northern hands. "He couldn't even make a pot of tea," recalled Woody Wood, one of his colleagues. "He'd eat all his meat raw because he was always hungry and couldn't be bothered cooking it—though he usually killed the animals first. I remember one time, Scotty shot an owl, and his wife cooked it because it was Christmas, and once served on a platter it looked a bit like turkey. When it was put in front of him, Scotty took one bite, and smacking his lips with pleasure said, 'Oy, it tastes like premasticated mouse meat to me.' I never had roast owl again."

not impressed. "It's all bunk about the North West Passage, it gives me a pain," said he. "We could have done it any time, and gone higher north. But that was no advantage to us. We were traders, and we went where the fur was. There was nobody to the north of us. What the hell good would it have done to run right through the Passage, when there were no Eskimos, and we didn't have any trade there?"

The *Nascopie* had not found easy passage because Prince Regent Inlet, which leads to the strait, was choked with blue ice that year. She had a tight margin of only seven days in which to reach Fort Ross, establish the post, and steam out again to free water. J.W. Anderson and Paddy Gibson, a Chief Trader normally in the Western Arctic, went ashore to select the site, having first paid silent tribute at the cairn left behind by McClintock, the Admiralty sailor who had made five futile attempts to sail through Bellot Strait nearly a century before. HBC carpenter Clem James, aided by two Company traders, Lorenz Learmonth and D.G. Sturrock (who had arrived the same day after a harrowing journey from Gjoa Haven, mainly on foot, carrying a sixteen-foot canoe), erected a store, staff building and warehouse. By the evening of September 7, the work had been nearly completed and the HBC flag was raised over the Company's last new post devoted to the fox trade. Learmonth stayed behind (with interpreter-trader Ernie Lyall) as Fort Ross's first manager. The *Nascopie* landed her Inuit passengers, and just before she was due to sail away an HBC hand named Donald Goodyear, incongruously dressed in a three-piece suit, topped off with a fedora (because he was on his way out on furlough), rowed himself ashore, determined to help Learmonth finish building the post. The *Aklavik* tooted her whistle and the *Nascopie* blew her horn as the ships parted, headed back to their separate oceans, knowing their meeting had made a four-hundred-year dream come true. On shore, Goodyear was waving his silly fedora and Lyall a dishcloth; Learmonth gave a salute. Fort Ross was in business.

But not for long. In 1942 and 1943 unusually thick pack ice prevented the *Nascopie* from resupplying Fort Ross, then manned by W.A. Heslop, his wife, Barbara, and a clerk named Darcy Munro, who also operated the post's new short-wave radio. "One evening in September [1943], we sighted the *Nascopie* about fifteen miles off shore," recalled Mrs Heslop. "We thought our worries were over; but it was not until later that we were to realize they were just beginning. For three days we saw her, or her smoke, on the horizon and it was evident she was having difficulty in the ice-pack. That was an anxious three days, but we didn't give up until we finally saw her heading north with black smoke belching from her funnel."* Food was so short that both HBC men spent most of their time hunting. By November, a U.S. Army Air Forces plane was sent in to rescue the staff and leave food for the Inuit.

The post was reactivated the following summer, but by 1947 it was clear that Fort Ross was too remote, too expensive and too risky to keep open. It was closed and its Inuit families were moved yet again, this time to Spence Bay, 180 miles to the south. Fort Ross vanished from the Hudson's Bay Company's rosters, but its memory survived. All those involved knew that they had for a brief time been part of a brave experiment on the very edge of the world. Lorenz Learmonth, long after he had retired from the HBC, managed to find commercial passage to Bellot Strait. For a week he rummaged around the ruins of that lonely little outpost, pining for the forgotten dreams of a land that seemed to exist north of hope.

CAPTAIN SMELLIE RETIRED IN 1945 and was succeeded by James Waters, who had served as the *Nascopie*'s first officer since 1941. On his second run, during the early afternoon of July 21, 1947, Waters was nosing the *Nascopie* into Cape Dorset when the ship struck an uncharted reef off Beacon Island. J.W. Anderson, then in charge of the fur trade's Eastern Arctic Division, was aboard and vividly remembered the grounding: "Dashing out on deck, I could see what had happened, but the tide was falling and notwithstanding the reversing of the engines she stuck fast in a perfectly upright position. Well, I thought, if this is going to be a shipwreck, it is quite a civilized one. . . ." Another witness was Peter Pitseolak, a local artist who had customarily piloted HBC ships into Dorset but on this, of all occasions, had been rebuffed by Waters, who thought he could outdo Smellie by bringing the ship in himself. A few hours after the vessel went aground, the captain ordered everyone ashore in lifeboats, but the mood was still buoyant because it was a beautiful windless day and except for her ten-degree list to stern, the ship seemed unharmed. Anderson and the other HBC managers expected the lightened vessel could be refloated at high tide. Helped by kedged anchors, that was exactly what happened—the ship worked her way off the reef. But in so doing, she grievously holed her hull. The Arctic waters rushed in,

---

*Captain Smellie had intended to stay longer, but on the afternoon of the third day, a group of crewmen led by two Newfoundland lightermen confronted him on the bridge. They issued an ultimatum: if he didn't turn the ship around by dusk, they would refuse to work it because they feared being frozen in for the winter. Smellie recognized the truth, if not the manner, of that advice, headed his ship back to sea, and did not lay any mutiny charges.

*Captain James Waters (left) and others take a last look at the sinking* Nascopie.

flooding her engine room. At 3 A.M. a gale came up, smashing the vessel into another rock. She was now down by her bow, her decks at a thirty-degree angle, her screw high out of the water, her bilge pumps useless. At 5 A.M. the order was given to abandon ship.

Captain Waters, standing on shore watching his doomed vessel, asked one of his mates, a colourful Newfoundlander named Willis Warren, to go back aboard and rescue some warm clothes for his wife, who had been travelling with him. "Willis got into a dory and rowed back to the ship, climbing up her stern on a jacob's ladder that had been left hanging there," the HBC's George Whitman said later. "This was all done to a gallery of smirking Inuit who had been watching the white men make fools of themselves, running their ship into a rock. Warren went below into the captain's cabin, vanished for a while, then stuck his head out a porthole and waving a pair of Mrs Waters's pink bloomers, yelled: 'Would these be what ye wants, Captain?' The assembly burst into laughter, with the Inuit dancing out their joy, jumping up and down, wildly clapping their hands. Then the ship lurched a little and Warren got out of there fast."

The *Nascopie* remained poised on the reef for an incredible three months. Battered by gales and ice, she showed off her seaworthiness one last time, finally slipping under at midnight on October 15, 1947. Peter Pitseolak, Cape Dorset's Inuit pilot, quoted her fitting epitaph, voiced by his friend Kululak: "Our big helper has hit the bottom."

*Furs being brought to the HBC post at Great Whale River*

# CHAPTER 12

# NORTHERN GRIDLOCK

*"There was a big war. It was between the Bay and the Germans. The Bay won."*

—Octave Sivanertok

A PAINTING OF THE NATIVITY that hung in the Anglican Cathedral in Aklavik until it burned down in 1975 depicted a crowd of Inuit celebrating the blessed event. Clearly identifiable among them were a missionary, a Mountie and an HBC Factor.

The theme and juxtaposition were entirely appropriate to the birth of the modern North except that in many of the really isolated Arctic posts, Bay managers frequently handled both spiritual and legal functions on top of their commercial mandates. "The real boss of each settlement was the local Bay man," recalled Ed Spracklin, who served in half a dozen posts. "Everybody came to you for advice, even on family and medical matters. I was also acting as commissioner of oaths and registrar for family allowances." Bay men were not medically trained and their stores carried only such nostrums as Minard's Liniment, Dodd's Kidney Pills, Perry Davis's Pain Killer (30 percent alcohol), Carter's Little Liver Pills and Gin Pills (which achieved little except to turn the urine green), but the Factors were often faced with medical emergencies. "One time, this Eskimo interpreter of ours at Cape Dorset got a nick in his left elbow, and it turned septic," recalled Chesley Russell, a veteran of the service. "There was a young fellow from Scotland with me as clerk, and we decided we'd take his arm off above the elbow. We put him on the kitchen table, and I found some morphine in the first-aid kit. It was outdated by a couple of years, so I

231

figured we'd give him a double dose. We overdosed the poor son of a gun and every hour or so we'd have a look to find out how bad it was. One of the symptoms was to watch his eyes and see how much they had contracted. His pupils got as small as pinpoints. He was really overdosed. The first-aid book said the remedy was to keep him moving. But he was out for the count. He couldn't move. So we got him off the table, and my clerk would roll the poor bugger across the kitchen floor one way, and I'd roll him back. Every once in a while we'd skin back the eyes to see if they were dilating, and we were just about exhausted when he began coming around. To hell with cutting his arm off after that. We forgot about it. In a day or two he started to get better. It was the exercise that had started up his circulation again. He came around. Otherwise, we'd have taken his arm off—we had the saws and everything ready. . . ."*

The best of the Bay men in the Arctic—characters like Ches Russell, Lorenz Learmonth, Scotty Gall, Sandy Lunan, Bert Swaffield, Jimmy Ford, John Stanners, Bob Cruickshank and J.W. Nichols—became true northerners, growing grey in the service, and as Leonard Budgell, who was one of them, remarked: " [We] accepted a more intimate responsibility for [our] customers. It was a good way to live, no matter what today's experts will tell you . . . we could not have existed without that paternal feeling . . . no one will ever convince me that it was not right in its time and place." Certainly that streak of paternalism characterized the HBC's dealings. P.A.C. Nichols, who for a time was in charge of the Arctic stores, referred to the Inuit as "these simple, primitive folk of the Arctic" who had remained "unspoiled" but some of whom could now "see no reason to struggle for survival if the wherewithal to live can be acquired with little effort" so that "the temptation to relax and be looked after often becomes too strong to conquer." That attitude was institutionalized in *The Eskimo Book of Knowledge*, published and distributed by the Company in 1931. Its author, an HBC Factor and Oxford graduate named George Binney, utilized biblical cadence to praise the Company not only as an agent of the British King but as a Divine presence. "Take heed," ran a typical passage aimed at the Inuit, warning them against

---

*Apart from their rough but ready medical skill, some of the post managers were unusually ingenious, even inventing a better mousetrap. "Using a large ten-gallon pail, half filled with water, I laid narrow pieces of board against it," recalled Hugh Mackay Ross. "Then I dangled a juicy piece of salt pork from a nail directly over the pail. When the mice smelled the pork, they ran up the boards to get at it, and overbalancing, fell into the water and drowned."

doing business with independent fur traders that threatened the HBC's monopoly, "strange traders will come among you seeking only your furs . . . these wanderers are like the drift-ice; today they come with the wind, tomorrow they are gone with the wind. Of these strangers some will be fairer than others, as is the nature of men; but whosoever they be, they cannot at heart possess that deep understanding of your lives through which our traders have learned to bestow the care of a father upon you and upon your children."

The northern field men may have been patronizing in their outlook and dictatorial in their methods, but they certainly weren't in the HBC's service for the money. "Sometimes we could be trading in the store for over twenty-four hours at a stretch without stopping," Ernie Lyall remembered. "We never got any overtime for this sort of thing, of course, or for any of the extra work we did evenings or weekends. . . . I was getting $120 a month when I started in Spence Bay in 1949, and $185 when I left the HBC in 1962."

The Company's influence grew in the first half of the second decade of the twentieth century, as the HBC became determined to take advantage of its monopoly by significantly expanding its northern presence. The move prompted Winnipeg's *Free Press* to comment approvingly: "The Company will make a last stand against civilization at the Arctic Ocean." But when the First World War disrupted European trade, the British government suspended London fur auctions, forcing pelt prices into dramatic, if temporary, decline. In the 1914–15 season, for the first time in its long history the Company halted its North American fur purchases, forbidding its traders to grant the natives new credit. Some of the HBC veterans ignored the sour directive and continued to distribute limited quantities of food and essential supplies to the Inuit and Indians, entering these shadowy transactions in "purgatory ledgers" that didn't show up in their posts' regular accounts. But enough aboriginals were deprived of rations for one deadly season that, as the HBC's Philip Godsell later observed, "I think any experienced trader will agree that the Hudson's Bay Company never fully regained their old-time prestige." In 1916, as the American fur market expanded, prices surged upward, more than doubling to $38 per white fox skin within the next four years, then nearly doubling again to $70 in 1928. The trade became so lucrative that in some posts along the Mackenzie, the HBC owed considerable amounts in trade goods to its customers. By 1924 the Inuit of Aklavik had purchased a private fleet of thirty-nine auxiliary-powered schooners and twenty-eight whaleboats, valued at $128,000.

The HBC was operating more than two hundred northern posts,

opening new stores as high in the Arctic as Gjoa Haven, where Amundsen had wintered during his traverse of the North West Passage, and for a time even maintaining a string of trading outlets in eastern Siberia. Despite this rapid expansion, or perhaps because of it, the HBC began behaving like a bloated dinosaur—big, awkward and almost totally disconnected from its shifting environment. Writing of the trade along the Mackenzie, Heather Robertson noted in her evocative memoir of the HBC's Richard Bonnycastle that "the Company had lost control in the north. The economy was changing: Imperial Oil was developing the oil field at Norman Wells; prospectors were searching for gold and silver; fly-by-night free traders had introduced a cash economy among the natives. The Company's political base, the Indians—once the proud wives and children of famous post factors, the loyal 'family' of a mighty patron—had been reduced to patients and pupils, cooks and chore boys; and the great factors themselves . . . once feared as demi-gods, were more often than not the objects of laughter and ridicule for their pompous manners and foolish brass hats. The unthinkable was happening—the Hudson's Bay Company was losing money."

It was a measure of the Company's fiscal desperation that its directors took seriously the suggestion of an old Arctic hand to turn a fortune in breeding reindeer as a cheap substitute for beef. Vilhjalmur Stefansson, the Icelandic-Canadian who became the Arctic's most accomplished non-Inuit sledge driver, won fame leading three daring expeditions that added one hundred thousand square miles to the maps of Canada's Far North, charting its last sizeable unknown islands. Like Samuel Hearne and John Rae before him, Stefansson was able to dash across the Arctic by adopting Inuit survival techniques instead of being burdened by what he derisively described as "the portable-boarding-house school" methods of British adventurers. Stefansson genuinely believed that exploration required less courage than driving a New York taxicab, with preparation and adaptability taking the place of mock heroics. "I know nothing whatever about courage," he was fond of pointing out. "Everything you add to an explorer's heroism you have to subtract from his intelligence." He predicted Canada's North could support thirty-five million reindeer because its grazing territory was superior to most semi-arid sheep lands—but nobody took him seriously except the HBC. In 1920, the Company approved his scheme to establish a subsidiary to breed the ungainly beasts on Baffin Island, purchased 14,000 Lapland reindeer in northern Norway, hired a dozen herders, and shipped the first contingent of 689 animals (plus 3,000 sacks of moss) across the

*Arctic explorer Vilhjalmur Stefansson*

Atlantic aboard the *Nascopie*. Only 550 reindeer were still alive by the time the ship anchored off Amadjuak on the south coast of Baffin Island, the spot chosen by one of Stefansson's associates as having the best moss. A storm immediately dispersed the seasick reindeer, and though there was indeed plenty of moss, it turned out to be the wrong variety. (The reindeer wanted to munch on *Cladonia rangeferina*, which grew out of the soil in Lapland and thus contained delicious nutrients; the Baffin moss, which sprouted out of bare rock, contained no nutritional equivalent.) "We soon found," reported Captain John Mikkelborg, the HBC official charged with the loony venture, "that the pastures would not permit us to keep a large herd under restraint; if we did, they would starve to death. Consequently, we had to divide them into flocks and let them spread over a wide area, after the style of the caribou. . . . Sometimes the caribou would come and mix with our reindeer—more often the reverse—and that was the last we would see of them." Only 210 animals survived the winter, and with expenses still mounting, HBC accountants calculated by the end of

1922 that each beast was now worth $80.22. The $200,000 venture was eventually written off, though the Hudson's Bay Reindeer Company was still on the HBC's books as late as 1956.

Because the HBC operated in an area virtually inaccessible to visitors, its spreading northern presence was immune to criticism; any outsider wanting to live in the Arctic depended on its supplies. That protection from censure was challenged in 1927 when Dr Frederick Banting, the co-discoverer of insulin, went on an Arctic expedition with his sketching companion, A.Y. Jackson, a founding member of the Group of Seven, whose work caught the enduring beauty of the Arctic's desolation. The two men went along as guests aboard the Department of the Interior's supply ship *Beothic* and visited most of the HBC's stations in the Eastern Arctic. Banting had embarked on the journey as an amateur painter badly in need of a vacation, but his medical training and essential humanity could not long be denied. His journal contained many astute observations, such as that "a native cannot live on white man's food or in white men's dress," a correct diagnosis of the unsuitability of woollen and cotton goods for Arctic wear and of salted and canned provisions for Arctic food. But he was harshest in his assessments of the HBC. "The company have systematically possessed themselves of this country," he noted. "They have at each post an interpreter who puts before the native the company's view & teaches them that the great company will look after them & is their savior. While at the same time they hire them at ten dollars per year to 'retain' them as their men. They buy their furs very cheap—in trade—tea—tobacco—woollens etc.—which are by no means as good for the native as his former life without these things. At this port [Arctic Bay] we took on 23 bales of fox furs & there are said to be one hundred skins per bale—They sell at $50 to $60 per skin. 2300 x 50 = $115,000. Now where does the native come in? He hunts $100,000 worth of furs & the Company takes the profits."

In a Toronto *Star* interview after his return (given to a reporter while he thought he was speaking off the record), Banting expanded on his criticism, charging that the Inuit were getting goods worth only $5,000 in exchange for fox skins marketed at $100,000 and that the natives' resistance to disease was being lowered by the diet the Company encouraged its northern customers to eat. In a subsequent letter to an official at the Department of the Interior, he recommended that the Canadian government "take over full control of the fur trade throughout Eskimo territory. From the profits of the trade, proper administration could be carried out and steps be taken to improve rather than destroy the chances of the Eskimo race." The doctor, who because of his Nobel Prize was one of the best-known and most trusted Canadians of his day, went on to comment that "the native should be encouraged to lay up a reserve of money or credit in time of plenty to take care of the inevitable lean years . . . generally speaking, the policy of the trader has been to keep the Eskimo in his debt."

In the face of this and Banting's many other criticisms, Governor Charles Vincent Sale wrote a twenty-seven-page letter to Deputy Minister W.W. Cory in which he denied the charges, claiming that "it is obvious that we must be interested in their [the Inuit] welfare since they are the people who, given reasonable opportunities, can best occupy and make use of the snow covered regions in which we operate, and where we have embarked so much of our capital." Banting's attack was a timely indication that the HBC could no longer insulate itself against outsiders questioning its divine right to rule. The North, especially the Arctic's western sector, was exploding with activity that would change the fur trade forever.

THE MACKENZIE RIVER HAD BECOME a comfortable superhighway through the Western Arctic, with the HBC's impressive fleet of thirteen ships leading the way. By 1927, the Company was offering tourists thirty-five-day round-trip cruises on the Mackenzie as far north as Aklavik for $325, including meals, and was unable to accommodate all the passengers who swarmed in every summer to take advantage of the journey, advertised as being "2000 MILES OFF THE BEATEN TRACK."* Ships such as the *Athabasca River* boasted a cruising speed of thirteen knots, electric lights, and luxury salon accommodation for fifty-eight passengers. Those were great days on the river. "You had time, for there was no schedule but the riverboat's own," recalled Laco Hunt, a former HBC Factor who took the journey many times. "You had time to muse on the legends you'd heard about the great Northern lakes whose names echoed with history; about the fur-trading forts and the men who'd fought to put them in the wilderness. . . . The long procession of days brought a new rhythm to your life; it seemed to fall in with the pattern made by the mornings and

---

*The meals the Company advertised received mixed reviews. When one of the steamer captains asked a passenger, the Reverend Gerald Card, to say grace, the Anglican minister refused. "Indeed, I won't," he thundered. "After paying the Hudson's Bay Company fifty cents for a meal, against which even my stomach registers the most vigorous and continual protests, I fail to see any reason why I should lift my voice in thanks to God!"

afternoons filled with the sounds of birds, and the swift undercurrents of water, dark blue with reflected sky."

That romantic vision was disrupted by construction of the Alberta and Great Waterways Railway, known to every northern hand as the Muskeg Limited, which tapped the Mackenzie Basin into the country's main transportation network. The most disturbing influence was the dramatic mineral strike in the region by a Toronto prospector named Gilbert LaBine. On the unseasonably cold morning of May 16, 1930, at a forlorn inlet on the eastern shore of Great Bear Lake, a day's walk from the Arctic Circle, he found a plum-sized glob of rock that turned out to be pure pitchblende. This would become the great Eldorado Mine, the source first of radium and later of the uranium that was used in the atomic bomb dropped on Hiroshima. The find, which trebled the world stock of radium (before LaBine's discovery, supplies of the precious metal amounted to only half a pound, worth $22 million), set off a mining rush. Would-be prospectors included a Russian prince who arrived with his princess, accompanied by a bearded valet, and an Arab sheikh who wandered aimlessly along the shores of Great Bear, his robes catching in the stunted conifers. The most ingenious method of discovering surface traces of the radioactive ore was that used by Tom Creighton, a veteran sourdough who had earlier helped stake the Flin Flon mine in northern Manitoba. He dropped undeveloped film on likely-looking rocky outcrops; the presence of pitchblende would show up as streaks of light.

At about the same time, major gold deposits were discovered at Beaverlodge, on the north shore of Lake Athabasca, while a Cominco prospector named Spud Arsenault struck gold at Yellowknife. Most of the bushwhackers and goldseekers who poured into every part of the North arrived by airplane. LaBine himself had first spotted the pitchblende deposit from the back seat of C.H. "Punch" Dickins's primitive biplane. Peering through the aircraft's humming shrouds, he noticed rocks smudged with the peach-red hues that indicated cobalt bloom, one of the clues associated with radium deposits—a mineral strike that would eventually create a world-scale mine. "I suddenly realized," he later recalled, "that I was in elephant country."

The first prospecting flight into the North had actually taken place a decade earlier, when Imperial Oil purchased two German-built 175-h.p. Junkers monoplanes to supply drilling crews during the oil rush at Norman Wells. The monoplanes got only as far as Fort Simpson, where one of them crash-landed, breaking its propeller. The aircraft was able to take off again after an HBC carpenter named Walter

*One of Imperial Oil's 175-h.p. Junkers that made the first prospecting flight into the Arctic*

Johnson fashioned a substitute out of toboggan boards held together with babiche—glue distilled from moose hoofs. Those early bush pilots became reluctant heroes as they peered over the sides of their open cockpits to verify their bearings, nervously checking their watches against fuel gauges, adjusting their goggles, praying that the far distant dot on the tundra for which they were heading was actually there. The Inuit, who had never seen a streetcar or automobile, could easily distinguish a Junkers from a Fokker, Norseman, Beechcraft, Gypsy Moth or Beaver, but as one of their elders at Chesterfield Inlet remarked when gazing for the first time at a flying machine, "That is a bad thing to know just a little about." In the tradition of the voyageurs who dared to tread where others only dreamed of going, the fliers, most of them beached veterans of Great War dogfights, transformed the North. Probably the most enterprising pilot on those early runs was Leigh Brintnell, whose tiny Mackenzie Air Service won the government mail contract for most of the Western Arctic. His arrangement with Ottawa called for him to be paid according to how many pounds of mail he delivered to each settlement. He had been granted the contract by drastically underbidding his rivals, who were certain he couldn't make a profit on existing traffic. They were right. But that didn't stop Brintnell. He purchased airmail subscriptions to the Edmonton *Journal* for nearly every log shack along the Mackenzie, automatically increasing his payload and trebling his income. W.R. "Wop" May, who had duelled with Germany's Red Baron and flown

*W.R. "Wop" May (right) tinkering with his Bellanca "Pacemaker,"*
*Fort Chipewyan, 1933*

under the High Level Bridge at Edmonton on a bet, became the first idol of Canada's air age, closely followed by Punch Dickins.

With its customary foresight, the HBC refused to participate in a new scheduled air service between Edmonton and the Mackenzie Valley. But it did employ Dickins on contract to fly bales of fur out of Fort Good Hope and in the winter of 1930 financed him on a medical mercy mission into Coppermine. The Company purchased its first plane—a twin-engined Beechcraft equipped with wheels, skis and floats—in 1939, only eleven years after nearly everyone else in its territories had taken to doing business by air. Paul Davoud, the HBC's first pilot, calculated that George Simpson's eighty-four-day dash by canoe in 1824 on his famous inspection tour from Lachine to the Pacific would now take only ten hours. Davoud flew HBC executives on their first aerial inspection tour in the summer of 1940, much to the unwelcome surprise of local store managers, used to getting warnings of visits by Company brass via the staff moccasin telegraph. "We landed at Fort Resolution at five in the morning," Davoud recalled. "The post manager, with about a five days' beard on him, was down on the dock, scratching his belly, wanting to know who I had aboard. When I told him I had 'the works'—the chief of the fur trade, head of Canadian operations, and the Governor, over from London—he groaned and was sure he'd be fired. He wasn't, but I don't think he was the same man after that." When the Beechcraft set down at Fort Rae, one of the local aboriginals was shown through it. Pointing at the plane's luxurious fittings, an HBC executive asked the visitor whether he admired the white man's marvel. "Sure," was the laconic reply. "We paid for it."

An incursion into the North of a very different sort was the railway built to Churchill, on Hudson Bay. Proponents of the railroad claimed that exporting grain through the Bay would force the CPR to reduce freight rates and cut the cost of trans-shipping Liverpool-bound goods at Montreal. The project had been kicking around Parliament since 1884, awaiting funds and legislative sanction. Nine charters were approved, but actual construction didn't start until 1910. The line was originally planned to terminate at Port Nelson, near York Factory, and a $6-million, seventeen-span steel bridge was erected to a man-made island, where the new harbour was to be built. The First World War intervened, and when the railway was finally completed in 1929, Churchill was its terminus, leaving Port Nelson abandoned, the sub-Arctic's most expensive white elephant. Two years later, the *Farnworth*, a tramp steamer out of Newcastle-on-Tyne, loaded Churchill's first commercial wheat shipment. For a time the harbour handled general goods, but soon its only customer was a reluctant Canadian Wheat Board, and the dream of building an alternative grain-export route faded.*

The failure of Churchill was partly due to its inauguration on the eve of the Depression, which also cut deeply into HBC profit and the fur trade in general. Arctic fox prices declined as much as 800 percent, and silver fox pelts plummeted in value from $450 in 1920 to only $9 by 1939. The problem with that luxurious variety was not only the Depression but the new customers it attracted. Nearly every prostitute in London and Paris suddenly decided she couldn't successfully walk the streets unless she was decked out in a silver fox stole—and with more and more tarts adopting the fur as a badge of office, the bottom fell out of the market. The Depression cut severely into Company budgets. Operational costs were dramatically reduced by the closing of a hundred stores. At one Arctic settlement, coal rations grew so short that the HBC manager had to dismantle and burn his warehouse to keep warm. The HBC's presence in the Western Arctic was reduced to only three posts: Coppermine, Cambridge Bay and Tuktoyaktuk.

---

*The train from Winnipeg to Churchill was still operating in the 1990s, but in a typical year it attracted only 5,616 passengers, so that a $11.5-million annual federal subsidy— or $2,047 a passenger for its thirty-four-hour run—was required. Adam Corelli of the *Financial Times of Canada* calculated that the same trip in a rented Mercedes limousine would cost only $1,566—if only there were a road.

The Depression only aggravated the Company's less than generous staff policies. Post managers were usually moved to lower-paying positions for the last few years of their tenures, so that the pensions due them, calculated as a percentage of their final years' pay, could be reduced. But the HBC's management did come up with the occasional generous and humane decision. When Hugh Mackay Ross was appointed manager of the Saskatchewan district, he wanted to pension off Jock Mathieson, the veteran post manager at Beauval, who hadn't many years to go in the service and was the main stumbling block to Ross's reorganization plans. Ross sent his recommendation to the Company's Canadian headquarters, where his request for removing the old trader was denied. "They had carefully studied Mr. Mathieson's dossier," he later recalled, "and had concluded that because his son was attending the local school, it would be a hardship for the family to be sent where no school was available. They further concluded that Mr. Mathieson's abilities as a competent post manager had always been in doubt, but no action had been taken by the Company. The fault, therefore, was the Company's, and not Mr. Mathieson's, and he should remain at Beauval until he reached full retirement." Ross pondered the ruling and after his initial disappointment had to admit that it was a wise decision, one that made him feel proud to be a "Bay man."

About the only improvement the Company made to its northern facilities during the 1930s was installation of short-wave transmitters that for the first time connected the isolated outposts with each other and the outside world. Except for the annual supply-ship visit and the occasional winter dog team, the Company's servants received no personal or corporate news until these radios were installed, starting with Arctic Bay, Leaf River, Cape Dorset and Cape Smith in 1937. The twelve-watt Morse code sets were powered by windmill-operated generators and twelve-volt storage batteries that were nursed like colicky babies, kept warm by claiming the place of honour behind each staff house stove. The network grew to fifty-four stations—the country's largest—and was eventually converted to single sideband, and later to voice and radio telephones.

A more daring departure was the first modern Canadian beaver preserve, established near Rupert House on James Bay. The area's beaver ponds had been almost totally trapped out, leaving the Cree with nothing to trade, when the local HBC manager, James Watt, and his wife, Maud, persuaded Company authorities to leave the few remaining beaver houses alone, so that the animals would have a

*HBC clerk Charles N. Stephen, with radio equipment at Lansdowne House, 1941*

chance to multiply. Quebec designated a 7,200-square-mile beaver sanctuary, which was so successful that by 1940 trapping could begin again.

During the Second World War several northern locations were used for temporary airfields, as staging areas for military manoeuvres and for Ferry Command operations. The largest undertaking was the great Canol project, which piped oil from Norman Wells on the Mackenzie River six hundred miles to a refinery built at Whitehorse for use in the North Pacific theatre of war. As the Arctic expert Graham Rowley noted, "In a country where old lard pails had been treasured, 45-gallon drums, not always empty, were discarded." One measure of the HBC's dominant influence among the Inuit at that time was this description of the Second World War, given by Octave Sivanertok of Repulse Bay in a 1979 interview with the CBC's Lorna Kusugak: "There was a big war. It was between the Bay and the Germans. The Bay won." Yet in at least one way, the war years were merely an extension of the Depression. The Canadian government, pressured by more urgent priorities, perpetuated its benign neglect of the North.

What changed all that was the precipitous dive of white fox prices from thirty-five dollars to three dollars between 1946 and 1948. With their only cash crop all but wiped out, the Inuit found their social and economic framework altered. They had abandoned their hunting ethic to become trappers, and now, cut off for at least a generation from living off the land, they could not subsist on the low fur prices. Epidemics of such white men's illnesses as measles, influenza, tuberculosis, diphtheria and venereal diseases were spreading across the North. Families were starving and sled dogs dying, further reducing the ability of the Inuit to hunt. There were some work opportunities, such as the opening of a nickel mine at Rankin Inlet, which operated between 1957 and 1962, employing up to eighty Inuit, and construction of the ninety-eight Distant Early Warning stations across the North in the mid-1950s. But they were too limited to have much impact. According to a 1960 survey, only 307 Inuit (out of a total population of about 12,000) had jobs that year, and only 63 of them worked for non-government agencies: 58 for North Rankin Nickel Mines Limited, 2 for missionaries and 3 for the Hudson's Bay Company. With such narrow employment opportunities, the Northerners grew increasingly dependent on government welfare. As Ottawa became more concerned about their ability to survive, the Inuit themselves were being urbanized, a process that significantly raised their individual and collective aspirations. Paradoxically, the most significant of these urbanizing influences was tuberculosis, which at one time afflicted a third of the Inuit population. "Endemic upper respiratory diseases like tuberculosis, emphysema, and bronchitis motivated movement of the people into white men's settlements, mainly to hospitals in the South," recalled R.G. Williamson, an anthropologist at the University of Saskatchewan. "New lifestyle expectations were created during their time at the treatment centres, as they watched television and visited white people's homes in Winnipeg, Brandon, Hamilton, Toronto, and Montreal. As material expectations were raised, the Hudson's Bay Company had to modernize its merchandising methods and expand its lines. It began to stock tailor-made cigarettes and moved from selling mainly high-protein foods to such high-carbohydrate (and high mark-up) items as sweet biscuits, soft drinks, candy, and other junk foods. That was a big change to the old fur trade posts, where keeping 2½-inch nails in stock was thought to be a bit of a luxury."

As the economic plight of the Inuit developed into a political issue and it became evident that the fur trade could no longer sustain them, Ottawa moved north with a vengeance, formally accepting the fact that education and welfare were its responsibilities. Well-intentioned teachers, nurses, doctors, welfare officers and administrators galore arrived in the Arctic. To monitor the behaviour of the new arrivals, the Royal Canadian Mounted Police increased its northern presence, being charged, among other duties, with distributing family allowances and old-age pensions.* Government handouts were issued not as cash, which was still not a generally accepted means of doing business in the North, but as entries in RCMP ledgers. The police would itemize precisely what goods the people could receive and send the tally over to the HBC store, which then handed out the merchandise. A typical 1945 monthly family ration consisted of fourteen pounds of flour, a pound of tea, three pounds of sugar, three pounds of rolled oats, two pounds of rice, six packages of Pablum and a gallon of coal oil. Not much to build a dream on, but better than starving. The notion of receiving goods free from HBC stores that had previously traded them for furs was disturbing and not always understood. "The Mountie told me I could go into the trading post and buy anything I needed because I had family allowance," recalled Matthew Innakatsik of Baker Lake. "It didn't make any sense because I had never

---

*Some of their patrols were amazingly infrequent. When an RCMP constable arrived in the Belcher Islands on April 11, 1940, it was the first police visit since 1919. Official calls too were rare. "When I went to the Belchers in 1969," said former Commissioner Stuart Hodgson, "it was the first public meeting that had ever been held there. As I recall, it was in a little one-room schoolhouse that had been dumped off in the southern end of the Belchers rather than the north. As a consequence, a few houses were built for the local people, as their children were going to school. Essentially, the main settlement was in the north end of the island. In any event, the meeting started about six o'clock and by midnight there were only myself and the interpreter left. The rest of our party had retired. At 2.00 A.M. as the meeting developed into a sort of lull, I asked the people (all the locals were there—grandparents, parents, children and babies—the entire settlement) if perhaps they would like to adjourn the meeting and they said, 'Oh, no.' At 2.30 I again put the question to them, 'Have you anything more to talk about?' and they said no. I said, 'Well, perhaps we should adjourn the meeting,' and they again replied no, to which I said, 'Why not?' The reply was both astounding and humorous. They simply said that they had never had a meeting before and they thought it was a lot of fun. I was up the next morning at six o'clock. We had breakfast and left at seven to see the people at the north end of the island. When the plane landed and I opened the door, I was astonished to see the same people. They asked, 'Are we going to have another meeting?' They had travelled fifty miles overland that night in order to be there for another meeting."

*Nurse at work in the Arctic*

received anything for free before and I was afraid to do it."*

The combination of nervousness about Canadian sovereignty, the paranoid influences of the Cold War, which gave the Arctic unexpected strategic significance, and the growing awareness in southern Canada that the Inuit were severely deprived lent impetus to the government's involvement. Free match-box houses were provided for Inuit families in the main settlements, with electricity and water at nominal cost. The North became fashionable. Experts arrived by the hour, it seemed—scientists and human manipulators,

---

*Relations between the Mounties and Inuit were not limited to welfare. "Almost all the single RCM Policemen had native girlfriends," observed F.G. Cooch, a Canadian government ornithologist who specialized in on-site Arctic studies. "It was no big deal. But I remember being told about a young constable posted to Pond Inlet who was a very fastidious individual and apparently afraid of women, behaving like a bashful monk. One time, when his senior colleague had to go on patrol to Arctic Bay, he was out about five hours when he remembered something and went back. He could hear noises from the ground-floor bathroom, so he looked in and there was the monk in the bathtub with one of the local girls, scrubbing her back. There was a candle and a bottle of wine beside them and my friend, Cliff, said he didn't have the heart to walk in and disturb them."

all eager to carry the white man's burden. Minnie Aodla Freeman, a wonderfully wise Inuit from Cape Hope Island, summed up the effect of the influx most succinctly when she commented that the ideal Arctic family now consisted of a husband and wife, four children and an anthropologist.*

After 1960, family allowances and old-age pensions were sent directly to the intended recipients. Not only did some managers insist that old debts be paid before they extended any credit to their customers (a policy the Company claimed was not contained in their directives), but natives who dared send order forms to Eaton's catalogue department or any other competitor claimed their letters were occasionally mislaid. Even when orders did get through, usually on a cash-on-delivery basis, they could not always be claimed. Jean Godsell, whose husband was stationed with the HBC in Fort Smith, recalled a typical scene when the long-expected mail-order goods finally arrived and the customers came to collect them: "One by one, they appeared at the wicket, their dusky faces wreathed in smiles which soon turned to black anger when they found they could not take the parcels off in debt, as was the case with the trading stores. . . . Naturally, most of the parcels went back, but others came in on the next plane; still more came in on the steamer, and it was quite some time ere the mail-order houses realized that Marie Chandelle, Rosalie Squirrel, Elsie Lame-Duck et al. were not, despite their substantial orders, the type of customers they desired."†

Best of the newcomers to the North was James Houston, a Toronto artist who spent fourteen years on Baffin Island under contract to the Department of Northern Affairs, teaching the Inuit how best to market their soapstone creations. Carving, an intrinsic skill of the Inuit, had been used to fashion out of bone, stone and ivory the snow goggles, parka toggles, harpoons, arrowheads, ice-chisels, spoons, fish spears, talismans and toys that were part of their everyday existence. In 1949, Houston, assisted by Norman Ross, the HBC store manager at Port Harrison, collected a test group of Inuit carvings for the Canadian Handicrafts Guild in Montreal, which successfully sold the items. Gradually a market was built up for the best of the pieces. After

---

*She married one—Milton Freeman, a professor of anthropology at the University of Alberta—and went on to write some of the best of the northern books, including *Survival in the South* and *Life Among the Qallunaat*.

†The men had their own problems with mail-order catalogues, especially those pages featuring women's underwear. One trapper, gazing with fascination at the suggestive layouts, wrote away for "the lady on the far right of page 59."

a false start trying to produce bookends, ash trays and such, the carvers, under Houston's guidance, let their imaginations soar. By the late 1950s, the carvings had achieved international stature. The work was so successful partly because the carvers' own longing for a return to their ancestors' hunting days, expressed in their art, coincided with the southern buyers' romantic notions of what "Eskimos" were all about. The native artists responded to the material they were working. Their sculptures were not as much artistic as ritualistic, the crystallization of moments in time. "These are not cold sculptures of a frozen world," Houston noted. "They reveal to us the passionate feelings of a people aware of all the joys and terrors of life. They also reveal an enormous freshness and ingenuity, a hunter's sense of observation." Once the soapstone trade was established, Houston and his then wife, Alma, moved to Cape Dorset. "Oshaweetok, a famous Eskimo carver ... sat near me one evening casually studying the sailor head trademarks on two identical packages of cigarettes," Houston later recalled. "He noted carefully every subtle detail of color and form, and he suggested to me that it must be tiresome for some person to sit and paint every one of the little heads with exact sameness on an endless number of packages. . . . Looking around to find some way to demonstrate printing, I saw an ivory walrus tusk that Oshaweetok had recently carved. . . . Taking an old tin of writing ink that had frozen and thawed many times . . . I dipped up the heavy black residue and smoothed it over the tusk. Taking a thin piece of toilet tissue, I laid it carefully on the inked surface and rubbed it lightly and quickly. Stripping the paper from the tusk, I saw that by good fortune we had a clear negative image of Oshaweetok's incised design. . . . 'We could do that,' he said. And so we did." That was how Cape Dorset's block printing and sealskin stencil printing industry was born, its evocative images later gracing museums and private collections the world over. By 1960, the HBC was buying forty tons of "Eskimo" carvings a year for resale in southern Canada.*

The prints and carvings grew so profitable that the following year a native-run West Baffin Eskimo Co-operative was opened at Cape

---

*A less serious Company sideline was the U-Paddle Canoe rental service for adventurous holidayers who wanted to spend part of their summers following the trade routes of the voyageurs or exploring the wilder shores of the continent's sub-Arctic rivers. The Company purchased twenty-eight seventeen-foot aluminum canoes in 1964 and distributed them to posts at likely locations. There were enough rentals (at twenty-five dollars a week) to allow the HBC to break even, and by the time the U-Paddle service was abandoned twenty years later, the Company had a fleet of eighty canoes, renting for a weekly $125.

*Artist and novelist James Houston*

Dorset to market the art. Nineteen similar outlets were soon opened in other communities, over stern protests from the HBC. "They were strongly against the move," recalled Ben Sivertz, then Commissioner of the Northwest Territories and a co-op advocate. "But the Eskimos took to it like ducks to water. We didn't have to tell them what to do. They took over from the Hudson's Bay post manager the business of setting carving prices. Jim Houston told me he was away when it happened, but when he got back to Cape Dorset he was invited to a meeting where everybody brought in their carvings. Each one was put on a table and all the carvers wrote down what they thought it should sell for; they then averaged that out, and that was the set price. They did that on their own in place after place. The pieces were sent to Ottawa, where we distributed them to the Handicrafts Guild and other merchandisers—in San Francisco, Paris, London and anywhere. The money was then sent back to the carvers, and that in fact was how cash on a large scale first came to the North—though it still had to be spent in Hudson's Bay Company stores."

As retailing competition grew more intense, so did the scrutiny of the HBC's methods and mark-ups. The Company maintained that its objective for mature northern stores (those established five years or more) was a 23-percent return on net assets (before interest and taxes). Some outlets exceeded that average and many others, particularly in the more remote areas, fell below it because of higher transportation costs. Testifying before the Northwest Territories

The Hunt, *engraving by Juanisialu, 1965*

Council on May 27, 1981, Marvin Tiller, then head of the HBC's northern operation, gave a rare insight into corporate pricing policies. The retail price of non-perishable goods, he stated, included a mark-up of up to 25 percent on top of landed costs, with the margin rising to one-third on most perishable items. He pointed out that stock in the North turned over only one and a half times a year, compared with eleven or twelve times in the South. Instead of trying to refute the accusation that perishables at the HBC's Frobisher Bay store were selling at 70 percent more than comparable items in Montreal, Tiller boasted that "to lay down fresh produce in Frobisher at only 70 percent more than Montreal prices is, in our view, a remarkable achievement of planning and organization." Goods at the HBC stores were—and are—expensive, but most of the added margin is accounted for by transportation costs. In 1981, a five-pound bag of potatoes at Pond Inlet, for example, sold for a ridiculous $7.10. But its actual freight cost was $5.15. "We are probably regarded as large and prosperous from money made out of the natives," Dick Murray, the HBC's managing director, complained in 1966. "The fact that in ninety-eight cases out of one hundred our men are able and dedicated, and work under conditions that most Canadians would refuse to work under for any length of time, is simply not taken into consideration."

Perception of the HBC was changing. Clearest summary of that evolution was the observation of Adrian Tanner of Memorial University, writing in *Queen's Quarterly*. "When I lived in an Arctic trading post community in the late 1950s, where trade with the Inuit was still conducted using Hudson's Bay Company tokens rather than cash, the two subjects which we learned to avoid at the segregated social gatherings of the white inhabitants were religion and impact of the Hudson's Bay Company on the native people. We who did not work for the Company found it remarkable that all Hudson's Bay employees, from the old-time traders to newest clerks who had just arrived from across the Atlantic, had a staunch and unquestioning loyalty to their employer and its past actions, and that when a subject like this was raised they seemed to quickly be reduced to irrational argument and wounded feelings. . . . By the time I went north again in the mid-1960s the Hudson's Bay Company fur trade and its effects on the native people had become something of a dead horse which the Canadian public was only too willing to flog, thanks to authors like Farley Mowat, and to some of the native political leaders. However, my own attitude to the recent situation, if not to the past history, had by then become less harsh. The Hudson's Bay Company's operation of its contemporary monopoly in the north seemed to be a model of benign responsibility, in comparison both to the European exploiters in other parts of the colonial world, and to the other 'marginal men' who were by then taking over power in the communities— government administrators, policemen, missionaries and teachers."*

"THE IMAGE OF THE CLASSIC ESKIMO is still that of Nanook of the North, the indomitable hunter clad in a sealskin anorak and polar-bear pants, his harpoon poised for the kill," concluded Sam Hall, an Arctic

---

*One of the major changes in the Arctic was the introduction in 1960 of legally sold liquor. Previously, with no legal booze available, some of the more desperate Arctic hands, both aboriginal and white, had been swilling Aqua Velva after-shave lotion, Lysol or anti-freeze. HBC employees for a while enjoyed a tastier and more literary potion. Because the ink used by store managers to mark ledger entries kept freezing in their unheated stores, an enterprising Boston manufacturer introduced a new variety of red ink that contained so much alcohol it didn't turn solid. Once the HBC field hands discovered they could drink the stuff as well as write with it, orders for the scarlet concoction multiplied rapidly. But the Company caught on and went back to filling inkwells with less delectable thirst-quenchers.

documentary film-maker, in a 1987 study. "In the Arctic today, this vision is as ludicrous as that of Caesar, his toga flowing behind him, a bunch of grapes in one hand and a silver chalice in the other, striding through a traffic jam in Rome." That's true enough, but the Inuit still live in both worlds. They left behind the last vestiges of the Stone Age only four decades ago; most were born in sealskin tents by the light of whale-oil lamps. The Inuit, caught between past and present, must find their refrigerators, VHS recorders and Yamaha trail buggies just as unreal as their fathers' and grandfathers' walrus-meat sledge runners, whalebone eye goggles and *iglus*. All those stately *kayaks*, *umiaks*, York boats and peterheads were displaced by functional 14- or 24-foot square-stern aluminum canoes, weighted down with 25- or 45-h.p. Evinrudes. For long journeys, there were the de Havilland Twin Otters operated by the many airlines criss-crossing the North; for short trips, snowmobiles.

That switch—from dogs to snowmobiles—was the final farewell to tradition. The few dog teams that remained were seldom used, except as rentals to film-makers or white tourists pretending they were Scott of the Antarctic. It was the whine of the snowmobiles' super-charged 250-cc motors that shattered the Arctic dream. Soon there were more skeletons of dead Ski-Doos than caribou carcasses around the community dumps. Local teenagers spent endless hours aimlessly racing the machines in and out of settlements, the unmuffled roar of their engines giving voice to their desperation and their anger.

In this troublesome context the HBC became a natural target for discontent. Despite the natives' steady incomes, from government handouts, it was a strict Company rule never to grant an Inuk a Bay credit card. At the same time, the Company came to be perceived as an agent of destruction of the old values. "The Hudson's Bay Company . . . helped the government practice genocide of Eskimo dogs, by providing the necessary hardware in which Inuit were to become assimilated into Canadian society," charged Josh Teemotee of Frobisher Bay. "This would also place the Inuit into a credit situation. Whether it was a commercial plot to assimilate Inuit is not known, but it seems coincidental that civil service posts would open up where Hudson's Bay stores located." Billy Diamond, Grand Chief of the Grand Council of the Cree of Quebec, complained that as late as 1970 the HBC store at Rupert House was not paying interest on funds it was holding for its customers—yet charging interest on credit overdrafts. "I was just starting out as Chief at Rupert," he recalled, "and you had to buy everything at the Bay store. After your furs had been auctioned off by the Company, the money went directly to the store and they told you how much your furs had been worth, though there was no way of verifying it. Then you dealt for goods, but the store kept the balance and paid no interest. Even if you deposited money for safekeeping with the Bay—and I heard of people who had $25,000 with the Company—you got no interest. . . . It was only my generation that said, 'Listen, there's much more to life than the Hudson's Bay Company. There's a world out there!' "

Reduced in their function to local supermarkets, the stores began to expand their merchandise racks, featuring such southern specialties as soft-porn magazines, canned lobster, Poly-fil parkas with Velcro pocket fasteners and every possible variety of junk food. The surfeit of Kool-Aid, Coca-Cola, chocolate, bubble gum and potato chips from the HBC store meant that most young Inuit lost their teeth by the time they were teenagers.*

The HBC's presence had radically altered the Inuit way of life, and while it was easy enough to be critical of the Company's impact, there was no permanent escape from the malignant forces of the white man's civilization. Within that context the Bay demonstrated remarkable restraint, and many of its local managers earned their reputations for fair treatment of their customers. "I got to know probably twenty or thirty of the Bay managers and I never knew one who was a rascal," recalled Ben Sivertz. "It was life of a specialized kind and I think that the rectitude and decency of the Bay men was remarkable, though I'm not talking now about sexual relations with Eskimo women. That's one aspect that needs special interpretation. But all that stuff about how mean they were about the prices they paid for fur, that was Company policy. I am not sure there was any other way to do it." Even Billy Diamond relented in his criticism of the modern HBC. "The Company took a look at our needs and has tried to adapt to what we're doing up there and at the same time they're trying to give us a chance to take control of a lot of things," he admitted. "They used to be the only guys selling gas, outboards and Ski-Doos. We've taken over all that and the local trappers' association is ordering its own canoes and supplies. The Hudson's Bay Company really streamlined its operations to bringing in the groceries, appliances and clothing. It's no longer a credit outlet." Nellie Cournoyea, an Inuk born in Aklavik and currently Minister of Health, Minister of Energy, Mines and Petroleum Resources and Minister of Public Works in the Northwest Territories, agrees: "I'm indifferent to the Bay. To us it is just

---

*The 500-year-old remains of an Inuit woman found in 1978 in a Greenland cave had a near-perfect set of teeth.

another store with no particular significance."

Under the HBC's—and later the government's—sponsorship, life was certainly better for the old and the sick, and having a box of matches was an improvement on rubbing sticks together to light a fire. But the argument about whether the Inuit were happier then or now can never be resolved. "I know people were happier in the old days," said William Kuptana, an elder at Sachs Harbour. "But I know for sure they were not happy every day." Former Commissioner Stuart Hodgson recalled asking Jimmy Kilabuk at Pangnirtung the same question. "I don't know," was the reply. "But I'll tell you this: when I was a young man, I can never, ever remember being warm."

Minnie Aodla Freeman, the Inuit author, placed the Company in its proper perspective when she told a 1980 conference that it had "made easier lives for Inuit since 1670. They were in my home area of James Bay long before I was born, fur trading with my ancestors. . . . I think one of the reasons why Inuit welcomed the Hudson's Bay Company was the fact that the Company never tried to change Inuit ways of behaving or thinking. Yes, they changed our equipment, to better steel knives, steel saws, steel nails, steel axes and manufactured cloth. Inuit understood it was the furs that the Hudson's Bay Company were after. Inuit hunters had employment through the Hudson's Bay Company. It was the familiar job Inuit enjoyed. We still hear older Inuit today saying that the Hudson's Bay Company is most useful in Inuit lands. . . . Hudson's Bay Company sold Fort Garry tea to Inuit first, before it was sold in Bytown . . . pity!"

# III MERCHANT PRINCES

*Delivery teams at the HBC Winnipeg store, 1914*

# CHAPTER 13

# THE LORDS AND THE GOOD OLD BOYS

*"In England we gave them knighthoods; in Winnipeg they became directors of the Hudson's Bay Company."*

—Joe Links, HBC Director

THE TRANSITION OF THE BAY MEN from merchant adventurers to merchant princes was slow, painful and absolute. By the end of that long cycle, the Hudson's Bay Company had become a major retailing empire with no sense of privilege or feeling for history. But in the half-century leading up to that lapsed state of grace, the Company's top management went through a series of stops and starts, serious internal wrangling and several boardroom convulsions.

The protagonists in this jousting for control were the governors, deputy governors and their ennobled retinues trying to *rule* the Company from London pitted against a group of fiercely proud, down-home Good Old Boys trying to *run* the Company from Winnipeg. The two groups did battle with the obdurate conviction of crusaders, each side serving the righteousness of its cause.

On the surface, it seemed an uneven contest. The British lords and knights were exquisitely aware of the subtleties of their clout and class. Their authority was so persuasive because it flowed not from any divine right or self-proclaimed sense of superiority. They really *were* the best and the brightest in the upper crust of a society that took breeding and intelligence for granted, and they genuinely represented the interests of the HBC's shareholders, 97 percent of whom were domiciled within the United Kingdom.

Arrayed against these British proprietors and their distinguished proconsuls was a tightly knit posse of Winnipeg's finest. Midwestern squires, they were good if limited men, frontier-tough and damned if they were going to kowtow to these haughty strangers wearing spats and with handkerchiefs up their sleeves. Yet they loved being involved with the Company that had once ruled the West and eventually viewed themselves as a kind of apostolic succession, smoothly following one another as members of the HBC's Canadian Committee. That tenure became such a desirable badge of office among the local business élite that Joe Links, the British board's wittiest member, once quipped: "In England we gave them knighthoods; in Winnipeg they became directors of the Hudson's Bay Company."

In a very real way, Canadianization of the Hudson's Bay Company was part of the decolonization of the British Empire. Victory through gradualism. In the fifty-eight years between formation of the first Canadian Advisory Committee in 1912 and permanent transfer of the Company's charter across the Atlantic in 1970—between the governorships of Lord Strathcona and Lord Amory—a sequence of tippy-toe measures was reluctantly taken to shift authority from London to Winnipeg. Although provision of a domestic registry for Canadian shareholders had been suggested as early as 1908, it wasn't until forty-five years later, in 1953, that it was actually put into effect. On October 16, 1958, the Hudson's Bay Company board convened in Winnipeg, the first time its directors had met outside London in 288 years. It took another half-decade before the British shares were listed on the Toronto Stock Exchange. A year later, for the first time the Company's dividend cheques were paid to Canadian shareholders in Canadian dollars instead of British pounds, and it was 1970 before the annual report was printed in Canada.

The transfer of substantive decision-making authority didn't really begin until 1930, when Winnipeg was granted power of attorney to deal with the Company's day-to-day operations. In 1957, the Canadian Committee's members became directors of the mother firm, though it took a further six years before they were allowed to outnumber their British colleagues. "The Canadians were always trying to grab more authority," remembered Peter Wood, for thirty-eight years the Company's senior financial officer, "but the Brits kept hanging on, putting little roadblocks in the way, standing about with long faces, stressing the risks and disadvantages, so that it was difficult to be enthusiastic. They were such a distinguished and respected group that it was hard to ignore them. Besides, they held the power."

HBC *Board of Directors' meeting, Winnipeg, October 16, 1958*

The nature of that power was limited at best, authority and responsibility being divided between two continents, with London possessing the former but unable to impose the latter. It was one thing to draft policies in the hush of the HBC's City boardroom but quite another to police how—or whether—those directives had been followed in the field. Accountability was always the pivotal issue, yet making orders stick was never satisfactorily resolved. The mesmerizing effect of the HBC's unique history made everyone cautious about allowing authority to be dispersed too quickly or too widely. The Canadian Committeemen had the local knowledge but not the breadth of experience to run a major trading company; the London directors possessed the necessary expertise but were too far removed from the trenches to have much practical input.

The operating heads of the Company in Canada quickly realized that their main leverage lay in how much or how little data they transmitted across the Atlantic, and being astute about it—knowing full well that rationing performance statistics would only make

London suspicious—they tried to overwhelm the HBC's British head-quarters with tidal waves of facts. Sheaves of weekly returns enumerated each post's fur intake and each department store's inventory of socks; every transaction was meticulously documented and transmitted overseas. What went missing was any feeling about the exciting new economy sprouting up north of the 49th parallel.

That omission was less by design than by the character of the Canadian operation. The Committee, in fact, knew very little about the new Canada evolving outside Winnipeg's municipal boundaries. Its members stubbornly resisted lifting their sights beyond regional concerns, leaving others, as they haughtily declared, "to go whoring in the East." The dynamics of delay ruled the Company's affairs.

THE TENSION THAT PERMEATED RELATIONS between the British directors and Canadian Committeemen even touched their social lives. Sir Eric Faulkner recalled his first visit to Winnipeg in the mid-1950s when he was the HBC's Deputy Governor: "I was viewed with enormous suspicion by the Canadians and subsequently learned they were told to invite me to their houses for a drink, but under no circumstances to serve me a meal until they'd taken my measure. I went to have a drink with Stu Searle, who turned out to be a delightful man. After a whisky, he suddenly exclaimed, 'Do you realize I'm not allowed to ask you to dinner? This is bloody nonsense, but since there's no food in the house, let's go out and eat.' We finally changed our minds and had scrambled eggs while sitting on his living-room floor, and that was the beginning of a friendship that lasted all our lives."

In a letter to the last British Governor, Lord Amory, the last Chairman of the Winnipeg Committee, David Kilgour, betrayed the Canadians' real feeling about the visitations of London dignitaries. "I confess," he wrote, "we are probably unduly annoyed by individuals who have that austere superiority which we Western Canadians ascribe to some Englishmen. . . ." Joe Harris, one of the Canadian Committeemen, was more blunt. "When a North American wants to insult you," he explained to Amory, "he calls you a son of a bitch, laughs with you about it over a drink at lunch, and forgets it by evening. A Britisher, on the other hand, does it in the most thoughtful courteous language that can be devised—and writes it into the Minutes."

The Canadians' standoffish attitude was demonstrated in the smallest gestures. Most of the Winnipeggers owned lodges in the duck-hunting marshes northwest of Winnipeg, and even though the aristocratic visitors loved shooting, invitations were seldom forthcoming. "It was soon clear that ... the Winnipeg Establishment didn't want them at their lodges and sent them out to Delta for me to take care of," wrote Al Hochbaum, then in charge of the local waterfowl research station. "I remember especially what fine specimens of the human race were Tony Keswick [the HBC's Governor] and Sir Henry Benson [then Deputy Governor]. I kept wondering why Winnipeg society didn't wish to have them for a weekend. They shot like gentlemen, drank like gentlemen, swore like gentlemen—and didn't mind the outdoor toilets." The British visitors tended to be overpolite, slightly patronizing and more than a little puzzled by the Winnipeg-gers' provincialism. "I once asked Con Riley, the first time I met him after he was appointed to head the Canadian Committee," Keswick recalled, "exactly what Winnipeg was famous for. I've never forgotten his answer. He said very quietly, without looking left or right, 'Nice people,' and left it at that."

Both groups were so internally cohesive it was difficult for either side to comprehend the other. Except for one attempted *coup d'état* in 1963, the British directors were so compatible they didn't bother taking votes on any significant issue. "I was going to say we never voted on anything," recalled Joe Links, a twenty-eight year board member, "but we actually did hold one vote when we were getting some new china for serving tea in the boardroom. Some of us wanted green, some wanted yellow. I think the yellows had it."

The British directors received virtually no perks, and none of them needed either the prestige or the token stipend (£500 annually). Yet there never seemed to be a shortage of top-drawer candidates. "We frankly had the pick of the best men in the City," boasted Lord Amory. "I don't remember any directors whom we thought of turning us down, no matter how high their calibre. Whereas the Canadian Committee people were big men only in Manitoba, but had little contact with the rest of Canada."

The executive committee of the British board met at noon every Tuesday (with the entire directorate attending once a month); sherry was served at quarter to one, though several of the more robust members would have preferred gin and tonic. Seated under the portraits of past Governors and surrounded by silver objects, some dating back to 1670, they discussed Company business, mainly reports of the Canadian Committee, which met each previous Thursday. Over lunch they would lapse into a wider discussion of public affairs, occasionally touching some such tangent as dismissing the latest biography of Lord Keynes for being the work of an Oxford man struggling to understand a Cambridge mind. The east wall of the

*Sir Edward Peacock*

walnut-panelled boardroom was covered with a map showing the
Company's posts and operations, visited yearly by the Governor or his
deputy. Most shareholders' annual meetings (still called "Courts")
were quick and tame affairs; an elapsed time of seventeen minutes in
1957 was the record for speed. "One frail old proprietor," recalled
Links, "used to refer at the annual Court to the previous speaker,
equally frail, as 'the adventurer who has just sat down,' probably
correctly, since we were 'the Governor and Company of Adventurers
of England, trading into Hudson's Bay.' "

Immediately after the Second World War, bankers became significant on the HBC board, mainly in the person of Sir Eric Faulkner (later
chairman of both Lloyds Bank and Glyn, Mills). He had won a
football Blue at Cambridge, participated in the retreat at Dunkirk,
fought against Rommel, done all the important things expected of an
all-round English gentleman of his generation, yet he regarded his
dozen years with the HBC as very special. "During the 1930s when I
first went to Glyn's," he recalled, "I thought that if I ever did succeed
in getting up the ladder and was allowed to take outside directorships
I would love to be invited one day to join the board of the Hudson's
Bay Company. By chance fate dealt the cards that way. I well remember saying laughingly at one of our board meetings, 'God, what a
Company this is, never a moment of peace. There is always turbulence somewhere.' " Sir Martin Jacomb, another distinguished
banker who also served on the HBC board, reached a similar conclu-

sion. "Some institutions," he said, "although they are only legal entities, do have real organic personalities. The Bay transmits that feeling to anyone who comes in contact with it."

One of the HBC's great strengths was the active interest in its financial welfare displayed by the Bank of England. The Old Lady of Threadneedle Street had actually been founded twenty-four years *after* the Hudson's Bay Company—a fact successive central bank governors were never allowed to forget—but the two institutions remained very close. Half a dozen Bank of England governors and directors had been either governors or directors of the HBC, including Sir John Henry Pelly, Henry Hulse Berens, George Joachim Goschen, Sir Robert Molesworth Kindersley, Sir Patrick Ashley Cooper, Lord Cobbold and, above all, Sir Edward Peacock. The Canadian-born financier had for two decades been a dominant figure in the Bank of England and later became senior partner of Barings, the London money house the Duc de Richelieu, premier of France, had in 1818 dubbed Europe's "Sixth Great Power," alluding to the continent's economic order being ruled by England, France, Prussia, Austria, Russia and Baring Brothers. Peacock, who became an HBC director in 1931 and stayed on the board for the next nineteen years, was also an adviser to the Royal Family and had been intimately involved in matters financial and otherwise concerning Edward VIII's abdication. His influence on the HBC's economic deliberations over two crucial decades was considerable, and it was highly conservative.

Because of existing tax laws, the English shareholders much preferred capital gains to income, so that stock splits were more desirable than dividends. The Company's capital funds were grossly inadequate to keep it expanding along with the Canadian economy because until 1960 the HBC refused to borrow. "We all hated borrowing and considered any loan a blister on the balance sheet," Keswick confirmed. "Mum told us you mustn't overspend your allowance, and that was the British discipline. We were against borrowing because we saw all around us people borrowing tremendously and getting into difficulties, and we didn't want our beloved Hudson's Bay Company to get into trouble. We may have missed some tricks, but we were old-timers and had seen accidents happen before."

The real paradox was that despite their "blister on the balance sheet" attitude and the rigid corporate directives that flowed from that bias, the London directors were often less averse to risk than the Winnipeggers. "It always seemed to me that we were more anxious than the Canadians to modernize and keep up with the times," Faulkner recalled. "Few of the Winnipeg directors got around the country or the Company, and so were inclined to miss opportunities. We could never persuade them to travel much outside Winnipeg. They might have a look-in at the Vancouver store if they happened to be there, but we'd often add a week or two to our tours and go to the really remote places, into the Saguenay country or way up into the Arctic, where we were welcomed by the staff who were delighted to see a director, even an English one."

THE DICHOTOMY OF THE MENTALITIES at work in Winnipeg and London reached far deeper than that. The Canadian West is a land of long memories. At the turn of the century, Winnipeggers had felt at the very forefront of Canadian civilization. The *Winnipeg Telegram* proudly reported in its January 29, 1910, edition that the city had nineteen millionaires, pointedly adding that Toronto, many times its size, had only twenty-one. An American journalist who arrived the following year waxed enthusiastic about the Manitoba capital as the Chicago of the North, "a gateway through which all the commerce of the east and the west, and the north and the south, must flow. No city, in America at least, has such absolute and complete command over the wholesale trade of so vast an area. It is destined to become one of the greatest distributing commercial centres of the continent as well as a manufacturing community of great importance."

Instead, completion of the Panama Canal gradually eliminated Winnipeg as the transportation and distribution linchpin of the Canadian economy's spread to the Pacific coast, although the population of Vancouver surpassed that of Winnipeg only in 1931.* No longer a potential Chicago, Winnipeg became Canada's Vienna—a city-state without an empire. Geared to supply a hinterland half a continent wide, it became an economic backwater, its geographical

---

*The Panama Canal was only one factor in Winnipeg's decline, though a major one. Also at fault was the post-war collapse of the local wholesale business, when prosperity allowed carload lots to be shipped across the West instead of being broken up by wholesalers in Winnipeg, which meant that the three provinces west of Manitoba began to deal directly with the large eastern companies and institutions. As that trend intensified, Winnipeg tapered off to being a provincial capital, even though more cultured than most. At the same time, the financial functions of Winnipeg changed. First, British Columbia banking executives were allowed to report directly to head office in Montreal or Toronto. Later, because of the 1947 oil boom, the same became true of Alberta. The service industries, especially insurance, followed the pattern of the banks. Until the late 1940s Winnipeg was the regional centre of the entire West for these industries, but it declined rapidly after that.

significance drastically reduced by history's tides. Most Winnipeggers responded to the change by leaving or sending their children to carve out lives and careers elsewhere; certainly the city's most valuable export was its people. Those who stayed either accustomed themselves to living in a pleasant, unspectacular place or—like the Hudson's Bay Committeemen—scarcely acknowledged Winnipeg's demise. Bound together by fear of their own irrelevance, the Bay men dug in. W.L. Morton, the Manitoba historian who understood his province better than anyone else, concluded that the local business community—from which the Hudson's Bay Company's Committeemen had been drawn—was "cautious, canny, reactionary, untravelled, fearful of ideas and of imagination."

The most unyielding point of dispute between London and Winnipeg directors was location of the Canadian headquarters. In the mid-1930s the British Governor hinted that a move to Toronto might be desirable, to take better advantage of the country's future opportunities. The Winnipeg Committee immediately threatened to resign *en masse*, and a lame compromise of naming a few token non-Manitoba directors was finally accepted. Still, the Winnipeggers howled in anger and frustration—even though the appointees ranked among Canada's best-connected businessmen. J.W. McConnell, for example, was a dominant figure in St Lawrence Sugar, Ogilvie Flour Mills, the Bank of Montreal, CPR, Canada Steamship Lines, Brazilian Traction, Dominion Bridge, Sun Life, Inco, Royal Trust and later the *Montreal Star*, while another, D.C. Coleman, was senior vice-president of the CPR (as well as a director of Metropolitan Life and Canadian Marconi) and had only recently moved away from Winnipeg. The then resident HBC managing director assured London that these two Eastern members were "of no practical value to the Company" and that "in any case, it was impossible to justify paying them the same fees as the Winnipeg members who did all the work" so that "if the Board wished to keep them, their fees should be reduced to $50 a meeting." As late as 1966, the Canadian managing director, Richard Murray, wrote a four-page, closely spaced memorandum to the then Governor, Lord Amory, explaining that the HBC's headquarters had to stay in Winnipeg "both now and in the future" because it was Canada's geographical centre, had adequate Telex and air services, and that even if executives had to be paid a premium for being willing to relocate there, it meant lower turnover because there would be less "job hopping." What Murray failed to mention was that this was true mainly because there was nowhere to hop to—and that maintaining headquarters in Winnipeg almost guaranteed being out of touch with the mainstream of Canada's business community. "The actual benefits from such contacts," he huffed, "are intangible, vary with individuals, and are impossible to calculate ... [but] this affects a very small portion of the total number of executives and thus cannot be given too much weight."

Not only did the HBC's Canadian pastorate limit itself to a Winnipeg parish but its membership was circumscribed by directorships in a handful of local companies. A dozen HBC Committeemen who held office between 1913 and 1970 were also directors of Great-West Life Assurance, for example, and David Kilgour, who was the head of both concerns, once assured the British Governor that "the Canadian Committee of the Hudson's Bay has perhaps very parallel objectives so that it is wholly natural that there should be some duplication between the two Companies." The other Winnipeg-based firms that spawned succeeding generations of HBC Committeemen included Monarch Life, Beaver Lumber, Northern Trusts, Canadian Indemnity, Manitoba Bridge & Iron Works, Osler, Hammond & Nanton and, most important of all, the Richardson group. The successive generations of Winnipeg Establishment men who ran these commercial concerns were entwined corporately, socially and even genetically. The Hudson's Bay Company in Canada was run by a clique of buddies with limited horizons and a common mentality. Part of that mindset was their determination to break the hold on the West of St James Street in Montreal and Bay Street in Toronto by establishing strong corporate principalities in Winnipeg. Local control of the HBC was an essential element in that strategy.

BETWEEN 1911 AND 1926, THE HUDSON'S BAY COMPANY built or purchased its fleet of flagship downtown department stores in Victoria, Vancouver, Edmonton, Calgary, Saskatoon and Winnipeg, opening smaller versions in Kamloops, Vernon, Nelson, Macleod, Lethbridge, Yorkton and Kenora, all of them initially successful as the transcontinental railways deposited tens of thousands of new customers on their doorsteps.* Despite the proliferation of department stores across the country, their share of the retail dollar remained constant—at 10.23 percent in 1923 and exactly the same percentage three decades later,

---

*The HBC was actually a latecomer among Canadian department stores. As well as the major Eaton's and Simpsons chains originating in Toronto, there were Jas. A. Ogilvy's, Morgan's and Dupuis Frères in Montreal; Bowring's in St John's; Wood Brothers in Halifax; Manchester, Robertson, Allison in Saint John; Paquet's and Pollack's in Quebec City; Charles Ogilvy's in Ottawa; Robinson's in Hamilton; Smith's in Windsor; Goudie's in Kitchener; Smallman and Ingram's in London; Williams's in Regina; Spencer's in Victoria; and Woodward's in Vancouver.

which meant fierce competition among the existing players and minimal profit margins. Figures released by Harry Stevens's 1934 Royal Commission on Price Spreads showed that only the HBC's coal sales were keeping the retail operation in the black, and Peter Wood estimated that the stores had actually never made a profit.*

By the time Lord Strathcona had completed his interminable governorship in 1914, the HBC was accurately described as being "more of an historical curiosity than a vital enterprise, because it had failed dismally to keep pace with the Dominion." Although London retained its power under Strathcona's immediate successors (Sir Thomas Skinner and Sir Robert Kindersley), the Canadian Advisory Committee named in 1912 had no authority beyond helping London keep in touch with local conditions. It included Sir William Whyte, the Winnipeg-based retired vice-president of the CPR's western division, and George Galt (a nephew of Sir Alexander Tilloch Galt, one of the Fathers of Confederation), who had established Blue Ribbon Limited, a Winnipeg wholesale grocery house, and become a director of three of the city's touchstone companies: Great-West Life, Northern Trusts and Manitoba Bridge & Iron Works. The Galt family lived at 460 Wellington Crescent, described as "the finest house from Fort William to the coast," and George Galt remained on the Canadian Committee until 1928. Augustus Nanton, the third of the original Committee members, was a central figure in Winnipeg financial circles who served on the boards of Great-West Life and Manitoba Bridge & Iron Works and turned the investment firm of Osler, Hammond & Nanton into a major player in prairie land and resource ventures.†

Nanton could not exercise much Canadian influence on the HBC because the land and fur-trade commissioners reported directly to

---

*HBC earnings between 1947 and 1983, for example, totalled $897.5 million, while income from all non-merchandise sources (including land sales, fur auctions and oil royalties) amounted to $954.2 million. That meant a *loss* of $56.7 million attributable to the department stores in thirty-seven years. (The calculation assumed the stores had to finance their own debt loads and did not take into account the fact that operating the outlets increased their real-estate values.)

†The extent of Nanton's participation showed up in the fact that twelve western towns and cities have streets named after him, and there is still a Nanton, Alberta, between Calgary and Fort Macleod. An early nationalist, Nanton protested when an American firm was hired to make a film commemorating the HBC's 250th anniversary in 1920 and prohibited the abbreviation U.S.A. from appearing anywhere in the presentation. When Nanton became a key animator in the citizens' committee organized in 1919 to quash the General Strike, his farm was a target for demonstrators, who burned down the stable.

London. Even worse, the key department-store operation was run by Herbert E. Burbidge, whose father headed Harrods and was a London-based director of the Bay. Only thirty years old when he was handed responsibility for the Canadian retail outlets, clearly modelled on the Harrods Brompton Road department store, the young Burbidge moved the headquarters of the retailing division to Vancouver, where he was comfortably settled, and allowed the individual units to fend for themselves. This meant giving up the advantage of mass buying, with the manager of every department in each store free to set his own mark-ups and credit policies. The chain soon became unmanageable—even if in 1914 its profit (£63,757) for the first time surpassed that of the fur department (£55,008). By 1919, Burbidge, who turned out to be allergic to hard work, was fired and later supplanted by Edward Fitzgerald, a former CPR assistant purchasing agent, who was appointed the Canadian Committee's full-time Deputy Chairman. He had little merchandising experience, found himself the pawn of games played between Winnipeg and London, and within six years returned to the relative calm of railroading. His main legacy was that during his stewardship the Canadian Advisory Committee (from now on simply called the Canadian Committee) was granted slightly more authority, including the naming of some senior appointees, but the Company had meanwhile acquired a much more profitable sideline.

SIR ROBERT MOLESWORTH KINDERSLEY, who served as Governor from 1915 to 1925, was also chairman of the London affiliate of Lazard Frères, the Anglo-French merchant bank, and it was through his Paris connections that the HBC gained a unique opportunity. Using Jean Monnet, wartime organizer of the French government's emergency International Supply Committee (and later father of the Treaty of Rome that spawned Europe's Common Market), as a go-between, he negotiated appointment of the Hudson's Bay Company as the French government's transportation agency for the duration of the First World War.* The contract would eventually net the Company £1,265,000 for five years' involvement, the most profitable single transaction in its long history, but it took a lot of doing. Thrown into disarray by the initial German advances, the French government had moved to Bordeaux and was desperately seeking a way of supplying its

---

*As a reward, Monnet later was granted a £40,000 "loan," most of which was written off. Its existence was not mentioned in Monnet's memoirs or in the HBC's annual reports.

population with foodstuffs and its troops with ammunition. There being no effective French merchant marine available, Alexandre Millerand, France's war minister, named the HBC the country's chief purchasing agent to arrange international credits and charter the ships required to deliver the goods.

The Company's 1-percent commission on these transactions was well earned. The Bay Steamship Company, a hastily set-up subsidiary, chartered 286 merchant ships totalling 1.58 million tons deadweight, which carried 13 million tons of supplies to French ports. In addition to grains from Canada, Argentina, Algeria and Australia and sugar from Cuba, Java and Martinique, their cargoes included coal from England and the United States, groundnuts and palm-kernels from Morocco, and airplane parts from Casablanca.

By war's end, the Company was operating the world's third-largest merchant fleet, loading 11,000 tons of goods daily—the equivalent of the *Nonsuch*'s cargo every seven minutes.* It had been contracted to carry out similar supply missions for Romania and the White Russian Army (following the Bolshevik Revolution), through an agency at Archangel. The Company's house flag—the Red Ensign with the letters HB.C. on the fly—became a recognized and proud symbol in ports the world over, the more so since German submarines, storms, icebergs and fires at sea sank 110 of the Bay ships. The maritime commerce was highly profitable but horrendously complicated. Towards the end of 1917, for example, the HBC undertook management of four large Russian liners capable of carrying 13,000 passengers that became international ferries, taking Central Europeans, Belgians, Romanians and Argentines out of Russia before collapse of the Tsarist regime. The German steamer *Prinz Heinrich*, interned in Portugal where she had been requisitioned by the government, was chartered by the British government, then sublet to the French government, which turned her over to be operated by the HBC. The Company used her to repatriate Russian Jews who preferred returning home to service in the British Army. (Each passenger had to be provided with kosher rations for the long railway trip from Murmansk to Petrograd.)

---

*One problem was that the Company soon ran out of titles for its expanded fleet and began using such forms as *Bayford, Baykerran, Bayfield, Baymount, Baysoto, Baychattan* and so on. The names, one of the HBC's senior officials explained to Jean Monnet, should be limited to "10 letters, that is including the first three [Bay], the reason being that they can then be telegraphed as one word, and this, over the course of a year, makes quite a little economy compared with the names which cost two or three words."

*The HBC's* Baytigern *at Brest during the First World War*

Co-ordinating such complex arrangements and handling assignments for the Company's 145 purchasing agents went far beyond the HBC's existing knowledge or established facilities. The London staff was expanded from 10 to 120, and to head the operation Kindersley hired, as the HBC's full-time Deputy Governor, Charles Vincent Sale, president of his family's firm of coal shippers, F.G. Sale & Sons, whose unoriginal motto was "Coals to Newcastle." Sale and Kindersley had swung many deals together, providing rails to the Japanese for construction of the Manchurian Railway as well as trading arms, cotton, coal and metals between the United States, Belgium and the Orient. Both men were close to Lord Cowdray, Minister for Air in Lloyd George's wartime cabinet, and had made friends with Sir John Anderson, who as Lord Waverley would subsequently become an HBC director. A tall, pink-faced workaholic, complete with white military moustache, bowler hat and wing collar, Sale was pompous and could be fussy. Dora Darby, who was his secretary, recalled that he sometimes came into the HBC offices on Saturdays and "checked the girls' work stations searching for cosmetics. He put any he found on their desks to indicate they did not belong in an office. He was very strait-laced, and when he was in charge, every stenographer knew not to cross her legs in front of a man while taking dictation." Bob Chesshire, who worked for the Company at the time, remarked, "He was a peculiar sort of chap who suffered from a tropical liver and was quite likely to pick up a dictionary and heave it at someone he didn't like."

THE SHARPEST BREAK IN THE CONTINUITY of the old executive system in the Company was caused by the war. The immense profits from the French engagement perpetuated the illusion of management by the London Governor and directorate while the end of the temporary profits eventually made all too plain the dilapidation of its Canadian affairs.*

Ignoring this underlying weakness, the Company chose this very moment to stage the most elaborate and most expensive pageant in its history. The Hudson's Bay Company celebrated its 250th birthday on May 2, 1920, and Sir Robert Kindersley decided to visit Canada— only the second reigning Governor ever to do so.† Each Company unit, including every northern post, was given a grant to join in the festivities and every employee received a month's extra wages.‡ Philip Godsell, an imaginative veteran who after joining the Company in 1906 had travelled more than 100,000 miles by dog team, snowshoe and canoe, was placed in charge of planning the celebration. It was to be the last great Company occasion, and Godsell made the most of it.

On May 1, 1920, Kindersley addressed the Winnipeg staff at a gala dinner in the Hotel Fort Garry. He quickly got the guests on side by announcing a relatively generous non-contributory pension plan and pledged $1,225,000 to its trust fund. "I look to the future of the fur trade with a feeling of utmost confidence," he declared. "The last three years have shown the best results of any years in the history of the Company." The speech prompted loud cheers, several choruses of "For He's a Jolly Good Fellow," and a new Company song to the tune of "There's a Long, Long Trail A-Winding." The fur traders, ships' captains, department store managers, clerks and servants formed a

---

*One business that briefly flourished around that time was bootlegging. Canadian provinces had passed laws prohibiting the sale though not the manufacture of alcoholic beverages, but since each province could enforce laws only within its own borders, booze could easily be transported for sale in other jurisdictions. The HBC immediately established a dozen mail-order houses from Kenora to Revelstoke and installed a Winnipeg bottling plant, capable of turning out four hundred cases daily, to supply its own brands to these outlets. Income peaked in 1917 at $2,260,627.

†The other had been Lord Strathcona, his last predecessor but one, though that was a special case because Strathcona had been the only Governor in the Company's history to work his way up through the HBC's Canadian service.

‡The Company's assets at the time consisted of eleven major department stores, six wholesale houses, three hundred fur-trading posts, eighty-six steam and motor vessels, twelve hundred canoes, six hundred sledge dogs and 2.5 million acres of desirable prairie agricultural land.

happy, chanting line, marching around the dining-room enmeshed in nets of paper streamers.*

Climax of the Canadian celebrations was the great spectacle Godsell staged at Lower Fort Garry, once the proud domicile of Sir George Simpson. Indian chiefs and their retinues came from every corner of the HBC's former empire—Swampy Cree from Hudson and James bays, Saulteaux from Lake Winnipeg, Ojibwas from the Nipigon country, Sioux from the Portage Plains, and mighty warriors from the Peace and Athabasca valleys. "For a while," Godsell noted, "the atmosphere of earlier and more picturesque days hovered about the Old Stone Fort. Silhouetted against the painted tepee covers at night the shadowy figures carried the mind back to days of long ago. . . . Within the walls all was quiet and silent though the tent occupied by the two Mounted Policemen who kept watch was dimly lighted with a coal-oil lantern. An occasional light flickered from the Governor's residence and there was a peculiar tranquillity permeating the old fort and its surroundings, so different from the bustle of the city but a few short miles away." The following morning the Governor took the salute as birchbark canoes, York boats and dugouts sailed by the great stone fort, and cheering Winnipeggers lined the riverbanks. Salute guns boomed, the Governor's flag snapped in the wind, and Godsell introduced each tribal chief to the six-foot-six Governor, who looked exactly the way a benign despot should look. Godsell had arranged for the Company interpreter to censor the Indians' comments, so that when the Chief of the York Factory Cree, for instance, complained because the Company was not feeding his dogs, the comment was translated into a flowery tribute to "the Great Master of the Company." Long into the night could be heard the screech of fiddles and the tattoo of moccasined feet stamping out the Red River Jig and Eightsome Reel. "As I gazed at the flickering lights of the tepees and watched the shadowy forms of the old Indians passing the pipe once more from hand to hand," Godsell lamented, "I realized with a keen pang that history had been made that day, and that, with its passing, the old fort and the traditions which surrounded it had taken another long step towards antiquity."

The most important legacy of the celebrations was Kindersley's decision to establish *The Beaver*, a magazine "Devoted to the Interests

---

*At a dinner for the London staff, Deputy Governor Sale gave a similar oration, handing out 134 long-service medals. One warehouse worker topped the list with sixty years of servitude. In Winnipeg, John George McTavish Christie was presented with a special medal; his family had served a combined 238 years with the Company.

*HBC celebrations at Lower Fort Garry, May 1920*

of Those Who Serve the Hudson's Bay Company." It eventually became a superb journal of record chronicling the history of the Northwest. But under its first editor, a Chicago advertising man named Clifton Moore Thomas, *The Beaver* limited itself mainly to a hodgepodge of curling scores from the Saskatoon store, news of an engagement in Kamloops, photos of an office picnic in Victoria, the results of a pie-eating competition at Fort à la Corne, word of new tennis and quoits courts for the Winnipeg staff—all interwoven with hair-raising fur-trade accounts and glued together with bad Irish jokes and harmless homilies on how to increase sales.*

Kindersley also signed a contract with Bruno Weyers, a New York business agent who'd had previous dealings with the Company, to produce films. The subsidiary eventually purchased two Hollywood studios and during the next decade produced thirty-seven two-reel films featuring such stars as Buster Keaton, Helen Morgan, James Melton, the Easy Aces and the Pickens Sisters. Some of the films premiered in Broadway's best first-run houses, but the advent of the

---

* *The Beaver*'s scope and quality improved dramatically under its subsequent editors, Robert Watson, Douglas MacKay, Clifford Wilson, Malvina Bolus, Helen Burgess and Christopher Dafoe.

big Hollywood productions killed the business, and the HBC wrote off its investment.*

THE PROFIT WINDFALL from its shipping operations had camouflaged its financial instability, but the Company could not compete in the volatile post-war market because its traditional methods emphasized conservative mark-up policies instead of customer-enticing price cuts and quality of service ahead of high volume. Charles Vincent Sale took over as Governor from Kindersley in 1925 and a year later the new Winnipeg super-store was opened. It covered an entire city block and had all the latest equipment. Its two massive banks of six elevators each faced one another on the street floor in a concave configuration. "The consequence of this layout," noted James Bryant, who worked there at the time, "was that every customer wishing to visit any floor other than the main one, congregated in the elevator lobby. It was so restricted in size and shape that even small crowds caused utter confusion. . . . Customers ran back and forth to catch elevators, only to have doors close as they reached them. Many became convinced that all the elevators on one side only went up and those on the other side only went down, an idea encouraged by some management trainees who, despite the scarcity of jobs, were not above having a little joke at the customers' expense."

Sale, who enjoyed risk and knew the Company desperately needed to diversify, had entertained an unusual visitor in his London offices before coming to Canada for his annual inspection tour in 1926. He was Ernest Whitworth Marland, born at Pittsburgh in 1874 when oil was $2.70 a barrel, who had struck his first gusher in West Virginia and soon founded his own Marland Oil company with headquarters in Ponca City, Oklahoma. Applying his practical grasp of petroleum geology and his natural instinct for the hunt, he hit it big in 1911 with the ninth well drilled on land owned by Willie Cries-for-War near the Osage Indian Reservation. He went on to develop Marland Oil into a major company but spent his money even faster than he made it.

Marland fenced in a tract of four hundred acres near Ponca and turned it into a pseudo-upper-class British estate, complete with polo fields, peacocks, ponies and hounds. Across the savage prairie of

---

*The Company commissioned a forgettable eight-reeler about itself called *The Romance of the Fur Country*, and jealously guarded its reputation. When another film-maker produced a shoddy thriller entitled *The Lure of the North*, the HBC's lawyers got changes made in the print depicting a heroic-looking free trader being crushed by a brutal (unnamed, but British) fur monopoly whose agents burned his shack, stole his provisions, then dispatched him across something ominously called The Long Traverse.

*Elevator lobby at Winnipeg's new super-store*

Oklahoma Marland and his pals would spend long afternoons, mounted on British hunters, following British hounds on the scent of British foxes. The son of a Scottish mother and an English father, Marland was so infatuated with Anglophile values that he went to grade school dressed in a kilt, and arrived in the wild Indian country during his oil-hunting days wearing a belted tweed jacket, knickerbockers and spats. He often visited London to recharge these pretensions and on one such trip made a deal with the Hudson's Bay Company to exploit the mineral rights it had retained (from 1910 onwards) on 4.5 million acres of the Canadian West, checkerboarded across Manitoba, Saskatchewan and Alberta.

Sale and Marland worked out a simple arrangement: in return for providing the technical knowledge and paying all exploration expenses, Marland was granted a twenty-five-year option to lease any parcel of land for drilling purposes, with the HBC receiving a royalty on any oil or gas produced.* Three years later, when Marland's

---

*Significantly, the partnership missed leasing the Athabasca tar sands, said to hold the world's largest oil reserves, because it viewed them only as a substitute for asphalt in road building. The two companies opened only one filling station, near the HBC's Winnipeg store, which sold Marland lubricating products but gasoline supplied by Imperial Oil.

personal spending habits caught up with him and he had to amalgamate his company with Continental Oil, the two concerns formed Hudson's Bay Oil & Gas (HBOG), with the HBC owning 25 percent (later reduced to 21.9 percent) of the stock.

By the mid-1920s, when the shift from Kindersley to Sale took place, chairmanship of the Canadian Committee passed from Nanton to George Allan, who was soon joined by such Winnipeg worthies as James Armstrong Richardson, Robert Gourley, Conrad Riley and Hugh Lyall. They had all the required credentials: Richardson was president of his family's firm, head of the Winnipeg Grain Exchange, a director of the CPR and the Canadian Bank of Commerce, and in the decade that ended in 1929 accumulated one of Canada's great fortunes. Richardson's horizons, unlike those of most other HBC Committeemen, reached far beyond Winnipeg. The Richardsons have always had all of Canada for a playground.* Gourley was the animating force in Beaver Lumber and a director of such other Winnipeg touchstone companies as Monarch Life and Manitoba Bridge & Iron Works, and had been Canadian curling champion. Riley had worked for seven years on the Northern Pacific Railway before moving to Winnipeg to take a job in his father's Canadian Fire Insurance Company. He was, of course, also a director of Beaver Lumber and Great-West Life. Lyall had slightly different connections, being one of the rare HBC Committeemen who was not a director of either Monarch or Great-West, but he did establish Manitoba Bridge & Iron Works, was on the board of Northern Trusts, and president of Dominion Tanners, both companies controlled by the Rileys. George Allan, who had been a Committee member since 1914, remained Chairman until 1940. True to form, he was a director of Great-West Life and Northern Trusts, but unlike his predecessors and successors, he devoted most of his time to the Company's affairs. A graduate of Upper Canada College and Trinity University in Toronto, he had cofounded one of Winnipeg's largest law firms (Munson & Allan) and had been responsible for channelling millions of dollars' worth of British investment into the Canadian West. A Conservative MP from 1917 to 1921, he was a political traditionalist, once complaining in a letter to London that "democracy has its valuable and strong features, but it certainly has its weak ones. I suppose it is natural that during a long drawn out period, activities of crooks, cranks, university professors, school masters and a clergyman with extreme socialistic views

---

*When Richardson died of a heart attack at sixty-four in 1939, the *Winnipeg Free Press* lowered the flags on its building to half-mast.

[J.S. Woodsworth], miracle workers and pedlars of paradise, should have their innings and their place under the sun, and that the product of their combined efforts should be a Social Credit Party, a CCF Party, a Communist Party and a Labour Party."

London, too, had been undergoing important physical and personnel changes. Governor Sale was coming under increasingly virulent attack for the Company's inability to turn adequate earnings on its huge department stores. Despite these uncertainties, the Company invested the bulk of its wartime profits in a new head office building on Great Trinity Lane, opposite the famed Church of St Ethelburga the Virgin in Bishopsgate.* Designed by Oscar Faber, Hudson's Bay House was a curious, turreted edifice that needed a large formal garden around it to bring out its lines. The Company also built Beaver House on Garlick Hill in the 1920s, and for the first time in two centuries, the HBC's fur auction could once again be held at its own premises. Inside, there was refrigerated storage space for two million pelts and large fur-grading rooms under double windows with a northern exposure.† The halls and boardroom were decorated with paintings of former governors, narwhal tusks and ship models in cases. After the Hudson's Bay House building was sold, this structure also accommodated the Company offices.

In Canada, the Company's stores were being transformed. Through the direct intervention of Deputy Governor Sir Frederick Henry Richmond, managing director of Debenhams, a large London department store, the HBC's retailing outlets were placed in the charge of P.J. Parker, a former Boston merchandiser who had set up his own store across the road from the HBC's Calgary outlet and had been bought out to obtain his services. A tiny creature who appeared to have walked straight out of the pages of *Pickwick Papers*, he had rosy cheeks and always wore gloves and matching spats. But Parker was a misanthropic presence who angered his fellow employees with his fusty ways, and he lasted for less than a year. In his place was appointed an obscure British accountant named Philip Chester, who would exercise almost as significant an impact on the Hudson's Bay Company as had Sir George Simpson a century earlier.

---

*It was at this stone sanctuary, dating back at least to 1430, that Henry Hudson received communion on April 19, 1607, before setting off on the voyage of exploration that would eventually provide the Company with its initial base of operations.

†To prevent any variation in light quality, the walls and floors of these grading chambers were glazed with sand-blasted non-reflecting battleship-grey tiles.

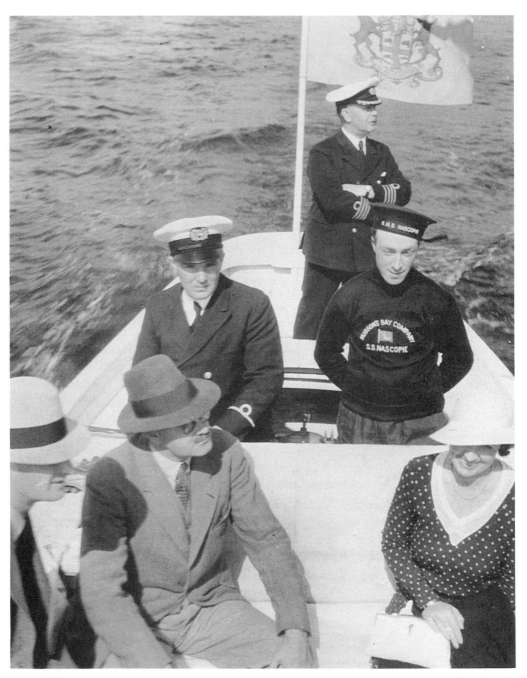

*Governor Patrick Ashley Cooper (middle front) and Mrs. Cooper go ashore at Cartwright, Labrador, 1934*

# CHAPTER 14

# TRANS-ATLANTIC BLOOD FEUD

*The Governor and the HBC's Canadian General Manager understood
that, like two scorpions in a bottle, only one would emerge the victor.*

WHILE PHILIP CHESTER WOULD TURN OUT to be the dominant force in
creating the modern Hudson's Bay Company, neither his tenure nor
its success would have been possible without the operational matrix set
down by Charles Vincent Sale. Eventually deposed as the HBC's
Governor in a shareholder revolt triggered by charges of self-dealing,
during his sixteen years in the Company's two top jobs Sale turned its
operations upside down. Not only was he largely responsible for
generating the wartime profit that financed its growth through the
uncertain 1920s but he also transformed the HBC from mainly a fur-
trading house and general-store business into a mass retailer. Unlike
most of his predecessors, he took more than a passing interest in
Canada, spending three months of every year touring the Company's
stores, and, as a parting gesture, granted the Canadian Committee
most of the authority it had always wanted. At the same time, he
widened the Company's horizons by throwing its archives open to
historians and hiring a young Oxford zoologist (Charles Elton) as a
consultant to study fluctuations in Arctic animal populations.

What really brought Sale down was the Depression. The great
department stores he had built across the West were transformed
almost overnight from luxurious merchandising palaces into drafty
nightmares with huge overheads. The new Winnipeg store alone
had an annual carrying charge of $3.3 million, while Vancouver, at

$2.6 million, was nearly as expensive. Gross margins had to be increased to 38.5 percent of selling price just to meet overhead costs, making it difficult to turn any profit. Between 1929 and 1931, operating losses in the retail division jumped from $182,000 to more than $2 million. Sale's plight was aggravated by shareholder expectations. "Many of them had acquired their shares in the same confidence of steady returns with which they would have opened a savings account," wrote HBC archivist Anne Morton, and, "bitterly disappointed, were now out for blood. Sale was the obvious scapegoat."

London's initial response to the Depression's onset was to dispatch Lord Ebury, one of its senior directors, to Canada for a first-hand report.* He was appalled at the laxness of some of the staff, condemning P.J. Parker, then in charge of stores, as being unfit for the job. "Amongst his chief weaknesses—apart from Drink—are a tendency to jump into action without proper forethought," Ebury reported. "He fails to appreciate the supreme importance of . . . living up to agreements and promises, and he is inclined to be a bit of a 'slick.'"

In contrast, Ebury had nothing but praise for Philip Alfred Chester, who had been assigned to Canada by Sale as Chief Accountant in 1925 after having joined the London staff as a junior two years previously. "Mr. Chester," wrote Ebury, "is, in my opinion, brilliantly clever and certainly one of the quickest thinking men I have come across in a long time." The visiting peer added a prophetic footnote: "He suffers from high blood pressure and needs careful nursing; one of the drawbacks of Winnipeg is that this man is never free of his work, or thinking or talking shop." Ebury strongly recommended that the Canadian Committee, then headed by George Allan, be given power to deal with the Company's staff appointments and daily operations. His suggestion was confirmed at the Court of proprietors on June 27, 1930, and put into effect by Sale himself during a Winnipeg visit shortly afterwards.

The essential element in the reorganization that followed was the appointment of Chester as General Manager for Canada, at an

---

*Francis Egerton Grosvenor, 4th Lord Ebury, was one of the most-decorated officers of the Canadian Expeditionary Force in the First World War. He came out from England and spent the early years of the century in the Kootenays as an assayer for smelters at Trail and Nelson, and after 1910 worked on the Duke of Sutherland's land-settlement plan in Alberta. He joined the 29th Battalion CEF (Tobin's Tigers) in Vancouver in 1914, and won the DSO and bar, the MC and bar, and the Croix de Guerre with palm. He was mentioned in dispatches five times, was wounded, and ended the war staff officer with the 4th Canadian Division. He served on the board of the HBC and another City institution, the Royal Exchange Assurance.

annual salary of $20,000. Although the London board's resolution had conferred on the Canadian Committee "full powers of attorney" and all necessary arrangements "for the due exercise thereof," the true meaning of these phrases would be argued over for the next forty years. "There seemed afterwards to be some misconception of what was really arranged with the then Governor on this side of the water and what apparently was the conception at head office," admitted Allan in a speech to his Calgary staff, "but that was very soon washed away. . . . As I put it, if they desired us to relieve them and take over the management, administration and control, that it might as well be one hundred percent, and that the horns had better go with the hide."

The HBC's affairs were clearly in crisis, and its proprietors began demanding a drastic shakeup. In London, the fight to unseat Sale and his board was led by a solicitor named Charles Louis Nordon. A highly effective campaigner on behalf of minority shareholders' rights and dividend incomes, he was incensed with the Hudson's Bay Company's dismal earnings record and eventually fought the Company of Adventurers to a standstill. "My father considered it to be one of his greatest legal triumphs," recalled Keith Nordon of his father's clash with the HBC, "in that he was well and truly up against not only an enormous Company but also against almost the whole of the City of London in that, in the big dispute, the City naturally sided with the powerful Hudson's Bay." At one point, things got so nasty that Nordon (who held 740 shares in 1927 and whose family had been investing in HBC stock since 1873) was physically barred from one of the HBC's annual Courts and had to sneak in through a fire escape.

Nordon had first challenged Sale on the fact that between 1920 and 1925, the Company had sold land worth £1,987,738 while paying out £1,750,922 in taxes—a levy which, when added to administrative expenses, meant the land sales had been a futile waste of potential future assets. It was a perfectly reasonable criticism, but Sale chose to ignore it because Nordon was too insignificant a shareholder. Nordon continued to bombard the directors with meticulously researched queries in the later 1920s so that even proprietors who had at first considered him a noisy nuisance began to pay attention. He was particularly incensed by the revelation that in 1927, which was not an especially bad year, the Company had been able to earn only £151,909 on its £6,779,656 investment in the fur trade and sales shops.

Having been barred from corresponding with the Company, Nordon began issuing a series of circulars condemning its fiscal performance and the integrity of its directors. He organized a shareholders' vigilante group that included several major investors including

Captain Victor Alexander Cazalet (the HBC's largest stockholder with 40,500 shares), who demanded action.* The shareholders were particularly frustrated by the Company's practice of diverting profits to something called a "dividend equalization fund," which was really a reserve account, preventing more generous dividend distribution.

But it was Nordon's pointed attacks on the Governor's integrity that finally broke Sale's hold and reputation. Nordon had accused Sale of self-dealing in the 1920 purchase by the HBC, for £60,000, of a 15-percent interest in the Merchant Trading Company, owned mostly by the Sale family. Used during the Great War as a purchasing agency for the shipping operation, the firm had continued in business but returned the HBC almost no dividends. Although it was never identified as such, the HBC acquisition of Sale's shares had been more in the nature of an interest-free loan to reward the then Deputy Governor for his wartime services. Sale's great mistake was to pretend that it had been a legitimate business transaction, thus trapping himself into defending the indefensible.

At the 1930 annual Court, Nordon asked that an internal committee be set up to investigate the Company's affairs. Its report, tabled five months later, vindicated Sale but suggested the HBC's stores be run by a newly established, Canadian-domiciled HBC subsidiary. Since Sale had just approved a similar arrangement, or at least granted the Canadian Committee all the authority it could handle, there seemed to be no reason for him to resign. Yet he left the governorship just before publication of the report, leading contemporary observers to believe there had been a secret deal: that Sale would be officially exonerated from the accusations of self-dealing by his peers in return for clearing up all the suspicion surrounding the Company by agreeing to abandon his post.

The resignation took place during an extraordinary Court, held at the City Terminus Hotel on Cannon Street on January 16, 1931. Company records pointed to a loss of £746,334 for the fiscal year, which meant there would be no cash for dividends. With the worth of its assets reduced by an astonishing £2 million in the previous twelve months—and facing the prospect of an extended economic downturn—the Company seemed well on its way to technical bankruptcy.

---

*Four times the British (and once the Canadian) squash champion, Cazalet had attended Eton and Oxford (where he earned four Blues), fought with distinction in the trenches during the Great War, and was later elected a Member of Parliament. He inherited the HBC stake from his father. He was killed with General Wladyslaw Sikorski, the Polish premier in exile, in the crash of a Liberator bomber off Gibraltar in 1943.

Shareholders nearly went berserk, calling for the resignation of the entire board and nominating members of the Nordon committee to take their place. Chaired by Deputy Governor Sir Frederick Richmond, the noisy meeting would not allow Sale to speak. When he rose briefly to reassert his innocence in the Merchant Trading affair, he was shouted down and could barely be heard, lamenting: "For my shortcomings I ask your forgiveness." Five other directors eventually stepped down, and were replaced by three Nordon nominees, including Cazalet. A new board was elected, led by the redoubtable Edward Peacock, but the most important item on the agenda was the appointment of a new governor.

THE MAN PICKED TO RESCUE THE COMPANY at this difficult moment was Patrick Ashley Cooper, and his selection was no accident. In an act of direct, almost brutal intervention unprecedented in the HBC's long history, Montagu Norman, Governor of the Bank of England, personally assigned Cooper to the job, then went on to choose Sir Alexander Murray, one of the City's ablest financiers, to be Cooper's Deputy.* In case there might be any doubt about the weight of authority behind his nominations, Norman sent a letter to C.L. Nordon not only affirming his personal regard for Cooper but placing the Company of Adventurers in its appropriate context. "I alone selected Mr. Patrick Ashley Cooper and recommended him as suitable for the Governorship of the Hudson's Bay Company," he wrote. "I am not concerned with the affairs of the Hudson's Bay Company except as regards the Governorship and that owing to the prestige and imperial importance of the Company." Norman stressed the same historical link during a private briefing with Cooper. "Your task," said the Governor of the Bank of England to the Governor of the Hudson's Bay Company, "is to rebuild a bridge of Empire."

A tall, awkward Scot with round tortoise-shell glasses and a crisp military moustache, Cooper could be kind and approachable, though he never softened his attitude of trying to run the firm like the headmaster of a rowdy boys' school. With the sombre suits he favoured draped over his six-foot-four frame, he commanded instant attention—and got it. Born in middle circumstances at Aberdeen,

---

*Yet another of those peripatetic Scottish financiers who held the Empire together, Murray had spent three decades in India, occupying most of its important administrative positions, including a five-year stint as Governor of the Imperial Bank of India. He later became a director of Lloyds Bank and the Bank of London and South America, remaining a solid influence on the Hudson's Bay board until 1946.

Cooper attended Fettes College in Edinburgh (Scotland's Eton), then read law at Aberdeen and went on to Trinity Hall, Cambridge, where his long arms helped him win an oar. Badly wounded in the back while serving as an infantry major during the Great War, he became a City accountant and did so well that the Bank of England began asking him to act on its behalf in helping salvage near-defunct British companies around the globe. At forty-three and married to the beautiful Welsh heiress Kathleen Spickett, he became an important figure in London society, having won kudos for successfully liquidating the Banco Italo-Britannica in Milan and rescuing the Primitiva Gas Company of Buenos Aires. He had accepted the difficult job of turning the Hudson's Bay Company around in the bearpit of the Depression on condition that his initial salary of £5,000 be raised when the economy improved. Despite his relatively meagre stipend, Cooper brought the July 1931 proprietors' Court to its feet with the offer to reduce his pay by 10 percent. "Are we to devote ourselves," he demanded, "to searching in the past or building for the future?"

"Both!" cried out an Adventurer.

"No. It cannot be both. You must make up your minds whether you are going to ask us to dig into the past, or go forward into the future, and *that* is the decision I shall ask you to make." It was a clever ploy because the Company's proprietors had become so mesmerized by recent troubles they had lost sight of the future. For the next three years that future was grim indeed, with losses totalling £3.6 million. Cooper threw himself into his new job, leaving almost immediately for Canada, eager to meet Philip Chester, the new General Manager.

The omens were not good. Just before he left England, Cooper was informed by the Canadian Committee that henceforth communications to London would be dispatched monthly instead of weekly and that, oh yes, P.J. Parker, the Canadian operation's highest-ranking executive in charge of stores, had just been fired. In reporting these changes to the Governor, Chester—speaking through Canadian Committee Chairman George Allan—lamely apologized for not having first consulted or even notified the London board. "It was purely an oversight," Allan explained, ". . . caused by very great stress of work at the time."

Cooper arrived in Montreal on September 3, 1931, and the first entry in his private diary reflected his sour mood: "Went to Ritz-Carlton. General Manager of the HBC in the Hotel and still in bed." His outlook didn't improve at the breakfast he had next morning in the Windsor Hotel. He ordered "a pot of tea. Dry toast, butter on the side. *English* marmalade and two eggs boiled three minutes . . .

three minutes precisely." When the waiter arrived, all was as requested, but there was only one eggcup with *one* egg perched on it. Cooper, according to his breakfast companion, berated the hotel employee mercilessly, calling him a "stupid colonial" and similar epithets. He stopped only when the waiter, with white-gloved hand and beatific smile, lifted the eggcup to reveal the missing egg, boiled three minutes precisely.

The Governor's mood brightened considerably when he was summoned to Ottawa for a private meeting with the Prime Minister, only to find that the Right Honourable R.B. Bennett was, as Cooper confided to his journal, "cordial and helpful, but most critical of the Company, its higher personnel and policy." Still, he stayed at Rideau Hall, the Governor General's official residence, with the Earl of Bessborough and went swimming in the Chateau Laurier pool wearing a bathing suit borrowed from CNR Chairman Sir Henry Thornton that had "room for myself and two others." In Toronto he met most of the men who mattered—Sir Joseph Flavelle, Sir John Aird, E.R. Wood, W.E. Rundle—and was shown around Eaton's (by R.Y. Eaton) and Simpsons (by C.L. Burton). He then went off to Winnipeg and a tour of the Company's retail operation, at one point "driving down the main street of Kamloops to examine our competitors' windows." By the time he left, two months later, Cooper was not at all pleased with what he had seen. "I was dismayed at what I found," he noted. "As soon as I arrived in Winnipeg, it was perfectly obvious to me that the state of misunderstanding and tension between London and Winnipeg had almost reached an open breach. . . ." Later, Cooper summarized the areas of serious concern he had uncovered. He had found not one department or subsidiary operation that wasn't losing money; "great and thoughtless extravagance in all directions," he noted in his diary, "a sense of unthinking security throughout the whole staff," and "no general comprehension that the Company was nearing complete collapse. . . ." As if that diagnosis wasn't gloomy enough, Cooper wisely concluded that his main problem would be learning to live with Chester, the thirty-five-year-old General Manager installed under Sale. Chester, the Governor felt, should have a different attitude towards London, one that would show loyalty to the British board and shareholders.

Fat chance.

MOST FACES BETRAY THE CHARACTER of their owners, reflecting the balance between their generous natures and niggardly emotions. But Chester's facial features were smooth and uncommunicative, like those of the masked man in *The Phantom of the Opera*—not ugly, but expressionless, designed to evoke in others emotions complementary to his own. His eyes were as blank as gun barrels, tinted pewter-grey, revealing nothing. His three-piece suits were all the same: immaculately tailored (by Lloyd Brothers in Toronto or one of the bespoke shops in Savile Row), but interchangeable; no one ever remembered anything he wore. Even his handshake was bereft of feeling. "Like taking hold of a piece of cold fish," one Bay employee recalled. "There was no squeeze. You let go quickly, because you got no response."

He grew up in a harsh and sterile place—Long Eaton, an industrial town in the working-class region of Derbyshire, where his mother (a Rhinelander) worked as a governess and his father as an intermittently employed millhand. In 1914, Philip, who was then barely eighteen, volunteered for the King's Royal Rifle Corps. The day he was set to leave for the Front—already dressed in his uniform and ready to board the troop train—his mother wanted to snap a picture of him with her Brownie. She aimed the camera, but young Philip's grandmother smashed it out of her hands with the admonition: "Not on the Sabbath!"

Chester won a field commission (to Staff Captain) and was severely wounded, both times on January 10, first in France and later on the Isonzo Front in northern Italy. He saved his gratuities and had just enough money to put himself through accounting school, then joined the Hudson's Bay Company's London office. He grew to love the Company, but his feelings were poisoned by his intense awareness that no matter what he did, no matter how successful within the HBC's hierarchy he might become, its upper-class directors would make him feel he didn't quite measure up, that he was of lowly birth, a man who had emigrated to make his way in a former colony. "However nice they are to you, they'll never accept you, because they know where you came from by the sound of your voice," Frank Walker, his executive assistant and later editor of the *Montreal Star*, had warned Chester after he had been fêted at a social function by members of the London board. Years later, Lady Cooper, Sir Patrick's widow, confirmed that diagnosis. "Socially," she recalled, "Chester wasn't in the same group as the other people he worked with. They were all on a higher plane in London. He thought they were always looking down on him, which made him feel mad. He was absolutely off his head. My husband was being invited to stay at Sandringham ... the King would invite him to go down. Then he was made a director of the Bank of England, and Chester hated him more than ever. He'd never even *met* the Governor of the Bank of England. My husband was moving in those circles—miles above Philip."

*Philip Alfred Chester, Managing Director, HBC*

But Chester knew the rules of the game and how it was played. Confronted by the icy nuances of the British class system, he decided to find a suitable exit. He couldn't change his birthplace, but he could fix his speech, and eventually he did. He invented a new persona for himself to bypass the upper-class English habit of accepting or dismissing individuals on the basis of their accents. His voice, melodious, incongruously rich coming through those pursed lips, marked him as a certified gentleman. "He never achieved the 'oink' of an old Etonian," remembered Charles Loewen, the Bay Street broker who married Chester's daughter, Susanne. "His became an unidentifiable English accent, a sort of Alistair Cooke inflection."

That transformation, as significant as it may have been to his future, had to be put on hold until Chester could deal with the crisis of confidence at the Company's Canadian headquarters and impose discipline on an organization that had spun out of control. Chester began a major reorganization of the fur department under the direction of Ralph Parsons and later Bob Chesshire, while Western Arctic Manager Dudley Copland winnowed the number of posts from nineteen to fourteen. He had Company engineers experiment with and use insulation materials for the northern posts, masterminded development of a radio medical network and initiated research into permafrost. In charge of retail operations he placed a Massachusetts-born merchandising specialist named Francis F. Martin. It was not a popular choice. "He was a rude, ruthless, egoistical despot," recalled John Enright, then in charge of the sewing machine department. "Even dress regulations were laid down, with salesladies expected to wear conservative black or navy and short sleeves permitted only if they were at least four inches below the armpit." Chester and Martin would reassign the coal-department manager from one store to run the corset department of another.

Even if his methods were crude, Chester shook up the stores' bureaucratic lethargy and moved them into the twentieth century. He insisted that the Company be a leader in personnel and wage administration policies; the HBC was one of the first national companies to name a woman ( Joan Whiting) to an executive post. Chester was responsible for starting a preparatory course in merchandising in the Company. Advertising was increased; selection and variety became as important as mark-ups; self-service food floors were introduced; executive salaries were raised; training and profit-sharing became part of senior employees' fringe benefits. The unprofitable Lethbridge store was sold, and the cost-benefit ratio of each outlet was examined and re-examined. A strict rule against hiring relatives of existing employees was put into effect. Decentralized purchasing and consolidated management techniques allowed individual store managers freedom to match their merchandise selection more closely with their own communities' needs, while the central buying office in Winnipeg handled such staples as HBC blankets, sheets, towels, dried fruit and so on. To collect its bills from hard-pressed customers, the HBC employed its own bailiffs. Fred Herbert, who occupied that office in Vancouver, boasted that he was kindness personified while repossessing unpaid-for articles: "If there's kids in the house, I'll never take a stove, but I'll take a radio or gramophone goddamn quick."

Within a year of Chester's appointment, store profits were up 60 percent, and by 1937, though the Depression had hardly abated, most divisions had begun to prosper again.* What Chester achieved

---

*Not so lucky was the HBC's oil investment. Chester had tried unsuccessfully to sell the Company's share in Hudson's Bay Oil & Gas to the Anglo-Ecuadorian Oilfields Company, and further investment funds in oil and gas exploration were cut off after September 1931. Three years later, HBOG signed a deal with the Northwest Company, a subsidiary of Imperial Oil, and eventually renewed it to June 1951, to allow the Esso subsidiary to explore the Company's holdings in return for a 50-percent share in the findings.

was to break the psychology, widespread among Company executives when he arrived, that it was their right to demand the trade of the public. The HBC's monopoly had been dead for more than half a century, but they had yet to react to the news.

Chester's store inspections were legendary. "He was positively vicious," recalled Bob Chesshire. "He would raise so much hell, you wouldn't know whether you were standing on your head or your feet. He wouldn't miss a thing, find ten things wrong on every floor, had everybody scared out of their wits, because we were all hanging on to our jobs by our eyebrows at the time. He used to place a lot of emphasis on cleanliness of toilets, and one poor store manager got into deep trouble because he hadn't finished having the washrooms painted, so Chester couldn't get in to see if they passed muster." Another time, in the Calgary store, Chester happened to pass a suggestion box. He asked how often it was cleared, and when he was assured it was at least once a day, demanded it be opened. He read every suggestion, found one two weeks old, and sacked the store supervisor on the spot.

"Why must I be surrounded by bloody fools?" he often complained to anyone in range of his wrath. One senior executive who had momentarily displeased Chester was astounded to find the General Manager staring at him for a long moment, then pronouncing his verdict: "You know, whenever I look at you, I think we're a man short." George Weightman, who worked at head office at the time, had been assigned to produce an inventory of HBC blankets. He had trouble collecting the necessary documentation and one afternoon found that Chester had quietly stolen up behind him. "He stood looking silently on for a few minutes and then said: 'You know what's the matter with you, Weightman? You've got more records than we have blankets.'" Chesshire remembered being summoned into Chester's office (known as the holy of holies) only to find his temper in full flight. "*You!*" Chester began, an accusing finger pointed at Chesshire. "*You!* I *told* you what to do and they've buggered up the whole thing! Now you're just sitting there, with nothing to say!" Chesshire, one of the few head-office functionaries not actively terrified of Chester, calmed him down by investigating the situation and reporting back. "Chester made a lot of preposterous statements to deliberately get under your hide," he observed, "because he felt that it was sometimes the only way to get all the facts."

Chester was always testing people. Almost every conversation became an interrogation. But anyone brave enough to face him down usually won. "He was sitting in my office when I accused him of not having told me the truth about something," recalled Frank Walker. " 'Are you calling me a liar?' he demanded. I calmly replied that to be a liar, he would have had to make a habit of not telling me the truth. Well, he marched out of there, and I didn't see him again until next morning, when he came in to apologize. I said there was no need to apologize; all he had to say was that he hadn't told me the truth. That got him fired up all over again, and he stormed out. He had been willing to be decent, but I was being a son of a bitch and had brought the issue up again. Finally, he came in just before lunch and mumbled, 'That's all you want me to say, that I didn't tell you the truth?' I told him that he didn't really have to say anything, so he shot back: 'All right, I didn't tell the truth'—and marched out of my office in high dudgeon, for the *third* time."

"There's no question that Chester used his outbursts to get precisely what he wanted, especially from the British board," mused John de B. Payne, the HBC official who had hired Walker as one of Chester's executive assistants. "His temper was never vindictive, never personal, just temper really, as in, 'I've got an idea and this is the way I'm going to fight for it.' He was driven by an obsession for excellence and in seeking it was as harsh on himself as with others." Chester himself, looking back on his stewardship, wrote to E.F. Newlands, secretary of the Canadian Committee: "While I was a tough bird—perhaps too tough on many occasions—it was because of my constant urge to keep a first-class office and to be an example for the rest of the old Company. I had seen and lived in the sad Winnipeg H[ead] O[ffice] of the late twenties, which was a disgrace and a big contributor to the mess in which the Company found itself in those years."

While most HBC employees (who made up a new translation for the Company's initials as "Here Before Chester") viewed him as "living on Mount Olympus, occasionally hurling a thunderbolt," they were fairly often exposed to his exquisite political tactics. "He used to brief a group of us before each Canadian Committee meeting," recalled Pete Buckley, who worked with Chester at the time, "and we'd have to rehearse everything he wanted us to say, so that by the time we presented our case the Committee members could only agree. It kind of shocked me."

THE MAIN VICTIM OF CHESTER'S TEMPER TANTRUMS was Patrick Ashley Cooper, a target so perfect that if he hadn't existed he would have to have been made up. The Governor and the HBC's Canadian General Manager understood that, like two scorpions in a bottle, only one would emerge the victor. Once the Company had been turned around, the blood feud between Chester and Cooper over corporate territoriality took on the extra dimension of competing to get the credit for its hard-won return to profitability. For Chester, the great advantage of having Cooper to shoot at was that the British Governor had little sense of humour and never really understood his opponent. He genuinely believed that Chester's mood swings were physiological rather than tactical and could never figure out any way of controlling or silencing his Canadian colleague—apart, perhaps, from somehow court-martialling him or challenging him to a duel. The British Governor and the Canadian Manager both became obsessed with keeping one another at bay, studying every nuance of every letter they exchanged— the slant of the signature, the way the paper was folded—as though it were written in hieroglyphics signalling a wealth of hidden motives and meanings. Each was convinced that only his way of doing things was correct and that anyone who strayed one inch from his particular path to righteousness was a write-off. "They just didn't get along," recalled Cooper's widow. "They disagreed about everything, and each prickled when the other was near. Chester set out to run the Company from Canada, and my husband, from the moment he heard that, put his foot down, saying, 'Never. Over my dead body. It was founded by Prince Rupert. It has always been in London and will always be in London!' They were poles apart."

"Chester is so changeable," Cooper bitterly complained to his diary (August 2, 1934). "When he is in control of himself, a pleasure and anxious to do what he can for us . . . but then again, swept by brain storms, he takes a ridiculous attitude almost amounting to open opposition to London, fighting over every detail." The diary bristles with complaints about Chester's behaviour. *November 27, 1936*: "Long talk with Chester. If the English language means anything, he was entirely reasonable and satisfactory. I fancy it was all eyewash." *January 7, 1943*: "Chester's behaviour abominable. He sat with a face black as thunder and contributed nothing except one or two outbursts . . . he was very narrow minded and difficult. I was glad however that his ill temper and bad manners were exposed to the board." On his first trip to London as General Manager for Canada, Chester expressed his contempt for the annual Court proceedings. "I was given a seat on the rostrum so that I could look over a selection of our proprietors," he wrote to Allan, "and to me, the gathering resembled that of the representatives of a Diocese assembled together for the induction of a new Archbishop, rather than a bunch of intelligent and disturbed shareholders."

The two men had little in common except that they happened to have been born on the same island. Winnipeg was such a long way from London in those days, and the Governor seemed untouchable. He led a charmed life. Hexton Manor, his country seat near Hitchin, in Hertfordshire, dates back to 1030, is mentioned in the Domesday Book and has been occupied by only sixteen different families since. If, as Noel Coward once pointed out, the stately homes of England existed to prove that the upper classes still had the upper hand, Cooper's home was a grand example of the genre. Set on a private lake in a 4,000-acre estate, it had twenty-eight rooms and that feeling of elegance-as-a-throwaway-gesture that marks the British gentry. The Coopers were invited to dine with the Prince of Wales at St James's Palace ("Another milestone!" he triumphantly noted in his diary on February 21, 1934); he was named a director of the Bank of England ("From now onwards I enter the Bank as of right, and have a peg on which to hang my hat with my name over it!"—April 6, 1932); and on January 16, 1935, he and Kathleen went to Sandringham—the first HBC Governor to be invited to a royal residence since Sir Bibye Lake in 1713. ("Down to dinner where I met . . . Sir Herbert and Lady Fetherstonhaugh. Lady Meade-Fetherstonhaugh's first husband was Hesketh Pritchard who was at Fettes 7 years before me. I sat on the Queen's left. . . . When the ladies left the room the King called me around to sit by him and was full of questions about the Eskimos.")

Into the early 1950s, the HBC was still reckoned as something of a viceregal presence among Canadian companies, and the Governor's tours resembled a royal procession, with the Coopers treated like visiting heads of state, accompanied by flag-bearers and trailed by a retinue of flustered flunkies.* They would cross the Atlantic aboard one of the great liners, occupying a suite of two bedrooms, sitting room and bathroom on A deck, being seated nightly at the Captain's table. In Montreal, Cooper called on the greatest capitalists of the day, including Sir Herbert Holt, Sir Charles Gordon, Sir Edward Beatty and Arthur Purvis, the head of Canadian Industries Limited, the first Canadian executive to have a private airplane, who won the admiration of his peers for having chaired meetings in Montreal, Ottawa and

---

*One of the stranger legacies of Cooper's stewardship was his insistence that *The Beaver* publish photographs of him on safari. The magazine regularly featured candid shots of the Governor "shooting crocodile from the roof of a launch on the Kafue River in Northern Rhodesia" or the Governor "setting out on a duck expedition in the swamps of the Zambesi at Lealui village, ruled by King Yeta III." Exactly how this was supposed to raise the morale of the fur traders freezing their butts off at Baker Lake wasn't clear.

Toronto on the same day.* Then on to Ottawa. "We were received by the Prime Minister, provincial premiers, and, of course, stayed at Government House—with the Bessboroughs, Tweedsmuirs, Athlones and Alexanders," recalled Lady Cooper. "They would lend us their private railway cars to travel in, and my husband had nicknames for all the young aides who worked at Rideau Hall. It was charming."†

After a triumphal stopover in Toronto (lunch at the Toronto Club with Principal W.L. Grant of Upper Canada College and calls, as always, on the heads of Simpsons and Eaton's), the caravan would roll into Winnipeg. The usual sparring with Chester and the Canadian Committee was followed by a visit to the Manitoba Club, where he gave a yearly address. "There were 63 present including the lieutenant governor, the premier, and almost everyone in Winnipeg of any importance," he noted of his visit on October 7, 1932. "George Allan introduced me with a speech of 35 minutes which was of unnecessary length, the first 25 minutes being taken up with sheer irrelevancies and before the end of his speech people were getting fairly restive. I rose in this atmosphere but was fortunate to find that I was able instantly to claim their attention and I thought that I held it without a break to the end." While in Canada, Cooper believed that he had the right to communicate directly with any Company official, which often caused annoyance, confusion and misunderstanding. "One thing that particularly riled Mr. Chester," remembered Winifred Archer, his loyal secretary, "was that when Governor Cooper visited Canada and was with, say, the manager of a large store, he would question the Canadian executive on matters not under the control of London. Mr. Chester felt this was not only unfair to himself, but also unfair to

*On his 1939 visit, Cooper took a detour to meet Maurice Duplessis, the Union Nationale premier, in Quebec City. "The whole performance and atmosphere of his office was very like a provincial government office in the Argentine," he disdainfully noted in his diary [July 18, 1939]. "Unshaven secretaries sitting about and smoking innumerable cigarettes . . . I went in and found the typical young Latin politician. He made it evident that he had no time to waste on me, for he kept one of the members of parliament with him. . . . During our short talk he made a few of his facetious remarks accompanied by winks, for which he is so famous."

†Cooper was happy to borrow His Ex's rail car but would far rather have had his own. Repeated entreaties to have the Canadian Committee purchase or lease one for him were manfully rebuffed by George Allan, who patiently explained that "we are, of necessity, driving our rank and file pretty hard these days of reduced salaries and wages . . . and my own hunch is [that you should avoid] a breath of criticism by any member of the staff, no matter how Bolshevistic he might be. . . . Democracy in Canada has made great advances and Canadians . . . are critical of people of importance from Great Britain and other countries visiting Canada. . . ."

the manager." That didn't stop Cooper, and he always made a special point of inspecting the Winnipeg store. On one such occasion, his wife expressed a desire to view the competing Eaton's store, then managed by Bill Palk. "How do you like it?" Palk politely inquired, after she and Mrs Conrad Riley had spent some time touring several departments.

"Well," Kathleen Cooper replied, equally politely, "actually, I don't like it at all. We've just been all through the Hudson's Bay Company store and it's nice and quiet. You can do your shopping in peace. But here, the aisles are crowded and everyone is pushing you around all the time." Palk, who read the riot act to any department manager whose aisles weren't crowded enough to force him and his assistant to walk through in single file, knew at that moment why Eaton's was outselling the Bay.

The first Governor to undertake northern inspection tours by air, Cooper posed a special problem for his keepers. The Governor insisted that his official flag be fluttering *before* he arrived at any Company post.* Many stores, especially in the North, didn't have one, or it had been eaten by rats, and often the HBC Beechcraft kept circling for some time. Chesshire recalled being stuck in just such a situation, trying to land the HBC plane against an incoming low-pressure front, when Cooper exclaimed: "I can't see the Governor's flag flying!"

"But Sir," Chesshire replied, "they don't have a flag."

"Well, they should have."

"What good would it do?"

"The Indians would know the Governor's in town," explained Cooper. Chesshire had no answer for that except to shrug and turn his eyes heavenward.

Cooper inspected not just every store but every warehouse. While at Fort Chipewyan, he once found "numbers of horse collars, horse shoes although I ascertained that there were only two horses in the whole district. These have been written off the books but it is an obvious weakness that they are not moved somewhere where they can be sold" [September 16, 1932]. One problem with Cooper's northern sojourns was that he demanded a full press corps reception when he returned to Winnipeg. Local journalists obliged the first time but soon found more interesting copy. Murray Turner, then in charge of public relations, solved the problem by recruiting eight tea and coffee salesmen from the wholesale department, handing them cameras—

---

*This was the Company's coat of arms on a white field, which today flies from all HBC stores.

*Patrick Ashley Cooper and others, with the first airplane purchased by the Hudson's Bay Company. Left to right: Harold Winny, Pilot; Patrick Ashley Cooper; Duncan McLaren, Mechanic; Paul Davoud, Manager, Transportation; Philip A. Chester, General Manager, HBC; Bob Chesshire, New Manager, Fur Trade Department.*

but not film—from the retail store, and telling them to pretend they were photographing the Governor's every limb movement as he descended from the aircraft. That made Cooper very happy, but every year when he returned to London, he would puzzle about it. "Extraordinary," he would say. "I have lots of photographs taken when I'm in Canada—and they never let me see them . . ."

COOPER'S MOST NOTABLE—and most bizarre—adventure was his 1934 journey into Hudson Bay. "1933 was a year of depression and losses," Chester noted when the Governor's decision to go North the following summer was being debated. "Within the Company the prospect of an Arctic pageant was received with misgivings and hopes that nothing would come of it. But as events quickly proved, such hopes were reducing the man and his plan to too simple a simplicity, as in no time at all London and Canada were organizing a voyage that would be the talk of Arctic circles for years to come." The *Nascopie* was turned over to a shipyard for reconfiguration of her passenger space to accommodate the Governor and his retinue. Bronze commemorative medals were struck featuring the profile of Cooper; hundreds of hunting knives were inscribed "From P. Ashley Cooper, Governor of the Hudson's Bay Company, 1934" on one side and "Be happy while you hunt" on the other; and an extra stock of Governor's flags was ordered.

On July 7, 1934, Cooper boarded the ship at her home berth in Montreal. With him were his wife, her maid, his secretary (G.R. Macdonald), a piper from the Black Watch of Canada (Pipe Sergeant Hannah) and Michael Lubbock, who was to act as Cooper's executive assistant and speech writer.* Aboard also were Ralph Parsons, the Company's Fur Trade Commissioner, a King's Scout (one a year was awarded the trip by the HBC), eight Mounties and several new HBC clerks, an archaeologist, an astronomer, an ornithologist and a news-reel production team. A thousand spectators lined the dock as the thirtieth Governor of the Hudson's Bay Company was piped aboard his ship for a six-week voyage into the Company's original territory that none of his predecessors had ever bothered to make.

The *Nascopie*, her pennants flying, steamed along the north shore of the St Lawrence, through the Strait of Belle Isle, then up the rocky coast of Labrador to Cartwright and later Port Burwell. The piper first did a round of the decks, frightening the caged chickens and sheep, then climbed into the bow of the ship's cutter and began playing "Oh where, tell me where, is my Highland laddie gone?" He was followed down the ladder by the Governor and his wife, Captain Smellie of the *Nascopie* and Parsons. "Sir George Simpson in his 30-foot canoe, with his beaver hat, piper and singing voyageurs, made no braver picture than this," rhapsodized R.H.H. Macaulay, a Company scribe. "A white motor boat of trim line—amidships, on a high-backed seat, the Governor and Mrs. Cooper, by the Governor's side the Commissioner. At the small wheel immediately behind the seat stood the 3rd mate in uniform, and by his side a uniformed seaman to tend the motor. Behind them, standing with arms folded, was the Captain, with his gold ribbon and oak leaves, and aft the Governor's

---

*The highly educated son of a director of the Bank of England and a former director of the HBC, Lubbock was not unduly fond of Cooper. "He was almost illiterate," Lubbock claimed, "so that whenever I wanted him to express rather loftier sentiments, I would insert, 'as the seventeenth-century writer said'—and then put in my own words. I even got quoted in a number of papers, and I knew he'd never dare ask me who the writer was."

flag. In the bow . . . the piper keeping time to his 'Highland Laddie' with one brogued and buckled foot, the ribbons decorating his pipes flying in the breeze." The Coopers inspected the tiny settlement, handed out the inscribed knives to the hunters, and mouth organs, toques, beads and rattles to the children, then officiated at the laying of a cornerstone for a new Bay store.* "It is no exaggeration to say," Macaulay reported with all the paternalism he could muster, "that those Eskimos were overcome by this unprecedented shower of gifts; never before in their lives had such a thing happened, and, in consequence, they could only sit and look at their presents, touching them gently every now and then to see that they were real, and, finding that they were, giving delighted little laughs."

As he would at all his stops, Cooper then showed his Inuit audience a film of King George reviewing the trooping of the colour, explaining through an interpreter that this was *their* King too. There is no record of local reactions to the movie—the first they had ever seen—or to the notion that somebody who usually went around on a horse was their King, but everybody's attention was soon distracted by a kayak race, a square dance and fireworks.† Next morning, as the *Nascopie* struck her anchor and pulled out of Cartwright on the way to Port Burwell, Cooper got ready for the broadcasts he intended to give just before his arrival or just after his departure at each stop. He would rush to the radio room and, sitting in front of a large microphone, drone on about how glad he was to be here, how the Eskimos should be more diligent in trapping foxes, how it had taken "many moons travelling" to reach them, and how they must always be loyal subjects of the King who was sponsoring this message. Then, straining even his own considerable limits of condescension, the Governor would conclude with the admonition: "We . . . leave you with confidence that you will work with our post manager as one large happy family, you following his advice as if he were your father, for he does the things which I tell him and I want you to do the things which he tells you."

---

*"Possibly arranged," as Chester later noted, "by the Post manager to express hopes for a new building; but after the *Nascopie* left, the ceremonial platform and inscribed cornerstone (a wooden crate filled with rocks and covered with concrete) were sadly dismantled."

†At Stupart Bay, the Governor gamely climbed into a kayak, got his balance, and paddled around the cove until his legs got cold. One highlight of the journey, recalled by Michael Lubbock, was stopping off at Lake Harbour, where the piper started to wail for a group of elderly Inuit. "I noticed they were in a sort of ring, shuffling around, and it suddenly struck me that they were going through the rudiments of a Scottish reel. It was a most curious spectacle, but of course the Dundee whalers used to come here regularly, and they were doing what they had been taught so many, many years ago."

*Patrick Ashley Cooper and Mrs Cooper posing on the ice
during the Hudson Bay tour, 1934*

There were three problems with the Governor's broadcasts:

1. Each settlement had only one radio receiver, usually in the store manager's staff house, so that the chances of an Inuk's actually hearing Cooper were remote.
2. He spoke in English, so that any Inuit who did listen would not understand a word Cooper was saying.
3. When Ottawa objected to an HBC official's speaking to Canadian subjects on behalf of the King, the plug was pulled on Cooper's microphone amplifier. As a result, his carefully rehearsed speeches were never heard outside the little shipboard studio. "They kind of went up in the air and never came down," Captain Smellie later confessed with a mischievous twinkle in his eye.

Cooper was not aware of any of this—then or later—and earnestly continued to perform his daily stint. The post managers had meanwhile been carefully briefed to praise him for his non-existent broadcasts wherever he appeared.

The voyage's most historic event was commemoration of Henry Hudson's voyage of discovery into the Bay, 324 years earlier. Cooper had been charged by Lord Jellicoe of the Royal Empire Society in London to cast a specially prepared wreath (which had been preserved in a huge block of ice) upon the waters near the spot where Hudson was thought to have been abandoned in a lifeboat by his mutinous crew. The previous evening the Captain had asked Arthur Reed, his Chief Steward, to prepare the wreath for launching. It could not be found, and Reed finally concluded it had mistakenly been left behind. "Make a wreath," ordered the skipper, adding, "by tomorrow morning." To create a circle of flowers held together by red ribbon on a supply ship in the middle of Hudson Bay might have daunted a lesser man, but Reed produced a realistic facsimile within twelve hours. It had been fashioned out of artificial blooms painted on and cut out of toilet paper by one of the passengers, mounted in moss that had been brought aboard by one of the scientists. Cooper delivered one of his windier speeches, then solemnly heaved the contraption into the sea, while his piper appropriately played "Flowers of the Forest."

"On his triumphant return to Winnipeg the Governor gave a dinner for the Canadian Committee," Chester noted, barely able to rein in his sarcasm. "And after speaking about the great value which the Company, the C.C., and the Fur Trade Department would reap from his efforts, he called up each member to be pinned with one of his medals. To climax the subsequent silence ... G.W. Allan remarked: 'Governor, by God, never before in my long life have I received a medal and I shall always treasure this memorable occasion.' "

IN DRAMATIC CONTRAST TO COOPER'S CHIVALROUS if extravagant approach, Chester's life in Winnipeg was remarkably routine. He lived on River Avenue, had an account with Bradley's Taxi, but usually walked to work and taxied home. He spent most of his limited spare time at the Manitoba Club, either playing bridge or trading gossip with members of the Sanhedrin. They were an informal group of thoughtful Winnipeggers led by John W. Dafoe, the great editor of the *Free Press* who customarily huddled in a corner of the club lounge (which always seemed redolent of ox blood), to dissect world events, talk up free trade, and spread the gospel of Manchester Liberalism. They resented the restraints placed on western development by the Montreal-Ottawa-Toronto axis and fervently believed that a prosperous West, exercising its financial independence, would strengthen Confederation. They were also an insular and extremely conservative bunch; having weathered the Depression, they vowed not to owe anybody anything ever again, encouraging Chester in his determination that the HBC should not borrow money to finance a move into Eastern Canada. When Owen Funnell, the ambitious and capable manager of the Calgary store, formulated plans for the Company to open a branch at the head of the Great Lakes in the grain-export town of Port Arthur, Chester cut off the discussion by proclaiming the community would not grow because the St Lawrence Seaway would never be built.

Chester's wife, Isabel, was an Ivey, the youngest child of a wealthy family from London, Ontario, who had made their fortune in Empire Brass and later branched out into life insurance and packaging. She had been planning to spend a season in Paris when she met Chester during a Great Lakes steamboat excursion, and they decided to marry. Their honeymoon at Beaver Point, the Ivey family summer compound on Ahmic Lake, near Burk's Falls, northwest of Huntsville, was an appropriate portent of things to come. The happy couple arrived in style and were met by the bride's two maids, but within two days Chester had decided they were not good enough and fired them both. Chester eventually bought the place and spent six weeks every summer there. "Beaver Point had a magnificent main house with six bedrooms, an enormous stone fireplace, and its own electricity generating plant," recalled son-in-law Charles Loewen. "Chester kept pretending it was just a little country cottage and got very cross when some Boy Scouts, who had paddled the lake in a canoe, came to borrow a can opener and asked: 'Sir, what's the name of this hotel?' He did things with reasonable style, so that at breakfast, for example, there were always ten pots of different jams and you had to go through the ceremony of choosing one. I remember particularly one day having lunch with him on the dock. He was sipping champagne and offered me some. When I told him I'd rather have beer, he looked at me and exclaimed, 'Helot!' Now, that was interesting, because he was calling me a peasant but granting me the recognition that I was an educated one, and would know the Helots had been Spartan serfs. He had a fairly sophisticated sense of humour."

Life at the Chesters' was not always that placid. They had adopted a son in England named David Andrew, a sensitive, artistic child. He was sent to Trinity College School at Port Hope, was a good student in art, literature and jazz piano, but worked only intermittently as a journalist. So displeased was the father with his intellectual son that Chester kept him at an emotional distance. David's attractive wife, from whom he would later become estranged, was a trained speech therapist but had to take jobs as a cleaning lady to pay the grocery bills. Young David's recurring nightmare was his memory of the time his father forced him to eat some jelly dessert that he was allergic to. When he got so upset he threw up, Chester insisted he eat everything on his plate, including the vomit—but his mother intervened.

Despite his frustrations with the British overlords, Chester loved his visits to London. He would arrive on the *Queen Mary*, stay in a suite at the Dorchester, lunch at the Savoy Grill, and be the dinner guest at various functions hosted by resident directors. The trips tapered off during the Second World War, as nearly everyone was pressed into service. Chester himself served briefly as Acting Master General of Ordnance in Canada's suddenly mobilized defence department but left Ottawa two months later, frustrated by the impenetrable maze of regulations. When he returned to Winnipeg, his wife gave a celebratory dinner party for their friends. As the guests sat down to eat, they found each serving tied up in red tape, and they had to fill out forms in triplicate before they could begin the meal.

Cooper also served his country, as Director-General of Finance in the Ministry of Supply, and in 1944 was knighted for his efforts. The Company's London office was never hit by German bombs, but they came close. More than one directors' meeting was concluded with the directors crouching under the boardroom table, and the annual Court in 1944 was disrupted three times by buzz-bombs landing nearby. A spice warehouse just behind Beaver House was hit and burned for a week, giving off a terrible smell. Several fire bombs landed on the front steps and roof of the Company building, but they didn't go off.*

The staff spent most nights huddled in the building's underground fur-storage vaults, occasionally relieving the tension by chuckling through one of the least authentic Hollywood films ever made.† Although there was a wartime embargo on importing fur, the HBC maintained the continuity of its operations by auctioning the pelts of

---

*A typical wartime incident was the near escape of a Company employee named A.J. Pullen, who woke up in his southeast London house one Saturday evening just as a hundred-pound bomb penetrated his roof and buried itself in an upstairs floor. He borrowed a saw, removed enough floor boards to free it, attached it to a wire cable, and dragged it over his garden railings into the street. He then hoisted the bomb—still ticking loudly in his ear—on his shoulder and carried it towards a bomb disposal dump. He was accompanied in this perilous journey by his seventeen-year-old son, Harry, who explained to neighbours that he was along in case his father dropped it. When Pullen finally reached the dump, he was arrested and fined three pounds (which the Company paid) for "removing and tampering with a bomb dropped from enemy aircraft."

†*Hudson's Bay*, a clinker produced in 1940 by Twentieth Century Fox, starred Gene Tierney (as a beautiful Indian princess), Vincent Price (as Charles II), Virginia Field (as Nell Gwyn), Paul Muni (as Pierre Radisson) and a 309-pound Laird Cregar (as Médard Chouart, Sieur Des Groseilliers). The movie's grasp of Canadian geography was as real as the canvas canoes, painted to resemble birchbark, in which most of the action took place.

British wild rabbits, used in the hat trade. On February 25, 1946, regular sales resumed, with £200,000 in turnover the first day alone. The HBC was back in business.

Cooper celebrated the end of hostilities by revamping his board. Much to everyone's surprise, but prompted by his directors, he named Chester a British director (replacing Victor Cazalet) and upgraded his title from General Manager to Managing Director for Canada. The Governor also recruited as new board members some of the war's most distinguished graduates. They included Field Marshal the Right Honourable the Viscount Alanbrooke, who had served as Chief of the Imperial General Staff and, according to the American general Douglas MacArthur, was "the greatest soldier that England has produced since Wellington"; Sir John Anderson, later Lord Waverley, one of Britain's most distinguished public servants, who had served as Governor of Bengal (where he earned the reputation of being the most shot-at man in the world) and wartime Chancellor of the Exchequer;* and William "Tony" Keswick, a brigadier on the staff of General Montgomery's planning group for the Normandy invasion, whose family controlled Jardine, Matheson & Company, a Far Eastern trading company.

The most interesting new post-war recruit was Joe Links, the head of his own firm of furriers that had been chosen by Royal Appointment Furrier to the Royal Household. A spritely and cultured gentleman with all the social graces and a novelist's eye for detail, he had written authoritative studies of Venice, Canaletto and the fur trade. Links made light of the fact that he was the first Jew to be invited on the board, and when asked whether he had encountered any preju-

---

*Alanbrooke's honours and decorations: Knight of the Garter, Knight Grand Cross of the Bath, Order of Merit, Knight Grand Cross of the Royal Victorian Order, Distinguished Service Order (he was twice a DSO—in 1917 and 1918). He also held the French, Belgian and Czechoslovak Croix de Guerre and the Distinguished Service Medal from the United States, and his wife was from an old HBC family: a great-granddaughter of Sir John Henry Pelly, Deputy Governor 1812–22 and Governor 1822–52. Waverley's honours: Privy Councillor, Knight Grand Cross of the Bath, Order of Merit, Knight Grand Commander of the Star of India, Knight Grand Commander of the Indian Empire, Fellow of the Royal Society. He attended the universities of Edinburgh and Leipzig, and held an MA and a BSc. He was Home Secretary in the early years of the 1939–45 war, and the little air-raid shelters that dotted British gardens were known as Andersons after him. After the war he became chairman of the Port of London Authority and a director of the CPR. The Order of Merit is limited in number to twenty-four members, with provision for honorary foreign members. General Dwight Eisenhower was made an honorary OM in 1945. The Bath is a much larger order, with many degrees, including several of knighthood.

dice, replied, "Of course not, neither then nor at any other time in my life. It's not so much that I was the only Jewish director, I was the *English* one—the only Englishman among six Scots or sons of Scots. So, perhaps I cannot acquit my colleagues altogether of prejudice." Described by a later Governor as "the most useful board member, his mind worked like lightning and he would always ask the kind of awkward questions that made us wonder why we had never thought of what he had just brought up," Links served on the board for twenty-eight years, an invaluable source of wisdom, humour and plain good sense.

The Canadian Committee also underwent drastic changes. In 1940, Charles Dunning, who had become Premier of Saskatchewan at thirty-six and later served as federal minister of finance, was invited to join. Chancellor of Queen's University, chairman of Ogilvie Flour Mills and a director of eleven other major companies, he was one of the few distinguished non-Winnipeggers to join the HBC Committee. In Winnipeg itself, the Company's corporate traditions carried on through the appointment of Perley Banbury (Beaver Lumber), Stewart Augustus Searle (Searle Grain, and a director of Monarch Life), Colonel Hugh F. Osler (head of Osler, Hammond & Nanton and a director of Great-West Life) and Joe Harris (Canada Packers, Great-West Life and a director of Beaver Lumber).* Originally an executive in his father's meat packing-house (later merged into Canada Packers), Harris was a candid character who had the disconcerting habit of ending most lunches by pushing back his chair and, as he was turning to leave, informing his fellow diners: "Got to get back to the abattoir and stick a piggy."

After George Allan's death in 1940, the Canadian Committee chairmanship went to Conrad Stephenson Riley, an unassuming but effective financier who could divert most of Cooper's aggressive ploys with the simple: "Yes, Patrick, I'm sure that would be very nice. But no." A noted oarsman who became a member of Canada's Sports Hall of Fame, he succeeded his father as president of Northern Trusts and was a director of such Winnipeg touchstone companies as Great-West Life and Beaver Lumber. Under Riley, the Cooper-Chester feud quieted down a bit, with the Winnipeg Managing Director temporarily becalmed because of his new title and London appointment,

---

*A prominent member of a well-established Winnipeg grain family, Searle stayed on the Committee for fifteen years, but when he developed the habit of spending every winter in Florida, and thus missing an increasing number of meetings, he was not invited to stand for re-election.

while the British Governor, savouring his new knighthood, felt vindicated and slightly more immune to the Canadian's little plots.*

Within a decade, Riley was succeeded by J. Elmer Woods, who would run the Canadian Committee from 1950 to 1964. While he was cut from the same pattern as every other Winnipeg Committeeman (he was president of Monarch Life and a director of Beaver Lumber), Woods was an original. He was the ultimate insider, so trusted by Manitoba's political and economic élite that for a brief time he was chief bagman for both the provincial Liberal and Conservative parties at one and the same time. He took on the HBC Chairmanship determined to move the Company's head office to its proper address, on Winnipeg's Main Street, and though he didn't succeed, he put in place most of the necessary groundwork. Prompted by Chester, he also reactivated the Hudson's Bay Oil & Gas operation. By the spring of 1943, the firm owned a dozen wells in Turner Valley, representing 10 percent of the field's production. Within the decade, the HBC had invested $8 million in exploration and HBOG had become the second-largest holder of known gas reserves (4.3 million acres) in Alberta, with eighty producing wells. A major exploration agreement was signed with Continental Oil, to expire June 30, 1951. That proved to be a bonanza because Continental at about this time named as its president L.F. McCollum, one of the great Texas oilmen, who invested $300 million in land acquisition and oil exploration in the next two decades.

A continuing controversy of the 1950s concerned the desirability of moving retail operations into Ontario and Quebec and whether or not the HBC should join other department stores in establishing satellite branches in suburban shopping centres. Chester's position, strongly supported by Elmer Woods, was nothing if not clear: he would never "go whoring in the East," and there was no point going into shopping centres because sales in such urban fringes would only reduce the core business of the Bay's magnificent downtown department stores. "If there were fuddy-duddies in the Company, they were to be found in Canada rather than London," claimed Joe Links. "Chester was instinctively opposed to buying other companies, believing the HBC could perfectly well build up any business it wanted and 'crucify' its competitors. Above all, Chester wanted the HBC to stay in the West— certainly to make itself competitive, to enlarge its big downtown stores, to build parkades, and open up new stores in unexploited

---

*Chester was so relaxed that he even took on an outside directorship (his only one), naturally choosing the Great-West Life Assurance Company.

areas, but not to challenge 'those whores in the East,' where an honest trader with Western Canadian principles would only get his fingers burnt. We in London felt the shopping centre movement gave HBC opportunities with its expertise in operating retail stores of widely differing sizes. Chester's argument that anything that might weaken our downtown stores must weaken the Company was an interesting reversal of a situation that arose in the HBC's pioneering days. When the French took to opening trading posts upriver in order to catch the Indians before they reached the HBC posts with their furs, the Bay men on the spot sought authority from London to go still farther upriver. But London foresaw a limitless leap-frogging and decided instead that better prices for furs and better trade goods would do more for the Company's reputation. I once reminded Chester of this story and saw him momentarily waver. If what he was saying had been said by those London bastards of the eighteenth century, then perhaps he might be wrong after all. But he was comforted by the thought that twentieth-century London didn't agree with him: this confirmed that he *must* be right." Peter Wood, the HBC's Treasurer, verified this: "If the London people had been overtly against the suburban stores, Chester would have been vehemently for them."

It was a costly dispute. Sears in the United States had opened its first suburban store at Aurora, a Chicago suburb, in 1928, and by the early 1950s shopping centres with department stores at each end were sprouting up all over America. Woodward's opened Canada's first shopping-centre store at West Vancouver's Park Royal in 1950 after the HBC had turned down an offer from the Guinness family, the centre's developers, to be the anchor store. Four years later Canada's initial double department store plaza was launched in a suburb of Hamilton, with Morgan's and Simpsons-Sears as anchor tenants. Eaton's put its first branch into Oshawa in 1956. George Weightman, a thirty-year Bay man who eventually became manager of market research, still laments the lost opportunities. "I wrote a long précis summing up the prospects for the Company and made a convincing argument, but when I finished my presentation, Chester just said, 'Young man, you can't see the woods for the trees,' and I thought to myself, 'Well, there you are.' " Part of the problem was that Chester was an atrocious driver, seldom drove his car and was not aware of the effect of people's new mobility on North American cities.

BY THE EARLY 1950S, Sir Patrick Ashley Cooper, now nearing his sixty-fifth birthday, began to send out feelers about having his term as

Governor extended beyond normal retirement. He had a good case and made certain that it was promulgated in the Company's 1951 report. Share values, he reminded the proprietors, had fallen from 131*s* 3*d* in 1928 to 22*s* 6*d* in 1930, but since 1932 the Company had distributed £3 million in dividends and ploughed £8.5 million back into its treasury, raising assets from £10.7 million to £66.8 million. Cooper had introduced many enlightened policies, such as stressing promotion from within. He established the Hudson's Bay Record Society to take over publication of the Company's historic documents. He was the first Governor to hold summer picnics for the London staff at his home, and even demonstrated a sense of humour when he read out to an annual Court a letter he had received. "I got your letter about what I owe," wrote the troubled HBC customer. "Now be pachant. I ain't forgot you. Please wait. When I have the money I will pay you. If this was the Judgement Day and you was no more prepared to meet your maker than I am to meet your account you sure would go to hell. Trusting you will do this."

"I kind of liked Sir Patrick," remarked Scotty Gall, the old Arctic hand, who met the Governor several times. "He loved the feudal system, behaved like a baron coming around to inspect his serfs. But he was a keen businessman, too. He knew the right side of the dollar and gave nothing away." That was true enough, and there was no doubt that Cooper had rescued the Company from the Depression. But the post-war era demanded other qualities, and even if it was mostly Chester's fault, relations between Winnipeg and London had deteriorated beyond repair, so that no concerted expansion plan could be put into effect. Cooper's exaggerated sense of personal vanity had become even less endearing to Canadians than it was to the Londoners, and his Churchillian refrain, that he had not become Governor of the HBC in order to preside over its dissolution, was a brave stance but hardly a policy.

During his tenure at Beaver House, Cooper had acquired a collection of silver pieces made in 1670, the year of the Company's founding, and had special carpets woven in Kidderminster by four artisans especially chosen for the job. He also had his portrait painted, and as was then the custom, an extra copy was done for a record of the original. Cooper borrowed the copy to hang in his country house and one summer weekend in 1952 told R.A. Reynolds, the Company secretary, he was taking the original home to compare the two canvases. Reynolds had placed a secret mark on the primary painting and was not too surprised when Cooper returned on Monday morning, passing off the copy as the real thing.

It was a tiny incident, but it raised questions about Cooper's approach. There had been rumours that he was charging his London flat to the Company and that he accepted generous expense-account advances but seldom reported on them. Whether or not this amounted to any serious abuse of his fiscal responsibilities, it certainly was true that after more than two decades in the Governor's chair Cooper had lost the ability to differentiate between his personal considerations and those of the Company. There were, in those days, very tight foreign exchange controls in Britain, to the extent that executives travelling abroad were allocated ridiculously small spending allowances. The Bank of England agreed to grant Cooper, as HBC Governor, a special exemption to finance his journeys and required entertainments, yet Company auditors discovered that he was withdrawing a similar amount from the Winnipeg office but sending his bills through to be paid in London. Cooper made his own rules and at one time even imported a tractor for his farm with the allowance granted him by the British central bank. The London board members deputized Lord Waverley to persuade Cooper that he should resign. The final confrontation, attended by Tony Keswick (by then promoted to Deputy Governor) and Waverley, left Cooper no escape.

Keswick recalled later, "We just said: 'The staff have lost confidence; it's no use trying to build it up. It must come to an end. There must be a change.'"

"Do I understand what that means?" asked a distraught Cooper.

"You understand what it means."

"Yes, I understand what it means. We won't discuss it any more."

And so, on November 19, 1952, Sir Patrick Ashley Cooper resigned as thirtieth Governor of the Hudson's Bay Company.

Chester had won.

*Lord Amory*

# CHAPTER 15

# CANADIAN AT LAST

*"The British have the rigidity of red hot pokers without their warmth."*

—Lord Amory

TONY KESWICK, WHO HAD BEEN BROUGHT on the board by Cooper in the mid-1940s, now took over as Governor, and his presence introduced a whiff of China Seas buccaneering to the HBC's deliberations. "He was a big man in every sense, a sharp trader, and I thoroughly enjoyed working with him," reminisced Eric Faulkner, who was for a time his Deputy, "although there were moments when one had to slightly pull on the reins and say, 'Tony, you're going a bit too far. There's too much bullshit in that, you *must* be more careful.'"

To such admonitions, mild as they were, Keswick preferred to reply with a parable and a fact. The fact was that during his steward-ship, HBC profits climbed 320 percent; the parable had something to do with a mythical creature known as the Arctic Robin. "It had been snowing for a long, long time," went his oft-told tale, "and the poor bird, having had nothing to eat, said to himself, 'I think I'll turn up my toes and pack it in.' Just then, a farmer let his bull out of its pen near where the Arctic Robin was sitting. The bull had been overfed and after a while deposited an enormous pile, which allowed the Robin to have a delicious hot breakfast. The bird, feeling perky again, flew up a tree and started singing so loudly that it attracted the attention of the farmer's son, who fetched a catapult, took aim, and killed the Arctic Robin stone dead." The point of the story, as Keswick loved to explain through snorts of belly-pumping laughter,

309

was that "if you get to the top with the aid of bullshit, you shouldn't sing about it."

Keswick came by his merchant adventurer's calling honestly, having been associated for most of his business life with Jardine, Matheson, the Hong Kong trading house. "Both companies, at different times and different places, lived dangerously and had to struggle against larger forces," he pointed out. "Whatever else, the life of a merchant adventurer is full of incidents." One such incident that illustrated Keswick's approach to life and adventure made good his claim that he may have been the only politician ever shot for making a budget speech. In the winter of 1940–41, when he was working for Jardine's along the South China coast, the invading Japanese had hived most of the surviving foreign community into the International Settlement, the European quarter of Shanghai. Elected head of the municipal council, Keswick was presenting his annual budget at an outdoor arena in Shanghai filled with five thousand ratepayers when Yukichi Hayashi, a Japanese radical opposed to the foreign presence, rushed on stage, took out a revolver and began firing at him. The first bullet went through his rib cage, causing Keswick to feel genuinely annoyed. "I told the Japanese fellow, 'For God's sake, stop that.' Then I fell on top of the little chap. Nearly killed him. He tried to send another bullet up my nose and took three fingers off the interpreter's left hand with his last shot. Seemed *very* upset."

His would-be assassin was hailed as a hero in Tokyo while Keswick escaped with only superficial wounds and eventually boarded the last plane to leave Singapore before the Japanese invasion. He had a good war, and later spent most of two decades as a director of the Bank of England. His many honours included membership in the Royal Company of Archers. "We're the Queen's bodyguard whenever she's in Scotland," he explained. "We have bows, arrows and little swords and stomp about protecting her." Scotland was also the site of his grouse moor, on a 6,000-acre estate in Dumfriesshire, sixty miles south of Glasgow. It was stocked not only with game birds, sheep and cattle but also with statues. Haunted by memories of Buddhas spotted in the Far Eastern landscape, Keswick planted, at strategic viewpoints throughout his estate, works of some of the twentieth century's most famous sculptors: two Rodins, Epstein's famous *Madonna* and half a dozen Henry Moores, including his resplendent *King and Queen*. "I have all the big boys," he allowed, "and they look very well in their natural surroundings against the sky—better than seeing them in some damn museum."

*Sir William J. "Tony" Keswick*

Perhaps because Keswick had such a powerful sense of self-worth and came to the HBC without having to prove anything, his thirteen years as Governor were very different from the stewardships of his predecessors. Unlike Cooper, Keswick placed the greatest emphasis on cultivating the staff, trying to raise morale by re-igniting their pride in the Company. "He used to come around and sit in my office," recalled Arthur Frayling, who was in charge of London fur sales, "and say, 'Arthur, we're having a bad year, can you do anything for us?' I'd tell him that we would make a decent kick, and he'd put his hand on my shoulder and reply, 'We're counting on you.' That pompous old bugger Cooper would never have done that. He would have sent out four memorandums on how to reorganize the fur division." After his annual trips to Canada, Keswick would write a hundred or more personal letters to the Bay employees he'd met, and eventually knew nearly all of them by their first names.

Keswick's most serious assignment was to protect the Company against an attempted takeover by Max Bell of Calgary and H.R. Milner of Edmonton. The episode was referred to in the HBC's secret internal files as "The Bullfight" because the tactics employed by the Alberta investors were similar to those used in the takeover of the Matador Land & Cattle Company, a venerable Texas land outfit that had struck oil. The idea, novel at the time, was to seek representation on the board of the desired company and, with the information obtained, promote an offer to shareholders for control. Once their goal was achieved, the new owners would then sell off parts of the company to pay for their acquisition expenses. Had Bell succeeded, he would have spun off the HBC's retail stores to Simpsons or Eaton's and, in effect, obtained the HBC's petroleum reserves for nothing. An athletic-looking gent with a sporty brushcut, Bell had made an early fortune in the Alberta Oil Patch, purchased half a dozen daily newspapers, and become a well-known horse breeder and racer. A fitness devotee, he would disconcert employees who had come to see him for a pay increase by walking across the office floor on his hands, urging them to state their case as money poured out of his upside-down trouser pockets. He owned the luxury yacht *Campana*, a pair of islands up the B.C. coast and several vacation palaces but had Spartan eating habits. "Max's idea of real debauchery," claimed his friend the sports-writer Jim Coleman, "is to have three flavours of ice-cream in the same dish."

There had been heavy buying of HBC stock on American stock exchanges in early 1952 and rumours began to grow that a New York syndicate, organized and headed by S.G. Warburg & Company, the British merchant bankers, would attend that year's annual Court to grab control of the Company. Because both the Canadian and the U.S. groups were attracted by the HBC's oil leases, Company management immediately began to negotiate a new long-term agreement with its exploration partner, Continental Oil, locking the two companies into joint ventures until 1999. Within a year of its original push, the Warburg group decided to unite with Max Bell. That gave the combined group sway over more than 200,000 shares (out of 2.5 million shares outstanding), nowhere near a control position but enough to worry management. Keswick decided to deal first with Siegmund Warburg. "I put on a clean white shirt and went to have tea with Mr. Warburg in the interest of 'shareholder relations,' " he wrote to Canadian Committee Chairman Elmer Woods. "After a sip of very indifferently made tea I took the opportunity of expressing my own views on the breaking up of the companies or selling off limbs, especially those with long histories and established success. I left him with no doubt that in principle I would find it very difficult to agree to any such policy and that I personally believed ardently in maintaining the united strength of our grand old Company."

After prolonged discussion and some bickering, Warburg agreed to vote his proxies with the board, but Bell held out. He had drawn up a forty-four-page report suggesting how the HBC could improve its profit potential, particularly in oil operations, and on March 17, 1953, Bell and Keswick met face to face. "At times he shouted like an undisciplined or spoilt boy unable to get his way too easily," Keswick recalled. "Curiously enough, the question of taxation never arose as a major criticism, nor did transfer, other than his recommendation that I should transfer myself over and settle down like a broody hen on top of the Canadian Committee. . . . It could all be summed up in one generalization: that Mr. Bell feels that we lack drive and progressive management; we do not make the most of our assets; and that if we did we could treble and quadruple our profits. . . . It is good that we have shareholders as keen as this but I am glad there are not too many of them." Bell quite rightly concluded he was not being taken seriously and soon afterwards sold his HBC stock—at a $500,000 profit. The main impact of his raid was to bring a substantial block of stock across the Atlantic.

PERHAPS IT HAD SOMETHING TO DO with celebrating his victory over Bell, the first colonial to challenge London's vested authority, but more likely it was Keswick's intuition that his beloved Company could not much longer resist the pull westward and would soon be domiciled in Canada, that prompted him to stage one final, glorious pageant. Who better as the centrepiece of such a grand occasion than the most eminent Englishman of the century, Sir Winston Churchill? The wartime Prime Minister's ancestor John Churchill (later first Duke of Marlborough) had during his seven-year reign as the HBC's third Governor restored the Company to glory. Nine generations later, the eighty-one-year-old Sir Winston had reluctantly retired from active politics in 1955, and allowed Anthony Eden to succeed him with the immortal comment: "I must retire soon. Anthony won't live forever." He was working on his masterpiece *The Second World War*, and while his intellect seemed undiminished his health was poor and he was feeling left out of things. Word had come from Chartwell, his country house, that he might be open to an invitation to join the HBC in some manner because he felt there was no other commercial enterprise with which he could align himself without drawing criticism for favouritism. Lord Waverley had suggested the entirely honorific but appropriately

*Sir Winston Churchill at Beaver Hall, April 27, 1956*

historic title "Grand Seigneur of the Company of Adventurers of England Trading into Hudson's Bay," which had the advantage of playing up to Churchill's approach to the British Empire: its details had always bored him, but he was much attached to its ideal—"the spectacle of that immense estate enhancing the grandeur of England," as Jan Morris described it.

Churchill accepted Keswick's invitation but Winnipeg did not. When the Governor mentioned the idea to the Canadian Committee, Elmer Woods replied that he thought "any such position would be incompatible with the stature of Sir Winston. By the unthinking public it would be construed as a form of publicity, with unfavourable reactions. . . ." Keswick forwarded copies of the Woods letter to his fellow British directors with the notation: "I have received the attached somewhat typical and ungracious unanimous disapproval," and paid scant attention to the Canadians. He decided the title would be conferred at a ceremony in Beaver Hall, followed by luncheon at Skinners' Hall on April 27, 1956, with the top layer of Britain's social, economic and political establishments invited to attend.*

"We had a hell of a job getting him up the Skinners' Hall steps," Faulkner recalled. "He appeared deathly pale and we had seats with little tables every fifty yards or so, equipped with helpings of Hudson's Bay fifty-year-old cognac. He would take a little slug of it and go on, so that by the time he got into the hall there was colour in his cheeks and he was happily coherent." Another HBC director, Lord Alan-brooke, who had been Churchill's senior military commander, was astonished at the transformation. "He is a marvel," the former Chief of the Imperial General Staff told Lord Moran, Churchill's physician, who was at the luncheon. "Before the Election in 1945 I said to myself: He is finished. I could not get him to decide anything. . . . He was burnt out. . . . That was eleven years ago, and look at him now."

Keswick and Sir Edward Peacock proposed glowing toasts to the old man, praising his magnificent accomplishments, pretending the office of Grand Seigneur was more than just a grandiose title. The former Prime Minister went along with the game. He rose to his feet, looking a trifle strange in what he must have imagined was a Grand Seigneur's uniform—a smoking jacket over a dress shirt decorated by a bright green bow-tie with large white polka dots—and mis-chievously told his delighted audience: "I must be very careful how I use the great power that has been placed at my disposal at this very agreeable and memorable function. If I were perhaps to interpret it too literally, it might need a lengthy explanation and I might not receive the full accord which it is in all cases desirable should be given to it and also given to the Grand Seigneur. I will not, therefore, attempt any strong action as a result of the post to which you have called me until and unless I have had further experience. . . ."

Churchill concluded his remarks with a touching benediction. "This honour will be appreciated all my—," there was a long pause and his voice tightened, "—all my remaining life." Sensing they might not see him again, members of the audience grew still. The Grand Seigneur turned to leave. He stepped gingerly from the speaker's dais and, when he reached the bottom stair, faced the hall and gave everyone present a long, searching look; then his features

---

*The banquet was catered by Ring & Brymer at forty-two shillings a head, with the menu consisting of Scotch salmon with hollandaise sauce; long fillet of beef with new potatoes and French beans; lemon posset and Savoy fingers—and two wine varieties to wash it down: Forster Fleckinger Riesling Auslese, 1953, and Château Léoville Poyferré, 1934. Warre's Port, 1927, accompanied dessert, and Fine Old Cognac was served with the coffee.

broke into a cherubic smile. The ovation was deafening, lasting the long moments it took for the head table party to escort Sir Winston down to his car.*

HAVING VANQUISHED BELL and toasted Churchill, Keswick's main pre-occupation became getting along with Chester. His style was certainly more accommodating than Cooper's. After visiting London late in 1952, the Winnipeg-based executive sent the Governor a comforting note. "I cannot attempt to describe the wonderful contrast of my first visit under your reign," he wrote; "it was so happy and enjoyable that I'll hop over any time, even for forty-eight hours." But Chester had by then been battling London for nearly a quarter-century, and his suspicion of British motives had marinated his brain, so that despite his early good intentions he could not stop fighting. "It was easy to follow Cooper," Keswick recalled, "because he was a puffed-up hot-air merchant. But my main task was handling Chester, who was very able, a piledriver intolerant of people not willing to work twenty-four hours a day, but he had a great capacity for sulking. At some of our board meetings, I could see him starting to lose his temper, and I'd say, 'Phil, you're turning black.' It was enormous fun." On one occasion while en route from Toronto to Vancouver, the plane in which the Governor was travelling experienced extreme turbulence in an air pocket over Winnipeg. "We all had to fasten our lap straps," Keswick recalled, "and the passenger next to me, who must have known who I was but hadn't uttered a word during the flight, said out of the side of his mouth: 'Phil Chester must be down below.' "

Even the London board members who admired Chester found him difficult. Deputy Governor Faulkner complained that "on his black-face-days, he was almost impossible to deal with." Yet Faulkner also believed that "Chester had saved the Company. He was a difficult man to like but easy to respect." That was a generous verdict because Faulkner's introduction to Chester had not been promising. "When I first went on the board, I arrived in Montreal and had breakfast with

---

*After the ceremony, Churchill wanted to know if he could do anything for the Company. Asked whether he might donate one of his paintings, the former Prime Minister replied that this would be difficult since he'd given them all to his wife. When Joe Links went to see Lady Churchill, she explained that while Sir Winston had painted about six hundred canvases, only twenty-five of them were any good, and she didn't want to give the Company either one of his bad ones or a very good one. They finally settled on "the twenty-sixth or twenty-seventh," a Marrakesh street scene that still hangs in the HBC Governor's office, now in the Simpson Tower at the corner of Bay and Queen streets in downtown Toronto.

Chester at the Ritz-Carlton," he remembered—only too well. "I needed to blow my nose, so I drew a handkerchief from my left sleeve, where I always carried it. Chester saw me and said: 'It may offend you deeply, but for Christ's sake, don't wear those suede shoes in Canada, because the only people who wear suede shoes here are not the sort of people we would have as directors of the Hudson's Bay Company. Secondly, last week four Royal Canadian Navy captains returned from a course in the United Kingdom. They went on television, and when one of them blew his nose into a handkerchief he'd taken out of his sleeve, Canada went up in smoke, thinking this man's been corrupted. So, don't keep your handkerchief there and take off those shoes.' I remember thinking to myself, 'My God, what have I walked into?' "

Still, the Company under Chester's regime prospered. On August 29, 1946, he had been promoted to Managing Director and granted a $15,000 bonus, but not even that show of confidence satisfied him. "He would chip away at London's authority, chip away at it the whole time," HBC financial officer Peter Wood remembered. "They always said, 'We'll give in on the little things, but we're not going to give in on the main points.' By the time Chester had chipped away a hundred times, he had grabbed a fair amount of authority."

Records of the time reveal that despite Chester's constant complaining, he made not a single policy proposal that wasn't eventually approved by London, while the British directors seldom pressed him to do anything against his will. Yet the feud continued unabated. The enlarged Canadian membership on the London board—in 1957 and 1960—required new appointments that dramatically improved the calibre of the Canadian Committee. C. Gordon Smith, the scion of a well-known grain family with the appropriate Winnipeg credentials (directorships in Beaver Lumber and Monarch Life) joined the board, as did James Richardson, who became chairman and the fourth-generation member to head the family grain firm. (This particular Richardson later became minister of national defence in the Trudeau cabinet.) Two other previously named Committeemen, Stewart Searle and Joe Harris, joined the parent board.

But the most significant catch was Graham Towers, the former (and first) governor of the Bank of Canada, who during his twenty-year reign at the central bank had become universally recognized as the country's most respected economic thinker. In his time, Towers had preserved an unsullied reputation for business prescience, but he never lost his shy and self-depreciating presence. At one time he found himself at a Maritimes hotel without enough cash to settle his account. When a suspicious cashier demanded identification before he would cash a cheque, the Bank of Canada Governor tried with considerable embarrassment to avoid revealing who he was, but finally pulled out a dollar bill and reluctantly showed the startled hotel employee his signature, then decorating Canada's paper currency.

As the Canadian Committee grew in stature, the British board was undergoing a similar metamorphosis. The distinguished but largely decorative Lords Waverley and Alanbrooke departed, while J.E.H. Collins, a thirty-six-year-old financier who later headed Morgan, Grenfell, the London banking firm, moved in, as did Henry (later Lord) Benson and Lord Heyworth. Collins put in a useful decade and a half on the board, questioning policies with youthful vigour, but it was Benson and Heyworth who caused the most trouble—and, in retrospect, the most regret. A distinguished Coopers & Lybrand accountant who had served as a colonel in the Grenadier Guards, Benson was a born troubleshooter, having chaired three dozen commissions and inquiries. Tough and unsentimental, he took a good look at the HBC and decided the make-up of its non-executive board of directors was all wrong. To help him with what he felt were the required reforms, he recruited to the board Lord Heyworth, the recently retired head of Unilever, one of the world's great trading companies. Heyworth had worked for the Anglo-Dutch soap and food multinational in Canada, had married a Canadian and was vitally interested in improving the HBC's administration.

The pair set down the necessary steps to reorient a firm whose earnings and performance record they felt had been deplorable. They recommended that the Company's most able operating executives be appointed to a revamped board that would include half a dozen Canadians of Graham Towers's stature; that the Company be immediately Canadianized by transfer of its charter across the Atlantic; and that the HBC's Canadian headquarters be moved from Winnipeg to Montreal or Toronto. The hidden item on their agenda was that Keswick, whom they considered too old-fashioned and too compassionate to wield a broad enough axe, be shoved aside and replaced by Heyworth as a full-time Governor with clear executive powers to modernize the Company and turn it Canadian. The rest of the board demurred, and even if nearly all of the directors would later admit that Benson and Heyworth had been right, not much happened.

What brought the impasse to a head was the move by Keswick to fill a British board vacancy with Lord Cobbold, the retiring governor (1949–61) of the Bank of England. A subsequent Lord Chamberlain of the Royal Household and later a permanent Lord in Waiting to the

Queen, Cameron Fromanteel Cobbold was the perfect personification of the trend Benson and Heyworth had been protesting against: perpetuation of the Company's creaky command structure by the naming of yet another distinguished non-executive director with little knowledge of Canada and less of retailing to a board already top-heavy with such creatures. "Benson and Heyworth," Links later recalled, "argued that far from adapting ourselves to change, we were determined to perpetuate the traditional, decorative, and entirely ineffective board of the past. All of us agreed there was much to be said about the approach of appointing executive directors, but little to be done about it until the right people could be found. Interestingly, the Canadian members were aghast at the prospect and demanded that Benson and Heyworth resign immediately. There was no difficulty about this—neither of them wanted to stay under existing conditions. Heyworth just walked out of the board meeting but Benson, cerebrally superior to any of us, stayed behind to tell us not what he thought of the Canadians but what the Canadians thought of us, one by one. There was no malice in this, nothing more than a sense of duty to ensure that we did not continue under any delusions."

Keswick won that round ("They had no notion of the strength of the man they were up against," his wife later declared). It was a remarkable reflection on both men that after it was all over, Benson remained Keswick's personal accountant. Yet it was a hollow victory. Looking back on Benson's thwarted *coup d'état*, Peter Wood enthusiastically sided with the departed renegades. "They were absolutely right," Wood maintained. "If their advice had been followed, the Company would have moved to Canada ten years earlier and it would have been very different. For one thing, we could have got into the first instead of third generation of shopping centres, which would have meant grabbing a lot of the most desirable locations. We could never do that as long as Chester was around."

HAVING CONSOLIDATED HIS POWER and position, by the late 1950s Chester had changed. The provocative complainer of the Cooper period had been replaced by a far more equable and cultured presence who had become a fervent Canadian nationalist. He regarded his past battles with London as having been a microcosm of Canada's struggle to free itself from foreign domination, and in Winnipeg's case to become less dependent on the overwhelming influence of central Canadian bankers. He was part of the small but powerful circle of

Manitoba capitalists—the Richardsons, the Rileys, the Gourleys and others—dedicated to halting at Winnipeg the flow of money eastward from British Columbia and the Prairies, which was why they launched financial service institutions and insurance companies.

Within that context Chester grew frustrated by his confinement to his Winnipeg circle and, incongruous as it seemed, enjoyed nothing so much as his semi-annual visits to London. Corporately, he desperately wanted to be the architect of the Company's patriation to Canada, realizing that it had become silly to have the HBC run from London. But personally, he loved the stays in his suite at the Dorchester Hotel, his dinners with the cultured members of the HBC board at Claridge's and the St James's Street clubs, or at Greenwich. He enjoyed especially spending weekends at the country home of Joe Links, playing poker and discussing modern art. "He was totally dedicated to the HBC and everybody, both in London and Canada, knew it and respected him for it," Links reminisced. "We all liked his company, and above all, trusted him."

Chester did not plan to attend the Company's May 1959 Court because most of the board was due to be in Winnipeg during July in connection with the Queen's visit for the Rent Paying Ceremony. He did, however, go to London in February and either caught pneumonia or suffered a mild stroke. On his way home, he convalesced at Toronto's Park Plaza Hotel for a week. On July 23 at a Canadian Committee meeting in Winnipeg, one of the subjects discussed was enlargement of the Company board that would have made more room for Canadians while retaining the requirement that eight directors—including the Governor and Deputy Governor—should be U.K. residents. Chester stood alone in opposing the restriction, and when he recognized there would be no movement on the issue, orally submitted his resignation.

He was on the platform at the Rent Paying Ceremony at Assiniboine Park the next day and even gave a large garden party at his home immediately afterwards. Although his resignation did not officially take effect until September 30, he never again set foot in Hudson's Bay House.*

---

*Chester's final bonus and pension payment amounted to $505,000. The pressures of work removed, Chester lived another seventeen years. Although he resolutely stayed away from the HBC and didn't even shop at its Winnipeg store, in 1976, when he knew he was dying, Chester returned to the Company fold. He requested that his burial service be celebrated by Jack Dangerfield and Joan Whiting, HBC executives who had become Anglican priests. And so it was.

RICHARD MURRAY, WHO NOW BECAME the HBC's Managing Director, possessed the one quality that could never have been ascribed to Chester: he was a diplomat. High-strung, romantic and compassionate, with a wideranging mind and a set of beliefs stronger than the discipline required to contain them, he tended to be indecisive and dithering. Yet Murray was, in a way, the perfect trans-Atlantic gentleman—in awe of the Establishments on both sides of the ocean, yet their willing and capable instrument. He got along with the Canadians who mattered as well as with Keswick, and after one of the Governor's Canadian visits wrote him a typically effusive letter: "The atmosphere was indeed extraordinary when you arrived; in fact, it defied description or analysis. Your direct, constructive and friendly approach to all issues and personalities in the short time you were with us did a tremendous amount of good." Murray was a true Bay man, outrageously proud of working for what he described as "the most hellishly modern old-fashioned company in the world," and boasted that the Winnipeg headquarters staff often came to work at 7:45 in the morning, although the office didn't officially open until 8:30, just to get an early start.* He wasn't a retailer, and swore he never would be, but loved what he called "the trading part" of the Company and was known to comfort employees complaining about their jobs with the slightly incongruous sally: "How would you like instead to be a vice-president of General Motors in charge of designing tail lights?"

A graduate in liberal arts and law from McGill University, Murray volunteered for the Royal Canadian Navy and served as a corvette signals officer, then joined External Affairs and was almost immediately posted to the Canadian Embassy in Washington. He worked under Lester Pearson, Hume Wrong, Clifford Clark, Norman Robertson, Wynne Plumptre and John Deutsch, the intellectual giants who dominated Canada's post-war recovery, and emerged from that magic apprenticeship as both a patriot and a Liberal.†

Unable to meet the expenses of his growing family on an External

---

*Murray fitted right in with the Company's Scottish traditions, although he had been born in Winnipeg. When he was out driving, he not only tried hard to make sure that the money he put into parking meters covered only his required time, but if he miscalculated and returned before the meter had expired, he'd sit in his car until it did.

†During the 1962 general election, when the upstart Quebec wing of the Social Credit party threatened the Liberal party's bastion, Murray was watching the outcome on television in the viceregal suite of the Royal York Hotel in Toronto with a group of HBC executives. As a news flash appeared on the screen that a Créditiste had captured the traditionally *Rouge* seat of Quebec East, Murray jumped to his feet and shouted, "It's a national disgrace!"

*J.R. "Dick" Murray, Managing Director,* HBC

salary, Murray joined the HBC's fur department in Montreal and within two years was named head of the New York fur-sales operation. Thrust among the street-wise Jewish traders of Seventh Avenue, he surprised everyone, including himself, by successfully turning the HBC's auction house into a major profit centre that set the trade's pace and prices. By 1955, he had been transferred to Winnipeg as Chester's chief of staff and heir apparent.

Murray's first major move as Managing Director was his 1960 decision to purchase Henry Morgan & Company, a Montreal-based, family-owned department store with ten outlets and annual sales of $48 million. The move, financed with a rights issue and an increase in equity share capital, broke Chester's most sacred commandment that the Company not go "whoring in the East." Since Morgan's owned five shopping-centre branches, the purchase signalled the Bay's first venture into the suburbs, a move that Chester had also vehemently opposed. Morgan's staff organization and downtown store turned out to be riddled with problems and neglect, while Montreal's carriage trade, which had sustained the main store, promptly switched to shopping at Ogilvy's. "Those wheat farmers from Winnipeg moved in and catered to a wider market," Aird Nesbitt, who then owned Ogilvy's, disdainfully declared. "Now the Morgan family buys in *our* store."*

Despite its bold steps eastward, the Hudson's Bay Company retained its reputation as "the sick man of the Canadian retail business," its image tarnished by age and conservatism. There was growing evidence that the acquisition had been a desperately costly way to break into the East; $12 million had been spent to modernize its stores, and the chain had still to produce any profit. "A stroll through any Bay [department store unit] in the 1950s and 1960s indicated that the ingrained and rigid policies of the 1930s were not about to be abandoned overnight," reported James Bryant, a department store chronicler. "In a Bay store in the Boulevard Shopping Centre in the east end of Montreal, six years after the Bay had taken it over from Morgan's, the luggage department consisted of one camper's trunk and one suitcase. On them leaned a lonesome bicycle, the total stock in that category." Murray hired a top U.S. retailing consultant, Alfred H. Daniels, a former head of Federated Department Stores, to survey the scene. He found deep variances between both stores and departments. "There were no common denominators," Daniels reported. "You could have a fairly good shoe department in Vancouver, and the world's worst in Winnipeg. The Victoria store should have been sunk; it was a disgrace. None of the tricks of merchandising that had been developed in the previous decade were being used, or even heard of in many instances. They didn't know how to make a profit—the whole emphasis was on cost control. Don't spend a cent. They didn't even have records on profitability, so that prominent space in a store might be given to toothpaste and shaving cream, on which you hardly made a dime, while cosmetics, on which you can make billions, were in the rear corner or some goddamn place. The Bay had no understanding of the fashion business. They had a lot of klutzy guys who could have been there or at Rupert's Landing, and had almost no important women or Jews in the Company. Yet they had the best name in the business, and problems that were both definable and rectifiable."

One of the rectifiable factors was finally moving the Bay into the shopping centres sprouting outside Canada's main cities. The rush to

---

*A condition of the purchase was that Bart Morgan, the chain's chairman, be allowed to join the HBC board. He was welcomed, but Morgan seldom showed up, attending only 13 out of 147 HBC board meetings between April 13, 1961, and November 1, 1968, mainly the annual all-expenses-paid trips to the London annual Court. He almost never went to Winnipeg and was eventually dropped.

the suburbs had dramatically reversed the long-term dip in department stores' sales, so that by 1967, more than a third of their increased
turnover was coming out of the suburbs. Apart from the Morgan's
acquisitions, the Hudson's Bay Company's first shopping-centre
branch—a Morgan's—was opened at Eglinton Square in Metro
Toronto in 1963, but it was a further six years before the first western
suburban store went on stream, in Richmond, outside Vancouver.
That store turned a profit in its first year, but it almost wasn't built.
George Weightman, a Company marketing executive, had taken
Murray on a tour of Richmond, parts of which lie very close to sea
level and in those days had ditch drainage. "There were these wide
canals along the sides of each road, perpetually filled with water, and
every house had a footbridge for access," Weightman recalled. "After I
had been driving Dick Murray around for a few hours through the
rain between these canals, he drew himself up to his full height, gazed
at the watery view, and declared, 'As long as I'm Managing Director
of this Company, we'll never build a store in this swamp!' "*

At about this time, Murray presided over a sad historical event.
York Factory, the great tidewater headquarters on Hudson Bay where
the HBC had perfected the fur trade as a world-scale enterprise and the
base from which the first trader-explorers had set out to probe the
Company's inland empire, was turned over to the federal government
as a national historic site. The object of a major naval engagement,
invasions and bloody battles, York Factory had changed hands between the French and English ten times, eventually becoming not
only the centre of the fur trade but also the venue for the annual
meeting of the Council of the Northern Department of Rupert's
Land, the body charged with governing the greater part of what
would later become Canada. At one time, the depot had consisted of
more than thirty buildings that included a haberdashery, ironmon-

---

*The Company followed up its free-standing suburban store in Richmond by opening
later the same year its first western shopping-centre outlet at Lougheed Mall in
Burnaby, also adjoining Vancouver, and in 1973 it built a shopping mall around its
Richmond store. The failure to turn a profit at Morgan's made Murray gun-shy of any
further expansion and inhibited any move to the suburbs. The Eglinton Square store
was an exception—complete with a "parkade," which now sits useless and dilapidated.
Murray was finally persuaded to add another Montreal suburban store in Châteauguay.
It was approved by the Canadian Committee, and Murray, who was going to the United
Kingdom for the annual Court, decided to stop off in Montreal on the way and look at
the site. He was appalled by what he saw—a sparse collection of blue-collar housing
developments bordering the Mohawk reserve—and he pulled the item off the agenda for
the Board meeting in London. Châteauguay ruined his appetite for further suburban
expansion and lowered his confidence in the judgment of Bay retail management.

gery and even a perfumery, but in the 1930s all the structures but one were torn down for firewood. All that remained was the three-storey depot building, the "Big House" on the shore of the Hayes River, its hundred vacant windows yawning in the early sunsets. After 275 years of trading, the Company had abandoned the post in 1957, and now it was cutting the final ties. Even the handing-over ceremony didn't disturb York Factory's hibernation: it was conducted at Lower Fort Garry, more than five hundred miles to the southwest.

But York Factory couldn't entirely shed its heritage. The government did next to nothing with it, and the Big House started to be overrun with looters and loiterers, duck hunters who would come in off the Bay and set up bowling alleys on its main floor, using leftover cannon balls and empty beer bottles as pins. There was always the danger of fire; above all, it didn't seem right that this ghost of a wilderness metropolis should be given up to neglect and the ravages of nature. At least that was the feeling of Doug MacLachlan, a Winnipegger who had served briefly as an HBC apprentice clerk at York Factory in the late 1930s. A tight-end on the Blue Bomber championship football team of 1947, MacLachlan later ran his own fur-trading post at St Theresa Point on Island Lake in northern Manitoba, but his heart belonged to York Factory. After Ottawa took over, he became the desolate post's only permanent resident, tending the place, collecting relics (more than five thousand of them—candlesticks, strap-on skates, scissors and guns), guiding visitors, trapping to keep alive and setting up a chapel on the depot's second floor. "Sometimes you arrive at a place, and you feel as if you'd been there before," MacLachlan reminisced. "When I first got to York Factory, I knew where everything was, even the location of buildings no longer standing. It was kind of peculiar, but I felt that it should be properly protected, that there was something valuable here for the whole country." When the Canadian fur-trade historian Arthur J. Ray visited York Factory in the summer of 1982, he was discouraged by what he saw: "This summer marked the 300th anniversary of the founding of the first York Factory. At the end of each century the post has faced crises. In 1782 it was sacked and burned by the Comte de La Pérouse. In 1882 it was experiencing the trauma of readjusting to new economic and environmental circumstances. . . . In 1982 it is the heritage of the post that is threatened. Unless an aroused (and interested) public makes a concerted effort to make sure that appropriate actions are taken to save the architectural and archaeological heritage, too little will be done too late. I am not optimistic. I have a sinking feeling that the post is in its twilight years."

At the government turnover ceremony, Murray had joked about the absence of either adventure or profit in the exchange, but another decision caused a lot more harm to the Company's historical reputation. His management committee, concerned about lack of a national identity—Morgan's in the East, the Bay in the West—and a reputation for high prices and unfriendly service, persuaded Murray to hire a team of New York image-makers to come up with a solution. The result was the replacement of an inconsistent collection of mainly green signs and grey bags proclaiming in Old English script "Hudson's Bay Company" with a bright yellowish ochre designation in modern typeface that flatly stated "The Bay." An executive recalls that Murray had to be dragged along, protesting about tradition, and he personally vetoed a scheme for Beatle-influenced psychedelically coloured trucks.

By the mid-1960s, Murray had a more serious worry. His friend and mentor, Tony Keswick, decided to retire from the Governorship (though not yet the board) because, as he told friends, he would not personally preside over the Company's departure from Britain. Such a transfer had become an urgent necessity. Canadians on the British board had been officially notified on October 26, 1961, that none of the London members opposed the transfer except Keswick, who wished to go as soon as the time seemed propitious. Apart from the obvious efficiencies in having the Company run from the country where it transacted 90 percent of its business, tax considerations required the shift. At the 1965 annual Court, his last, Keswick bewailed the fact that under new British regulations on overseas trading companies, taxes on dividends would increase by about £800,000 a year, affecting shareholders' pockets in both the United Kingdom and Canada.* Having given his farewell address to the shareholders, Keswick would not allow anyone to tender him a retirement dinner as was the custom with departing Governors. He wrote to Murray that he was remaining on the board, but wanted to leave the Governorship "as quietly and as innocently as possible without any fuss whatsoever."

In Keswick's place arrived Lord Amory, destined to be the Hudson's Bay Company's last British Governor. Recently retired as British High Commissioner in Canada, Derick Heathcoat Amory had spent most of three lively decades in Conservative politics, having been

---

*Company documents revealed that in the preceding twenty years the HBC had suffered a tax disadvantage of approximately £2,500,000 by retaining its United Kingdom tax residence. If those taxes had been reinvested in the Company at 6 percent, its earnings would have been £3,750,000 higher.

minister of pensions in the post-war Churchill government and chancellor of the exchequer under Harold Macmillan. He had a distinguished military record that included twenty years in the Devon Yeomanry, where he trained as an expert in airborne warfare and during the dark days of the Second World War broke his leg in a parachute jump at the siege of Arnhem in the Netherlands. Taken prisoner, Amory was about to have his left leg amputated when the Nazi doctor noted a pin identifying the Englishman as a master of the hunt. The two men swapped foxhunting stories as the German worked to save the limb.*

Amory lived modestly in a drab sixteen-guinea-a-week bachelor flat at Marsham Court, where he ironed his own shirts and made his own breakfast, although he could have afforded much more as chairman and part-owner of a large textile firm, John Heathcoat & Company. Shy and naturally secretive, he delivered a stern lecture to Roy Hodson of the *Financial Times* for "sensationalizing" news of his appointment to the HBC Governorship because the story had run under a two-column headline.

He loved limericks and could deliver amusing speeches.† Eric Faulkner remembered the first time Amory was asked to speak at a Canadian HBC function: "We'd had about ten speeches already and everyone was absolutely speech-drunk when somebody called on Lord Amory, and to my horror he got to his feet. He had a habit of nibbling at the corner of his handkerchief and he started in his owlish way to talk about visiting our Montreal store and having had some difficulty disengaging himself from the chap who sold socks. Nobody knew how to react; there was a deathly hush, and I thought, 'Oh God, it's the first time the Canadians are seeing him. What are they going to make of him?' But he went on and on, talking about the sock salesman until some chaps began to realize he was pulling their legs, and there were

---

*The wound never completely healed, and in November 1967 Amory had an emergency hip replacement. While still in hospital, he wrote to Murray: "I am now coming to life again with a new hip designed on most modern lines—stainless steel with plastic embellishments. I shall no doubt leave a trail of sparks behind me as I stride along unless I carry a grease gun for lubrication."

†His favourite was one of his own:
  There was a young lady of Kent,
  Who knew very well what it meant,
  When asked out to dine,
  Given cocktails and wine.
  She knew what it meant, but she went.

a few titters. Soon the whole place was rocking with laughter. They made him go on for twenty minutes and after that, he had the whole top Bay executive in the palm of his hand. It was an extraordinary performance by a cunning old man."

Amory had been put in place because his influence with British politicians would grease the ways for the HBC's transfer. In that transaction, Dick Murray turned out to be an essential partner. The Canadian Managing Director had first demonstrated his political clout in 1960 when the Diefenbaker government introduced a 15-percent tax on dividends paid by branches of foreign companies operating in Canada. By quietly nurturing his contacts, Murray got the bill altered to exclude companies carrying on trade in Canada before July 1, 1867—an amendment that applied only to the HBC.

Circumstances were conspiring to accelerate the Company's trans-Atlantic shift: a 14-percent devaluation of the British pound to $2.40 made the investment in HBC shares more attractive to Canadian shareholders, and the prospect of British membership in the European Economic Community, now that the Germans supported Britain against the continuing French veto, had loosened Westminster's iron grip on the status quo. The Company's three hundredth anniversary, May 2, 1970, was chosen as the ideal symbolic date for patriation. Peter Wood moved temporarily to London and soon had all of the Company's accounting ledgers and systems transferred to Winnipeg.

At Amory's request, Joe Links did much of the preliminary negotiating with the Privy Council Office, conferring with lawyers and stock-exchange officials concerning the 92.6 percent of HBC shares then held in the United Kingdom. He recalled stalking the corridors of the Treasury—not his first visit, "but first as emissary of a former Chancellor of the Exchequer; it made a difference. The question we always asked ourselves was to whom control should be transferred, once permission was granted. To have transferred to a weak board and management would inevitably have resulted in a takeover followed by a breakup of the Company's assets, so that it would have ceased to exist. Could the Company have continued and prospered without a takeover bid, or fended one off, under the management available before 1970? We shall never know, but it did not seem likely to us. Why, then, did we not find the management we could hand over to, or go to Canada and run the Company ourselves? On this, perhaps, we shall be judged, as well as the wisdom of vesting control in a board of non-executive, part-time directors. As is so often the case with anomalous, unplanned developments, success or failure must be judged by whether they work. The HBC was certainly not a failure. For most of the twenty-five post-war years it was a success. Had we taken a different course it might have been more successful still. But the risk of failure was too daunting to contemplate."

When Lord Amory was taking the final poll on whether or not to go for transfer, he asked each board member for his views, and they agreed—but as Amory went around the table, all eyes were on Keswick, still a director and known for his antipathy to allowing the Company to leave England. The former Governor sat up a little straighter in his seat, tugged at the handkerchief in his sleeve, and in a clear, strong voice gave the verdict: "Mr. Governor, I would go. I would go *now*."*

Although double taxation was held out publicly as the main reason for the transfer, several other factors contributed to the move. Despite the British board's reservations about the quality of Canadian management, it was increasingly ludicrous to believe that an absentee board of part-timers could direct a modern retailing operation an ocean and half a continent away. It had become obvious that to stay in the race, the HBC would have to expand its retail operations significantly, which meant undertaking some serious public financing. In such transactions, the Company's dual citizenship was sure to depress credit ratings. Since no British trading company with a royal charter had ever moved abroad—and since the Canadian directors didn't really wish to lose that privileged status—some new corporate formula had to be discovered.

The man who found it was David Guest, a senior partner at Blake, Cassels & Graydon, the Toronto legal factory, who drew up a new Canadian Charter (to be granted by Elizabeth II in her capacity as Head of State of the United Kingdom and Canada) that would simultaneously keep the Company incorporated under the Royal Charter of 1670 and turn it into a Canadian corporation, subject to

---

*Keswick, who was knighted in 1972, later reminisced about that momentous day. "I had very mixed feelings. It was a bit like your child departing, you feel sad, but only momentarily because you know it's the right thing to do. I recognized that it should be done but didn't feel politically competent to handle the transfer to Canada. Politics is not my game. I'm just a dirty little merchant adventurer, with an eye on the main chance." In fact, Tony Keswick would probably not have voluntarily sanctioned the departure of his beloved Company for foreign parts in a thousand years. He retired from the board not long after the fatal vote and sold all his stock but never left the Company in spirit. Of all the modern HBC Governors, he alone magnified the grandeur of the HBC's past without using it to reflect glory on himself.

*Joe Links*

nearly all the standard provisions of the Canada Corporations Act.*
Outlining the effect of Guest's approach, Murray wrote to Amory that
it meant the "transfer is a historical move with certain economic
consequences, rather than an economic move with historical consequences." That wonderfully meaningless phrase appealed to the
Governor's sense of irony; he immediately wanted it translated into
Latin and used on the crest of the new Canadian incorporation.

Before Guest had thought through his formula, both Michael
Pitfield, the Clerk of the Privy Council in Ottawa, and Britain's
Solicitor-General, the Right Honourable Sir Dingle Foot (eldest
brother of Michael Foot, later leader of the Labour Party), had
considered transfer impossible without winding up the Company in

---

*The Queen granted a new Charter, the old one remaining but with a supplementary
charter attached. The crucial work was done by the Clerk of the Privy Council in
London. The Company's main exemption from the Canada Corporations Act was that
the HBC would never have to use the word "Limited" in its name, because it is not and
never was just another incorporated enterprise with limited liability. In his search for
precedents, Guest found that the Victorian Order of Nurses and the Dominion Drama
Festival had been granted similar privileged status.

England first, which would have disrupted its continuity, cost much in new incorporation expenses and had dire tax consequences. When initially confronted by HBC officials advocating the transfer, the two men, who up to that time had not spoken, used the same metaphor to describe why they thought it could never be done. As if on cue, they said it was not technically feasible because it would be "like trying to reverse the immaculate conception." Following that rebuff, Murray recalled going to see Pitfield with the Guest opinion. "I had never met him before, and I stumbled into his office, as I often do, without having organized my sentences, but when I showed him Guest's letter, he read it, and like Rex Harrison in *My Fair Lady* telling Eliza Doolittle that she's got it, he said, 'My God, he's right. It can be done.'"

Prime Minister Lester Pearson had written a personal letter (drafted by Murray) to Prime Minister Harold Wilson advocating the HBC's transfer, and most of the outstanding questions seemed to be resolved when a new issue came up. Sam Bronfman, acting through Harris & Partners, a Toronto investment dealer, launched a takeover attempt to acquire 100 percent of the HBC's stock. Murray met the Bronfmans' intermediary, Noah Torno, who had become a minor partner in the Seagram business when his Danforth Wines was bought out in 1948, and told him that on no account would the Canadian government countenance a takeover of the HBC. Torno backed off, but the incident triggered a series of unexpected events.*

To prevent other takeover attempts, Murray started to lobby Ottawa for a special amendment that would not allow any investor to hold more than 10 percent of the Company's stock for a five-year period. A comparable ownership rule already existed for Canadian banks, but no other private-sector company enjoyed a similar privilege. The board had reluctantly accepted the notion, but there was one holdout: David Kilgour, who had succeeded Elmer Woods as head of the Canadian Committee in 1964. President of Great-West Life, son of a judge, father-in-law of a future prime minister and a pillar of the Winnipeg Establishment, Kilgour was debonair and worldly yet obstinately ambitious. During his three decades at Great-West, he had

---

*It was not the first time the Bronfmans had taken a run at the HBC. In 1952, Allan Bronfman, Sam's younger brother, approached Governor Cooper to buy Hudson's Bay Oil & Gas for Royalite Oil, which then managed most of the family's energy investments. Cooper turned him down but described the encounter in his diary: "The Bronfmans, who began as bartenders and bootleggers, have made a fantastic fortune and they seem to buy new companies almost every day. . . . I liked him and would have asked him to lunch, but Elmer Woods has advised me that Phil Chester hated him so much, he would have been most unhappy" [May 30, 1952].

become used to behaving like a Chief Executive Officer and saw no reason to change his ways when he took on the HBC's Canadian Committee chairmanship. That quickly brought him into conflict with Dick Murray, who as Managing Director was charged with running the Canadian operation. The rift between the two men soon widened beyond repair.* Operational difficulties aside, their positions had hardened on the 10-percent ownership rule. Murray was now dedicated to achieving the five-year limit, while Kilgour had dug in at a full ten years and was personally lobbying John Turner, then the federal minister of justice, who had married his daughter Geills.

That not only subverted Murray's efforts at working through the proper Ottawa channels but also roused the ire of Amory because he and other board members were convinced Kilgour's real motive for backing the longer term was to guarantee himself a quiet decade as the HBC's first Canadian Governor. Amory had already indicated that a Canadian would be named to head the Company immediately after patriation, but no one had yet been picked. Kilgour considered himself the ideal candidate, being familiar with the HBC's Canadian workings—and being dangerously close to the end of his stewardship at Great-West Life. (Control of the Company had been purchased by Power Corporation in 1969, and Paul Desmarais, the Montreal conglomerate's chairman, was known to be unhappy with Kilgour's style of management.)

After Kilgour had been involved in several minor attempts at trying to usurp the authority of both the Canadian Managing Director and the British board, Murray's patience broke, and on February 14, 1970, he wrote to Amory requesting that Kilgour be immediately dismissed because he "had not only failed in his responsibilities as a director and as Chairman of the Canadian Committee, but had indeed violated the trust placed in him as the premier of the Canadian directors charged with special responsibilities for loyalty and cooperation with the Governor of this Company." Two weeks later Amory wrote to the Canadian Committee Chairman, demanding that he submit his resignation at a forthcoming Montreal board meeting because, as he put it, "not only is there a lack of mutual confidence between you and the Managing Director but increasingly between you and me." Kilgour refused to quit. Amory got tough. He

---

*Their relationship turned so nasty that Amory called a special board meeting in the viceregal suite of the Windsor Hotel in the autumn of 1969 to discuss the impasse. Most of the directors backed Murray. The two men reluctantly shook hands; but nothing was really resolved.

sent a cable informing the recalcitrant Chairman that if he didn't offer his resignation he would be retired involuntarily. Kilgour kept his peers on edge until the last minute. They had misjudged their man. He may have overreached himself, but he was too proud to be humiliated by the swarm of former colleagues now baying for his blood. So as the first order of business at the March 6, 1970, directors' meeting he resigned with a flourish, wishing the Company a long, happy future, and walked out.

Not quite. A week later he wrote a stinging rebuke to Amory, denying all of Murray's accusations. "We reached exactly the right conclusion," he wrote, "but I was unhappy with the 'saturation bombing' you felt was required in getting there.... There was an amusing cartoon in the *New Yorker* a few years ago of a mild little man sitting at a Board room table with about a dozen big, red-faced, blustery Directors. He was shown breaking into their debate with the remark, 'Haven't you forgotten that I own 51 percent of the stock?' Some of us at times forget that in the Hudson's Bay Company Britishers own over 90 percent." Amory, ever the gentleman, replied: "During the unheroic years in which I served in the Army, I was taught that when in doubt deploy maximum fire power! However, I hated doing it and if I did overestimate, I can only ask you to forgive me.... It was, I think, one of your fellow countrymen who said that 'the British have the rigidity of red hot pokers without their warmth.' " Both men agreed to consign their vitriolic exchange "to the flames" so that it would not, someday, turn up in the Company Archives. When Amory made that request of Murray, who had been sent copies of the correspondence, the Managing Director enthusiastically agreed. "Your 'for the fire and ashes' exchange of letters with David Kilgour was waiting for me when I got home. They are returned for shredding in Mrs. Harron's hungry little machine," he wrote to the Governor.

There remained only the matter of choosing an appropriate farewell gift to the departing Canadian Chairman. Having been asked what he would prefer, Kilgour suggested a Canadian painting and a trip to the Arctic with his wife, Mary. In response, Murray immediately set a $2,000 limit on any canvas that might be purchased and had cost accountants do runs on what kind of expense would be involved in the northern expedition. "I am not too happy to have Mr. and Mrs. Kilgour go on a working trip," he wrote to Amory, "since [his] views on the English directors are so embittered.... I would prefer to see him go on a goose hunt in our Grumman Goose."

Kilgour was not thrilled about the wild-goose chase because he was told he couldn't take Mary along, and suggested that the two of them accompany a regular northern inspection trip. That idea threw Murray into a total panic. "It is incredible," he wrote to Amory, "but he can be as difficult (almost) in retirement as he was before. He has written to request a trip to the North with his wife—we thought we had gone rather far with the Goose Hunt offer."

Murray eventually got an auditor's opinion that any northern journey by the retiring chairman would be a taxable benefit, and in a curt letter on July 8 he withdrew the offer. Kilgour replied in kind: "God forbid that I should be involved in over-generosity by the HBC. I am going north, but completely happily on my own, and a painting from HBC would, on reflection, not be something I would welcome—so please forget it."

Kilgour's stormy departure left open the issue of who would succeed Amory and become the Company's first Canadian Governor. The clear choice of board members had been Donald Gordon, the dynamic former Bank of Canada deputy governor and chairman of Canadian National Railways, who had joined the HBC board in 1967. But he died within two years of his arrival, and the Bay insiders had to look elsewhere. In 1970, after only three hundred years, the Hudson's Bay Company recognized the existence of Toronto and appointed its first director from that trading post, A.J. MacIntosh, a senior partner in Blake, Cassels & Graydon. And it was from Toronto that the majority of the British directors wanted to recruit their first Canadian Governor. He was Allen Thomas Lambert, the high-school drop-out who had joined a Victoria branch of the Bank of Toronto at sixteen and was now chairman of the Toronto-Dominion Bank. "Lord Amory approached me and it was not something you would turn aside lightly," Lambert recalled. "I would have had to give the Company at least 40 percent of my time and I wasn't able to resolve in my own mind how I could do that and still be fair to the bank." Other suggested candidates included Senator Hartland de Montarville Molson, the former chairman of his family's brewing company, and Major-General A. Bruce Matthews, chairman of Excelsior Life Insurance, but in the end the job went to yet another Winnipegger: George Taylor Richardson.

The sixth Richardson to head the family business, he was a tall, imperial man who exuded a kind of easy institutional grace. Although he seemed on the surface to be the ultimate corporate bureaucrat, whose proudest boast was how many members of his company's twenty-five-year club were third-generation Richardson employees, there was an adventurous side to him as well, known only to his closest associates. An experienced helicopter pilot, Richardson would guide his Bell Jet Ranger across the Canadian landscape, swooping down on some lonely HBC post, skimming over the nocturnal terrain of the endless prairie, following the moving lights on highways and train tracks, hopping across the Rockies, and finally, like some giant mechanical hummingbird, dip his skids in the Pacific. A Bay man even as a youngster, Richardson ran a trapline near his old family home on St Mary's Road at St Germain, near Winnipeg, catching and skinning ermine, mink and the odd coyote, which he sold to the HBC. He lived there with his elegant wife, Tannis, hunting, riding his horses and puffing his Rea Belvedere cigars—guarded all the while by a rainbow of peacocks, gugalating trumpeter swans and a domesticated flight of ptarmigan.

The governance issue having been settled (though Richardson was not sworn into office until November 26, 1970), the Canadianization of the Company moved into its final phase. The cabinet in Ottawa had stamped the terms of the transfer (including a five-year, 10-percent ownership clause) on February 26, 1970, and two months later Lord Amory had received notification from the U.K. Treasury approving the move. On May 28, the British proprietors convened at Beaver House for the last time. The HBC had been founded on May 2, 1670, in Whitehall Palace, when Charles II handed Prince Rupert the Charter, naming him and his fellow Adventurers "true lords and proprietors" of all the sea and lands of Hudson Bay and its drainage system—a grant that turned out to enclose a land empire of 1.5 million square miles, 40 percent of modern Canada plus several states of the northern United States. Now, three centuries later, the Company still mattered (it ranked fifty-sixth among U.K. firms in 1970) and, more than that, its uninterrupted existence was a reminder of the days when Britain had been great—just as its departure served notice that Britain was not quite so great any more.

"The die is cast, we're on our way to Canada!" exclaimed one of the elderly Adventurers after Amory proclaimed the transfer to Winnipeg; only four hands had been raised in protest when the Governor called for a vote. That evening, the directors adjourned to Nelson's Tavern at Greenwich, where the supply ships that ventured to York Factory had once been waved farewell. Joe Links had devised a menu replicating those early feasts; many toasts were proposed and many more were drunk, and while there may have been personal regrets, the mood was one of exhilaration. They had kept the faith, these quirky Scotsmen and their English cousins who privately respected history while publicly appearing to exist only for profit, kept the faith and dispatched the Company to its modern domicile, intact, ready to benefit from the breath of fresh life in a new world.

THAT SAME DAY IN OTTAWA, Governor General Roland Michener had been host to a small ceremony at Government House at which the HBC's new Canadian Charter was signed into law. Because the move required simultaneous proclamation on both sides of the Atlantic, there was some concern about delays. Ron Basford (born in Winnipeg, of course), who was Registrar-General of Canada at the time, asked his executive assistant, Tex Enemark, to handle the details, including the business of affixing the Great Seal of Canada on the new Charter. Enemark telephoned Louis McCann, the Deputy Registrar-General, who explained that he could get the charter from Government House, once it had been signed by Michener, and bring it back to his office to imprint the Seal, then return it for Basford's signature. "I asked McCann how long it would take," Enemark recalled, "and he said perhaps forty-five minutes at the outside, but that would have meant that the Hudson's Bay Company would have been homeless for most of an hour, so I said, 'Well, why don't you take the Great Seal up to Government House and make the impression there?' "

"Because it's bolted down," McCann replied, never having been confronted with such an order before.

"Why not unbolt it?"

"It weighs 350 pounds!"

"So, get a truck."

Although McCann firmly believed that the security of Canada depended squarely on the Great Seal's remaining bolted in place on the twelfth floor of the Canadian Building in downtown Ottawa, he did recognize that this was a special occasion and agreed—though he insisted the entire operation be classified as top secret and an armoured vehicle be rented from Brink's for the transfer. The HBC was represented at the brief ceremony by Graham Towers, the former Bank of Canada Governor who had served on the board; David Guest, the lawyer who had thought up the patriation formula, was also present. There, too, was the Great Seal of Canada, resting on top of the Governor General's writing desk, which was almost collapsing under its weight. "At this point, a noticeable change overtook McCann," Enemark remembered. "Here was a middle-level civil servant who had spent his whole life immersed in the monotony of the shuffling of the paperwork of officialdom.... Now, suddenly, there was this great national event wherein the oldest incorporated company in the world was going through the metamorphosis from being British to being Canadian, and there was Karsh's brother, Malak, taking pictures, while Louis was telling the Governor General, the Registrar-General and the former Bank of Canada Governor about where to sign. Mc-Cann became quite animated, showing His Excellency how to turn the screw on the Great Seal with such zest that I thought the desk would collapse for sure. After several attempts, the impression of the Seal was placed on the document, and the job was done."*

And that was how the Hudson's Bay Company came to Canada at last.

---

*At the date of its Canadian incorporation, the HBC's assets consisted of nine ships, three airplanes, 585 trucks, 33 large and medium-sized department stores, 218 northern stores, three of the world's largest fur-auction houses, merchandise worth $65 million, a payroll of 15,000, plus a 21.9-percent interest in 41 million acres of oil and gas rights across the Prairies. That was a considerable increase from its original stake in the country, three hundred years earlier, when the Company's total assets consisted of a leaky ketch, one abandoned canoe, three pair of used snowshoes and fourteen employees. But then it also owned 38.8 percent of Canada—compared with only .0017 percent by 1970. It took a further four years for the Hudson's Bay Company Archives to be transferred from London. Shirlee Smith, the Keeper of the Archives, was posted to London in October 1973 and supervised the transfer of 4,200 linear feet of records, which were shipped in six twenty-ton containers, divided among different ships for safety across the Atlantic. In the fall of 1974 the documents were deposited in the Provincial Archives of Manitoba, where they are housed in an environmentally controlled vault on the second floor of the Manitoba Archives Building. This significant archive is consulted by national and international scholars and the odd journalist.

*Donald S. McGiverin*

# CHAPTER 16

# McGIVERIN'S RUN

*He altered the HBC's corporate culture forever.*

ONE OF THE UNWRITTEN CONDITIONS set by London before agreeing to the HBC's transfer was that a top retailer be hired to run what had become the Company's core business. No one was more anxious to recruit the right person than Dick Murray. The managing director was a great Bay man but a lousy merchandiser. Murray's restless energy and infectious enthusiasm had guided the smooth Canadianization of the Company, but it had also burned him out. (Suffering from nervous exhaustion, he signed himself into the Mayo Clinic but soon recovered.) More dedicated to the glorious *idea* of the Company than its often grubby daily realities, he began to have trouble making decisions. He would get his staff to work up proposals for construction of a shopping centre branch, approve their submission, then take it to the board and vote against the project. At the same time, he was facing an internal dilemma about the leveraging staff accountants were injecting into the Company's balance sheets. (Borrowing charges, instead of being shown under merchandising costs, were attributed to the overall operation, which made the retailing results look far better than they actually were.)

Murray's choice to head the department stores—though he must have known he was also picking his own successor—was Donald Scott McGiverin, then a Winnipeg-based group vice-president with Eaton's, who joined the Bay as Managing Director, Retail Stores, in

September 1969. Born in Calgary (where his father spent the best part of his fifty-three years with Dominion Rubber, which later became Uniroyal) and educated in Winnipeg, McGiverin began working at Eaton's (selling men's shoes at $1.85 a day) on weekends and holidays, leaving only to earn an MBA at Ohio State. He was never good at sports. Referring to his lack of co-ordination, his father once remarked that his son "ran like a crowd." In Toronto, Donald quickly worked his way up the Eaton's corporate ladder, becoming a protégé of Chairman John David Eaton, and in 1961, at only thirty-seven, was appointed to the company's board, the youngest non-Eaton ever to be so favoured. Five years later he was transferred to Winnipeg and placed in charge of western operations.

One reason McGiverin worked so hard was his tragic home life. He married Margaret Ann Weld in 1950, and they had a son (Richard) and a daughter (Mary). In 1957, they were living just north of Toronto in Thornhill, which at that time had run-off ditches paralleling the streets. Richard, who was then four, had dressed up to celebrate his grandfather's birthday and went out to watch the water flow by. He lost his footing and drowned while his mother watched helplessly from a kitchen window. She never got over it and died eleven years later. Mary suffered from a rare disease of the spine called scoliosis that required special care including years in a body cast. Though she later fully recovered, her condition took its toll on McGiverin's spirit.

In Winnipeg, McGiverin at first had little intention of taking the Bay offer because he assumed he would have a shot at the top slot in Eaton's. But in the spring of 1969, when John David Eaton retired, his sons instead picked R.J. Butler, who was far less experienced. McGiverin took his daughter on a long European cruise aboard the *Michelangelo*, and somewhere under the Mediterranean moon decided that the Hudson's Bay Company was his destiny. That option was made considerably easier by an offer from Eaton's to work for Butler in a newly created but ill-defined post as vice-president, corporate development. "These guys were sending me east to do something I wasn't interested in," he told a friend. "I'm a sock salesman, after all. Corporate development, what's that? It probably meant dealing in property, but I did only two real-estate deals in my life—when I sold my houses in Thornhill and Winnipeg, and lost money on both—so I didn't feel qualified."

McGiverin and Murray worked well together, each glad he wasn't doing the other's job. During the next three years the Company purchased the A.J. Freiman department-store operation in Ottawa as well as 49.9 percent of the G.W. Robinson firm in Hamilton, and eight suburban stores were opened.

In the fall of 1972, after an Edmonton board meeting of Hudson's Bay Oil & Gas, Murray was called into the hotel suite of HBC Governor George Richardson and his Deputy, Alex MacIntosh, a tough Toronto lawyer named to the board in 1969.* They uncere- moniously presented Murray with a memorandum that not only listed in precise, almost hourly detail the newly outlined duties of the job he had held for thirteen years but also spelled out in humiliating terms that he was henceforth not allowed to discuss any aspect of retailing with anyone except McGiverin, and that, effective immediately, he couldn't even enter an HBC department store without McGiverin's permission. On a recent visit to Montreal, Murray had entertained at lunch a French-Canadian executive who had just been hired by the Morgan's subsidiary. It had been a friendly, welcoming gesture, especially so since Murray was the only HBC executive who could speak French, and he wanted the newcomer to feel at home. But Richardson and MacIntosh used that incident as proof of his inter- ference in the retail department. "It was grubby, grubby," Murray recalled. "So I just said, 'Oh, for God's sake, I quit.' "†

On November 17, 1972, McGiverin was appointed president of the Hudson's Bay Company. He hit the ground running. "At our first management meeting," he recalled, "we committed ourselves to be- coming the pre-eminent department store in Canada." The Company had a long way to go. The year McGiverin took over, retail sales generated per square foot of store space were a dismal $57, compared with $88 for Woodward's and $100 for Simpsons. The stores were run according to a pathetically outmoded decentralized buying and distribution system, with each major unit having its own warehouse and purchasing agents. The HBC was very much the weak sister of Canadian retailing.

A born-again pragmatist with little concern for the Company's traditional survival syndrome, McGiverin set out on a massive ac- quisition spree to establish The Bay as *the* leading national retailer. Trying to catch up on two decades of hesitation, he projected the HBC's

---

*MacIntosh's family motto is "Touch not the cat without a glove."

†Murray later became head of the government's Foreign Investment Review Agency and, later still, president of the Federal Business Development Bank. He then retired as a gentleman adventurer, dividing his year between seaside dwellings in Maine and British Columbia. But the Company is not forgotten; above the bathtub in each of his houses hangs a full-colour painting of the *Nonsuch*, the ship that started it all.

presence into suburban malls by accepting nearly every developer's proposal that came along. At the same time, he took over a major real-estate company (despite his self-confessed ignorance of the subject) and began to assemble and build his own shopping centres and shake up the HBC's oil investments in a huge gamble that almost paid off. In the decade and a half of his dominance he expanded Company sales tenfold from $502 million to $4,829 million, and even if the impact of his stewardship was muffled by the recession of the 1980s, he altered the HBC's corporate culture forever.

But the bill was staggering. McGiverin, fully supported by the board, which was loaded with financial experts, leveraged the Company to the hilt so that its once modest "blister on the balance sheet" became a festering boil. Under McGiverin, the HBC's debt grew exponentially from $70 million to $2.5 billion while the number of issued shares nearly doubled. The pain resulting from the huge debt became intense when prime interest rates peaked at 22¾ percent in September 1981.*

McGiverin's priority assignment was to create a major retailing presence in Toronto, the country's largest marketplace. One problem was that he alone among his planning staff had ever lived there, and everyone except for his comptroller (Donald Wood, who was from Montreal), was a Winnipegger, totally unaware of the Ontario city's retailing geography. "We wanted to be at Yonge and Bloor because we would then be sitting on the crossroads of the subway system," Wood recalled, "but market research was of little help because they gave us a potential sales range of $15 million to $30 million. We opted for a $60-million, 260,000-square-foot flagship department store and made the final decision in the recreation room of Don McGiverin's house on a Sunday morning in the fall of 1971, with most of us not quite sure where Bloor and Yonge actually was."† That dramatic choice meant that McGiverin himself had to move to be near his massive investment, and that in turn meant the end of Winnipeg as the Company's operational head office.

---

*In early 1973, three Canadian brokerage houses, Richardson Securities, Harris & Partners and Wood Gundy Limited managed a syndicate that floated $100 million in convertible HBC debentures. The proceeds were delivered to McGiverin in the form of a huge cheque embossed on the back of a stretched beaver pelt, certified by the Canadian Imperial Bank of Commerce (see illustration on page 343).

†The final decision on Bloor and Yonge made by the HBC board on November 19, 1971, was not unanimous. Rolph Huband, Company Secretary, recalls that "in my thirty years of attending Board and Canadian Committee meetings, almost all decisions have been by consensus with no opposition, but a vote was taken on both Bloor and Yonge and on the Freiman purchase, with three directors voting against in each case."

*When underwriters for a new $100-million debenture for The Bay made payment on July 21, 1973, they appropriately chose a beaver pelt on which to write the huge cheque. Left to right: Irwin Nightingale, Assistant Treasurer, HBC; Lionel Goffart, Blake, Cassels & Graydon; Donald Fraser, Richardson Securities; Iain Ronald, Treasurer, HBC; Peter Wood, Vice-President, Finance, HBC; Howard Bennett, Richardson Securities; Jim Pitblado, Harris & Partners; Donald McGiverin, President, HBC; Pat Vernon, McCarthy & McCarthy; John O'Brian, Harris & Partners.*

Completion of the giant Toronto unit was celebrated to the rocking cadence of the Grease Ball Boogie Band on August 1, 1974. At the official opening a week later, so many customers jammed in to inspect the first downtown department store opened in the Ontario capital in forty-four years that after two hours the doors had to be shut and escalators closed down.* McGiverin subsequently expanded the Company's national activities by purchasing the 30,000 credit-card accounts of Montreal's bankrupt department store Dupuis Frères, creating an HBC travel agency, establishing a sixty-three-outlet catalogue-store operation under the Shop-Rite banner, and acquiring 35 percent of Eaton's life insurance and mutual fund marketing agency, renamed Eaton Bay Financial Services Limited. But the most interesting non-retail diversification was the deal in 1973 with Siebens Oil & Gas.

Through a subsidiary, the Company still held mineral rights on

---

*The HBC honoured the launch by promising to donate three black beavers to the Metropolitan Toronto zoo. But the Company's trappers had done such a thorough job that none of the subspecies could be found in Canada's backwoods. Three animals were finally located at a breeding ranch near Salt Lake City, Utah. They were purchased for $200 and shipped north.

4.5 million prairie acres; but depletion allowances had run out, and McGiverin decided on a potentially more profitable—though much more risky—investment. It involved turning the HBC's rights income over to Siebens, a company then active in North Sea exploration, in return for 3.2 million Siebens shares (35 percent of the total), mainly to come from its treasury. A brainchild of Don Mackenzie, a savvy Calgary oil consultant who had joined the HBC board a year earlier, the deal caught investors' imaginations because it gave The Bay, which had money but few proven oil reserves, the chance to share in a big potential strike, and it gave Siebens, which had potential oilfields but little money, more cash for exploration.

Not long afterwards, McGiverin purchased control of Mark-borough Properties, which owned a real-estate portfolio worth at least $100 million. In a dramatic last-minute struggle with Robert Camp-eau, McGiverin outbid the developer from Sudbury mainly because hysterical Markborough shareholders wanted anybody but Campeau to buy their company. They kept The Bay in the bidding and stormed Royal Trust offices five minutes before closing to get back the stock they had already pledged to the swashbuckling financier.

Ironically, McGiverin, whose hiring as a first-rate retailer had been a condition of the U.K. directors for transferring the Company to Canada, was soon spending most of his time on corporate affairs, acquisitions and strategy, while Ronald Sheen, an uninspired executive who had been bypassed for McGiverin in 1969, ran The Bay department stores through most of the 1970s. By the spring of 1978, McGiverin had gathered around him a top-flight takeover team of financial experts including Peter Wood, John McIntyre, Iain Ronald, Donald Wood, Rolph Huband, Peter Nobbs and Douglas Mahaffy, while Marvin Tiller, aided by George Whitman, provided locomotion for the Northern Stores Division. McGiverin himself, usually jacketless, feet up on his desk and incessantly puffing on Camel cigarettes, had grown into the job, running the Company with good humour but little charisma. Dependent more on logic than emotion, he conducted the business not so much by issuing orders as by making suggestions—and repeating them if they weren't followed up. Irish in manner rather than Scottish—outgoing and breezy, not introspective and gloomy—he liked to pretend that he was really a small-town boy, hitching his pants up towards his armpits, telling stories with a grin on his lived-in face and rhapsodizing about the weekends he spent "getting a little plastered" at his "hut in a swamp" at Palgrave, Ontario. (He actually lived in a luxury apartment in the Manulife Centre in Toronto's upscale Bloor and Bay retailing district, and much preferred spending weekends at the Lyford Cay resort in Nassau, where he had a house.) One of his few eccentricities was that he never sold any of his cars, which he considered old friends. He still had his first purchase, a 1930 Ford coupe, but mostly drove his 1963 Falcon, his 1962 Cadillac convertible or the 1972 Lincoln—bought to celebrate his appointment as the HBC's president. He never got caught up in the Company's history except as a source for after-dinner anecdotes, and stoutly maintained that "you don't make money by reflecting on a glorious past. . . . There are no muskrat traps hanging from the rafters any more."

THE YEAR OF THE BIG CHANGE WAS 1978. McGiverin's acquisitive impulses reached their crescendo as, in a series of stunning corporate coups, he more than doubled the Company's revenues—as well as its longterm debt.

There were a few disposals: the sale of a minority interest in Glenlivet Distillers of Scotland to Seagrams for $6 million, realizing $4.4 million in profit; sale of the HBC's 35-percent interest in Siebens Oil & Gas to Dome Petroleum at $38.50 a share, generating a $94-million gain for a five-year hold, though the dream of striking it rich in the North Sea never materialized.

In early June, word came through from George Richardson's Vancouver office that Joe Segal, chairman of Zellers Limited, which operated cut-rate department stores, wanted to discuss some new merchandising concepts with McGiverin. When the two men met, Segal came right to the point: his great merchandising idea was to buy the Hudson's Bay Company. He proposed purchasing 51 percent of the issued shares at $28, about $7 over current market, though part of the value would be in Zellers shares. An astonished McGiverin replied that any offer would have to be for 100 percent, and all cash. Shortly afterwards, Jim Pitblado, chairman of Dominion Securities, the country's largest brokerage house, phoned McGiverin to inform him that Dominion Securities would be acting for Segal, but only if it was a friendly takeover. Then came the kicker: Segal informed McGiverin that he had consulted his associates and that a 100-percent, all-cash offer was on its way. Segal matter-of-factly confirmed that he had the necessary funds ($450 million), and agreed to meet McGiverin in Winnipeg on July 7 to complete the takeover.

The Company of Adventurers went ape. Flying to that meeting (aboard the Company's new HS-125-400 $2-million jet), McGiverin and his advisers hurriedly pored over intelligence reports they had gathered about Segal. Born in Vegreville, Alberta, he had dropped out of school at fifteen to work in the Credit Arcade clothing store in Edmonton ("a quarter down and a quarter a week"), was a labourer during construction of the Alaska Highway, then lost his entire savings in an all-night poker game. After two years in the army, he was demobbed in Vancouver and launched a small army and navy surplus outlet, starting with some naval exhaust fans built to operate through portholes. He sold them off to tailor shops willing to have round exhaust holes cut in their store fronts. Subsequently he opened a clothing outlet called Fields near Woodward's main store. That was the beginning of a highly successful western chain that later included a hardware operation (Marshall Wells). He eventually used his Fields holdings for a reverse takeover of Zellers, a Canadian variety chain that had been sold in the 1950s to W.T. Grant, a U.S. marketing giant. At the time, Canada's business Establishment thought so little of Segal that the news of his takeover pushed down Zellers' already depressed stock $2.00 to a new low of $2.50. But within two years, Zellers was in fine shape and Segal was wealthy enough to purchase Vancouver's most beautiful house.*

Before he left Toronto for the Winnipeg meeting, McGiverin had tried to find out who was backing Segal and soon traced the Bank of Montreal as the most likely suspect. When he got Fred McNeil, the Montreal's chairman, on the telephone, nearly everything McGiverin asked was met with stone-cold silence.

Finally the HBC president demanded, "May I assume that your bank is behind this takeover bid?"

"If I were in your position," McNeil replied, "that is the assumption I would make. But I didn't say it."

The Winnipeg meeting began warily. McGiverin and his advisers had concluded that only one move would defuse Segal's takeover strategy: a pre-emptive bid for Zellers.

"I recognized the Hudson's Bay Company as a sleeping giant with a tremendous, understated balance sheet," Segal later recalled. "The Company would have been the greatest leveraged buyout in history. Its breakup value was huge, except that I wouldn't have broken it up but would have maximized the value of its assets—and that meant merging it with Zellers to create the largest retailing entity in Canada.

---

*Rio Vista, his palace at 2170 Southwest Marine Drive (sold to a Singapore billionaire in 1990), had its own terraced Italian garden, waterfall, tranquillity ponds and galleried conservatory where he grew grapefruit-sized lemons and melon-sized grapefruit. The mansion itself had ten fireplaces, eleven bathrooms, a sunken ballroom, a full-sized tavern with suede walls, not to mention a banquet-sized dining chamber, a billiards room decorated in tartan, a full-scale spa and so on—all done up in a mongrel mixture of elegance and Disneyland.

*Joe Segal, principal HBC shareholder for a time*

I didn't particularly care which of the two companies emerged on top, as long as it was done."

About halfway through Segal's presentation, his financial man, John Levy, mused—as if he'd just then thought of it—"Of course the real way to do it is for The Bay to take over Zellers."

McGiverin was delighted the suggestion—which was to have been his trump card—had been made. Three months later, on October 3, 1978, The Bay bought 57.1 percent of Zellers for the equivalent of $10 a share, with Segal receiving 452,177 HBC shares and a lump of cash for his 13-percent holding in the chain. For his $76-million purchase price, McGiverin obtained control of the 155-store Zellers and the 61-unit Fields chain. The transaction temporarily made the Vegreville entrepreneur the HBC's largest shareholder; becoming the first Jewish Governor of the Hudson's Bay Company was within his grasp.

But in two months, Zellers and Segal were overshadowed by the largest deal in the HBC's history.

SIMPSONS AND THE HBC had always been one another's favourite buyout targets. They each specialized in quality merchandise, considered themselves the country's best department stores, but unlike Eaton's had no national customer constituencies. To combine the western dominance of The Bay with the eastern presence of Simpsons seemed a perfect match. Back in the 1920s, Sir Augustus Nanton of the HBC's Canadian Committee had approached Sir Joseph Flavelle on the possibility of a merger, but the Simpsons chairman declined on the grounds that he was reluctant at his age to launch new ventures. In October 1936, Philip Chester and George Allan, then running the Canadian operation, were hastily summoned to London by Governor Patrick Ashley Cooper. When they arrived, Cooper informed them he was about to complete negotiations for a merger with Simpsons and that the Toronto department store's chairman, Charles Burton, and its investment adviser (also a major shareholder), Harry Gundy, were on the way to London with the documents, ready to be signed. At a meeting the following morning, also attended by HBC director Sir Edward Peacock, Chester made a fervent plea against any such move. "I talked for about forty minutes," he recalled, "about Simpsons, the HBC Stores, the ruinous effect of the deal upon the future of HBC in Canada, and so forth. . . . As we filed out, Peacock called me aside and, putting his arm around my shoulder, said 'Don't you worry,' and left. A few days later Burton and Gundy arrived and proceeded to Hudson's Bay House to see Cooper. By accident or design, they were left in a small anteroom cooling their heels for well over an hour, saw Cooper for a few minutes, and left in a state of fury and consternation."*

The next attempt, in 1968, was much more sophisticated, involving G. Allan Burton, who had that year succeeded his brother Edgar as chairman of Simpsons, and Lord Amory, the HBC's last British Governor. Dick Murray had brought the two men together, and Amory felt quite excited by the prospect, since the combined chains would account for 22 percent of Canadian department-store sales. "There might be something really big for our old Company here," he wrote to Murray. "Anyway, if we do not like it, we can sing in Elizabethan style, 'With a hey nay ninny nonny-no!' "

Simpsons then had a market value of $280 million compared to The Bay's $320 million. In the minds of the HBC executives, there was no question whether this should be a merger; it was to be a takeover, pure and simple. Two main problems had to be overcome. The first was corporate. In 1953, Simpsons had signed an agreement with Sears, Roebuck & Company of Chicago to form a new enterprise, Simpsons-Sears Limited, which took over Simpsons' mail-order operation and launched an intensive drive to open branches in suburban

---

*The following notation appears in Chester's unpublished history of the Company: "Some years later Charlie Burton wrote the story of his business life [*A Sense of Urgency*, published by Clarke, Irwin in 1952]. He told me it contained a chapter on these events with HBC and I urged him with all the power at my command to cut this out. . . . When the book was published I was thankful to see he had done so."

malls. Among the many conditions of the partnership (which included a provision that Simpsons-Sears could not operate stores within twenty-five miles of a Simpsons outlet) was a firm undertaking that no Simpsons shares could be transferred without Sears' permission. When Burton visited Chicago, Sears executives granted him a hunting licence to follow up the possibilities but also made it clear they would retain veto power over the results.

The other problem was personal. Allan Burton, DSO, CM, ED, LLD, OSJ, KCLJ, had a proud pedigree, overdeveloped social graces and a keen sense of his own importance. His love of horses (he was Joint Master of the Eglinton Hunt for twenty-three years) led him to a commission with the Governor General's Horse Guards.* He fought with the regiment in the Second World War (winning a Distinguished Service Order on the Italian front) and later took over command.† Burton transferred his sense of military precision to Simpsons, trying, not always successfully, to operate his main store like divisional headquarters and its branches like outlying regiments—and he was not about to give up command easily. He ran Simpsons as a family concern, even though the Burtons and all the directors and senior officers together owned a mere 1.8 percent of the shares.

Burton saw The Bay offer as a way of both increasing his company's retail reach and making the combination so powerful it could never be overshadowed by Sears. The two sides decided to meet in secret on neutral ground at the Waldorf-Astoria Hotel in New York on January 15, 1969. Their venue was a large dining-room decorated like the Hall of Mirrors at Versailles, with a long green baize table down the middle and delegations seated on either side, as if they were negotiating a peace treaty. Burton had written out several "military appreciations" of the situation, and concluded that the new retailing giant emerging out of the deal should include all of the HBC's operations and be owned 40 percent each by Simpsons and the HBC, with Sears tacked on for the remaining 20 percent. The Bay executives wanted to include only their stores, combining them with those of Simpsons and Simpsons-Sears into a package—owned 40 percent by The Bay, 40 percent by Simpsons-Sears and 20 percent by the

---

*The Burtons were pivotal members of the Canadian Establishment. Their youngsters played department store together with the Eaton boys in their Forest Hill recreation rooms, running a pretend shop named the Seaton Company.

†"The war toughened me up a great deal," he maintained. "For one thing, I overcame my quite noticeable stutter. That was from talking on a field wireless sixteen, seventeen hours a day. When I first started in action, I used to have to write out every single message before I tried to transmit it."

*Simpsons Chairman Allan Burton*

Canadian public—all operating under the Hudson's Bay Company banner. Those deep differences guaranteed failure, and when it came, Burton blamed the impasse on the HBC's unwillingness to include its oil and gas holdings in the deal. In fact, the idea had been killed by Sears executives in Chicago who insisted they would not go along with any arrangement that didn't guarantee them 50 percent of voting shares.

A decade later, in 1978, coming off his successful takeover of Zellers, McGiverin examined Simpsons afresh. That had been a banner year for Burton. Simpsons-Sears was celebrating its silver anniversary, and in June he had entertained his twenty-five-year employees with a Sunday picnic at his country home. A month later he was host to an anniversary dinner for Edward Telling, chairman of Sears, Roebuck, the world's largest retailer with annual sales of $18 billion. During dessert, Burton brought up the fact that he felt his company was vulnerable to takeovers and that it might be best to move towards an outright amalgamation of Simpsons with Simpsons-Sears. Six weeks later Telling agreed, and on August 16 the merger was announced. The new company, with assets of $3.2 billion, would be Canada's seventh largest, and although Sears, Roebuck would retain a controlling interest, Burton would remain Chairman and Chief Executive Officer well past retirement age. The scheme required only the approval of the Foreign Investment Review Agency, which then had to confirm all major takeovers, before being implemented.

"There was really no alternative for The Bay but to try and buy Simpsons because had that merger been completed, Canada's retail trade would forever have been dominated by Sears," recalled HBC Governor George Richardson. "The timing was not our own, but it was now or irrevocably never, even if it extended The Bay more than we would prudently have done had the circumstances not been forced on us." McGiverin and Peter Wood were enthusiastic, but some of the acquisition team, notably Iain Ronald and Doug Mahaffy, as well as his top merchant, Evan Church, were opposed, pointing out that most of the earnings increases of Simpsons were attributable to Simpsons-Sears, while Simpsons itself had grown weary, top-heavy and unprofitable.* Martin Jacomb, a British director, strongly opposed the idea of further borrowing and the overheated expansion, although he supported the proposed takeover. Richardson phoned Russ Harrison, chairman of the Canadian Imperial Bank of Commerce, and instantly secured a standby credit line of $70 million.†

Burton had initiated the merger talks with Sears to protect himself and his family against a takeover. Watching the HBC's rampaging growth, he realized that his store might be the next target. It was. At eight o'clock on the cloudy morning of November 17, the telephone rang at Limestone Hall, the four-hundred-acre farm that was the Burtons' main residence, near Milton, Ontario. The Simpsons chairman and his wife, the broadcaster Betty Kennedy, were about to leave for Florida. "Allan," said McGiverin, "this is Don. We're going to be making an announcement this morning, and I wanted to speak to you first. Our board has authorized The Bay to make an offer for your company. The specific terms will be made available on Monday." Good soldier that he was, Burton pressed his clipped white moustache into the mouthpiece, and calmly replied, "Thanks for letting me know."

---

*Joe Segal, who was opposed to the acquisition of Simpsons and whose position in the HBC would be diluted by the shares issued under the takeover, resigned from the HBC board shortly after the deal's completion.

†An influential factor was a McLeod Young Weir report by Ray Bettridge claiming that Simpsons shares were severely undervalued, with the stock market assessing the firm as being worth $241 million ($5.13 a share) while the real value of the Simpsons-Sears stock alone held by Simpsons was $248 million—and that took no account of the department store's impressive facilities and valuable real estate.

McGiverin had actually been trying to get through to Burton for the past ten hours. He couldn't trust anyone else to place the call and seemed unable to find the number or to dial the right combination of digits when he finally got it. "What do you do?" Burton later complained to a friend. "A guy calls you up at eight in the morning and says he's going to take you over. . . . It screwed up the whole day."

Thoughts of Florida forgotten, Burton rushed downtown to confer with what he had already named his "war cabinet," which included lawyer Jim Tory, and Ian Sinclair, Tom Bell and several other top company directors. He reached Earle McLaughlin just as the Royal Bank chairman was boarding his jet for Bermuda and asked him for a $500-million credit line. McLaughlin's reply was brisk and to the point: "Canadian or American?"

Coming from the Company that had said nothing public for most of three hundred years, McGiverin's tactics were refreshing. He announced the details of The Bay's $310-million offer for Simpsons (at $8.27 a share, 27 percent over market price) on CTV's *Canada AM* and made himself constantly available to the media, which quickly became caught up in the "Store Wars" battle for control.* Each side issued earnings figures, equity and growth potentials, and lobbied hard in Ottawa to influence the Foreign Investment Review Agency.

In an imaginative defensive move, on December 11 Simpsons declared a dividend payable December 14 consisting of its entire holdings of Simpsons-Sears. This was supposed to blow the HBC bid out of the water as it reduced the value of the Simpsons shares to less than one-third of the HBC bid of $8.27 (Simpsons shares hit a low of $2.35 in December 1978). But in their haste to pay out the dividend, the Simpsons group had violated stock-exchange rules on notice of dividends and got themselves in trouble with the regulators. The Toronto Stock Exchange normally sets an ex-dividend date five days before payment, but Simpsons paid the dividend only three days after its declaration, which was clearly against the rules. Trading in Simpsons shares was suspended on December 14.†

---

*Three of Toronto's most prestigious law firms were engaged in the Store Wars battle, but with a twist. When Don McGiverin phoned Alex MacIntosh to line up Blake, Cassels for The Bay, he was sheepishly told that not expecting a Bay move, they had some months earlier agreed to represent Sears in its merger negotiations. So McGiverin recruited McCarthy & McCarthy—Peter Beattie for the corporate work and Donald Macdonald, a former Liberal cabinet minister and later High Commissioner to the United Kingdom, for government relations. Tory, Tory acted for Simpsons.

†Burton wrote in his private diary that evening: "I no longer feel in charge because there are just too many legal manoeuvres going on from several directions at the same time. We must put our faith in Jim Tory and God . . ."

On the same day, Trade and Commerce Minister Jack Horner announced the FIRA approval of the merger. McGiverin didn't miss a step, sweetening his offer (to $388 million by including the dividend as well as the Simpsons shares) and declaring he was still going after Simpsons and to hell with Ottawa.

Then, in the final hours of Sunday night, December 17, just before the hearings into the Simpsons irregularities by the Montreal and Toronto stock exchanges, Chicago torpedoed Colonel Burton. "In terms of an alternate merger proposal," Simpsons lawyer Jim Tory told a surprised group of reporters before the hearings started, "a disagreement with our American partners could not be resolved. It's a sad day for us." Burton, for once abandoning his code that the worse things are the more cheerful the commanding officer must look, could only gasp: "The toughest blow . . . a partnership of twenty-five years, out the window. . . ." He went home to Limestone Hall that night, walked among the pawing horses in his stables, watched the Canada geese bed down between the big stone house and the pond, and saw the moonlight glistening cold and blue on the icy fields. Then he went to bed but just lay there, wondering what had happened to the world of loyalty and civilized behaviour that had sustained him until now.

What had happened was not simple to explain or understand. Certain conditions had been attached to the original deal, allowing Sears, Roebuck to back out. The main escape clause stated that if any third party accumulated more than 10 percent of the merged company's stock, Sears could withdraw its approval for the merger. Burton and his family had started out owning less than 2 percent of Simpsons, and he had diluted his position by the dividend so it was entirely likely that a financial institution such as Royal Trust could—even inadvertently— accumulate 10 percent and activate the escape clause. Without Sears reversing its conditions, the deal was not feasible, and Burton lacked the clout—or shares—to persuade Chicago.

Burton and Tory did their best. The Simpsons chairman was on the phone almost constantly with Sears chairman Ed Telling, all but begging him to lift the 10-percent restriction or at least give the issue a breather until after Christmas, when the Simpsons chairman could formulate fresh defence strategies. Tory meanwhile had been calling Jack Kincannon, known in the company as "a professional son of a bitch," then Sears' chief financial officer. By early Monday morning, Tory was tracking Kincannon and several other Chicago executives on their car phones as they were driving to work, making desperate appeals to have "that damn provision" waived. "We couldn't get them to move," he recalled. "We kept postponing the hearing to ten and then eleven o'clock, but at the end I told them, 'Okay, look, if you're not going to support us, we're walking away from the hearing, and we'll take what we get.' "

What Simpsons got was the dubious privilege of running up the white flag and surrendering to Don McGiverin.

Sears insiders gave a slightly different version of this dramatic exchange, pointing out that they had used the 10-percent provision as a handy escape clause because they lacked confidence in Burton, in Canada and in the idea of trying to run downtown department stores. They were angry that under the agreement Simpsons reached with the FIRA, their voice in Canadian retailing would have been considerably diminished. Just as in 1968, they were happy to have Simpsons' management do anything it wanted—providing Chicago had the final veto power. They had used The Bay's raid as an excuse to cut their links with Simpsons, convinced that a free-standing Sears operation in Canada meant less trouble and more profit.

Allan Burton's life was never the same after that. "It's different," he wrote in his diary. "I've been my own boss for thirty years, roughly, and I think that once you're not in the public eye and not in a top position, there is a very subtle erosion of power that you didn't even dream you had. . . . I don't think wealth can buy happiness or peace of mind, or anything else. But having the means to produce situations of happiness for yourself and other people is a very satisfying thing. I can conceive being happy within a cabin. I don't need all this. I'd like to have a nice wife like Betty; and I'd like to have a good horse, and a few things . . ."

Just before Christmas, 1978, the final handover was completed. By the end of that year, Donald McGiverin had achieved his goal. The Hudson's Bay Company had become Canada's pre-eminent retailer. Now he could enjoy his new corporate stature, consolidate things, get back to walking around the floors of his stores chatting up the staff, have some fun. Little did he suspect that the Company he had built into the country's retailing giant was about to fall under the tight-fisted control of a most unexpected outsider—Lord Thomson of Fleet.

# IV FAREWELL TO GLORY

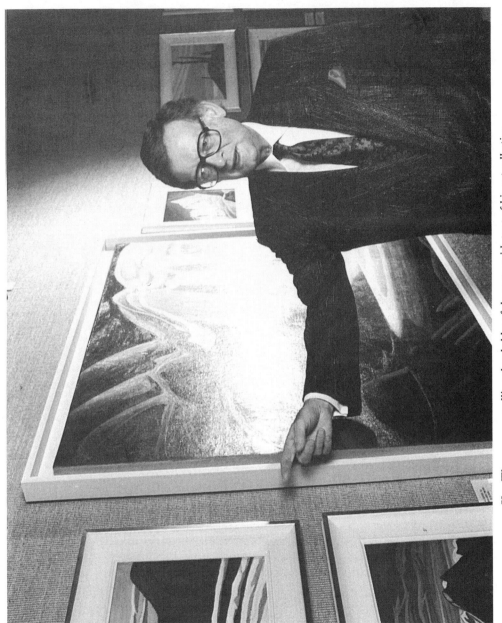

*Ken Thomson, controlling shareholder of the HBC, with part of his art collection*

# CHAPTER 17

# YOUNG KEN

*The world's eighth-richest individual . . . Thomson acts and looks*
*as if he were a small-town bank-teller living near the poverty line.*

HE SHAMBLES THROUGH LIFE, his limb movements a study in awkward-
ness, doing none of the things one would expect a man of his means
and opportunities to venture and enjoy. Deferential to the point of
absurdity—and stingy to a point far beyond that—Ken Thomson has
turned self-effacement into an art form.

His astonishing communications empire swirls about him, throwing off $4.4 million a week into his personal dividend account, em-
ploying 105,000 on four continents, and threatening to become the
world's largest media company. It already ranks fourth—after Germany's Bertelsmann, Capital Cities/ABC and Time Warner. Thomson publishes 175 newspapers (with a daily circulation of 4.5 million)
—more than any other firm—and sells an incredible 40,000 other
editorial products, including 145 magazines, 188 weeklies, and as-
sorted books, directories, newsletters and softwear packages.

There's no corporate kingdom quite like it anywhere. Besides the
Hudson's Bay Company and his publishing holdings, Thomson owns
a real-estate arm (Markborough, with assets of $2.3 billion) and an
overseas travel subsidiary that accounts for 40 percent of England's
package tour business and owns five hundred Lunn Poly "holiday
shops." He also is sole proprietor of Britannia Airways, the United
Kingdom's second-largest airline, which last year carried six million
passengers aboard forty jets. (Sixteen more are on order.) Because the

Thomson companies' debt ratios are unusually low and their credit lines are virtually unlimited, Ken is in the enviable position of being able to buy any $5-billion competitor. That would overnight make him the world's media king.

By mid-1991, Thomson's personal equity holdings were worth $7.7 billion. The July 22, 1991, issue of *Forbes*, which annually tallies the wealthy, ranked him as the world's eighth-richest individual. The listing placed Thomson well ahead of Gerald Grosvenor, sixth Duke of Westminster, who is England's richest man, and such celebrated moneybags as Italy's Giovanni Agnelli, Hong Kong's Li Ka-shing, the Gettys, the Rothschilds and the Bronfmans. He is also the richest Canadian—a reckoning that excludes Toronto's Reichmann brothers because their holdings are divided among three families.

Unlike these and other worldly figures who qualify as rich and famous—and behave as if they were—Thomson acts and looks as if he were a small-town bank-teller living near the poverty line. He spends virtually no money on himself and divulges no public clues to his private thoughts or personal motivations. Compulsively shy of personal publicity and seldom interviewed except about his art (and for this book), he would much prefer to be invisible, and he in fact almost is. "The lowest profile," he contends, "is the very best to have."

Although he seems scarcely aware of it, Thomson is caught in a time warp between the high-tech world of his communications conglomerate and the unbending Baptist ethic of rural Ontario where he simmered up. "We were raised on the principle that you kept yourself to yourself and that only the members of your close family were your true friends," recalls his niece Sherry Brydson, who grew up with Ken. "You played it close to your chest and believed that only with family could you let your hair down. Ken has taken it a step further. He's got to the point where he doesn't let his hair down with anybody."

Thomson, even in his dealings with longtime business colleagues, demonstrates that air of impenetrable reserve. It is entirely in character that his office, on the top floor of the Thomson Building at the corner of Queen and Bay streets in downtown Toronto, has a vertical moat. Public elevators run to the twenty-fourth floor, but only pre-screened and thoroughly vouched-for visitors are allowed into the private elevator that ascends to the twenty-fifth level, shared by Ken Thomson and John Tory, his chief corporate strategist. Thomson's office houses part of his art collection, including most of the 204 canvases by the Dutch-Canadian artist Cornelius Krieghoff that he owns—hanging there, looking about as comfortable as nuns in a discothèque.

Gathering Krieghoffs is Ken Thomson's most visible dedication,

*Ken Thomson and his hero Hank Snow (centre)*

but his real cultural hero is a somewhat less exalted artist in a very different discipline: Clarence Eugene "Hank" Snow, the Nova Scotia-born country singer. Thomson regularly visits Hank at the Grand Ole Opry in Nashville, owns all his records, has been to Snow's house in Tennessee, and once presented him with a gold Hamilton pocket-watch that had been a family heirloom.

Ken Thomson's psyche is so difficult to penetrate because he behaves like an accomplished actor, able to detach himself from whatever crisis might be occupying his mind. Occasionally, very occasionally, a show of passion will flicker across his shuttered face, only to be withdrawn quickly, like a turtle's head back into its protective shell. Exceptions to his customary reticence come unexpectedly.

A FEW SEASONS AGO, Posy Chisholm, a sophisticated and vivacious Toronto socialite who looks smashing in hats, has a profoundly developed sense of the absurd and possesses a remarkable memory, found herself at Heathrow, about to board British Airways Flight 93 to Toronto. When she spotted Ken, the two acquaintances decided to travel together, though Chisholm had to trade down a class, wondering why Thomson was too cheap to travel in style and comfort.

"You know why I'm flying home?" Thomson asked, when they were settled in their narrow seats.

"No, I don't, not really," Posy replied.

"To give Gonzo his evening meal," the press lord matter-of-factly explained. "I've been away from my dog for five days now, and I miss him so terribly. We were half an hour late leaving London, and I'm really nervous they might give him dinner without me."

"Oh, Ken," Chisholm tried to reassure her agitated companion, "they'll make up time across the ocean."

"Gonzo is crazy in many ways, but very, very lovable," Thomson went on as Posy, crammed into steerage beside the fretting billionaire, began looking longingly down at the heaving Atlantic. "Gonzo is the sweetest dog. He's everybody's pal, especially mine. He's a Wheaton terrier, the colour of wheat, off-white. Actually, he's got a little apricot."

"How about some champagne, Ken? No? Oh well . . . "

"Gonzo leads a good life. I plan my trips abroad around him. I never go to annual meetings unless I've got him covered. I couldn't put him in a kennel; he's a member of the family. He seems to have an understanding of what's happening all the time. We communicate. We know what the other is thinking. We love each other."

"I suppose you take him walking . . ."

"Oh, I take him out all the time. Early in the morning, late at night, and every time I can in between. If I can't get home for lunch, my man goes up and walks him. He might be there right this minute. Gonzo's got to have his exercise."

"Doesn't he have a garden?" asked Posy, grasping for relevance.

"He doesn't want to stay out all day. Gonzo's a people dog. He likes walking in the park and then he wants to come back inside."

It was going to be a long flight.

Chisholm remembered a friend's joking that if she was ever reincarnated, she wanted to come back as Ken Thomson's dog. So Posy told him, hoping the idea might amuse the single-minded tycoon.

"Well, she'd be well looked after," was the serious reply. "I tell you, Gonzo's a big part of my life. I know that sounds awfully funny. But it's a fact. I think of him all the time. I look after him like a baby."

"What about your wife—does Marilyn love Gonzo too?"

"One time, I was looking at Gonzo, and I said to Marilyn, 'Geez, he wants something.'

"She said, 'We all want something.'

"'Yes, but he can't go to the refrigerator and open the door. Gonzo can't tell you he's got a pain in his tummy. We've got to look after him, anticipate everything he wants. It might be a bit of food he needs, maybe to go out or just a show of affection.' "

At this point Thomson leaned forward to emphasize the significance of what he was about to reveal. "I tried to figure what Gonzo was really after," he confided. "It's a game we play."

"So, what did Gonzo end up wanting?" Posy Chisholm halfheartedly inquired—purposefully fumbling under her seat, hoping that was where they kept the parachutes.

"A bikkie!" exclaimed the world's eighth-richest man. "That's what Gonzo wanted—a bikkie!"

There followed a lengthy silence. Thomson seemed satisfied there was little point trying to top that remarkable bit of canine mind-reading.

About half an hour out of Toronto, he started to get restless because the 747 had been unable to make up the original delay and was not going to arrive at 1735, as scheduled. He put on his coat and complained so bitterly he might miss getting home in time for his dog's feeding that Chisholm suggested she take his luggage through customs and drop it off at his house—while he dashed through the terminal, bound for Gonzo.

KEN THOMSON SIGHTINGS ARE LIKE THAT. If he knows and trusts the person he's with, he will talk about his dog or his art collection, but that's it. He leaves few contrails. "The smartest thing those who have more than anybody else can do is not to flaunt it," he says. "It's resented and it's in terribly bad taste. It shows a poor sense of priority.

"Everybody has their own ways of doing things," he allows. "It's all a matter of temperament. A lot of people who make money fast spend it fast. It's very difficult to live a simple life and love your dog as much as I do. I spend as much time as I can with my family, walking Gonzo, watching a fair bit of television. I like to get in my car and fill it up with gas. So if you add up running the business with all the personal things I do, there's not an awful lot of time and energy left after that. I am as happy as can be."

Walking your dog and filling your car with gas may well be the path to eternal happiness, but those who know Thomson best insist that he is not as content as he claims. "He's not a man doing his choice of things," insists his niece. "If he had two or three brothers, he would never have chosen—or been chosen—to run the family empire. I get the impression of someone doing his duty. He is intensely loyal and was very attached to his father, so when my grandfather said, 'I'm going to start a dynasty and you're going to carry it on,' Ken said, 'Right.' It didn't really matter that he might have preferred to be the curator of an art museum—and now he's training his son David to take over, just as his father wished. He's doing it with good will but not much joy. Every morning when he wakes up he must say to himself, 'I'm unhappy being a businessman, but wait a minute, it's bringing me all this other stuff like my art collection that I couldn't otherwise have—so it's a trade-off.' "

Everything Ken Thomson says and does is to underline that he's fundamentally decent, that he would be quite happy to have his epitaph read: "What a Nice Guy." He *is* a nice guy, but he is much more than that—and despite his pose as the ultimate *innocente*, his self-assurance can be devastating. For instance, he readily conceded in early 1980 that "there is a limit to how many papers one man, or company, should own," insisting that his own firm had yet to grow to such "ludicrous" extremes. "We will know ourselves if and when we do," he reassured the dubious commissioners on the 1980 Royal Commission on Newspapers. Thomson then controlled one of the largest concentrations of press ownership in any democratic country.

The best evidence of Ken Thomson's success in perpetuating his anonymity is that most Canadians, even fairly sophisticated business-men, still regard him as the youthful and untried inheritor of the publishing empire built up by his father, Roy Thomson. They dismiss the current press lord as "Young Ken," an immature figurehead whose main accomplishment was to be his father's only son.

"Young Ken" is in fact sixty-eight years old. "I'm not young any more, but I don't really mind being called 'Young Ken,' " says he. "My dad was such an unusual individual that nobody can expect to be anywhere near a carbon copy of him. He was one of a kind. He channelled his ambition in a single direction and everything ema-nated from that. Now it's a different world we live in."

Ken has force-fed his father's business empire from annual reve-nues of $725 million in 1976, when he took over, to $11.5 billion a decade and a half later. The total equity value of the companies he controls has sky-rocketed from less than $1 billion to more than $11 billion, exponentially surpassing Roy Thomson's impressive rate of annual growth.

In 1989, following sale of the Thomson Group's North Sea oil holdings for $670 million, its publishing and travel assets were com-bined into an umbrella organization (the Thomson Corporation). Ken uncharacteristically boasted that it would allow him to set his sights on any target. "I can't imagine any publishing company anywhere in the world that would be beyond our ability to acquire," he gloated.

KEN THOMSON LEADS A DOUBLE LIFE, and enjoys neither. In England—
and most of non-North America where titles still mean something—
he is Baron Thomson of Fleet of Northbridge in the City of Edinburgh, the peerage bestowed on his father on January 1, 1964, two
days before he lost his Canadian citizenship for accepting a British
title. "I regret giving up Canadian citizenship," Roy Thomson said at
the time, "but I had no choice. I didn't give it up. They took it away
from me. They gave me the same reward you give a traitor. If I had
betrayed my country, that's the reward I would get—taking away my
citizenship. Canada should allow titles. If you get a title from the
Pope, there's no trouble accepting that."*

During their visits to England, Lord and Lady Thomson live in a
four-bedroom flat (purchased for £90,000 in 1967) in Kensington
Palace Gardens, off Bayswater Road.† A secluded street with extra
police protection, this is where many of the ambassadors to the Court
of St. James's have their residences. While abroad, the introverted
Ken and Marilyn Thomson of Toronto are transformed into the
introverted Lord and Lady Thomson of Fleet, using their titles, with
two sets of clothing and accessories as well as stationery and visiting
cards. "I lead a dual life and I'm getting away with it," Thomson
declares. "It actually works."

One place it doesn't work is in the House of Lords. Ken has never
taken up his father's seat in Westminster's august Upper Chamber,
nor does he intend to. The older Thomson glowed with pride the day
he received his title. After celebrating by queuing up at Burberrys for
a cashmere coat reduced from £75 to £40, he had his official coat of
arms‡ carved on his office door, and when one elderly London
dowager persisted in calling him "Mr Thomson," he barked,

---

*Roy Thomson turned down Prime Minister John Diefenbaker's 1959 offer to appoint
him Governor General of Canada. "It wouldn't have suited me very well because I'm
too much of an extrovert for that," Roy declared at the time. "I can't conceal my feelings
very easily. I talk too much, everybody says, but I talked myself into more deals than I
ever talked myself out of, so I'm still ahead of the game. At any rate, it worked out for the
best. Since then, I've got a hereditary peerage. And I'm a Knight Grand Cross of the
Order of the British Empire, that's a GBE, which is the highest degree of the Order of the
British Empire. That entitles you to be 'Sir.' If I hadn't got a peerage I'd be Sir Roy, so
I'm right at the top of the heap."

†During the Second World War the flat was used for interrogating high-ranking
Nazi officers.

‡It features the bizarre image of a beaver blowing an Alpine horn under the motto,
"Never a Backward Step."

"Madam, I've paid enough for this goddamn title, you might have the good grace to use it."*

Having been elevated to the House of Lords, Thomson seldom attended its sessions and didn't particularly enjoy it when he did. "I've made a lot of money, but I'm not the brightest guy in the world, by a hell of a long ways," he once commented. "I've found that out since I've been in the House of Lords. About 90% of the things they discuss there, I'm a complete ignoramus about. I've got a one-track mind, but I bloody well know my own business."

"For Dad, the title symbolized what he had achieved from nothing, and he made me promise I wouldn't give it up," Ken recalls. "He told me he'd like to see me carry it on because he rightly suspected I was the type of person who might not want to. I remember telling him, 'Well, Dad, I think you're a little naughty to ask me to do that. Because everybody should have the right to make his own decisions in this world. But after what you've done for me, if you really want me to, I'll make you that promise.' Now, I didn't promise him I'd use the title in Canada or that I'd take up my seat in the House of Lords. So now I'm happy to have it both ways."

Another of the inheritances from his father was the attitude that while making money was holy, spending it was evil. The Thomson style of penny-pinching—father and son—goes well beyond sensible parsimony. "Nobody has any sympathy for a rich man except somebody that's richer again," Roy once ruminated. "I mean, hell, I eat three meals a day and I shouldn't. I should probably eat two. And I only have so many suits of clothes, and I'm not very particular about my dress anyway, and I can't spend, oh, not a small fraction of what I make, so what the hell am I doing? I'm not doing it for money. It's a game. But I enjoy myself. I love work. I like to be successful. I like to look at another paper and think, Jesus, if only that was mine. Let's have a look at the balance sheet."

Roy Thomson's approach to spending was best summed up in the marathon bargaining sessions he staged when he was renting space for his Canadian head office at 425 University Avenue in downtown Toronto. The landlord, a promoter who had a Scrooge-like reputation of his own to uphold, despaired of reaching any reasonable rental agreement because Thomson's offer was so far below rates charged for

---

*The reason for the granting of a title is never promulgated, but in Thomson's case it was thought to have been mainly for his initiative in donating £5 million to establish a foundation to train Third World journalists. It is still active and recently helped revive the *New China Daily*.

*1st Lord Thomson of Fleet*

comparable space elsewhere. When the press lord finally wore him down, the building's owner gasped in reluctant admiration, "Mr Thomson, you really are cheap!" To which an indignant Roy Thomson responded, "I'm not cheap! You're cheap! I'm cheap cheap!"

The photographs of the original Lord Thomson weighing his baggage so he wouldn't have to pay extra on his economy flights across the Atlantic, going to work on London's underground, or lining up for cafeteria lunches created a comic mask that somehow took the hard edge off his business deals. His outrigger spectacles, with lenses as thick as Coke-bottle bottoms, magnified his glinting blue eyes as he peered at the world with Mister Magoo-like good humour, hiding his touch of icy cunning. Thomson carefully cultivated the image of himself as the living embodiment of the profit motive on the hoof. Seated next to Princess Margaret at a fashion show, he spotted a lamé gown on one of the models. "My favorite color," he told the Princess. "Gold!" During Thomson's much-publicized 1963 encounter with Nikita Khrushchev, the Russian dictator teasingly asked what use his money was to him. "You can't take it with you," said Khrushchev. "Then I'm not going," shot back a determined Thomson.

Ken Thomson's scrimping habits are equally mingy, if less well known. Although he is a member of six of Toronto's most exclusive clubs—the York, Toronto, National, York Downs, Granite and Toronto Hunt—he prefers to have lunch by himself at a downtown yogurt bar, if he's not home walking Gonzo, that is.* He does most of his shopping on department-store bargain days. Murray Turner, a former HBC executive who knows Thomson slightly, was shopping in the Loblaws store at Moore and Bayview when he heard a shout, "Murray! Murray!" and saw Thomson beckoning to him. As he reached the side of the world's eighth-richest man, it was obvious that Thomson could hardly contain himself. "Lookit," he exclaimed, "lookit this. They have hamburger buns on special today. Only $1.89! You must get some." Turner looked in disbelief at Thomson's shopping cart, and sure enough, there were six packages of buns, presumably for freezing against a rainy day. "I'd walk a block to save a dime at a discount store," Thomson readily admits. On the same day he spent $641 million on a corporate takeover, Thomson met George Cohon, the Canadian head of McDonald's, and asked him for a toy Ronald McDonald wristwatch. Cohon sent him one of the free timepieces (used mainly for internal promotions), but the very next day Thomson's secretary was on the phone claiming the watch had gained four minutes over the past twenty-four hours and asking where His Lordship could get it fixed. Cohon ordered another watch sent to him, but the messenger had strict orders to bring back the original gift.

The press lord appears to dress well (his shoes are from Wildsmith's on London's swank Duke Street), but his suits are made for him by a cut-rate tailor in Toronto's Chinatown at $200 apiece from the discounted ends of bolts he picks up during his journeys to Britain. He lives in a twenty-three-room mansion behind a set of handsome gates at the top of Rosedale's Castle Frank Road, built in 1926 by Salada Tea Company president Gerald Larkin. A prime example of Ontario Georgian-style architecture, the dwelling is run down, its curtains left over from its first owner. The Thomsons (Marilyn's parents live with them in a coach-house) usually eat in the kitchen to save electricity, and the family is unable to retain housekeepers because of the low pay. Even the help's food is rationed. Most cookies are kept in a box with the Thomson name lettered on it. A strict

---

*He occasionally frequents fancier restaurants but takes the uneaten portions home in a Gonzo-bag.

allocation of two of Mr Christie's best is placed on a separate plate to feed the rotating parade of disillusioned cleaning women.*

Thomson owns a Mercedes 300-E but usually drives his ancient Oldsmobile ("it clunks around but it's the car that Gonzo prefers") and once purchased a red Porsche turbo. ("Honestly, not one of my more practical expenditures. I was thrilled at first but I hardly use it—I've probably driven not more than twenty-five miles in it this summer." The car is for sale.) The Thomsons never entertain and seldom go out. When they do, preparations include discreet calls to find out precisely what other guests have been invited, whether any-one will be smoking or drinking, how soon they might comfortably leave, and so on.

The world's eighth-richest man is one of the country's most reluc-tant philanthropists. When Toronto-Dominion Bank chairman Dick Thomson (no relation) and Fred Eaton, head of his family's depart-ment store chain, called on Thomson to solicit funds for the Toronto General Hospital, a favourite Establishment charity, they were warned by a mutual friend that the only way they would get any money was to pledge construction of a veterinary wing to treat Gonzo. They thought it was a joke, and came back almost empty-handed.

There has been much argument among his headquarters staff over how much cash Ken Thomson actually spends per week. Some insiders claim it's twenty dollars; others insist it's at least forty. No one bids any higher. He has credit cards but seldom if ever uses them. "It's an idiosyncrasy," says John Tory, his chief confidant. "It's just very difficult for Ken to put his hand in his pocket and spend money. Yet he's extremely kind and generous. When we're rushing to a meeting and we're late, if he sees a blind man, he'll stop, miss a couple of lights, and help him cross the street." Tory didn't need to add that the blind man gets no money. Thomson himself won't discuss his spending habits. "I agree with my father that you should use only a small portion of your money on yourself and that you have some kind of obligation to do something useful with the balance. He thought the most beneficial thing you could do with money was to invest and reinvest it, to keep it growing—and so do I."

---

*Besides the London flat, the only other Thomson residence is in Barbados, where he owns the Southern Palms Hotel. To maximize profits, Ken and Marilyn stay in a third-floor walk-up apartment whenever they visit instead of occupying one of the more luxurious main-floor suites. Toronto travel impresario Sam Blyth has occasionally booked them aboard West Indies cruises on a travel agent's discount.

Ken's only excursion into philanthropy was his successful 1982 effort to have Toronto's premier concert hall, the magnificent structure designed by Arthur Erickson, named after his father. He gave $4.5 million to the project, the largest donation ever granted the performing arts in Canadian history. "Dad would have been thrilled," he says. "I'm so proud to hear it on the radio sometimes— Roy Thomson Hall, my dad's name being mentioned—or see it in the *Globe* and *Star*. He was born on Monteith Street and loved Toronto. He even tried to use Lord Thomson of Toronto as his title, but the government wouldn't let him." Still, a cultural—especially musical— edifice hardly seemed an appropriate monument. "I could do without culture," Roy Thomson once confided. "I haven't got any, particularly. And I could do without art. I can do without the theatre. I can do without all these things. . . . Some people love culture. They live on it. They appreciate it and I rather envy them in a way. But, not for me. My favorite music is about the level of *Gigi*. I like tunes like the 'Blue Danube' waltz, 'Sailing Down the River,' and *South Pacific*."

The naming of Roy Thomson Hall caused a furore. Of the $39 million required to finance the building's construction, $26.5 million had been allocated by the federal, provincial and municipal governments; a further $12.5 million had been raised from corporate donors and individuals. The Thomson contribution was a welcome but hardly essential windfall to be used for future improvements, which to many minds did not warrant naming of the hall after Roy. Accountants quickly calculated that the magnificent gift would not cost Ken very much. The $4.5-million donation was divided into five annual instalments of $900,000, paid through a Thomson subsidiary. As well as saving Thomson $450,000 a year in deductible taxes, the delayed instalments earned annual interest of more than half a million dollars at the high rates prevailing at that time, leaving the benefactor to scrape up only $2 million.*

THE SAGA OF ROY HERBERT THOMSON, the Toronto barber's son who quit school at fourteen to become a five-dollar-a-week clerk and in 1931 leased a fifty-watt radio station in North Bay, Ontario, and another later at Timmins—so he could sell the radios he was lugging along country roads—is one of the sustaining legends of Canadian capitalism. Less well known is the way the hardships of the Great Depression

---

*That's not all. When they attend Roy Thomson Hall concerts, Ken and Marilyn regularly phone down for free house seats—and get them.

permanently imprinted themselves on generations of the Thomson clan. "I'm still horrified by people who don't make soup stock out of meat scraps," says Ken's niece Sherry, who spent her youth in the communal Thomson home at Port Credit, just west of Toronto. "And if you were making a custard with three egg yolks, you could have knocked me over with a feather the first time I saw a woman throw the egg whites down the drain. That just wouldn't occur to me; the whites are tomorrow's dessert. You used everything and got into the rhythm of making your own jam and freezing your vegetables."

The Port Credit household, which for a time included not only Ken but also his sisters, Irma (Sherry's mother) and Phyllis Audrey, and most of their children, was run according to stern, puritanical precepts. "Granddad loved us very much," Sherry recalls, "but the affection was always very gruff. It was a staunch, didn't-come-from-much kind of family, so that signs of affection came out almost by accident, as asides." It was a stern upbringing. She remembers her mother being locked out by Roy, the family patriarch, if she ventured home after midnight. This was not when Irma was a teenager but well into her thirties, divorced, with a nine-year-old daughter, and dating again. Luckily the family had German shepherds and a dog porthole had been cut into the sunroom door. Irma's dating partners still recall having to push her, 1940s dirndl and all, through the dog door after their goodnights. "They could only do that in the summer," according to Sherry, "because in other seasons, the ground got too wet. When I became a teenager I was locked out by my mother in turn, and had to climb up the trellis."

Young Ken had attended elementary school in North Bay, where he worked summers as a disc jockey in his father's radio station, CFCH. His main job was to play background noises meant to evoke the crowd sounds and clinking glasses of a ballroom, while big-band dance numbers were on the air, but he also fell in love with the music of Hank Snow and dreamed someday of actually meeting him. When the family moved to Toronto, young Ken was enrolled in Upper Canada College. After an unsuccessful year at the University of Toronto, he joined the Royal Canadian Air Force but was never promoted beyond Leading Aircraftman, the equivalent of an army lance-corporal, spending most of his time as an editorial assistant on *Wings Abroad*, a propaganda weekly. He took his discharge in London and spent two years at Cambridge, though the university had no discernible effect on him. After spending a year on the editorial staff of his father's Timmins *Daily Press*, he moved back to Southern Ontario where Roy Thomson had acquired the Galt *Evening Reporter* as one of four dailies he picked up in 1944. His five-year apprentice-ship there was an important formative influence, as were the week-ends he spent at the Port Credit house.

Roy Thomson had moved to Scotland in 1954 but returned to the family homestead in summer and at Christmas. The elder Thomson held court while watching the TV set in front of him, listening to the radio beside him, petting the Scottie dog at his feet, eating fruit with a little paring knife, all the while reading a murder mystery. Ken loved frightening his nieces and nephews, especially when they slept in garden tents during the summer. "He'd put a sheet over his head and ghost us," Sherry recalled. "Or he'd hide behind a bush and make fake owl noises. But we always knew it was him and we'd yell, 'Oh Kenny, stop it!' He was very much the tease."

By the late 1950s, Roy Thomson had not only acquired the prestigious *Scotsman* but had also won control, in what was the world's first reverse takeover bid, of the huge Kemsley chain that included London's influential *Sunday Times*.* Roy's lucky streak broke in 1967, when he acquired *The Times*, Britain's great journal of record.† *The Times* may not have lost its lustre under Thomson, but it lost him bags of money.

Thomson had by this time become a fixture among British press lords. He could always be depended upon to say something mildly outrageous and to pose for yet one more photograph showing off his skinflint habits. "They say business is the law of the jungle," was a typical sally. "I think it's the law of life. . . . If you want to prosper, you've got to be ambitious. . . . You've got to be ready to sacrifice leisure and pleasure, and you've got to plan ahead. I was forty years old before I had any money at all. But these things don't happen overnight. Now how many people are there that will wait that long to be successful, and work all the time? Not very many. Maybe they're right. Maybe I'm a bloody fool. But I don't think I am."

American tycoons J. Paul Getty and Armand Hammer ap-proached Thomson in 1973, offering a 20-percent share in their Occidental consortium preparing to drill in the North Sea where Phillips Petroleum had already found valuable indications. Roy bet his family's (as opposed to his company's) fortune on the play, though

---

*At about that time his daughter Irma had to canvass funds from neighbours to get the roof of the Thomson house fixed because Roy refused to spend the money.

†The extent of *The Times*' authority was best summed up in a *Punch* cartoon, depicting a secretary walking into a British company president's office to announce: "Sir, the gentleman from *The Times* and the press are here."

oil was then worth only $3.60 a barrel. When Occidental struck the giant Piper field and later the Claymore—and prices climbed to $14 a barrel—Thomson almost overnight earned $500 million.

By 1976, Roy Thomson was in his eighty-second year and not at all well. Ken, who by then had married a graceful model named Nora Marilyn Lavis, had been brought across the Atlantic to assist the old man.* "Most people would say, 'I wouldn't want to do what you've done, even for your success,' " Roy reminisced in one of his last interviews. "They'd say, 'You've missed a lot out of life and success hasn't made it all worthwhile.' But it has to me. It's just a matter of ambition and determination, you keep plugging away. I learn more from my failures than I learn from my successes, because I learn bloody well not to do them again. Nothing has ever happened to me in my life that hasn't been for the best, now I accept death. I lost my wife. I lost a daughter, but those things, I mean, you can't measure them in terms of happiness or success or failure. I'm a very imperfect individual, and I've done a lot of things I shouldn't have done, but I honestly am not a person who caused anybody any suffering if I could help it."

Henry Grunfeld, former chairman of S.G. Warburg, the London merchant bankers who had helped finance Thomson, remembered his last conversation with Roy in the bank's Terrace Room at its Gresham Street headquarters. "It was about three weeks before his death and we both knew it was the last time we would meet. He told me he was worth about $750 million, or whatever it was, and complained bitterly how much he wished he could have made a billion. 'Why, haven't you got enough, Roy?' I remember asking, especially since he was so obviously very ill. He looked surprised, as if he had never considered the question, and shrugged, 'Henry, it's just for the fun of it . . .' It was pathetic."

Thomson died on August 7, 1976, and Ken was suddenly in charge. His father had passed away both too soon, because the younger Thomson was not ready to take over, and too late—because Ken was by this time fifty-three years old and had spent most of his adult life following his father, a tactful step behind like a commercial version of

---

*Theirs is a wonderful marriage. But Ken seems to be deferential at home as well as the office. In an impromptu 1988 telephone exchange with a reporter from the *Financial Post*, Thomson admitted that he saved barbers' bills by having his wife cut his hair, but made the transaction sound curiously self-demeaning. "My wife made me have it cut commercially lately," he admitted, "but if I behave myself, she'll do it for me. I'd just as soon have her cut my hair. Nobody does it as nicely as Marilyn. The cost is for me to be nice to her for a few days."

Prince Philip. Inheriting a father's business is difficult; succeeding an individual as powerful and articulate as Roy Thomson—recognized as a folk hero of capitalism—was impossible. Ken tried valiantly to turn himself into an extrovert but soon conceded that it was a mission impossible. "The nice thing about my dad was that he was so unusual. No one in his right mind could expect me to be the same. I'd be happy to go unnoticed. I've tried to be a good, sound businessman in my quiet way, but I can't say I've been a slave to business. I've tried to strike more of a balance between my personal and business lives." His father's friend and adviser, Sidney F. Chapman, summed up the situation more succinctly: "When you live in the shadow of a legend, you don't go flashing mirrors."

Ken's first major decision was to cut family ties with *The Sunday Times* and *The Times*, where union problems had forced suspension of publication for eleven months. During their stewardship the Thomsons, father and son, had poured £100 million into the properties without any significant return. Their loyalty to those great institutions without any apparent fiscal controls was totally out of character. Thomson sold the two papers for the value of the land and buildings to Rupert Murdoch, and gradually moved his businesses back to Canada.

The company owned forty-three daily and eleven weekly Canadian newspapers at the time. They ranged geographically from the Nanaimo *Daily Free Press* on Vancouver Island to the *Evening Telegram* in St John's, Newfoundland. What they had in common, apart from ownership, was a blandness so pervasive that no self-respecting fish could bear being wrapped in one of their pages. "Disliking Ken Thomson, let alone detesting him, is wholly impossible," confessed Richard Gwyn, a leading Canadian commentator who once worked for him. "He radiates niceness from every pore, down to the holes in the soles of his shoes. He's self-effacing, shy, unpretentious, soft-spoken. He peppers his conversations with engaging archaisms, like 'golly' and 'gee whiz.' But then you stop feeling sympathetic, because you realize that his innocence is just a synonym for timidity. And you realize at the same instant that the reason Thomson newspapers are bland is that they are led by the bland."

The Thomson operational code had been set down by Roy but it didn't initially change much under Ken. Both Thomsons regarded editors as expendable eccentrics, and Clifford Pilkey, then president of the Ontario Federation of Labour, once called their company "a vicious organization, certainly not compatible with what I describe as decent, honourable labour relations."

Reporters did not receive free copies of their own newspapers, and earnest bargaining went on to deprive delivery kids of half a cent in their meagre take-home pay. Most positions had fixed salary limits, so that anyone performing really well would inevitably work himself or herself out of a job. In pre-computer days, Thomson papers sold their used page mats to farmers as chicken-coop insulation and Canadian Press printers were adjusted from triple to double spacing to save paper. Each newsroom telephone had a pencil tied to it, so there would be no wasteful stubs floating around. "God help us if they ever realize there are two sides to a piece of toilet paper," one publisher was heard to whisper at a management cost-cutting meeting. In a thesis he wrote for the Carleton School of Journalism, Klaus Pohle, the former managing editor of the Lethbridge *Herald*, documented the Thomsonization of his former paper and coined the name for a sadly relevant and increasingly frequent process.

In January 1980, Thomson had used some of his North Sea oil proceeds to purchase, for $130 million, a major Canadian newspaper chain, FP Publications Limited, but that projected him into new and unfamiliar territory. FP had fielded an impressive Ottawa news bureau under the inspired direction of Kevin Doyle (later the editor of *Maclean's*) that included such stars of Canadian journalism as Allan Fotheringham, Walter Stewart and Doug Small. The bureau regularly beat the Parliamentary Press Gallery to the news, but it didn't fit in with Thomson's usual barebones operation. When FP's Edmonton bureau chief, Keith Woolhouse, who was working out of his one-bedroom apartment, asked for a wastebasket, that was enough to trigger the cost-efficiency instincts of Thomson's executive vice-president, Brian Slaight. Doyle tried to defuse the situation by offering to send out an extra wastebasket from the Ottawa office.

"Is it excess to the Ottawa bureau?" Slaight, ever the champion of independent editorial control, sternly demanded.

Doyle, about to break the news of Prime Minister Pierre Trudeau's resignation, calmly replied, "Well, if you mean, do we need it, no, we don't."

At last, a triumph for head office. Slaight could barely contain himself. "We have a truck that goes from Ottawa to Toronto to Winnipeg, then on to Edmonton. If we put the wastebasket on the truck, it will hardly take up any room, and won't cost us a cent!"

So the wastebasket journeyed jauntily across the country, and it took only a week and a half to reach its destination. But the Edmonton Bureau's troubles were far from over. Woolhouse wanted to rent an office and needed furniture. Slaight vetoed the initial $1,600 estimate but later approved a bid of $1,100 from a local repossession centre.

That didn't save Woolhouse. He permanently blotted his copy book by purchasing his pens and paper clips on the open market instead of from the repossession house. The Edmonton bureau was soon closed, as was the entire FP news operation.

The FP purchase had also thrown the Thomson organization into the unusual position of having to operate newspapers against local competition, especially in Ottawa, where its *Journal* was up against the Southam-owned *Citizen*; in Winnipeg, where its *Free Press* was head to head with Southam's *Tribune*; and in Vancouver, where its *Sun* had to compete with Southam's *Province*. That ran strictly against Thomson's publishing philosophy, which perpetuated his father's dictum that what's important "isn't the circulation of one's own newspaper, it's the circulation of the opposition's. Even second-largest is no good. Only the largest is worth buying." The dilemma was neatly resolved on August 27, 1980, when Southam's closed the Winnipeg *Tribune* while Thomson shut the Ottawa *Journal*—throwing eight hundred employees on the street—and Southam's bought out Thomson's interest in the *Vancouver Sun*. The Ottawa move was particularly puzzling because the *Journal*'s circulation had climbed 25 percent in the previous six months and its advertising linage was the highest in eight years. But looking back on that Black Wednesday, Thomson wouldn't change a thing. "Nobody likes to see people lose their jobs," he says. "We didn't take any satisfaction in that. But the situation at the *Journal* was hopeless and it was never going to get any better. We couldn't give the paper away for a dollar. We tried nine different buyers. Nobody else wanted it. Somebody had to draw the curtain. So when Gordon Fisher of Southam's told us he was going to close his paper in Winnipeg, he suggested we close them both on the same day. I thought it was a good idea because I knew if he closed his paper first, people would come to me and ask, are you going to close yours, and I didn't want to lie to them. So when he said, 'Why don't we do it the same day?' I said, 'Oh boy, we'll be in real trouble—but let's do it.'"

Trouble came in the form of a Royal Commission, headed by Tom Kent, a former *Economist* and *Winnipeg Free Press* editor, who labelled the Thomson publications as "small-town monopoly papers [that] are almost without exception, a lacklustre aggregation of cash-boxes" and suggested the organization be forced to sell its flagship publication in Toronto, the *Globe and Mail*, purchased in 1980. The recommendation was not followed up, but the hearings brought into the public consciousness Thomson's utilitarian code of editorial independence. "We run our newspapers in a highly decentralized manner, delegating operating authority to publishers," Ken Thomson told the Commission's opening session. "We have vested in our publishers the responsibility and the autonomy to decide what news, information and comment should be published daily in their newspapers." That was true enough, and there was no more eloquent witness to that philosophy than Harold Evans, the former editor of both *The Times* and *The Sunday Times*, who wrote in his memoirs that the difference in ownership between the Thomsons and Rupert Murdoch was "a transition from light to dark." Neither of the Thomsons have, in fact, cast much of an editorial shadow over their publications. The problem is that editorial budgets ultimately decide any publication's content, and that was— and is—how the Thomsons exercise control. Since the Kent hearings, John Tory has impressively improved both the quality of Thomson papers and the working conditions under which they're produced.

The severest test of Thomson's hands-off attitude was the *Globe* story about the newspaper closings written by Arthur Johnson, quoting the press lord's heartless comment on the plight of those who had lost their jobs: "Each one has to find his own way in this world." Johnson firmly stuck to his version, but Thomson categorically denies having made the comment. "I explained for twenty minutes how we had gone way beyond our statutory obligations in severance arrangements, but that we were not prepared to see the company's assets dissipated because we didn't have the guts to face up to the flak. I never said anything about everyone having to make his own way in the world, even though that quote will go down in history with me. I would never say that. I know I'm not brilliant, but even I can figure that one out." He didn't phone the *Globe* to complain, but six weeks later he met publisher Roy Megarry at a Royal York Hotel reception and let him have it. "Jesus, Roy, the *Globe* misquoted me terribly," he complained. "They put the worst words in my mouth. I never phoned you about it, but I wish I had."

"Geez, Ken," Megarry replied, "I wondered at the time why you'd make such a statement and I talked it over with the editor involved, but he insisted that you had said it."

"You'll have to take my word for it. I didn't. I'm not that stupid."

Megarry, who persuaded Thomson to invest $65 million in turning the *Globe* into a national newspaper, insists there has been no editorial interference from the Thomson head office, a few blocks away. "It's one thing to own the Barrie *Examiner* and not interfere editorially," he says. "It's another to own the *Globe* in the city where you reside and resist the temptation to put on pressure. But they

*Southam's Gordon Fisher consoles*
*Ken Thomson during the 1981*
*Royal Commission on Newspapers*

haven't." On Thomson's sixtieth birthday, Megarry edited a special
one-copy issue of the *Globe*, substituted on his doorstep for the real
thing, that had a front page with Ken's picture on it and several
feature stories about Gonzo. "That morning, Ken did phone me,"
Megarry recalls, and said, "'What are you doing, you rascal?'—he
frequently refers to me as a rascal—and admitted he had been
stunned, because for a split second he thought it really was that day's
*Globe*. 'It was a cute thing to do,' he told me, 'but I hope it didn't cost
the company too much money.' "

DURING THE LATE 1970S, Ken Thomson enjoyed a unique problem. With
oil prices up to as much as $34 a barrel, his share in the North Sea
fields purchased by his father was throwing off annual revenues of
$200 million. That's not the kind of sum you keep in a savings
account. Tax reasons plus the wish to get into hard assets dictated new
acquisitions, but the chain had run out of cities, towns and even
villages where they could maintain monopolies. Thomson went shopping for a safe, timeless investment for his family.

While on a flight to London, John Tory passed over to Ken an annual report of the Hudson's Bay Company, with the comment, "This is one you should think about." That struck Thomson as a weird coincidence because he *had* been thinking about The Bay, ever since Fred Eaton at a party had mentioned that the HBC was lucky because so much of its profit flowed from non-merchandising sources. "It was like mental telepathy," Thomson recalled of the airplane conversation.* At first glance, the Hudson's Bay Company seemed a perfect takeover target. It certainly carried the kind of historic pedigree that would please a British-Canadian lord, it was widely held with no control blocks that would have demanded premium prices, and it was a well and conservatively managed enterprise, ideal for the Thomson habit of acquiring companies that turned decent profits without requiring day-to-day involvement. "It looked to me like a business that in the inflationary environment of that time would do quite well, because the top line was pushed up by price increases while many of the costs, including store leases, were fixed," John Tory recalled. "Also I knew that Simpsons, which they had just taken over, was not well managed, so that a turnaround would have impressive bottom-line results."

On March 1, 1979, Ken Thomson and John Tory called on Don McGiverin to announce they were bidding $31 a share—36 percent over market value—for 51 percent of the Hudson's Bay Company. At The Bay's board meeting two weeks later, Governor George Richardson reported that in a meeting with Thomson the previous Sunday evening he had failed to persuade him to buy less than 51 percent. The board decided that the premium offered for control was not high enough and that $37 to $40 would have been a more appropriate amount. That consideration was aborted by the sudden entry into the bidding of grocery magnate Galen Weston, offering $40 for the same percentage, though part of it would have been payable in stock. Unlike Thomson, Weston hinted that he intended to fire most of the HBC executives, replacing them with his own.

In typical Establishment fashion, the first telephone call Thomson received after word of his intended takeover leaked out was from Fred Eaton. "I wish you luck. Welcome to the world of merchandising." The second was from Galen Weston, advising him of the competing

---

*There is another theory why Thomson settled on The Bay. He walked Gonzo most often through Craigleigh Gardens, near his Rosedale home, and at night the most visible object from the shrubbery is the ochre neon sign at Yonge and Bloor, announcing "The Bay! The Bay!"

bid.* By April 2, Thomson and Tory had raised their bid to $35 for 60 percent of the HBC stock. Weston countered with an improved offer ($40 for 60 percent), but once Thomson came in with an unconditional cash offer of $37 for 75 percent of the shares—$276 million more than he had originally been willing to pay (although for 75 percent of the shares rather than the original 51 percent)—the bidding was over. The Bay board met on April 4 to approve the takeover formally. The Thomson group made only three demands: a pledge that its equity position wouldn't be diluted by the issue of extra treasury shares; two seats on The Bay board for Thomson and Tory; and alteration of the Company's banking arrangements so that the two banks on which they sat as directors—the Toronto-Dominion and the Royal, which had financed the deal—could get some of the business. There was so little board discussion on these issues that when Richardson pointed out it was Don McGiverin's fifty-fifth, the directors burst into "Happy Birthday."

Ironically, this all happened just five weeks short of the ten-year limit that Canadian Committee Chairman David Kilgour had wanted to include in the Company's patriation arrangements. "I don't like all this bloody publicity," was Ken Thomson's only public comment.†

KEN THOMSON DID LITTLE TO ENJOY his position as the HBC's proprietor, neither becoming its Governor nor taking part in any of its rituals. One exception was a summer journey he took to Baffin Island and Hudson Bay with his wife, Marilyn, two of their children, Lynne and Peter, and George Whitman, the Company's Vice-President of Public Affairs, a Second World War pilot who had fought in the Battle of

---

*It was a project the fathers of both men had desired. Galen's father, Garfield, had purchased 200,000 HBC shares in preparation for making his own bid, just before he died; Roy Thomson had told his sidekick Sid Chapman and his granddaughter Sherry that he someday wanted to own the Hudson's Bay Company.

†There was one strange incident in the takeover. George Richardson made a personal profit of more than $15 million by buying—through his own firm, Richardson Securities—1,059,800 shares of HBC stock in twenty-one separate deals between February 6 and 23, 1979, at an average price of $22.50, nearly $15 below the amount for which he traded them in six weeks later to Thomson. "Lucky George," as he quickly became known, defended his amazing good fortune and the Ontario Securities Commission cleared him of any wrongdoing. But he was worried enough about accusations of insider trading that he devoted half his speech as Governor before the 1979 annual meeting to defending his actions.

Britain and had since earned a cross-Canada reputation as a social animator. They had just finished lunch at Ross Peyton's tiny hotel at Pangnirtung, on Baffin Island, and Whitman was relaxing on a small rise overlooking the town when up puffed Marilyn and said, "George, I want to do some shopping at that co-op you told me about. You got any money? Here I am, married to the richest man in the country, and he won't allow me to have any credit cards or anything like that. Can I borrow a hundred dollars? But don't tell Ken about it."

Whitman peeled off the bills and she skipped off down to the co-op. Just as she disappeared from view, as if on cue, the world's eighth-richest man came up the hill with the same request. "George, I want to go up to the Bay store and buy some fishing tackle. Can you lend me a hundred dollars?" Later that day, as they were fishing, Ken began to eye Whitman's down-filled vest so wistfully that the Bay man finally told him to take off his Eddie Bauer finery and slip it on. "If you like it, it's yours," Whitman offered, happily expecting to agree with Thomson's refusal. Instead, the press lord held out his hand and said: "Let's shake on it." And that was the last Whitman ever saw of the vest that had been his Linus blanket on many a northern expedition.

Later that day something significant happened, best recorded in Whitman's diary: "We were fishing on the Kulik River and I had gone back to the boat with a double handful of char, when I heard Paul McIlwain, one of our pilots, shouting: 'George! George! Marilyn's hurt bad!' She was down between two river rocks and had a deep cut between her eyes and down her nose. I pulled my shirt and T-shirt off and bound up her head in them. I carried her to the boat where we met Ken and our Inuit guide. We started across the mile and three-quarters of iceberg-studded water to the first-aid station at Pang, Marilyn in the bow, weeping and still in a state of shock. Me on the motor, Ken amidships and the old Inuk, in front with Marilyn, telling her a story.

" 'In the Kulik River, there's a big mother fish,' he was saying, 'but this year the fish was going to die and there would be no more char in the Kulik. But today you put some of your blood in that river and the mother fish is going to live and we'll always have char.' Having used a little applied psychology, the Inuk moved back and stood between Ken and me. He gave me a nudge with his elbow and, pointing at Ken, asked: 'He good man?'

"I didn't reply for about fifteen seconds because to have given a token response to a deeply personal question like that would have been perceived as flippant. So I waited, and then said, 'Yes, he's a very good man.'

"The Inuk, who was one of Pang's elders, turned to Ken, and carefully crafting his thoughts, said: 'You don't go home. You stay. We take boat, we go down Kingnait Fiord. You come. You catch big char, see polar bear, caribou. We live on the land. You stay with us, my wife, my family, George too.'

"Ken was absolutely mesmerized. He tried to mumble something, but nothing came out. He leaned over and whispered to me, 'Does he really mean it?'

" 'Of course he means it.'

" 'Well, I can go anywhere. I can go anywhere in the world for a holiday.'

" 'Yes, but Ken, there are things that money can't buy. You've just been paid the most tremendous compliment that one man can give another. He's offering to share his life with you.'

"Poor Ken," Whitman noted in his journal, "that kind of generous gesture was completely outside his conceptual frame of reference —that some person from another culture would comfort his wife with a beautiful little made-up fairy tale and pay him the highest tribute that a person in a tribal society can extend to someone who comes from away. . . ."

IF THERE IS ONE SANCTUARY where Ken Thomson can find peace it's in the private world of his art objects. Within these hushed precincts he can build his own aesthetic universe, indulging his whims without the budgetary problems that inhibit most collectors. He richly deserves his reputation as the premier collector of *habitant* scenes by Krieghoff (some selling for as high as $275,000), all of them magically revivified by one of England's best restorers. "He knows every picture the artist painted or attempted to paint and is constantly improving his collection," according to the Earl of Westmorland, a director of Sotheby's in London. "He's got a great eye and a passionate love of art," echoes Christina Orobetz, the president of Sotheby's Canadian company.

The best of his Canadiana collection (conservatively estimated as worth $20 million) is now displayed in a 5,000-square-foot gallery on the top floor of Toronto's main Bay store. "I've reached a plateau," he says. "I've got my collection basically together and have reached the point where I can be very selective with gathering my *objets d'art*." They include the only wood carving Michelangelo ever did, stunning boxwood and ivory carvings and some incredible miniatures by Octavio Jenilla. Death is a recurring theme of his collection, which includes any number of realistically rendered skulls—the carving of a sleeping child using a skull as a pillow, the tableau of a starving wolf being strangled by a skeleton, and a pearwood skull hinged to reveal a miniature Adam and Eve on one side and the Crucifixion on the other. The most unusual—and most treasured—objects in his collection are the ship models carved by French prisoners in British jails during the Napoleonic era. They carved to keep from going insane in their dungeons but had few tools or materials, so most of the hulls are fashioned out of the bones of their dead, the rigging braided out of their hair.

As with most enterprises, Ken Thomson's art collection is not exactly what it seems. It's controlled by Thomson Works of Art Limited, a company owned by his three children so the increase in value of the collection will be exempted from taxes on his death. The Krieghoff paintings offer their owner an extra incentive: every Christmas, Ken lends one or two canvases to Hallmark, which sends him free Christmas cards bearing the imprint of his painting in return. "They give me a thousand cards free and another four hundred wholesale," he admits.*

IN RUNNING HIS COMPLEX OPERATION, Thomson of course enjoys the advantages of proprietorship, so that he can be wrong without triggering any adverse consequences. He also has the supreme luxury of belonging to a dynasty, so that financial results— good and bad—can be spread over generations instead of having to meet quarterly projections. The HBC's stock values didn't climb back to their original purchase price for more than a decade, but there was never a thought of liquidating or seeking other drastic remedies. "We never have to keep looking over our shoulders at people taking over any of our companies," John Tory points out. "Even when we make major acquisitions that have an initially negative impact on our profitability, in the longer term we'll have a broader base on which we're able to grow. It's really that simple."

Not quite. Tory's real function in the Thomson hierarchy is a source of constant conjecture within and without the organization. "I'm a professional and I never worry about my image," Tory says. "As a business person you can have too high a profile and there's no upside to that whatsoever. When we bought the Hudson's Bay Company there was a big fuss, but we didn't say much; when it was

---

*The Thomson Christmas card list has carefully noted beside each name the year when it will be removed from his mailings.

down for the count we said even less; and when it recovered we said nothing." Tory refuses to play the Bay Street game. "I don't need the kind of glory others seek," he says.

It's too easy to speculate that John Tory is the brains behind Ken Thomson, because that wouldn't be fair to either of them. Thomson is smarter than that and Tory is not that self-effacing. As president of most of the family holding companies, Tory exercises enormous influence. He acts as a kind of secretary-general of the $11-billion corporate confederacy, prodding, solving, appointing, acquiring, divesting, trouble-shooting—running the damn thing—but never quite making the ultimate decision by himself. He is not exactly a surrogate because when he speaks no one knows whether it's really with his voice or Ken's. Veterans of the Thomson organization know that it's usually both, and leave it at that.

Tory reads at least two books a year that have nothing to do with business, loves to parse balance sheets, is happy to work sixteen-hour days, plays some golf and tennis, and skis, but when a friend asked him to go sailing discovered he didn't own a suitable short-sleeved shirt. The centre of his life is his family—four super-bright children (John, Jennifer, Jeffrey, Michael) and ten grandchildren. He plays a mean "After You've Gone" on a barrel-house piano and dabbles in bridge, but his most serious hobby is keeping up with his wife, Liz, Toronto's shrewdest and busiest social animator. As well as his Thomson responsibilities he is a director of Sun Life, Rogers Communications, Abitibi-Price and, for the past twenty years, the Royal Bank of Canada. "If you asked almost anyone on the Royal board who was the most brilliant guy there," says former deputy chairman John Coleman, "they'd say John Tory. He asks the most pertinent questions and can see through a deal most quickly."

Thomson himself doesn't just admire Tory; he worships the man. "If you take the best qualities of the best people in all the different fields of business and roll them into one—that's John Tory," he says. "It's the same pleasure for him to work, the way I collect paintings and walk my dog. Above all, he's got a great wife, family and good friends. They have fun together."

That emphasis on family governs Thomson's own life. "He has so much love and affection with the family and Gonzo," says his son David, "we get so much pleasure just seeing him and trying to make him happier." David likes to quote the maxim of Meyer Guggenheim, the Swiss-born American industrialist who maintained a family dynasty by handing each of his sons a stick and asking him to break it. Each did. He then gave each a bundle of sticks, which none of them could break. "Stand alone, and you will be broken," he told them. "Stand together and no one will break you." The Thomson family very much sticks together; they are proud and protective of one another, especially in tragic circumstances.

Just two weeks before Christmas 1990, Gonzo died.

"I've had the loss of dear ones, human beings," Ken lamented, "but I've never experienced anything that shook me more than his death. Gonzo slept with me the last night. I held the little guy in my arms and I thought, I can't really stand this. I left the room and then I thought, no, he really needs me. I've got to be there. I felt him expire. I don't want ever, ever to go through such a thing again . . ."

*John Tory, Ken Thomson's chief strategist*

# CHAPTER 18

# Disaster and Deliverance

*"There are no merchants here.
You're all a lot of bookkeepers."*
> —Harvard Professor Walter Salmon,
> speaking to an HBC executive think-tank

FOR MOST OF THE FIRST TWO YEARS after they had attained control of the Hudson's Bay Company, Ken Thomson and John Tory were ecstatic about their new purchase. Contrary to everyone's expectations, they seldom intervened in board decisions, and Thomson evidenced no desire to become the Company's Governor. "I'm not on any ego trip," he said after George Richardson left the post and was succeeded by Don McGiverin. "I've got so much in my life that I'm grateful for and so much to be occupied with, that I don't need or want to be Governor. The future of the Company is largely in Don McGiverin's hands. He's an awfully nice guy. Nobody could represent the Company better. I'm much happier to have him do it than myself."

Thomson and Tory joined the board but, with one exception, seemed happy merely to be consulted, their input limited mainly to deciding the extent of dividend payouts and monitoring major capital expenditures. The exception was Tory's concern about Simpsons. The first item on his agenda was to advise McGiverin to merge the twenty-three-unit department-store chain with The Bay.* "We're absolutely delighted with our long-term investment ... happy with

---

*Had Tory's advice been followed, $500 million in operating losses and $600 million in interest carrying costs over the next decade might have been avoided.

management and very hopeful the year's results will be quite satisfactory," Tory told the *Financial Post* in 1979, when the Company's operations showed a net of $104 million on sales of $3.4 billion.

By the early 1980s, inventory was turning over more slowly and interest rates had started to climb. That was a serious matter. The interest payments necessary to cover the $2.3-billion debt McGiverin and his board had incurred expanding the retailing empire quickly overwhelmed every other balance-sheet item. By 1982, The Bay had moved into a serious negative earnings position (a net loss of $128 million), and at a directors' meeting on June 22, Tory finally stepped in. "We can't keep growing by incurring more and more debt," he warned the board, threatening drastic measures if there was no bottom-line improvement by the end of the year.

What Tory came to realize was that the Company's management had become obsessed with expanding its share of market at the expense of profit. The quest for greater sales became a *jihad*. The Company, which had once confined its special pricing to semi-annual Bay Days, launched Super Dollar Days, In-Store Warehouse Sales, Big Deals, Scratch and Save Days, Price Blow-Outs and quarterly Bay Days each of which lasted two weeks. Customers reacted by cherry-picking the merchandise that was deeply discounted (up to 50 percent) and passing over the items with big mark-ups. To heighten the impression of a stock of bargain goods that had to be moved quickly, stores were over-inventoried; the typical sales floor looked like an untidy warehouse, with merchandise left in cartons to block the aisles. As they were picked over, the items usually spilled onto the floor, where they were trampled on—or stolen.* The pressure to produce advertising flyers promoting the many sales grew so intense that their pages were crammed with mistakes. A four-page HBC flyer published on August 20, 1989, for example, contained thirty-seven errors that had to be corrected in subsequent newspaper ads.

Such tactics proved costly in terms of both immediate profit and the HBC's long-term reputation. Richard Sharpe, who then ran the competing Simpsons-Sears (later Sears Canada) chain, reacted by issuing orders that his company would not even try to match the HBC price cuts. "We ignored them," he says. "They were giving the goods away and losing pailfuls of money. We lost some market share, but we

---

*There was a story going the rounds of Toronto's fashion district about the sales manager of a dress supply house, who told his staff, "There's a Bay buyer coming in this afternoon to see our line; lay it out on the floor, so she'll know what it will look like when it gets into the store."

were *making* money." Still, no expense was spared in trying to pump up the HBC's sales totals, which in 1984 had climbed by $1.4 billion since the Thomson purchase—while earnings of $104 million for 1979 had turned into a loss of $107 million in 1984. When one high-ranking Company executive defended that strategy of continual growth and praised the merits of spreading overhead costs through continual expansion, Tory shot back, "You can't eat market share—and you can't eat overhead, either." Not being a retail merchant, Tory didn't really know what was possible in the department-store trade, but he did know that as desirable as a growing market share might be, profit was much better—particularly since current cash flows were not enough to service existing debts.

FOR A TIME, THE COMPANY was barely under control, lacking direction or sensible forward momentum. Its executives had been taught how to expand the business, not how to change it. The Company's troubles were so serious that everyone was looking inward to prevent collapse, instead of outward to trigger resurrection. Most of the organization men who were moved in to run various departments had the necessary know-how, but they lacked soul. Walter Salmon, who taught retailing at the Harvard Business School, said as much, addressing the HBC's executives at a 1982 think-tank. "The problem with this company," he declared, gazing at the gathered suits, "is that there are no merchants here. You're all a lot of bookkeepers."

Sir William Keswick, the retired British Governor, observing the tribulations of his beloved Hudson's Bay Company from his retirement at Theydon Bois, shook his head in disbelief: "We handed over the Company in apple-pie order, and they went wild with it. If you borrow money at a certain percentage and invest at half that percentage, sooner or later it doesn't work. That's sort of elementary. But that was what they did."

"They imbued the staff with the notion that fiscal accountability was the highest virtue, and forgot that retailing is really showbiz," complained Shirley Dawe, a brilliant marketer who had joined the HBC as a trainee and rose to be a vice-president. "Don McGiverin had a wonderful rapport with everybody," she fondly remembered, "but he kept getting further and further away from the action."

One problem was The Bay's inability to keep up with the changing tastes of Canadian consumers. The Company still behaved as if its main competitors were other department stores when retailing was being fragmented in new directions, with specialty marketers such as

Dylex, the Grafton Group, Leon's, The Brick and thousands of imaginative independents winning sales. Despite the Herculean efforts to raise it, between 1978 and 1984 The Bay's market share of Canadian retail sales actually declined to 5.3 percent from 5.7 percent—while profits plummeted at the same time. The Company did a lot of silly things, such as abandoning its pharmacy counters, which may not have produced an especially high gross (9 percent) but had been great traffic builders. Some areas—like the cosmetics department at the Winnipeg store with its $12-million face-lift—were overbuilt; others, such as the untidy, often filthy main floor in the Victoria store, were ignored. "If there is an example of abrogated opportunity in the history of corporate Canada," concluded a 1983 study of the HBC by Toronto's Yorkton Securities, "surely it is the Hudson's Bay Company."

The HBC became so obsessed with cutting costs that the basic rationale for its department stores—friendly service and a wide selection of merchandise—was lost. The Bay stores switched almost entirely into soft goods, emphasizing fashion at a time when more and more families were nesting in their homes, stocking many of the hard goods the HBC was abandoning. Even the fashion-driven clothing business faced an uncertain future. "Nobody knows what women want to wear any more," commented Marilyn Brooks, a leading Toronto fashion designer. Service at most Bay stores became virtually non-existent as thousands of knowledgeable and loyal employees were laid off and part-timers took their places. The temporary substitutes may have been untrained and disinterested, but unlike permanent employees they cost the company no pensions, paid statutory holidays, vacation times or other fringe benefits. Barry Wilson, manager of The Bay at Yonge and Bloor in Toronto, reported a 43-percent staff turnover at his store in 1987.

It was not always easy for Bay management to dismiss longtime employees. One of the mainstays of the downtown Vancouver store, for instance, was Helen Carson, who had managed the wool department for twenty-eight years and had a large following of local knitters. The Bay wanted to fire her because her salary had reached the maximum, but that would have cost a considerable severance allowance. Since she refused to quit, she was transferred to the children's wear department, where she had to move heavy boxes. Carson eventually injured her lower back and had to resign for medical reasons, leaving behind an untended—and unfrequented—wool department. Lynn Scully, who successfully built up the same store's book department, had taken great pride in her work. "My grandfather was a fur trapper and the whole family was excited when I got the job. We loved The Bay and I remember when it was a prestige store and people would actually come in just to buy our shopping bags." But Scully left, as so many other department managers did, because not only had unrelenting cost-cutting made effective merchandising impossible but the Company had also turned into an impassive and uncaring bureaucracy. In her last year at The Bay, Scully was reporting to *nineteen* different managers.*

All through this time, the head-office bureaucracy continued to balloon. D.G. (Pete) Buckley, a Bay vice-president, once burst into McGiverin's office to dramatize the point. "Look, Don," he told the Governor, "when I first arrived at your head office, we had an internal phone directory five pages long. This one, published today, has two hundred pages and that doesn't include the whole data-processing group. We've got a problem."

"I was absolutely appalled by many of the attitudes and directions within the HBC," recalls David Thomson, Ken's elder son, who was training on the job in the HBC organization at the time. "There seemed to be a distinct separation between the people who felt themselves visionaries and the line operators facing the customer. The latter were less involved in the decision-making process, which in fact they were funding. The world was turned on its head. The system had come to a great human impasse."

Pierre Mignault, a brilliant merchandiser and later president of the Price Club of Canada but then head of the HBC's Quebec region, felt a similar frustration with "the grids of people coming at me from all angles out of that humongous Toronto head office. It was unreal. You didn't even know who to call about anything important. The Company became too big and too fat and didn't have the human-resource structure to handle its rapid expansion." Mignault experienced a good example of Bay bureaucracy in 1983 when the roof of the Place Vertu store started leaking. He had to put twenty buckets on the

---

*Many people left the Company with understandable bitterness, none more so than Mark Blumes, who later started the successful Mark's Work Wearhouse chain. Blumes had been forced out of his job as a junior manager at the Calgary store because his many ideas and ambitions didn't fit the HBC mould. This diverted him from his objective of becoming the youngest—and only Jewish—senior executive of The Bay. He was not pleased. "For many years afterwards," he recalls, "if I felt a little lazy, and was thinking, 'Geez, I'm not going to bother opening up in Quebec,' or something like that, I'd drive down to the Bay store and just ride the escalators. The hate would wash over me and would fuel up my emotions, remembering all the times I had answered the page 'Blumes, call 555,' only to have my nose rubbed in it. So I'd come back and tell my staff, 'Let's go for it!' "

shop floor to catch the water whenever it rained, but couldn't find the appropriate vice-president in charge of fixing leaky roofs. Even though the local fire department temporarily closed the store because of the danger of the ceiling's collapsing, Mignault never did get head office to sanction repairs to the building. He gave up the attempt after a year and ordered it done on his own. "Of course it cost much more than it would have originally," he recalls, "because after a year of dripping water, the carpets had to be replaced and I had to buy huge fans to get rid of the musty smell. It was awful. It was embarrassing."

To offset the neglect and losses, the Company launched an internal money-raising program that took the form of disposing of the balance of its Simpsons-Sears stock for $211 million to Sears, Roebuck, realizing a $48-million profit, and cashing in—for $455 million—the 7.7 million preferred shares in Dome Resources it had received in 1981 on the sale to the Calgary company's parent of its remaining interest in Hudson's Bay Oil & Gas.

That Dome transaction was a milestone in Canadian business history, because it was ultimately responsible for the toppling of the high-flying Calgary energy company and its even higher-flying chairman, Jack Gallagher. Dome had grown from a one-man operation in the early 1950s to a major energy player, but its corporate behaviour remained dominated by that same man, Jack Gallagher, whose dreams of grandeur knew no limits. At the heart of his fantasies was the desire to make Dome larger in Canada than Imperial Oil. To achieve that goal, in 1981 Gallagher went after Hudson's Bay Oil & Gas, a subsidiary of Conoco, the former Continental Oil, based in Stamford, Connecticut. He easily won control (53 percent) of HBOG but only by doubling Dome's debt load to $5.3 billion, a level that required interest payments of an agonizing $3 million a day. To lighten that load he desperately needed access to HBOG's $300-million annual cash flow, and that meant buying out all the minority shareholders, including the largest single block—the 10.1 percent still owned by the HBC.

Just before Gallagher had made his move on Conoco, he had offered Tory, through a Bay Street intermediary, $27 a share for the Company's HBOG stock. Tory, who had done his own calculations, considered it to be worth at least $50, though he had at one time been willing to sell HBC's position at $40 to $45. Now he dug in. Tory seldom loses his temper, but he still turns red thinking about that $27 bid, particularly since it was made just three days before Gallagher offered Conoco the equivalent of $52 for its HBOG stock. "That really stiffened our backbone," he recalls, "and when I met Gallagher I told him in no uncertain terms that I thought this was not the way ethical businessmen operated." He refused a trade of Dome shares for HBC's stake and would accept only a complicated retractable preferred-stock formula that made the HBC's 7.7 million Dome shares worth $57.50 each on or before December 31, 1984, with the money paid out of an escrow account that Dome management couldn't touch in the interval. Gallagher later claimed the deal was largely responsible for Dome's downfall, but for HBC the 1983 Dome redemption provided a badly needed infusion of $455 million in cash.*

By 1984, the HBC's pre-tax losses over the preceding four years amounted to more than $320 million. Thomson and Tory had grown exasperated with management's intransigence. One of the big problems was that the cost of the money involved in the HBC's expansions was never included in profit projections. Regional and departmental managers would make presentations to the board forecasting glowing revenues and operating profits for new store expansions without even mentioning returns on capital invested, interest costs, cash flows or tax considerations. At 5 P.M. on November 29, 1984, Tory, who had brought up the issue so many times he was fed up with bleating about it, arrived late at a Bay committee meeting attended by Governor Don McGiverin and HBC vice-presidents Wally Evans, Rolph Huband, Marvin Tiller, Don Wood, Al Guglielmin and Lorne Klapp. The outside directors present included Ian Barclay of Vancouver, Marcel Bélanger of Montreal and Dawn McKeag of Winnipeg. They had met to hear the presentation of C.W. "Chuck" Gerhart, then general manager of the Ottawa region, who reviewed his area's retail growth, projected sales and operating profits five years into the future, cheerfully predicting a net increase from $3.5 million to $12.1 million by 1989 — this for a district that had a profit peak of $5 million in the past and had not recently been reaching its own sales targets.

For Tory, that was it. Keeping himself under tight control, he politely inquired whether Gerhart cared to acknowledge the fact that current profits had been realized only after investment of about $30 million to improve the main Ottawa store, linking it to the Rideau Centre, and pointed out that this expenditure had involved considerable financing costs. When the Ottawa manager replied with the equivalent of a shrug, Tory gave him a stern lecture about the impact

---

*The HBC's only remaining oil investment was the small Calgary-based Canadian Roxy Petroleum (named after the Roxy Arcade, a New York roller-skating rink where its promoter, Robert Peters, had spent an enjoyable evening), bought in 1980 and sold seven years later to Westcoast Transmission for $82 million at a small profit.

of financing charges on cash flows and bottom-line profits. "It really wasn't Gerhart's fault," he later admitted. "He was just part of the HBC's corporate culture. They were living in a dream world—only looking at operating profits and pretending everything else would take care of itself."

The next day, just after a revised quarterly profit outlook was tabled showing a further $50-million dip in a rapidly accelerating financial slide (the loss for the nine months ended October 31, 1984, was $7.67 a share, compared with $4.20 the year before), Tory addressed the Company's full board. It was the toughest speech he'd ever given, and would in retrospect become recognized as a watershed in the Hudson's Bay Company's long history. "When we acquired HBC," one of the directors recalls his saying, "it had just taken over Simpsons. I thought HBC was well managed and could help Simpsons, which had inferior management. Instead, the Bay's management screwed up Simpsons, and I've lost confidence in the HBC management. The major shareholder would not consider investing another cent in HBC at this time. I will review the situation with Ken and our people and will have recommendations for the Board at our next meeting in January." He stressed that the continued existence of the HBC was at risk because nobody seemed to be focusing on the real problem—that the Company simply wasn't generating enough cash to cover its daily requirements. An immediate freeze was placed on capital spending; drastic cuts in corporate overhead were ordered; new guidelines were established to focus objectives on cash flows and net earnings rather than sales totals and operating profits.

"When you look back," Thomson later ruminated, "it's a legitimate question to ask why we let it go so long. When we made the investment, we believed the HBC was a well-managed company, and there was very little reason for us to think otherwise, as profits grew in the first few years. Then, all of a sudden, with the downturn in business and upturn in interest rates, the sins of the past came home to roost. Now *that* doesn't make for a passive investment. Professional management was failing to meet budget objectives by increasingly wide margins. When I said the management of the HBC is great, I was right—I just got the tense wrong. Don McGiverin and his people had done a superb job, but the Company had turned into a sort of ivory-tower bureaucracy. We could have tried to get a hot-shot retailer from the States to take his place, but that wouldn't have been right. We could have sold off The Bay's real estate and broken up the Company, but I didn't want to do that. We could have merged the HBC with

Thomson Newspapers, but that wouldn't have been fair to the share-holders who had invested in our publishing abilities. No, the best thing was to stick with it, and build it up again."

Right after that November 30 meeting, Tory had an encounter with McGiverin over costs of the Company's computer operation, which were climbing at an alarming 20 percent annually. Tory wanted independent cost-control experts to review the computer systems, but McGiverin refused to allow them access. Tory and Thomson quickly realized that the Governor's head would have to be included in any effective reform package. "I don't really think management realized how desperate the financial situation had become," Ken Thomson recalls. "They thought, 'Here's a 300-year-old company, and nothing will happen'—so they just kept doing things as before. We had waited and waited and waited, but finally we had to take action. Lookit, out of respect for the kind of person he is and what he had done in the past, we didn't want to hurt Don McGiverin. But he had to go, and he was gentlemanly enough, big enough to realize changes had to be made. We were able to maintain our mutual respect and friendship."

And so the merchant prince was stripped of his crown, if not his title. Feeling prouder of his run than bloodied because of the way it had ended, McGiverin lost not an ounce of dignity in the process of giving up his authority. "I hung in too long, I really did," he told a friend on the morning after his demotion. "But then, not every person's built for all seasons. If I had thought there was a better way of doing things, I'd have done it. God, I've been forty-five years in this thing, and I've been at it twenty hours a day. Still, the Chief Executive Officer can never have a bullet-proof vest. I've had a good run, and when they asked me to stay on as Governor, I told them I'd be delighted."

At a crucial board meeting on January 25, 1985, Tory, speaking on Thomson's behalf, announced that McGiverin had relinquished his post as Chief Executive Officer but would continue as Governor in a non-executive capacity. In his place, two executive vice-presidents— Iain Ronald and George Kosich—were being appointed to run the Company, with the former to be in charge of Zellers, wholesale, furs, real estate, the northern stores and the disposal of non-strategic assets, while the latter would take over control of the HBC's department stores including Simpsons as well as credit and information services. The directors (except Ronald and Kosich) thought this was a silly idea because the Company would not have a single responsible executive.

They only approved the new structure subject to Tory's taking on the chairmanship of the management committee of the board, thus effectively turning himself into the Company's CEO, since neither Ronald nor Kosich could implement major policy shifts without first checking with him. For the next half-decade, John Tory, in effect, ran the HBC. It was a stormy five years, but in the end he saved the Company.

THE TORY-DOMINATED RONALD-KOSICH PARTNERSHIP represented a dramatic shift in direction, since Don McGiverin had by then been running the Company for fifteen years. While few had ever questioned his skills as a retailer, McGiverin had, since 1978, opted out of his chosen profession, spending nearly all his time and energy on takeovers. As a result of that neglect—plus the effects of the recession and the Company's astronomical debt load—the HBC's credit ratings were downgraded from AAA to a humiliating B. Between 1980 and 1982, operating profits declined 97 percent.*

Apart from cutting costs of its existing retail operations, The Bay under both McGiverin and Tory had also drastically trimmed the number of its operations. The Shop-Rite catalogue stores were closed in 1982 and its Marshall Wells hardware subsidiary was sold in 1985. Its travel business and its share of Eaton Bay Financial Services, Computer Innovations, Hudson's Bay Distillers and Toronto Credits were disposed of the same year.† In the summer of 1987, The Bay sold off its wholesale division, established in 1907 to handle liquor as well as grocery distribution, later adding candies and tobacco. With annual sales of $800 million, it was a big operation, but it never made much profit. After a partnership between Norman Paul, brother of a former president of Zellers, and Jimmy Kay (then chairman of Dylex) bought it for $133 million (about half of it down), the pair took not quite a year to run it into the ground, forcing its 1,200 employees on to the street and causing a $45-million writedown on the HBC's books, though much of it was later recovered.

Late on a Friday evening in January 1987, Marvin Tiller, head

---

*At one point in 1986, things got so tight that the Company applied to take a $35-million surplus out of its employee pension fund. The application was withdrawn only when the Pension Commission of Ontario warned that it would be refused.

†The Bay's real-estate holdings, except those buildings occupied by its stores, were folded into its subsidiary Markborough Properties in 1984 and six years later Markborough was turned into a separate public company through the spinning off of its shares to the HBC's stockholders. With 78.4 percent of the parent company's stock, Ken Thomson could claim the same percentage of Markborough, which allowed him to realize a tax-free $315-million capital gain.

*Iain Ronald, Executive Vice-President,* HBC

of the Northern Stores Division in Winnipeg, got a call from Iain Ronald, the HBC's executive vice-president, advising him to be in his office at 8:30 A.M. the following Monday. "When I got there, Ronald abruptly advised me that the Northern Stores Division had been sold and that the new owners would be arriving in half an hour," Tiller recalls. "I told him that we'd like to have done an employee buyout, but sure enough, thirty minutes later Ian Sutherland and Raymond Doré, representing Mutual Trust of Waterloo, Ontario, rolled in, ready to take over."

Sale of the Company's historic Northern Stores Division had first been discussed at a management committee meeting on September 12, 1986. Ronald reported that he had been approached by a group of investors organized by Mutual Trust and that while profits for the operation might reach $35 million, it didn't have much opportunity for expansion. The item came up again at a January 23 meeting, where the selling price was set at $8 million over book value, with an 80-percent cash advance. Approval to jettison this most historic of the HBC's departments—the territory for which it had received its Charter 317 years earlier—was granted at the directors' meeting on January 28, 1987. The official minute hardly does that momentous decision justice: "The Board discussed the pros and cons of such a sale. On the one hand N.S.D. is profitable and represents to Canadians the heritage and pioneering spirit of the company. On the other hand, it operates in a total welfare environment with considerable risks of government intervention, it requires capital for modernization and has little growth potential. On balance, given the over-riding need to substantially reduce debt, the Board decided to approve the sale."

Strangely, no outside directors attended that meeting, though they were polled by telephone. Only four executives, who also served on the board, were there to vote on the fateful motion to cut the ties with the HBC's own history.* "My recollection," recalled J.W. "Bud" Bird, one of the directors who was telephoned on the issue, "was of feeling a sense of loss, that we were really changing the character of the Company, but that it was sort of a side-battle in the mission to establish three main retailing giants and to concentrate where the volumes were and the super-store kinds of activity. The preservation of the origins of the Company was no longer commercially attractive to the main mission of the Company."

That seemed more of a retroactive rationalization than a reason. Northern Stores had been a dependable money-maker, clearing $28 million in operating profit on a $400-million sales volume the year the division was sold. Spinning the 178 stores off for $189 million reduced the parent company's debt by a net $150 million, about 6 percent of the total it then owed, which didn't make any material difference. Tiller was as puzzled by the decision as anyone. "I couldn't fathom how they could possibly come to that decision," he said, "particularly since we had a five-year profit trend that was right on target and was marching on and on. The most difficult experience for me was having to face my people, who all have an HBC stamped on their backsides, and tell them about it."

Rolph Huband, the HBC's vice-president and secretary, was the only Company executive who took note of the sale's historic dimensions. "The heritage and adventuring spirit of the Company is gone," he lamented. Dick Murray, the former managing director, came out of retirement to thunder: "Only unpardonable cowardice and incompetence could lead the Canadian owners of this great historic company to throw away these jewels in their crown. The Company now abandons the Canadian North; it severs generations of a trusting and respectful relationship between native peoples and traders—it deletes the words and discards the heart of its historic name: Company of Adventurers. One might just as well take the RCMP and sell it to Pinkertons." These sentiments were shared by former Deputy Governor Sir Eric Faulkner, who mourned: "If the HBC is alive three

---

*They were: Don McGiverin, George Kosich, Iain Ronald, and Gary Lukassen. All the directors polled by telephone agreed to the sale.

hundred years from now, it will be neither the fault of the Thomsons or of the Bay directors from 1970 on. If we had foreseen what would follow . . . would we all have been persuaded to transfer to Canada?"*

On May 2, 1987, precisely 317 years after the Company of Adventurers had taken up Charles II's Charter to exploit the upper half of the North American continent, Derek Riley, the Winnipeg businessman who had been elected chairman of the offshoot company, folded the Governor's flag that had flown over the posts of the HBC's northern division and handed it back to Don McGiverin. Suddenly it was over—317 years of history cut adrift as if they had never happened. Ken Thomson's main interest in the transfer was to claim for the HBC the art works collected by the northern division, taking three-quarters of the Inuit sculptures, prints and historical paintings.

He felt very much more strongly about getting rid of the Company's fur business. "I was just praying the Company would sell it," he confided after the decision had been made. "I think it's an anachronism. We don't need to kill animals to feed our vanity. They may not be a high order of life, but animals have the same right to live as we have. They can say what they like about animals being humanely trapped—it's not true. You can't kill an animal without making it suffer. So why should we kill creatures who are out there trying to survive? That's all they're doing, trying to survive. Over the coming years, people are just not going to be wearing fur coats. It's a dying business. I know that somebody else is still doing it, but it has nothing to do with my family." That was a revealing statement, because it was the one aspect of current HBC operations that Thomson really felt passionately about (except, of course, for losing all that money), yet he himself did nothing about it, allowing the Company's executives to work their way towards his conclusion on the issue—but only eight years after he became the Company's principal proprietor.

His son David confirms his father's reluctance to apply the force of his authority, even in a cause he feels passionately about. "My father has never wished to dictate his will to the business operators," says he. "Power is always perceived; when it is used, it ceases to be. He had believed that the people within HBC supported the business and that it was beneficial to the Company. Although he made his personal feelings very clear on numerous occasions, he would never unilaterally end the fur business within the HBC."

---

*The last of the great British directors, Sir Martin Jacomb, expressed his views of the sale by quietly investing in the successor company to the Northern Stores Division, which at George Whitman's suggestion became known as the North West Company.

The Canadian fur-sale operations near the Toronto airport were sold for $45 million to Len Werner, the previous manager. Disposing of the British facilities at London's Beaver House was a much more complicated affair. Hugh Dwan, the president of the HBC's British fur unit, received a phone call from Iain Ronald ordering him to be at the London offices of Morgan Stanley a day or two later to hear the details pertaining to the sale of his company. Dwan, who had up to then received no notice of the move, was just as puzzled as Marvin Tiller had been about jettisoning the northern stores, particularly since the auction house had been turning good profits and he had just recently submitted (and had approved) his optimistic budgets. The sale—to the Finnish Fur Sales Company, for $37.5 million—had been negotiated without his knowledge or consent. "They told me that selling the auction house would enable the Company to concentrate on their core business," he recalls. "In fact, the fur business in England was no drain at all on Canadian management because we didn't need them. The debt reduction benefits were a drop in the bucket. To me, their decision seemed like chopping up the kitchen furniture to feed the fire, and then finding out you have no place to sit. . . . They sold the company in the face of fast-rising fur prices, so if they had waited one more year, they could have got several million dollars more. It was an undignified scramble to get out."

Dwan had a devil of a time persuading London's fur traders that the HBC move was serious. Three centuries is a long time. "They thought it was some kind of reverse takeover for tax reasons and that the HBC would end up owning the Finnish co-operative," Dwan remembers. "There was strong feeling that the Company had let them down. In furs, the HBC was a mark of confidence all over the world." After his day at Morgan Stanley, going over the dreary details of the sale, Dwan walked to Earls Court, then took a taxi home. "I turned on the TV news," he recalls, "and there was young David Thomson, who had just purchased a Constable for £2 million, saying that as its new owner he was anxious the United Kingdom not lose its heritage, and that he therefore might not take it out of the country. I thought to myself, 'They've just sold out the best trading name in the world,' and I cried."

On January 31, 1988, the fur men held a wake on the auction floor at Beaver House. It had been on January 24, 1672, that the first London HBC fur auction was held at Garraway's coffee house, near the Royal Exchange, where tea from dried leaves imported by the East India Company had originally been brewed. That first sale was a very special event attended by the Company's founder, Prince Rupert, his cousin, the Lord High Admiral, the Duke of York (who would become the HBC's second Governor and, as James II, King of England) and the poet John Dryden. Now it was all over, and from seven in the evening to midnight, a lot of rum was tasted, songs were sung, and stories told. Special arrangements had been made to transmit the Company's farewell telegrams and telephone calls that day, presuming there would be some form of official farewell wishes sent to mark the end of the Company's founding department. Incredibly, no message ever came. "They didn't even know we still existed," said a bitter Arthur Frayling, Dwan's predecessor and a sixty-eight-year veteran of the fur trade. "The greetings from head office in Canada were as they had been for some years previous—zero. They had actually established in their minds that the Company's great background and tradition was, in fact, a drawback. Now that I can't take. I'm sorry, I can't bloody well take it."*

The British fur trade ended with Frayling, well over six feet tall and with the bearing of the infantry colonel he once was, standing on the bidding stage at Beaver House and leading the mourners in song:

> Dear old pals,
> jolly old pals
> all in together
> in all sorts of weather.
> Dear old pals,
> jolly old pals,
> Give me the solace
> of dear old pals . . .

THE RULE OF THE TORY-KOSICH-RONALD triumvirate ended on July 1, 1987, with the appointment of George Kosich as the HBC's president and chief operating officer. A University of British Columbia Commerce grad, he had spent twenty-seven years with The Bay, and even though his cutbacks had earned him the nickname George Carnage, he was a capable retailer with energy to burn, and brought to his position an optimistic outlook and determination to dismantle the

---

*Having divested itself of its northern stores and fur trade, the Company went on a kind of scorched-earth rampage, getting rid of the very last historic symbol it possessed. This was the collection of silver objects minted in 1670, the year of its incorporation, that had been gathered by various Governors and kept at Beaver House. The thirty hallmarked pieces were shipped without notice to New York for sale by Christie's, so that some of the former British HBC directors had less chance to buy them, or, as one former Governor intended, to donate them to the city of London.

deadening sanctions of head office.* Kosich's—and the HBC's—good fortune was to have at his side Gary Lukassen, the Company's chief financial officer, who became a key man in its resurrection.

Kosich was tough and as single-minded as a mountain mule, which didn't enhance his popularity. On October 24, 1988, an anonymous petition was circulated at the HBC's head office, asking executives whether they respected Kosich's style of management. "Do you believe that the removal of George Kosich [as chief operating officer and president] would return the Company to a more stable and productive environment?" the questionnaire demanded. At the first management committee meeting after its distribution, John Tory began the proceedings by turning to Kosich and, with mock seriousness, explaining, "Before we start the business of the meeting, there is an announcement I have to make. It concerns the questionnaire that was circulated to the executive staff. We've tabulated the results. There were 175 replies that came in. Six percent voted for Ed Broadbent [then NDP leader], about 15 percent were undecided, and the others said they didn't know who George Kosich was." One of Kosich's problems in dealing with staff morale was his vocabulary. He was always talking about M.B.W.A. (which meant Management By Walking About—a reference to mingling with customers), eliminating T.N.M.J. (the That's Not My Job syndrome, when it came to helping close sales by using a little extra effort) and in a gush of participles, defined his formula for success as "downsizing, rationalizing, fine-tuning and refocusing."

With Ken Thomson's and John Tory's active backing, Kosich turned the Company inside out, closing unprofitable units but supporting success with ambitious retailing plans. The deliverance of the HBC was not nearly as dramatic as its near disintegration. It was largely a matter of rationalization and reorganization—the gradual reintroduction of the Company to its natural retailing audience.

Kosich eliminated layers of middle management and centralized buying and sales promotion to cut expenses. He used computer technology to provide better data for buying decisions and his merchandising flair to pick commodity winners, then spent money backing those premium items with more inventory and upgraded locations in the

---

*Iain Ronald resigned the same day Kosich was appointed, later becoming president of administration for the Canadian Imperial Bank of Commerce. "I just couldn't stay at The Bay a moment longer, because I have to look at myself in the mirror every day and can't shave with my eyes shut," he told a friend just after he quit. Doug Mahaffy, the HBC's senior vice-president, finance, also resigned within a few weeks of the Kosich appointment.

*George Kosich, President, HBC*

stores. At the same time he restored flagship downtown units to some semblance of their former glory by installing colourful, contemporary environments for housewares and women's and men's fashions.

It was at Zellers, the discount store that Joe Segal saved from bankruptcy and Don McGiverin bought at gunpoint, that Kosich and the HBC enjoyed their most spectacular success. When he and David Thomson took over Zellers in 1987, it was experimenting with an upscale format to distinguish itself from its discount competitors. Kosich declared that a discount store must look like a discount store and ordered the newly installed partitions and carpeting removed. He also insisted that in discounting, expenses are everything and put into effect the lowest operating costs in the industry. This allowed Zellers to reduce its prices and trumpet that at its stores "the lowest price is the law." Customers responded, driving sales up, expense rates down, and prices still lower. As a result, Zellers' operating profits tripled in the four years of the Kosich presidency and for the first time since the Thomson takeover, the owners opened the pursestrings in November 1990 to purchase the fifty-store Towers chain. By mid-April 1991, Kosich had their carpets removed, their expense rates reduced, and new Zellers signs installed.

In the meantime the Company had completed its transformation from a conglomerate to a retailer. "Disposal of the fur and northern departments was required to correct the daring excesses of the 1970s," maintains Rolph Huband, the Company's vice-president and corporate secretary. "The necessary corrections having been made, the HBC reset the course originally plotted in 1970—to become the most successful of Canadian business enterprises." With the distribution in August 1990 of Markborough Properties shares to its own stockholders, the HBC was for the first time since 1870 mainly in one line of business—retailing.

The only unit that never stopped bleeding was Simpsons. That upscale, Toronto-centred department store had proved a disaster since Don McGiverin had taken it over in the late 1970s. Simpsons had suffered through the tenures of eight presidents in a decade: Ted Burton, Charles MacRea, George Kosich, Al Brent, Bob Peter, David Thomson, Paul Walters and Bob Peter again. None of them could resurrect the sleeping elephant. The store had lost its audience. HBC management tried going first upscale and then downscale, firing sales personnel over thirty-five years of age, publishing yuppie ads, shutting down the Montreal and Regina units, combining purchasing offices, amalgamating advertising departments, putting in the country's— probably the continent's—most expensive food hall (in the basement), but nothing worked. The upscale shoppers didn't get upscale service— and so they stayed away. At any rate, there weren't enough of them to turn Simpsons into a northern Bloomingdale's. Even internally, Simpsons was treated as a joke, with Bay executives referring to its main Toronto store as "the Panty Palace." The Company became fed up with throwing people and money at the troublesome Simpsons division and finally in the summer of 1991 closed it down.

But that was all anti-climax. By the spring of 1989, the HBC's balance sheets reflected the dramatic turnaround that Tory had masterminded and Kosich had engineered: profits at $144 million were up 389 percent from the previous year's. The Company's salvation had been slow and painful but, against all odds, it had been achieved and its credit ratings had been restored. The Hudson's Bay Company was once more safely in the black.

*Ken Thomson (left) with John Tory prior to the annual meeting of Thomson Corporation at Roy Thomson Hall, Toronto, 1991*

*David Thomson, Deputy Chairman of The Woodbridge Company Limited*

# CHAPTER 19

# LAST LORD OF THE BAY

*"I become excited at the thought of measuring myself in varied situations, alongside Wellington in India or being in a fighter, attacking a formation of bombers and being vastly outnumbered. It's an interesting way to test yourself because you set your own limits."*

—David Thomson

THE RICH DON'T HAVE CHILDREN; they have heirs. For the first-born male, growing up is a brief interval during which he matures into becoming his father's Son, with all the baggage of continuity and shedding of spontaneity that such a rite of passage implies. Youth involves being wafted through Father's private school and enrolled in his clubs at birth, experiencing all the right things (doing drugs means two Aspirins at bedtime), earning a Harvard MBA, and spending languid vacations at large summer homes on the manicured shores of cool green lakes.

These precocious progeny learn at their daddies' knees how to exude that air of besieged innocence that marks the Canadian Establishment's young—a mixture of being well bred and mentally inert. As a group, they seldom have an original idea, think it's daring to use an adverb and believe that culture means attending a Pavarotti gala in a tux. They are dull to the point of banality.

And then there is David Kenneth Roy Thomson.

His very name evokes the three-generation dynasty he represents, and he is, by quite a wide margin, the most fascinating of Canada's inheritors, being his own kind of pensive rebel and a recognized art connoisseur to boot. At thirty-four, David Thomson is Deputy Chairman of Woodbridge, the holding company that controls the family assets. The trust set up by Roy Thomson, who died in 1976 at

405

eighty-two, having amassed a corporate flush then worth at least $750 million, appointed David, Ken's elder son, to be the next head of the Thomson Organization. He will also assume his grandfather's title, which will give him a seat in the House of Lords, never claimed by Ken. "David, my grandson, will have to take his part in the running of the Organization, and David's son, too," the dying Thomson wrote, spelling out the rules. "For the business is now all tied up in trusts for those future Thomsons, so that death duties will not tear it apart. . . . These Thomson boys that come after Ken are not going to be able, even if they want to, to shrug off these responsibilities. The conditions of the trust ensure that control of the business will remain in Thomson hands for eighty years."*

The scenario is predictable; its leading man is not. The young Thomson marches to his own drum corps. He is as private as Conrad Black—his only intellectual rival among Canada's young rich—is public. He has climbed to the second-highest position within the Thomson Organization with no profile, has yet to grant his first newspaper, television or any other interview (except for this book), and is so circumspect that his 1988 marriage to a fashion buyer for Simpsons was missed by Toronto's social columnists and not detected even by the nosy Rosedale mavens who surround his home. His conversation, which is what he must mainly be judged by, since he has yet to exercise much visible power, is an improbable mixture of introspective genius and post-industrial babble. Tall and wispy, with curly sandy hair and frigid blue eyes, he is light on both feet, betraying the easy grace born of his training in the martial arts. Intensity characterizes all his thoughts and actions. Ask him the meaning of life or the time of day and the brows furrow into deep scars (the forehead is too youthful to show supporting wrinkles), the eyes grow reflective, and the brain cells almost audibly start churning; there is never any small talk.

---

*Ken Thomson has two other children: Lynne, eighteen months younger than David, a stunning brunette who graduated from the acting faculty at Harvard and is currently in Hollywood, working with a producer, and Peter, eight years David's junior, who participates in Southern Ontario racing circuits and dirt-rally events, practising his driving four or five hours a day. A graduate of the University of Western Ontario, he owns a substantial interest in a Toronto cable-TV company and is beginning his career inside the Thomson Organization. To avoid succession duties, Roy Thomson's will stipulated that his personal fortune would be divided among his seven grandchildren. Roy Thomson's trust is administered by his son, Ken, his surviving daughter, Phyllis Audrey Campbell (the other daughter, Irma, died in 1966), his former chief of staff, Sidney Chapman, and John Tory.

DAVID THOMSON WAS EDUCATED at The Hall School in England and Toronto's Upper Canada College. He was (and is) painfully shy, staying away from the sports and military training in which both schools specialize. "I never understood the emphasis on playing games as the only forum for exhibiting manliness," he recalls. "The Upper Canada College Battalion was an unnecessary and wasteful commitment, illustrating the shallow nature of so many contemporaries in early life. As a chore, it was counter to the deep emotional issues which I sought to begin my journey." Not your average prom-date jock.

He read history at Cambridge, specializing in studies of the civil service in India from the late eighteenth to the mid-nineteenth centuries, particularly under Mountstuart Elphinstone, who rose from aide-de-camp to Colonel Arthur Wellesley (later the Duke of Wellington) to governor of Bombay and was one of the chief founders of state education in India. "My classmates were more interested in military battles," he remembers, "and I must say Wellington fought tactically superb engagements, greater by far than any of his European campaigns, including Waterloo. His tactics were similar to Hannibal's against the Romans after his crossing of the Alps, when he gained the higher ground at the battle of Lake Trasimene. But I was much more fascinated with the mundane aspects of how the British were able to educate and develop an infrastructure of modern government in that huge land mass. Legalities are very important and represent absolute regulation, constrictive and formal. I prefer frameworks to guidelines, because you're able to be creative within them. My mind works with associations and ideas. History taught me this above all else. At an early age, I realized that to not understand these life experiences would lessen my ultimate success and enjoyment in life." To lighten the academic load, Thomson played left wing on the 1976 Cambridge hockey team that beat Oxford for only the fourth time since 1930. "I like to think I was on the team because of my abilities," he laughs, "but I owned a Volvo, which afforded me a constant place."

David believes his most significant formative influence was the weekends he spent with his grandfather at Alderbourne Arches in Buckinghamshire. "He was very lonely and we conversed for hours about business and people," the young Thomson reminisces. "His curious mind was always questioning why things were done in a particular way, seeking to understand the forces that affect people's judgments. Granddad would relate his experiences with various personalities: Chou En-lai, Mao, Khrushchev, Beaverbrook, competitors, social companions, family. He always admired those people who could laugh at themselves amidst the negative circumstances that surrounded their lives. He was an optimist with an uncanny ability to seize opportunities that others could not see. This approach was in complete parallel to my own nature." There was another parallel: Roy Thomson unleashed the random thoughts that he credited with helping him resolve the most complex corporate problems by guessing the murderer in the dozen Agatha Christie and other whodunits he devoured every week. Those mystery stories were for him what art would become to his grandson, less an escape than a way to sharpen and exercise the mind for managing the exponential growth of the family fortune. (Every morning of every day David still puts on the copper bracelet Roy Thomson wore to ward off arthritis, as a reminder of the old man's spirit.)

It was at this time that his serious interest in painting took root. "Art came to mean more and more as I became involved with the lives of the artists and came to better understand the context in which they lived. For me, art has never been a financial or social game." Aware that any cultural hobby pursued by a rich kid was bound to be dismissed as dilettantish, David put in a long and arduous apprenticeship under Hermann Baer, who ran a small shop on London's Davies Street that rented antique props to the film industry and was also an articulate expert in medieval art. The other mentor in art has been his father, whose collection, David claims, "should be celebrated in its completeness; even the frame mouldings are harmonious. He has distilled his vision of a few artists into a handful of works by each. The result is sincere and compelling."

"David gets feelings that I never get from pictures," admits his father, Ken. "He never misses the technical aspect of art. He sees when something is well executed and when it's not so well executed. He talks about the soul, the true message of a painting and can sort of read what the artist had in his mind when he did it. I'm not that good. I can't figure those things out. He gets signals that I don't even understand. I just get an instant message that's probably much more shallow than David's." The relationship between the two men is close but not cloying, with the senior Thomson occasionally wondering if his son is tuned in to worldly business realities. "Our private discussions evoke mixed emotions, but once agreed, we tackle issues with a single-minded tenacity," David insists. "I love him deeply, would do anything for him, and I am not alone. Many of my cohorts would defend him to the death." Of his son, Ken Thomson says, "He's a fine young man. The same sensitivity that he relates to his paintings, he relates to people and business. It worries him if somebody isn't being treated right and all that sort of stuff. He relates to quality. When he's involved in something he wants it to be the best, but of course we can't always have the very best. In his position, he could have just taken what's coming and enjoyed it, but that would have been more shallow than his thinking. It wouldn't have been as satisfying."

DAVID THOMSON WORKS on the eighteenth floor of the Thomson Building across the street from Toronto City Hall. A visitor entering the private headquarters of his personal holding company, Lavis Incorporated (after his mother's maiden name), is struck by the sight of three incongruous objects: the large-scale model of a 1920s U.S. Post Office monoplane, painted every colour of the rainbow, that looks as if it had just landed out of a *Peanuts* cartoon; an exquisite, life-sized thirteenth-century French limestone figure that appears to be bending towards its owner in an attitude of gentle benediction; and the dark green seat from a Second World War Nazi Luftwaffe fighter. The office walls are covered with the striking canvases of Patrick Heron, a controversial contemporary British artist who specializes in jarring colour patterns.

David usually works gazing out the window opposite his desk on which are mounted several transparencies. "That one," he explains, "is a Constable, an oil sketch he painted on his honeymoon in November 1816 of Weymouth in Dorset, along England's south coast. These two are by Cy Twombly, the most compelling of modern artists, who left the States in the 1950s and now lives in Rome. That small transparency is a marvellous limestone figure from about 1260 and represents the beginning of sculpture in the full round. One must travel backwards to pagan times before one encounters full relief sculpture."

In the same mood he produces out of his desk a coin from the Dark Ages, a Merovingian gold Tremissis struck in Lyons about 675 A.D., modelled after the Roman currency of the Emperor Justinian: "Hundreds of moneyers minted crude coinage in the manner of Imperial Rome, inscribing their names and cities on the reverse legend. The effigies are extraordinary in their vivid line and spontaneous gesture; they evoke a most wonderful sense of expression and power. For me, they are the beginnings of the small entrepreneur in the history of coinage—they were created amidst the most barbaric circumstances by a people in constant motion and are amongst the few objects that remain from those distant days."

Thomson's most valuable acquisition was J.M.W. Turner's magnificent *Seascape, Folkestone*, which Lord Clark, the former director of the National Gallery (who once owned the painting), described as "the best picture in the world." David bought it at auction in 1984 for $14.6

million, outbidding the National Gallery of Scotland; five years later it was officially valued at $50 million. But his real obsession is with John Constable, the miller's son who with Turner dominated English landscape painting in the nineteenth century. Thomson's first purchase, at nineteen, was a page out of the artist's 1835 Arundel sketchbook, and his current collection of twenty major works and eighty-six of his drawings, as well as oil sketches, watercolours and letters, ranks as the world's finest private representation of Constable's art.

Thomson has recently published a lavishly printed and illustrated 328-page study, *Constable and his Drawings* (with text by Ian Fleming-Williams, Britain's leading Constable expert), which has been highly praised by English art critics. "In sharp contrast to formal art history monographs," he notes, "one can read this book without having studied fifteen previous works. This is about pure observation, not terribly different to the art itself. Constable's sensibility has had a strong influence on my personal philosophy, which I carry forward in all walks of life, including the business. So few people allow themselves to openly see and question scenes and events as he did. All too often subjects are viewed from a narrow perspective, with strong conclusions drawn in advance. Being possessed by imagination, curiosity and such dreamlike qualities doesn't mean one is incapable of pragmatism and tough decision-making. Whenever you lose that sense of idealism, you lose your reason for being. Constable for me has always represented the search for truth."

THAT SEARCH HAS TAKEN THOMSON into the soggy pastures of existentialism, at least in the sense that he believes men and women are diminished by not meeting the challenges they set for themselves. Intensely attracted by war and danger, because those circumstances force people to harness the peak of their physical and emotional energies, he owns a large library documenting first-hand experiences of aerial combat and the uses of camouflage ("creating patterns and colour combinations that transformed each aircraft into a work of art"). He often imagines himself in battle. ("I become excited at the thought of measuring myself in varied situations, alongside Wellington in India or being in a fighter, attacking a formation of bombers and being vastly outnumbered. It's an interesting way to test yourself because you set your own limits.")

Among his favourite documents is one of the last letters written by Antarctic explorer Robert Falcon Scott, found beside his frozen body in 1912, that Thomson regularly rereads as an example of an undaunted spirit facing death. "The existential idea of life's journey is very important," he contends. "It's all too easy to become cynical and to forget that we are all children at heart, that when you leave those youthful dreams behind you leave a great part of your being forever, you abandon your sense of wonder and astonishment, the idea that you can be spiritually moved by something or someone."

That sense of wonder is best caught in his house, an architect's jewel on a dead-end street in Rosedale where he finds sanctuary. He lives there with his wife, a pre-Raphaelite beauty named Mary Lou La Prairie, and their daughter, Thyra Nicole. He met Mary Lou in 1988 at Simpsons where she worked as a fashion buyer for young contemporary women's wear. ("Our love for one another was instantaneous. It was a fairy-tale romance. It has changed my life.")

David drives a 1984 Audi and owns a *pied-à-terre* in New York and a house in the Highbury district of London. His main interest is the collection at his Toronto house, which is less a home than an art gallery with a kitchen and some bedrooms attached. Every wall is crammed with paintings. The total effect is less than the sum of its parts because individual pictures have so little room to breathe; the eye cannot feast on any one canvas without being distracted by those on either side of it. Edvard Munch, Sir Stanley Spencer, Ilya Chasnik, Piet Mondrian, Eugene Jansson, Picasso, Ivan Kluin, Roger Hilton, Cy Twombly, Joseph Beuys, Ferdinand Hodler, Ernst Ludwig Kirchner, Mark Rothko, Paul Klee and a dozen other artists of equal international renown are represented. Strangely, except for a small drybrush by David Milne, there are no Canadian paintings. (Not a Krieghoff in sight.)

"I look forward to the day," he says, "when I can hang a room of empty frames. What an extraordinary experience that would be. Nothing can be more perfect than a frame and one's perception of balance and space, within and without its running pattern. This is sculpture. Immediately one thinks of the classic argument about what one chooses to leave out as opposed to what one puts back in. As with business, it is what we end up not expending that returns far more in the long run, well beyond any immediate cost savings or profits."

And then there are his art objects: a rare book on coloured fifteenth-century woodcuts, among the earliest printed and hand-coloured images in the history of art; facsimiles of the original texts of T.S. Eliot's *The Waste Land* and George Orwell's *1984*, showing the authors' corrections in ink; a study of fences from the Middle Ages ("one of the finest ways of dating objects and understanding the social order of those times"); an animation cell from Dr Seuss's *The Grinch*

*Who Stole Christmas*; an Ethiopian book of holy scriptures in hippopotamus-hide binding from the year 1500; an original Schulz cartoon of Charlie Brown; a small woodcut from Lower Swabia, dated 1420; an eighteenth-century African bronze from Benin; and a magnificent depiction in wood of the Crucifixion, mounted on its original cross, which was the focal point of an unidentified church in South Germany during the last quarter of the twelfth century.

David and a visitor gaze at this icon. "The agony of Christ is pronounced with the hips slightly tilted," he explains. "The profile of Jesus' head is quite spectacular. In this piece, one confronts the beginnings of Gothic carving and the tremendous expressionism of the northern world . . ."

"Look at those nails," the overwhelmed visitor offers helpfully, "how honest and raw they are . . ."

"Well, no, actually I put them there myself; they're what the cross is hanging on."

The gallery is constantly being expanded but its paintings will probably never be exhibited. "One does not form an art collection to then have a representative of *Architectural Digest* come by and write an article that invades one's privacy," Thomson insists. He maintains an intelligence network in New York and London to hunt down the works he seeks. "The art world has taught me harsh lessons on human nature," he confesses. "Money does not open every door. A real collector will rarely sell a work unless he can replace it with something even greater that has more personal meaning. Sometimes the issue can only be resolved by a trade or an exchange. I rely on a few people to update me and avidly peruse books and catalogues. I'll take three or four volumes with me to bed every night. It's no different from my grandfather reading all those spy and detective novels."

Almost hidden from view in the basement of the Rosedale house are a few exquisitely fine pencil-lead drawings—of a fish pond, an oak tree, water lilies, wrecked cars. These are some of David Thomson's own. He has been drawing to express his innermost thoughts since childhood. One British critic who saw them while on a visit noted they were "very good indeed, highly detailed, well observed," but they will never be shown. "I sometimes say to Mary Lou, 'I must draw a tree now,' and go away into my world for several hours. I have to. I am absolutely compelled to follow my feelings, or I forfeit the right to live."

Thomson makes little effort to separate his passion for art from his devotion to business. In his mind, these twin strands are forever intertwined: "I take art so seriously because it's one of the few pursuits in which I can totally unravel my soul. For me, the act of creation comes through in a better appreciation of business.... I measure great achievements in information publishing [the Thomson newspapers] in the same way as I view a compelling work of art." He dismisses the criticism that Thomson newspapers fill the spaces between their ads with the cheapest boiler-plate copy available as being out of date. Instead, he praises employees such as Peter Kapyrka, publisher of the Barrie *Examiner*, for furthering his company's organic growth by adding a weekly real-estate supplement.

There is, according to the youthful inheritor, almost no aspect of art that can't be related to some section of the Thomson Organization's operational code. "If you look at Limoges and Mosan, two of the great French workshops producing art in the twelfth century, you might think, 'What the hell does that have to do with business?' " he says. "Limoges in central France made fantastic reliquaries and chalices for churches and cathedrals with very few variables. But the Mosan craftsmen were different. They worked the market between Liège and Cologne. Their representatives sat down directly with the local bishop and asked what he wanted to see in the holy shrine. They were, in effect, forming the first customer focus groups and producing castings that were far superior to the Limoges enamels. You can't do anything well in publishing without a highly developed sense of audience."

David's spiritual bible is a remarkable book-length essay entitled *Happiness: An Exploration of the Art of Sleeping, Eating, Complaining, Postponing, Sympathising, and, Above All, Being Free*, by Theodore Zeldin, an Oxford don who portrays Everyman's journey into paradise, comparing what he encounters with what he expected to find. "The book," Thomson summarizes, "is about having the courage to dream in a highly structured society and the corporate world. It's about having faith in one's intuition, about preserving one's childhood vision and curiosity, about the fact that dissent requires great moral courage, and that failure is as important as success." He is mesmerized by the fact that in his position and state of development he is free to make mistakes and believes that this may be the greatest privilege bestowed on him by wealth. It's the errors in judgment that really accelerate his learning curve; he takes the correct decisions for granted.

That learning curve received its most valuable spurt during the decade he spent with the Hudson's Bay Company.

DAVID THOMSON'S DEDICATION to the HBC seems incompatible with his artistic temperament and search for mental stimuli. Yet he spent ten years in the service of the Company—between the ages of twenty-four and thirty-four, his most productive business apprentice-ship—as a full-time retailer, right down to a term of selling socks at The Bay's downtown Toronto department store.

In the summer of 1982, when Ken Thomson took his family on a second northern journey to view the HBC's Arctic kingdom, their guide was once again the Company's George Whitman. The party was encamped on the Belcher Islands in the middle of Hudson Bay when Whitman bluntly asked the elder Thomson why he had bought the Hudson's Bay Company. When Ken explained that he had a sense of Canadian history and he did not want to see the Company swapped around, sold off, or allowed to disappear, Whitman turned to David and said, "It would really be nice to hope that someday you might become the Governor. How do you feel about that?" David, who was then looking for a place to light, allowed that he would indeed be interested but that he knew nothing about retailing. Sensing the young man's excitement, Whitman talked for hours about the Com-pany's glorious history and its magical presence in the Canadian wilderness. He suggested to Ken that David not be parachuted into some senior position where he would be usurping the succession of staff climbing through the system but that a comprehensive training program be put together that would expose the young Thomson to the Company's inner workings, and vice versa.

"People were very careful about what they'd say to me and were told to be so, anticipating that I would not stay long," David recalls. "But this didn't happen because I became enthralled with many areas of the Company's then disjointed business potential. I have always been fascinated by how one motivates people in a negative situation. My business focus was entirely retail, and to learn it well I allowed myself no distractions or meanderings. I committed myself to the cause of making the HBC a great Company again." He began in the main Toronto retail store, then spent a year commuting to Quebec, Saskatchewan, Alberta (where he once forgot his pyjamas in a motel at Medicine Hat) and British Columbia in addition to the fur divi-sions in New York and Montreal.

Probably his most moving experience was the time he spent at a fur-trading post in Prince Albert. "The juxtaposition was dramatic," he recalls. "On July 4, 1980, I bid successfully for a Munch wood-block; the following week I was in Prince Albert, and I remember being taken to the post's backyard where ten bear claws were posi-tioned on the cement floor, with fresh bloodstains and tissue intact. One fellow proceeded to demonstrate the various new traps and took me through the back room, where numerous shiny models were hanging. He hinged several in open positions and tossed a branch into

*Ken Thomson, David Thomson and George Kosich at the 1988 HBC annual meeting*

the claw. I shall never forget the powerful crescendo of the folding pincers. For one of the first times I enjoyed a completely unfettered response to life, isolated from big cities and the diversions of money. We drove along dirt roads, watched sunsets, merchandised the store, went fishing and talked of our childhoods. The experience was unforgettable and I developed a deep respect and empathy towards those real people."

That warm feeling described his reaction to the Company as a whole. During his travels, he kept a private journal, recording his thoughts—among them:

> *On store fixtures*: Chrome is poor choice. For specialty men's store in Toronto, would buy old barns which farmers glad to get rid of and refurbish our departments completely in cedar.
>
> *On display*: Spotlight the ring on a model's finger in a downtown window . . . use all senses, including the aroma of good cooking.
>
> *On old stock*: Things never die. One item from an unsuccessful line will become so popular, it becomes one itself.
>
> *On expansion*: To build a new shopping centre or store is an analytical decision with no feelings. Yet selling decisions are all feelings.
>
> *On selling*: Merchandising is the last frontier of the untrained intelligence.
>
> *On Zellers*: Slop it up. Far too clean.
>
> *On Fred Eaton*: Talk to any time. Get in touch. Ball is in my court.

In the course of his training, he spent twelve months with one of the HBC's most troubled units, Shop-Rite, which ran five dozen discount catalogue outlets, mostly in Southern Ontario, and was losing about $2 million a year. Pete Buckley, who then ran the division, recalls that David was an effective junior manager, particularly as a member of Shop-Rite's ball-hockey team, which challenged the company's warehousemen to a match. "I was the referee and it got pretty rowdy," he recalls. "As soon as the warehousemen saw David, I could hear them muttering, 'Get that sucker.' But he was the most competitive guy in there and just beat the hell out of some of them." The admiration was mutual. "I have a lot of respect for Buckley," Thomson says. "He told me on one occasion, 'David, do you know how to better understand your consumer? I'll tell you. At one time I lived in an apartment building and at night, using binoculars, I would scan people's apartments, to see what goods they were using.' I said, 'You're a bloody genius! That's so simple!' "

David's next and most important step, in July 1983, was his appointment as manager of the HBC's suburban Toronto Cloverdale store, which he ran for a year, raising its operating profit to 8.9 percent, among the chain's highest. He established a Grandmother's Boutique ("a fine opportunity to cater to all the empty-nesters in Cloverdale's trading area"), reduced inefficiencies and soon found other managers copying his methods. "For many, it made no sense that David Thomson would need to work, and I think it was a surprise because no one had ever seen me perform alone," he recalls. "That year's journey made me acutely aware of the pressures and discomforts some people felt from the mere thought of my presence." But he persisted, and the time at Cloverdale established his independent reputation among Bay executives. There followed a stint with Simpsons, where he became assistant to George Kosich, who, a year later, would be promoted to run both Simpsons and The Bay. They quickly formed a duo, cruising the HBC retailing empire's inner and outer limits, cutting costs, closing stores, laying off employees, recasting its merchandising philosophy. (What annoyed staffers most was that when Thomson and Kosich would arrive at a store, obviously preparing to wield the axe, they first spent a day walking around each department handing out jujubes.) "The system was at an impasse," David remembers, "and its dismal financial results mirrored my feelings, as did many conversations and pieces of information that came my way. I had clandestine meetings under stairwells in shopping malls and other places, as employees, torn between what they knew in their hearts was right and the security of their employment, confided to me about basic merchandising issues that were not being addressed. I felt the ground swell beneath me as I realized how passionately these people cared about the Company."

Others were critical of his methods, accusing him of grilling underlings about their superiors' performance, then attacking those in charge on the basis of what he'd heard. They claimed that he could operate at only two speeds, full throttle or total indifference, and recalled an HBC management meeting where he grew bored, slumped at his desk, and finally started reading a book. "David used to phone from Liechtenstein on a Sunday night and say, 'Hey boss, can I get Monday off?' " complained Marvin Tiller, then in charge of the HBC's Northern Stores, where the young Thomson put in some time.

Early in 1987, he had to decide whether to continue with retailing or switch to publishing. He flew to London, took a long walk on Hampstead Heath, and opted for the presidency of Zellers. That meant moving to Montreal and taking on his first major executive assignment. "David was only twenty-nine years old, an unknown quantity, his apparent qualifications confined to his shareholdings," recalls J.W. "Bud" Bird, an HBC director at the time. "We made the appointment, knowing it was an innovative move that could have a lot of precarious circumstances." With one exception, the investment community was not impressed. "I don't think it's appropriate," an investment analyst charged anonymously in the *Financial Times of Canada*. "He should not be allowed such a position just because of his father's influence, to take over such a large chain without working his way to the top." The exception was Don Tigert, an analyst with Burns, Fry, who commented, "I was very impressed with the guy. He said he was going to whack $80 million out of Zellers' expense structure and in just six months he did precisely that."

According to David, the franchise had to be brought back down to its pedestrian fundamentals, which had governed its earlier success, because its stores and merchandise were becoming too expensive and head office, in particular, needed some brutal trimming. "In the initial week," he recalls, "I summoned the head-office staff and announced my decision to lay off 250 employees who, in fact, were standing in that room. I remember someone questioning me about having butchered the Simpson organization a couple of years earlier. I always appreciated blunt opinions, and this was no exception."

He had a brief but spectacular success at Zellers (he raised operating profit by 45 percent), although some attribute a good deal of the credit to the influence of his mentor, George Kosich, who was now president of the HBC. It was followed by a frustrating term as president of Simpsons which, unlike Zellers, was no easy turnaround, and after a year he was discreetly promoted to part-time chairman and sixteen months later resigned to pursue his other business interests. Although his relations with Kosich have cooled noticeably and some question his continuing interest in retailing, he remains a director of the HBC and attends its Executive Committee meetings. "I have asked my father on many occasions," says he, "where the family might find a great franchise equal to the Hudson's Bay Company."

Most if not all Thomson employees who have come into contact with David respect him but eventually become overdosed on his intensity and his lingo. He told one dissatisfied British staff member that perhaps he should consider leaving the firm, that there were certain disadvantages and anxieties involved in working for someone like him. "But at the end of the day," he added, "you may say: 'You know, it's interesting working for David. Even if he's mad.' If that means I'm not normal, I'm perfectly happy with that. That's the type of dialogue I really enjoy because it not only gives me strength but allows so many wonderful initiatives to occur in the business."

DAVID THOMSON IS VOLATILE, as unpredictable as a hailstorm. He could become the leader of the new generation of Canada's Establishment, or he might seek permanent refuge in his art. He is just beginning his run, with each new experience providing the bounce that will determine his ultimate direction.

Not at all like the father he loves but very close to the grandfather he respects, he faces a future limited only by his ability to survive his own intensity. Perhaps he had an inkling of the fact that nothing could stop him except himself when he chose the quote to accompany his picture in the Upper Canada College 1975 graduation yearbook: "We are never so much the victims of another as we are the victims of ourselves."

Meanwhile, he goes on pontificating, turning dollars and flexing his expanding authority. "I wish," he says, "to prolong those inspired moments in life and see them continually manifested in all areas of endeavour. . . . My search is always to create new wealth."

Once a Thomson, always a Thomson.

*The Bay store at Bloor and Yonge, Toronto*

# EPILOGUE

*The Hudson's Bay Company is permanently woven into the marrow and the dreams of this country. Its geography became Canada, its history the new nation's dowry.*

TWO DECADES INTO ITS FOURTH CENTURY OF EXISTENCE, the Hudson's Bay Company has seldom been spiritually weaker or economically stronger. When Ken Thomson decided to wash his hands of the fur trade and jettison its northern operations, the Company lost its soul. Yet by abandoning its founding territory and rejecting its past as the basis of its future, he inadvertently set the Company free.

For most of three hundred years the HBC's prevailing ethic could be summed up in one word: survival. Such a benign state of endurance was, of course, squarely within the Canadian experience, since the country prided itself on nothing so much as just being there. The resultant mindset was best caught by Margaret Atwood in her seminal work, *Survival*, and by Harry J. Boyle, the Canadian broadcaster who rhapsodized about "the soul-sharpening satisfaction that comes from being a survivor." While survivors are the winners in any game, standing by is not enough. The problem with survival is that it too often produces an over-respectful, timorous mentality. Hypnotized by the extraordinary history of the institution they represented, the Bay men turned inward and became marginal to the country growing up around them—in it, but not of it.

Their obsessive concern with durability governed nearly every stage of the Company's evolution from a one-fort trading operation on Hudson Bay to its modern incarnation as a $5-billion merchandising conglomerate. Reading the Bay men's journals, one is struck by the strong sense of obligation they felt to those who had gone before or would come after; they behaved as if one wrong step might wipe out the HBC's history. They didn't seem to realize that history is not a disposable commodity, that the future cannot erase the past.

The Hudson's Bay Company is permanently woven into the marrow and the dreams of this country. Its geography became Canada, its history the new nation's dowry. More important, the Company's frontier presence spawned the country's founding ethic.

All those early forts and trading posts were really Company towns, demanding deference to authority from inhabitants inside their ramparts and deference to nature beyond them. That orderly attitude—stressing collective survival instead of individual excellence—became the country's prevailing ideology, and it still colours what Canadians do and especially don't do. That was very different from the American frontier, where authority was challenged rather than deferred to, and the hunt was on for "life, liberty and the pursuit of happiness" instead of "peace, order and good government." One expression of those dissimilar approaches was the treatment of aboriginals. The Americans conquered their frontier, sharpshooters against tomahawks, with first the mountain men slaughtering Indians for their furs, followed by the U.S. Cavalry, which fought sixty-nine Indian wars, often killing "Injuns" just to "watch 'em spin."

In contrast, the HBC established a long-term commercial relationship with the natives across the territory that would later become Canada. Its traders never shot their customers. It was the Indians (and later the Inuit) who provided the furs swapped for imported goods at the Company stores. The terms of trade were not always fair, but being exploited was not as bad as being shot. In a curious way, it was a form of mutual exploitation because the Indians and Inuit were able to trade near-worthless pelts (they had previously killed animals mainly as food) for axes, guns, blankets, tea kettles and the many other desirable goods that made wilderness life easier.

While it is impossible to generalize about any large group of employees—especially when their tenure stretched over three centuries—the Hudson's Bay Company traders were more saints than sinners. Keeping in mind the fact that they ruled a large slice of the earth's territory for a dozen generations—with virtually no accountability—the Governors, officers and servants cannot be charged with any great burden of shame. They were mostly good men, some better than others, who led expedient lives in harsh surroundings, and lived to tell the tale.

As well as deference to authority, the most significant strain they injected into the Canadian character was the Presbyterian notion of stressing life's sombre virtues. Mostly Scots, the early Bay men rejected creativity and joy, replacing these qualities with stoicism and the notion that hard work was the Lord's eleventh commandment. In contrast to the exuberant individualism of the American West, the idea was to be plainly dressed and plain spoken, never too free with one's money or emotions.

Until its Canadianization in 1970, perpetuating the HBC as a corporate entity often seemed less a means to desirable financial goals (such as shareholder dividends or capital reinvestment) than an end in itself. That very special onus flowed from its genesis as a royally chartered trading company and the prestige of its early governors—Prince Rupert, the Duke of York, the Duke of Marlborough—and the imposing peers and knights who followed. The influence of these personages, plus the never-denied rumour that the Royal Family still owned its stock, marked the Company as an untouchable colonial agency. Imperial troops and fleets of the Royal Navy were dispatched to defend its flanks; the Bank of England coddled its treasury, lending it credit and the occasional Governor.

Within its North American domain, the HBC became a significant instrument of empire, its explorers probing the West and North, planting across the frontier the necklace of forts that kept the American annexationists at bay, and laying down the commercial matrix for a national economy. "The honoured old initials HBC have been interpreted facetiously as meaning 'Here Before Christ,' " noted W. Kaye Lamb, the fur-trade historian; "instead, they might more fittingly be taken as signifying 'Here Before Canada.' And if this had not been so, it is unlikely that Canada as we know it today would now exist." The Company acted as a volunteer surrogate of the British Empire, occupying the territories beyond its founding North American colonies until Canada's own aspirations stretched across to the Pacific and up to the Arctic oceans.

The writ of the HBC's offbeat mercenary army of fur traders ran across the continent. By canoe, York boat, steamship and Red River cart, on snowshoes and aboard the backs of pack-ponies, they eventually established the viability of a transcontinental state. This was all heady stuff and it was no wonder that the Company's employees felt they were a very special breed, developing an almost canine loyalty to the HBC. It was as if signing on with the Bay included an unspoken contract that in return for accepting relatively low pay and inadequate working conditions they could enter the faith—become adventurers and merchant princes. An essential element of that belief system required their acceptance of the notion that the Company had to be protected at all costs—human and fiscal—so that it would go on forever. Because the first duty of any faith is to perpetuate itself, that creed paralysed the HBC's policy planners. They took occasional risks, but they never bet the Company. At those moments when an intuitive leap was required to advance the HBC into fresh and potentially lucrative economic jurisdictions, its decision-makers almost always opted for safety and survival.

THERE ARE TWO WAYS TO VIEW the history of the Hudson's Bay Company's first three hundred and twenty years: what it did, and what it might have done.

What it did, as this three-volume study of the Bay documents, was to endure and endure comfortably—to survive considerably longer than any of history's many chartered trading companies. Its traders moved across the empire of the Bay like assault platoons of an inland regiment, ready to defend the faith wherever it might be threatened.

There is nothing wrong with an organization determined to preserve itself; many more daring commercial enterprises have long since vanished from contention. Yet in strictly commercial terms, the Company's marathon was something of a bust. Its dividend record indicates that after an initial fourteen years without paybacks it earned a 50-percent dividend in 1684 and a similar rate four years later. It then took more than *two centuries* of modest profits averaging well under 10 percent before the 50-percent rate was achieved again, for one year, in 1913. Despite its glorious history, the HBC was a spectacular financial underachiever, yet few of the Company's guiding spirits were willing to admit just how mediocre their performance had really been.

One exception was Sir Henry Benson (later Lord Benson), who resigned in a huff as the HBC's Deputy Governor in 1962 to become senior adviser to the Governor of the Bank of England. "I remember giving enormous offence to the Canadians when I said it was extraordinary how little the Company had achieved, bearing in mind that it had by then been in existence for nearly three hundred years," he vividly recalled. "This was taken to be, quite wrongly, a reflection on the then management. I didn't mean that at all. I meant it was surprising that a company in existence for three centuries still only had assets of whatever they were at the time. This caused enormous offence, but it was true. I don't think that it used its position and its advantages very well for long periods in its history. Looking back, it still surprises me that it wasn't a much greater trading corporation, operating all over Canada. It was asleep." John Ernest Harley Collins, a former naval captain (DSC and bar) who rose to head Morgan, Grenfell, one of England's leading merchant banks, and spent seventeen years as an HBC director, put the case more succinctly: "We fell into a *folie de grandeur*, became too conservative, allowed things to bumble on, just because it was the HBC."

Although it owned the world's most valuable land monopoly—a third of the still-to-be-explored northern part of the American continent—the Company spent most of the eighteenth century huddled in a handful of insignificant posts around Hudson Bay, trading a few pelts but doing almost nothing to claim the economic benefits of the great land mass at its back door. Between 1693 and 1714 it maintained only twenty-seven men on the Bay at a time when free traders from Quebec were ranging far inland in their quest for furs. (By 1688 the *coureurs de bois* had penetrated past Lake Superior nearly to the present site of Winnipeg.) Joseph Robson, an early HBC surveyor stationed on Hudson Bay, was dead right when he charged that "the Company have for eighty years slept at the edge of a frozen sea." This isolation was no accident. It was such strict corporate policy that when an HBC trader named John Butler wanted to send his son inland to learn the Indian language, he was ordered to have the boy stay put. The Company didn't establish its first inland trading post until 1774 and in the next four decades was almost wiped out by the rampaging traders of Montreal's North West Company. The Nor'Westers sarcastically praised the Company of Adventurers for providing such a useful "cloak to protect the trade from more active opponents."

Except for the occasional jolt of imagination, the Company operated at its maximum effectiveness mainly during the four-decade span when Sir George Simpson ran it, from 1821 to 1860. Unlike his predecessors, Simpson expanded its geographical limits and pushed it well beyond furs into trading lumber, cranberries, frozen salmon and even North Pacific icebergs and glaciers. (His crews sawed off chunks of the appropriate size and loaded them aboard a fleet of leased ships for a quick journey to San Francisco, where the ice was sold for refrigerating meat.) Acting with the hauteur of a man in charge of his private universe, Simpson did any damn thing he pleased and in the process temporarily transformed the HBC into a dynamic and imaginative enterprise.

APART FROM ITS PREOCCUPATION with survival, the Hudson's Bay Company suffered from three centuries of being run on a part-time basis by well-connected (and well-intentioned) London financiers who didn't know the going rate for stamina in the Canadian bush. They were the ultimate absentee landlords. Nothing was more symbolic of their stewardship than the fact that it took 264 years before any Governor of the Hudson's Bay Company—Sir Patrick Ashley Cooper, the twenty-ninth man to hold the office—actually visited Hudson Bay. At nearly every major turning point, the Company's London godfathers, not quite trusting their colonial appointees in Canada to do the right thing, chose to do as little and as late as possible. With a few enlightened exceptions, the British overlords seemed mainly concerned with not becoming agents of the HBC's demise. They neither granted their Canadian administrators full authority nor exercised it themselves—except at the beginning, when the stakes were too small to matter.

The Hudson's Bay Company was confronted by so many dazzling business opportunities it refused to exploit that it's a miracle it didn't founder out of a sense of corporate shame. Here was a company that dominated the world's fur trade for most of three hundred years yet never made a single fur coat. Here was a company that pioneered Canada's transportation arteries (even the Trans-Canada Highway runs along the old canoe routes) and for two centuries exercised a transportation monopoly in the West and later in the North, yet when it came time to build a transcontinental railway, opted out of the process. Here was a company that had the only functioning infrastructure in the Prairies and owned seven million acres of prime real estate, much of it along the new railway route, yet did little to capitalize on these invaluable assets except to sell off the land. Here was a company that established a world-wide market for its "Best Procurable" Scotch, for its high-quality gin and rye, but instead of continuing to distil its popular house brands turned the business over to Seagrams, harvesting no advantage from its good reputation in this high mark-up industry. "The Company could surely have developed more of the country in so many imaginative ways," complained Walter Rose, a former head of both the Fur Sales and Wholesale departments at the HBC. "They had all that land, had been there for two centuries before the European immigrants arrived, and all they ever did was sell the raw acreage and take out dividends."

Even in its modern retailing phase, the Company, having had the money and opportunity to snare most of the desirable shopping-centre sites across western Canada, concentrated instead on the miniature versions of Harrods it had built in provincial capitals, nurturing these masonry mausoleums even when they seemed as obsolete as trans-Atlantic ocean liners. While other department-store chains were busy constructing the suburban shopping malls that would capture the bulk of the retail business, the HBC was throwing up grand concrete parking garages next to its downtown retail palaces.

The HBC's most obvious dereliction of opportunity was the failure to capitalize on its potential oil and gas reserves. In the mid-1920s the Company still held mineral rights on 4.5 million acres checkered across the Prairies. Rather than exploit that invaluable asset, described by *Fortune* as "an oilman's dream," the HBC leased the entire package to Marland Oil of Ponca City, Oklahoma (and its successor, Continental), retaining only a 21 percent interest. By the late 1960s, the joint venture ranked as Canada's third-largest oil and gas producer, with 1,606 wells in production and 11.2 million acres under licence. Its earnings were twice as high as those of the HBC and its equity worth four times as much—even though the Company received less than a quarter of the royalties. "Instead of leasing out all those oil and gas lands," Alexander MacIntosh, Deputy Governor of the HBC, lamented, "we should have held on to them like the CPR."

L.F. McCollum, former chairman of Continental Oil and a director of Hudson's Bay Oil & Gas, was more blunt: "They were years of lost opportunity. I felt sorry for the HBC. They had great assets and did nothing about them. They should have created their own oil company and, if they didn't want to keep it going, spun it off to the stockholders rather than allowing the benefits to flow to somebody else. The Hudson's Bay people used to tell me how proud they were to be the oldest company in the western hemisphere and I'd tell them, 'So what? What have you done? Continental Oil is only twenty-five years old and our assets are worth ten times as much as yours, so please don't brag to me.'"

FOR MORE THAN THREE HUNDRED YEARS, the HBC men were content to bask in the comforting faith that the Company of Adventurers was too old, too big and too important ever to disappear. They were right. The Company still exists, even if it has changed more dramatically in the past two decades than in the two previous centuries.

Although it was the 1979 purchase of the Hudson's Bay Company by Ken Thomson that eventually shuffled its components beyond recognition, the fundamental shift in the Company's character occurred with its transfer to Canada nine years earlier. Before 1970, the HBC had been a very British company, its managing directors in Canada being English (like Philip Chester) or Anglophiles (like Dick Murray) who expended most of their energies defending their decisions, large and small, to the London board, which was composed of distinguished City men whose common strain was that they refused to think like North Americans. The appointment of Don McGiverin as president and later as governor changed all that. As North American as they come, he launched a dramatic sequence of risky takeovers that created one of the world's great retailing empires whose potential impressed Ken Thomson enough to buy in.

By mid-1991, the HBC had become a business like any other, except for the tug of its memories. Having buried its past and shed its glory, it had become an aggressive and successful retailing colossus, ready to jump into the United States if that seemed an appropriate tactic.

Like Canada, the Hudson's Bay Company has always shuttled between unstoppable momentum and impending collapse—a great might-have-been Company in a great might-have-been country, both facing an unpredictable future.

# Acknowledgements

THE ORIGINAL IMPULSE to establish the Hudson's Bay Company in the mid-seventeenth century had come from London, and it was there that the mysterious sources of its astonishing longevity had to be traced. That involved several journeys to England, where many interviews—some lasting most of a day—altered my preconceived notions of the British business mentality. I understood at last how the Company's huge domain could have been run with such enduring results for three centuries by men who seldom set foot in it.

Wry thoughts came to mind as I made my appointed rounds through the City, London's bustling financial district, meeting the dozen remarkable men who had been the Company's last British overlords. In few former seats of empire is there so much to occupy the eye, the imagination and the memory. The men who built London's magnificent office structures, and whose descendants still occupy them, brought a touch of civility to the rough-and-tumble world of commerce. Former U.S. Secretary of State Dean Acheson, who knew his history, once remarked that he could think of no more delightful period or place in which to have lived than mid-nineteenth-century England, when the country was run by a small group of highly intelligent and largely disinterested individuals. I know precisely what he meant, even if the merchant adventurers I met were anything but disinterested. Their involvement with the Hudson's Bay Company had been a magic moment in their successful professional lives.

Interviewing them was no simple task. Steeped in discretion, they pleaded everything except ignorance to avoid my questions, and it took several visits before they felt at ease with me and my tape recorder. (One former Governor kept eyeing the machine with suspicion, certain that whatever kind of contraption it was, the thing might explode in his face at any moment.) Though they eventually proved to be far more helpful and forthcoming than their Canadian counterparts, their initial demeanour was reminiscent of John le Carré's astute comment that "your extrovert Englishman or woman of the supposedly privileged classes ... can have a Force Twelve nervous breakdown while he stands next to you in the bus queue, and you may be his best friend, but you'll never be the wiser."

That impression of reticence stayed with me as I visited a Royal Bank of Canada safehouse near Buckingham Palace. The site was so historic that I vaguely wondered what century I had blundered into;

then, catching a glimpse of a 747 in a holding pattern above Hyde Park, I stepped inside. The tight-lipped guests included Lord Adeane, financial adviser to the Queen; Jocelyn Hambro, a leading merchant banker and chairman of the Phoenix Assurance Company; Hugh Dwan, Managing Director in London for the HBC; Geoff Styles, in charge of the Royal Bank's British operations; and Lord Tweedsmuir. I had heard rumours that the Royal Family still owned the HBC stock their ancestors had acquired three hundred years before, so I asked Lord Adeane whether they had a special interest in the Company. "Yes," was the discreet reply—that, and not another word.*

Lord Tweedsmuir, son of John Buchan, first Baron Tweedsmuir of Elsfield and Canada's fifteenth Governor General, turned out to be the most interesting guest of all. He had spent fourteen months as a trader for the Hudson's Bay Company at Cape Dorset on the south-western tip of Baffin Island. That had been forty-one years earlier, but when he spoke about "our flag" he meant not the Union Jack but the HBC's house pennant. "I am a Scottish adventurer, and we do not change much with the centuries," he told me, recalling that the year at Dorset had been the happiest of his life, that the Company was a great link of empire, and that the Scots were its perfect servants.

THE HOUSE OF LORDS—repository for many former HBC characters—is a geriatric paradise, a venue out of time and place, with elderly dukes, earls, countesses, barons and bishops sitting about looking at one another, whispering in mildewed tones of past triumphs, terrified of dying with empty appointment books. Their inflexible graces are still in place but they look as if they would get winded playing chess. In a nearby lounge, I spotted Lord Home, Harold Wilson and James Callaghan, former Prime Ministers all, who looked like Tussaud replicas of themselves. ("In his dotage, sorry to say. Makes no sense at all," somebody breathed, pointing at Wilson, nodding in a corner with a fixed smile on his face.)

My host was the fourth Lord Strathcona and Mount Royal, a great-grandson of the Labrador fur trader who had been associated for seventy-five years with the Company, twenty-five of them as its

---

*When I returned to Canada, I asked Donald McGiverin, the HBC's current Governor, the same question. His reply was slightly more illuminating. "I don't really know," he said, "because no record of royal stockholdings is published. But the last time I saw the Duke of Edinburgh during the Canadian royal tour in 1977, he took me aside and whispered, 'Tell me, how are *we* doing?' "

Governor. The current Strathcona turned out to be a tall, vital and charming gentleman with a great white beard and hair growing all over him, sprouting out of his shirt cuffs and collar. "I'll risk the beef," he said, as we settled into the Peers' Dining Room, a setting straight out of an Alexander Korda extravaganza, with silver serving dishes and waiters who look as if they had been carved out of Pears soap. A graduate in engineering from McGill University and a former minister of state for defence in Margaret Thatcher's cabinet, he lived on one of his ancestor's many estates, on the Isle of Colonsay in the Inner Hebrides. He finally cleared up the mystery of what happened to the CPR's original last spike and produced some fascinating new evidence about his great-grandfather's relations with the HBC.

IN THE CORNER OF THE LORDS' TEA-ROOM sat Viscount Amory, who was first appointed to cabinet by Winston Churchill, had served as Chancellor of the Exchequer under Harold Macmillan, and was the last British Governor of the Hudson's Bay Company (1965–70). Derick Heathcoat Amory resembled a mellow and very wise owl. But his eyes were alive with that special look of absorbed experience that only a man with a million miles on his meter can convey. We chatted away the afternoon, looking at the barges heading along the Thames towards Ratcliffe Wharf, where HBC supply ships had once been loaded for their ocean crossings. He was intrigued by my tape recorder ("Isn't that amazing—all in that little black box!") and spoke with barely concealed puzzlement about Lord Thomson, the Canadian billionaire who had acquired control of the HBC following his tenure. "I was amazed he put so many eggs in one basket," he said, "but he is a man of honour, and the last time I met him he became quite sentimental about the Company. He told me at dinner, almost with tears in his eyes, 'Derick, you may think of me as a hard-faced Canadian financier who wants to see what he can get out of this Company. If ever you catch me at that game, let me know. You will never find me doing that!' "

My final visit was to Beaver House, the HBC's London headquarters, and lunch at the Strathcona Restaurant on Garlick Hill with Arthur Frayling. Then head of the HBC's fur auction house—the world's largest—he had spent fifty-eight years with the Company yet could still muster the enthusiasm of a boy on the first day of summer camp. Munching Trout Cleopatra, he described his obsession with the Bay. "It's not a job, it's a calling," said he. "To be a Bay man has always caused me to feel that one is working for a Company with a fairly big foot in history. Where is the value commercially in such a feeling? There is none. But I always felt, as did most old-time Hudson's Bay employees, that I was contributing to something a little outside the ordinary commercial run. I can't really put it into words, because I can't see too much sense in it. But that's the way I feel."

THAT'S THE WAY I FEEL too, and it was while touring Canada's Arctic — between my British visits — that I came closest to touching the Company's spirit. The HBC then operated a string of 173 stores and fur-trading posts in Canada's Arctic. In a series of airborne sweeps, into Baffin Island, up to Resolute and around the great arcs of James and Hudson bays, I interviewed many of these Bay men and their aboriginal clients, the Indians and Inuit who people this volume.

The time-worn faces of these fur-trade veterans, durable mercenaries out of Scotland, Newfoundland, Nova Scotia and New Brunswick, were permanently leathered from lifetimes spent outdoors. Even if the real glory days were long gone, it still meant something to work for the Company in Canada's North. Management's cloying paternalism, poor pay and the frustration of being a cog in the machinery of an often comatose bureaucracy were tempered by the idea of being part of a tradition as grand as the Royal Navy's.

Canada's North is a state of mind, having more to do with attitude than with latitude. Even official definitions of the Arctic differ, some restricted to territory above the Arctic Circle, an arbitrary line at 66.32° north, while others place its limits somewhere beyond the tree-line, a boundary that dips 870 miles below the Arctic Circle at James Bay and rises 220 miles above it at Horton River. The outrageous dimensions of Arctic geography — 1.3 million square miles, spread over five time zones — dwarfed yet enchanted the Bay men. The best of them saw it as an empty land filled with wonders, even if they recognized that it offered only a temporary truce with their presence. Others regarded their surroundings as a prison where cold and wind erased the hope of meaningful human endeavour. But most of the HBC field hands, at least those who stayed, viewed the North as a place with its own natural laws, where they could get to know their true feelings on a first-name basis. "Hell," I was told by James Deyell, then head of the HBC's Ungava District, who had arrived in 1965 from the Shetlands, "I was born the equivalent of three hundred miles *north* of here. I came right out of grammar school at seventeen because the only other choice I had at home was joining the merchant navy or living off my father. I was getting $2,500 a year, which I thought was marvellous—an unheard-of salary in the Shetlands for a trainee. Since I arrived here, I've never had time for an identity crisis. When you're surrounded by silence, you find out in a hurry who you are. Once the life grabs you, it's permanent and it never lets you go. Certainly working for the Bay is more than just a job; for some reason, you perform above your imagined capacity. At the end of the day, you can certify that you were *there*, that you made a difference."

The Canadian Arctic has only two seasons, winter and August, its weather varying from clear, sparkling heat waves to white-outs that reduce visibility to the inside of a dwelling and the human comfort zone to the immediate circumference of its stove. The cold is unimaginable. One HBC trader described how he and his companion managed to survive a typical winter in their Company house: "The weather grew colder and colder and, at Jim's suggestion, I moved from my room upstairs down to the kitchen, where I slept on top of the table. Then came the day when even Jim was forced to leave his bedroom to sleep with me in the kitchen. Then the living room, and finally the office, became uninhabitable. . . . If I had to go only to the store I would dress as though I was going on a hunting trip." Another HBC Factor, W.O. Douglas at Baker Lake, loved eggs and imported a few chickens every summer. In winter, he not only had to bring them indoors but ended up knitting little duffel coats for them.

The resident Bay traders lived and worked in a strange world. In summer, the northern sun never sets; then for eight months it seldom rises. For two-thirds of each winter the moon remains below the horizon. During those gloomy intervals, the main natural light source is the shimmering Aurora Borealis, hanging over the polar horizon like a spangled theatre curtain. Winter temperatures drop below -55°F, causing steel to snap like celery stalks, tires to become as brittle as glass and to detonate. Human senses are stretched to their outer limits as the moisture in the atmosphere freezes, breaking down into countless ice particles that attack exposed skin. Ptarmigans make the sound of tearing silk as they painfully propel themselves through the frigid atmosphere.


NORWAY HOUSE, NEAR THE TOP of Lake Winnipeg, was the inland rallying point for the HBC's canoe brigades on their way to tidewater at York Factory on Hudson Bay. The Company's Northern Council met here intermittently between 1821 and 1860, and the ghost of Sir George Simpson still haunts the place. It was here, too, in 1875, that Treaty Number Five was negotiated by which the Saulteaux and

Swampy Cree ceded to Canada their possessory rights over the surrounding hundred thousand square miles, one of the worst deals the Indians ever made. While on one of my northern probes, I met Adam Dick, Chief of the War Lake Indian Band, born in a tepee seven miles northwest of Split Lake in 1897, then living at Norway House. He had started trapping beaver and snaring rabbits at the age of eight. "My dad made me a bow and arrow and snowshoes, and my mum made me a bag," he recalled. "When I began hunting by myself, I caught one rabbit and four prairie chickens. Later, I worked twenty-three years for the Hudson's Bay as a cribber, freighting supplies by dog team or canoe to twelve trappers' camps. They paid me sixty-five dollars a month. I never got a raise and never got a pension. I brought them lots of furs but I didn't get anything from them." The chief, who was eighty-seven when I saw him and had yet to acquire his first grey hair, had only one kind thought about the Company. "There was never any room in the sled for me because they piled all the space up with supplies. So I had to run behind it . . . I guess that's why I'm so healthy." Before leaving Norway House, I asked how nearby Bull Island got its name. I wish I hadn't. When a bull gored a local Bay man named Isbister, the animal was smeared with tar, taken by boat to the small rocky outcrop, and set on fire. Nobody ever goes to Bull Island now.

At Fort Severn, I spent a long afternoon with Manasseh Munzie Albany, aged ninety-seven, a hunter and ship's pilot who used to lug seven bags of mail to York Factory and back every winter, and his friends Reverend Jeremiah Albany and Abel Bluecoat. They told me about life at Fort Severn: gasoline costs $6 a gallon, there is no electricity, and it's $9 for a four-litre can of naphtha that lights a cabin for three nights. Nearly everybody is on welfare, barely getting by. Only 270 people live at Severn, but the Bay store's annual sales top $350,000, with average mark-ups of 40 percent. Not so long ago a ninety-foot freighter loaded with eighty tons of foodstuffs for the Bay, operated by an Inuk named Lewis Voisey, ran aground nearby, and the weather turned so nasty the ship had to be abandoned for the winter. Next spring, when she was refloated, not a single item of the vessel's cargo was missing except six cans of pop, consumed by the captain while cleaning out the bilge. He paid the HBC for the six-pack.

Rupert House, where I spent a fascinating two days, is the oldest of the Bay settlements, built in 1668 by Médard Chouart, Sieur Des Groseilliers, who led the first trading expedition into the Bay. There is palpable tension here between the HBC and its captive customers. The Cree measure their feelings for the Company by the price it pays for muskrat and beaver skins. "Why do they need to make me pay back my lousy $25 credit, when they arrive here in a $2-million plane?" is a common complaint. (Twenty whites and a thousand Cree live here, and there's enough traffic to fill a DC-3 four times a week.) A local Indian named Isaiah Salt, who spent forty years working for the HBC, told me the most he ever made was $25 a month. This is Billy Diamond country, and it is he, as Grand Chief of the Cree, and not some Company functionary, who reigns supreme.

It was at Cape Dorset that the artist James Houston spent a decade introducing the Inuit to print-making. I had always been mystified by how such luminous artistry could flourish in a climate that a Company trader once described as being so cold that "people are born with jumper cables as umbilical cords." Houston, who had learned the graceful alchemy of print-making in Japan, inspired the local stone carvers to try this new art form, which quickly brought the best of them world fame. I remembered Houston's wonderful story about the time he gathered his artists for an early-morning pep-talk because he wanted them not only to produce prints of great originality but to make enough money to support their families in what was then a cashless society. He made his point by slapping down several dollar bills on the print-room table. "When I returned to the shop late that night," he told me, "I found one of our most talented print-makers just completing a stone-cut of his version of a Canadian dollar bill. He had cut it oversize, he said, to increase its value."

The going rate for marijuana joints at Broughton Island is fifty dollars, and the market is brisk. The HBC used to buy 30,000 sealskins a season here, but Brigitte Bardot's protests killed all that. The only remaining cash crop was selling hunting tags to American tourists who wanted to shoot polar bears; the local quota was twenty-two tags, and they fetched $3,000 each. When I cornered an Inuk and asked how fair the HBC's prices really were, he was lost for an answer because there was no alternative outlet to match quotes against. Head lettuce was selling at $2.98, which didn't seem unreasonable. One of the minor ironies of the Arctic these days is that it's the visitors who wear the furs while the Inuit keep warm in army-surplus down-filled parkas. Dog teams have all but disappeared; teenaged Inuit with mirror sunglasses race their snowmobiles in endless circuits of the settlement's one street.

Resolute Bay, Canada's second-most-northern community, had lost its horizon when I arrived; the sky was the same pitted-pewter hue as the land. Hugging the 74th parallel and about a thousand miles from the North Pole, Resolute has the worst climate and the worst economy in Canada. I couldn't interview Mayor George Eckalook because he was busy. One of the few people with a job, he was driving the settlement's only garbage truck. The place was dotted with snow-mobile skeletons and boarded-up houses, including a complex of Ottawa-sponsored apartment buildings that had to be abandoned because the plumbing was embedded in the north wall, where it froze for good. An earlier bureaucratic initiative moved Inuit families here from Port Harrison and Pond Inlet. They were told the hunting would be better, but nobody notified the animals. The Resolute Inuit are proud and independent. In 1982, when the Bay store burned to the ground and its credit records were destroyed in the blaze, within hours, every Inuk at Resolute had reported his or her outstanding credit to the local manager. A quick check with head office confirmed that the total tallied precisely with the Company's figures.

HAVING COME TO THE END of the nearly ten years devoted to this three-volume study of the Hudson's Bay Company, I find myself surrounded by literary debts. The half-million words contained in *Company of Adventurers* (1985), *Caesars of the Wilderness* (1987) and *Merchant Princes* (1991)—plus the illustrated *Empire of the Bay* (1989)—were my own, but their inspiration sprang from many sources.

My prime obligation is to the five hundred or so men and women I interviewed about the HBC. Most of these resource people are listed in the appendices of the three books. I have donated the tapes and transcripts of the interviews to the Provincial Archives of Manitoba in Winnipeg, where, after a decent interval, they will be publicly available. At the same time, I'm grateful to the Company's current owners and executives for allowing me unrestricted access to archives and files without demanding even a glance at my manuscript.

These books could never have been written without the inspired determination of Shirlee Smith, who until recently was head of the HBC Archives in Winnipeg. She not only encouraged the idea of a popular history of the HBC but her personal readings of my chapters proved invaluable. Anne Morton of the Archives has also been tre-mendously helpful. John de B. Payne, a former HBC executive and political alchemist, was of immense assistance.

I have greatly benefited from generous professional advice and personal support of such distinguished scholars as Tim Ball, Abe Rotstein, Blair Stonechild, Alan Wilson, Hartwell Bowsfield, W. Kaye Lamb, John S. Galbraith and the late Richard Glover. They and others encouraged this project because they understood what I was trying to accomplish and subscribed to my notion that truth is not necessarily the sum of all the ascertainable facts.

The preparation of the sections of this book dealing with the North was greatly assisted by the wisdom of Stu Hodgson, the former Commissioner of the Northwest Territories, NWT cabinet ministers Nellie Cournoyea and Gordon Wray, Senator Willie Adams and Peter Ernerk. Their advice was particularly appreciated. Janet Craig and Martin Lynch, who have edited all my books, performed their usual magic, bravely attempting to make my overheated prose more comprehensible. George Whitman and the late Al Hochbaum became my friends during the research for these volumes. Their grace and kindness, their sharing of perceptions and knowledge made it worthwhile. I regret that Sir William "Tony" Keswick passed away before this volume was published.

Thanks go also to Cynthia Good, publisher at Penguin Canada, whose dedication and contribution to this series I gratefully acknowledge; Mary Adachi, for her fabulous copy editing; Kathryn Dean, for choosing and captioning the books' illustrations; Chris Blackburn, for compiling the indexes and the Chronology of the present volume; Neil West and Jim Gordon, for their conscientious word processing; Hilda Earl, for assistance with the Chapter Notes, Bibliography and Resource People; and, above all, Pat Harding, my loyal and indefatigable assistant, for putting up with me, co-ordinating my untidy life as well as my hectic work schedule. As always, a salute to the bravura Artistry in Rhythm of Stan Kenton, who kept me alive and kicking.

When I started work on *Company of Adventurers*, it seemed like an uncomplicated excursion into Canadian history. Now, so many words and years later, I leave the project, happy to have resurrected, however briefly, many heroes and villains whose existence had too long been ignored by Canadians convinced their country's history is dull.

It isn't, and it never was. Trying to re-create 320 years of history has been a tough assignment; attempting, as I have, to write it in the manner of an itinerant story-teller has been harder still. It is done as well as I could do it.

This book owes its existence to many people; the responsibility for its many imperfections is fully my own.

Cordova Bay and Deep Cove, B.C.                                    P.C.N.
August 1, 1987–August 1, 1991

# APPENDICES

# Chronology

**1867**
British North America Act provides for the admission of Rupert's Land and the North West Territories to the new Confederation.

**1869**
Donald A. Smith is in charge of the Labrador and Montreal districts of the Hudson's Bay Company. The Canadian government agrees to purchase Rupert's Land from the Company. William McDougall is appointed Lieutenant-Governor of Rupert's Land and the North West Territories, but is refused entry to Red River by a National Committee of the Métis, objecting to sale of the HBC's lands without their consent.

**1870**
Métis under Louis Riel meet to discuss the proposals from Ottawa brought to Red River by Donald A. Smith. The Manitoba Act, forming the new province of Manitoba and including provisions for Métis rights, is passed by the Canadian government. Smith is elected to the Manitoba legislature.

**1871**
Donald Smith gains a seat in the House of Commons. He negotiates new Deed Poll to compensate HBC Chief Factors and Chief Traders: in return for a settlement, the officers agree to give up any share of future land-sales profits. British Columbia joins Confederation on the promise of a railway link with eastern Canada. Smith recommends the use of steamboats to improve HBC transportation.

**1873**
Smith's vote is crucial in "Pacific Scandal" debate: he goes against Macdonald's government, which resigns. Formation of the North West

Mounted Police. Red River incorporated as Winnipeg.

**1874**
Rt. Hon. George Goschen appointed Governor of HBC. Smith elected a Liberal M.P.

**1875**
Federal government begins construction of Pacific Railways.

**1876–1878**
Recession leads to a decline in HBC share values. No dividends paid in 1877 or 1878.

**1879**
Smith and partners form the St Paul, Minneapolis and Manitoba Railway. As the link with Winnipeg is completed, the line gains a temporary monopoly on western Canadian freight. Smith resigns as HBC Land Commissioner but continues to buy stock.

**1880**
Eden Colvile appointed HBC Governor. Main Canadian office moved from Montreal to Winnipeg. Land boom in Winnipeg over next three years. CPR syndicate is formed and signs contract with government.

**1881**
HBC opens retail store in Winnipeg. Simpsons moves to Queen Street location in Toronto.

**1883**
Smith elected to HBC Board as major shareholder.

**1885**
North West Rebellion under Louis Riel. Last spike of the CPR is driven.

**1886**
Smith knighted.

**1887**
HBC retail store opens in Vancouver. Smith returns to federal

parliament as a Tory. Hislop and Nagle fur company creates competition with HBC.

1889
Donald Smith appointed Governor of HBC, serving until 1914. HBC co-operates with CPR and government to promote prairie settlement.

1891
Beginning of three-year recession. HBC reorganizes and pushes land sales.

1893
Deed Poll extinguished: HBC officers now receive only a salary.

1894
Hislop and Nagle open Arctic posts.

1896
HBC stores and land sales develop, lessening importance of fur trade. Smith appointed High Commissioner for Canada.

1897
Old North West Territories achieve responsible government. HBC establishes stores in Yukon to supply prospectors. Donald Smith becomes Lord Strathcona and Mount Royal. Red River flood. Queen Victoria's Diamond Jubilee is celebrated.

1898
Yukon becomes a separate territory, with its own government.

1899
Revillon, furrier from France, competes with HBC in Hudson Bay and Northwest.

1900
Job Bros. opens fishing station in Labrador (later bought out by HBC). Furs are in fashion in Europe. Many Inuit succumb to disease.

1901
Marconi sends first wireless signals across the Atlantic, opening access for independent fur traders to latest market information. Competition continues from Hislop and Nagle and from Revillon.

1902
The Boer War ends. British victors helped by Strathcona's gift of a regiment of roughriders.

1903
Alaska Boundary Dispute, and establishment of the Alaska-Canada boundary. HBC complains about U.S. whalers trading with Canadian Inuit. Amundsen begins his voyage across the Arctic (to 1906), as the Far North gradually opens up.

1905
The provinces of Alberta and Saskatchewan are created. Great increase in immigration to the West means buyers for HBC land.

1906
Beginning of eight years of high dividends as the HBC profits from land sales. Lord Strathcona announces that HBC will retain mineral rights on lands sold.

1909
Strathcona becomes chairman of newly formed Anglo-Persian Oil Company, which enters into a supply agreement with the British Admiralty. HBC establishes its first trading post in the Eastern Arctic. Richard Burbidge of Harrods examines HBC stores for the Board.

1910
Stockholders' group challenges Strathcona's control over the Board, and wins significant influence. The HBC is divided into three departments: land, stores and furs. Expansion of department stores in western cities begins.

1911
First HBC post established on Baffin Island; Chesterfield Inlet post opened. Northern Trading Company established, in competition with HBC and Revillon. Strathcona commissions construction of *Nascopie*.

1912
HBC names Canadian Advisory Committee.

1913
The Northern Trading Company buys out Hislop and Nagle Company. HBC dividend reaches an unprecedented 50 percent.

1914
Death of Lord Strathcona, "the greatest figure in the history of the Hudson's Bay Company." Sir Thomas Skinner becomes Governor. North American fur purchases halted by war conditions; many aboriginals deprived of food and supplies.

1915–1919
HBC contracts with French government to transport goods and munitions by steamship in war zone.

1916
Opening of the Panama Canal, with eventual adverse effect on Winnipeg's position as a commercial centre. Sir Robert Molesworth Kindersley appointed Governor of the HBC.

1917
Northwest Game Act attempts to regulate the fur trade and to protect musk ox and caribou.

1918
Greatly increased competition from Lamson and Hubbard. HBC land sales continue at rising prices.

1919
HBC directors note the company is subject to both U.K. and Canadian taxation, while competition pays only Canadian tax. Considers moving some operations to Canada.

1920
Celebration of HBC's 250th anniversary. Governor Kindersley visits Canada. First issue of HBC magazine, *The Beaver*, appears. Competition with Revillon continues.

1920–1929
HBC continues the development of its general retail stores; opens a Newfoundland fishing and packing industry; sells whaling products; and explores for oil in western Canada. Offices are opened in Paris and New York. Fifteen new posts are established in the Canadian Arctic.

1922
First domesticated beaver bred. Standardization of thirty-five "house brands," e.g., Fort Garry tea and coffee. Talks with Simpsons regarding merger come to nothing.

1924
After years of competition, HBC buys out Lamson and Hubbard and its subsidiary, the Alberta and Arctic Transportation Company.

1925
Establishment of HBC Overseas Settlement Ltd. in partnership with Cunard Lines and with the cooperation of the CPR. Charles Vincent Sale appointed HBC Governor. *Bayeskimo* sinks with a year's supplies for northern posts; passengers rescued by *Nascopie*. Beaver House opened in London for fur sales.

1926
HBC agreement with Marland Oil Co. to explore for oil on prairie lands. Opening of new Winnipeg store. Concern that trading posts are adversely affecting caribou migrations.

1927
First northern air-freight planes sent to Churchill, and two railways reach Hudson Bay. The splendid new HBC steamship *Bayrupert* is wrecked off Labrador. Frederick Banting criticizes HBC's treatment of Inuit.

1928
Sale and his Board come under attack from C.L. Nordon and other shareholders for the company's poor earnings record. The Imperial Privy Council decides that gold and silver on HBC lands belong to the federal government.

1929
The federal government transfers to the provincial governments control

of natural resources in Manitoba and Saskatchewan. HBC fulfils its obligation to discover a North West Trading Passage by the interlocking voyages of three of its trading vessels across the Canadian Arctic. Hudson's Bay Oil & Gas Company formed.

1930
Depression affects HBC, and many posts are closed.

1931
Philip Chester appointed General Manager for Canada, and more authority is delegated to the Canadian Committee. Sale resigns as Governor; Patrick Ashley Cooper appointed in his place. Cooper is not pleased with his findings on a visit to Canada.

1932
Chester sets out to shake up Canadian operations. British Governor and Canadian Manager are frequently in disagreement over the next two decades.

1934
Cooper undertakes an inspection tour of Hudson Bay.

1936
Purchase of Revillon's Canadian assets.

1937
Shares in Revillon sold off. First organized commercial use of North West Passage. Short-wave radio transmitters installed at northern posts.

1938
Dividends resumed after seven years. HBC purchases Northern Traders Ltd. and Canalaska Trading Company, adding to its posts and transportation system.

1940
Many Arctic posts eliminated. Amalgamation of C.M. Lampson with HBC.

1943
Interest in Job Bros. sold.

1945
Chinchilla ranching started. Radio telephone replaces radio telegraph in North. Purchase of wholesale tobacco businesses of John Erzinger Ltd. and Scales and Roberts Ltd.

1946
Board reorganized. Philip Chester given seat on English Board, and named Managing Director for Canada.

1947
Hudson's Bay Oil & Gas has 50 percent interest in five producing oil wells at Leduc, Alberta, and makes many more productive oil and gas discoveries over the next two decades. *Nascopie* strikes an uncharted reef off Cape Dorset, and sinks with a one-year supply of trade goods and provisions for the Eastern Arctic. Christian Dior's "New Look" signals a decline in furs as a fashion item.

1948
White fox prices reach a new low, causing hardship for Inuit dependent on trapping.

1950
HBC assists efforts to promote sales of Inuit carvings. Woodward's opens Canada's first suburban shopping-centre store, but HBC turns down opportunities to move into shopping centres through the 1950s.

1952
Cooper resigns, and William Johnston (Tony) Keswick is appointed HBC Governor. He introduces a more personal approach to management.

1953
Max Bell of Calgary attempts to acquire control of HBC. Henry Benson becomes an HBC Director. Benson and Lord Heyworth begin attempts to reorient the firm, but their progressive proposals are turned down by the rest of the Board.

1956
Sir Winston Churchill is awarded the title "Grand Seigneur of the Company of Adventurers."

1957
Canadian Committee members become HBC directors.

1958
The HBC Board convenes in Winnipeg, meeting in Canada for the first time.

1959
Richard Murray succeeds Philip Chester as Managing Director for Canada.

1960
HBC buys the Montreal-based Henry Morgan department-store chain.

1962
Hudson's Bay Oil & Gas has a major gas strike north of Edmonton —the largest gas field in Canada.

1963
HBC begins move to suburban shopping malls.

1965
The HBC adopts "The Bay" designation. Viscount Derick Heathcote Amory appointed Governor.

1968–1969
Hudson's Bay Oil & Gas plans exploration for oil on extensive properties in the Arctic.

1968
York Factory, closed since 1957, is transferred to the federal government as a national historic site.

1969
An attempted merger of Simpsons, Simpsons-Sears, and the HBC falls through. Donald Scott McGiverin joins The Bay as Managing Director, Retail Stores.

1970
May 2—300th anniversary. Headquarters are moved from London, England, to Winnipeg.

George T. Richardson appointed HBC Governor.

1972
HBC acquires A. J. Freiman Ltd. and Middlesex Warehouse Ltd. McGiverin appointed President of the HBC. More suburban stores opened.

1973
The Bay acquires a majority interest in Markborough Properties Ltd., a real-estate firm. A deal involving HBC mineral rights is made with Siebens Oil & Gas.

1974
Toronto store opens at Bloor and Yonge. HBC operational headquarters move to Toronto.

1978
The Bay adds more department stores: first the Zellers chain, with the Fields chain, and then the Simpsons stores. The HBC is now Canada's leading retailer.

1979
Kenneth Thomson buys 75 percent of The Bay for $641 million. The Bay acquires large interest in Dome Petroleum.

1980
HBC buys major interest in Roxy Petroleum Ltd.

1981
Dome Petroleum wins control of Hudson's Bay Oil & Gas.

1982
McGiverin appointed Governor of the HBC. The Bay moves into automation, testing a video shopping service. Losses for the year come to $122 million.

1983
The HBC sells its preferred shares in Dome Petroleum.

1984
Another year of big losses for The Bay. Under McGiverin, sales have increased, but so has debt. The high interest rates of the early 1980s have created a crisis. John Tory, speaking

for Ken Thomson, orders drastic
changes in management direction.

1985
McGiverin resigns as president but
remains Governor. A three-man
team of John Tory, George Kosich
and Iain Ronald takes over top
management.

1987
The Bay sells its northern stores, and
fur auction house, ending 317 years
of connection with the Canadian
North. George Kosich becomes
president, and imposes stern
standards for profit achievement.

1989
First profit since 1979, thanks to
big gains in merchandising and real
estate.

1990
The Bay spins off Markborough
Properties Inc. and acquires Towers
department stores. Retail sales
revenues increase, but the Simpsons
stores remain a disaster.

1991
Simpsons Division is closed down:
seven net Simpsons stores are sold
to Sears Canada, and the remaining
seven are merged into The Bay.
To take advantage of lower taxes
and operating costs, The Bay is
considering the move of some
operations to the U.S.

# Resource People

During research for the three volumes of *Company of Adventurers*, nearly a thousand men and women who were either part of the HBC, or had been touched by its activities, were interviewed. They are listed as Resource People in the Appendices of all three books. Many of these interviews were done by Camilla Turner, and I am most grateful for her wise and imaginative contributions. The tapes and transcripts of all the recorded interviews have been donated to the Provincial Archives of Manitoba, and will eventually be opened for public perusal.

N.H. (Nick) Abramson
Vancouver

Senator Willie Adams
The Senate
Ottawa

John C. Ames
Vice-president and secretary
Canadian Pacific Ltd.
Montreal

Virginia Baldwin
Virginia Baldwin Company
Toronto

Timothy Ball
Department of Geography
University of Winnipeg
Winnipeg

Ian Barclay
Director, HBC
Ian A. Barclay & Associates
Vancouver

John C. Barrow
Former chairman of the board,
CEO, and director
Simpsons-Sears Ltd.
Toronto

Hon. Ron Basford
Former Minister of Consumer and
Corporate Affairs
Ottawa

Dave Bowker
Sales manager
Westrade Wholesale Ltd.
Victoria

Dr Hartwell Bowsfield
Professor
York University
Toronto

Allan W. Brent
Former president
Simpsons Ltd.
Victoria

Sherry Brydson
Toronto

D.G. (Pete) Buckley
Former head, Shop-Rite Stores
White Rock, B.C.

Al Burrows
Former head, HBC Wholesale
Division
Victoria

G. Allan Burton
Former chairman and CEO
Simpsons Ltd.
Toronto

J.R. Cavers
Professor Emeritus
University of Guelph
Guelph, Ontario

Syd Chapman
Former financial adviser to Lord
Thomson
Toronto

Robert (Bob) Chesshire
Former manager, HBC Northern
Stores Division
Former general manager, HBC Fur
Trade Department
Kingston

Elizabeth Chester
Daughter-in-law of Philip Chester
Vancouver

Posy Chisholm
Toronto and New York

Freeman Clowery
Archivist
Bank of Montreal
Sherbrooke, Quebec

W.L. Cobb
Former assistant general manager,
Northern Stores Department, HBC
Now residing in Shediac Cape, N.B.
and Victoria, B.C.

Alan Cooke
Director
Hochelaga Research Institute
Montreal

Hon. Nellie Cournoyea
Minister of the Government of
N.W.T.
Yellowknife

Al Daniels
Former consultant to HBC
San Francisco

Dora F. Darby
Former secretary to Governors Sir
Patrick Ashley Cooper and Sir
William Keswick
(Retired from HBC London in 1969
after 41 years of service)
Now residing in Beckenham, Kent,
England

Paul Davoud
Chief pilot, HBC
Kingston, Ontario

Chief Billy Diamond
Former Grand Chief of the Grand
Council of the Crees (of Quebec)
Val d'Or, Quebec

Hugh Dwan
Former head of Fur Sales, HBC
London

Tex Enemark
Former president
B.C. Mining Association
Vancouver

John A. English
Former vice-president, personnel,
HBC
Toronto

John Enright
Retired HBC accountant
Vancouver

Peter Ernerk
M.L.A., Government of N.W.T.
Yellowknife

Charles Waldron Evans
Former president of The Bay
Thornhill, Ontario

Sir Eric Faulkner
Deputy governor, HBC, 1952-1955
Director, HBC, 1950-1972
Former chairman, Glyn, Mills & Co.
London

Arthur Frayling
General manager, Fur Sales, HBC
London

Professor Milton Freeman
Department of Anthropology
University of Alberta
Edmonton

E.J. (Scotty) Gall
Head of transport, Western Arctic,
HBC, 1923-1966
Now residing in Victoria

Rita Green and staff
Statistics Canada
Advisory Services, Pacific Region
Vancouver

Brian Gross
Treasurer, HBC
Toronto

David Guest
Blake, Cassels & Graydon
(Lawyer involved in transfer of
HBC from London to Winnipeg)
Toronto

A.A. Guglielmin
Executive vice-president
Bay/Simpsons Merchandise Services
Toronto

Hon. Elijah Harper
Minister of Northern and Native
Affairs, Manitoba
Winnipeg

Pierre Henry
Missionary, Oblate of Mary
Immaculate, Apostle of the Inuit
N.W.T.

H. Albert Hochbaum
Artist and Naturalist
Delta, Manitoba

Stuart Hodgson
Chairman
British Columbia Ferry Corp.
Former commissioner, N.W.T.
Victoria

Rev. Dr Gerald Hutchinson
Thorsby, Alberta

Marie Ibell
Director, Legal Services
HBC
Victoria

Ted Johnson
Former head of The Bay Buying
Office
Toronto

Sir William Keswick
Governor, HBC, 1952-1965
Chairman, Matheson & Co. Ltd.
London

George Kosich
President, HBC
Toronto

Martin Lennon
Leicester, England

John Levy
Former president, Zellers
Vancouver

J.G. Links
Former director, HBC
Calman Links Ltd., Furrier to Her
Majesty The Queen
London

Charles B. Loewen
President
Loewen, Ondaatje, McCutcheon
Son-in-law of former HBC
managing director Philip Chester
Toronto

Michael Lubbock
Former HBC employee
Ottawa

L.F. McCollum
Director, Hudson's Bay Oil &
Gas Co.
(Former chairman, Continental Oil
Co.; chairman emeritus, Mercantile
Texas)
Dallas, Texas

Donald McGiverin
Governor, HBC, 1982-
Toronto

Alexander J. MacIntosh
Former deputy governor
Toronto

John McIntyre
Former vice-president, Real Estate,
HBC
Toronto

W.D.C. (Don) Mackenzie
W.D.C. Mackenzie Consultants
Former HBC director
Calgary

Doug MacLachlan
Guardian
York Factory
Winnipeg

Hugh MacLennan
Author
Montreal

D.W. Mahaffy
Senior vice-president, Finance and
Administration, HBC
Toronto

Roy Megarry
Publisher, *Globe and Mail*
Toronto

James Melville
Vice-president and director
The Woodbridge Company Limited
Toronto

Pierre Mignault
Former head, Quebec Division,
HBC
Price Club of Canada
Montreal

James Richard (Dick) Murray
Managing director, HBC, 1959-1972
Now residing in Victoria

E.F. (Ed) Newlands
Vancouver

Peter F.S. Nobbs
Vice-president, Corporate Finance
Midland Bank Canada
Former HBC treasurer
Toronto

Miyoko Okino
The Woodbridge Company Limited
Toronto

John de B. Payne
Public relations director,
HBC, 1947-1957
Montreal

D.H. (Des) Pitts
Former head of Northern Stores,
HBC
Winnipeg

Diane Rajh
Researcher
Deep Cove, B.C.

George Richardson
Governor, HBC, 1970-1983
(President, James Richardson &
Sons Ltd.)
Winnipeg

Lord Roll of Ipsden
S.G. Warburg and Co. Ltd.
London

Iain Ronald
Former executive vice-president,
HBC
Toronto

Larry Rowe
Vice-president, Information
Services, HBC
Toronto

Chesley Russell
Former HBC employee
Sidney, B.C.

Lynn Scully
HBC Retail
Vancouver

Joe Segal
Kingswood Capital Corp.
Vancouver

Ron Sheen
Former HBC employee
Victoria

Ian D. Sinclair
Chairman, CPR
Toronto

Ben Sivertz
Former commissioner, N.W.T.
Victoria

Jack Skolnick
New York

E.J. Spracklin
Former district manager, Keewatin
District
Northern Stores Department, HBC
Winnipeg

Herb Stovel
Heritage Trust
Toronto

Lord Strathcona and Mount Royal
(Descendant of Donald A. Smith,
1st Baron Strathcona and Mount
Royal)
London

Josh Teemotee
Inuit Tapirisat of Canada
Frobisher Bay, N.W.T.

David Thomson
President, Lavis Inc.
Toronto

Kenneth R. Thomson
Thomson Newspapers Ltd.
Proprietor, 76 percent, HBC
Toronto

J. Donald Tigert
Former director, Burns Fry Ltd.
Toronto

Marvin Tiller
Former head, Northern Stores, HBC
Winnipeg

Jim Tory
Lawyer and former director
Simpsons Ltd.
Toronto

John Tory
President and director
Thomson Corp. Ltd.
Toronto

Liz Tory
Governor, Shaw Festival,
Niagara-on-the-Lake
(Animator *extraordinaire*)
Toronto

Joy Turner
Documentalist, Canadian Plains
Research Centre
University of Regina
Regina

Frank Walker
Executive assistant to Philip Chester
of the Canadian Committee, HBC,
1951-1959
Montreal

George E. Weightman
Former manager, Market Research,
HBC, and Member Retail
Management Committee
Victoria

Bernie Weston
Trader and retailer
Skin & Bones
Toronto

Bill Wilder
Former director, Simpsons Ltd.
Toronto

R.G. Williamson
Professor of Anthropology
Department of Anthropology and
Archaeology
University of Saskatchewan
Saskatoon

Professor Alan Wilson
North West Cove
Hubbards, Nova Scotia

J.J. (Woody) and Kay Wood
Former HBC Factor and his wife
Victoria

Peter Wood
Former executive vice-president,
HBC
Toronto

Hon. Gordon Wray
Minister of the Government of
N.W.T.
Yellowknife

Jordan Zinovich
Fur-trade historian
New York

# Chapter Notes

CHAPTER 1
THE MAN WHO BECAME A
COUNTRY

P. 4. *As a Canadian:* Peter C.
Newman, *Flame of Power*, p. 49.

P. 4. *The Smith syndicate:* ibid.

P. 6. *the world's jumping-off place:*
W.T.R. Preston, *The Life and Times of
Lord Strathcona*, p. 15.

P. 7. *"Who is Smith?":* quoted in W.R.
Richmond, *The Life of Lord Strathcona*,
pp. 182–83.

P. 8. *All his life Smith was attended:*
James [Jan] Morris, *Heaven's
Command*, p. 347.

P. 9. *Apart from their illegibility:* Alan
Wilson, Introduction, in Hartwell
Bowsfield, ed., *The Letters of Charles
John Brydges 1879–1882*, p. xvii.

P. 9. *"races struggling to emerge":* Lord
Carnarvon, quoted in R.G. Moyles
and Doug Owram, *Imperial Dreams
and Colonial Realities*, p. 14.

P. 10. *There were always others:*
Preston, *Life and Times of Lord
Strathcona*, p. 265.

P. 10. *"What a strange creature":*
George Stephen, quoted in Albro
Martin, *James J. Hill and the Opening
of the Northwest*, p. 436.

P. 10. *He loved the solitude of a crowd:*
John Macnaughton, quoted by E.A.
Collard, Montreal *Gazette*, 10 May
1976, p. 6.

P. 12. *"To rest is to rust":* W.L.
Morton, unpublished MS biography
of Donald A. Smith, Ch. V
epigraph.

P. 12. *Scotland's history:* John Keegan,
*Six Armies in Normandy*, p. 167.

P. 13n. *Scottish puritanism . . . :* Hugh

MacLennan, in interview with
author, 18 September 1984.

P. 13. *"wife is said to have":* quoted in
Pierre Berton, *The Last Spike*,
pp. 353–54.

CHAPTER 2
GROWING UP COLD

P. 17. *Her voice was low:* Beckles
Willson, *The Life of Lord Strathcona
and Mount Royal*, p. 6.

P. 17. *without error, pause or confusion:*
ibid., p. 7.

P. 18. *"I have already visited":* Donald
A. Smith, quoted ibid., pp. 24–25.

P. 18. *"Canada is a country":* Evans,
quoted in Peter C. Newman, *Flame
of Power*, p. 52.

P. 20. *"took a friendly interest":* quoted
in Willson, *Life of Lord Strathcona*,
p. 50.

P. 21. *"any upstart, quill-driving
apprentices":* George Simpson, quoted
ibid.

P. 21. *"You would have to travel":*
Donald A. Smith, quoted ibid.,
p. 59.

P. 22. *"Your counting house department":*
George Simpson, quoted in W.L.
Morton, "Donald A. Smith and
Governor George Simpson," *The
Beaver*, Autumn 1978, p. 5.

P. 22. *"Let them go, too,":* Donald A.
Smith, quoted in Willson, *Life of
Lord Strathcona*, p. 63.

P. 22n. *"Hang Donald S.!":* quoted
ibid., p. 56.

P. 23. *"the most suspicious and faithless
set":* Nicol Finlayson, HBCA B38/
e/1/2 and B38/e/1/2d.

P. 25. *"He is all fire":* Richard

449

Hardisty, quoted in W.L. Morton, unpublished MS biography of Donald A. Smith, Ch. IV, p. 9.

P. 26. *"no command of his passions":* Donald A. Smith in letter to George Simpson, quoted ibid., p. 14.

P. 26. *has [very] much to learn:* Donald A. Smith in letter to George Simpson, quoted ibid.

P. 27. *It is just possible:* Donald A. Smith in letter to George Simpson, quoted ibid., pp. 14–15.

P. 27. *"A man who has been frozen":* Donald A. Smith, quoted in Willson, *Life of Lord Strathcona*, Vol. I, p. 122n.

P. 28. *Because the HBC controlled:* Alan Cooke in interview with author.

P. 29. *Indians starving to death:* Alan Cooke, *A History of the Naskapi of Schefferville*, p. 87.

P. 29. *no matter how poor the post:* W.R. Richmond, *The Life of Lord Strathcona*, p. 66.

P. 30. *"To-day we all assembled":* quoted in Willson, *Life of Lord Strathcona*, Vol. I, p. 133.

P. 30. *Then the astonished ear:* Charles Hallock, "Three Months in Labrador," Part II, *Harper's New Monthly Magazine*, 22, no. 132, 1861, p. 759.

P. 31. *"Smith . . . was about forty years old":* Sir Leopold McClintock, quoted in Willson, *Life of Lord Strathcona*, Vol. I, p. 157.

P. 31. *"I believe":* Donald A. Smith to George Simpson, quoted in Newman, *Flame of Power*, p. 55.

P. 31. *"When you want to bring":* George Simpson to Donald A. Smith, quoted in Morton, "Donald A. Smith and Governor George Simpson," p. 9.

P. 32. *"Smith, the officer in charge":* Eden Colvile to Curtis Lampson, quoted in Willson, *Life of Lord Strathcona*, Vol. I, pp. 194–95.

P. 32. *"I myself am becoming":* Donald A. Smith, quoted in Douglas MacKay, *The Honourable Company*, p. 290.

P. 33. *"The object I most wanted":* Donald A. Smith, quoted in Willson, *Life of Lord Strathcona*, Vol. I, p. 204.

P. 33. *"Really, why should Mr. Stephen":* Isabella Smith, quoted ibid., p. 207.

P. 34. *"I called today":* HBC Factor, quoted in Richmond, *Life of Lord Strathcona*, p. 81.

## CHAPTER 3
## BRINGING LOUIS RIEL TO HEEL

P. 38. *The plains were as thousands:* W.L. Morton in "A Century of Plain and Parkland," in R. Douglas Francis and Howard Palmer, *The Prairie West*, p. 19.

P. 39n. *"a haven of warmth":* quoted in Eric Wells, *Winnipeg, Where the New West Begins: An Illustrated History*.

P. 40. *"the incubus of the Company's monopoly":* James Ross, quoted in Frank Rasky, *The Taming of the Canadian West*, p. 202.

P. 40. *"the greedy London directory":* William Mactavish, quoted ibid., p. 202.

P. 40. *"a stoker in hell":* William Mactavish, quoted in *Dictionary of Canadian Biography*, Vol. IX, p. 530.

P. 40n. *"I will not speak":* William Mactavish, quoted in Beckles Willson, *The Life of Lord Strathcona and Mount Royal*, Vol. I, pp. 281–82.

P. 42. *"You go no farther":* Louis Riel, quoted in Joseph Howard, *Strange Empire, a Narrative of the Northwest*, p. 98.

P. 43. *"to keep those wild people quiet":* Sir John A. Macdonald, quoted in Frank Rasky, *The Taming of the Canadian West*, pp. 203–4.

P. 44. *"prompt display of vigour":* William McDougall, quoted ibid, p. 205.

P. 44. *"done his utmost"*: Sir John A. Macdonald, quoted in Sandra Gwyn, *The Private Capital*, p. 117.

P. 45. *"a dead man"*: William Mactavish, quoted in Willson, *Life of Lord Strathcona*, Vol. I, p. 284n.

P. 45n. *"an injustice to the people"*: John Bruce, quoting William Mactavish, in House of Commons *Debates*, 1876, pp. 811–12.

P. 46. *The tendency of North American events:* New York *Sun*, quoted in Peter C. Newman, *Flame of Power*, pp. 56–57.

P. 46. *"to volunteer to correct"*: Donald A. Smith, quoted in Willson, *Life of Lord Strathcona*, p. 182.

P. 47. *"If no settlement occurs"*: Donald A. Smith, quoted ibid., Vol. I, p. 307.

P. 49. *"Imperial Government has no intention"*: Sir John Young's proclamation, quoted in W.R. Richmond, *The Life of Lord Strathcona*, pp. 106–7.

P. 50. *"I am here to-day"*: Donald A. Smith, quoted ibid.

P. 51. *"We must make Canada respect us"*: Louis Riel, quoted in Hartwell Bowsfield, *Louis Riel, The Rebel and the Hero*, p. 49.

P. 52. *"Oh, let me out of this"*: Thomas Scott, quoted in Willson, *Life of Lord Strathcona*, Vol. I, p. 363.

P. 52. *"The secret of Thomas Scott's burial"*: Alexandre Nault, quoted in Winnipeg *Tribune*, 6 March 1961, p. 12.

P. 52n. *"We tried Riel"*: juror quoted in G.F.G. Stanley, "Louis Riel and the Prairie Uprising," p. 193.

P. 55. *"benevolent constabulary"*: Col. Garnet Wolseley, quoted in James [Jan] Morris, *Heaven's Command*, p. 350.

P. 55. *"Hope Riel will have bolted"*: Col. Garnet Wolseley, quoted in Frank Rasky, *The Taming of the Canadian West*, pp. 207–8.

P. 55. *"more suitable for"*: R.G. MacBeth, quoted in Robert Stewart, *Sam Steele: Lion of the Frontier*, p. 24.

P. 56. *"banditti"*: Howard, *Strange Empire*, p. 208.

P. 57. *"I yield up to you"*: Donald A. Smith and Adams G. Archibald, quoted in Richmond, *Life of Lord Strathcona*, p. 143.

P. 57. *"our just rights"*: Louis Riel, quoted in Willson, *Life of Lord Strathcona*, Vol. I, p. 354.

P. 57. *"I congratulate"*: Louis Riel, quoted in Morris, *Heaven's Command*, p. 349.

P. 58. *He was a man of intelligence:* Bowsfield, *Louis Riel: The Rebel and the Hero*, p. 7.

CHAPTER 4
THE GREAT FIRE CANOES

P. 62. *"A corporation has no conscience"*: W.F. Butler, quoted in Beckles Willson, *The Life of Lord Strathcona and Mount Royal*, Vol. I, p. 155.

P. 62. *"The sudden withdrawal"*: William Mactavish, letter, in Correspondence Inward, D 10/1, #145, Mactavish to Joseph Howe, 16 May 1870, p. 167, HBCA-PAC.

P. 63. *"Gentlemen, this Company"*: HBC shareholder, quoted in Arthur Ray, "Adventurers at the Crossroads," *The Beaver*, April/May 1986, p. 10.

P. 65. *"coolly turned the boat"*: *Manitoban*, quoted in Theodore Barris, *Fire Canoe*, p. 30.

P. 65. *"Hey! You put"*: Steamboat captain, quoted in Bruce Wishart, "Paddle Wheels on the Prairies," *The Beaver*, Dec. 1989/Jan. 1990, p. 31.

P. 66. *"We go from one bank"*: Lady Dufferin, quoted in Barris, *Fire Canoe*, p. 37.

P. 67. *"was trying to waltz"*: Manitoba *Free Press*, quoted in Wishart, "Paddle Wheels on the Prairies," p. 32.

P. 67. *Horses with buckskin riders:*
Barris, *Fire Canoe*, p. 20.

P. 68n. *"the greatest marine disaster":*
Saskatoon newspaper, quoted ibid.,
p. 191.

P. 72. *"O my God":* Louis Riel,
quoted ibid., p. 85.

P. 73n. *now beckons a congregation:*
ibid., p. 256.

CHAPTER 5
PROGRESSION AND BETRAYAL

P. 76. *"Our immediate destiny":* HBC
Factor quoted in Douglas MacKay,
*The Honourable Company*, pp. 285–86.

P. 78. *"If we had insisted":* Roderick
McKenzie quoted in Beckles
Willson, *The Life of Lord Strathcona
and Mount Royal*, Vol. I, p. 516.

P. 78. *"It is all very well":* James
Lockhart quoted ibid., Vol. I,
pp. 521–22.

P. 80. *"The Chief Commissioner cares":*
James Lockhart, quoted ibid.,
Vol. I, 521.

P. 80. *"It may not be out of place":*
Donald A. Smith, letter, in Hardisty
Papers, G-A1A-file 76, Donald
Smith to Richard Hardisty, 31 May
1873, Glenbow Institute, Calgary.

P. 82. *"Where every man's a liar":*
quoted in Grant MacEwan, *Between
the Red and the Rockies*, p. 29.

P. 84. *If ever an organization:* Michael
Bliss, *Northern Enterprise*, pp. 194–95.

P. 85. *Looking to the small amount:*
William Armit to Donald A. Smith,
HBCA, A6/51, fos. 225–226,
London, 19 June 1878.

P. 86. *His arrival in Winnipeg:* Alan
Wilson and R.A. Hotchkiss in
*Dictionary of Canadian Biography*,
Vol. XI, p. 124.

P. 87n. *"the symbol of success":* W.L.
Morton, quoted in Peter C.
Newman, *The Canadian Establishment*,
Vol. II, *The Acquisitors*, p. 303.

P. 87n. *"in the progress women have
made":* E. H. Macklin, quoted ibid.,

p. 302.

P. 88. *"The office now is"* [and]
*"Bedlam let loose":* Charles J. Brydges
to William Armit, HBCA, A12/21,
fo. 40 and fos. 122–23.

P. 88. *were more crowded:* Merrill
Denison, *Canada's First Bank*, Vol. II,
p. 210.

P. 89. *"I am satisfied":* Charles J.
Brydges to G.J. Goschen, quoted in
Alan Wilson, Introduction in
Hartwell Bowsfield, ed., *The Letters
of Charles John Brydges 1879–1882*,
p. xlin.

P. 89. *Armed with:* Alan Wilson,
ibid., p. lxxxiv.

P. 91. *erred on the side:* John S.
Galbraith, "Land Policies of the
Hudson's Bay Company,
1870–1913," *Canadian Historical
Review*, 32, no. 1 (March 1951), p. 9.

P. 91. *"We . . . trace all these":* Sir John
Rose to Sir John A. Macdonald,
quoted in Shirlee A. Smith, "A
Desire to Worry Me Out," *The
Beaver*, Dec. 1987/Jan. 1988, p. 8.

P. 91. *"My long connection":* Donald A.
Smith, quoted in *The Times*, 28 Nov.
1883.

P. 92. *Smith's actions:* Shirlee A.
Smith, "A Desire to Worry Me
Out," pp. 8–9.

P. 92. *"every appearance of":* Charles J.
Brydges, letter to Sir John A.
Macdonald, quoted ibid., p. 11.

P. 93. *"I . . . see no prospect":* James L.
Cotter, letter of 10 July 1886, quoted
in Willson, *Life of Lord Strathcona*,
Vol. II, pp. 39–40.

P. 94. *While competent in the woods:*
George McTavish, *Behind the
Palisades*, p. 238.

P. 95n. *"I have a pain here":* Robert
Campbell, quoted in Clifford
Wilson, *Robert Campbell*, p. 175.

P. 97. *This very startling information:*
N.M.W.J. McKenzie, *The Men of the
Hudson's Bay Company*, p. 46.

P. 97. *Here was a great:* ibid., p. 137.

P. 97. *"I have waited"*: J. Ogden Grahame, letter of 21 May 1891, quoted in Willson, *Life of Lord Strathcona*, Vol. II, p. 185.

P. 97. *"The fiat has gone forth . . ."*: Roderick Ross, quoted ibid., p. 186.

P. 97. *"the prince of humbugs"*: letter, PAC, Roderick MacFarlane papers, MacArthur to Duncan MacFarlane, 15 Feb. 1878.

CHAPTER 6
STEAL OF EMPIRE

P. 99. *For forty years:* characterization of Donald A. Smith, W.T.R. Preston, *The Life and Times of Lord Strathcona*, pp. 13-14.

P. 100. *His philosophical disposition:* on Donald A. Smith, ibid., p. 175.

P. 101. *"a curse to the country"*: Dr John C. Schultz in House of Commons *Debates*, 18 April 1877, and *Manitoba Free Press*, 21 April 1877.

P. 101. *a mixture of putty:* description of Winnipeg, quoted in Pierre Berton, *The National Dream*, p. 225.

P. 101. *"Winnipeg and Barrie"*: report, quoted in W.L. Morton, *Manitoba: A History*, p. 171.

P. 104. *"Upon you and the influence"*: Sir John A. Macdonald to Donald A. Smith, quoted in Peter C. Newman, *Flame of Power*, p. 60.

P. 105. *"We first noticed"*: Angus McKay's journal, quoted in J.G. MacGregor, *Senator Hardisty's Prairies, 1849–1889*, p. 108.

P. 106. *"To the health"*: MPs, quoted in Preston, *Life and Times of Lord Strathcona*, p. 84.

P. 107. *"I would be most willing"*: Donald A. Smith, quoted in Newman, *Flame of Power*, p. 60.

P. 107. *"Donald A. has"*: Parliamentary page, quoted in Preston, *Life and Times of Lord Strathcona*, p. 85.

P. 107. *"I could lick"*: Sir John A. Macdonald, quoted in Newman, *Flame of Power*, p. 61.

P. 107. *"Sir John is dead"*: Liberals in House of Commons, 5 Nov. 1873, quoted in Sandra Gwyn, *The Private Capital*, p. 131.

P. 107. *"Mr. Smith was a representative"*: Charles Tupper's Orangeville speech, reported in House of Commons *Debates*, 1878, Vol. V, p. 2560, as quoted in Preston, *Life and Times of Lord Strathcona*, p. 307.

P. 108. *The key to Smith's actions:* David Cruise and Alison Griffiths, *Lords of the Line*, p. 72.

P. 108. *"We are now simply"*: Eden Colvile to James A. Grahame, 5 June 1874, HBCA A.7/4, fos. 198–99.

P. 108. *"Few figures in political history"*: regarding Donald A. Smith, Gustavus Myers, *A History of Canadian Wealth*, Vol. I, p. 266.

P. 111. *"It is impossible"*: Lord Dufferin letter, PAC, Mackenzie Papers, Dufferin to Mackenzie, 10 Aug. 1877.

P. 111. *"put money in"*: Sir John A. Macdonald, House of Commons *Debates*, 1878, Vol. IV, pp. 1690–91.

P. 112. *"which would put a stop"*: Sir John A. Macdonald, House of Commons *Debates*, 1878, Vol. V, pp. 2556–57.

P. 112. *Finally . . . Black Rod entered:* W.T.R. Preston, *My Generation of Politics and Politicians*, pp. 112–14, quoted in Cynthia M. Smith with Jack McLeod, *Sir John A.: An Anecdotal Life of John A. Macdonald*, pp. 72–73.

P. 112. *Tory members:* Preston, *My Generation of Politics and Politicians*, p. 112, quoted ibid.

P. 112. *"That fellow Smith"*: Sir John A. Macdonald, quoted in Donald Creighton, *John A. Macdonald: The Old Chieftain*, p. 240.

P. 113. *Now, Sir John:* Dr John C. Schultz, letter, PAC, Macdonald Papers, Schultz to Macdonald, 28 May 1878.

P. 113. *"the primary object of the railway"*: Donald A. Smith, quoted in *Manitoba Free Press*, 20 Aug. 1878.

P. 113. *keep the Company neutral:* William Armit to James A. Grahame, HBCA, A1, Grahame to Secretary, 10 Aug. 1878, and reply.

P. 113. *"no favour to ask":* Donald A. Smith, quoted in Preston, *Life and Times of Lord Strathcona*, pp. 119–20.

P. 114. *"I am sorry to say":* Donald A. Smith and a supporter, election of 1878, quoted in Newman, *Flame of Power*, p. 50.

P. 114. *A new current was in motion:* Ralph Allen, *Ordeal by Fire*, p. 13.

P. 115. *The immensity of the treeless Prairie:* W.L. Morton, in unpublished MS biography of Donald A. Smith.

P. 115. *This was the climate:* Pierre Berton, *The National Dream*, p. 336.

P. 116. *"the most stupendous contract":* Preston, quoted in Newman, *Flame of Power*, p. 67.

P. 118. *"We did not like him":* J.H.E. Secretan of Van Horne, quoted ibid., p. 80.

P. 118. *"It may be that":* Donald A. Smith to George Stephen, quoted in *McGill News,* Montreal, March 1932, p. 31.

P. 118. *"HAVE NO MEANS":* W.C. Van Horne to Donald A. Smith, quoted in Newman, *Flame of Power*, p. 64.

P. 119. *"for the planet Jupiter":* Sir John A. Macdonald to George Stephen, quoted ibid.

P. 119. *"an idle, ice-bound":* Liberal critic, quoted ibid., p. 83.

P. 119. *He was the great:* Donald A. Smith described in Preston, *Life and Times of Lord Strathcona*, p. 133.

P. 120. *Once again the partnership:* Creighton, *John A. Macdonald: The Old Chieftain*, pp. 397–98.

P. 120. *"It's to the government":* Donald A. Smith to George Stephen, quoted in Newman, *Flame of Power*, p. 64.

P. 120. *"The day the CPR busts":* a CPR director, quoted ibid.

P. 121. *"The time has now come":* Louis Riel, quoted in Hartwell Bowsfield, *Louis Riel, The Rebel and the Hero*, p. 7.

P. 124. *"All supplies furnished":* Joseph Wrigley, quoted in J.E. Rea, "The Hudson's Bay Company and the North-West Rebellion," *The Beaver*, Summer 1982, p. 47.

P. 124. *"We tossed up chairs":* William Van Horne, quoted in David Cruise and Alison Griffiths, *Lords of the Line*, p. 155.

P. 124. *"the Canadian Pacific Railway":* Sir Charles Tupper, describing Sir Donald A. Smith, quoted in Beckles Willson, *The Life of Lord Strathcona and Mount Royal*, Vol. II, p. 132.

P. 124n. *bonification:* PAC MG 29, A5, vol. 22, IV, p. 52, Letter from F.A. McKenzie to Mr Garson, 22 June 1915.

P. 125. *"The last spike":* William Van Horne, quoted in Pierre Berton, *The Last Spike*, p. 413.

P. 125. *"It seemed":* Sandford Fleming, quoted in Lawrence Burpee, *Sandford Fleming, Empire Builder*, p. 118.

P. 125. *"the work has been done":* William Van Horne, quoted in Berton, *The Last Spike*, p. 416.

P. 126. *"All aboard":* quoted ibid.

P. 126n. *The last spike was an ordinary nail:* Lord Strathcona, in letter to author, 10 March 1989.

P. 127. *The Canadian Pacific Railway:* Michael Bliss, *Northern Enterprise*, p. 195.

P. 127n. *"They didn't tell us":* CPR employee, quoted in Peter C. Newman, "An Unseemly End to the Railway Saga," *Maclean's*, 5 Feb. 1990.

P. 128. *"Building that railroad":* William Van Horne, quoted in John Robert Colombo, *Colombo's Canadian*

*Quotations*, p. 611.

P. 128. *"Now, there's a very neat place":* Donald A. Smith, quoted in Willson, *Life of Lord Strathcona*, Vol. II, p. 125.

P. 128n. *"How much does the stable boy":* story about William Van Horne, Newman, *Flame of Power*, p. 88.

P. 129. *"Remember, James":* Donald A. Smith, quoted in Newman, *Flame of Power*, p. 51.

CHAPTER 7
CANADA IN A SWALLOW-TAIL COAT

P. 133. *"There is one man":* Sam Hughes, quoted in Beckles Willson, *The Life of Lord Strathcona and Mount Royal*, Vol. II, p. 154.

P. 134. *"I have no claim":* Sir Donald A. Smith, quoted ibid.

P. 135n. *"A Canadian soldier":* British housewife to High Commissioner Vincent Massey, quoted in Norman Webster, "Massey's War," *Globe and Mail*, 10 July 1980, p. 1.

P. 135n. *"Canada has been modest":* Sir Wilfrid Laurier, speech, quoted in John Robert Colombo, *Colombo's Canadian Quotations*, p. 332.

P. 136. *There were Rajput princes:* James [Jan] Morris, *Farewell the Trumpets*, pp. 21–22.

P. 136. *The British as a whole:* Morris, *Farewell the Trumpets*, p. 30.

P. 136. *"the dervishes of Anglo-Saxondom":* O.D. Skelton, *The Life and Letters of Sir Wilfrid Laurier*, p. 60.

P. 137. *As a warm darkness fell:* June Callwood, *The Naughty Nineties*, p. 21.

P. 138. *"The All-Red Line":* Sir Sandford Fleming, quoted in Lawrence Burpee, *Sandford Fleming, Empire Builder*, p. 199.

P. 138. *"Now we must attend":* doctor to Lord Strathcona, quoted in Willson, *Life of Lord Strathcona*, Vol. II, p. 406.

P. 140. *"yielding to the earnest entreaties":* Sir Thomas Shaughnessy on Lord Strathcona, quoted in W.R. Richmond, *The Life of Lord Strathcona*, p. 226.

P. 140. *"The Sabbath is over":* Lord Strathcona, quoted in Peter C. Newman, *Flame of Power*, p. 66.

P. 140n. *"I still remember vividly":* Dr Wilfred Grenfell, of Lord Strathcona, quoted in Willson, *Life of Lord Strathcona*, Vol. II, p. 479.

P. 141. *"Lord Strathcona presides":* Gaspard Farrer, quoted in Heather Gilbert, *Awakening Continent*, pp. 163–64.

P. 143. *"Give the gentleman":* Lord Strathcona, quoted in Newman, *Flame of Power*, p. 68.

P. 144. *"His Labrador Lordship":* Queen Victoria, of Lord Strathcona, quoted in Willson, *Life of Lord Strathcona*, Vol. II, p. 316.

P. 144. *"Uncle Donald":* Edward VII, quoted ibid., p. 427.

P. 145. *"Let the watch fires be lit":* Sir Wilfrid Laurier, quoted in Callwood, *Naughty Nineties*.

P. 145. *"the useless ruffians":* Lord Minto, quoted in Robert Stewart, *Sam Steele: Lion of the Frontier*, pp. 239–40.

P. 147. *"Of all the regiments":* *Daily Express*, quoted ibid., p. 251.

P. 147. *"The occasion of his own toast":* *The Times*, quoted in Newman, *Flame of Power*, p. 67.

P. 147. *"He arrived a bit tight":* Agar Adamson, quoted in Sandra Gwyn, *The Private Capital*, p. 363.

P. 148. *"it was very difficult":* S. Macnaughtan, *My Canadian Memories*, p. 94.

P. 148. *"He is Canada":* A.G. Gardiner, quoted in Newman, *Flame of Power*, p. 65.

CHAPTER 8
THE RECKONING

P. 152. *remarkable vitality: Economist*, 2 June 1906.

P. 152. *"to aid in doing the right thing"*: Roderick MacFarlane to an HBC director, quoted in Beckles Willson, *The Life of Lord Strathcona and Mount Royal*, Vol. II, p. 201.

P. 152. *an historical concern:* HBC director, quoted ibid.

P. 153. *"all Hell for a basement"*: Rudyard Kipling, quoted in W.L. Morton, unpublished MS biography of Donald A. Smith.

P. 153. *It little mattered:* R.G. Moyles and Doug Owram, *Imperial Dreams and Colonial Realities*, p. 42.

P. 154. *"Caleb would stand"*: Martha Ostenso, quoted in David C. Carpenter, "Matriarchs and Patriarchs in Canadian Prairie Fiction," in Howard Palmer, *The Settlement of the West*, p. 167.

P. 156. *"The arrogance of the Canadian"*: *Hamburger Nachrichten*, quoted in Willson, *Life of Lord Strathcona*, Vol. II, p. 294.

P. 158. *"the Hudson's Bay Company by their dealings"*: Lord Strathcona to shareholders, quoted in HBC, "Report of the Governor and Committee of the Hudson's Bay Company to be laid before Shareholders, 6 July 1908," p. 12.

P. 159. *"Company policies were not changed"*: Philip Chester, "The First 250 Years," unpublished MS history of the Hudson's Bay Company, p. 4.

P. 163. *"[Lord Strathcona] was most kind"*: R.L. Borden quoted in Willson, *Life of Lord Strathcona*, Vol. II, p. 432.

P. 164. *"on every rock"*: Sydney Smith, quoted in James [Jan] Morris, *Pax Britannica*, p. 429.

P. 164. *"That would never have happened"*: quoted in *Pax Britannica*, p. 425.

P. 165. *"It was not as a mercantile company"*:

Lord Strathcona quoted in R.W. Ferrier, *The History of the British Petroleum Company*, Vol. I, p. 159.

P. 165. *"detachment of manner"*: Ethel Hurlbatt, quoted in Willson, *Life of Lord Strathcona*, Vol. II, p. 475.

P. 166. *The whole scene:* J.W. Pedley, *Biography of Lord Strathcona and Mount Royal*, p. 168.

P. 166n. *"Lord Strathcona"*: Drs Barlow and Pasteur on last words of Lord Strathcona, quoted in W.L. Morton, unpublished MS biography of Donald A. Smith.

P. 167. *"We need not fear"*: Sir Charles Davidson, of Lord Strathcona, quoted in Willson, *Life of Lord Strathcona*, Vol. II, p. 460.

P. 167. *"Since Sir John Macdonald's time"*: Sir Wilfrid Laurier, of Lord Strathcona, quoted in Pedley, *Biography of Lord Strathcona*, pp. 182–83.

P. 167. *With no advantages: The Times*, 22 January 1914.

P. 167. *"In sorrowful memory"*: tribute of Dowager Queen Alexandra, quoted in Willson, *Life of Lord Strathcona*, Vol. II, p. 463.

P. 168. *"I remit and cancel"*: will of Lord Strathcona, quoted in W.T.R. Preston, *The Life and Times of Lord Strathcona*, pp. 272-73.

CHAPTER 9
ON THE TRAIL OF THE ARCTIC FOX

P. 172n. *to prevent the United States:* British Colonial Office, quoted in David Judd, "Canada's Northern Policy: Retrospect and Prospect," *Polar Record*, 14, no. 92 (May, 1969), p. 593.

P. 172. *For at least 150 years:* William G. Watson, "A Southern Perspective on Northern Economic Development," in Michael S. Whittington, co-ordinator, *The North*, p. 8.

P. 172. *At one time:* Bob Chesshire in interview with author.

P. 173n. *What's so difficult about that:*

story of Father Henri from Stuart Hodgson, in interview with author.

P. 173. *The Eskimo makes his or her appearance:* Hugh Brody, *Living Arctic: Hunters of the Canadian North*, p. 19.

P. 174. *The "Eskimo" smiles:* Brody, *Living Arctic*, p. 19.

P. 174. *The Eskimos were very smart:* J.J. Wood in interview with author.

P. 176. *One could look across:* Archie Hunter, *Northern Traders: Caribou Hair in the Stew*, p. 60.

P. 176. *"The sooner the caribou are gone":* trader quoted in Philip Godsell, *Arctic Trader: The Account of Twenty Years with the Hudson's Bay Company*, p. 274.

P. 176. *a case of the Indian:* ibid.

P. 176. *I have made it my study:* George Simpson, letter to London Committee, 1822, quoted in *Caesars of the Wilderness*, p. 226.

P. 178. *So fond are these poor people:* Graham, in *Andrew Graham's Observations on Hudson's Bay, 1767–91*, p. 237.

P. 178. *It was not some primitive blood lust:* Daniel Francis in *Arctic Chase: A History of Whaling in Canada's North*, pp. 11–12.

P. 179. *There is something extremely painful:* William Scoresby, from *An Account of the Arctic Regions*, Vol. I, p. 472, quoted in Daniel Francis, *Arctic Chase*, p. 1.

P. 180. *a paradise of those who reject all restraint:* Hudson Stuck, *A Winter's Circuit of Our Arctic Coast*, p. 320, quoted in Morris Zaslow, *The Opening of the Canadian North, 1870–1914*, p. 258.

P. 180. *when girls were not obtainable:* C.E. Whittaker, *Arctic Eskimo*, pp. 234–35, quoted ibid., p. 259.

P. 181. *"They were so innocent a people":* Klengenberg, quoted in R.A.J. Phillips, *Canada's North*, p. 75.

P. 182. *Mine, a single, had a hay tick:* Elizabeth Taylor, quoted in Grace Lee

Nute, "Paris to Peel's River in 1892," *The Beaver*, March 1948, p. 20.

P. 184. *Snowing fast, very tough wind:* Ralph Parsons, quoted in Larry Gingras, *Medals, Tokens and Paper Money of the HBC*, p. 80.

P. 186. *He was naturally reserved:* Ralph Parsons described in A.L. Fleming, *Perils of the Polar Pack*, p. 331.

P. 186. *The Company is a hard taskmaster:* of Ralph Parsons, Henry Toke Munn, *Prairie Trails and Arctic Byways*, p. 271.

P. 189. *a Man, preeminently:* in Gontran de Poncins, *Kabloona*, p. 25.

P. 190. *I'd go in there:* E.J. Gall, in interview with author.

P. 191. *the market value of a rifle:* Philip Godsell, *Arctic Trader*, p. 273.

P. 191. *The man would answer:* Duncan Pryde in *Nunaga: Ten Years of Eskimo Life*, p. 215.

P. 192. *It sold good rifles:* Albert Hochbaum, in interview with author.

P. 193. *The new barter economy:* Diamond Jenness, quoted in Brody, *Living Arctic*, p. 23n.

P. 193. *It was the accepted thing to do:* E.J. Gall, in interview with author.

P. 193. *The Eskimos were just as jealous:* Chesley Russell, in interview with author.

P. 194. *Harris' wives were quite a mixed lot:* on Inuit-white marriages, in Sydney A. Keighley, *Trader, Tripper, Trapper: The Life of a Bay Man*, p. 100.

P. 194. *"What would happen if I asked":* de Poncins, in *Kabloona*, pp. 127–28.

P. 195. *Far from being the casual and promiscuous affair:* Ernest Burch, in "Marriage and Divorce Among the North Alaskan Eskimos," in Paul Bohannan, ed., *Divorce and After: An Analysis of the Emotional and Social Problems of Divorce*, pp. 152–53.

P. 197. *So here we were:* J.W. Anderson, in *Fur Trader's Story*, p. 80.

P. 198. *The northern traders' loyalty:* Bob Chesshire, in interview with author.

P. 198. *God was the Company:* and story of Jim Deckers as told by W.L. Cobb in interview with author.

P. 198. *it disappeared into him:* Ray Price, *The Howling Arctic: The Remarkable People Who Made Canada Sovereign in the Farthest North*, p. 213.

P. 200. *Most masters of the Company's posts:* Annie Redsky, quoted in Edith May Griffis, "The Lady of the Bay," *The Beaver*, Winter 1960, p. 48.

P. 200. *When I was in charge of a post:* Cornwallis King, quoted in *Trader King (as told to Mary Weekes)*, p. 178.

P. 200. *"Your ability to keep this book":* quoted in Heather Robertson, ed., *A Gentleman Adventurer: The Arctic Diaries of R.H.G. Bonnycastle*, p. 1.

P. 200. Story of Pierre Mercredi and the oxen: from Barbara Hunt, ed., *Rebels, Rascals & Royalty*, p. 54.

P. 201. *It was a pretty primitive existence:* W.L. Cobb, in interview with author.

P. 202. *One day this fellow:* Stuart Hodgson, in interview with author.

P. 202. *When things were not going well:* Senator Charlie Watt, quoted in "A Short History of Outside Contact," *Taqralk* (Inuit Magazine), Jan.–Feb. 1978, pp. 30–32.

P. 202. *The Bay* would *grubstake people:* Stuart Hodgson, in interview with author.

## CHAPTER 10
## KILLING THE COMPETITION

P. 205. *Growing numbers of fur buyers and traders:* Arthur Ray, *The Canadian Fur Trade in the Industrial Age*, p. 50.

P. 207. *I remember one time:* John Montague, quoted in "Fur Traders," in *Them Days,* 1973, p. 25.

P. 207. *They were considered outlaws:* Jordan Zinovich on Hislop and Nagle personnel, in interview with author.

P. 210. *"When the tide fell":* George Venables, quoted in L.F.S. Upton, "The Wreck of the *Eldorado*: Strange Tale of Shipwreck," *The Beaver*, Autumn 1968, p. 28.

P. 210. *"When we got up each morning":* George Venables, quoted ibid., p. 30.

P. 210. *"as unknown to the party":* Globe, quoted ibid., p. 31.

P. 211. *Only those who have worked:* Philip Godsell, in *Arctic Trader*, p. 158.

P. 211. *To open up a store against the Bay:* W.L. Cobb, in interview with author.

P. 212. *I just asked him who won:* R.J. Renison, quoted by Walter Gordon in interview with author.

P. 212. *that showed a profit:* Wallace Laird, quoted in R.H. Cockburn, "Revillon Man." *The Beaver*, February/March 1990, p. 15.

P. 212. *Arrangements should be definitely made:* background of HBC takeover of Revillon Frères, in HBC internal memo, HBCA, Unclassified, DD, 176-Revillon Frères.

P. 212. *After more and more consideration on the subject:* Jean Revillon, in letter to Patrick Ashley Cooper, 5 December 1935, ibid.

P. 213. *we have good grounds to claim:* Jean Revillon, in letter, 16 December 1935, ibid.

P. 214n. *Months later:* Clarence Birdseye, in "The Birth of an Industry," *The Beaver*, September 1941, p. 24, reprinted Autumn 1980, p. 12.

## CHAPTER 11
## THE *NASCOPIE* CHRONICLES

P. 217. *Signifying many things to many people:* Henny Nixon, "SS/RMS *Nascopie*, 1912–1947: A Biography of a Ship," *Argonauta: The Newsletter of the Canadian Nautical Research Society*, 4. no. 3, 1987, p. 4.

P. 218. *There may have been some "luck" about it:* Roland Wild, *Arctic Command: The Story of Smellie of the Nascopie*, p. viii.

P. 219. *"Would you like anything to eat?":* ibid., pp. 3–4.

P. 220. *When the Port inspectors made their routine check:* ibid., pp. 90–91.

P. 220. *When we arrived no one from shore dared:* Archie Hunter, in *Northern Traders*, p. 8.

P. 220. *At every port where we stopped:* Ernie Lyall, in *An Arctic Man: Sixty-Five Years in Canada's North*, p. 40.

P. 220. *The sight of these great vessels:* Alootook Ipellie, quoted in Penny Petrone, ed., *Northern Voices*, p. 246.

P. 224. *A strange spectacle the decks presented:* Isobel Hutchinson, quoted in Heather Robertson, ed., *A Gentleman Adventurer: The Arctic Diaries of R.H.G. Bonnycastle*, pp. 211–13.

P. 224. *Pity. She still had:* E.J. Gall, in interview with author.

P. 226. *I knew where all the reefs were:* E.J. Gall, in interview with author.

P. 226. *The current was running pretty fast:* E.J. Gall, in interview with author.

P. 227. *It's all bunk about the North West Passage:* E.J. Gall, in interview with author.

P. 227. *One evening in September:* Barbara Heslop, in "Arctic Rescue," *The Beaver*, March 1944, p. 9, reprinted Autumn 1980, p. 71.

P. 228. *Dashing out on deck:* J.W. Anderson, quoted in *Fur Trader's Story*, p. 242.

P. 229. *Willis got into a dory and rowed back:* George Whitman, on the wreck of the *Nascopie*, in interview with author.

P. 229. *"Our big helper has hit the bottom":* quoted in Penny Petrone, ed., *Northern Voices*, p. 166.

CHAPTER 12
NORTHERN GRIDLOCK

P. 231. *The real boss of each settlement:* E.J. Spracklin, in interview with author.

P. 231. *One time this Eskimo interpreter:* Chesley Russell, in interview with author.

P. 232n. *Using a large ten-gallon pail:* H.M. Ross, in *The Apprentice's Tale*, p. 60.

P. 232. *[We] accepted a more intimate responsibility:* Leonard Budgell, quoted in "Recollections of Rigolet," *Them Days 60 Years Ago*, August 1975, p. 13.

P. 232. *"these simple, primitive folk"* and description of Inuit: P.A.C. Nichols, in "Enter . . . The Fur Traders," *The Beaver*, Winter 1954, p. 37.

P. 232. *Take heed: Eskimo Book of Knowledge*, quoted in Hugh Brody, *The People's Land*, p. 21.

P. 233. *Sometimes we could be trading:* Ernie Lyall, in *An Arctic Man: Sixty-Five Years in Canada's North*, pp. 210–11.

P. 233. *The Company will make a last stand: Winnipeg Free Press*, 24 Oct. 1913, quoted in Arthur J. Ray, *The Canadian Fur Trade in the Industrial Age*, p. 95.

P. 233. *purgatory ledgers:* ibid., p. 105.

P. 233. *I think any experienced trader:* Philip Godsell, quoted ibid., p. 96.

P. 234. *the Company had lost control in the north:* Heather Robertson, in *A Gentleman Adventurer: The Arctic Diaries of R.H.G. Bonnycastle*, pp. 14–15.

P. 234. *"the portable-boarding-house school":* Vilhjalmur Stefansson quoted in Frank Rasky, *The North Pole or Bust: Explorers of the North*, p. 386.

P. 235. *We soon found:* John Mikkelborg, in "Reindeer from Lapland," *The Bay*, 1949–50, p. 37.

P. 236. *"a native cannot live on white man's food":* Dr Frederick G. Banting's observations on the Inuit, quoted in Michael Bliss, *Banting: A Biography*, p. 173.

P. 236. *take over full control of the fur trade:* Banting, in letter to O.S. Finnie, HBCA A-92/Can./251.

P. 237. *the native should be encouraged:* Banting, ibid.

P. 237. *It is obvious:* Governor Charles Sale, letter to W. W. Cory, 28 Feb. 1928, HBCA A-92/Can./251.

P. 237. *2000 MILES OFF:* advertisement in *The Beaver*, March 1933, p. 249.

P. 237n. *Indeed, I won't:* Rev. Gerald Card, quoted in Jean Godsell, *I Was No Lady*, p. 190.

P. 237. *You had time:* Laco Hunt, in Barbara Hunt, ed., *Rebels, Rascals & Royalty*, p. 2.

P. 238. *I suddenly realized:* Gilbert LaBine, quoted in Peter C. Newman, *Flame of Power*, p. 156.

P. 239. *"That is a bad thing":* an Inuk, quoted in Maja Van Steensel, ed., *People of Light and Dark*, p. 57.

P. 240. *We landed at Fort Resolution:* Paul Davoud, in interview with author.

P. 241. *Sure. We paid:* an Inuk at Fort Rae, quoted in Richard Finnie, *Canada Moves North*, p. 103n.

P. 242. *They had carefully studied:* H.M. Ross, in *A Manager's Tale*, p. 184.

P. 243. *In a country where old lard pails:* Graham Rowley, quoted in photo display at Northwest Territories Pavilion, Expo 86, Vancouver.

P. 243. *There was a big war:* Octave Sivanertok, quoted in photo display at Northwest Territories Pavilion, Expo 86, Vancouver.

P. 244. *Endemic upper respiratory diseases:* R.G. Williamson, in interview with author.

P. 245. *The Mountie told me:* Matthew Innakatsik, quoted in photo display at Northwest Territories Pavilion, Expo 86, Vancouver.

P. 247. *One by one they appeared:* Jean Godsell, in *I Was No Lady*, p. 85.

P. 248. *These are not cold sculptures:* James Houston, in "Inuit Sculpture: The Spirit in the Stone," *Town and Country*, May, 1984.

P. 248. *Oshaweetok, a famous Eskimo carver:* Houston, quoted in Sol Littman, "The Souvenir That Grew," *Maclean's*, September 1975, 68C–68D.

P. 249. *They were strongly against the move:* Ben Sivertz, in interview with author.

P. 250. *to lay down fresh produce:* Marvin Tiller, in Presentation to the N.W.T. Council, 27 May, 1981.

P. 250. *We are probably regarded:* Richard Murray, in letter to Lord Amory, 2 Dec. 1966, HBCA, Unclassified, DD G7B.

P. 251. *When I lived in an Arctic trading post:* A. Tanner, in "The End of Fur Trade History," *Queen's Quarterly*, 90, no. 1 (Spring 1983).

P. 251. *"The image of the classic Eskimo":* S. Hall, in *The Fourth World: The Heritage of the Arctic and Its Destruction*, p. 122.

P. 252. *The Hudson's Bay Company . . . helped the government:* Josh Teemotee, in undated letter to author.

P. 252. *I was just starting out as Chief at Rupert:* Chief Billy Diamond, in interview with author.

P. 253. *I got to know:* Ben Sivertz, in interview with author.

P. 253. *The Company took a look at our needs:* Diamond, in interview with author.

P. 254. *"I know people were happier in the old days":* William Kuptana, quoted in photo display at Northwest Territories Pavilion, Expo 86, Vancouver.

P. 254. *"I don't know":* Jimmy Kilabuk, quoted by Stuart Hodgson, in interview with author.

P. 254. *The Hudson's Bay Company made easier lives:* Minnie Freeman, in "Living in Two Hells," *Inuit Today*,

8, Oct. 1980, reprinted in M. Zaslow, ed., *A Century of Canada's Arctic Islands, 1880–1980*, p. 272.

## CHAPTER 13
## THE LORDS AND THE GOOD OLD BOYS

P. 260. *to go whoring in the East:* Richard Murray, quoting Philip Chester, in interview with author.

P. 260. *I confess we are:* David Kilgour, in letter to Lord Amory, 25 Nov. 1966, David Kilgour personal files.

P. 260. *When a North American:* Joe Harris, quoted in David Kilgour letter to Lord Amory, 2 March 1966, David Kilgour personal files.

P. 261. *It was soon clear:* Albert Hochbaum, in letter to author, 31 May 1985.

P. 261. *I once asked:* Sir William Keswick, in interview with author.

P. 261. *I was going to say:* J.G. Links, in interview with author.

P. 261. *We frankly had:* Lord Amory, in interview with author.

P. 262. *One frail old proprietor:* Links, in interview with author.

P. 262. *During the 1930s:* Sir Eric Faulkner, in interview with author.

P. 263. *We all hated borrowing:* Sir William Keswick, in interview with author.

P. 264. *a gateway through which:* William E. Curtis, in *Chicago Record Herald*, quoted in Peter C. Newman, *The Canadian Establishment*, Vol. II, *The Acquisitors*, p. 299.

P. 265. *cautious, canny, reactionary:* W.L. Morton, *Manitoba: A History*, p. 501.

P. 265. *of no practical value:* Philip Chester, in letter to Patrick Ashley Cooper, 10 June 1940, HBCA Unclassified.

Pp. 265–66. *The actual benefits:* Richard Murray, in letter to Lord Amory, 12 Dec. 1966, HBCA Unclassified DDG 7B.

P. 266. *the Canadian Committee of the Hudson's Bay:* Kilgour, in letter to Lord Amory, 28 Dec. 1966, David Kilgour personal files.

P. 267. *more of an historical curiosity:* Philip Chester, in letter to William Keswick, 11 Aug. 1955, HBCA Unclassified DD CG2.

P. 269n. *10 letters, that is including the first three:* C.V. Sale, letter to Jean Monnet, 7 Jan. 1916, AFG 5/629.

P. 270. *checked the girls' work stations:* Dora Darby, in interview with author.

P. 270. *He was a peculiar sort of chap:* Bob Chesshire, in interview with author.

P. 271. *I look to the future:* Sir Robert Kindersley, quoted in Philip Godsell, *Arctic Trader*, p. 175.

P. 272. *For a while:* ibid., pp. 166–67.

P. 272. *As I gazed at the flickering lights:* ibid., p. 172.

P. 274. *The consequence of this layout:* James Bryant, *Department Store Disease*, pp. 183–84.

Pp. 276–77. *democracy has its valuable and strong features:* G.W. Allan, quoted in Allan Levine, unpublished MS on George Allan, p. 6.

## CHAPTER 14
## TRANS-ATLANTIC BLOOD FEUD

P. 280. *Many of them had acquired:* Anne Morton, "Charles Elton and the Hudson's Bay Company," *The Beaver*, Spring 1985, p. 25.

P. 280. *Amongst his chief weaknesses:* comment on P. J. Parker in Lord Ebury, Report to C.V. Sale, 8 July 1930, HBCA Unclassified 1-7-1 Admin NA.

P. 280. *Mr Chester is, in my opinion:* ibid.

P. 281. *full powers of attorney . . . for the due exercise thereof:* Memo to Canadian Committee from C.V. Sale, 27 Aug. 1930, Unclassified CC Vol. X10, fo. 118.

P. 281. *There seemed afterwards to be some misconception:* George Allan,

Calgary Speech, 28 Dec. 1931, Unclassified CCO files 1-7-1 Admin NA Cdn Committee.

P. 283. *For my shortcomings:* C.V. Sale, quoted in Anne Morton, "The Looking-Glass Vision: The Minute Books of the Hudson's Bay Company, 1914–1931."

P. 283. *I alone selected:* Montagu Norman to Charles L. Nordon, 29 June 1931, HBCA A 10 & 11.

P. 283. *Your task is to rebuild:* Montagu Norman to Patrick Ashley Cooper, quoted in London *Record*, 31 May 1952.

P. 284. *Are we to devote ourselves:* Patrick Ashley Cooper to General Court, 29 July 1931, pamphlet, p. 16.

P. 284. *No. It cannot be both:* Patrick Ashley Cooper, ibid, p. 17.

P. 284. *It was purely an oversight:* George W. Allan, letter to Ashley Cooper, 30 July 1931, HBCA DD GS3-Chairman, C.C. 1931–35.

P. 284. *a pot of tea:* Ashley Cooper, quoted in James Bryant, *Department Store Disease*, p. 108.

P. 285. *I was dismayed:* Ashley Cooper, quoted in Tom Mahony and Leonard Sloane, *The Great Merchants*, p. 213.

P. 285. *As soon as I arrived:* Ashley Cooper, "Memorandum of Canadian Visit - 1931," HBCA #1041292.

P. 285. *great and thoughtless extravagance:* Ashley Cooper, Unclassified, DD G3, P.A. Cooper 29/12/31, attached to P. A. Cooper to G.W. Allan, 21 Jan. 1932.

P. 286. *Like taking hold:* Frank Walker, describing Philip Chester, in interview with author.

P. 286. *Not on the Sabbath:* Elizabeth Chester regarding Philip Chester's family in interview with author.

P. 288. *If there's kids in the house":* Fred Herbert, bailiff, quoted by John Enright in interview with author.

P. 289. *Why must I be surrounded:* Philip Chester, quoted by Ron Sheen in interview with author.

P. 289. *You know, whenever I look at you:* Philip Chester, quoted ibid.

P. 289. You! You! *I told you what to do:* Philip Chester, quoted by Bob Chesshire, in interview with author.

P. 290. *While I was a tough bird:* Philip Chester, letter to E.F. Newlands, 7 Dec. 1960, HBCA E.135, Box 3, Chester's Misc. Correspondence, 1945–75.

P. 290. *living on Mount Olympus:* John English describing Philip Chester, in interview with author.

P. 290. *He used to brief:* Pete Buckley describing Philip Chester, in interview with author.

P. 291. *I was given a seat:* Philip Chester in letter to G.W. Allan, 6 May 1933, Series B.

P. 293n. *we are, of necessity:* George W. Allan in letter to Ashley Cooper, 9 Aug. 1933, HBCA DD G3 - Chairman, CC 1931–35.

P. 295. *Extraordinary. I have lots:* Ashley Cooper, quoted by Sir William Keswick, in interview with author.

Pp. 295–96. *1933 was a year of depression:* Philip Chester, "The First 250 Years," unpublished history of the Hudson's Bay Company.

Pp. 296–97. *Sir George Simpson in his 30-foot canoe:* R.H.H. Macaulay, *Trading into Hudson's Bay*, p. 19.

P. 297n. *Possibly arranged:* Philip Chester, unpublished history of the Hudson's Bay Company.

P. 297. *It is no exaggeration:* Macaulay, *Trading into Hudson's Bay*, p. 39.

P. 297. *we . . . leave you:* Ashley Cooper, quoted in R.A.J. Phillips, *Canada's North*, pp. 78–79.

P. 298. *They kind of went up:* Captain Thomas Smellie, quoted in Roland Wild, *Arctic Command*, p. 146.

P. 299. *Make a wreath:* Captain Thomas Smellie, quoted ibid., p. 142.

P. 299. *On his triumphant return:* Ashley Cooper described by Philip Chester, unpublished history of the Hudson's Bay Company.

P. 301n. *removing and tampering:* Pullen story from "London Letter," *The Beaver*, June 1941, p. 54.

P. 302. *the greatest soldier:* Viscount Alanbrooke, described in Robert Blake, "Key Figures of the Second World War" (review of biography of Alanbrooke), *Illustrated London News*, June 1982, p. 92.

P. 303. *Yes, Patrick, I'm sure:* Conrad S. Riley, quoted by Bob Chesshire in interview with author.

P. 304. *go whoring in the East:* Philip Chester, quoted by Richard Murray, in interview with author.

P. 306. *"I got your letter":* letter quoted in Tom Mahony and Leonard Sloane, *The Great Merchants*, p. 30.

CHAPTER 15
CANADIAN AT LAST

P. 312. *Max's idea of real debauchery:* Bell described by Jim Coleman, quoted in Jeannine Locke, "Max Bell," *Star Weekly*, 12 Feb. 1966, p. 16.

Pp. 312–13. *I put on a clean white shirt:* W.J. Keswick, in letter to Elmer Woods, 15 January 1953, HBCA Unclassified DD G8A.

P. 313. *At times he shouted:* Bell described by W.J. Keswick in letter to Elmer Woods, 18 March 1953, HBCA Unclassified, DD G8A.

P. 313. *I must retire soon:* Sir Winston Churchill, quoted in Richard Nixon, *In the Arena*, p. 361.

P. 314. *the spectacle of that immense estate:* James [Jan] Morris, *Farewell the Trumpets*, p. 547.

P. 314. *any such position would be incompatible:* Elmer Woods to W.J. Keswick, 30 June 1955, HBCA Unclassified DD G8A.

P. 314. *I have received the attached:* W.J. Keswick to HBC directors, HBCA Unclassified DD G8A.

P. 315. *He is a marvel:* Viscount Alanbrooke on Churchill, quoted in Lord Moran, *Winston Churchill: The Struggle for Survival, 1940-1965*, p. 695.

P. 315. *This honour will be appreciated:* Sir Winston Churchill, quoted in "Sir Winston, the Grand Seigneur, has to hesitate," Johannesburg *Star*, 28 April 1956.

P. 316. *I cannot attempt to describe:* Philip Chester to W.J. Keswick, 4 February 1953, HBCA DD G4A.

P. 321. *The atmosphere was indeed extraordinary:* Richard Murray to W.J. Keswick, 17 November 1959, HBCA DD G7.

P. 321. *the most hellishly modern:* Richard Murray, quoted in Seymour Freedgood, "Hudson's Bay: Return to Greatness," *Fortune*, August 1958.

Pp. 322–23. *Those wheat farmers from Winnipeg:* Aird Nesbitt, quoted in Robert Moon, "Nesbitt of Ogilvie's: Montreal taste maker," *Executive Magazine*, September 1966, p. 38.

P. 323. *the sick man:* HBC described in Roger Croft, "Retailing, with a dash of glamor oil: the new HBC is a longterm attraction," *Financial Times of Canada*, 5 Jan. 1967, p. 1.

P. 323. *A stroll through any Bay store:* The Bay described in 1950s and 1960s in James Bryant, *Department Store Disease*, p. 111.

P. 325. *This summer marked:* Arthur Ray, "York Factory: The Crisis of Transition, 1870–1880," *The Beaver*, Autumn 1982, p. 35.

P. 326. *as quietly and innocently as possible:* Sir William Keswick, letter to Richard Murray, 17 June 1964, HBCA Unclassified, DD G7A 1964.

P. 327. *I am now coming to life:* Lord Amory, letter to Richard Murray, 14 June 1967, HBCA Unclassified, DD G7C.

P. 330. *transfer is a historical move:* Richard Murray, letter to Lord Amory, 5 Dec. 1967, HBCA Unclassified DDCG 4.

P. 332. *had not only failed:* Richard Murray, letter to Lord Amory, 17 Feb. 1970, David Kilgour personal files.

P. 332. *not only is there a lack:* Lord Amory, letter to David Kilgour, 2 March 1970, David Kilgour personal files.

P. 333. *We reached exactly the right conclusion:* David Kilgour, letter to Lord Amory, 9 March 1970, David Kilgour personal files.

P. 333. *During the unheroic years:* Lord Amory, letter to David Kilgour, 12 March 1970, David Kilgour personal files.

P. 333. *Your "for the fire and ashes" exchange:* Richard Murray, letter to Lord Amory, 25 March 1970, David Kilgour personal files.

P. 334. *It is incredible:* Richard Murray, letter to Lord Amory, 27 June 1970.

P. 334. *God forbid that I should be involved:* David Kilgour, letter to Richard Murray, 13 July 1970.

P. 335. *The die is cast:* HBC Adventurer, quoted in Tom Green, "Company of Adventurers votes for New World," Winnipeg *Tribune*, 29 May 1970.

Pp. 336–37. *At this point:* Tex Enemark regarding the HBC Charter patriation ceremony, in letter to author, 7 Jan. 1983.

## CHAPTER 16
## McGIVERIN'S RUN

P. 348. *I talked for about forty minutes:* Philip Chester, "The First 250 Years," unpublished MS history of the Hudson's Bay Company [n.p.].

P. 348. *There might be something big:* Lord Amory in letter to Richard Murray, 21 Oct. 1968, HBCA Unclassified, DD CG7, Simpsons File.

P. 353. *a professional son of a bitch:* Donald R. Katz, *The Big Store: Inside the Crisis and Revolution at Sears*, p. 882.

## CHAPTER 17
## YOUNG KEN

P. 362. *"there is a limit":* Kenneth Thomson quoted in Robert Lewis, "Looking for missing links," *Maclean's*, 22 Dec. 1980, p. 16.

P. 362. *"I can't imagine":* Kenneth Thomson quoted in John Partridge and Dan Westell, "Thomson merger to create vast acquisition opportunities," *Globe and Mail*, 16 March 1989.

P. 363. *"I regret giving up":* Roy Thomson quoted in Peter C. Newman, "Table Talk of Roy Thomson," *Maclean's*, Dec. 1971, p. 41.

P. 363n. *"It wouldn't have suited me":* Roy Thomson quoted ibid.

P. 364. *"Madam, I've paid enough":* Roy Thomson quoted in Norman Peagam, "Canadian Dynasty: Like Father, Like Son? No, But All Goes Well in Thomson Empire," *Wall Street Journal*, 27 May 1980, pp. 1, 14.

P. 364. *"I've made a lot":* Roy Thomson quoted in Newman, "Table Talk of Roy Thomson."

P. 364. *"Nobody has any sympathy":* Roy Thomson quoted ibid.

P. 365. *"Mr Thomson, you really are cheap!":* Roy Thomson story from James B. Lamb, *Press Gang: Post-War Life in the World of Canadian Newspapers*, p. 166.

P. 365. *"My favorite color:"* Roy Thomson story from Newman, "Table Talk of Roy Thomson."

P. 368. *"I could do without culture":* Roy Thomson quoted ibid.

P. 370. *"They say business is the law":* Roy Thomson quoted ibid.

P. 371. *"Most people would say":* Roy Thomson quoted ibid.

P. 371. *"My wife made me":* Kenneth Thomson quoted in "The most cost-conscious executive," *Financial Post Magazine*, 18 Sept. 1988, p. 8.

P. 372. *Disliking Ken Thomson:* Richard Gwyn, "Dullness at the Top Dulls Many Thomson Papers," Toronto *Star*, 14 April 1981, p. 7.

P. 372. *a vicious organization:* Clifford Pilkey quoted in David MacFarland, "The Accidental Tycoon," *Saturday Night*, October 1980, p. 28.

P. 374. *isn't the circulation:* Russell Braddon, *Roy Thomson of Fleet Street*, p. 351.

Pp. 374–75. *"We run our newspapers":* Kenneth Thomson, testimony at Kent Commission hearings, 13 April 1981.

P. 375. *a transition from light:* Harold Evans, *Good Times, Bad Times*, p. 7.

P. 375. *"Each one has to find":* Kenneth Thomson quoted in Arthur Johnson, "Two papers die as Thomson, Southam tighten belts," *Globe and Mail*, 28 Aug. 1980, p. 2.

P. 377. *"I wish you luck":* Fred Eaton, quoted in "Store Wars" (script for TV show), p. 18.

P. 378. *"I don't like all this":* Kenneth Thomson, quoted in Richard Conrad, "Thomson closes big deal—for wine," Toronto *Star*, 5 April 1979, p. A1.

P. 379. *"George, I want to do some shopping":* Marilyn Thomson, quoted in George Whitman's unpublished journal; remainder of account of Thomsons' northern journey from same source.

CHAPTER 18
DISASTER AND DELIVERANCE

Pp. 385–86. *"We're absolutely delighted":* John A. Tory, quoted in Winifred Nobel, "The Bay tightens up inventories," *Financial Post*, 22 Dec. 1979.

P. 388. *If there is an example:* Yorkton Securities study quoted in *Investor's Digest*, 14 June 1983, p. 1138.

P. 388. *"Nobody knows what women":* Marilyn Brooks quoted in Barbara

Aarsteinsen, "Rough Times in the Rag Trade," *Report on Business Magazine*, Oct. 1988, p. 158.

Pp. 396–97. *If the HBC is alive:* Sir Eric Faulkner in letter to author, Easter Sunday, 1988.

P. 400. *Do you believe that the removal:* Barry Critchley and Brian Baxter, "HBC executives dipping their ballpoints in poison," *Financial Post*, 24 Oct. 1988.

CHAPTER 19
LAST LORD OF THE BAY

P. 406. *"David, my grandson":* Roy Thomson, quoted in Russell Braddon, *Roy Thomson of Fleet Street*, p. 356.

P. 409. *"the best picture in the world":* Lord Clark, quoted in Donn Downey, "British rue loss of art treasure to Canadian," *Globe and Mail*, 3 May 1989, p. A8.

P. 417. *"I don't think it's appropriate":* analyst quoted by Terry Brodie in "Shakeup at the Bay," *Financial Times of Canada*, 8 June 1987.

EPILOGUE

P. 420. *"the soul-sharpening satisfaction":* Harry J. Boyle quoted in Peter C. Newman, *Sometimes a Great Nation*, p. 21.

P. 422. *The honoured old initials:* W. Kaye Lamb quoted in Peter C. Newman, *Caesars of the Wilderness*, p. xxi.

P. 424. *"the Company have for eighty years":* Joseph Robson quoted in Peter C. Newman, *Company of Adventurers*, p. 145.

P. 424. *"cloak to protect the trade":* North West Company agent quoted in Newman, *Caesars of the Wilderness*, p. xix.

P. 426. *an oilman's dream:* "From Beaver Skins to Deep-Freezers and Oil," *Fortune*, Aug. 1958, p. 130.

ACKNOWLEDGEMENTS

P. 428. *"your extrovert Englishman or woman":* John Le Carré, *The Secret Pilgrim*, p. 120.

# Bibliography

This listing is a selection from the main texts and journal articles consulted during the writing of this volume. The Chapter Notes in Appendix Three provide further information for those pursuing research, or for readers curious about the sources of the quotes used in the book.

Allen, Ralph. *Ordeal by Fire: Canada, 1910–1945*. Canada History Series, Vol. 5. Toronto: Doubleday: Popular Library, 1961.

Anderson, James Watt. *Fur Trader's Story*. Foreword by Lord Tweedsmuir. Toronto: Ryerson Press, 1961.

Anderson, William Ashley. *Angel of Hudson Bay: The True Story of Maud Watt*. Toronto: Clarke, Irwin, 1961.

Annesley, Pat. "The Lady Awakens." *Equity,* November 1985: 108–10.

Artibise, Alan F. J. "Boosterism and the Development of Prairie Cities, 1871–1913." In R. Douglas Francis and Howard Palmer, eds., *The Prairie West: Historical Readings*. Edmonton: Pica Pica Press, 1985, pp. 408–34.

——— , ed. *Town and City: Aspects of Western Canadian Urban Development*. Canadian Plains Studies no. 10. Regina: Canadian Plains Research Centre, 1981.

Asch, Michael I. "Some Effects of the Late Nineteenth Century Modernization of the Fur Trade on the Economy of the Slavey Indians." *Western Canadian Journal of Anthropology,* 6, no. 4 [1976]: 7ff.

Atwood, Mae, ed. *In Rupert's Land: Memoirs of Walter Traill*. Toronto: McClelland and Stewart, 1970.

Baikie, Margaret. "Labrador Memories." In *Them Days* [n.d.].

Ballantyne, R.M. *Hudson's Bay, or Every-day Life in the Wilds of North America*. London: Blackwood, 1848.

Banfield, A.W.F. "The Barren-Ground Caribou." [Ottawa]: Canada, Department of Resources and Development, Northern Administration and Lands Branch, [n.d.].

Barr, William. "On to the Bay." *The Beaver,* Autumn 1985: 43–53.

Barris, Theodore. *Fire Canoe: Prairie Steamboat Days Revisited*. Toronto: McClelland and Stewart, 1977.

Batten, Jack. *Canada Moves Westward, 1880/1890*. Canada's Illustrated Heritage. Toronto: Jack McClelland/N.S.L. Natural Science of Canada, 1977.

"Beaver House." *The Beaver* [1928].

Beavis, L.R.W. "Titania, Queen of the Clippers." *The Beaver,* September 1942: 35–37.

Begg, Alexander. *History of the North-West*. 3 vols. Toronto, 1894.

Berger, Carl, ed. *Imperialism and Nationalism, 1884–1914: A Conflict in Canadian Thought*. Issues in Canadian History. Toronto: Copp Clark, 1969.

——— , and Ramsay Cook, eds. *The West and the Nation: Essays in Honour of W.L. Morton*. Toronto: McClelland and Stewart, 1976.

Berton, Pierre. *The Last Spike: The Great Railway, 1881–1885*. Toronto: McClelland and Stewart, 1971.

——— . *The National Dream: The Great Railway, 1871–1881.* Toronto: McClelland and Stewart, 1970.

——— , ed. *Historic Headlines: A Century of Canadian News Dramas.* Canadian Illustrated Library. Toronto: McClelland and Stewart, 1967.

"Bill Cobb Retires After 37 Years' Service." *Moccasin Telegraph,* June 1965: 26–27.

Birdseye, Clarence. "The Birth of an Industry." *The Beaver,* September 1941; reprinted, Autumn 1980: 12–13.

Bliss, Michael. *Northern Enterprise: Five Centuries of Canadian Business.* Toronto: McClelland and Stewart, 1987.

——— . *Banting: A Biography.* Toronto: McClelland and Stewart, 1984.

Bone, Jack. "Ernie Lyall, the 'Arctic Man.' " *Northwest Explorer,* 5, no. 4 (September 1986): 29–30.

Bonnycastle, R.H.G. *A Gentleman Adventurer: The Arctic Diaries of Richard Bonnycastle*: see entry under Robertson, Heather.

Bowle, John. *The Imperial Achievement: The Rise and Transformation of the British Empire.* Orig. publ. 1974. Harmondsworth, Middlesex, England: Penguin Books, 1977.

Bowsfield, Hartwell. *Louis Riel: The Rebel and the Hero.* Toronto: Oxford University Press, 1971.

——— , ed. *The Letters of Charles John Brydges, 1879–1882: Hudson's Bay Company Land Commissioner.* Introduction by Alan Wilson. HBRS, Vol. 31. Winnipeg: Hudson's Bay Record Society, 1977.

——— , ed. *The Letters of Charles John Brydges, 1883–1889: Hudson's Bay Company Land Commissioner.* Introduction by J.E. Rea. HBRS, Vol. 33. Winnipeg: Hudson's Bay Record Society, 1981.

——— , ed. *Louis Riel: Selected Readings.* New Canadian Readings. Toronto: Copp Clark Pitman, 1988.

Braddon, Russell. *Roy Thomson of Fleet Street.* Orig. publ. 1965. London and Glasgow: Collins/ Fontana Books, 1968.

Briggs, Asa. *A Social History of England.* Orig. publ. 1983. Harmondsworth, Middlesex, England: Penguin Books, 1985.

Brock, Paul. "She Prowls the Arctic." *The Skipper,* September 1965.

Brody, Hugh. *Living Arctic: Hunters of the Canadian North.* London/ Boston: Faber and Faber in collaboration with the British Museum and Indigenous Survival International, 1987.

——— . *The People's Land: Whites and the Eastern Arctic.* Harmondsworth, Middlesex, England: Penguin Books, 1975.

Brooks, J. Chadwick. "HBC and 'The Old Lady': The Company's Association with the Bank of England Has Been Continuous Through Two Hundred Years." *The Beaver,* March 1934: 32ff.

Bruce, Jean. *The Last Best West.* Toronto/Montreal/Winnipeg/ Vancouver: Fitzhenry & Whiteside in association with the Multiculturalism Programme, Department of the Secretary of State, 1976.

Bruemmer, Fred. *Seasons of the Eskimo: A Vanishing Way of Life.* Orig. publ. 1971. Paperback, Toronto: McClelland and Stewart, 1978.

Bryant, James. *Department Store Disease.* Toronto: McClelland and Stewart, 1977.

Bryce, George. *The Remarkable History of the Hudson's Bay Company.* London: Sampson Low, Marston, 1910.

Budgell, Leonard. "Recollections of Rigolet." In *Them Days 60 Years Ago* [ed. Doris Saunders], August 1975: 4–24.

Burch, Ernest S., Jr. "Marriage and Divorce Among the North Alaskan Eskimos." In Paul Bohannan, ed., *Divorce and After: An Analysis of the Emotional and Social Problems of Divorce.* Garden City, N.Y.: Doubleday & Co., 1970: 152–81.

Burgess, Lois M. "Influences Affecting the Transfer of Rupert's Land: Some Aspects of the Attitudes of Five Governments and Peoples to the Transfer of Rupert's Land from the Hudson's Bay Company to Canada, July 15th, 1870." Master's thesis, University of Ottawa, 1963.

Burpee, Lawrence J. *Sandford Fleming, Empire Builder.* London: Oxford University Press, 1915.

Burton, C.L. *A Sense of Urgency: Memoirs of a Canadian Merchant.* Toronto: Clarke, Irwin, 1952.

Burton, G. Allan. *A Store of Memories.* Toronto: McClelland and Stewart, 1986.

Butler, William Francis. *The Great Lone Land: A Narrative of Travel and Adventure in the North-West of America.* Reprint. Edmonton: Hurtig Publishers, 1968.

Callwood, June. *The Naughty Nineties, 1890/1900.* Canada's Illustrated Heritage. Toronto: Jack McClelland/N.S.L. Natural Science of Canada, 1977.

——— . *Portrait of Canada.* Garden City, N.Y.: Doubleday, 1981.

Campbell, Bruce D. *Where the High Winds Blow.* New York: Charles Scribner's Sons, 1946.

Campbell, Lydia. "Sketches of Labrador Life." In *Them Days,* 1980.

Campbell, Marjorie Wilkins. *The Saskatchewan.* Rivers of America Series. New York/Toronto: Rinehart, 1950.

Camsell, Charles. *Son of the North.* Toronto: Ryerson Press, 1954.

Carmichael-Galloway, Andrew Strome Ayers. "Who resembles the Scots? What a silly question." *Globe and Mail,* 26 November 1989.

Carter, Kim. "Remembering the 'Arctic Man.' " *Inuktitut,* no. 64, Fall 1986: 63–65.

Chalmers, John W. *Horseman in Scarlet: Sam Steele of The Mounties.* Frontier Books. Toronto: W. J. Gage, 1961.

——— , et al., eds. *The Land of Peter Pond.* Boreal Institute for Northern Studies, Occasional Publication no. 12. Edmonton: Boreal Institute for Northern Studies, 1974.

*Charters, Statutes, Orders in Council, &c., Relating to the Hudson's Bay Company.* London: Hudson's Bay Company, 1963.

"The Christie Family and H.B.C." *The Beaver,* August 1923: 1–17.

Coates, Kenneth. *Canada's Colonies: A History of the Yukon and Northwest Territories.* Canadian Issues Series. Toronto: James Lorimer, 1985.

——— , and William R. Morrison. *Land of the Midnight Sun: A History of the Yukon.* Edmonton: Hurtig Publishers, 1988.

Coats, Robert H., and R.E. Gosnell. *Sir James Douglas.* The Makers of Canada, Vol. 20. Toronto: Morang & Co., 1908.

Cobb, W. J. "Interesting Years with the HBC." *Moccasin Telegraph,* Winter, 1970: 25–27.

Cockburn, R.H. "Revillon Man: The Northern Career of A. Wallace Laird, 1924–1931." *The Beaver,* February–March 1990: 12–26.

Collins, Robert. *The Age of Innocence, 1870/1880.* Canada's Illustrated Heritage. Toronto: Jack McClelland/N.S.L. Natural Science of Canada, 1977.

Colombo, John Robert, ed. *Colombo's Canadian Quotations*. Edmonton: Hurtig Publishers, 1974.

"The Company in London." *The Beaver*, September 1935: 31–36.

Cooke, Alan. *A History of the Naskapi of Schefferville*. Montreal: Naskapi Band Council of Schefferville, 1976.

——— . *Naskapi Independence and the Caribou*. Montreal: Centre for Northern Studies and Research, McGill University, 1981.

——— . "The Montagnais." *The Beaver,* Summer 1985: 13–19.

——— . "The Ungava Venture of the Hudson's Bay Company, 1830–1843." Ph.D. thesis, Darwin College of Cambridge University, 1969.

Cooper, Mrs. [Anne] Ashley. *100 Years of Hexton*. [N.p.]: Mrs. Ashley Cooper, 1982.

Cooper, Patrick Ashley. *Trading into Hudson's Bay, A Narrative of the Visit of Patrick Ashley Cooper Thirtieth Governor of the Hudson's Bay Company to Labrador, Hudson Strait, and Hudson Bay in the Year 1934*. From the Journal of R.H.H. Macaulay. Winnipeg: Hudson's Bay Company, 1934.

Copland, A. Dudley. *Coplalook: Chief Trader, Hudson's Bay Company, 1923–1939*. Winnipeg: Watson & Dwyer Publishing, 1985.

Corley, T.A.B. *A History of the Burmah Oil Company 1886-1924*. London: Heinemann, 1983.

Cotter, H.M.S. "Famous H.B.C. Captains and Ships." *The Beaver,* June 1921: 32–33.

"The Cover Picture: Mount Everest and The Hudson's Bay Company." *The Beaver,* June 1933: 52.

Creighton, Donald. *John A. Macdonald: The Old Chieftain*. Toronto: Macmillan Company of Canada, 1955.

——— . *The Passionate Observer: Selected Writings*. Toronto: McClelland and Stewart, 1980.

Crowe, Keith J. *A History of the Original Peoples of Northern Canada*. Arctic Institute of North America. Orig. publ. 1974. Reprinted, Kingston/Montreal: McGill-Queen's University Press, 1982.

Cruise, David, and Alison Griffiths. *Lords of the Line*. New York: Viking Penguin, 1988.

"C.S. Riley Joins Canadian Committee." *The Beaver,* September 1928.

Dale, Tim. *Harrods: The Store and the Legend*. London: Pan Books, 1981.

Dalrymple, A.J. " 'Cap' Ross of the Saskatchewan." *The Beaver,* June 1944: 20–23.

De Coccola, Raymond, and Paul King. *The Incredible Eskimo: Life Among the Barren Land Eskimo*. Surrey, B.C./Blaine, WA: Hancock House Publishers, 1986.

*Deed Poll by the Governor and Company of Hudson's Bay, for Conducting Their Trade in North America, and for Defining the Rights and Prescribing the Duties of Their Officers*. London: Sir Joseph Causton and Sons, 1871.

Demaree, Allan T. "The Old China hands who know how to live with the new Asia." *Fortune,* November 1971: 132–34, 214, 216.

Denison, Merrill. *Canada's First Bank: A History of the Bank of Montreal*. 2 vols. Toronto: McClelland and Stewart, 1966, 1967.

den Otter, A. A. "The Hudson's Bay Company's Prairie Transportation Problem, 1870–85." In John E. Foster, ed., *The Developing West: Essays in Canadian History in Honor of Lewis H. Thomas*. Edmonton: University of Alberta Press, 1983.

*Dictionary of Canadian Biography*. Toronto: University of Toronto Press, (Vol. ix) 1976; (Vol. x) 1972; (Vol. xi) 1982.

Dunae, Patrick A. " 'Making Good': The Canadian West in British Boys' Literature, 1890–1914." *Prairie Forum*, 4, no. 2 (Fall 1979): 165ff.

Erasmus, Peter, as told to Henry Thompson. *Buffalo Days and Nights*. Introduction by Irene Spry. Calgary: Glenbow-Alberta Institute, 1976.

Ettagiak, Agnes, co-author. "Four Inuit Women." *Inuit Today*, 5, no. 6 (June 1976): 20–31.

Evans, Harold. *Good Times, Bad Times*. London: Weidenfeld and Nicolson, 1983.

Farb, Peter. *Man's Rise to Civilization: The Cultural Ascent of the Indians of North America*. 2nd rev. ed. New York: E.P. Dutton, 1968.

Ferrier, R.W. *The History of the British Petroleum Company*. Vol. 1: *The Developing Years, 1901–1932*. Cambridge: Cambridge University Press, 1959.

Ferris, Paul. *The City*. Orig. publ. 1960. Rev. ed. Harmondsworth, Middlesex, England: Penguin Books, 1965.

Finnie, Richard. *Canada Moves North*. New York: Macmillan, 1942.

——— . "Trading into the North-West Passage." *The Beaver,* December 1937: 46–53.

——— . "Stefansson and the Reindeer/Caribou Dream." *North*, 25, no. 3 (May/June 1978): 94.

Flanagan, Thomas. *Louis 'David' Riel: Prophet of the New World*. Orig. publ. 1979. Canadian Lives Series. Halifax: Goodread Biographies, Formac Publishing, 1983.

——— . *Riel and the Rebellion: 1885 Reconsidered*. Saskatoon: Western Producer Prairie Books, 1983.

——— , ed. *The Diaries of Louis Riel*. Edmonton: Hurtig Publishers, 1976.

Fleming, Archibald Lang. *Archibald the Arctic*. New York: Appleton-Century-Crofts, 1956.

——— . *Perils of the Polar Pack*. Toronto, 1932.

*Fort St. James Conceptual Development Objectives and Plan: Fort St. James National Historic Park, British Columbia*. [Ottawa]: Indian and Northern Affairs, 1975.

*Fort St. James National Historic Park: Provisional Development Plan*. [Ottawa]: National Historic Sites Service, Department of Indian Affairs and Northern Development, [1969–70].

Foster, John E., ed. *The Developing West: Essays in Canadian History in Honor of Lewis H. Thomas*. Edmonton: University of Alberta Press, 1983.

Francis, Daniel. *A History of World Whaling*. Markham, Ont.: Viking, 1990.

——— . *Arctic Chase: A History of Whaling in Canada's North*. A Breakwater Book in the Arctic and Northern Life Series. Canada: Breakwater Books, 1984.

——— . *Discovery of the North: The Exploration of Canada's Arctic*. Edmonton: Hurtig Publishers, 1986.

Francis, R. Douglas, and Howard Palmer, eds. *The Prairie West: Historical Readings*. Edmonton: Pica Pica Press of University of Alberta Press, 1985.

Freedgood, Seymour. "Hudson's Bay: Return to Greatness." *Fortune*, August 1958: pp. 72ff.

Freedman, Jim, and Jerome H. Barkow, eds. *Proceedings of the Second Congress, Canadian Ethnology Society*. National Museum of Man Mercury Series, Canadian Ethnology Service, Paper #28. Ottawa: National Museum of Canada, 1975.

"From Beaver Skins to Deep-freezers and Oil," *Fortune*, August 1958.

Frost, Stanley Brice. *McGill University: For the Advancement of Learning.* Vol. 1, *1801–1895;* Vol. 2, *1895–1971.* Kingston/Montreal: McGill-Queen's University Press, 1980, 1984.

Fry, Joseph N., and J. Peter Killing. *Canadian Business Policy: A Casebook.* Scarborough, Ont.: Prentice-Hall Canada, 1983.

Frye, Northrop. *Divisions on a Ground: Essays on Canadian Culture.* Edited, with a preface, by James Polk. Toronto: House of Anansi, 1982.

Fulford, Roger. *Glyn's, 1753–1953: Six Generations in Lombard Street.* London: Macmillan, 1953.

Fullerton, Douglas H. *Graham Towers and His Times: A Biography.* Toronto: McClelland and Stewart, 1986.

Galbraith, John Kenneth. *The Scotch.* Orig. publ. 1964. Baltimore, Maryland: Penguin Books, 1966.

Galbraith, John S. "The Hudson's Bay Land Controversy, 1863–1869." *Mississippi Valley Historical Review,* 36, no. 3 (December 1949): 457–78.

——— . "Land Policies of the Hudson's Bay Company, 1870–1913." *Canadian Historical Review,* 32, no. 1 (March 1951): 1–21.

——— . "A Note on the Mackenzie Negotiations with the Hudson's Bay Company, 1875–1878." *Canadian Historical Review,* 34, no. 1 (March 1953): 39–45.

Garrod, Stan. *Sam Steele.* The Canadians: A Continuing Series. Don Mills, Ont.: Fitzhenry and Whiteside, 1979.

"George F. Galt" [obituary]. *The Beaver,* June 1928: 6.

Getty, Ian A. L., and Antoine S. Lussier, eds. *As Long As the Sun Shines and Water Flows: A Reader in Canadian Native Studies.* Nakoda Institute Occasional Paper No. 1. Vancouver: University of British Columbia Press, 1975.

Gibbon, John Murray. *Canadian Mosaic: The Making of a Northern Nation.* Toronto: McClelland and Stewart, 1938.

Gibson-Jarvie, Robert. *The City of London: A Financial and Commercial History.* Cambridge: Woodhead-Faulkner with Commercial Union Assurance Co. Ltd., 1979.

Gingras, Larry. *Medals, Tokens and Paper Money of the Hudson's Bay Company.* [N.p.]: Canadian Numismatic Research Society, 1975.

Gilbert, Heather. *Awakening Continent: The Life of Lord Mount Stephen.* Vol. 1: *1829–91.* Aberdeen, Scotland: Aberdeen University Press, 1965.

——— . *The End of the Road: The Life of Lord Mount Stephen.* Vol. 2: *1891–1921.* Aberdeen, Scotland: Aberdeen University Press, 1977.

Godsell, Jean W. *I Was No Lady . . . I Followed the Call of the Wild: The Autobiography of a Fur Trader's Wife.* Toronto: Ryerson Press, 1959.

Godsell, Philip H. *Arctic Trader: The Account of Twenty Years with the Hudson's Bay Company.* Orig. publ. 1932. 6th ed. rev. Toronto: Macmillan of Canada, 1943.

Goldenberg, Susan. *The Thomson Empire.* New York: Beaufort Books; Toronto: Methuen, 1984.

Granatstein, J. L., Irving M. Abella, David J. Bercuson, R. Craig Brown, H. Blair Neatby. *Twentieth Century Canada.* Toronto/Montreal: McGraw-Hill Ryerson, 1986.

Gray, Earle. *The Great Canadian Oil Patch.* Toronto: Maclean-Hunter, 1970.

——— . "Born of English and U.S. Parents." *Oilweek,* 20, no. 28 (September 1969): 16–21.

Great Plains Research Consultants. *Fort St. James Costuming and Animation.* Microfiche Report Series 85. [Ottawa]: Parks Canada, 1983.

Gregor, Alexander. *Vilhjalmur Stefansson and the Arctic.* We Built Canada Series, ed. Keith Wilson. Agincourt, Ont.: Book Society of Canada, 1978.

Griffis, Edith May. "The Lady of the Bay." *The Beaver,* Winter 1960: 48.

Grover, S.H. "The Church of St Ethelburga the Virgin." *The Beaver,* June 1928: 8.

Gwyn, Sandra. *The Private Capital: Ambition and Love in the Age of Macdonald and Laurier.* Toronto: McClelland and Stewart, 1984.

Hall, Sam. *The Fourth World: The Heritage of the Arctic and Its Destruction.* New York: Alfred A. Knopf, 1987.

Hallock, Charles. "Three Months in Labrador." Part I. *Harper's New Monthly Magazine,* 22, no. 131 (1861): 577–99.

——— . "Three Months in Labrador." Part II. *Harper's New Monthly Magazine,* 22, no. 132 (1861): 743–65.

Harrington, Richard. *The Inuit: Life As It Was.* Edmonton: Hurtig Publishers, 1981.

Hedges, James B. *Building the Canadian West: The Land and Colonization Policies of the Canadian Pacific Railway.* New York: Macmillan, 1939.

Heslop, Barbara. "Arctic Rescue." *The Beaver,* March 1944, reprinted Autumn 1980: 70–76.

Hildebrandt, Walter. *The Battle of Batoche: British Small Warfare and the Entrenched Métis.* Studies in Archaeology, Architecture and History. Ottawa: National Historic Parks and Sites Branch, Environment Canada, 1985.

Homick, Teresa H. "A Social History of Fort St. James, 1896." [N.p.], 1984.

Houston, James A. "Inuit Sculpture: The Spirit in the Stone." *Town and Country,* May 1984: 110.

Howard, Joseph. *Strange Empire: Louis Riel and the Métis People.* Orig. publ. 1952. Toronto: James Lewis and Samuel, 1974.

*Hudson's Bay Company. A General Court of the Governor and Company of Adventurers of England Trading into Hudson's Bay was held on Wednesday, July 29, 1931, at Beaver House, Garlick Hill, London, E.C.* London: The Times Publishing Co. [1931].

Hughes, Stuart. *The Frog Lake "Massacre": Personal Perspectives on Ethnic Conflict.* Edited and with introduction by Stuart Hughes. Carleton Library no. 97. Toronto: McClelland and Stewart, 1976.

Humber, Charles J., ed. *Canada's Native Peoples.* Canada Heirloom Series, Vol. 2. Mississauga, Ont.: Heirloom Publishing, 1988.

Hunt, Barbara, ed. *Rebels, Rascals & Royalty: The Colourful North of Laco Hunt.* Yellowknife, N.W.T.: Outcrop, 1983.

Hunter, Archie. *Northern Traders: Caribou Hair in the Stew.* Victoria, B.C.: Sono Nis Press, 1983.

"In Celebration." *The Beaver,* May 1920.

Inglis, Alex. *Northern Vagabond: The Life and Career of J.B. Tyrrell.* Toronto: McClelland and Stewart, 1978.

Inkyo [pseud.]. *The Reflections of Inkyo on the Great Company.* London: London General Press, 1931.

Jackson, J.A., Gordon W. Leckie, and W.L. Morton, eds. *Papers Read before the Historical and Scientific Society of Manitoba.* Ser. 3, no. 6. Winnipeg: Advocate Printers, 1951.

Jackson, J.A., and W.L. Morton, eds. *Papers Read before the Historical and Scientific Society of Manitoba.* Ser. 3, no. 5. Winnipeg: Advocate Printers, 1950.

"James A. Richardson Joins Canadian Committee." *The Beaver,* March 1928: 153.

*Jardine, Matheson & Company: An Historical Sketch.* Hong Kong: Jardine, Matheson, [n.d.].

Jenness, Diamond. *Eskimo Administration: II. Canada.* Technical Paper no. 14. Montreal: Arctic Institute of North America, 1964.

——— . *Eskimo Administration: V. Analysis and Reflections.* Technical Paper no. 21. Montreal: Arctic Institute of North America, [n.d.].

Katz, Donald R. *The Big Store: Inside the Crisis and Revolution at Sears.* New York: Viking Penguin, 1987.

Keate, Stuart. *Paper Boy: The Memoirs of Stuart Keate.* Toronto/Vancouver: Clarke, Irwin, 1980.

Keegan, John. *Six Armies in Normandy: From D-Day to the Liberation of Paris.* Orig. publ. 1982. Harmondsworth, Middlesex, England: Penguin Books, 1983.

Keighley, Sydney Augustus, in collaboration with Renée Fossett Jones and David Kirkby Riddle. *Trader, Tripper, Trapper: The Life of a Bay Man.* Winnipeg: Rupert's Land Research Centre/Watson & Dwyer Publishers, 1989.

Kelly, L.V. "Lady in Distress." *The Beaver,* June 1951: 25–29.

Kemp, H.S.M. *Northern Trader.* Toronto: Ryerson Press, 1956.

Kerr, Donald. "Wholesale Trade on the Canadian Plains in the Late Nineteenth Century: Winnipeg and Its Competition." In R. Douglas Francis and Howard Palmer, eds., *The Prairie West: Historical Readings.* Edmonton: Pica Pica Press, 1985: pp. 130–7.

Keswick, Maggie, ed. *The Thistle and the Jade: A Celebration of 150 Years of Jardine, Matheson & Co.* London: Octopus Books, 1982.

Kilbourn, William. *The Making of the Nation: A Century of Challenge.* Canadian Illustrated Library. Orig. publ. 1965. Rev. ed. Toronto: McClelland and Stewart, 1973.

Klengenberg, Christian. *Klengenberg of the Arctic: An Autobiography*: see entry under MacInnes, Tom.

Knox, Olive. "The Question of Louis Riel's Insanity." In J. A. Jackson, Gordon W. Leckie, and W. L. Morton, eds., *Papers Read before the Historical and Scientific Society of Manitoba.* Ser. 3, no. 6. Winnipeg: Advocate Printers, 1951: 20–34.

Krech, Shepard, III. *Native Canadian Anthropology and History: A Selected Bibliography.* Winnipeg: Rupert's Land Research Centre, University of Winnipeg, 1986.

Lamb, James B. *Press Gang: Post-War Life in the World of Canadian Newspapers.* Toronto: Macmillan of Canada, 1979.

LeBourdais, D. M. "North West River." *The Beaver,* Spring 1963: 14–21.

Letourneau, Rodger. "The Grand Rapids Tramway." *The Beaver,* Autumn 1977: 47–54.

Levine, Allan G. "The London-Winnipeg Connection: The Management of the Hudson's Bay Company in the Early Twentieth Century" [paper].

——— . "Augustus Nanton, Western Canada's greatest financier!" *Manitoba Business,* [no date, no vol. number], pp. 34–35.

Links, J.G. *The Book of Fur.* [London]: James Barrie, 1956.

Littlejohn, Bruce, and Jon Pearce, eds. *Marked by the Wild: An Anthology of Literature Shaped by the Canadian Wilderness.* Toronto: McClelland and Stewart, 1973.

Littman, Sol. "The Souvenir That Grew Up." *Maclean's,* September 1975, 68c–68d.

"London Letter." *The Beaver,* June 1941: 54.

"Lord Waverley." *Illustrated London News*, June 1982.

Lopez, Barry. *Arctic Dreams: Imagination and Desire in a Northern Landscape.* New York: Charles Scribner's Sons, 1986.

Lower, J.A. *Canada: An Outline History.* Orig. publ. 1966. Rev. ed. Toronto: McGraw-Hill Ryerson, 1973.

——— . *Western Canada: An Outline History.* Vancouver/Toronto: Douglas & McIntyre, 1983.

Lyall, Ernie. *An Arctic Man: Sixty-five Years in Canada's North.* Orig. publ. 1979. Canadian Lives Series. Halifax: Goodread Biographies, Formac Publishing, 1983.

Macaulay, R.H.H. *Trading into Hudson's Bay:* see entry under Cooper, Patrick Ashley.

MacBeth, R.G. "Famous Forres." *The Beaver,* December 1929: 307–8.

——— . "Strathcona." *The Beaver,* September 1922: 3–5.

MacEwan, Grant. *The Battle for the Bay.* Saskatoon: Western Producer Book Service, 1975.

——— . *Between the Red and the Rockies.* Toronto: University of Toronto Press, 1952.

MacGregor, James G. *Edmonton Trader: The Story of John A. McDougall.* Toronto: McClelland and Stewart, 1963.

——— . *Senator Hardisty's Prairies, 1849–1889.* Saskatoon: Western Producer Prairie Books, 1978.

MacInnes, Tom, ed. *Klengenberg of the Arctic: An Autobiography.* London/Toronto: Jonathan Cape, 1932.

MacInnis, Joe. *The* Breadalbane *Adventure.* Montreal/Toronto: Optimum Publishing International, 1982.

Mack, Capt. G. Edmund. "Breaking the Ice for the Allies." *The Beaver,* December 1938: 20–25.

——— . "Nascopie Downs Submarine." *The Beaver,* June 1939: 19–21; reprinted, Autumn 1980.

MacKay, Donald. *The Square Mile: Merchant Princes of Montreal.* Vancouver/Toronto: Douglas & McIntyre, 1987.

MacKay, Douglas. *The Honourable Company: A History of the Hudson's Bay Company.* Toronto: McClelland and Stewart/Bobbs-Merrill, 1936.

McKenzie, N.M.W.J. *The Men of the Hudson's Bay Company, 1670 A.D.–1920 A.D.* Fort William, Ont.: The Author, 1921.

McLaren, Moray. *Understanding the Scots: A Guide for South Britons and Other Foreigners.* New York: Bell Publishing, 1956, 1972.

McLean, Don. *1885: Metis Rebellion or Government Conspiracy?* Winnipeg: Pemmican Publications, 1985.

Macleod, R.C. *The NWMP and Law Enforcement, 1873–1905.* Toronto/Buffalo: University of Toronto Press, 1976.

McNaught, Kenneth. *The Penguin History of Canada.* Orig. publ. 1969. Rev. and reprinted. London: Penguin Books, 1988.

Macnaughtan, S. *My Canadian Memories.* London: Chapman and Hall, 1920.

Macnaughton, John. *Lord Strathcona.* Makers of Canada Series, Anniversary Edition. London and Toronto: Oxford University Press, 1926.

McRae, Hamish, and Frances Cairncross. *Capital City: London As a Financial Centre.* Orig. publ. 1973. Rev. ed. London: Methuen, 1984.

McTavish, George Simpson. *Behind the Palisades: An Autobiography.* Sidney, B.C.: Evelyn Gurd, 1963.

Mahony, Tom, and Leonard Sloane. *The Great Merchants: America's Foremost Retail Institutions and the People Who Made Them Great.* Orig. publ. 1949. 2nd ed. rev. New York: Harper and Row, 1966.

Malcolm, Andrew H. *The Canadians.* Orig. publ. 1985. Toronto/New York: PaperJacks, 1986.

Martin, Albro. *James J. Hill and the Opening of the Northwest.* New York: Oxford University Press, 1976.

Mathews, John Joseph. *Life and Death of an Oilman: The Career of E. W. Marland.* Norman, Okla.: University of Oklahoma Press, 1951.

Mayles, Stephen. *William Van Horne.* The Canadians: A Continuing Series. Don Mills, Ont.: Fitzhenry & Whiteside, 1982.

Meilleur, Helen. *A Pour of Rain: Stories from a West Coast Fort.* Victoria, B.C.: Sono Nis Press, 1980.

"Merchandise to All the World." *The Beaver,* June 1933: 42–43.

Mikkelborg, John. "Reindeer from Lapland." *The Bay* [London Staff Magazine], 1949–50: 37ff.

Milne, Jack. *Trading for Milady's Furs: In the Service of the Hudson's Bay Company 1923–1943.* Saskatoon: Western Producer Prairie Books, 1975.

Mirsky, Jeannette. *To the Arctic! The Story of Northern Exploration from Earliest Times to the Present.* Introduction by Vilhjalmur Stefansson. Orig. publ. 1934. Chicago: University of Chicago Press, 1970.

Moberly, Henry John, in collaboration with William Bleasdell Cameron. *When Fur Was King.* London/Toronto: J. M. Dent and Sons, 1929.

Money, Anton. *This Was the North.* Toronto: General Publishing, 1975.

Montague, John, with Isaac Rich. "Fur Traders." In *Them Days,* 1973, [n.p.].

Moran, Lord. *Winston Churchill: The struggle for survival, 1940-1965.* Taken from the diaries of Lord Moran. London: Constable, 1966.

Morice, A.G. *The History of the Northern Interior of British Columbia.* Orig. publ. 1904. Reprinted Fairfield, WA: Ye Galleon Press, 1971.

Morley, William F.E. *Ontario and the Canadian North.* Canadian Local Histories to 1950: A Bibliography, Vol. 3. Toronto: University of Toronto Press, 1978.

Morris, James [Jan]. *Farewell the Trumpets: An Imperial Retreat.* Orig. publ. 1978. Harmondsworth, Middlesex, England: Penguin Books, 1979.

——— . *Heaven's Command: An Imperial Progress.* Orig. publ. 1973. Harmondsworth, Middlesex, England: Penguin Books, 1979.

——— . *Pax Britannica: The Climax of an Empire.* Harmondsworth, Middlesex, England: Penguin Books, 1968.

Morton, Anne. "Charles Elton and the Hudson's Bay Company." *The Beaver,* Spring 1985: 22–29.

——— . "The Looking-Glass Vision: the Minute Books of the HBC 1914–1931" [paper].

Morton, Desmond. *The Last War Drum: The North West Campaign of 1885.* Toronto: A.M. Hakkert, 1972.

——— . *A Short History of Canada.* Edmonton: Hurtig Publishers, [c.1983].

Morton, W.L. *Manitoba: A History.* Orig. publ. 1957. 2nd ed. Toronto: University of Toronto Press, 1967.

——— . "Donald A. Smith and Governor George Simpson." *The Beaver,* Autumn 1978: 4–9.

——— . Unpublished biography of Donald A. Smith.

Mowat, Farley. *Canada North.* Canadian Illustrated Library. Toronto: McClelland and Stewart, 1967.

——— . *Canada North Now: The Great Betrayal.* Toronto: McClelland and Stewart, 1976.

——— . *Tundra.* Toronto: McClelland and Stewart, 1973.

Moyles, R.G., and Doug Owram. *Imperial Dreams and Colonial Realities: British Views of Canada 1880–1914.* Toronto: University of Toronto Press, 1988.

Mulvaney, Charles Pelham. *The History of the North-West Rebellion of 1885 . . . .* Toronto: A. H. Hovey, 1885.

Myers, Gustavus. *A History of Canadian Wealth.* Vol. 1. Orig. publ. 1914. First Canadian ed. Introduction by Stanley Ryerson. Toronto: James Lewis & Samuel, 1972.

——— . *History of the Great American Fortunes.* Orig. publ. 1909. Modern Library ed. New York: A.S. Barnes, 1937.

"My Mother's Home." [The HBC Packet]. *The Beaver,* September 1933: 9.

Nanton, Paul. *Arctic Breakthrough: Franklin's Expeditions, 1819–1847.* Introduction by Trevor Lloyd. Orig. publ. 1970. Paperback, Toronto/ Vancouver: Clarke, Irwin, 1981.

Naylor, R.T. *The History of Canadian Business 1867–1914.* Vol. 1, *The Banks and Finance Capital.* Foreword by Eric Kierans. Toronto: James Lorimer, 1975.

Newman, Peter C. "A Vanished Heritage." Review of A. Dudley Copland, *Coplalook: Chief Trader, Hudson's Bay Company, 1923-1939.* In *The Beaver,* August/September 1986: 56–57.

——— . *The Canadian Establishment.* Vol. 2: *The Acquisitors.* Toronto: McClelland and Stewart, 1981.

——— . *Flame of Power: Intimate Profiles of Canada's Greatest Businessmen.* Orig. publ. 1959. Paperback, Toronto: McClelland and Stewart, 1965.

——— . *Sometimes a Great Nation: Will Canada Belong to the 21st Century?* Toronto: McClelland and Stewart, 1988.

——— . "The Table Talk of Roy Thomson." *Maclean's,* December 1971, 41.

Newth, A.M. *Britain and the World, 1789–1901.* Orig. publ. 1967. Rev. ed. Harmondsworth, Middlesex, England: Penguin Books, 1968.

Nichols, P.A.C. "Enter . . . The Fur Traders." *The Beaver,* Winter 1954: 37–38.

Nixon, Henny. "SS/HMS *Nascopie,* 1912–1947: A Biography of a Ship." *Argonauta: The Newsletter of the Canadian Nautical Research Society,* 4, no. 3, Sept. 1987.

Nixon, Richard. *In the Arena: A Memoir of Victory, Deceit and Renewal.* New York: Simon and Schuster, 1990.

*Northern Frontier, Northern Homeland.* Report of the Mackenzie Valley Pipeline Inquiry: Vol. 1 [Berger Inquiry]. Ottawa: Minister of Supply and Services Canada, 1977.

Nugent, Jo. "The World's Great Department Stores, since 1850, entertainers and friends of the family and community." *The Rotarian,* February 1982: 26ff.

Nute, Grace Lee. "Paris to Peel's River in 1892." *The Beaver,* Outfit 278, no. 4, March 1948: 19-23.

Oleson, Robert. "The Commissioned Officers of the Hudson's Bay Company and the Deed Poll in the 1870's, with Particular Emphasis on the Fur Trade Party, 1878-1879." Master's thesis, University of Manitoba, 1977.

———. "The Past Hundred Years." *The Beaver,* Spring 1970: 14-23.

"Opportunity in the Fur Trade." *The Beaver,* March 1928: 174-75.

Owram, Douglas. "The Myth of Louis Riel." In R. Douglas Francis and Howard Palmer, *The Prairie West: Historical Readings.* Edmonton: Pica Pica Press, 1985: 163-81.

Palmer, Howard. *The Settlement of the West.* Calgary: University of Calgary, Comprint Publ., 1977.

Pedley, J.W. *Biography of Lord Strathcona and Mount Royal.* Introduction by Sir John Willison. Toronto: J.L. Nichols, 1915.

Peel, Bruce. "First Steamboats on the Saskatchewan." *The Beaver,* Autumn 1964: 16-21.

Pelly, David F. *Expedition: An Arctic Journey Through History on George Back's River.* Toronto: Betelgeuse Books, 1981.

Petrone, Penny, ed. *Northern Voices: Inuit Writing in English.* Toronto: University of Toronto Press, 1988.

Phillips, Alan. *Into the 20th Century, 1900/1910.* Canada's Illustrated Heritage. Toronto: Jack McClelland/ N.S.L. Natural Science of Canada, 1977.

Phillips, R.A.J. *Canada's North.* Toronto: Macmillan of Canada, 1967.

Pinkerton, Robert E. *The Gentlemen Adventurers.* Introduction by Stewart Edward White. Toronto: McClelland and Stewart, 1931.

Pohle, Klaus. "The *Lethbridge Herald*: A Case Study in 'Thomsoniza- tion.'" Master of Journalism thesis, Carleton University, Ottawa, Ontario, 1984.

Poncins, Gontran de, in collaboration with Lewis Galantière. *Kabloona.* New York: Reynal & Hitchcock, 1941.

Pope, Maurice, ed. *Public Servant: The Memoirs of Sir Joseph Pope.* Toronto: Oxford University Press, 1960.

Porter, William A., and Bert Porter. *A Backward Look at the Forefolk of Lord Thomson of Fleet and North Bridge.* London: 1976 [privately printed].

Pratt, A.M., and John H. Archer. *The Hudson's Bay Route.* [N.p.]: Governments of Manitoba and Saskatchewan, 1953.

Prebble, John. *John Prebble's Scotland.* Orig. publ. 1984. Harmondsworth, Middlesex, England: Penguin Books, 1986.

Preston, W.T.R. *The Life and Times of Lord Strathcona.* Toronto: McClelland, Goodchild & Stewart, 1914.

———. *My Generation of Politics and Politicians.* Toronto: D.A. Rose, 1927.

———. *Strathcona and the Making of Canada.* New York: McBride, Nast, 1915.

Price, Ray. *The Howling Arctic: The Remarkable People Who Made Canada Sovereign in the Farthest North.* Toronto: Peter Martin Associates, 1970.

Priestley, J.B. *Victoria's Heyday.* Orig. publ. 1972. Harmondsworth, Middlesex, England: Penguin Books, 1974.

Pryde, Duncan. *Nunaga: Ten Years of Eskimo Life.* Orig. publ. 1972. New York: Bantam Books, 1973.

R.T.L. [Charles Vining.] *Bigwigs: Canadians Wise and Otherwise.* Toronto: Macmillan of Canada, 1935.

*Rangifer: Proceedings of the Fourth International Reindeer/Caribou Symposium, Whitehorse, Yukon, Canada, 22–25 August 1985.* Harstad, Norway: Nordic Council for Reindeer Research, 1986.

Rasky, Frank. *The North Pole or Bust: Explorers of the North.* Toronto: McGraw-Hill Ryerson, 1977.

———. *The Taming of the Canadian West.* Toronto: McClelland and Stewart, 1967.

Ray, Arthur. "Adventurers at the Crossroads: At Momentous and Stormy Summer Meetings in 1871 the Future of the Hudson's Bay Company Was Charted." *The Beaver,* April/May 1986: 4–12.

———. *The Canadian Fur Trade in the Industrial Age.* Toronto: University of Toronto Press, 1990.

———. "Rivals for Fur." *The Beaver,* April/May 1990: 30–39, from *The Canadian Fur Trade in the Industrial Age.*

———. "York Factory: The Crisis of Transition, 1870–1880." *The Beaver,* Autumn 1982: 27ff.

Rea, J.E. "The Hudson's Bay Company and the North-West Rebellion." *The Beaver,* Summer 1982: 43–57.

Rea, K.J. *The Political Economy of the Canadian North: An Interpretation of the Course of Development in the Northern Territories of Canada to the Early 1960s.* [Toronto]: University of Toronto Press in association with the University of Saskatchewan, 1968.

Reid, W. Stanford, ed. *The Scottish Tradition in Canada.* A History of Canada's Peoples. Toronto: McClelland and Stewart in association with the Multiculturalism Program, Department of the Secretary of State of Canada and the Publishing Centre, Supply and Services Canada, 1976.

*Report to the Proprietors of the Hudson's Bay Company, by the Special Committee appointed at an informal meeting of certain Proprietors held on 22nd July, 1930, to be Laid Before the Proprietors on 16th January, 1931.* London, 1930.

Reynolds, Thomas A. [Martin Hunter, pseud.]. *Canadian Wilds.* Columbus, Ohio: A.R. Harding, 1907.

Rich, E.E. "The Perpetual Governor." *The Beaver,* Autumn 1974: 18–22.

Richmond, W. R. *The Life of Lord Strathcona.* London/Glasgow: Collins, [n.d.]

*The Riel Rebellion — 1885.* A Frontier Book. Surrey, B.C.: Heritage House Publishing, 1984.

Roberts, Lance W. "Becoming Modern: Some Reflections on Inuit Social Change." In Ian A.L. Getty and Antoine S. Lussier, eds., *As Long As the Sun Shines and Water Flows: A Reader in Canadian Native Studies.* Vancouver: University of British Columbia Press, 1975: 299ff.

Robertson, Heather, ed. and comp. *A Gentleman Adventurer: The Arctic Diaries of R.H.G. Bonnycastle.* A Richard Bonnycastle Book 2. Toronto: Lester & Orpen Dennys, 1984.

Robin, O.B. "How the Fort St. James National Historic Park Came into Being." Unpublished manuscript. 1979.

Robinson, William M. *Novice in the North.* Surrey, B.C./Blaine, WA: Hancock House, 1984.

Ross, Hugh Mackay. *A Manager's Tale.* Winnipeg: Watson & Dwyer Publishing, 1990.

———. *The Apprentice's Tale.* Winnipeg: Watson & Dwyer Publishing, 1986.

Ross, W. Gillies. *Whaling and Eskimos: Hudson Bay 1860-1915.* National Museum of Man Publications in Ethnology, no. 10. Ottawa: National Museums of Canada, 1975.

Rostecki, Randy R. "Winnipeg Land Politics in the 1870s." *The Beaver,* Spring 1985: 42-48.

Royal Commission on Newspapers [Kent Commission]. *The Journalists.* Vol. 2, Research Publications. Ottawa: Minister of Supply and Services Canada, 1981.

Royal Commission on Price Spreads. *Report.* Ottawa: King's Printer, 1937.

Russell, Chesley. "The Devon Island Post." *The Beaver,* Spring 1978: 41-47.


Sampson, Anthony. *The New Europeans: A Guide to the Workings, Institutions and Character of Contemporary Western Europe.* London: Hodder and Stoughton, 1968.

Schooling, Sir William. *The Governor and Company of Adventurers of England Trading into Hudson's Bay during Two Hundred and Fifty Years 1670-1920.* London: Hudson's Bay Company, 1920.

Scoresby, William. *An Account of the Arctic Regions.* Vol. 1. Newton Abbot, Devon, England: David and Charles, 1969.

Sealey, Gary D. "History of the Hudson's Bay Company, 1870-1900." Master's thesis, University of Western Ontario (London), 1969.

Searle, Ronald, and Kildare Dobbs. *The Great Fur Opera: Annals of the Hudson's Bay Company, 1670-1970.* Toronto: McClelland and Stewart, 1970.

Selwood, John. "Mr Brydges' Bridges." *The Beaver,* Summer 1981: 14-21.

———, and Evelyn Baril. "The Hudson's Bay Company and Prairie Town Development, 1870-1888." In Alan F. J. Artibise, ed., *Town and City: Aspects of Western Canadian Urban Development,* Canadian Plains Studies no. 10. Regina: Canadian Plains Research Centre, 1981.

———. "Land Policies of the Hudson's Bay Company at Upper Fort Garry: 1869-1879." *Prairie Forum,* 2, no. 2 (November 1977): 101-19.

Sexé, Marcel. *Two Centuries of Fur-Trading, 1723-1923: Romance of the Revillon Family.* Paris, 1923.

Shortt, Adam, and Arthur G. Doughty, eds. *Canada and Its Provinces: A History of the Canadian People and Their Institutions by One Hundred Associates.* Vols. 1-23. Toronto: Glasgow, Brook, 1917.

Skelton, O. D. *The Life and Letters of Sir Wilfrid Laurier.* 2 vols. Toronto: S.B. Gundy, University of Toronto Press, 1921.

Skinner, Constance Lindsay. *Beaver Kings and Cabins.* New York: Macmillan, 1933.

Smith, Cynthia M., ed., with Jack McLeod. *Sir John A.: An Anecdotal Life of John A. Macdonald.* Toronto: Oxford University Press, 1989.

Smith, Shirlee Anne. " 'A Desire To Worry Me Out': Donald Smith's Harassment of Charles Brydges, 1879-1889." *The Beaver,* 67, no. 6. December 1987/January 1988: 4-11.

Sprenger, George H. "Coping with Competition: The Reorganization of the Hudson's Bay Company after the Monopoly." In Jim Freedman and Jerome H. Barkow, eds., *Proceedings of the Second Congress, Canadian Ethnology Society.* National Museum of Man Mercury Series, Canadian Ethnology Service, Paper #28, 1975.

Stanley, George F. G. *The Birth of Western Canada: A History of the Riel Rebellions.* Orig. publ. 1936. Toronto: University of Toronto Press, 1961.

——— . "The Fur Trade Party. Part 1: Storm Warnings." *The Beaver,* September 1953: 35–39.

——— . "The Fur Trade Party. Part 2: United We Stand . . ." *The Beaver,* December 1953: 21–25.

Steele, Harwood. *The Marching Call.* Foreword by Major-General Victor W. Odlum. Toronto: Thomas Nelson & Sons (Canada), 1955.

Steele, Samuel B. *Forty Years in Canada: Reminiscences of the Great North-west with Some Account of His Service in South Africa.* Orig. publ. 1920 [?]. Ryerson Archive Series. Toronto: McGraw-Hill Ryerson, 1972.

Stephenson, William. *The Store That Timothy Built.* Toronto: McClelland and Stewart, 1969.

Stevenson, Alex. "Arctic Fur Trade Rivalry." *The Beaver,* Autumn 1975: 46–51.

Stewart, Robert. *Sam Steele: Lion of the Frontier.* Toronto: Doubleday Canada, 1979.

Stewart, Walter, ed. *Canadian Newspapers: The Inside Story.* Edmonton: Hurtig Publishers, 1980.

Swinton, George. *Sculpture of the Eskimo.* Toronto: McClelland and Stewart/M. F. Feheley Arts Co. Ltd., 1972.

Tanner, Adrian. "The End of Fur Trade History." *Queen's Quarterly,* 90, no. 1 (Spring 1983): 176–91.

Thomas, Lowell. *Kabluk of the Eskimo.* London: Hutchinson [n.d.].

Thomson, David. *England in the Twentieth Century (1914–79).* Orig. publ. 1965. Enlarged and revised, with additional material by Geoffrey Warner. Pelican History of England, no. 9. Harmondsworth, Middlesex, England: Penguin Books, 1981.

Thomson of Fleet, First Baron [Roy H. Thomson]. *After I Was Sixty: A Chapter of Autobiography.* Toronto: Thomas Nelson & Sons Canada, 1975.

Tobin, Brian. "Hudson's Bay House: What goes on in the building that houses the headquarters of the Company in Canada." *The Beaver,* March 1944: 28–34.

Tolboom, Wanda Neill. *Arctic Bride.* Toronto: Ryerson Press, 1956.

"To The Arctic." *The Beaver,* March 1933: 249.

Tupper, Sir Charles. *Recollections of Sixty Years in Canada.* London: Cassell, 1914.

Tway, Duane C. "The Influence of the Hudson's Bay Company upon Canada, 1870–1889." Ph.D. dissertation, University of California at Los Angeles, 1963.

——— . "The Wintering Partners and the Hudson's Bay Company, 1863 to 1871." *Canadian Historical Review,* 33, no. 1 (March 1952): 50–63.

——— . "The Wintering Partners and the Hudson's Bay Company, 1867–1879." *Canadian Historical Review,* 41, no. 3 (September 1960): 215–23.

Tweedsmuir, 2nd Baron [John Norman Stuart Buchan]. *Hudson's Bay Trader.* London: Clerke & Cockeran, 1951.

Tyrrell, C.S. "The Strathcona Herd." *The Beaver,* March 1933: 191–93.

Upton, L.F.S. "The Wreck of the *Eldorado*: Strange Tale of Shipwreck." *The Beaver,* Autumn 1968: 27–31.

Usher, Peter J. *Fur Trade Posts of the Northwest Territories, 1870–1970.* [Report] Northern Science Research Group, Department of Indian Affairs and Northern Development. Ottawa: Department of Indian Affairs and Northern Development, 1971.

Valentine, Victor F., and Frank G. Vallee, eds. *Eskimo of the Canadian Arctic.* Carleton Library no. 41. Toronto: McClelland and Stewart, 1968.

Van Steensel, Maja, ed. *People of Light and Dark.* Foreword by H.R.H. Prince Philip; Introduction by R. Gordon Robertson. [Ottawa]: Department of Indian Affairs and Northern Development, 1966.

Voisey, Paul. "The Urbanization of the Canadian Prairies, 1871–1916." In R. Douglas Francis and Howard Palmer, eds., *The Prairie West: Historical Readings.* Edmonton: Pica Pica Press, 1985: pp. 383–407.

Voorhis, Ernest, comp. "Historic Forts and Trading Posts of the French Regime and of the English Fur Trading Companies." Mimeographed. Ottawa: Department of the Interior, 1930.

Watson, William G. "A Southern Perspective on Northern Economic Development." In Michael S. Whittington, co-ordinator, *The North.* Toronto: University of Toronto Press, 1985.

Weekes, Mary. *Trader King, as told to Mary Weekes. The thrilling story of forty years' service in the North-West Territories, related by one of the last of the old time* Wintering Partners *of the Hudson's Bay Company.* Regina and Toronto: School Aids and Text Book Publishing Co. Ltd., 1949.

Weil, Gordon L. *Sears, Roebuck, U.S.A.: The Great American Catalog Store and How It Grew.* Orig. publ. 1977. New York: Harcourt Brace Jovanovich, 1979.

Wells, Eric. *Winnipeg Where the New West Begins: An Illustrated History.* Burlington, Ontario: Winnipeg Chamber of Commerce/Windsor Publications, 1982.

Whittington, Michael S., co-ordinator. *The North.* Collected research studies. Toronto: University of Toronto Press in co-operation with the Royal Commission on the Economic Union and Development Prospects for Canada and the Canadian Government Publishing Centre, Supply and Services Canada, 1985.

Wild, Roland. *Arctic Command: The Story of Smellie of the* Nascopie. Foreword by Sir Patrick Ashley Cooper; Introduction by Dennis Jordan. Toronto: Ryerson Press, 1955.

Wilkinson, Doug. "A Vanishing Canadian." *The Beaver,* Spring 1959: 25–28, 62.

Wilkinson, Douglas. *The Arctic Coast.* Illustrated Natural History of Canada. Toronto: N.S.L. Natural Science of Canada, 1970.

Williams, J. "The Last Voyage of the Stork." *The Beaver,* September 1939: 44–47.

Willson, Beckles. *From Quebec to Piccadilly and Other Places: Some Anglo-Canadian Memories.* London: Jonathan Cape, 1929.

———. *The Life of Lord Strathcona and Mount Royal, G.C.M.G. G.C.V.O.* 2 vols. Boston and New York: Houghton Mifflin, 1915.

———. *The Life of Lord Strathcona and Mount Royal, G.C.M.G., G.C.V.O., (1820–1914).* London: Cassell, 1915.

Wilson, Alan. " 'In a Business Way': C.J. Brydges and the Hudson's Bay Company, 1879–89." In Carl Berger and Ramsay Cook, eds., *The West and the Nation: Essays in Honour of W.L. Morton.* Toronto: McClelland and Stewart, 1976: pp. 118–23.

Wilson, Clifford. *Campbell of the Yukon.* Toronto: Macmillan of Canada, 1970.

———. "The Emperor at Lachine." *The Beaver,* September 1934: 18–22.

———, ed. *Northern Treasury: Selections from* The Beaver. Introduction by Leonard W. Brockington. Toronto: Thomas Nelson & Sons (Canada) [n.d.].

———. "Private Letters from the Fur Trade. A Selection from the Correspondence of William McMurray . . . Between 1845 and 1871." In J. A. Jackson and W. L. Morton, eds. *Papers Read Before the Historical and Scientific Society of Manitoba.* Ser. 3, no. 5. Winnipeg: Advocate Printers, 1950: 19ff.

———. "Tadoussac, the Company and the King's Posts." *The Beaver,* June 1935: 8–12, 63, 66.

Winchester, Simon. *Their Noble Lordships: Class and Power in Modern Britain.* Orig. publ. 1981. New York: Random House, 1982.

Wishart, Bruce. "Paddle Wheels on the Prairies." *The Beaver,* December 1989/January 1990: 30–36.

Wissink, Renée. "The Quest for Ultima Thule." *Arctic Circle,* 1, no. 1, 1990: 16–21.

Wonders, William C., ed. *Canada's Changing North.* Carleton Library no. 55. Toronto: McClelland and Stewart, 1971.

Woodcock, George. *Gabriel Dumont: The Métis Chief and His Lost World.* Edmonton: Hurtig Publishers, 1975.

———. *Skinned.* North Falmouth, Mass.: International Wildlife Coalition, 1988.

Zaslow, Morris, ed. *A Century of Canada's Arctic Islands, 1880–1980.* Ottawa: Royal Society of Canada, 1981.

———. *The Northward Expansion of Canada, 1914–1967.* Canadian Centenary Series, no. 17. Toronto: McClelland and Stewart, 1988.

———. *The Opening of the Canadian North, 1870–1914.* Canadian Centenary Series, no. 16. Toronto: McClelland and Stewart, 1971; paperback, 1981.

Ziegler, Philip. *The Sixth Great Power: Barings, 1762–1929.* London: Collins, 1988.

# Illustration Credits

P. x
J. McDougall, Photographer;
Hudson's Bay Company Archives,
Provincial Archives of Manitoba,
HBCA Photograph Collection,
1987/13/152 (N8507)

P. 2
McCord Museum of Canadian
History, Notman Photographic
Archives, Photo no. 110, 266-II

P. 11
Hudson's Bay Company Archives,
Provincial Archives of Manitoba,
HBCA Photograph Collection,
1987/363-H-225 (N8505)

P. 14
Metropolitan Toronto Reference
Library, J. Ross Robertson
Collection, T33162

P. 16
Painting by William George
Richardson Hind; National
Archives of Canada C-33690

P. 19
From Beckles Willson, *The Life
of Lord Strathcona and Mount Royal
G.C.M.G., G.C.V.O. (1820–1914)*,
London: Cassell and Company Ltd.,
1915; Metropolitan Toronto
Reference Library

P. 20
From a lithograph of the drawing
by Coke Smyth; Hudson's Bay
Company Archives, Provincial
Archives of Manitoba, HBCA
Picture Collection, P-44 (N5256)

P. 28
From *A Woman's Way Through
Unknown Labrador*, Toronto: Ryerson
Press, 1908; Hudson's Bay Company
Archives, Provincial Archives of
Manitoba, HBCA Photograph
Collection, 1987/363-P-80 (N8514)

P. 35
McCord Museum of Canadian
History, Notman Photographic
Archives, Photo no. 66962-I

P. 36
Saskatchewan Archives Board,
R-A2294

P. 41
Provincial Archives of Manitoba,
Collection—Transportation—
Red River Cart 45

P. 45
Provincial Archives of Manitoba,
Collection—Transportation—
Red River Cart 5/Hall & Lowe,
Photographer

P. 53
Glenbow Archives, Calgary,
Alberta; file no. PB-540
(NA-1406-71a)

P. 59
National Archives of Canada C-1879

P. 60
Provincial Archives of Alberta,
Ernest Brown Collection, no. B-5631

P. 64
Provincial Archives of Manitoba,
Collection—Emerson 11

P. 70
Provincial Archives of Manitoba,
Collection—Transportation—
Railway—*Countess of Dufferin* 1

P. 72
National Archives of Canada C-3447

P. 74
Provincial Archives of Manitoba,
Collection—Immigration 15,
Photo no. N7934

P. 85
Provincial Archives of Manitoba,
Collection—Brydges, Charles
John 1

P. 88
Hudson's Bay Company Archives,
Provincial Archives of Manitoba,
HBCA Map Collection, G.3/847
(N8501)

P. 94
National Archives of Canada
C-1229

P. 96
Hudson's Bay Company Archives,
Provincial Archives of Manitoba,
HBCA Photograph Collection,
1987/289 (N8512)

P. 98
National Archives of Canada
PA-38667

P. 111
McCord Museum of Canadian
History, Notman Photographic
Archives, Photo no. 63, 346-I

P. 117
National Archives of Canada C-8549

P. 119
Provincial Archives of Alberta,
Ernest Brown Collection,
no. B-6220

P. 121
National Archives of Canada
PA-28853 (left); National Archives
of Canada C-27663 (right)

P. 123
Canadian Pacific Archives,
neg. no. 8997

P. 126
Glenbow Archives, Calgary,
Alberta, NA-1494-6

P. 131
Provincial Archives of Alberta,
Ernest Brown Collection,
no. B-5683

P. 132
National Archives of Canada
C-14100

P. 137
From *Maclean's*, 11 April 1959, p. 27;
Metropolitan Toronto Reference
Library

P. 142
McCord Museum of Canadian
History, Notman Photographic
Archives, Photo no. 4267-View

P. 146
Glenbow Archives, Calgary,
Alberta, NA-294-1

P. 149
National Archives of Canada
C-3841

P. 150
National Archives of Canada
C-9671

P. 155
Provincial Archives of Manitoba,
Collection — Events 14/3,
Photo no. N7615

P. 157
Miss A.H. Gamlin, Photographer;
Hudson's Bay Company Archives,
Provincial Archives of Manitoba,
HBCA Photograph Collection,
1987/363-P-8.3 (N8511)

P. 162
Hudson's Bay Company Archives,
Provincial Archives of Manitoba,
HBCA Photograph Collection,
1987/374/21 (N8459)

P. 170
Richard Harrington, Photographer;
Hudson's Bay Company Archives,
Provincial Archives of Manitoba,
HBCA Photograph Collection,
1987/51/H-109 (H-109)

P. 177
Canadian Museum of Civilization,
National Museums of Canada,
Ottawa, Canada, negative no. 39674

P. 180
Geological Survey of Canada,
Ottawa, Photo no. 199680

P. 185
Hudson's Bay Company Archives,
Provincial Archives of Manitoba,
HBCA Photograph Collection,
1987/363-C-510 (N82-295)

P. 188
Richard Harrington/National
Archives of Canada PA-112094

P. 192
Richard Harrington/National
Archives of Canada PA-143236

P. 204
Hudson's Bay Company Archives,
Provincial Archives of Manitoba,
HBCA Photograph Collection,
1987/363-F-29 (N8515)

P. 206
Hudson's Bay Company Archives,
Provincial Archives of Manitoba,
HBCA Photograph Collection,
1987/363-K-30

P. 209
Glenbow Archives, Calgary,
Alberta, NA-3006-3

P. 215
Glenbow Archives, Calgary,
Alberta, NA-3006-1

P. 216
Max Sauer, Photographer; Hudson's
Bay Company Archives, Provincial
Archives of Manitoba, HBCA
Photograph Collection, 1987/363-
N-7A (N73-156)

P. 219
National Archives of Canada
PA-102214

P. 221
Max Sauer, Photographer; Hudson's
Bay Company Archives, Provincial
Archives of Manitoba, HBCA
Photograph Collection, 1987/363-
C-38/16 (N8470)

P. 223
Hudson's Bay Company Archives,
Provincial Archives of Manitoba,
HBCA Photograph Collection,
1987/363-B-11/6 (N7934)

P. 225
Charles Stuart McEuen,
Photographer; National Archives
of Canada PA-145040

P. 229
Norman Ross, Photographer;
Hudson's Bay Company Archives,

Provincial Archives of Manitoba,
HBCA Photograph Collection,
1987/363-N-8D (N81-257)

P. 230
A.A. Chesterfield Collection,
Queen's University Archives,
Photo no. E1-1

P. 235
W. McKinlay, Photographer;
National Archives of Canada
C-71050

P. 239
R. Fullerton, Photographer;
National Aviation Museum,
Photo no. 10098

P. 240
National Archives of Canada
C-25087

P. 243
Glenbow Archives, Calgary,
Alberta, NA-3235-65

P. 246
Rosemary Gilliat, Photographer;
From *Pageant of the North*, Clifford
Wilson, ed., Toronto: The Ryerson
Press, 1957, p. 170; Metropolitan
Toronto Reference Library

P. 249
W. Doucette, Photographer;
National Archives of Canada
PA-160707

P. 250
Reproduced with the permission of
La Fédération des coopératives du
Nouveau-Québec/Canadian
Museum of Civilization, National
Museums of Canada, Ottawa,
Canada, negative nos. 91-161
(b & w) and S90-7745 (slide)

P. 256
Hudson's Bay Company Archives,
Provincial Archives of Manitoba,
HBCA Photograph Collection,
1987/363-W-312 (N8077)

P. 259
Hudson's Bay Company Archives,
Provincial Archives of Manitoba,

HBCA Photograph Collection,
1987/363-C-9/29 (N8893)

P. 262
Hudson's Bay Company Archives,
Provincial Archives of Manitoba,
HBCA Photograph Collection,
1987/363-P-9/1 (N8469)

P. 270
Hudson's Bay Company Archives,
Provincial Archives of Manitoba,
HBC Archives, Schooling, p. 121
(N8908)

P. 273
Provincial Archives of Manitoba,
Collection—Foote 858

P. 275
Hudson's Bay Company Archives,
Provincial Archives of Manitoba,
HBCA Album 79-10 (N7236)

P. 278
Hudson's Bay Company Archives,
Provincial Archives of Manitoba,
HBCA Photograph Collection,
Album 53/40 (F1370-26) (N8471)

P. 287
Hudson's Bay Company Archives,
Provincial Archives of Manitoba,
HBCA Photograph Collection,
1987/363-C-27/39

P. 295
Hudson's Bay Company Archives,
Provincial Archives of Manitoba,
HBCA Photograph Collection,
1987/363-C-52/342 (N7401)

P. 298
Hudson's Bay Company Archives,
Provincial Archives of Manitoba,
HBCA Album, 53/83 (L24-496)
(N8903)

P. 308
Hudson's Bay Company Archives,
Provincial Archives of Manitoba,
HBCA Photograph Collection,
1987/363-A-24/61 (N8518)

P. 311
Hudson's Bay Company Archives,
Provincial Archives of Manitoba,

HBCA Photograph Collection,
1987/363-K-21 (N8519)

P. 314
The Central Press Photos, Ltd.

P. 322
Hudson's Bay Company Archives,
Provincial Archives of Manitoba,
HBCA Photograph Collection,
1987/339/32 (N8905)

P. 330
Hudson's Bay Company Archives,
Provincial Archives of Manitoba,
HBCA Photograph Collection,
1987/363-L-11 (N8902)

P. 338
*The Financial Post*/J. Chris
Christiansen

P. 343
Gilbert A. Milne & Co. Limited,
Photography. Courtesy Hudson's
Bay Company

P. 347
Courtesy Hudson's Bay Company

P. 350
*The Financial Post*/D. Dowling

P. 356
Brian Willer

P. 359
*ITO World*, Christmas 1983/
New Year 1984, p. 39

P. 365
London Express, from *Roy Thomson
of Fleet Street*, by Russell Braddon,
Toronto: Collins, 1965, opposite
p. 208; Metropolitan Toronto
Reference Library

P. 376
Canapress Photo Service/
Peter Bregg

P. 384
Elizabeth Bilton Photography.
Courtesy Hudson's Bay Company

P. 395
Peter Caton, Gerald Campbell
Studios, File no. A 86-24-8.
Courtesy Hudson's Bay Company

P. 401
Hal Roth, Photographer. Courtesy
Hudson's Bay Company

P. 403
Canapress Photo Service/
Peter Redman

P. 404
Michael De Sadeleer, Photographer

P. 415
Erik Christensen/*The Globe and Mail*

P. 419
Courtesy Hudson's Bay Company

Endpapers and p. 102
Maps by Jonathan Gladstone/
J.B. Geographics

# INDEX